The
COLORADO
Kid

by **Stephen King**

A HARD CASE CRIME NOVEL

A HARD CASE CRIME BOOK
(HCC-013-I)
First Hard Case Crime edition: May 2019

Published by

Titan Books
A division of Titan Publishing Group Ltd
144 Southwark Street
London SE1 0UP

in collaboration with Winterfall LLC

ISBN 978-1-78909-155-7

Design direction by Max Phillips
www.maxphillips.net

Typeset by Swordsmith Productions

The name "Hard Case Crime" and the Hard Case Crime logo
are trademarks of Winterfall LLC. Hard Case Crime books
are selected and edited by Charles Ardai.

Printed and bound by CPI Group (UK) Ltd, Croydon, CR0 4YY

Visit us on the web at www.HardCaseCrime.com

Raves for Stephen King's
THE COLORADO KID!

"Richly textured...one of [King's] best efforts."
—*Chicago Tribune*

"An intriguing story...wry and lively [and] artfully detailed."
—*USA Today*

"A small masterpiece...[*The Colorado Kid*] deserves in both its conception and its execution a place beside the classic tales of Poe, Conan Doyle, Stevenson, and the 20th-century masters of pulps."
—*Village Voice*

"A taut tale filled with engaging characters and old-school suspense."
—*Christian Science Monitor*

"A daring experiment...King's prose is engaging and propulsive."
—*This Week*

"Something new in the genre: the anti-mystery...it's absolutely riveting."
—*Philadelphia City Paper*

"A mystery that isn't a mystery so much as a book that comments on mysteries...postmodern."
—*New York Times*

"[A] charming story…Mr. King has shown us a magic trick, an illusion, but, unlike most mystery writers, doesn't show us how it was done."
—*Otto Penzler, New York Sun*

"A riveting tale."
—*U.S. News & World Report*

"*The Colorado Kid* is Stephen King's existential despair, his *Nausea* or *Waiting for Godot*."
—*Los Angeles Times*

"King appears to be fumbling in his tackle box when, in fact, he's already slipped the hook into our cheeks and is pulling us inexorably toward the bemusing, maddening… final page. If it's ironic that King delivered an experiment to people who celebrate the art of formula, that's OK. One of the reasons the pulps remain popular is that, behind those uniformly lurid painted covers, there always lurked a few writerly surprises."
—*Booklist*

"King has a unique way of completely redefining genres, and his homage to the pulp mystery—a kind of deconstruction of the traditional blueprint—is no different…*The Colorado Kid* is a must-read for mystery aficionados as well as all those who call themselves Stephen King fans. It's an unusual and thought-provoking addition to the author's already mammoth body of work… *The Colorado Kid* will have readers speculating until the very last page—and long afterward."
—*Barnes & Noble*

"Compelling reading: The author has a matchless narrative gift, and the characters are beautifully drawn."
— *Ellery Queen's Mystery Magazine*

"One of King's best works to date…a small story with a big heart that transcends genre."
— *The Magazine of Fantasy & Science Fiction*

"One of his most intriguing books…the way it ends makes you think more than you will with most other novels."
— *Napierville Sun*

"The ending comes as a most daring shock…I loved it."
— *The Guardian (UK)*

"Though the tale may end in ambiguity, the storytelling is powerful and has real effect and impact."
— *The Daily Camera*

"This is the best kind of Americana, true regional writing, a yarn told in the bumpy eloquence of small-town talk."
— *Ed Gorman*

"A showcase for King's trademark skills—making the mundane seem ominous, creating characters who leap off the page."
— *Charlotte Observer*

"An exercise in pure storytelling, and a commentary on the nature of closure [by] a storyteller at his peak."
— *Cemetery Dance*

"Filled with local color, memorable characters, and well-realized details…It's an almost-perverse touch that King's contribution to a publisher honoring genre fiction would end with a hard kick against genre conventions. But in its own way, it's an appropriate touch…finding death and mystery in a nice peaceful place where such things aren't supposed to happen. Now, as in the crime paperback's heyday, the message remains the same: Be watchful. Wherever you make your home, evil and temptation will follow."
—*The A.V. Club*

"[This] volume will speak to those who appreciate good storytelling…Quintessential King."
—*Library Journal*

"Time and again, King has surprised readers with his range…those in search of good characters, excellent dialogue and skillful writing will find all these in abundance in *The Colorado Kid*."
—*Newark Star Ledger*

"King's hard-boiled tour de force [is] a sparse but psychologically taut and layered thriller."
—*Tampa Tribune*

"A gem of storytelling…thought-provoking."
—*Lansing State Journal*

"A fascinating piece of narrative…King has yet again done something new."
—*Chicago Sun-Times*

"It's a measure of how good King's storytelling is—no news there—that he's given us a mystery without a solution and not made us feel as if we've been cheated."
—*New York Newsday*

"A really gripping book...readers who value storytelling are going to have a blast...Once again King has done things his way and succeeded."
—*Kansas City Star*

"There came a morning in the spring—April, it would have been—when they spied a man sitting out on Hammock Beach. You know, just on the outskirts of the village."

Stephanie knew it well.

"He was just sittin there with one hand in his lap and the other—the right one—lying on the sand. His face was waxy-white except for small purple patches on each cheek. His eyes were closed and Nancy said the lids were bluish. His lips also had a blue cast to them, and his neck, she said, had a kind of puffy look to it. His hair was sandy blond, cut short but not so short that a little of it couldn't flutter on his forehead when the wind blew, which it did pretty much constant.

"Nancy says, 'Mister, are you asleep? If you're asleep, you better wake up.'

"Johnny Gravlin says, 'He's not asleep, Nancy.'

"Johnny reached down—he had to steel himself to do it, he told me that years later—and shook the guy's shoulder. He said he knew for sure when he grabbed hold, because it didn't feel like a real shoulder at all under there but like a carving of one. He shook twice. First time, nothing happened. Second time, the guy's head fell over on his left shoulder and the guy slid off the litter basket that'd been holding him up and went down on his side. His head thumped on the sand. Nancy screamed and ran back to the road, fast as she could... He caught up to her and put his arm around her and said he was never so glad to feel live flesh underneath his arm. He told me he's never forgotten how it felt to grip that dead man's shoulder, how it felt like wood under that white shirt..."

With admiration, for DAN J. MARLOWE,
author of The Name of the Game is Death:
Hardest of the hardboiled.

THE BIRTH (AND REBIRTH)
OF THE COLORADO KID

When I first heard the title, I had two thoughts: boxing story or western.

This was back in 2004. I'd first reached out to Stephen King early in the year (April 16th, my obsessive record-keeping reminds me), sending him some materials about a line of books called "Hard Case Crime" that a friend and I were creating. We hadn't published any books yet—our first titles wouldn't come out until September—but we had a couple in the can and we'd hired painters to paint some covers, and our goal was nothing less than to revive pulp fiction in all its lurid mid-century glory. Gorgeous dames in torn negligees, tough guys with guns and felt hats, action and excitement, doom and despair.

Our books were going to be paperbacks, and not 500-page doorstops either—the sort of slender volumes you could read in a sitting or two, maybe on the train heading to or from work or while waiting for your clothes to spin dry at the laundromat.

In terms of content, we'd publish stories written at high

velocity, typically by authors who had to keep one eye out for the bill collector as they pounded the typewriter keys. The books would be the sort that grabbed you by the throat on page one and didn't let go till a killer was unmasked or someone lay bleeding in a gutter a scant 200 pages later. We'd package up these old-fashioned yarns behind sexy covers, price 'em about the same as a movie ticket (just as, in the old days, you could get either a movie ticket or a paperback for a quarter), and sell them in bookstores, truckstops, newsstands, drugstores, and military PXs across the land.

An ambitious plan. A quixotic plan. Not to mince words, a crazy plan. What could possibly have made us think that anyone in 2004 would want books that looked like they'd been published (and in some cases actually *had* first been published) half a century earlier?

Well, all I can say in my own defense is that there was drinking involved. But somehow we'd found backing for the project and had a publisher lined up to print and distribute the things, so we were charging full-steam ahead.

The only problem was how to get readers to give our books a try. We wanted to give voice to a new generation of hardboiled writers and to revive the work of an earlier generation that had long since been forgotten, terrific writers from the 1940s and 50s like David Dodge and Day Keene and Wade Miller. But modern readers wouldn't be likely to pick up a book by an author they'd never heard of, even if the cover price was modest and the cover art made their knees tremble. And I thought, maybe there's a well-known writer out there who loves old-time pulp crime novels as much as we do and would be willing to write us a blurb that would help entice readers to give us a try.

So I wrote to Stephen King.

Why Stephen King? Well, I didn't know the man, but I knew he shared our passion for this sort of book. He'd said so publicly more than once. He'd gone on the record about his love for the paperback crime novels of writers like John D. MacDonald and Lawrence Block. Hell, he'd even named the evil pseudonym in his novel *The Dark Half* "George Stark" after Richard Stark, the dark half of one of the writers we were going to be reprinting, the great Donald E. Westlake.

So I wrote to Stephen King. And held my breath and crossed my fingers and told myself not to be surprised if I never heard back. The man was busy, after all, and had to get a ton of random inquiries from random people wanting random things. No reason to think ours would catch his eye.

Then about a month later I was minding my own business when a call came in from Steve's agent and long-time editor, Chuck Verrill. "Steve asked me to give you a call," he said. "He wanted me to let you know that he does not want to write you a blurb—"

"Of course," I said, "I understand completely. That's completely understandable."

"—because," Chuck went on, "he wants to write you a book instead."

I sat on the other end of the phone while this sank in and tried to sound cool, like this was the sort of phone call I got every day and twice on Fridays. But inside I was turning cartwheels.

To this day I don't remember what I said to Chuck. But I remember what he said to me. He said that the book would be called *The Colorado Kid*, and though it would contain a mystery, it wasn't necessarily a crime novel, certainly not a conventional one, and would not fall strictly within our genre.

And I remember thinking, *The Colorado Kid*, not strictly within our genre...?

It's gotta be a boxing story. Either that or a western.

As you'll see, *The Colorado Kid* is not a boxing story and it's not a western. It's not a hardboiled crime novel either, though it surely does present a "hard case"—perhaps the hardest we've had the privilege to publish, since at its core the mystery of the Colorado Kid is the mystery we all wrestle with in our real lives, the mystery of the unanswerable. *The Colorado Kid* is an unusual and ambitious book, a tale about frustration that some readers have found frustrating—to which I answer, *Yes, exactly, that's the whole point!*

It's also very much a part of the classical mystery tradition we set out to revive. On the back cover I wrote that the book had "echoes of Dashiell Hammett's *The Maltese Falcon*," a comment that won me some raised eyebrows from readers who went looking in vain for Sam Spade. No, there are no trenchcoated private eyes in *The Colorado Kid*—no dames in torn negligees either, though in the best pulp tradition we didn't let that stop us from sticking a real looker on the cover. But as I reminded my skeptical interlocutors, in *The Maltese Falcon* Sam Spade tells the story of an assignment he had once to search for a man named Flitcraft, who left his office one day to go to lunch and vanished—vanished, Spade says, "like a fist when you open your hand."

The Colorado Kid is Stephen King's take on the Flitcraft parable, and it's as chilling and heartbreaking a reminder as any I've read that our ordinary, orderly lives are just one small sideways step away from a world of violence and terror and tragedy, a world of darkness that we don't normally want to think about but sometimes find ourselves brushing up against, all unwilling. And if that's not a noir story, I don't know what is.

That was 2004, when we were all a lot younger than we are today. When we published *The Colorado Kid* the following year, it really put Hard Case Crime on the map. I have no doubt—zero—that our little publishing imprint would no longer be around today if not for this act of generosity on the part of a man who owed us nothing, who chose to do us a kindness beyond any we deserved. The book reached hundreds of thousands of readers, and millions more heard about it thanks to coverage on television and in newspapers and magazines. (The Internet wasn't such a big thing back then. Twitter didn't exist yet, and Facebook had only recently been founded. My old friend Jeff Bezos had already dreamed up Amazon.com, though, and he helped us out when the time came to announce the book. The story behind *The Colorado Kid* is one of kindness all around.)

In 2007, Pete Crowther brought out a set of beautifully packaged collectible hardcover editions of the book through his imprint PS Publishing in the UK. Simon & Schuster published it in audiobook and ebook editions, and various publishing houses around the world brought it out in German, Italian, Hebrew, Dutch and many other languages. It deserved it. As I wrote to Steve the day after I first read the manuscript, it's not just a good story, it's an important one. And important stories ought to get out to as many readers as possible in as many formats as possible.

The Colorado Kid even made it to television—sort of. The month after the book was published, I began talking with a young TV producer named Adam Fratto about the possibility of creating a Hard Case Crime TV series, along the lines of the old *Alfred Hitchcock Presents*, where we'd adapt a different book each week. While that never got off the ground, the one book we kept coming back to was *The Colorado Kid*, and after a year of working on the project with TV writers Jim Dunn and Sam Ernst, Adam and his colleagues sold a script based on the book to ABC. Hollywood being Hollywood, that script never got filmed—but after a few years we eventually got the rights back, re-sold the show to SyFy, and in 2010 it debuted there under the name *Haven*.

Haven ran for five seasons between 2010 and 2015— well, six, kinda; the fifth was twice the length of any previous season—and many fine writers and actors and producers and behind-the-scenes folk put their heart and soul into it. I worked on all 78 episodes, providing detailed notes on every script and even writing two or three episodes myself. It was a thrill to fly to L.A. each season to help kick off the writer's room and to the seaside village of Chester in Nova Scotia to watch the filming. When my daughter was born at the end of 2010, Jim and Sam even named the femme fatale in Season 2 after her, as a present. So I have a lot of fond memories of *Haven*. But just how much of *The Colorado Kid* made it into the show? Not a whole lot. The two elderly newspapermen you're about to meet were in there (reimagined as brothers), but the young newspaper intern Stephanie McCann was not, replaced by what the TV world felt was sexier and more interesting, a beautiful FBI agent named Audrey Parker. She acquired two handsome male foils, a good boy (Nathan, the local lawman) and a bad boy (Duke, modern-day pirate and proprietor of the Grey Gull), neither of whom has any counterpart in the book. The island off the coast of Maine where the story takes place was changed to a mainland town and renamed. And over the course of the five (six?) seasons, the dead body on the beach that's at the center of the plot eventually got thoroughly explained, the very outcome the book resists so mightily. And, oh, the whole thing became heavily supernatural, something the book ostensibly isn't (though Steve did hint to me once that his own solution to the mystery might just possibly involve supernatural intervention).

Was the show good? At its best, yes—the evidence being that fans to this day still stream episodes online and write fanfiction in which Duke and Nathan realize their true love was for each other all along. But was it *The Colorado Kid*? Only very, very obliquely.

That might, incidentally, be one of the reasons Steve chose to let the paperback edition of the book go out of print a decade ago—while the show was on the air, it seems to me he might not have wanted fans to pick up the book and be frustrated to discover that Audrey, Nathan and Duke weren't in it. But it has now been several years since the show ended, and it felt to both of us like the time was right to bring *The Colorado Kid* back. Just as we did the first time, we're publishing it as a good old-fashioned paperback, with a suitably pulpy cover painting, and for good measure we're adding a generous helping of interior art besides. (Including two lovely pieces by the painter Kate Kelton—who, by the way, is also an actress, one of whose acting credits was the part of Jordan on *Haven*. Given enough time, everything comes full circle, doesn't it?)

And so, the Colorado Kid returns home. Not to Colorado, but to Hard Case Crime, where he was born.

Dutch, Hebrew...audio, television...hardcover, Kindle... this little story has been through a mighty number of incarnations, and surely this one won't be its last. But paperback was the first way anyone ever read the story of the Colorado Kid, and you can tell me I'm biased if you like, but I still think it's the best.

Some stories are meant to live between embossed leather covers, some to be told around a crackling campfire, some projected on a movie screen, larger than life, at 24 frames per second.

And some were born to be hauled around town in your pocket, the pages bowed and the spine cracked.

Go on: dive in. If you don't finish in one sitting, you have my permission to dog-ear the page when your laundry's dry or your train's pulling into the station. The Kid'll be waiting for you when you come back, teasing your curiosity and reminding you that sometimes the stories that don't answer all your questions are the ones you remember for a lifetime.

Charles Ardai
New York City, 2019

THE COLORADO KID

I

After deciding he would get nothing of interest from the two old men who comprised the entire staff of *The Weekly Islander*, the feature writer from the Boston *Globe* took a look at his watch, remarked that he could just make the one-thirty ferry back to the mainland if he hurried, thanked them for their time, dropped some money on the table-cloth, weighted it down with the salt shaker so the stiffish onshore breeze wouldn't blow it away, and hurried down the stone steps from the Grey Gull's patio dining area toward Bay Street and the little town below. Other than a few cursory gleeps at her breasts, he hardly noticed the young woman sitting between the two old men at all.

Once the *Globe* writer was gone, Vince Teague reached across the table and removed the bills—two fifties—from beneath the salt shaker. He tucked them into a flap pocket of his old but serviceable tweed jacket with a look of unmistakable satisfaction.

"What are you *doing*?" Stephanie McCann asked, knowing how much Vince enjoyed shocking what he called "her young bones" (how much they both did, really), but in this instance not able to keep the shock out of her voice.

"What does it look like?" Vince looked more satisfied than ever. With the money gone he smoothed down the flap over the pocket and took the last bite of his lobster roll. Then he patted his mouth with his paper napkin and deftly caught the departed *Globe* writer's plastic lobster bib when another, fresher gust of salt-scented breeze tried to carry it away. His hand was almost grotesquely gnarled with arthritis, but mighty quick for all that.

"It looks like you just took the money Mr. Hanratty left to pay for our lunch," Stephanie said.

"Ayuh, good eye there, Steff," Vince agreed, and winked one of his own at the other man sitting at the table. This was Dave Bowie, who looked roughly Vince Teague's age but was in fact twenty-five years younger. It was all a matter of the equipment you got in the lottery, was what Vince claimed; you ran it until it fell apart, patching it up as needed along the way, and he was sure that even to folks who lived a hundred years—as he hoped to do—it seemed like not much more than a summer afternoon in the end.

"But *why*?"

"Are you afraid I'm gonna stiff the Gull for the tab and stick Helen with it?" he asked her.

"No...who's Helen?"

"Helen Hafner, she who waited on us." Vince nodded across the patio where a slightly overweight woman of about forty was picking up dishes. "Because it's the policy of Jack Moody—who happens to own this fine eating establishment, and his father before him, if you care—"

"I do," she said.

David Bowie, *The Weekly Islander*'s managing editor for just shy of the years Helen Hafner had lived, leaned forward and put his pudgy hand over her young and pretty one. "I know you do," he said. "Vince does, too. That's why he's taking the long way around Robin Hood's barn to explain."

"Because school is in," she said, smiling.

"That's right," Dave said, "and what's nice for old guys like us?"

"You only have to bother teaching people who want to learn."

"That's right," Dave said, and leaned back. "That's nice." He wasn't wearing a suit-coat or sport-coat but an old green sweater. It was August and to Stephanie it seemed quite warm on the Gull's patio in spite of the onshore breeze, but she knew that both men felt the slightest chill. In Dave's case, this surprised her a little; he was only sixty-five and carrying an extra thirty pounds, at least. But although Vince Teague might look no more than seventy (and an agile seventy at that, in spite of his twisted hands), he had turned ninety earlier that summer and was as skinny as a rail. "A stuffed string" was what Mrs. Pinder, *The Islander*'s part-time secretary, called him. Usually with a disdainful sniff.

"The Grey Gull's policy is that the waitresses are responsible for the tabs their tables run up until those tabs are paid," Vince said. "Jack tells all the ladies that when they come in lookin for work, just so they can't come whining to him later on, sayin they didn't know that was part of the deal."

Stephanie surveyed the patio, which was still half-full even at twenty past one, and then looked into the main dining room, which overlooked Moose Cove. There almost every table was still taken, and she knew that from Memorial Day until the end of July, there would be a line outside until nearly three o'clock. Controlled bedlam, in other words. To expect every waitress to keep track of every single customer when she was busting her ass, carrying trays of steaming boiled lobsters and clams—

"That hardly seems…" She trailed off, wondering if these two old fellows, who'd probably been putting out their paper before such a thing as the minimum wage even existed, would laugh at her if she finished.

"*Fair* might be the word you're lookin for," Dave said dryly, and picked up a roll. It was the last one in the basket.

Fair came out *fay-yuh*, which more or less rhymed with *ayuh*, the Yankee word which seemed to mean both *yes* and *is that so*. Stephanie was from Cincinnati, Ohio, and when she had first come to Moose-Lookit Island to do an internship on *The Weekly Islander*, she had nearly despaired…which, in downeast lingo, also rhymed with *ayuh*. How could she learn anything when she could only understand one word in every seven? And if she kept asking them to repeat themselves, how long would it be before they decided she was a congenital idiot (which on Moose-Look was pronounced *ijit*, of course)?

She had been on the verge of quitting four days into a four-month University of Ohio postgrad program when Dave took her aside one afternoon and said, "Don't you quit on it, Steffi, it'll come to ya." And it had. Almost overnight, it seemed, the accent had clarified. It was as if she'd had a bubble in her ear which had suddenly, miraculously popped. She thought she could live here the rest of her life and never talk like them, but understand them? Ayuh, that much she could do, deah.

"Fair was the word," she agreed.

"One that hasn't ever been in Jack Moody's vocabulary, except in how it applies to the weather," Vince said, and then, with no change of tone, "Put that roll down, David Bowie, ain't you gettin fat, I swan, soo-ee, pig-pig-pig."

"Last time I looked, we wa'ant married," Dave said, and took another bite of his roll. "Can't you tell her what's on what passes for your mind without scoldin me?"

"Ain't he pert?" Vince said. "No one ever taught him not to talk with his mouth full, either." He hooked an arm over the back of his chair, and the breeze from the bright ocean blew his fine white hair back from his brow. "Steffi, Helen's got three kids from twelve to six and a husband that run off and left her. She don't want to leave the island, and she can make a go of it—just—waitressin at the Grey Gull because summers are a little fatter than the winters are lean. Do you follow that?"

"Yes, absolutely," Stephanie said, and just then the lady in question approached. Stephanie noticed that she was wearing heavy support hose that did not entirely conceal varicose veins, and that there were dark circles under her eyes.

"Vince, Dave," she said, and contented herself with just

a nod at the pretty third, whose name she did not know. "See your friend dashed off. For the ferry?"

"Yep," Dave said. "Discovered he had to get back down-Boston."

"Ayuh? All done here?"

"Oh, leave on a bit," Vince said, "but bring us a check when you like, Helen. Kids okay?"

Helen Hafner grimaced. "Jude fell out of his treehouse and broke his arm last week. Didn't he holler! Scared me bout to death!"

The two old men looked at each other...then laughed. They sobered quickly, looking ashamed, and Vince offered his sympathies, but it wouldn't do for Helen.

"Men can laugh," she told Stephanie with a tired, sardonic smile. "They *all* fell out of treehouses and broke their arms when they were boys, and they all remember what little pirates they were. What they don't remember is Ma gettin up in the middle of the night to give em their aspirin tablets. I'll bring you the check." She shuffled off in a pair of sneakers with rundown backs.

"She's a good soul," Dave said, having the grace to look slightly shamefaced.

"Yes, she is," Vince said, "and if we got the rough side of her tongue we probably deserved it. Meanwhile, here's the deal on this lunch, Steffi. I dunno what three lobster rolls, one lobster dinner with steamers, and four iced teas cost down there in Boston, but that feature writer must have forgot that up here we're livin at what an economist might call 'the source of supply' and so he dropped a hundred bucks on the table. If Helen brings us a check that says any more than fifty-five, I'll smile and kiss a pig. With me so far?"

"Yes, sure," Stephanie said.

"Now the way this works for that fella from the *Globe* is that he scratches *Lunch, Gray Gull, Moose-Lookit Island* and *Unexplained Mysteries Series* in his little Boston *Globe* expense book while he's ridin back to the mainland on the ferry, and if he's honest he writes one hundred bucks and if he's got a smidge of larceny in his soul, he writes a hundred and twenty and takes his girl to the movies on the extra. Got that?"

"Yes," Stephanie said, and looked at him with reproachful eyes as she drank the rest of her iced tea. "I think you're very cynical."

"No, if I was very cynical, I would have said a hundred and *thirty*, and for sure." This made Dave snort laughter. "In any case, he left a hundred, and that's at least thirty-five dollars too much, even with a twenty percent tip added in. So I took his money. When Helen brings the check, I'll sign it, because the *Islander* runs a tab here."

"And you'll tip more than twenty percent, I hope," Stephanie said, "given her situation at home."

"That's just where you're wrong," Vince said.

"I am? *Why* am I?"

He looked at her patiently. "Why do you think? Because I'm cheap? Yankee-tight?"

"No. I don't believe that any more than I think black men are lazy or Frenchmen think about sex all day long."

"Then put your brain to work. God gave you a good one."

Stephanie tried, and the two men watched her do it, interested.

"She'd see it as charity," Stephanie finally said.

Vince and Dave exchanged an amused glance.

"What?" Stephanie asked.

"Gettin a little close to lazy black men and sexy French-men, ain'tcha, dear?" Dave asked, deliberately broadening his downeast accent into what was nearly a burlesque drawl. "Only now it's the proud Yankee woman that won't take charity."

Feeling that she was straying ever deeper into the socio-logical thickets, Stephanie said, "You mean she would take it. For her kids, if not for herself."

"The man who bought our lunch was from away," Vince said. "As far as Helen Hafner's concerned, folks from away just about got money fallin out of their…their wallets."

Amused at his sudden detour into delicacy on her account, Stephanie looked around, first at the patio area where they were sitting, then through the glass at the in-door seating area. And she saw an interesting thing. Many—perhaps even most—of the patrons out here in the breeze were locals, and so were most of the waitresses serving them. Inside were the summer people, the so-called "off-islanders," and the waitresses serving *them* were younger. Prettier, too, and also from away. Summer help. And all at once she understood. She had been wrong to put on her sociologist's hat. It was far simpler than that.

"The Grey Gull waitresses share tips, don't they?" she asked. "That's what it is."

Vince pointed a finger at her like a gun and said, "Bingo."

"So what do you do?"

"What I do," he said, "is tip fifteen percent when I sign the check and put forty dollars of that *Globe* fella's cash in Helen's pocket. She gets all of that, the paper doesn't get hurt, and what Uncle Sam don't know don't bother him."

"It's the way America does business," Dave said solemnly.

"And do you know what I like?" Vince Teague said, turning his face up into the sun. When he squinted his eyes closed against its brilliance, what seemed like a thousand wrinkles sprang into existence on his skin. They did not make him look his age, but they *did* make him look eighty.

"No, what?" Stephanie asked, amused.

"I like the way the money goes around and around, like clothes in a drier. I like watching it. And this time when the machine finally stops turning, the money finishes up here on Moosie where folks actually need it. Also, just to make it perfect, that city fellow *did* pay for our lunch, and he walked away with *nones*."

"Ran, actually," Dave said. "Had to make that boat, don'tcha know. Made me think of that Edna St. Vincent Millay poem. 'We were very tired, we were very merry, we went back and forth all night on the ferry.' That's not exactly it, but it's close."

"He wasn't very merry, but he'll be good and tired by the time he gets to his next stop," Vince said. "I think he mentioned Madawaska. Maybe he'll find some unexplained mysteries there. Why anyone'd want to live in such a place, for instance. Dave, help me out."

Stephanie believed there was a kind of telepathy between the two old men, rough but real. She'd seen several examples of it since coming to Moose-Lookit Island almost three months ago, and she saw another example of it now. Their waitress was returning, check in hand. Dave's back was to her, but Vince saw her coming and the younger man knew exactly what the *Islander*'s editor wanted. Dave reached into his back pocket, removed his wallet, removed two bills, folded them between his fingers, and passed them across the table. Helen arrived a moment later. Vince took the check from her with one gnarled hand. With the other he slipped the bills into the skirt pocket of her uniform.

"Thank you, darlin'," he said.

"You sure you don't want dessert?" she asked. "There's Mac's chocolate cherry cake. It's not on the menu, but we've still got some."

"I'll pass. Steffi?"

She shook her head. So—with some regret—did Dave Bowie.

Helen favored (if that was the word) Vincent Teague with a look of dour judgment. "You could use fattening up, Vince."

"Jack Sprat and his wife, that's me n Dave," Vince said brightly.

"Ayuh." Helen glanced at Stephanie, and one of her tired eyes closed in a brief wink of surprising good humor. "You picked a pair, Missy," she said.

36

"They're all right," Stephanie said.

"Sure, and after this you'll probably go straight to the *New York Times*," Helen said. She picked up the plates, added, "I'll be back for the rest of the ridding-up," and sailed away.

"When she finds that forty dollars in her pocket," Stephanie said, "will she know who put it there?" She looked again at the patio, where perhaps two dozen customers were drinking coffee, iced tea, afternoon beers, or eating off-the-menu chocolate cherry cake. Not all looked capable of slipping forty dollars in cash into a waitress's pocket, but some of them did.

"Probably she will," Vince said, "but tell me something, Steffi."

"I will if I can."

"If she didn't know, would that make it illegal tender?"

"I don't know what you—"

"I think you do," he said. "Come on, let's get back to the paper. News won't wait."

2

Here was the thing Stephanie loved best about *The Weekly Islander*, the thing that still charmed her after three months spent mostly writing ads: on a clear afternoon you could walk six steps from your desk and have a gorgeous view of the Maine coast. All you had to do was walk onto the shaded deck that overlooked the reach and ran the length of the newspaper's barnlike building. It was true that the air smelled of fish and seaweed, but everything on Moose-Look smelled that way. You got used to it, Stephanie had discovered, and then a beautiful thing happened—after your nose dismissed that smell, it went and found it all over again, and the second time around, you fell in love with it.

On clear afternoons (like this one near the end of August), every house and dock and fishing-boat over there on the Tinnock side of the reach stood out brilliantly; she could read the SUNOCO on the side of a diesel pump and the *LeeLee Bett* on the hull of some haddock-jockey's bread-winner, beached for its turn-of-the-season scraping and painting. She could see a boy in shorts and a cut-off Patriots jersey fishing from the trash-littered shingle below Preston's Bar, and a thousand winks of sun glittering off the tin flashing of a hundred village roofs. And, between Tinnock

Village (which was actually a good-sized town) and Moose-Lookit Island, the sun shone on the bluest water she had ever seen. On days like this, she wondered how she would ever go back to the Midwest, or if she even could. And on days when the fog rolled in and the entire mainland world seemed to be cancelled and the rueful cry of the foghorn came and went like the voice of some ancient beast…why, then she wondered the same thing.

You want to be careful, Steffi, Dave had told her one day when he came on her, sitting out there on the deck with her yellow pad on her lap and a half-finished Arts 'N Things column scrawled there in her big backhand strokes. *Island living has a way of creeping into your blood, and once it gets there it's like malaria. It doesn't leave easily.*

Now, after turning on the lights (the sun had begun going the other way and the long room had begun to darken), she sat down at her desk and found her trusty legal pad with a new Arts 'N Things column on the top page. This one was pretty much interchangeable with any of half a dozen others she had so far turned in, but she looked at it with undeniable affection just the same. It was hers, after all, her work, writing she was getting paid for, and she had no doubt that people all over the *Islander*'s circulation area—which was quite large—actually read it.

Vince sat down behind his own desk with a small but audible grunt. It was followed by a crackling sound as he twisted first to the left and then to the right. He called this "settling his spine." Dave told him that he would someday paralyze himself from the neck down while "settling his spine," but Vince seemed singularly unworried by the possibility. Now he turned on his computer while his managing editor sat on the corner of his desk, produced a toothpick, and began using it to rummage in his upper plate.

"What's it going to be?" Dave asked while Vince waited for his computer to boot up. "Fire? Flood? Earthquake? Or the revolt of the multitudes?"

"I thought I'd start with Ellen Dunwoodie snapping off the fire hydrant on Beach Lane when the parking brake on her car let go. Then, once I'm properly warmed up, I thought I'd move on to a rewrite of my library editorial," Vince said, and cracked his knuckles.

Dave glanced over at Stephanie from his perch on the corner of Vince's desk. "First the back, then the knuckles," he said. "If he could learn how to play 'Dry Bones' on his ribcage, we could get him on *American Idol*."

"Always a critic," Vince said amiably, still waiting for his machine to boot up. "You know, Steff, there's something perverse about this. Here am I, ninety years old and ready for the cooling board, using a brand new Macintosh computer, and there you sit, twenty-two and gorgeous, fresh as a new peach, yet scrawling on a yellow legal pad like an old maid in a Victorian romance."

"I don't believe yellow legal pads had been invented in Victorian times," Stephanie said. She shuffled through the papers on her desk. When she had come to Moose-Look and *The Weekly Islander* in June, they had given her the smallest desk in the place—little more than a grade-schooler's desk,

really—away in the corner. In mid-July she had been pro-
moted to a bigger one in the middle of the room. This
pleased her, but the increased desk-space also afforded
more area for things to get lost in. Now she hunted around
until she found a bright pink circular. "Do either of you
know what organization profits from the Annual End-Of-
Summer Gernerd Farms Hayride, Picnic, and Dance, this
year featuring Little Jonna Jaye and the Straw Hill Boys?"

"That organization would be Sam Gernerd, his wife,
their five kids, and their various creditors," Vince said, and
his machine beeped. "I've been meaning to tell you, Steff,
you've done a swell job on that little column of yours."

"Yes, you have," Dave agreed. "We've gotten two dozen
letters, I guess, and the only bad one was from Mrs. Edina
Steen the Downeast Grammar Queen, and she's completely
mad."

"Nuttier than a fruitcake," Vince agreed.

Stephanie smiled, wondering at how rare it was once
you graduated from childhood—this feeling of perfect and
uncomplicated happiness. "Thank you," she said. "Thank
you both." And then: "Can I ask you something? Straight
up?"

Vince swiveled his chair around and looked at her.
"Anything under the sun, if it'll keep me away from Mrs.
Dunwoodie and the fire hydrant," he said.

"And me away from doing invoices," Dave said. "Although
I can't go home until they're finished."

"Don't you make that paperwork your boss!" Vince said.
"How many times have I told you?"

"Easy for you to say," Dave returned. "You haven't looked inside the *Islander* checkbook in ten years, I don't think, let alone carried it around."

Stephanie was determined not to let them be sidetracked —or to let them sidetrack her—into this old squabble. "Quit it, both of you."

They looked at her, surprised into silence.

"Dave, you pretty much told that Mr. Hanratty from the *Globe* that you and Vince have been working together on the *Islander* for forty years—"

"Ayuh—"

"—and you started it up in 1948, Vince."

"That's true," he said. "'Twas *The Weekly Shopper and Trading Post* until the summer of '48, just a free handout in the various island markets and the bigger stores on the mainland. I was young and bullheaded and awful lucky. That was when they had the big fires over in Tinnock and Hancock. Those fires...they didn't *make* the paper, I won't say that—although there were those who did at the time— but they give it a good runnin start, sure. It wasn't until 1956 that I had as many ads as I did in the summer of '48."

"So you guys have been on the job for over fifty years, and in all that time you've *never* come across a real unexplained mystery? Can that be true?"

Dave Bowie looked shocked. "We never said that!"

"Gorry, you were *there*!" Vince declared, equally scandalized.

For a moment they managed to hold these expressions, but when Stephanie McCann only continued to look from one to the other, prim as the schoolmarm in a John Ford Western, they couldn't go on. First Vince Teague's mouth began to quiver at one corner, and then Dave Bowie's eye began to twitch. They might still have been all right, but then they made the mistake of looking right at each other and a moment later they were laughing like the world's oldest pair of kids.

3

"You were the one who told him about the *Pretty Lisa*," Dave said to Vince when he had gotten hold of himself again. The *Pretty Lisa Cabot* was a fishing boat that had washed up on the shore of neighboring Smack Island in the nineteen-twenties with one dead crewman sprawled over the forward hold and the other five men gone. "How many times do you think Hanratty heard that one, up n down this part of the coast?"

"Oh, I dunno, how many places do you judge he stopped before he got here, dear?" Vince countered, and a moment later the two men were off again, bellowing laughter, Vince slapping has bony knee while Dave whacked the side of one plump thigh.

Stephanie watched them, frowning—not angry, not amused herself (well…a little), just trying to understand the source of their howling good humor. She herself had thought the story of the *Pretty Lisa Cabot* good enough for at least one in a series of eight articles on, ta-da, Unexplained Mysteries of New England, but she was neither stupid nor insensitive; she'd been perfectly aware that Mr. *Hanratty* hadn't thought it was good enough. And yes, she'd known from his face that he'd heard it before in his

Globe-funded wanderings up and down the coast between Boston and Moose-Look, and probably more than once.

Vince and Dave nodded when she advanced this idea. "Ayup," Dave said. "Hanratty may be from away, but that doesn't make him lazy or stupid. The mystery of the *Pretty Lisa*—the solution to which almost certainly has to do with gun-happy bootleggers running hooch down from Canada, although no one will ever know for sure—has been around for years. It's been written up in half a dozen books, not to mention both *Yankee* and *Downeast* magazines. And, say, Vince, didn't the *Globe*—?"

Vince was nodding. "Maybe. Seven, maybe nine years ago. Sunday supplement piece. Although it might have been the Providence *Journal*. I'm sure it was the Portland Sunday *Telegram* that did the piece on the Mormons that showed up over in Freeport and tried to sink a mine in the Desert of Maine…"

"And the 1951 Coast Lights get a big play in the newspapers almost every Halloween," Dave added cheerfully. "Not to mention the UFO websites."

"And a woman wrote a book last year on the poisonin's at that church picnic in Tashmore," Vince finished up. This was the last 'unexplained mystery' they had hauled out for the *Globe* reporter over lunch. This was just before Hanratty had decided he could make the one-thirty ferry, and in a way Stephanie guessed she now didn't blame him.

"So you were having him on," she said. "Teasing him with old stories."

"No, dear!" Vince said, this time sounding shocked for

real. (*Well, maybe,* Stephanie thought.) "Every one of those is a *bona fide* unsolved mystery of the New England coast —our part of it, even."

"We couldn't be sure he knew all those stories until we trotted em out," Dave said reasonably. "Not that it surprised us any that he did."

"Nope," Vince agreed. His eyes were bright. "Pretty old chestnuts, I would have to agree. But we got a nice lunch out of it, didn't we? And we got to watch the money go around and come out right where it should...partly in Helen Hafner's pocket."

"And those stories are really the only ones you know? Stories that have been chewed to a pulp in books and the big newspapers?"

Vince looked at Dave, his long-time cohort. "Did I say that?"

"Nope," Dave said. "And I don't believe I did, either."

"Well, what other unexplained mysteries *do* you know about? And why didn't you tell him?"

The two old men glanced at each other, and once again Stephanie McCann felt that telepathy at work. Vince gave a slight nod toward the door. Dave got up, crossed the brightly lit half of the long room (in the darker half hulked the big old-fashioned offset printing press that hadn't run in over seven years), and turned the sign hanging in the door from OPEN to CLOSED. Then he came back.

"Closed? In the middle of the day?" Stephanie asked, with the slightest touch of unease in her mind, if not in her voice.

"If someone comes by with news, they'll knock," Vince said, reasonably enough. "If it's big news, they'll hammer."

"And if downtown catches afire, we'll hear the whistle," Dave put in. "Come on out on the deck, Steffi. August sun's not to be missed—it doesn't last long."

She looked at Dave, then at Vince Teague, who was as mentally quick at ninety as he'd been at forty-five. She was convinced of it. "School's in?" she asked.

"That's right," Vince said, and although he was still smiling, she sensed he was serious. "And do you know what's nice for old guys like us?"

"You only have to teach people who want to learn."

"Ayuh. Do *you* want to learn, Steffi?"

"Yes." She spoke with no hesitation in spite of that odd inner unease.

"Then come out and sit," he said. "Come out and sit a little."

So she did.

4

The sun was warm, the air was cool, the breeze was sweet with salt and rich with the sound of bells and horns and lapping water. These were sounds she had come to love in only a space of weeks. The two men sat on either side of her, and although she didn't know it, both had more or less the same thought: *Age flanks beauty*. And there was nothing wrong with the thought, because both of them understood their intentions were perfectly solid. They understood how good she could be at the job, and how much she wanted to learn; all that pretty greed made you *want* to teach.

"So," Vince said when they were settled, "think about those stories we told Hanratty at lunch, Steffi—the *Lisa Cabot*, the Coast Lights, the Wandering Mormons, the Tashmore church poisonings that were never solved—and tell me what they have in common."

"They're *all* unsolved."

"Try doin a little better, dearheart," Dave said. "You disappoint me."

She glanced at him and saw he wasn't kidding. Well, that *was* pretty obvious, considering why Hanratty had blown them to lunch in the first place: the *Globe*'s eight-installment

51

series (maybe even ten installments, Hanratty had said, if he could find enough peculiar stories), which the editorial staff hoped to run between September and Halloween. "They've all been done to death?"

"That's a little better," Vince said, "but you're still not breaking any new ground. Ask yourself this, youngster: *why* have they been done to death? Why does some New England paper drag up the Coast Lights at least once a year, along with a bunch of blurry photos taken over half a century ago? Why does some regional magazine like *Yankee* or *Coast* interview either Clayton Riggs or Ella Ferguson at least once a year, as if they were going to all at once jump up like Satan in silk britches and say something brand new?"

"I don't know who those people are," Stephanie said.

Vince clapped a hand to the back of his head. "Ayuh, more fool me. I keep forgettin you're from away."

"Should I take that as a compliment?"

"Could do; probably *should* do. Clayton Riggs and Ella Ferguson were the only two who drank the iced coffee that day at Tashmore Lake and didn't die of it. The Ferguson woman's all right, but Riggs is paralyzed all down the left side of his body."

"That's awful. And they keep interviewing them?"

"Ayuh. Fifteen years have rolled by, and I think everyone with half a brain knows that no one is ever going to be arrested for that crime—eight folks poisoned by the side of the lake, and six of em dead—but still Ferguson and Riggs show up in the press, lookin increasin'ly rickety:

52

'What Happened That Day?' and 'The Lakeside Horror' and...you get the idea. It's just another story folks like to hear, like 'Little Red Ridin Hood' or 'The Three Billy Goats' Gruff.' Question is...*why*?"

But Stephanie had leaped ahead. "There *is* something, isn't there?" she said. "Some story you didn't tell him. What is it?"

Again that look passed between them, and this time she couldn't come even close to reading the thought that went with it. They were sitting in identical lawn chairs, Stephanie with her hands on the arms of hers. Now Dave reached over and patted one of them. "We don't mind tellin you... do we, Vince?"

"Nah, guess not," Vince said, and once again all those wrinkles appeared as he smiled up into the sun.

"But if you want to ride the ferry, you have to bring tea for the tillerman. Have you ever heard that one?"

"Somewhere." She thought on one of her mom's old record albums, up in the attic.

"Okay," Dave said, "then answer the question. Hanratty didn't want those stories because they've been written to rags. Why have they been?"

She thought about it, and once again they let her. Once again took pleasure in watching her do it.

"Well," Stephanie said, at last, "I suppose people like stories that are good for a shiver or two on a winter night, especially if the lights are on and the fire's nice and warm. Stories about, you know, the unknown."

"How many unknown things per story, dear?" Vince

Teague asked. His voice was soft but his eyes were sharp.

She opened her mouth to say *As many as six, anyway,* thinking about the Church Picnic Poisoner, then closed it again. Six people had died that day on the shores of Tashmore Lake, but one whopper dose of poison had killed them all and she guessed that just one hand had administered it. She didn't know how many Coast Lights there had been, but had no doubt that folks thought of it as a single phenomenon. So—

"One?" she said, feeling like a contestant in the Final Jeopardy round. "One unknown thing per story?"

Vince pointed his finger at her, smiling more widely than ever, and Stephanie relaxed. This wasn't real school, and these two men wouldn't like her any less if she flubbed an answer, but she had come to want to please them in a way she had only wanted to please the very best of her high school and college teachers. The ones who were fierce in their commitments.

"The other thing is that folks have to believe in their hearts that there's a *musta-been* in there someplace, and they got a damn good idea what it is," Dave said. "Here's the *Pretty Lisa,* washed up on the rocks just south of Dingle Nook on Smack Island in 1926—"

"'27," Vince said.

"All right, '27, smarty-britches, and Teodore Riponeaux is still on board, but dead as a hake, and the other five are gone, and even though there's no sign of blood or a struggle, folks say *musta-been* pirates, so now there's stories about how they had a treasure map and found buried gold and the folks that were guarding it took the swag off them and who knows what-all else."

"Or they got fighting among themselves," Vince said. "That's always been a *Pretty Lisa* favorite. The point is, there are stories some folks tell and other folks like to hear, but Hanratty was wise enough to know his editor wouldn't fall for such reheated hash."

"In another ten years, maybe," Dave said. "Because sooner or later, everything old is new again. You might not believe that, Steffi, but it's actually true."

"I *do* believe it," she said, and thought: *Tea for the Tillerman, was that Al Stewart or Cat Stevens?*

"Then there's the Coast Lights," Vince said, "and I can tell you exactly what's always made that such a favorite. There's a picture of them—probably nothing but reflected lights from Ellsworth on the low clouds that hung together just right to make circles that looked like saucers—and below them you can see the whole Hancock Lumber Little League team looking up, all in their uniforms."

"And one little boy pointin with his glove," Dave said. "It's the final touch. And people all look at it and say, 'Why, that *musta-been* folks from outer space, droppin down for a little look-see at the Great American Pastime. But it's still just one unknown thing, this time with interestin pictures to mull over, so people go back to it again and again."

"But not the Boston *Globe*," Vince said, "although I sense that one might do in a pinch."

The two men laughed comfortably, as old friends will.

"So," Vince said, "we might know of an unexplained mystery or two—"

"I won't stick at that," Dave said. "We know of at least one for sure, darlin, but there isn't a single *musta-been* about it—"

"Well…the steak," Vince said, but he sounded doubtful.

"Oh, ayuh, but even *that's* a mystery, wouldn't you say?" Dave asked.

"Yah," Vince agreed, and now he didn't sound comfortable. Nor did he look it.

"You're confusing me," Stephanie said.

"Ayuh, the story of the Colorado Kid is a confusing tale, all right," Vince said, "which is why it wouldn't do for the Boston *Globe*, don'tcha know. Too many unknowns, to begin with. Not a single *musta-been* for another." He leaned forward, fixing her with his clear blue Yankee gaze. "You want to be a newswoman, don't you?"

"You know I do," Stephanie said, surprised.

"Well then, I'm going to tell you a secret almost every newspaper man and woman who's been at it awhile knows: in real life, the number of actual stories—those with beginnings, middles, and ends—are slim and none. But if you can give your readers just one unknown thing (two at the very outside), and then kick in what Dave Bowie there calls a *musta-been*, your reader will tell *himself* a story. Amazin, ain't it?

"Take the Church Picnic Poisonings. No one knows who killed those folks. What *is* known is that Rhoda Parks, the Tashmore Methodist Church secretary, and William Blakee, the Methodist Church *pastor*, had a brief affair six months before the poisonings. Blakee was married, and he broke it off. Are you with me?"

"Yes," Stephanie said.

"What's *also* known is that Rhoda Parks was despondent over the breakup, at least for awhile. Her sister said as much. A third thing that's known? Both Rhoda Parks and William Blakee drank that poisoned iced coffee at the picnic and died. So what's the *musta-been*? Quick as your life, Steffi."

"Rhoda must have poisoned the coffee to kill her lover for jilting her and then drank it herself to commit suicide. The other four—plus the ones who only got sick—were what-do-you-call-it, collateral damage."

Vince snapped his fingers. "Ayuh, that's the story people tell themselves. The newspapers and magazines never come right out and print it because they don't have to. They know that folks can connect the dots. What's against it? Quick as your life again."

But this time her life would have been forfeit, because Stephanie could come up with nothing against it. She was about to protest that she didn't know the case well enough to say when Dave got up, approached the porch rail, looked out over the reach toward Tinnock, and remarked mildly: "Six months seems a long time to wait, doesn't it?"

Stephanie said, "Didn't someone once say revenge is a dish best eaten cold?"

"Ayuh," Dave said, still perfectly mild, "but when you kill six people, that's more than just revenge. Not sayin it *couldn't* have been that way, just that it might have been some other. Just like the Coast Lights might have been reflections on the clouds...or somethin secret the Air Force was testin that got sent up from the air base in Bangor...or who knows, maybe it *was* little green men droppin in to see if the kids from Hancock Lumber could turn a double play against the ones from Tinnock Auto Body."

"Mostly what happens is people make up a story and stick with it," Vince said. "That's easy enough to do as long as there's only one unknown factor: one poisoner, one set of mystery lights, one boat run aground with most of her crew gone. But with the Colorado Kid there was nothing *but* unknown factors, and hence there was no story." He paused. "It was like a train running out of a fireplace or a bunch of horses' heads showing up one morning in the middle of your driveway. Not that grand, but every bit as strange. And things like that..." He shook his head. "Steffi, people don't like things like that. They don't *want* things like that. A wave is a pretty thing to look at when it breaks on the beach, but too many only make you seasick."

Stephanie looked out at the sparkling reach—plenty of waves there, but no big ones, not today—and considered this in silence.

"There's something else," Dave said, after a bit.

"What?" she asked.

"It's *ours*," he said, and with surprising force. She thought it was almost anger. "A guy from the *Globe*, a guy from away—he'd only muck it up. He wouldn't understand."

"Do you?" she asked.

"No," he said, sitting down again. "Nor do I have to, dear. On the subject of the Colorado Kid I'm a little like the Virgin Mary, after she gave birth to Jesus. The Bible says something like, 'But Mary kept silent, and pondered these things in her heart.' Sometimes, with mysteries, that's best."

"But you'll tell me?"

"Why, yes, ma'am!" He looked at her as if surprised; also—a little—as if awakening from a near-doze. "Because you're one of us. Isn't she, Vince?"

"Ayuh," Vince said. "You passed that test somewhere around midsummer."

"Did I?" Again she felt absurdly happy. "How? What test?"

Vince shook his head. "Can't say, dear. Only know that at some point it began to seem you were all right." He glanced at Dave, who nodded. Then he looked back at Stephanie. "All right," he said. "The story we didn't tell at lunch. Our very own unexplained mystery. The story of the Colorado Kid."

5

But it was Dave who actually began.

"Twenty-five years ago," he said, "back in '80, there were two kids who took the six-thirty ferry to school instead of the seven-thirty. They were on the Bayview Consolidated High School Track Team, and they were also boy and girlfriend. Once winter was over—and it doesn't ever last as long here on the coast as it does inland—they'd run cross-island, down along Hammock Beach to the main road, then on to Bay Street and the town dock. Do you see it, Steffi?"

She did. She saw the romance of it, as well. What she didn't see was what the "boy and girlfriend" did when they got to the Tinnock side of the reach. She knew that Moose-Look's dozen or so high-school-age kids almost always took the seven-thirty ferry, giving the ferryman—either Herbie Gosslin or Marcy Lagasse—their passes so they could be recorded with quick winks of the old laser-gun on the bar codes. Then, on the Tinnock side, a schoolbus would be waiting to take them the three miles to BCHS. She asked if the runners waited for the bus and Dave shook his head, smiling.

"Nawp, ran that side, too," he said. "Not holdin hands, but might as well have been; always side by side, Johnny Gravlin and Nancy Arnault. For a couple of years they were all but inseparable."

Stephanie sat up straighter in her chair. The John Gravlin she knew was Moose-Lookit Island's mayor, a gregarious man with a good word for everyone and an eye on the state senate in Augusta. His hairline was receding, his belly expanding. She tried to imagine him doing the greyhound thing—two miles a day on the island side of the reach, three more on the mainland side—and couldn't manage it.

"Ain't makin much progress with it, are ya, dear?" Vince asked.

"No," she admitted.

"Well, that's because you see Johnny Gravlin the soccer player, miler, Friday night practical joker and Saturday lover as *Mayor* John Gravlin, who happens to be the only political hop-toad in a small island pond. He goes up and down Bay Street shaking hands and grinning with that gold tooth flashing off to one side in his mouth, got a good word for everyone he meets, never forgets a name or which man drives a Ford pickup and which one is still getting along with his Dad's old International Harvester. He's a carica-ture right out of an old nineteen-forties movie about small-town hoop-de-doo politics and he's such a hick he don't even know it. He's got one jump left in him—hop, toad, hop—and once he gets to that Augusta lilypad he'll either be wise enough to stop or he'll try another hop and end up getting squashed."

"That is *so* cynical," Stephanie said, not without youth's admiration for the trait.

Vince shrugged his bony shoulders. "Hey, I'm a stereotype myself, dearie, only my movie's the one where the newspaper feller with the arm-garters on his shirt and the eyeshade on his forread gets to yell out 'Stop the presses!' in the last reel. My point is that Johnny was a different creature in those days—slim as a quill pen and quick as quicksilver. You would have called him a god, almost, except for those unfortunate buck teeth, which he has since had fixed.

"And she…in those skimpy little red shorts she wore… she was indeed a goddess." He paused. "As so many girls of seventeen surely are."

"Get your mind out of the gutter," Dave told him.

Vince looked surprised. "Ain't," he said. "Ain't a bit. It's in the clouds."

"If you say so," Dave said, "and I will admit she was a looker, all right. And an inch or two taller than Johnny, which may be why they broke up in the spring of their senior year. But back in '80 they were hot and heavy, and every day they'd run for the ferry on this side and then up Bayview Hill to the high school on the Tinnock side. There were bets on when Nancy would catch pregnant by him, but she never did; either he was awful polite or she was awful careful." He paused. "Or hell, maybe they were just a little more sophisticated than most island kids back then."

"I think it might've been the running," Vince said judiciously.

Stephanie said, "Back on message, please, both of you," and the men laughed.

"On message," Dave said, "there came a morning in the spring of 1980—April, it would have been—when they spied a man sitting out on Hammock Beach. You know, just on the outskirts of the village."

Stephanie knew it well. Hammock Beach was a lovely spot, if a little overpopulated with summer people. She couldn't imagine what it would be like after Labor Day, although she would get a chance to see; her internship ran through the 5th of October.

"Well, not exactly *sitting*," Dave amended. "Half-sprawling was how they both put it later on. He was up against one of those litter baskets, don't you know, and their bases are planted down in the sand to keep em from blowing away in a strong wind, but the man's weight had settled back against this one until the can was…" Dave held his hand up to the vertical, then tilted it.

"Until it was like the Leaning Tower of Pisa," Steffi said.

"You got it exactly. Also, he wa'ant hardly dressed for early mornin, with the thermometer readin maybe forty-two degrees and a fresh breeze off the water makin it feel more like *thirty*-two. He was wearin nice gray slacks and a white shirt. Loafers on his feet. No coat. No gloves.

"The youngsters didn't even discuss it. They just ran over to see if he was okay, and right away they knew he wasn't. Johnny said later that he knew the man was dead as soon as he saw his face and Nancy said the same thing, but of course they didn't want to admit it—would you? Without making sure?"

"No," Stephanie said.

"He was just sittin there (well…half-sprawlin there) with one hand in his lap and the other—the right one—lying on the sand. His face was waxy-white except for small purple patches on each cheek. His eyes were closed and Nancy said the lids were bluish. His lips also had a blue cast to them, and his neck, she said, had a kind of *puffy* look to it. His hair was sandy blond, cut short but not so short that a little of it couldn't flutter on his forehead when the wind blew, which it did pretty much constant.

"Nancy says, 'Mister, are you asleep? If you're asleep, you better wake up.'

"Johnny Gravlin says, 'He's not asleep, Nancy, and he's not unconscious, either. He's not breathing.'

"She said later she knew that, she'd seen it, but she didn't want to believe it. Accourse not, poor kid. So she says, 'Maybe he is. Maybe he is asleep. You can't always tell when a person's breathing. Shake him, Johnny, see if he won't wake up.'

"Johnny didn't want to, but he also didn't want to look like a chicken in front of his girlfriend, so he reached down—he had to steel himself to do it, he told me that years later after we'd had a couple of drinks down at the Breakers—and shook the guy's shoulder. He said he knew for sure when he grabbed hold, because it didn't feel like a real shoulder at all under there but like a carving of one. But he shook it all the same and said, 'Wake up, mister, wake up and—' He was gonna say *die right* but thought that wouldn't sound so good under the circumstances (thinkin a little bit like a politician even back then, maybe) and changed it to '—and smell the coffee!'

"He shook twice. First time, nothing happened. Second time, the guy's head fell over on his left shoulder—Johnny had been shakin the right one—and the guy slid off the litter basket that'd been holding him up and went down on his side. His head thumped on the sand. Nancy screamed and ran back to the road, fast as she could…which was fast, I can tell you. If she hadn't've stopped there, Johnny probably would've had to chase her all the way down to the end of Bay Street, and, I dunno, maybe right out to the end of Dock A. But she *did* stop and he caught up to her and put his arm around her and said he was never so glad to feel live flesh underneath his arm. He told me he's never forgotten how it felt to grip that dead man's shoulder, and how it felt like wood under that white shirt."

Dave stopped abruptly, and stood up. "I want a Coca-Cola out of the fridge," he said. "My throat's dry, and this is a long story. Anyone else want one?"

It turned out they all did, and since Stephanie was the one being entertained—if that was the word—she went after the drinks. When she came back, both of the old men were at the porch rail, looking out at the reach and the mainland on the far side. She joined them there, setting the old tin tray down on the wide rail and passing the drinks around.

"Where was I?" Dave asked, after he'd had a long sip of his.

"You know perfectly well where you were," Vince said. "At the part where our future mayor and Nancy Arnault, who's God knows where—probably California, the good ones always seem to finish up about as far from the Island as they can go without needing a passport—had found the Colorado Kid dead on Hammock Beach."

"Ayuh. Well, John was for the two of em runnin right to the nearest phone, which would have been the one outside the Public Library, and callin George Wournos, who was the Moose-Look constable in those days (long since gone to his reward, dear—ticker). Nancy had no problem with that, but she wanted Johnny to set 'the man' up again first. That's what she called him: 'the man.' Never 'the dead man' or 'the body,' always 'the man.'

"Johnny says, 'I don't think the police like you to move them, Nan.'

"Nancy says, 'You *already* moved him, I just want you to put him back where he was.'

"And *he* says, 'I only did it because you told me to.'

"To which *she* answers, '*Please*, Johnny, I can't bear to look at him that way and I can't bear to *think* of him that way.' Then she starts to cry, which of course seals the deal, and he goes back to where the body was, still bent at the waist like it was sitting but now with its left cheek lying on the sand.

"Johnny told me that night at the Breakers that he never could have done what she wanted if she hadn't been right there watchin him and countin on him to do it, and you know, I believe that's so. For a woman a man will do many things that he'd turn his back on in an instant when alone; things he'd back away from, nine times out of ten, even when drunk and with a bunch of his friends egging him on. Johnny said the closer he got to that man lying in the sand—only lying there with his knees up, like he was sitting in an invisible chair—the more sure he was that those closed eyes were going to open and the man was going to make a snatch at him. Knowing that the man was dead didn't take that feeling away, Johnny said, but only made it worse. Still, in the end he got there, and he steeled himself, and he put his hands on those wooden shoulders, and he sat the man back up again with his back against that leaning litter basket. He said he got it in his mind that the litter basket was going to fall over and make a bang, and when it did he'd scream. But the basket didn't fall and he didn't scream. I am convinced in my heart, Steffi, that we poor humans are wired up to always think the worst is gonna happen because it so rarely does. Then what's only lousy seems okay—almost good, in fact—and we can cope just fine."

"Do you really think so?"

"Oh yes, ma'am! In any case, Johnny started away, then saw a pack of cigarettes that had fallen out on the sand. And because the worst was over and it was only lousy, he was able to pick em up—even reminding himself to tell George Wournos what he'd done in case the State Police checked for fingerprints and found his on the cellophane—and put em back in the breast pocket of the dead man's white shirt. Then he went back to where Nancy was standing, hugging herself in her BCHS warmup jacket and dancing from foot to foot, probably cold in those skimpy shorts she was wearing. Although it was more than the cold she was feeling, accourse.

"In any case, she wasn't cold for long, because they ran down to the Public Library then, and I'll bet if anyone had had a stopwatch on em, it would have shown a record time for the half-mile, or close to it. Nancy had lots of quarters in the little change purse she carried in her warmup, and she was the one who called George Wournos, who was just then gettin dressed for work—he owned the Western Auto, which is now where the church ladies hold their bazaars."

Stephanie, who had covered several for Arts 'N Things, nodded.

"George asked her if she was sure the man was dead, and Nancy said yes. Then he asked her to put Johnny on, and he asked Johnny the same question. Johnny also said yes. He said he'd shaken the man and that he was stiff as a board. He told George about how the man had fallen over, and the cigarettes falling out of his pocket, and how he'd put em back in, thinking George might give him hell for that, but he never did. *Nobody* ever did. Not much like a mystery show on TV, was it?"

"Not so far," Stephanie said, thinking it *did* remind her just a teensy bit of a *Murder, She Wrote* episode she'd seen once. Only given the conversation which had prompted this story, she didn't think any Angela Lansbury figures

would be showing up to solve the mystery…although someone must have made *some* progress, Stephanie thought.
Enough, at least, to know where the dead man had come
from.

"George told Johnny that he and Nancy should hurry on
back to the beach and wait for him," Dave said. "Told em
to make sure no one else went close. Johnny said okay.
George said, 'If you miss the seven-thirty ferry, John, I'll
write you and your lady-friend an excuse-note.' Johnny
said that was the last thing in the world he was worried
about. Then he and Nancy Arnault went back up there to
Hammock Beach, only jogging instead of all-out runnin
this time."

Stephanie could understand that. From Hammock Beach
to the edge of Moosie Village was downhill. Going the other
way would have been a tougher run, especially when what
you had to run on was mostly spent adrenaline.

"George Wournos, meanwhile," Vince said, "called Doc
Robinson, over on Beach Lane." He paused, smiling re-
membrance. Or maybe just for effect. "Then he called me."

6

"A murder victim shows up on the island's only public beach and the local law calls the editor of the local newspaper?" Stephanie asked. "Boy, that really *isn't* like *Murder, She Wrote*."

"Life on the Maine coast is rarely like *Murder, She Wrote*," Dave said in his driest tone, "and back then we were pretty much what we are now, Steffi, especially when the summer folk are gone and it's just us chickens—all in it together. That doesn't make it anything romantic, just a kind of…I dunno, call it a sunshine policy. If everyone knows what there is to know, it stops a lot of tongues from a lot of useless wagging. And murder! Law! You're a little bit ahead of yourself there, ain'tcha?"

"Let her off the hook on that one," Vince said. "We put the idea in her head ourselves, talkin about the coffee poisonins over in Tashmore. Steffi, Chris Robinson delivered two of my children. My second wife—Arlette, who I married six years after Joanne died—was good friends with the Robinson family, even dated Chris's brother, Henry, when they were in school together. It was the way Dave says, but it was more than business."

He put his glass of soda (which he called "dope") on the railing and then spread his hands open to either side of his face in a gesture she found both charming and disarming. *I will hide nothing*, it said. "We're a clubby bunch out here. It's always been that way, and I think it always will be, because we'll never grow much bigger than we are now."

"Thank *God*," Dave growled. "No friggin Wal-Mart. Excuse me, Steffi."

She smiled and told him he was excused.

"In any case," Vince said, "I want you to take that idea of murder and set it aside, Steffi. Will you do that?"

"Yes."

"I think you'll find that, in the end, you can't take it off the table or put it all the way back on. That's the way it is with so many things about the Colorado Kid, and what makes it wrong for the Boston *Globe*. Not to mention *Yankee* and *Downeast* and *Coast*. It wasn't even right for *The Weekly Islander*, not really. We *reported* it, oh yes, because we're a newspaper and reporting is our job—I've got Ellen Dunwoodie and the fire hydrant to worry about, not to mention the little Lester boy going to Boston for a kidney transplant—if he lasts long enough, that is—and of course you need to tell folks about the End-Of-Summer Hayride and Dance out at Gernerd Farms, don'tcha?"

"Don't forget the picnic," Stephanie murmured. "It's all the pie you can eat, and folks will want to know that."

The two men laughed. Dave actually patted his chest with his hands to show she had "gotten off a good one," as island folk put it.

"Ayuh, dear!" Vince agreed, still smiling. "But sometimes a thing happens, like two high school kids on their mornin run finding a dead body on the town's prettiest beach, and you say to yourself, 'There must be a *story* in that.' Not just reporting—what, why, when, where, and how, but a *story*—and then you discover there just *isn't*. That it's only a bunch of unconnected facts surrounding a *true* unexplained mystery. And that, dear, is what folks don't want. It upsets em. It's too many waves. It makes em seasick."

"Amen," Dave said. "Now why don't you tell the rest of it, while we've still got some sunshine?"

And Vince Teague did.

7

"We were in on it almost from the beginning—and by *we* I mean Dave and me, *The Weekly Islander*—although I didn't print what I was asked by George Wournos not to print. I had no problem with that, because there was nothing in that business that seemed to affect the island's welfare in any way. That's the sort of judgment call newspaper folk make all the time, Steffi—you'll make it yourself—and in time you get used to it. You just want to make sure you never get comfortable with it.

"The kids went back and guarded the body, not that there was a lot of guardin to be done; before George and Doc Robinson pulled up, they didn't see but four cars, all headed for town, and none of em slowed down when they saw a couple of teenagers joggin in place or doin stretchin exercises there by the little Hammock Beach parkin lot.

"When George and the Doc got there, they sent Johnny and Nancy on their way, and that's where they leave the story. Still curious, the way people are, but on the whole glad to go, I have no doubt. George parked his Ford in the lot, Doc grabbed his bag, and they walked out to where the man was sitting against that litter barrel. He

75

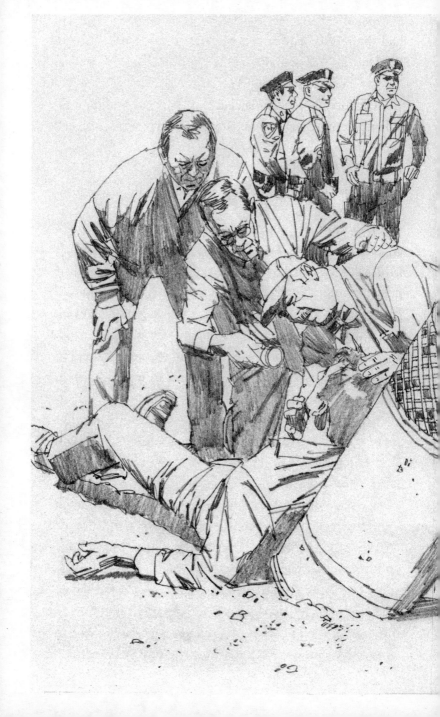

had slumped a little to one side again, and the first thing the Doc did was to haul him up nice and straight.

"'Is he dead, Doc?' George said.

"'Oh gorry, he's been dead at least four hours and probably six or more,' Doc says. (It was right about then that I came pulling in and parked my Chevy beside George's Ford.) 'He's as stiff as a board. *Rigor mortis.*'

"'So you think he's been here since…what? Midnight?' George asks.

"'He coulda been here since last Labor Day, for all I know,' Doc says, 'but the only thing I'm absolutely *sure* of is that he's been dead since two this morning. Because of the *rigor. Probably* he's been dead since midnight, but I'm no expert in stuff like that. If the wind was coming in stiff from offshore, that could have changed when the *rigor* set in—'

"'No wind at all last night,' I says, joining them. 'Calm as the inside of a churchbell.'

"'Well lookit here, another damn country heard from,' says Doc Robinson. 'Maybe you'd like to pronounce the time of death yourself, Jimmy Olsen.'

"'No,' I says, 'I'll leave that to you.'

"'I think I'll leave it to the County Medical Examiner,' he says. 'Cathcart, over in Tinnock. The state pays him an extra eleven grand a year for educated gut-tossin. Not enough, in my humble opinion, but each to his own. I'm just a GP. But…ayuh, this fella was dead by two, I'll say that much. Dead by the time the moon went down.'

"Then for maybe a minute the three of us just stood

there, looking down on him like mourners. A minute can be an awful short space of time under some circumstances, but it can be an awful long one at a time like that. I remember the sound of the wind—still light, but starting to build in a little from the east. When it comes that way and you're on the mainland side of the island, it makes such a lonely sound—"

"I know," Stephanie said quietly. "It kind of hoots."

They nodded. That in the winter it was sometimes a terrible sound, almost the cry of a bereft woman, was a thing she did not know, and there was no reason to tell her.

"At last—I think it was just for something to say—George asked Doc to take a guess as to how old the fella might be.

"'I'd put him right around forty, give or take five years,' he says. 'Do you think so, Vincent?' And I nodded. Forty seemed about right, and it occurred to me that it's too bad for a fella to die at forty, a real shame. It's a man's most anonymous age.

"Then the Doc seen something that interested him. He went down on one knee (which wasn't easy for a man of his size, he had to've gone two-eighty and didn't stand but five-foot-ten or so) and picked up the dead man's right hand, the one that'd been lying on the beach. The fingers were curled a little, as if he'd died trying to make them into a tube he could look through. When Doc held the hand up, we could see some grit stuck to the insides of the fingers and a little more dusted on the palm.

"'What do you see?' George asks. 'Doesn't look like anything but beach-sand to me.'

"'That's all it is, but why's it sticking?' Doc Robinson asks back. 'This litter basket and all the others are planted well above the high-tide line, as anyone with half a brain would know, and there was no rain last night. Sand's dry as a bone. Also, look.'

"He picked up the dead man's left hand. We all observed that he was wearing a wedding ring, and also that there was no sand on his fingers or palm. Doc put that hand back down and picked up the other one again. He tipped it a little so the light shone better on the inside. 'There,' he says. 'Do you see?'

"'What is that?' I ask. 'Grease? A little bit of grease?'

"He smiled and said, 'I think you win the teddy bear, Vincent. And see how his hand is curled?'

"'Yuh—like he was playin spyglass,' George says. By then we was all three on our knees, as if that litter basket was an altar and we were tryin to pray the dead guy back to life.

"'No, I don't think he was playing spyglass,' Doc says, and I realized somethin, Steffi—he was excited in the way people only are when they've figured something out they know the likes of them have no *business* figuring out in the ordinary course of things. He looked into the dead man's face (at least I thought it was his face Doc was lookin at, but it turned out to be a little lower than that), then back at the curled right hand. 'I don't think so at all,' he says.

"'Then what?' George says. 'I want to get this reported to the State Police and the Attorney General's Office, Chris. What I *don't* want is to spend the mornin on my knees while you play Ellery Queen.'

"'See the way his thumb is almost touching his first finger and middle finger?' Doc asks us, and of course we did. 'If this guy had died looking through his rolled-up hand, his thumb would have been *over* his fingers, touching his middle finger and his third finger. Try it yourself, if you don't believe me.'

"I tried it, and I'll be damned if he wasn't right.

"'This isn't a tube,' Doc says, once again touching the dead man's stiff right hand with his own finger. 'This is a *pincers*. Combine that with the grease and those little bits of sand on the palm and the insides of the fingers, and what do you get?'

"I knew, but since George was the law, I let him say it. 'If he was eatin somethin when he died,' he says, 'where the hell is it?'

"Doc pointed to the dead man's neck—which even Nancy Arnault had noticed, and thought of as puffy—and he says, 'I've got an idea that most of it's still right in there where he choked on it. Hand me my bag, Vincent.'

"I handed it over. He tried rummaging through it and found he could only do it one-handed and still keep all that meat balanced on his knees: he was a big man, all right, and he needed to keep at least one hand on the ground to keep himself from tipping over. So he hands the bag over to me and says, 'I've got two otoscopes in there, Vincent— which is to say my little examination lights. There's my everyday and a spare that looks brand-new. We're going to want both of them.'

"'Now, now, I don't know about this,' George says. 'I

thought we were gonna leave all this for Cathcart, on the mainland. He's the guy the state hired for work like this.'

"'I'll take the responsibility,' Doc Robinson said. 'Curiosity killed the cat, you know, but satisfaction brought him back snap-ass happy. You got me out here in the cold and damp without my morning tea or even a slice of toast, and I intend to have a little satisfaction if I can. Maybe I won't be able to. But I have a feeling...Vincent, you take this one. George, you take the new one, and don't drop it in the sand, please and thank you, that's a two hundred-dollar item. Now, I haven't been down on all fours like a little kid playin horsie since I was I'm gonna say seven years old, and if I have to hold the position long I'm apt to fall on top of this fella, so you guys be quick and do just what I say. Have you ever seen how the folks in an art museum will train a couple of pin-spots on a small painting to make it look all bright and pretty?'

"George hadn't, so Doc Robinson explained. When he was done (and was sure George Wournos got it), the island's newspaper editor knelt on one side of that sittin-up corpse and the island's constable knelt on the other, each of us with one of the Doc's little barrel-lights in hand. Only instead of lighting up a work of art, we were going to light up the dead man's throat so Doc could take a look.

"He got himself into position with a fair amount of gruntin and puffing—woulda been funny if the circumstances hadn't been so strange, and if I hadn't been sort of afraid the man was going to have a heart-attack right there —and then he reached out one hand, slipped it into the guy's mouth, and hooked down his jaw like it was a hinge. Which, accourse, when you think about it, is just what it is.

"'Now,' he says. 'Get in close, boys. I don't think he's gonna bite, but if I'm wrong, I'll be the one who pays for the mistake.'

"We got in close and shone the lights down the dead man's gullet. It was just red and black in there, except for his tongue, which was pink. I could hear the Doc puffin and grunting and he says, not to us but to himself, 'A little more,' and he pulled down the lower jaw a little further. Then, to us, 'Lift em up, shine em straight down his gullet,' and we did the best we could. It changed the direction of the light just enough to take the pink off the dead man's tongue and put it on that hanging thing at the back of his mouth, the what-do-you-call-it—"

"Uvula," Stephanie and Dave said at the same time.

Vince nodded. "Ayuh, that. And just beyond it, I could see somethin, or the top of somethin, that was a dark gray. It was only for two or three seconds, but it was enough to satisfy Doc Robinson. He took his fingers out of the dead man's mouth—the lower lip made a kind of plopping sound as it went back against the gum, but the jaw stayed down pretty much where it was—and then he sat back, puffing away six licks to the dozen.

"'You boys are going to have to help me stand up,' he says when he got enough wind so he could talk. 'Both my legs are asleep from the knees on down. Damn, but I'm a fool to weigh this much.'

"'I'll help you up when you tell me,' George says. 'Did

you see anything? Because I didn't see anything. What about you, Vincent?'

"'I thought I did,' I says. The truth is I knew friggin well I did—pardon, Steff—but I didn't want to show him up.

"'Ayuh, it's back there, all right,' Doc says. He still sounded out of breath, but he sounded satisfied, too, like a man who's scratched a troublesome itch. 'Cathcart'll get it out and then we'll know if it's a piece of steak or a piece of pork or a piece of something else, but I don't see that it matters. We know what matters—he came out here with a piece of meat in his hand and sat down to eat it while he watched the moonlight on the reach. Propped his back up against this litter basket. And choked, just like the little Indian in the nursery rhyme. On the last bite of what he brought to snack on? Maybe, but not necessarily.'

"'Once he was dead, a gull could have swooped in and taken what was left right out of his hand,' George says. 'Just left the grease.'

"'Correct,' Doc says. 'Now are you two gonna help me up, or do I have to crawl back over to George's car and pull myself up by the doorhandle?'"

8

"So what do you think, Steffi?" Vince asked, taking a throat-cooling swallow of his Coke. "Mystery solved? Case closed?"

"Not on your granny!" she cried, and barely registered their appreciative laughter. Her eyes were sparkling. "The cause-of-death part, maybe, but…what *was* it, by the way? In his throat? Or would that be getting ahead of the story?"

"Darlin, you can't get ahead of a story that doesn't exist," Vince said, and his eyes were also sparkling. "Ask ahead, behind, or sideways. I'll answer anything. Same with Dave, I imagine."

As if to prove this was indeed so, *The Weekly Islander*'s managing editor said: "It was a piece of beef, probably steak, and very likely from one of your better cuts—your tenderloin, sirloin, or filet mignon. It was cooked medium-rare, and *asphyxiation due to choking* was what went on the death certificate, although the man we have always called the Colorado Kid also had suffered a massive cerebral embolism—your stroke, in other words. Cathcart decided the choking led to the stroking, but who knows, it might have been vicey-versa. So you see, even the cause of death gets slippery when you look at it right up close."

"There's at least one story in here—a little one—and I'm going to tell it to you now," Vince said. "It's about a fella who was in some ways like you, Stephanie, although I like to think you fell into better hands when it came to putting the final polish on your education; more compassionate ones, too. This fella was young—twenty-three, I think— and like you he was from away (the south in his case rather than the Midwest), and he was also doing graduate work, in the field of forensic science."

"So he was working with this Dr. Cathcart, and he figured something out."

Vince grinned. "Logical enough guess, dear, but you're wrong about who he was workin with. His name...what *was* his name, Dave?"

Dave Bowie, whose memory for names was as deadly as Annie Oakley's aim with her rifle, didn't hesitate. "Devane. Paul Devane."

"That's right, I recall it now you say it. This young man, Devane, was assigned to three months of post-graduate field work with a couple of State Police detectives out of the Attorney General's office. Only in his case, *sentenced* might be the better word. They treated him very badly." Vince's eyes darkened. "Older people who use young people badly when all the young people want is to learn—I think folks like that should be put out of their jobs. All too often, though, they get promotions instead of pink-slips. It has never surprised me that God gave the world a little tilt at the same time He set it spinning; so much that goes on here mimics that tilt.

"This young man, this Devane, spent four years at some place like Georgetown University, wanting to learn the sort of science that catches crooks, and right around the time he was coming to bud the luck of the draw sent him to work with a couple of doughnut-eating detectives who turned him into little more than a gofer, running files between Augusta and Waterville and shooing lookie-loos away from car-crash scenes. Oh, maybe once in awhile he got to measure a footprint or take flash photos of a tire-print as a reward. But rarely, I sh'd say. Rarely.

"In any case, Steffi, these two fine specimens of detection—and I hope to God they're long out to pasture—happened to be in Tinnock Village at the same time the body of the Colorado Kid turned up on Hammock Beach. They were investigating an apartment-house fire 'of suspicious origin,' as we say when reporting such things in the paper, and they had their pet boy, who was by then losing his idealism, with them.

"If he'd drawn a couple of the *good* detectives working out of the A.G.'s office—and I've met my share in spite of the goddam bureaucracy that makes so many problems in this state's law enforcement system—or if his Department of Forensic Studies had sent him to some other state that accepts students, he might have ended up one of the fellas you see on that *CSI* show—"

"I like that show," Dave said. "Much more realistic than *Murder, She Wrote*. Who's ready for a muffin? There's some in the pantry."

It turned out they all were, and story-time was suspended

until Dave brought them back, along with a roll of paper towels. When each of them had a Labree's squash muffin and a paper towel to catch the crumbs, Vince told Dave to take up the tale. "Because," he said, "I'm getting preachy and apt to keep us here until dark."

"I thought you was doin good," Dave said.

Vince clapped a bony hand to his even bonier chest. "Call 911, Steffi, my heart just stopped."

"That won't be so funny when it really happens, old-timer," Dave said.

"Lookit him spray those crumbs," Vince said. "You drool at one end of your life and dribble at t'other, my Ma used to say. Go on, Dave, tell on, but do us all a favor and swallow, first."

Dave did, and followed the swallow with a big gulp of Coke to wash everything down. Stephanie hoped her own digestive system would be up to such challenges when she reached David Bowie's age.

"Well," he said, "George didn't bother cordoning off the beach, because that just would have drawn folks like flies to a cowpie, don'tcha know, but that didn't stop those two dummies from the Attorney General's office from doin it. I asked one of em why they bothered, and he looked at me like I was a stark raving natural-born fool. 'Well, it's a crime scene, ain't it?' he says.

"'Maybe so and maybe no,' I says, 'but once the body's gone, what evidence do you think you're gonna have that the wind hasn't blown away?' Because by then that easterly had gotten up awful fresh. But they insisted, and I will admit it made a nice picture on the front page of the paper, didn't it, Vince?"

"Ayuh, picture with tape reading CRIME SCENE in it always sells copies," Vince agreed. Half of his muffin had already disappeared, and there were no crumbs Stephanie could see on his paper towel.

Dave said, "Devane was there while the Medical Examiner, Cathcart, got a look at the body: the hand with the sand on it, the hand with none, and then into the mouth, but right around the time the Tinnock Funeral Home hearse that had come over on the nine o'clock ferry pulled up, those two detectives realized he was still there and might be getting somethin perilously close to an education. They couldn't have that, so they sent him to get coffee and doughnuts and danishes for them and Cathcart and Cathcart's assistant and the two funeral home boys who'd just shown up.

"Devane didn't have any idea of where to go, and by then I was on the wrong side of the tape they'd strung, so I took him down to Jenny's Bakery myself. It took half an hour, maybe a little more, most of it spent ridin, and I got a pretty good idea of how the land lay with that young man, although I give him all points for discretion; he never told a single tale out of school, simply said he wasn't learning as much as he'd hoped to, and seeing the kind of errand he'd been sent on while Cathcart was doing his *in situ* examination, I could connect the dots.

"And when we got back the examination was over. The body had already been zipped away in a body-bag. That didn't stop one of those detectives—a big, beefy guy named

O'Shanny—from giving Devane the rough side of his tongue. 'What took you so long, we're freezin our butts off out here,' on and on, yatta-yatta-yatta.

"Devane stood up to it well—never complain, never explain, someone surely raised him right, I have to say—so I stepped in and said we'd gone and come back as fast as anyone could. I said, 'You wouldn't have wanted us to break any speed laws, now would you, officers?' Hoping to get a little laugh and kind of lighten the situation, you know. Didn't work, though. The other detective—his name was Morrison—said, 'Who asked you, Irving? Haven't you got a yard sale to cover, or something?' His partner got a laugh out of that one, at least, but the young man who was supposed to be learning forensic science and was instead learning that O'Shanny liked white coffee and Morrison took his black, blushed all the way down to his collar.

"Now, Steffi, a man doesn't get to the age I was even then without getting his ass kicked a number of times by fools with a little authority, but I felt terrible for Devane, who was embarrassed not only on his own account but on mine, as well. I could see him looking for some way to apologize to me, but before he could find it (or before I could tell him it wasn't necessary, since it wasn't him that had done anything wrong), O'Shanny took the tray of coffees and handed it to Morrison, then the two sacks of pastries from me. After that he told Devane to duck under the tape and take the evidence bag with the dead man's personal effects in it. 'You sign the Possession Slip,' he says to Devane, like he was talking to a five-year-old, 'and you make sure nobody else so much as touches it until I take it back from you. And keep your nose out of the stuff inside yourself. Have you got all that?'

" 'Yes, sir,' Devane says, and he gives me a little smile. I watched him take the evidence bag, which actually looked like the sort of accordion-folder you see in some offices, from Dr. Cathcart's assistant. I saw him slide the Possession Slip out of the see-through envelope on the front, and...do you understand what that slip's for, Steffi?"

"I think I do," she said. "Isn't it so that if there's a criminal prosecution, and something found at the crime scene is used as evidence in that prosecution, the State can show an uncorrupted chain of possession from where that thing was found to where it finally ended up in some courtroom as Exhibit A?"

"Prettily put," Vince said. "You should be a writer."

"Very amusing," Stephanie said.

"Yes, ma'am, that's our Vincent, a regular Oscar Wilde," Dave said. "At least when he's not bein Oscar the Grouch. Anyway, I saw young Mr. Devane sign his name to the Possession Slip, and I saw him put it back into the sleeve on the front of the evidence bag. Then I saw him turn to watch those strongboys load the body into the funeral hack. Vince had already come back here to start writin his story, and that was when I left, too, telling the people who asked me questions—quite a few had gathered by then, drawn by that stupid yellow tape like ants to spilled sugar—that they could read all about it for just a quarter, which is what the *Islander* went for in those days.

"Anyway, that was the last time I actually saw Paul Devane, standing there and watchin those two widebodies load the dead man into the hearse. But I happen to know Devane disobeyed O'Shanny's order not to look in the evdence bag, because he called me at the *Islander* about sixteen months later. By then he'd given up his forensic science dream and gone back to school to become a lawyer. Good or bad, that particular course correction's down to A.G. Detectives O'Shanny and Morrison, but it was still Paul Devane who turned the Hammock Beach John Doe into the Colorado Kid, and eventually made it possible for the police to identify him."

"And we got the scoop," Vince said. "In large part because Dave Bowie here bought that young man a doughnut and gave him what money *can't* buy: an understanding ear and a little sympathy."

"Oh, that's layin it on a little thick," Dave said, shifting around in his seat. "I wa'nt with him more than thirty minutes. Maybe three-quarters of an hour if you want to add in the time we stood in line at the bakery."

"Sometimes maybe that's enough," Stephanie said.

Dave said, "Ayuh, sometimes maybe it is, and what's so wrong about that? How long do you think it takes a man to choke to death on a piece of meat, and then be dead forever?"

None of them had an answer to that. On the reach, some rich summer man's yacht tooted with hollow self-importance as it approached the Tinnock town dock.

9

"Let Paul Devane alone awhile," Vince said. "Dave can tell you the rest of that part in a few minutes. I think maybe I ought to tell you about the gut-tossing first."

"Ayuh," Dave said. "It ain't a story, Steff, but that part'd probably come next if it was."

Vince said, "Don't get the idea that Cathcart did the autopsy right away, because he didn't. There'd been two people killed in the apartment house fire that brought O'Shanny and Morrison to our neck of the woods to begin with, and they came first. Not just because they died first, but because they were murder victims and John Doe looked like being just an accident victim. By the time Cathcart *did* get to John Doe, the detectives were gone back to Augusta, and good riddance to them.

"I was there for that autopsy when it finally happened, because I was the closest thing there was to a professional photographer in the area back in those days, and they wanted a 'sleeping ID' of the guy. That's a European term, and all it means is a kind of portrait shot presentable enough to go into the newspapers. It's supposed to make the corpse look like he's actually snoozin.'"

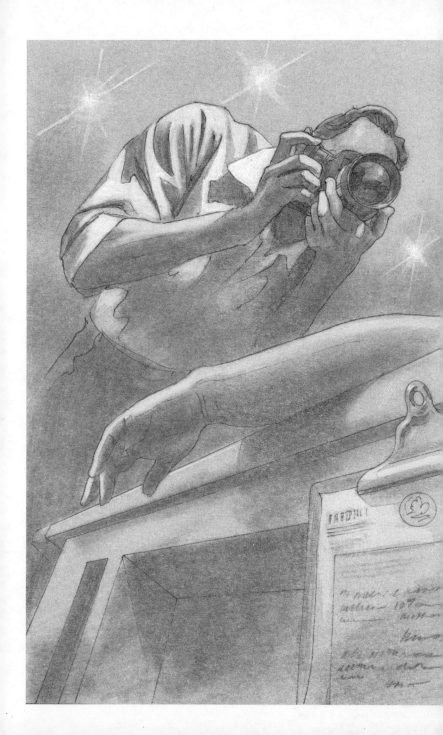

Stephanie looked both interested and appalled. "Does it work?"

"No," Vince said. Then: "Well…p'raps to a kid. Or if you was to look at it quick, and with one eye winked shut. This one had to be done before the autopsy, because Cathcart thought maybe, with the throat blockage and all, he might have to stretch the lower jaw too far."

"And you didn't think it would look quite so much like he was sleeping if he had a belt tied around his chin to keep his mouth shut?" Stephanie asked, smiling in spite of herself. It was awful that such a thing should be funny, but it *was* funny; some appalling creature in her mind insisted on popping up one sicko cartoon image after another.

"Nope, probably not," Vince agreed, and he was also smiling. Dave, too. So if she was sick, she wasn't the only one. Thank God. "What such a thing'd look like, I think, would be a corpse with a toothache."

Then they were all laughing. Stephanie thought that she loved these two old buzzards, she really did.

"Got to laugh at the Reaper," Vince said, plucking his glass of Coke off the railing. He helped himself to a sip, then put it back. "Especially when you're my age. I sense that bugger behind every door, and smell his breath on the pillow beside me where my wives used to lay their heads— God bless em both—when I put out my light.

"*Got* to laugh at the Reaper.

"Anyway, Steffi, I took my head-shots—my 'sleeping IDs'—and they came out about as you'd expect. The best one made the fella look like he mighta been sleepin off a bad drunk or was maybe in a coma, and that was the one we ran a week later. They also ran it in the Bangor *Daily News*, plus the Ellsworth and Portland papers. Didn't do any good, of course, not as far as scarin up people who knew him, at least, and we eventually found out there was a perfectly good reason for that.

"In the meantime, though, Cathcart went on about his business, and with those two dumbbells from Augusta gone back to where they came from, he had no objections to me hangin around, as long as I didn't put it in the paper that he'd let me. I said accourse I wouldn't, and accourse I never did.

"Working from the top down, there was first that plug of steak Doc Robinson had already seen in the guy's throat. 'That's your cause of death right there, Vince,' Cathcart said, and the cerebral embolism (which he discovered long after I'd left to catch the ferry back to Moosie) never changed his mind. He said that if the guy had had someone there to perform the Heimlich Maneuver—or if he'd performed it on himself—he might never have wound up on the steel table with the gutters running down the sides.

"Next, Contents of the Stomach Number One, and by that I mean the stuff on top, the midnight snack that had barely had a chance to start digesting when our man died and everything shut down. Just steak. Maybe six or seven bites in all, well-chewed. Cathcart thought maybe as much as four ounces.

"Finally, Contents of the Stomach Number Two, and here I'm talking about our man's supper. This stuff was pretty much—well, I don't want to go into details here; let's just say that the digestive process had gone on long enough so that all Dr. Cathcart could tell for sure without extensive testing was that the guy had had some sort of fish dinner, probably with a salad and french fries, around six or seven hours before he died.

"'I'm no Sherlock Holmes, Doc,' I says, 'but I can go you one better than that.'

"'Really?' he says, kinda skeptical.

"'Ayuh,' I says. 'I think he had his supper either at Curly's or Jan's Wharfside over here, or Yanko's on Moose-Look.'

"'Why one of those, when there's got to be fifty restaurants within a twenty-mile radius of where we're standin that sell fish dinners, even in April?' he asks. 'Why not the Grey Gull, for that matter?'

"'Because the Grey Gull would not stoop to selling fish and chips,' I says, 'and that's what this guy had.'

"Now Steffi—I'd done okay through most of the autopsy, but right about then I started feeling decidedly chuck-upsy. 'Those three places I mentioned sell fish and chips,' I says, 'and I could smell the vinegar as soon as you cut his stomach open.' Then I had to rush into his little bathroom and throw up.

"But I was right. I developed my 'sleeping ID' pictures that night and showed em around at the places that sold fish and chips the very next day. No one at Yanko's recognized him, but the take-out girl at Jan's Wharfside knew him right away. She said she served him a fish-and-chips basket, plus a Coke or a Diet Coke, she couldn't remember

97

which, late on the afternoon before he was found. He took it to one of the tables and sat eating and looking out at the water. I asked if he said anything, and she said not really, just please and thank you. I asked if she noticed where he went when he finished his meal—which he ate around five-thirty—and she said no."

He looked at Stephanie. "My guess is probably down to the town dock, to catch the six o'clock ferry to Moosie. The time would have been just about right."

"Ayuh, that's what I've always figured," Dave said.

Stephanie sat up straight as something occurred to her. "It was April. The middle of April on the coast of Maine, but he had no coat on when he was found. Was he wearing a coat when he was served at Jan's?"

Both of the old men grinned at her as if she had just solved some complicated equation. Only, Stephanie knew, their business—even at the humble *Weekly Islander* level— was less about solving than it was delineating what *needed* to be solved.

"That's a good question," Vince said.

"Lovely question," Dave agreed.

"I was saving that part," Vince said, "but since there's no *story*, exactly, saving the good parts doesn't matter...and if you want answers, dear heart, the store is closed. The take-out girl at Jan's didn't remember for sure, and no one else remembered him at all. I suppose we have to count our-selves lucky, in a way; had he bellied up to that counter in mid-July, when such places have a million people in em, all wanting fish-and-chips baskets, lobster rolls, and ice cream sundaes, she wouldn't have remembered him at all unless he'd dropped his trousers and mooned her."

"Maybe not even then," Stephanie said.

"That's true. As it was, she *did* remember him, but not if he was wearing a coat. I didn't press her too hard on it, either, knowin that if I did she might remember somethin just to please me…or to get me out of her hair. She said 'I seem to recall he was wearing a light green jacket, Mr. Teague, but that could be wrong.' And maybe it *was* wrong, but do you know…I tend to think she was right. That he was wearing such a jacket."

"Then where was it?" Stephanie asked. "Did such a jacket ever turn up?"

"No," Dave said, "so maybe there *was* no jacket…although what he was doing outside on a raw seacoast night in April without one certainly beggars *my* imagination."

Stephanie turned back to Vince, suddenly with a thousand questions, all urgent, none fully articulated.

"What are you smiling about, dear?" Vince asked.

"I don't know." She paused. "Yes, I do. I have so god-damned many questions I don't know which one to ask first."

Both of the old men whooped at that one. Dave actually fished a big handkerchief out of his back pocket and mopped his eyes with it. "Ain't that a corker!" he exclaimed. "Yes, ma'am! I tell you what, Steff: why don't you pretend you're drawin for the Tupperware set at the Ladies Auxiliary Autumn Sale? Just close your eyes and pick one out of the goldfish bowl."

"All right," she said, and although she didn't quite do that, it was close. "What about the dead man's fingerprints? And his dental records? I thought that when it came to identifying dead people, those things were pretty much infallible."

"Most people do and probably they are," Vince said, "but you have to remember this was 1980, Steff." He was still smiling, but his eyes were serious. "Before the computer revolution, and *long* before the Internet, that marvelous tool young folks such as yourself take for granted. In 1980, you could check the prints and dental records of what police departments call an unsub—an unknown subject—against those of a person you thought your unsub might be, but checkin em against the prints or dental records of all the wanted felons on file in all the police departments would have taken years, and against those of all the folks reported disappeared every year in the United States? Even if you narrowed the list down to just men in their thirties and forties? Not possible, dear."

"But I thought the armed forces kept computer records, even back then…"

"I don't think so," Vince said. "And if they did, I don't believe the Kid's prints were ever sent to them."

"In any case, the initial ID didn't come from the man's fingerprints or dental work," Dave said. He laced his fingers over his considerable chest and appeared almost to preen in the day's late sunshine, now slanting but still warm. "I believe that's known as cuttin to the chase."

"So where *did* it come from?"

"That brings us back to Paul Devane," Vince said, "and I *like* coming back to Paul Devane, because, as I said, there's a story there, and stories are my business. They're my *beat*, we would have said back in the old, old days. Devane's a little sip of Horatio Alger, small but satisfying. *Strive and Succeed. Work and Win.*"

"*Piss and Vinegar*," Dave suggested.

"If you like," Vince said evenly. "Sure, ayuh, if you like. Devane goes off with those two stupid cops, O'Shanny and Morrison, as soon as Cathcart gives them the preliminary report on the burn victims from the apartment house fire, because they don't give a heck about some accidental choking victim who died over on Moose-Lookit Island. Cathcart, meanwhile, does his gut-tossing on John Doe with yours truly in attendance. Onto the death certificate goes *asphyxiation due to choking* or the medical equivalent thereof. Into the newspapers goes my 'sleeping ID' photo, which our Victorian ancestors much more truthfully called a 'death portrait.' And no one calls the Attorney General's Office or the State Police barracks in Augusta to say that's their missing father or uncle or brother.

"Tinnock Funeral Home keeps him in their cooler for six days—it's not the law, but like s'many things in matters of this sort, Steffi, you discover it's an accepted custom. Everybody in the death-business knows it, even if nobody knows *why*. At the end of that period, when he was still John Doe and still unclaimed, Abe Carvey went on ahead and embalmed him. He was put into the funeral home's own crypt at Seaview Cemetery—"

"This part's rather creepy," Stephanie said. She found she could see the man in there, for some reason not in a coffin (although he must surely have been provided with some sort of cheap box) but simply laid on a stone slab with a sheet over him. An unclaimed package in a post office of the dead.

"Ayuh, 'tis, a bit," Vince said levelly. "Do you want me to push on?"

"If you stop now, I'll kill you," she said.

He nodded, not smiling now but pleased with her just the same. She didn't know how she knew that, but she did.

"He boarded the summer and half the fall in there. Then, when November come around and the body was still un-named and unclaimed, they decided they ought to bury him." In Vince's Yankee accent, *bury* rhymed with *furry*. "Before the ground stiffened up again and made digging particularly hard, don't you see."

"I do," Stephanie said quietly. And she did. This time she didn't sense the telepathy between the two old men, but perhaps it was there, because Dave took up the tale (such tale as there was) with no prompting from the *Islander*'s senior editor.

"Devane finished out his tour with O'Shanny and Mor-rison to the bitter end," he said. "He probably even gave them each a tie or something at the end of his three months or his quarter or whatever it was; as I think I told you, Stephanie, there was no quit in that young fella. But as soon as he was finished, he put in his paperwork at what-ever his college was—I *think* he told me Georgetown, but you mustn't hold me to that—and started back up again, taking whatever courses he needed for law school. And except for two things, that might have been where Mr. Paul Devane leaves this story—which, as Vince says, isn't a story at all, except maybe for this part. The first thing is that Devane peeked into the evidence bag at some point, and looked over John Doe's personal effects. The second is that he got serious about a girl, and she took him home to meet her parents, as girls often do when things get serious, and this girl's father had at least one bad habit that was more common then than it is now. He smoked cigarettes."

Stephanie's mind, which was a good one (both of the men knew this), at once flashed upon the pack of cigarettes that had fallen onto the sand of Hammock Beach when the dead man fell over. Johnny Gravlin (now Moose-Look's mayor) had picked it up and put it back into the dead man's pocket. And then something else came to her, not in a flash but in a blinding glare. She jerked as if stung. One of her feet struck the side of her glass and knocked it over. Coke fizzed across the weathered boards of the porch and dripped between them to the rocks and weeds far below. The old men didn't notice. They knew a state of grace perfectly well when they saw one, and were watching their intern with interest and delight.

"The tax-stamp!" she nearly shrieked. *"There's a state tax-stamp on the bottom of every pack!"*

They both applauded her, gently but sincerely.

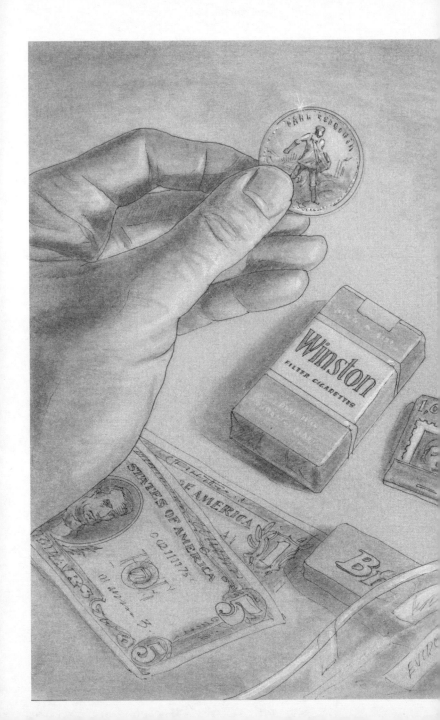

10

Dave said, "Let me tell you what young Mr. Devane saw when he took his forbidden peek into the evidence bag, Steffi—and I have no doubt he took that look more to spite those two than because he actually believed he'd see anything of value in such a scanty collection of stuff. To start with, there was John Doe's wedding ring; a plain gold band, no engraving, not even a date."

"They didn't leave it on his…" She saw the way the two men were looking at her, and it made her realize that what she was suggesting was foolish. If the man was identified, the ring would be returned. He might then be committed to the ground with it on his finger, if that was what his surviving family wanted. But until then it was evidence, and had to be treated as such.

"No," she said. "Of course not. Silly me. One thing, though—there must have been a Mrs. Doe somewhere. Or a Mrs. Kid. Yes?"

"Yes," Vince Teague said, rather heavily. "And we found her. Eventually."

"And were there little Does?" Stephanie asked, thinking that the man had been the right age for a whole gaggle of them.

"Let's not get stuck on that part of it just now, if you please," Dave said.

"Oh," Stephanie said. "Sorry."

"Nothing to be sorry about," he said, smiling a little. "Just don't want to lose m'place. It's easier to do when there's no… what would you call it, Vincent?"

"No through-line," Vince said. He was smiling, too, but his eyes were a little distant. Stephanie wondered if it was the thought of the little Does that had put that distance there.

"Nope, no through-line t'all," Dave said. He thought, then proved how little he'd lost his place by ticking items rapidly off on his fingers. "Contents of the bag was the deceased's weddin-ring, seventeen dollars in paper money —a ten, a five, and two ones—plus some assorted change that might have added up to a buck. Also, Devane said, one coin that wasn't American. He said he thought the writing on it was Russian."

"Russian," she marveled.

"What's called Cyrillic," Vince murmured.

Dave pressed ahead. "There was a roll of Certs and a pack of Big Red chewin gum with all but one stick gone. There was a book of matches with an ad for stamp-collectin on the front—I'm sure you've seen that kind, they hand em out at every convenience store—and Devane said he could see a strike-mark on the strip across the bottom for that purpose, pink and bright. And then there was that pack of cigarettes, open and with one or two cigarettes gone. Devane thought only one, and the single strike-mark on the matchbook seemed to bear that out, he said."

"But no wallet," Stephanie said.

"No, ma'am."

"And absolutely no identification."

"No."

"Did anyone theorize that maybe someone came along and stole Mr. Doe's last piece of steak *and* his wallet?" she asked, and a little giggle got out before she could put her hand over her mouth.

"Steffi, we tried that and everything else," Vince said. "Including the idea that maybe he got dropped off on Hammock Beach by one of the Coast Lights."

"Some sixteen months after Johnny Gravlin and Nancy Arnault found that fella," Dave resumed, "Paul Devane was invited to spend a weekend at his lady-friend's house in Pennsylvania. I have to think that Moose-Lookit Island, Hammock Beach, and John Doe were all about the last things on his mind just then. He said he and the girlfriend were going out for the evening, to a movie or somethin. Mother and Dad were in the kitchen, finishin the supper dishes—'doin the ridding-up' is what we say in these parts— and although Paul had offered to help, he'd been banished to the living room on the grounds of not knowin where anything went. So he was sittin there, watchin whatever was on the TV, and he happened to glance over at Poppa Bear's easy-chair, and there on Poppa Bear's little endtable, right next to Poppa Bear's *TV Guide* and Poppa Bear's ash-tray, was Poppa Bear's pack of smokes."

He paused, giving her a smile and a shrug.

"It's funny how things work, sometimes; it makes you

wonder how often they *don't*. If that pack had been turned a different way—so the top had been facing him instead of the bottom—John Doe might have gone on being John Doe instead of first the Colorado Kid and then Mr. James Cogan of Nederland, a town just west of Boulder. But the bottom of the pack *was* facing him, and he saw the stamp on it. It was a *stamp*, like a postage stamp, and that made him think of the pack of cigarettes in the evidence bag that day.

"You see, Steffi, one of Paul Devane's minders—I disremember if it was O'Shanny or Morrison—had been a smoker, and among Paul's other chores, he'd bought this fella a fair smack of Camel cigarettes, and while they also had a stamp on them, it seemed to him it wasn't the same as the one on the pack in the evidence bag. It seemed to him that the stamp on the State of Maine cigarettes he bought for the detective was an *ink* stamp, like the kind you sometimes get on your hand when you go to a small-town dance, or...I dunno..."

"To the Gernerd Farms Hayride and Picnic?" she asked, smiling.

"You got it!" he said, pointing a plump finger at her like a gun. "Anyway, this wa'nt the kind of thing where you jump up yelling 'Eureka! I have found it!', but his mind kep' returnin to it over and over again that weekend, because the memory of those cigarettes in the evidence bag bothered him. For one thing, it seemed to Paul Devane that John Doe's cigarettes certainly *should* have had a Maine tax-stamp on them, no matter where he came from."

"Why?"

"Because there was only one gone. What kind of cigarette smoker only smokes one in six hours?"

"A light one?"

"A man who has a full pack and don't take but one cigarette out of it in six hours ain't a light smoker, that's a *non-*smoker," Vince said mildly. "Also, Devane saw the man's tongue. So did I—I was on my knees in front of him, shining Doc Robinson's otoscope into his mouth. It was as pink as peppermint candy. Not a smoker's tongue at all."

"Oh, and the matchbook," Stephanie said thoughtfully. "One strike?"

Vince Teague was smiling at her. Smiling and nodding. "One strike," he said.

"No lighter?"

"No lighter." Both men said it together, then laughed.

11

"Devane waited until Monday," Dave said, "and when the business about the cigarettes still wouldn't quit nagging him—wouldn't quit even though he was almost a year and a half downriver from that part of his life—he called me on the telephone and explained to me that he had an idea that maybe, just *maybe*, the pack of cigarettes John Doe had been carrying around hadn't come from the State of Maine. If not, the stamp on the bottom would show where they *had* come from. He voiced his doubts about whether John Doe was a smoker at all, but said the tax-stamp might be a clue even if he wasn't. I agreed with him, but was curious as to why he'd called me. He said he couldn't think of anyone else who still might be interested at that late date. He was right, I *was* still interested—Vince, too—and he turned out to be right about the stamp, as well.

"Now, I am not a smoker myself and never have been, which is probably one of the reasons I've attained the great age of sixty-five in such beautiful shape—"

Vince grunted and waved a hand at him. Dave continued, unperturbed.

"—so I made a little trip downstreet to Bayside News and asked if I could examine a package of cigarettes. My request was granted, and I observed that there was indeed an *ink* stamp on the bottom, not a postage-type stamp. I then made a call to the Attorney General's Office and spoke to a fellow name of Murray in a department called Evidence Storage and Filing. I was as diplomatic as I could possibly be, Stephanie, because at that time those two dumbbell detectives would still have been on active duty—"

"And they'd overlooked a potentially valuable clue, hadn't they?" Steff asked. "One that could have narrowed the search for John Doe down to one single state. And it was practically staring them in the face."

"Yep," Vince said, "and no way could they blame their intern, either, because they'd specifically told him to keep his nose out of the evidence bag. Plus, by the time it became clear that he'd disobeyed them—"

"—he was beyond their reach," she finished.

"You said it," Dave agreed. "But they wouldn't have gotten much of a scolding in any case. Remember, they had an actual murder investigation going over in Tinnock— manslaughter, two folks burned to death—and John Doe was just a choking victim."

"Still…" Stephanie looked doubtful.

"Still dumb, and you needn't be too polite to say it, you're among friends," Dave told her with a grin. "But the *Islander* had no in'trest in makin trouble for those two detectives. I made that clear to Murray, and I also made it clear that this wasn't a criminal matter; all I was doing was tryin my best to find out who the poor fella was, because someplace there were very likely people missin him and wantin to know what had befallen him. Murray said he'd have to get back to me on that, which I kinda expected, but I still had a bad afternoon, wonderin if maybe I should have played my cards a little different. I could have, you know; I could have had Doc Robinson make the call to Augusta, or maybe even talked Cathcart into doing it, but the idea of using either of them as a cat's paw kind of went against my grain. I s'pose it's corny, but I really do believe that in nine cases out of ten, honesty's the best policy. I was just worried this one might turn out to be the tenth.

"In the end, though, it came out all right. Murray called me back just after I'd made up my mind he wasn't going to and had started pullin on my jacket to go home for the day—isn't that the way things like that usually go?"

"A watched pot never boils," Vince said.

"My gosh, that's like poitry, give me a pad and a pencil so I can write it down," Dave said, grinning more widely than ever. The grin did more than take years off his face; it knocked them flying, and she could see the boy he had been. Then he grew serious once more, and the boy disappeared again.

"In big cities evidence gets lost all the time, I understand, but I guess Augusta's not that big yet, even if it is the state capital. Sergeant Murray had no trouble whatsoever finding the evidence bag with Paul Devane's signature on the Possession Slip; he said he had it ten minutes after we got done talking. The rest of the time that went by he was trying to get permission from the right person to let me know what was inside it…which he finally did. The cigarettes were Winstons, and the stamp on the bottom was just the way Paul Devane remembered: a regular little stick-on type that said COLORADO in tiny dark letters. Murray said he'd be turning the information over to the Attorney General's office, and they'd appreciate knowing 'in advance of publication' if we got anywhere in identifying the Colorado Kid. That's what he called him, so I guess you could say it was Sergeant Murray in the A.G.'s Evidence Storage and Filing Department who coined the phrase. He also said he hoped that if we *did* have any luck identifying the guy, that we'd note in our story that the A.G.'s office had been helpful. You know, I thought that was sort of sweet."

Stephanie leaned forward, eyes shining, totally absorbed. "So what did you do next? How did you proceed?"

Dave opened his mouth to reply, and Vince put a hand on the managing editor's burly shoulder to stop him before he could. "How do you *think* we proceeded, dear?"

"School is in?" she asked.

"'Tis," he said.

And because she saw by his eyes and the set of his mouth (more by the latter) that he was absolutely in earnest, she thought carefully before replying.

"You…made copies of the 'sleeping ID'—"

"Ayuh. We did."

"And then…mmm…you sent it with clippings to—how many Colorado papers?"

He smiled at her, nodded, gave her a thumbs-up. "Seventy-eight, Ms. McCann, and I don't know about Dave, but I was amazed at how cheap it had become to send out such a number of duplications, even back in 1981. Why, it couldn't have come to a hundred bucks total out-of-pocket expense, even with the postage."

"And of course we wrote it all off to the business," said Dave, who doubled as the *Islander*'s bookkeeper. "Every penny. As we had every right to do."

"How many of them ran it?"

"Every frickin one!" Vince said, and fetched his narrow thigh a vicious slap. "Ayuh! Even the Denver *Post* and the Rocky Mountain *News*! Because *then* there was only one peculiar thing about it and a *beautiful* through-line, don't you see?"

Stephanie nodded. Simple and beautiful. She did see.

Vince nodded back, absolutely beaming. "Unknown man, maybe from Colorado, found on an island beach in Maine, two thousand miles away! No mention of the steak stuck halfway down his gullet, no mention of the coat that might have gotten off Jimmy-Jesus-knows-where (or might not have been there at all), no mention of the Russian coin in his pocket! Just the Colorado Kid, your basic Unexplained Mystery, and so, sure, they *all* ran it, even the free ones that are mostly coupons."

"And two days after the Boulder newspaper ran it near the end of October 1981," Dave said, "I got a call from a woman named Arla Cogan. She lived in Nederland, a little way up in the mountains from Boulder, and her husband had disappeared in April of the previous year, leaving her and a son who had been six months old at the time of his disappearance. She said his name was James, and although she had no idea what he could possibly have been doing on an island off the coast of Maine, the photograph in the *Camera* looked a great deal like her husband. A great deal, indeed." He paused. "I guess she knew it was more than just a passin resemblance, because she got about that far and then began to cry."

12

Stephanie asked Dave to spell Mrs. Cogan's first name. In Dave Bowie's thick Maine accent, all she was hearing was a bunch of *a*-sounds with an *l* in the middle.

He did so, then said, "She didn't have his fingerprints—accourse not, poor left-behind thing—but she was able to give me the name of the dentist they used, and—"

"Wait, wait, wait," Stephanie said, putting her hand up like a traffic cop. "This man Cogan, what did he do for a living?"

"He was a commercial artist in a Denver advertising agency," Vince said. "I've seen some of his work since, and I'd have to say he was a pretty good one. He was never going to go nationwide, but if you wanted a quick picture for an advertising circular that showed a woman holdin a roll of toilet tissue up like she'd just caught herself a prize trout, Cogan was your man. He commuted to Denver twice a week, on Tuesdays and Wednesdays, for meetings and product conferences. The rest of the time he worked at home."

She switched her gaze back to Dave. "The dentist spoke to Cathcart, the Medical Examiner. Is that right?"

"You're hittin on all cyclinders, Steff. Cathcart didn't

have any X-rays of the Kid's dental work, he wasn't set up for that and saw no reason to send the corpse out to County Memorial where dental X-rays could have been taken, but he noted all the fillings, plus the two crowns. Everything matched. He then went on ahead and sent copies of the dead man's fingerprints to the Nederland Police, who got a tech from the Denver P.D. to go out to the Cogan residence and dust James Cogan's home office for prints. Mrs. Cogan—Arla—told the fingerprint man he wouldn't find anything, that she'd cleaned the whole works from stem to stern when she'd finally admitted to herself that her Jim wasn't coming back, that he'd either left her, which she could hardly believe, or that something awful had happened to him, which she was *coming* to believe.

"The fingerprint man said that if Cogan had spent 'a significant amount of time' in the room that had been his study, there would still be prints." Dave paused, sighed, ran a hand through what remained of his hair. "There were, and we knew for sure who John Doe, also known as the Colorado Kid, really was: James Cogan, age forty-two, of Nederland, Colorado, married to Arla Cogan, father of Michael Cogan, age six months at the time of his father's disappearance, age going on two years at the time of his father's identification."

Vince stood up and stretched with his fisted hands in the small of his back. "What do you say we go inside, people? It's commencing to get a tiny bit chilly out here, and there's a little more to tell."

13

They each took a turn at the rest room hidden in an alcove behind the old offset press that they no longer used (the paper was now printed in Ellsworth, and had been since '02). While Dave took his turn, Stephanie put on the Mr. Coffee. If the story-that-was-not-a-story went on another hour or so (and she had a feeling it might), they'd all be glad of a cup.

When they were reconvened, Dave sniffed in the direction of the little kitchenette and nodded approvingly. "I like a woman who hasn't decided the kitchen's a place of slavery just because she works for a livin."

"I feel absolutely the same way about a man," Stephanie said, and when he laughed and nodded (she had gotten off another good one, two in one afternoon, a record), she tilted her own head toward the huge old press. "*That* thing looks like a place of slavery to me," she said.

"It looks worse than it ever was," Vince said, "but the one before it was a horror. That one'd take your arm off if you weren't careful, and make a damn good snatch at it even if you were. Now where were we?"

"With the woman who'd just found out she was a widow," Stephanie said. "I presume she came to get the body?"

"Yep," Dave said.

"And did one of you fetch her here from the airport in Bangor?"

"What do you think, dear?"

It wasn't a question Stephanie had to mull over for very long. By late October or early November of 1981, the Colorado Kid would have been very old business to the State of Maine authorities…and as a choking victim, he had been very minor business to begin with. Just an unidentified dead body, really.

"Of course you did. You two were really the only friends she had in the state of Maine." This idea had the odd effect of making her realize that Arla Cogan had been (and, somewhere, almost certainly still was) a real person, and not just a chess-piece in an Agatha Christie whodunit or an episode of *Murder, She Wrote*.

"I went," Vince said, speaking softly. He sat forward in his chair, looking at his hands, which were clasped in a driftwood gnarl below his knees. "She wasn't what I expected, either. I had a picture built in my head, one based on a wrong idea. I should have known better. I've been in the newspaper business sixty-five years—as long as my partner in crime there's been alive, and he's no longer the gay blade he thinks he is—and in that length of time, I've seen my share of dead bodies. Most of em would put all that romantic poetry stuff—'I saw a maiden fair and still'— out of your head in damn short order. Dead bodies are ugly things indeed, by n large; many hardly look human at all anymore. But that wasn't true of the Colorado Kid. He looked almost good enough to be the subject of one of those romantic poimes by Mr. Poe. I photographed him before the autopsy, accourse, you have to remember that, and if you stared at the finished portrait for more'n a second or two, he still looked deader than hell (at least to me he did), but yes, there was something kinda handsome about him just the same, with his ashy cheeks and pale lips and that little touch of lavender on his eyelids."

"Brrr," Stephanie said, but she sort of knew what Vince was saying, and yes, it was a poem by Poe it called to mind. The one about the lost Lenore.

"Ayuh, sounds like true love t'me," Dave said, and got up to pour the coffee.

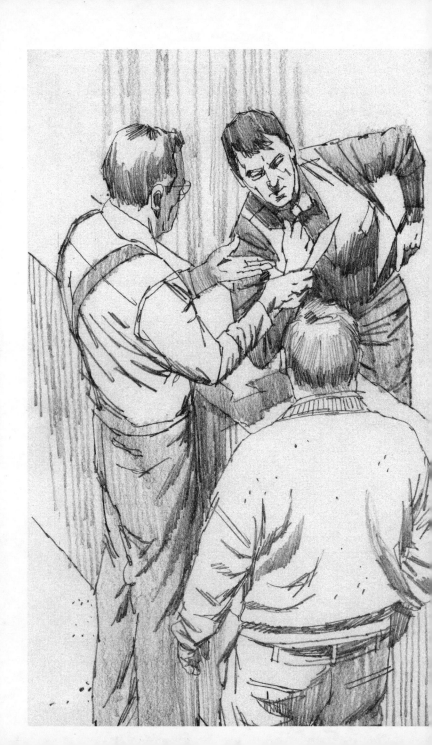

14

Vince Teague dumped what looked to Stephanie like half a carton of Half 'N Half into his, then went on. He did so with a rather rueful smile.

"All I'm trying to say is that I sort expected a pale and dark-haired beauty. What I got was a chubby redhead with a lot of freckles. I never doubted her grief and worry for a minute, but I sh'd guess she was one of those who eats rather than fasts when the rats gnaw at her nerves. Her folks had come from Omaha or Des Moines or somewhere to watch out for the baby, and I'll never forget how lost n somehow alone she looked when she came out of the jet-way, holdin her little carry-on bag not by her side but up to her pouter-pigeon bosom. She wasn't a bit what I expected, not the lost Lenore—"

Stephanie jumped and thought, *Maybe now the telepathy goes three ways.*

"—but I knew who she was, right away. I waved and she came to me and said, 'Mr. Teague?' And when I said yes, that's who I was, she put down her bag and hugged me and said, 'Thank you for coming to meet me. Thank you for everything. I can't believe it's him, but when I look at the picture, I know it is.'

"It's a good long drive down here—no one knows that better than you, Steff—and we had lots of time to talk. The first thing she asked me was if I had any idea what Jim was doing on the coast of Maine. I told her I did not. Then she asked if he'd registered at a local motel on the Wednesday night—" He broke off and looked at Dave. "Am I right? Wednesday night?"

Dave nodded. "It would have been a Wednesday night she asked about, because it was a Thursday mornin Johnny and Nancy found him on. The 24th of April, 1980."

"You just *know* that," Stephanie marveled.

Dave shrugged. "Stuff like that sticks in my head," he told her, "and then I'll forget the loaf of bread I meant to bring home and have to go out in the rain and get it."

Stephanie turned back to Vince. "Surely he *didn't* register at a motel the night before he was found, or you guys wouldn't have spent so long calling him John Doe. You might have known him by some other alias, but no one registers at a motel under *that* name."

He was nodding long before she finished. "Dave and I spent three or four weeks after the Colorado Kid was found —in our spare time, accourse—canvassin motels in what Mr. Yeats would have called 'a widenin gyre' with Moose-Lookit Island at the center. It would've been damn near impossible during the summer season, when there's four hundred motels, inns, cabins, bed-and-breakfasts, and assorted rooms to rent all competing for trade within half a day's drive of the Tinnock Ferry, but it wasn't anything but a part-time job in April, because seventy percent of em are shut down from Thanksgiving to Memorial Day. We showed that picture everywhere, Steffi."

"No joy?"

"Not a bit of it," Dave confirmed.

She turned to Vince. "What did she say when you told her that?"

"Nothing. She was flummoxed." He paused. "Cried a little."

"Accourse she did, poor thing," Dave said.

"And what did you do?" Stephanie asked, all of her attention still fixed on Vince.

"My job," he said, with no hesitation.

"Because you're the one who always has to know," she said.

His bushy, tangled eyebrows went up. "Do you think so?"

"Yes," she said. "I do." And she looked at Dave for confirmation.

"I think she nailed you there, pard," Dave said.

"Question is, is it *your* job, Steffi?" Vince asked with a crooked smile. "*I* think it is."

"Sure," she said, almost carelessly. She had known this for weeks now, although if anyone had asked her before coming to the *Islander*, she would have laughed at the idea of deciding for sure on a life's work based on such an obscure posting. The Stephanie McCann who had almost decided on going to New Jersey instead of to Moose-Lookit off the coast of Maine now seemed like another person to her. A flatlander. "What did she tell you? What did she know?"

Vince said, "Just enough to make a strange story even stranger."

"Tell me."

"All right, but fair warning—this is where the through-line ends."

Stephanie didn't hesitate. "Tell me anyway."

15

"Jim Cogan went to work at Mountain Outlook Advertising in Denver on Wednesday, April the 23rd, 1980, just like any other Wednesday," Vince said. "That's what she told me. He had a portfolio of drawings he'd been working on for Sunset Chevrolet, one of the big local car companies that did a ton of print advertising with Mountain Outlook— a very valuable client. Cogan had been one of four artists on the Sunset Chevrolet account for the last three years, she said, and she was positive the company was happy with Jim's work, and the feeling was mutual—Jim liked working on the account. She said his specialty was what he called 'holy-shit women.' When I asked what that was, she smiled and said they were pretty ladies with wide eyes and open mouths, and usually with their hands clapped to their cheeks. The drawings were supposed to say, 'Holy shit, what a buy I got at Sunset Chevrolet!'"

Stephanie laughed. She had seen such drawings, usually in free advertising circulars at the Shop 'N Save across the reach, in Tinnock.

Vince was nodding. "Arla was a fair shake of an artist herself, only with words. What she showed me was a very decent man who loved his wife, his baby, and his work."

"Sometimes loving eyes don't see what they don't want to see," Stephanie remarked.

"Young but cynical!" Dave cried, not without relish.

"Well, ayuh, but she's got a point," Vince said. "Only thing is, sixteen months is usually long enough to put aside the rose-colored glasses. If there'd been something going on— discontent with the job or maybe a little honey on the side would seem the most likely—I think she would have found sign of it, or at least caught a whiff of it, unless the man was almighty, almighty careful, because during that sixteen months she talked to everyone he knew, most of em twice, and they all told her the same thing: he liked his job, he loved his wife, and he absolutely idolized his baby son. She kept coming back to that. 'He never would've left Michael,' she said. 'I know that, Mr. Teague. I know it in my soul.'" Vince shrugged, as if to say *So sue me*. "I believed her."

"And he wasn't tired of his job?" Stephanie asked. "Had no desire to move on?"

"She said not. Said he loved their place up in the mountains, even had a sign over the front door that said HERNANDO'S HIDEAWAY. And she talked to one of the artists he worked with on the Sunset Chevrolet account, a fellow Cogan had worked with for years, Dave, do you recall that name—?"

"George Rankin or George Franklin," Dave said. "Cannot recall which, right off the top of my head."

"Don't let it get you down, old-timer," Vince said. "Even Willie Mays dropped a pop-up from time to time, I guess, especially toward the end of his career."

Dave stuck out his tongue.

Vince nodded as if such childishness was exactly what he'd come to expect of his managing editor, then took up the thread of his story once more. "George the Artist, be he Rankin or Franklin, told Arla that Jim had pretty much reached the top end of that which his talent was capable, and he was one of the fortunate people who not only knew his limitations but was content with them. He said Jim's remaining ambition was to someday head Mountain Outlook's art department. And, given that ambition, cutting and running for the New England coast on the spur of the moment is just about the last thing he would have done."

"But she thought that's what he *did* do," Stephanie said. "Isn't it?"

Vince put his coffee cup down and ran his hands through his fluff of white hair, which was already fairly crazy. "Arla Cogan's like all of us," he said, "a prisoner of the evidence.

"James Cogan left his home at 6:45 AM on that Wednesday to make the drive to Denver by way of the Boulder Turnpike. The only luggage he had was that portfolio I mentioned. He was wearing a gray suit, a white shirt, a red tie, and a gray overcoat. Oh, and black loafers on his feet."

"No green jacket?" Stephanie asked.

"No green jacket," Dave agreed, "but the gray slacks, white shirt, and black loafers were almost certainly what he was wearing when Johnny and Nancy found him sittin dead on the beach with his back against that litter basket."

"His suit-coat?"

"Never found," Dave said. "The tie, neither—but accourse if a man takes off his tie, nine times out of ten he'll stuff it into the pocket of his suit-coat, and I'd be willin to bet that if that gray suit-coat ever *did* turn up, the tie'd be in the pocket."

"He was at his office drawing board by 8:45 AM," Vince said, "working on a newspaper ad for King Sooper's."

"What—?"

"Supermarket chain, dear," Dave said.

"Around ten-fifteen," Vince went on, "George the Artist, be he Rankin or Franklin, saw our boy the Kid heading for the elevators. Cogan said he was goin around the corner to grab what he called 'a real coffee' at Starbucks and an egg salad sandwich for lunch, because he planned to eat at his desk. He asked George if George wanted anything."

"This is all what Arla told you when you were driving her out to Tinnock?"

"Yes, ma'am. Taking her to speak with Cathcart, make a formal identification of the photo—'This is my husband, this is James Cogan'—and then sign an exhumation order. He was waiting for us."

"All right. Sorry to interrupt. Go on."

"Don't be sorry for asking questions, Stephanie, asking questions is what reporters *do*. In any case, George the Artist—"

"Be he Rankin or Franklin," Dave put in helpfully.

"Ayuh, him—he told Cogan that he'd pass on the coffee, but he walked out to the elevator lobby with Cogan so they could talk a little bit about an upcoming retirement party for a fellow named Haverty, one of the agency's founders. The party was scheduled for mid-May, and George the Artist told Arla that her mister seemed excited and looking forward to it. They batted around ideas for a retirement gift until the elevator came, and then Cogan got on and told George the Artist they ought to talk about it some more at lunch and ask someone else—some woman they worked with—what *she* thought. George the Artist agreed that was a pretty good idea, Cogan gave him a little wave, the elevator doors slid closed, and that's the last person who can remember seeing the Colorado Kid when he was still in Colorado."

"George the Artist," she almost marveled. "Do you suppose any of this would have happened if George had said, 'Oh, wait a minute, I'll just pull on my coat and go around the corner with you?'"

"No way of telling," Vince said.

"Was *he* wearing his coat?" she asked. "Cogan? Was he wearing his gray overcoat when he went out?"

"Arla asked, but George the Artist didn't remember," Vince said. "The best he could do was say he didn't *think* so. And that's probably right. The Starbucks and the sandwich shop were side by side, and they really *were* right around the corner."

"She also said there was a receptionist," Dave put in, "but the receptionist didn't see the men go out to the elevators. Said she 'must have been away from her desk for a minute.'" He shook his head disapprovingly. "It's *never* that way in the mystery novels."

But Stephanie's mind had seized on something else, and it occurred to her that she had been picking at crumbs while there was a roast sitting on the table. She held up the forefinger of her left hand beside her left cheek. "George the Artist waves goodbye to Cogan—to the Colorado Kid—around ten-fifteen in the morning. Or maybe it's more like ten-twenty by the time the elevator actually comes and he gets on."

"Ayuh," Vince said. He was looking at her, bright-eyed. They both were.

Now Stephanie held up the forefinger of her right hand beside her right cheek. "And the counter-girl at Jan's Wharf-side across the reach in Tinnock said he ate his fish-and-chips basket at a table looking out over the water at around five-thirty in the afternoon."

"Ayuh," Vince said again.

"What's the time difference between Maine and Colorado? An hour?"

"Two," Dave said.

"Two," she said, and paused, and said it again. "*Two.* So when George the Artist saw him for the last time, when those elevator doors slid shut, it was already past noon in Maine."

"Assuming the times are right," Dave agreed, "and assume's all we can do, isn't it?"

"Would it work?" she asked them. "Could he possibly have gotten here in that length of time?"

"Yes," Vince said.

"No," Dave said.

"Maybe," they said together, and Stephanie sat looking from one to the other, bewildered, her coffee cup forgotten in her hand.

16

"That's what makes this wrong for a newspaper like the *Globe*," Vince said, after a little pause to sip his milky coffee and collect his thoughts. "Even if we wanted to give it up."

"Which we don't," Dave put in (and rather testily).

"Which we don't," Vince agreed. "But if we did...Steffi, when a big-city newspaper like the *Globe* or the *New York Times* does a feature story or a feature series, they want to be able to provide *answers*, or at least suggest them, and do I have a problem with that? The hell I do! Pick up any big-city paper, and what do you find on the front page? Questions disguised as news stories. Where is Osama Bin Laden? We don't know. What's the President doing in the Middle East? *We* don't know because *he* don't. Is the economy going to get stronger or go in the tank? Experts differ. Are eggs good for you or bad for you? Depends on which study you read. You can't even get the weather forecasters to tell you if a nor'easter is going to come in from the nor'east, because they got burned on the last one. So if they do a feature story on better housing for minorities, they want to be able to say if you do A, B, C, and D, things'll be better by the year 2030."

"And if they do a feature story on Unexplained Mysteries,"

Dave said, "they want to be able to tell you the Coast Lights were reflections on the clouds, and the Church Picnic Poisonings were probably the work of a jilted Methodist secretary. But trying to deal with this business of the time…"

"Which you happen to have put your finger on," Vince added with a smile.

"And of course it's outrageous no matter *how* you think of it," Dave said.

"But I'm willing to be outrageous," Vince said. "Hell, I looked into the matter, just about dialed the phone off the damn wall, and I guess I have a right to be outrageous."

"My father used to say you can cut chalk all day, yet it won't never be cheese," Dave said, but he was also smiling a little.

"That's true, but let me whittle a little bit just the same," Vince said. "Let's say the elevator doors close at ten-twenty, Mountain Time, okay? Let's also say, just for the sake of argument, that this was all planned out in advance and he had a car standin by with the motor running."

"All right," Stephanie said, watching him closely.

"Pure fantasy," Dave snorted, but he also looked interested.

"It's farfetched, anyway," Vince agreed, "but he was *there* at quarter past ten and at Jan's Wharfside a little more than five hours later. That's also farfetched, but we know it's a fact. Now may I continue?"

"Have on, McDuff," Dave said.

"If he's got a car all warmed up and waiting for him, maybe he can make it to Stapleton in half an hour. Now he surely didn't take a commercial flight. He could have paid cash for his ticket and used an alias—that was possible back then—but there were no direct flights from Denver to Bangor. From Denver to anyplace in Maine, actually."

"You checked."

"I did. Flying commercial, the best he could have done was arrive in Bangor at 6:45 PM, which was long after that counter-girl saw him. In fact at that time of the year that's after the last ferry of the day leaves for Moosie."

"Six is the last?" Stephanie asked.

"Yep, right up until mid-May," Dave said.

"So he must have flown charter," she said. "A charter *jet*? Are there companies that flew charter jets out of Denver? And could he have afforded one?"

"Yes on all counts," Vince said, "but it would've cost him a couple of thousand bucks, and their bank account would have shown that kind of hit."

"It didn't?"

Vince shook his head. "There were no significant withdrawals prior to the fella's disappearance. All the same, that's what he must have done. I checked with a number of different charter companies, and they all told me that on a good day—one when the jet stream was flowing strong and a little Lear like a 35 or a 55 got up in the middle of it—that trip would take just three hours, maybe a little more."

"Denver to Bangor," she said.

"Denver to Bangor, ayuh—there's noplace closer to our part of the coast where one of those little burners can land. Not enough runway, don'tcha see."

She did. "So did you check with the charter companies in Denver?"

"I tried. Not much joy there, either, though. Of the five companies that flew jets of one size n another, only two'd even talk to me. They didn't have to, did they? I was just a small-town newspaperman lookin into an accidental death, not a cop investigating a crime. Also, one of em pointed out to me that it wasn't just a question of checking up on the FBOs that flew jets out of Stapleton—"

"What are FBOs?"

"Fixed Base Operators," Vince said. "Chartering aircraft is only one of the things they do. They get clearances, maintain little terminals for passengers who are flyin private so they can *stay* that way, they sell, service, and repair aircraft. You can go through U.S. Customs at lots of FBOs, buy an altimeter if yours is busted, or catch eight hours in the pilots' lounge if your current flyin time is maxed out. Some FBOs, like Signature Air, are big business—chain operations just like Holiday Inn or McDonald's. Others are seat-of-the-pants outfits with not much more than a coin-op snack machine inside and a wind-sock by the runway."

"You did some research," Stephanie said, impressed.

"Ayuh, enough to know that it isn't just Colorado pilots and Colorado planes that used Stapleton or any other Colorado airport, then or now. For instance, a plane from an FBO at LaGuardia in New York might fly into Denver with passengers who were going to spend a month in Colorado visiting relatives. The pilots would then ask around for passengers who wanted to go back to New York, just so they wouldn't have to make the return empty."

"Or these days they'd have their return passengers all set up ahead of time by computer," Dave said. "Do you see, Steff?"

She did. She saw something else as well. "So the records on Mr. Cogan's Wild Ride might be in the files of Air Eagle, out of New York."

"Or Air Eagle out of Montpelier, Vermont—" Vince said.

"Or Just Ducky Jets out of Washington, D.C.," Dave said.

"And if Cogan paid cash," Vince added, "there are quite likely no records at all."

"But surely there are all sorts of agencies—"

"Yes, ma'am," Dave said. "More than you could shake a stick at, beginning with the FAA and ending with the IRS. Wouldn't be surprised if the damn FFA wasn't in there somewhere. But in cash deals, paperwork gets thin. Remember Helen Hafner?"

Of course she did. Their waitress at the Grey Gull. The one whose son had recently fallen out of his treehouse and broken his arm. *She gets all of it,* Vince had said of the money he meant to put in Helen Hafner's pocket, *and what Uncle Sam don't know don't bother him.* To which Dave had added, *It's the way America does business.*

Stephanie supposed it was, but it was an extremely troublesome way of doing business in a case like this one.

"So you don't know," she said. "You tried your best, but you just don't know."

Vince looked first surprised, then amused. "As to tryin

my best, Stephanie, I don't think a person ever knows that for sure; in fact, I think most of us are condemned—damned, even!—to thinking we could have done just a little smidge better, even when we win through to whatever it was we were tryin to get. But you're wrong—I *do* know. He chartered a jet out of Stapleton. That's what happened."

"But you said—"

He leaned even further forward over his clasped hands, his eyes fixed on hers. "Listen carefully and take instruction, dearheart. It's long years since I read Sherlock Holmes, so I can't say this exactly, but at one point the great detective tells Dr. Watson somethin like this: 'When you eliminate the impossible, whatever is left—*no matter how improbable*—must be the answer.' Now we know that the Colorado Kid was in his Denver office buildin until ten-fifteen or ten-twenty on that Wednesday morning. And we can be pretty sure he was in Jan's Wharfside at five-thirty. Hold up your fingers like you did before, Stephanie."

She did as he asked, left forefinger for the Kid in Colorado, right forefinger for James Cogan in Maine. Vince unlocked his hands and touched her right forefinger briefly with one of his own, age meeting youth in midair.

"But don't call this finger five-thirty," he said. "We needn't trust the counter-girl, who wasn't run off her feet the way she would have been in July, but who was doubtless busy all the same, it bein the supper-hour and all."

Stephanie nodded. In this part of the world supper came early. Dinner—pronounced *dinnah*—was what you ate from your lunchpail at noon, often while out in your lobster boat.

"Let this finger be six o'clock," he said. "The time of the last ferry."

She nodded again. "He had to be on that one, didn't he?"

"He did unless he swam the reach," Dave said.

"Or chartered a boat," she said.

"We asked," Dave said. "More important, we asked Gard Edwick, who was the ferryman in the spring of '80."

Did Cogan bring him tea? she suddenly found herself wondering. *Because if you want to ride the ferry, you're supposed to bring tea for the tillerman. You said so yourself, Dave. Or are the ferryman and the tillerman two different people?*

"Steff?" Vince sounded concerned. "Are you all right, dear?"

"I'm fine, why?"

"You looked…I dunno, like you came over strange."

"I sort of did. It's a strange story, isn't it?" And then she said, "Only it's not a story at all, you were so right about that, and if I came over strange, I suppose that's why. It's like trying to ride a bike across a tightrope that isn't there."

Stephanie hesitated, then decided to go on and make a complete fool of herself.

"Did Mr. Edwick remember Cogan because Cogan brought him something? Because he brought tea for the tillerman?"

For a moment neither man said anything, just regarded her with their inscrutable eyes—so strangely young and sweetly lad-like in their old faces—and she thought she might laugh or cry or do something, break out somehow just to kill her anxiety and growing certainty that she had made a fool of herself.

Vince said, "It was a chilly crossing. Someone—a man—brought a paper cup of coffee to the pilot house and handed it in to Gard. They only passed a few words. This was April, remember, and by then it was already going dark. The man said, 'Smooth crossing.' And Gard said, 'Ayuh.' Then the man said 'This has been a long time coming' or maybe 'I've been a long time coming.' Gard said it might have even been '*Lidle*'s been a long time coming.' There is such a name; there's none in the Tinnock phone book, but I've found it in quite a few others."

"Was Cogan wearing the green coat or the topcoat?"

"Steff," Vince said, "Gard not only didn't remember whether or not the man was wearing a coat; he probably couldn't have sworn in a court of law if the man was afoot or on hossback. It was gettin dark, for one thing; it was one little act of kindness and a few passed words recalled a year and a half downstream, for a second; for a third...well, old Gard, you know..." He made a bottle-tipping gesture.

"Speak no ill of the dead, but the man drank like a frickin fish," Dave said. "He lost the ferryman job in '85, and the Town put him on the plow, mostly so his family wouldn't starve. He had five kids, you know, and a wife with MS. But finally he cracked up the plow, doin Main Street while blotto, and put out all the frickin power for a frickin week in February, pardon my frickin *français*. Then he lost that job and he was on the town. So am I surprised he didn't remember more? No, I am not. But I'm convinced from what he *did* remember that, ayuh, the Colorado Kid came over from the mainland on the day's last ferry, and, ayuh, he brought tea for the tillerman, or a reasonable facsimile thereof. Good on you to remember about that, Steff." And he patted her hand. She smiled at him. It felt like a rather dazed smile.

"As you said," Vince resumed, "there's that two-hour time difference to factor in." He moved her left finger closer to her right. "It's quarter past twelve, east coast time, when Cogan leaves his office. He drops his easygoing, just-another-day act the minute the elevator doors open on the lobby of his building. The very *second*. He goes dashin outside, hellbent for election, where that fast car—and an equally fast driver—is waitin for him.

"Half an hour later, he's at a Stapleton FBO, and five minutes after that, he's mounting the steps of a private jet. He hasn't left this arrangement to chance, either. Can't have done. There are people who fly private on a fairly regular basis, then stay for a couple of weeks. The folks who take them one-way spend those two weeks attending to other charters. Our boy would have settled on one of those planes, and almost certainly would have made a cash arrangement to fly back out with them. Eastbound."

Stephanie said, "What would he have done if the people using the plane he planned to take cancelled their flight at the last minute?"

Dave shrugged. "Same thing he would've done if there

was bad weather, I guess," he said. "Put it off to another day."

Vince, meanwhile, had moved Stephanie's left finger a little further to the right. "Now it's getting close to one in the afternoon on the east coast," he said, "but at least our friend Cogan doesn't have to worry about a lot of security rigamarole, not back in 1980 and especially not flyin private. And we have to assume—again—that he doesn't have to wait in line with a lot of other planes for an active runway, because it screws up the timetable if he does, and all the while on the other end—" He touched her right finger. "—that ferry's waitin. Last one of the day.

"So, the flight lasts three hours. We'll say that, anyway. My colleague here got on the Internet, he loves that sucker with a passion, and he says the weather was good for flying that day and the maps show that the jet-stream was in approximately the right place—"

"But as to how *strong* it was, that's information I've never been able to pin down," Dave said. He glanced at Vince. "Given the tenuousness of your case, partner, that's probably not a real bad thing."

"We'll say three hours," Vince repeated, and moved Stephanie's left finger (the one she was coming to think of as her Colorado Kid finger) until it was less than two inches from her right one (which she now thought of as her James Cogan–Almost Dead finger). "It can't have been much longer than that."

"Because the facts won't let it," she murmured, fascinated (and, in truth, a little frightened) by the idea. Once, while in high school, she had read a science fiction novel called *The Moon Is A Harsh Mistress*. She didn't know about the moon, but she was coming to believe that was certainly true of time.

"No, ma'am, they won't," he agreed. "At four o'clock or maybe four-oh-five—we'll say four-oh-five—Cogan lands and disembarks at Twin City Civil Air, that was the only FBO at Bangor International Airport back then—"

"Any records of his arrival?" she asked. "Did you check?" Knowing he had, of course he had, also knowing it hadn't done any good, one way or another. It was that kind of story. The kind that's like a sneeze which threatens but never quite arrives.

Vince smiled. "Sure did, but in the carefree days before Homeland Security, all Twin City kept any length of time were their account books. They had a good many cash payments that day, includin some pretty good-sized refueling tabs late in the afternoon, but even those might mean nothing. For all we know, whoever flew the Kid in might have spent the night in a Bangor hotel and flown out the next morning—"

"Or spent the weekend," Dave said. "Then again, the pilot might have left right away, and without refueling at all."

"How could he do that, after coming all the way from Denver?" Stephanie asked.

"Could have hopped down to Portland," Dave said, "and filled his tank up there."

"Why would he?"

Dave smiled. It gave him a surprisingly foxy look that

was not much like his usual expression of earnest and slightly stupid honesty. It occurred to Stephanie now that the intellect behind that chubby, rather childish face was probably as lean and quick as Vince Teague's.

"Cogan might've paid Mr. Denver Flyboy to do it that way because he was afraid of leaving a paper trail," Dave said. "And Mr. Denver Flyboy would very likely have gone along with any reasonable request if he was being paid enough."

"As for the Colorado Kid," Vince resumed, "he's still got almost two hours to get to Tinnock, get a fish-and-chips basket at Jan's Wharfside, sit at a table eating it while he looks out at the water, and then catch the last ferry to Moose-Lookit Island." As he spoke, he slowly brought Stephanie's left and right forefingers together until they touched.

Stephanie watched, fascinated. "Could he do it?"

"Maybe, but it'd be awful goddamned tight," Dave said with a sigh. "*I'd* have never believed it if he hadn't actually turned up dead on Hammock Beach. Would you, Vince?"

"Nup," Vince said, without even pausing to consider.

Dave said, "There's four dirt airstrips within a dozen miles or so of Tinnock, all seasonal. They do most of their trade takin up tourists on sight-seein rides in the summer, or to look at the fall foliage when the colors peak out, although that only lasts a couple of weeks. We checked em on the off-chance that Cogan might have chartered him a second plane, this one a little prop-job like a Piper Cub, and flown from Bangor to the coast."

"No joy there, either, I take it."

"You take it right," Vince said, and his grin was gloomy rather than foxy. "Once those elevator doors slide closed on Cogan in that Denver office building, this whole business is nothing but shadows you can't quite catch hold of…and one dead body.

"Three of those four airstrips were deserted in April, shut right down, so a plane *could* have flown in to any of em and no one the wiser. The fourth one—a woman named Maisie Harrington lived out there with her father and about sixty mutt dogs, and she claimed that no one flew into their strip from October of 1979 to May of 1980, but she smelled like a distillery, and I had my doubts if she could remember what went on a *week* before I talked to her, let alone a year and a half before."

"What about the woman's father?" she asked.

"Stone blind and one-legged," Dave said. "The diabetes."

"Ouch," she said.

"Ayuh."

"Let Jack n Maisie Harrington go hang," Vince said impatiently. "I never believed in the Second Airplane Theory when it comes to Cogan any more than I ever believed in the Second Gunman Theory when it came to Kennedy. If Cogan had a car waiting for him in Denver—and I can't see any way around it—then he could have had one waiting for him at the General Aviation Terminal, as well. And I believe he did."

"That is just so far-fetched," Dave said. He spoke not scoffingly but dolefully.

"P'raps," Vince responded, unperturbed, "but when you get rid of the impossible, whatever's left…there's your pup, scratchin at the door t'be let in."

"He could have driven himself," Stephanie said thoughtfully.

"A rental car?" Dave shook his head. "Don't think so, dear. Rental agencies take only credit cards, and credit cards leave paper trails."

"Besides," Vince said, "Cogan didn't know his way around eastern and coastal Maine. So far as we can discover, he'd never been here in his life. You know the roads by now, Steffi: there's only one main one that comes out this way from Bangor to Ellsworth, but once you get to Ellsworth, there's three or four different choices, and a flatlander, even one with a map, is apt to get confused. No, I think Dave is right. If the Kid meant to go by car, and if he knew in advance how small his time-window was going to be, he would have wanted to have a driver standin by and waitin. Somebody who'd take cash money, drive fast, and not get lost."

Stephanie thought for a little while. The two old men let her.

"*Three* hired drivers in all," she said at last. "The one in the middle at the controls of a private jet."

"Maybe with a copilot," Dave put in quietly. "Them are the rules, at least."

"It's very outlandish," she said.

Vince nodded and sighed. "I don't disagree."

"You've never turned up even one of these drivers, have you?"

"No."

She thought some more, this time with her head down and her normally smooth brow furrowed in a deep frown. Once more they did not interrupt her, and after perhaps two minutes, she looked up again. "But *why*? What could be so important for Cogan to go to such lengths?"

Vince Teague and Dave Bowie looked at each other, then back at her. Vince said: "Ain't *that* a good question."

Dave said: "A *rig* of a question."

Vince said: "The *main* question."

"Accourse it is," Dave said. "Always was."

Vince, quite softly: "We don't know, Stephanie. We never have."

Dave, more softly still: "Boston *Globe* wouldn't like that. Nope, not at all."

17

"Accourse, we ain't the Boston *Globe*," Vince said. "We ain't even the Bangor *Daily News*. But Stephanie, when a grown man or woman goes completely off the rails, every newspaper writer, big town or small one, looks for certain reasons. It don't matter whether the result is most of the Methodist church picnic windin up poisoned or just the gentlemanly half of a marriage quietly disappearin one weekday morning, never to be seen alive again. Now—for the time bein never mindin where he wound up, or the improbability of how he managed to get there—tell me what some of those reasons for goin off the rails might be. Count them off for me until I see at least four of your fingers in the air."

School is in session, she thought, and then remembered something Vince had said to her a month before, almost in passing: *To be a success in the news business, it don't hurt to have a dirty mind, dear.* At the time she'd thought the remark bizarre, perhaps even borderline senile. Now she thought she understood a little better.

"Sex," she said, raising her left forefinger—her Colorado Kid finger. "I.e., another woman." She popped another finger. "Money problems, I'm thinking either debt or theft."

"Don't forget the IRS," Dave said. "People sometimes run when they realize they're in hock to Uncle Sam."

"She don't know how boogery the IRS can be," Vince said. "You can't hold that against her. Anyway, according to his wife Cogan had no problems with Infernal Revenue. Go on, Steffi, you're doin fine."

She didn't yet have enough fingers in the air to satisfy him, but could think of only one other thing. "The urge to start a brand-new life?" she asked doubtfully, seeming to speak more to herself than to them. "To just...I don't know ...cut all the ties and start over again as a different person in a different place?" And then something else *did* occur to her. "Madness?" She had four fingers up now—one for sex, one for money, one for change, one for madness. She looked doubtfully at the last two. "Maybe change and madness are the same?"

"Maybe they are," Vince said. "And you could argue that madness covers all sorts of addictions that people try to run from. That sort of running's sometimes known as the 'geographic cure.' I'm thinking specifically of drugs and alcohol. Gambling's another addiction people try the geographic cure on, but I guess you could file that problem under money."

"Did he have drug or alcohol problems?"

"Arla Cogan said not, and I believe she would have known. And after sixteen months to think it over, and with him dead at the end of it, I think she would have told me."

"But, Steffi," Dave said (and rather gently), "when you consider it, madness almost *has* to be in it somewhere, wouldn't you say?"

She thought of James Cogan, the Colorado Kid, sitting dead on Hammock Beach with his back against a litter basket and a lump of meat lodged in his throat, his closed eyes turned in the direction of Tinnock and the reach beyond. She thought of how one hand had still been curled, as if holding the rest of his midnight snack, a piece of steak some hungry gull had no doubt stolen, leaving nothing but a sticky pattern of sand in the leftover grease on his palm. "Yes," she said. "There's madness in it somewhere. Did *she* know that? His wife?"

The two men looked at each other. Vince sighed and rubbed the side of his blade-thin nose. "She might have, but by then she had her own life to worry about, Steffi. Hers and her son's. A man up and disappears like that, the woman left behind is apt to have a damn hard skate. She got her old job back, working in one of the Boulder banks, but there was no way she could keep the house in Nederland—"

"Hernando's Hideaway," Stephanie murmured, feeling a sympathetic pang.

"Ayuh, that. She kept on her feet without having to borrow too much from her folks, or anything at all from his, but she used up most of the money they'd put aside for little Mike's college education in the process. When we saw her, I should judge she wanted two things, one practical and one what you'd call…spiritual?" He looked rather doubtfully at Dave, who shrugged and nodded as if to say that word would do.

Vince nodded himself and went on. "She wanted to be

shed of the not-knowing. Was he alive or dead? Was she married or a widow? Could she lay hope to rest or did she have to carry it yet awhile longer? Maybe that last sounds a trifle hard-hearted, and maybe it is, but I should think that after sixteen months, hope must get damned heavy on your back—damned heavy to tote around.

"As for the practical, that was simple. She just wanted the insurance company to pay off what they owed. I know that Arla Cogan isn't the only person in the history of the world to hate an insurance company, but I'd have to put her high on the list for sheer intensity. She'd been going along and going along, you see, her and Michael, living in a three- or four-room apartment in Boulder—quite a change after the nice house in Nederland—and her leaving him in daycare and with babysitters she wasn't always sure she could trust, working a job she didn't really want to do, going to bed alone after years of having someone to snuggle up to, worrying over the bills, always watching the needle on the gas-gauge because the price of gasoline was going up even then…and all the time she was sure in her heart that he was dead, but the insurance company wouldn't pay off because of what her heart knew, not when there was no body, let alone a cause of death.

"She kept asking me if 'the bastards'—that's what she always called em—could 'wiggle off' somehow, if they could claim it was suicide. I told her I'd never heard of someone committing suicide by choking themselves on a piece of meat, and later, after she had made the formal identification of the death-photo in Cathcart's presence, he told her the same thing. That seemed to ease her mind a little bit.

"Cathcart pitched right in, said he'd call the company agent in Brighton, Colorado, and explain about the fingerprints and her photo I.D. Nail everything down tight. She cried quite a little bit at that—some in relief, some in gratitude, some just from exhaustion, I guess."

"Of course," Stephanie murmured.

"I took her across to Moosie on the ferry and put her up at the Red Roof Motel," Vince continued. "Same place you stayed when you first got here, wasn't it?"

"Yes," Stephanie said. She had been at a boarding house for the last month or so, but would look for something more permanent in October. If, that was, these two old birds would keep her on. She thought they would. She thought that was, in large part, what this was all about.

"The three of us had breakfast the next morning," Dave said, "and like most people who haven't done anything wrong and haven't had much experience with newspapers, she had no shyness about talking to us. No sense that any of what she was sayin might later turn up on page one." He paused. "And accourse very little of it ever did. It was never the kind of story that sees much in the way of print, once you get past the main fact of the matter: Man Found Dead On Hammock Beach, Coroner Says No Foul Play. And by then, that was cold news, indeed."

"No through-line," Stephanie said.

"No *nothing*!" Dave cried, and then laughed until he coughed. When that cleared, he wiped the corners of his eyes with a large paisley handkerchief he pulled from the back pocket of his pants.

"What did she tell you?" Stephanie asked.

"What *could* she tell us?" Vince responded. "Mostly what she did was ask questions. The only one I asked her was if the *chervonetz* was a lucky piece or a memento or something like that." He snorted. "Some newspaperman I was that day."

"The *chevron*—" She gave up on it, shaking her head.

"The Russian coin in his pocket, mixed in with the rest of his change," Vince said. "It was a *chervonetz*. A ten-ruble piece. I asked her if he kept it as a lucky piece or something. She didn't have a clue. Said the closest Jim had ever been to Russia was when they rented a James Bond movie called *From Russia With Love* at Blockbuster."

"He might have picked it up on the beach," she said thoughtfully. "People find all sorts of things on the beach." She herself had found a woman's high-heel shoe, worn exotically smooth from many a long tumble between the sea and the shore, while walking one day on Little Hay Beach, about two miles from Hammock.

"Might've, ayuh," Vince agreed. He looked at her, his eyes twinkling in their deep sockets. "Want to know the two things I remember best about her the morning after her appointment with Cathcart over in Tinnock?"

"Sure."

"How *rested* she looked. And how well she ate when we sat down to breakfast."

"That's a fact," Dave agreed. "There's that old sayin

about how the condemned man ate a hearty meal, but I've got an idea that no one eats so hearty as the man—or the woman—who's finally been up and pardoned. And in a way she had been. She might not have known why he came to our part of the world, or what befell him once he got here, and I think she realized she might not ever know—"

"She did," Vince agreed. "She said so when I drove her back to the airport."

"—but she knew the only important thing: he was dead. Her heart might have been telling her that all along, but her head needed proof to go along for the ride."

"Not to mention in order to convince that pesky insurance company," Dave said.

"Did she ever get the money?" Stephanie asked.

Dave smiled. "Yes, ma'am. They dragged their feet some—those boys have a tendency to go fast when they're putting on the sell-job and then slow down when someone puts in a claim—but finally they paid. We got a letter to that effect, thanking us for all our hard work. She said that without us, she'd still be wondering and the insurance company would still be claiming that James Cogan could be alive in Brooklyn or Tangiers."

"What kind of questions did she ask?"

"The ones you'd expect," Vince said. "First thing she wanted to know was where he went when he got off the ferry. We couldn't tell her. We asked questions—didn't we, Dave?"

Dave Bowie nodded.

"But no one remembered seein him," Vince continued. "Accourse it would have been almost full dark by then, so there's no real reason why anyone should have. As for the few other passengers—and at that time of year there aren't many, especially on the last ferry of the day—they would have gone right to their cars in the Bay Street parkin lot, heads down in their collars because of the wind off the reach."

"And she asked about his wallet," Dave said. "All we could tell her was that no one ever found it...at least no one who ever turned it in to the police. I suppose it's possible someone could have picked it out of his pocket on the ferry, stripped the cash out of it, then dropped it overside."

"It's possible that heaven's a rodeo, too, but not likely," Vince said drily. "If he had cash in his wallet, why did he have more—seventeen dollars in paper money—in his pants pocket?"

"Just in case," Stephanie said.

"Maybe," Vince said, "but it doesn't feel right to me. And frankly, I find the idea of a pickpocket workin the six o'clock ferry between Tinnock and Moosie a touch more unbelievable than a commercial artist from a Denver advertising agency charterin a jet to fly to New England."

"In any case, we couldn't tell her where his wallet went," Dave said, "or where his topcoat and suit-jacket went, or why he was found sittin out there on a stretch of beach in nothin but his pants and shirt."

"The cigarettes?" Stephanie asked. "I bet she was curious about those."

Vince barked a laugh. "Curious isn't the right word. That pack of smokes drove her almost crazy. She couldn't understand why he'd have had cigarettes on him. And we didn't need her to tell us he wasn't the kind who'd stopped for awhile and then decided to take the habit up again. Cathcart took a good look at his lungs during the autopsy, for reasons I'm sure you'll understand—"

"He wanted to make sure he hadn't drowned after all?" Stephanie asked.

"That's right," Vince said. "If Dr. Cathcart had found water in the lungs beneath that chunk of meat, it would have suggested someone trying to cover up the way Mr. Cogan actually died. And while that wouldn't have proved murder, it would've suggested it. Cathcart *didn't* find water in Cogan's lungs, and he didn't find any evidence of smoking, either. Nice and pink down there, he said. Yet someplace between Cogan's office building and Stapleton Airport, and in spite of the tearing hurry he had to've been in, he must've had his driver stop so he could pick up a pack. Either that or he had em put by already, which is what I tend to believe. Maybe with his Russian coin."

"Did you tell her that?" Stephanie asked.

"No," Vince said, and just then the telephone rang. "'Scuse me," he said, and went to answer it.

He spoke briefly, said *Ayuh* a time or three, then returned, stretching his back some more as he did. "That was Ellen Dunwoodie," he said. "She's ready to talk about the great trauma she's been through, snappin off that fire hydrant and 'makin a spectacle of herself.' That's an exact quote, although I don't think it will appear in my pulse-poundin account of the event. In any case, I think I'd better amble over there pretty soon; get the story while her recollection's clear and before she decides to make supper. I'm lucky she n her sister eat late. Otherwise I'd be out of luck."

"And I've *got* to get after those invoices," Dave said. "Seems like there must be a dozen more than there were when we left for the Gull. I swan to goodness when you leave em alone atop a desk, they breed."

Stephanie gazed at them with real alarm. "You can't stop now. You can't just leave me hanging."

"No other choice," Vince said mildly. "*We've* been hanging, Steffi, and for twenty-five years now. There isn't any jilted church secretary in this one."

"No Ellsworth city lights reflected on the clouds down-east, either," Dave said. "Not even a Teodore Riponeaux in the picture, some poor old sailorman murdered for hypo-thetical pirate treasure and then left dead on the foredeck after all his shipmates had been tossed overside—and why? As a warning to other would-be treasure-hunters, by gorry! Now *there's* a through-line for you, dearheart!"

Dave grinned…but then the grin faded. "Nothing like that in the case of the Colorado Kid; no string for the beads, don't you see, and no Sherlock Holmes or Ellery Queen to string em in any case. Just a couple of guys running a news-paper with about a hundred stories a week to cover. None of em drawin much water by Boston *Globe* standards, but stuff people on the island like to read about, all the same. Speakin of which, weren't you going to talk with Sam Gernerd? Find out all the details on his famous Hayride, Dance, and Picnic?"

"I was…I am…and I *want* to! Do you guys understand

that? That I actually *want* to talk to him about that dumb thing?"

Vince Teague burst out laughing, and Dave joined him.

"Ayuh," Vince said, when he could talk again. "Dunno what the head of your journalism department would make of it, Steffi, he'd probably break down n cry, but I know you do." He glanced at Dave. "*We* know you do."

"And I know you've got your own fish to fry, but you must have *some* ideas…some *theories*…after all these years…" She looked at them plaintively. "I mean…don't you?"

They glanced at each other and again she felt that telepathy flow between them, but this time she had no sense of the thought it carried. Then Dave looked back at her. "What is it you really want to know, Stephanie? Tell us."

18

"Do you think he was murdered?" *That* was what she really wanted to know. They had asked her to set the idea aside, and she had, but now the discussion of the Colorado Kid was almost over, and she thought they would allow her to put the subject back on the table.

"Why would you think that any more likely than accidental death, given everything we've told you?" Dave asked. He sounded genuinely curious.

"Because of the cigarettes. The cigarettes almost had to have been deliberate on his part. He just never thought it would take a year and a half for someone to discover that Colorado stamp. Cogan believed a man found dead on a beach with no identification would rate more investigation than he got."

"*Yes,*" Vince said. He spoke in a low voice but actually clenched a fist and shook it, like a fan who has just watched a ballplayer make a key play or deliver a clutch hit. "Good girl. Good job."

Although just twenty-two, there were people Stephanie would have resented for calling her a girl. This ninety-year-old man with the thin white hair, narrow face, and piercing blue eyes was not one of them. In truth, she flushed with pleasure.

"He couldn't know he'd draw a couple of thuds like O'Shanny and Morrison when it came time to investigate his death," Dave said. "Couldn't know he'd have to depend on a grad student who'd spent the last couple of months holdin briefcases and goin out for coffee, not to mention a couple of old guys puttin out a weekly paper one step above a supermarket handout."

"Hang on there, brother," Vince said. "Them's fightin words." He put up his elderly dukes, but with a grin.

"I think he did all right," Stephanie said. "In the end, I think he did just fine." And then, thinking of the woman and baby Michael (who would by this time be in his mid-twenties): "So did she, actually. Without Paul Devane and you two guys, Arla Cogan never would have gotten her insurance money."

"Some truth to that," Vince conceded. She was amused to see that something in this made him uncomfortable. Not that he'd done good, she thought, but that someone *knew* he had done good. They had the Internet out here; you could see a little Direct TV satellite dish on just about every house; no fishing boat set to sea anymore without the GPS switched on. Yet still the old Calvinist ideas ran deep. *Let not thy left hand know what thy right hand doeth.*

"What exactly do you think happened?" she asked.

"No, Steffi," Vince said. He spoke kindly but firmly. "You're still expectin Rex Stout to come waltzin out of the closet, or Ellery Queen arm in arm with Miss Jane Marple. If we knew what happened, if we had any idea, we would have chased that idea til we dropped. And frig the Boston *Globe*, we would have broken any story we found on page one of the *Islander*. We may have been *little* newspapermen back in '81, and we may be little *old* newspapermen now, but we ain't *dead* little old newspapermen. I still like the idea of a big story just fine."

"Me too," Dave said. He'd gotten up, probably with those invoices on his mind, but had now settled on the corner of his desk, swinging one large leg. "I've always dreamed of us havin a story that got syndicated nationwide, and that's one dream I'll probably die with. Go on, Vince, tell her as much as you think. She'll keep it close. She's one of us now."

Stephanie almost shivered with pleasure, but Vince Teague appeared not to notice. He leaned forward, fixing her light blue eyes with his, which were a much darker shade—the color of the ocean on a sunny day.

"All right," he said. "I started to think something might be funny about how he died as well as how he got here long before all that about the stamp. I started askin myself questions when I realized he had a pack of cigarettes with only one gone, although he'd been on the island since at least six-thirty. I made a real pest of myself at Bayside News."

Vince smiled at the recollection.

"I showed everyone at the shop Cogan's picture, including the sweep-up boy. I was convinced he must have bought that pack there, unless he got it out of a vendin machine at a place like the Red Roof or the Shuffle Inn or maybe Sonny's Sunoco. The way I figured, he must have finished his smokes while wanderin around Moosie, after gettin off the ferry, then bought a fresh supply. And I *also* figured that if he got em at the News, he must have gotten em shortly before eleven, which is when the News closes. That would explain why he just smoked one, and only used one of his new matches, before he died."

"But then you found out he wasn't a smoker at all," Stephanie said.

"That's right. His wife said so and Cathcart confirmed it. And later on I became sure that pack of smokes was a message: *I came from Colorado, look for me there*."

"We'll never know for sure, but we both think that's what it was," Dave said.

"Jee-*sus*," she almost whispered. "So where does that lead you?"

Once more they looked at each other and shrugged those identical shrugs. "Into a land of shadows n moonbeams," Vince said. "Places no feature writer from the Boston *Globe* will ever go, in other words. But there are a few things I'm sure of in my heart. Would you like to hear em?"

"Yes!"

Vince spoke slowly but deliberately, like a man feeling his way down a very dark corridor where he has been many times before.

"He knew he was goin into a desperate situation, and he knew he might go unidentified if he died. He didn't want that to happen, quite likely because he was worried about leaving his wife broke."

"So he bought those cigarettes, hoping they'd be over-looked," Stephanie said.

Vince nodded. "Ayuh, and they were."

"But overlooked by *who*?"

Vince paused, then went on without answering her question. "He went down in the elevator and out through the lobby of his building. There was a car waitin to take him to Stapleton Airport, either right there or just around the corner. Maybe it was just him and the driver in that car; maybe there was someone else. We'll never know. You asked me earlier if Cogan was wearing his overcoat when he left that morning, and I said George the Artist didn't remember, but Arla said she never saw that overcoat no more, so maybe he was, at that. If so, I think he took it off in the car or in the airplane. I think he also took off his suit-coat jacket. I think someone either gave him the green jacket to wear in their place, or it was waitin for him."

"In the car or on the plane."

"Ayuh," Dave said.

"The cigarettes?"

"Don't know for sure, but if I had to bet, I'd bet he already had em on him," Dave said. "He knew this was comin along…whatever *this* was. He'd've had em in his pants pocket, I think."

"Then, later, on the beach…" She saw Cogan, her mind's-eye version of the Colorado Kid, lighting his life's first cigarette—first and last—and then strolling down to the water's edge with it, there on Hammock Beach, alone in the moonlight. The midnight moonlight. He takes one puff of the harsh, unfamiliar smoke. Maybe two. Then he throws the cigarette into the sea. Then…what?

What?

"The plane dropped him off in Bangor," she heard herself saying in a voice that sounded harsh and unfamiliar to her.

"Ayuh," Dave agreed.

"And his ride from Bangor dropped him off in Tinnock."

"Ayuh." That was Vince.

"He ate a fish-and-chips basket."

"So he did," Vince agreed. "Autopsy proves it. So did my nose. I smelled the vinegar."

"Was his wallet gone by then?"

"We don't know," Dave said. "We'll never know. But I think so. I think he gave it up with his topcoat, his suit-coat, and his normal life. I think what he got in return was a green jacket, which he also gave up later on."

"Or had taken from his dead body," Vince said.

Stephanie shivered. She couldn't help it. "He rides across to Moose-Lookit Island on the six o'clock ferry, bringing Gard Edwick a paper cup of coffee on the way— what could be construed as tea for the tillerman, or the ferryman."

"Yuh," Dave said. He looked very solemn.

"By then he has no wallet, no ID, just seventeen dollars and some change that maybe includes a Russian ten-ruble coin. Do you think that coin might have been…oh, I don't know…some sort of identification-thingy, like in a spy novel? I mean, the cold war between Russia and the United States would have still been going on then, right?"

"Full blast," Vince said. "But Steffi—if you were going to dicker with a Russian secret agent, would you use a *ruble* to introduce yourself?"

"No," she admitted. "But why else would he have it? To show it to someone, that's all I can think of."

"I've always had the intuition that someone gave it to *him*," Dave said. "Maybe along with a piece of cold sirloin steak, wrapped up in a piece of tinfoil."

"Why?" she asked. "Why would they?"

Dave shook his head. "I don't know."

"Was there tinfoil found at the scene? Maybe thrown into that sea-grass along the far edge of the beach?"

"O'Shanny and Morrison sure didn't look," Dave said. "Me n Vince had a hunt all around Hammock Beach after that yella tape was taken down—not specifically for tinfoil, you understand, but for anything that looked like it might bear on the dead man, anything at all. We found nothing but the usual litter—candy-wrappers and such."

"If the meat was in foil or a Baggie, the Kid might very well have tossed it into the water, along with his one cigarette," Vince said.

"About that piece of meat in his throat…"

Vince was smiling a little. "I had several long conversations about that piece of steak with both Doc Robinson and Dr. Cathcart. Dave was in on a couple of em. I remember Cathcart saying to me once, this had to've been not more than a month before the heart attack that took his life six or seven years ago, 'You go back to that old business the way a kid who's lost a tooth goes back to the hole with the tip of his tongue.' And I thought to myself, yep, that's exactly right, exactly what it's like. It's like a hole I can't stop poking at and licking into, trying to find the bottom of.

"First thing I wanted to know was if that piece of meat could have been jammed down Cogan's throat, either with fingers or some sort of instrument like a lobster-pick, after he was dead. And that's crossed *your* mind, hasn't it?"

Stephanie nodded.

"He said it was possible but unlikely, because that piece of steak had not only been chewed, but chewed enough to be swallowed. It wasn't really meat at all anymore, but rather what Cathcart called 'organic pulp-mass.' Someone else could have chewed it that much, but would have been unlikely to have planted it after doing so, for fear it would have looked insufficient to cause death. Are you with me?"

She nodded again.

"He *also* said that meat chewed to a pulp-mass would be hard to manipulate with an instrument. It would tend to break up when pushed from the back of the mouth into the throat. Fingers could do it, but Cathcart said he believed he would have seen signs of that, most likely straining of the jaw ligatures." He paused, thinking, then shook his head. "There's a technical term for that kind of jaw-poppin, but I don't remember it."

"Tell her what Robinson told you," Dave said. His eyes were sparkling. "It didn't come to nummore'n the rest in the end, but I always thought it was *wicked* int'restin."

"He said there were certain muscle relaxants, some of em exotic, and Cogan's midnight snack might have been treated with one of those," Vince said. "He might get the first few bites down all right, accounting for what was found in his stomach, and then find himself all at once with a bite he wasn't able to swallow once it was chewed."

"That must have been it!" Stephanie cried. "Whoever dosed the meat sat there and just watched him choke! Then, when Cogan was dead, the murderer propped him up against the litter basket and took away the rest of the steak so it could never be tested! It was never a gull at all! It…" She stopped, looking at them. "Why are you shaking your heads?"

"The autopsy, dear," Vince said. "Nothing like that showed up on the blood-gas chromatograph tests."

"But if it was something exotic enough…"

"Like in an Agatha Christie yarn?" Vince asked, with a wink and a little smile. "Well, maybe…but there was also the piece of meat in his throat, don't you know."

"Oh. Right. Dr. Cathcart had that to test, didn't he?" She slumped a little.

"Ayuh," Vince agreed, "and did. We may be country mice, but we *do* have the occasional dark thought. And the closest thing to poison on that chunk of chewed-up meat was a little salt."

She was silent for a moment. Then she said (in a very low voice): "Maybe it was the kind of stuff that disappears."

"Ayuh," Dave said, and his tongue rounded the inside of one cheek. "Like the Coast Lights after an hour or two."

"Or the rest of the *Lisa Cabot*'s crew," Vince added.

"And once he got off the ferry, you don't know where he went."

"No, ma'am," Vince said. "We've looked off n on for over twenty-five years and never found a soul who claims to have seen him before Johnny and Nancy did around quarter past six on the morning of April 24th. And for the record—not that anyone's keepin one—I don't believe that anyone took what remained of that steak from his hand after he choked on his last bite. I believe a seagull stole the last of it from his dead hand, just as we always surmised. And gorry, I really *do* have to get a move on.'"

"And I have to get with those invoices," Dave said. "But first, I think another little rest-stop might be in order." That said, he lumbered toward the bathroom.

"I suppose I better get with this column," Stephanie said. Then she burst out, half-laughing and half-serious: "But I almost wish you hadn't told me, if you were going to leave me hanging! It'll be *weeks* before I get this out of my mind!"

"It's been twenty-five years, and it's still not out of ours," Vince said. "And at least you know why we didn't tell that guy from the *Globe*."

"Yes. I do."

He smiled and nodded. "You'll do all right, Stephanie. You'll do fine." He gave her shoulder a friendly squeeze, then started for the door, grabbing his narrow reporter's notebook from his littered desk on his way by and stuffing it into his back pocket. He was ninety but still walked easy, his back only slightly bent with age. He wore a gentleman's white shirt, its back crisscrossed with a gentleman's suspenders. Halfway across the room he stopped and turned to her again. A shaft of late sunlight caught his baby-fine white hair and turned it into a halo.

"You've been a pleasure to have around," he said. "I want you to know that."

"Thank you." She hoped she didn't sound as close to

tears as she suddenly felt. "It's been wonderful. I was a little dubious at first, but...but now I guess it goes right back at you. It's a pleasure to be here."

"Have you thought about staying? I think you have."

"Yes. You bet I have."

He nodded gravely. "Dave and I have spoken about that. It'd be good to have some new blood on the staff. Some young blood."

"You guys'll go on for years," she said.

"Oh yes," he said, off-handedly, as if that were a given, and when he died six months later, Stephanie would sit in a cold church, taking notes on the service in her own narrow reporter's book, and think: *He knew it was coming.* "I'll be around for years yet. Still, if you wanted to stay, we'd like to have you. You don't have to answer one way or another now, but consider it an offer."

"All right, I will. And I think we both know what the answer will be."

"That's fine, then." He started to turn, then turned back one last time. "School's almost out for the day, but I could tell you one more thing about our business. May I?"

"Of course."

"There are thousands of papers and *tens* of thousands of people writing stories for em, but there are only two types of stories. There are news stories, which usually aren't stories at all, but only accounts of unfolding events. Things like that don't *have* to be stories. People pick up a newspaper to read about the blood and the tears the way they slow down to look at a wreck on the highway, and then they move on. But what do they find inside of their newspaper?"

"Feature stories," Stephanie said, thinking of Hanratty and his unexplained mysteries.

"Ayuh. And those *are* stories. Every one of em has a beginning, a middle, and an end. That makes em happy news, Steffi, always happy news. Even if the story is about a church secretary who probably killed half the congregation at the church picnic because her lover jilted her, that is happy news, and why?"

"I don't know."

"You better," Dave said, emerging from the bathroom and still wiping his hands on a paper towel. "You better know if you want to be in this business, and understand what it is you're doin." He cast the paper towel into his wastebasket on his way by.

She thought about it. "Feature stories are happy stories because they're over."

"That's right!" Vince cried, beaming. He threw his hands in the air like a revival preacher. "They have *resolution*! They have *closure*! But do things have a beginning, a middle, and an end in real life, Stephanie? What does your experience tell you?"

"When it comes to newspaper work, I don't have much," she said. "Just the campus paper and, you know, Arts 'N Things here."

Vince waved this away. "Your heart n mind, what do they tell you?"

"That life usually doesn't work that way." She was thinking of a certain young man who would have to be dealt with if she decided to stay here beyond her four months…and that dealing might be messy. Probably *would* be messy.

Rick would not take the news well, because in Rick's mind, that wasn't how the story was supposed to go.

"I never read a feature story that wasn't a lie," Vince said mildly, "but usually you can make a lie fit on the page. This one would never fit. Unless…" He gave a little shrug.

For a moment she didn't know what that shrug meant. Then she remembered something Dave had said not long after they'd gone out to sit on the deck to sit in the late August sunshine. *It's ours,* he'd said, sounding almost angry. *A guy from the* Globe, *a guy from away—he'd only muck it up.*

"If you'd given this to Hanratty, he *would've* used it, wouldn't he?" she asked them.

"Wasn't ours to give, because we don't own it," Vince said. "It belongs to whoever tracks it down."

Smiling a little, Stephanie shook her head. "I think that's disingenuous. I think you and Dave are the last two people alive who know the whole thing."

"We were," Dave said. "Now there's you, Steffi."

She nodded to him, acknowledging the implicit compliment, then turned her attention back to Vince Teague, eyebrows raised. After a second or two, he chuckled.

"We didn't tell him about the Colorado Kid because he would have taken a true unexplained mystery and made it into just another feature story," Vince said. "Not by changin any of the facts, but by emphasizing one thing—the concept of muscle-relaxants making it hard or impossible to swallow, let's say—and leavin something else out."

"That there was absolutely no sign of anything like that in this case, for instance," Stephanie said.

"Ayuh, maybe that, maybe something else. And maybe he would have written it that way on his own, simply because making a story out of things that ain't quite a story on their own gets to be a habit after a certain number of years in this business, or maybe his editor would have sent it back to him to do on a rewrite."

"Or the editor might've done it himself, if time was tight," Dave put in.

"Yep, editors have been known to do that, as well," Vince agreed. "In any case, the Colorado Kid would most likely have ended up bein installment number seven or eight in Hanratty's Unexplained Mysteries of New England series, something for people to marvel over for fifteen minutes or so on Sunday and line their kitty-litter boxes with on Monday."

"And it wouldn't be yours anymore," Stephanie said.

Dave nodded, but Vince waved his hand as if to say *Oh, pish-tush.* "That I could put up with, but it would've hung a lie around the neck of a man who ain't alive to refute it, and that I *won't* put up with. Because I don't have to." He glanced at his watch. "In any case, I'm on my horse. Whichever one of you's last out the door, be sure to lock it behind you, all right?"

Vince left. They watched him go, then Dave turned back to her. "Any more questions?"

She laughed. "A hundred, but none you or Vince could answer, I guess."

"Just as long as you don't get tired of askin em, that's fine." He wandered off to his desk, sat down, and pulled a stack of papers toward him with a sigh. Stephanie started back toward her own desk, then something caught her eye on the wall-length bulletin board at the far end of the room, opposite Vince's cluttered desk. She walked over for a closer look.

The left half of the bulletin board was layered with old front pages of the *Islander*, most yellowed and curling. High in the corner, all by itself, was the front page from the week of July 9th, 1952. The headline read **MYSTERY LIGHTS OVER HANCOCK FASCINATE THOUSANDS**. Below was a photograph credited to one Vincent Teague—who would have been just thirty-seven back then, if she had her math right. The crisp black-and-white showed a Little League field with a billboard in deep center reading **HANCOCK LUMBER ALWAYS KNOWS THE SCORE!** To Stephanie the photo looked as if it had been snapped at twilight. The few adults in the single set of sagging bleachers were standing and looking up into the sky. So was the ump, who stood straddling home plate with his mask in his right hand. One set of players—the visiting team, she assumed—was bunched tightly together around third base, as if for comfort. The other kids, wearing jeans and jerseys with the words **HANCOCK LUMBER** printed on the back, stood in a rough line across the infield, all staring upward. And on the mound the little boy who had been pitching held his glove up to one of the bright circles which hung in the sky just below the clouds, as if to touch that mystery, and bring it close, and open its heart, and know its story.

THE END

Afterword

Depending on whether you liked or hated *The Colorado Kid* (I think for many people there'll be no middle ground on this one, and that's fine with me), you have my friend Scott to thank or blame. He brought me the news clipping that got it going.

Every writer of fiction has had somebody bring him or her a clipping from time to time, sure that the subject will make a wonderful story. "You'll only have to change it around a little," the clipping-bearer says with an optimistic smile. I don't know how this works with other writers, but it had never worked with me, and when Scott handed me an envelope with a cutting from a Maine newspaper inside, I expected more of the same. But my mother raised no ingrates, so I thanked him, took it home, and tossed it on my desk. A day or two later I tore the envelope open, read the feature story inside, and was immediately galvanized.

I have lost the clipping since, and for once Google, that twenty-first century idiot savant, has been of no help, so all I can do is summarize from memory, a notoriously unreliable reference source. Yet in this case that hardly matters, since the feature story was only the spark that lit the little fire that burns through these pages, and not the fire itself.

What caught my eye immediately upon unfolding the clipping was a drawing of a bright red purse. The story was of the young woman who had owned it. She was seen one day walking the main street of a small island community off the coast of Maine with that red purse over her arm. The next day she was found dead on one of the island beaches, *sans* purse or identification of any kind. Even the cause of her death was a mystery, and although it was eventually put down to drowning, with alcohol perhaps a contributing factor, that diagnosis remains tentative to this day.

The young woman was eventually identified, but not until her remains had spent a long, lonely time in a mainland crypt. And I was left again with a smack of that mystery the Maine islands like Cranberry and Monhegan have always held for me—their contrasting yet oddly complimentary atmospheres of community and solitariness. There are few places in America where the line between the little world Inside and all the great world Outside is so firmly and deeply drawn. Islanders are full of warmth for those who belong, but they keep their secrets well from those who do not. And—as Agatha Christie shows so memorably in *Ten Little Indians*—there is no locked room so grand as an island, even one where the mainland looks just a long step away on a clear summer afternoon; no place so perfectly made for a mystery.

Mystery is my subject here, and I am aware that many

readers will feel cheated, even angry, by my failure to provide a solution to the one posed. Is it because I had no solution to give? The answer is no. Should I have set my wits to work (as Richard Adams puts it in his forenote to *Shardik*), I could likely have provided half a dozen, three good, two a-country fair, and one fine as paint. I suspect many of you who have read the case know what some or all of them are. But in this one case—this very *hard* case, if I may be allowed a small pun on the imprint under whose cover the tale lies—I'm really not interested in the solution but in the mystery. Because it was the mystery that kept bringing me back to the story, day after day.

Did I care about those two old geezers, gnawing ceaselessly away at the case in their spare time even as the years went by and they grew ever more geezerly? Yes, I did. Did I care about Stephanie, who's clearly undergoing a kind of test, and being judged by kind but hard judges? Yes—I wanted her to pass. Was I happy with each little discovery, each small ray of light shed? Of course. But mostly what drew me on was the thought of the Colorado Kid, propped there against that trash barrel and looking out at the ocean, an anomaly that stretched even the most flexible credulity to the absolute snapping point. Maybe even a little beyond. In the end, I didn't care how he got there; like a nightingale glimpsed in the desert, it just took my breath away that he *was*.

And, of course, I wanted to see how my characters coped with the fact of him. It turned out they did quite well. I was proud of them. Now I will wait for my mail, both e- and of the snail variety, and see how *you* guys do with him.

I don't want to belabor the point, but before I leave you, I ask you to consider the fact that we live in a *web* of mystery, and have simply gotten so used to the fact that we have crossed out the word and replaced it with one we like better, that one being *reality*. Where do we come from? Where were we before we were here? Don't know. Where are we going? Don't know. A lot of churches have what they assure us are the answers, but most of us have a sneaking suspicion all that might be a con-job laid down to fill the collection plates. In the meantime, we're in a kind of compulsory dodgeball game as we free-fall from Wherever to Ain't Got A Clue. Sometimes bombs go off and sometimes the planes land okay and sometimes the blood tests come back clean and sometimes the biopsies come back positive. Most times the bad telephone call doesn't come in the middle of the night but sometimes it does, and either way we know we're going to drive pedal-to-the-metal into the mystery eventually.

It's crazy to be able to live with that and stay sane, but it's also beautiful. I write to find out what I think, and what I found out writing *The Colorado Kid* was that maybe—I just say *maybe*—it's the beauty of the mystery that allows us to live sane as we pilot our fragile bodies through this demolition-derby world. We always want to reach for the lights in the sky, and we always want to know where the Colorado Kid (the world is full of Colorado Kids) came from. Wanting might be better than knowing. I don't say that for sure; I only suggest it. But if you tell me I fell down on the job and didn't tell all of this story there was to tell, I say you're all wrong.

On that I *am* sure.

Stephen King
January 31, 2005

If You Enjoyed
THE COLORADO KID

You'll Love
JOYLAND

College student Devin Jones took the summer job at Joyland hoping to forget the girl who broke his heart. But he wound up facing something far more terrible: the legacy of a vicious murder, the fate of a dying child, and dark truths about life—and what comes after—that would change his world forever.

A riveting story about love and loss, about growing up and growing old—and about those who don't get to do either because death comes for them before their time—JOYLAND is Stephen King at the peak of his storytelling powers. With all the emotional impact of King masterpieces such as *The Green Mile* and *The Shawshank Redemption*, JOYLAND is at once a mystery, a horror story, and a bittersweet coming-of-age novel, one that will leave even the most hard-boiled reader profoundly moved.

"Immensely appealing."
— Washington Post

"Tight and engrossing...a prize
worth all your tokens and skeeball tickets."
— USA Today

Read on for a preview—
or get a copy today
from your favorite
local or online bookseller!

♥

I had a car, but on most days in that fall of 1973 I walked to Joyland from Mrs. Shoplaw's Beachside Accommodations in the town of Heaven's Bay. It seemed like the right thing to do. The only thing, actually. By early September, Heaven Beach was almost completely deserted, which suited my mood. That fall was the most beautiful of my life. Even forty years later I can say that. And I was never so unhappy, I can say that, too. People think first love is sweet, and never sweeter than when that first bond snaps. You've heard a thousand pop and country songs that prove the point; some fool got his heart broke. Yet that first broken heart is always the most painful, the slowest to mend, and leaves the most visible scar. What's so sweet about that?

♥

Through September and right into October, the North Carolina skies were clear and the air was warm even at seven in the morning, when I left my second-floor apartment by the outside stairs. If I started with a light jacket on, I was wearing it tied around my waist before I'd finished half of the three miles between the town and the amusement park.

I'd make Betty's Bakery my first stop, grabbing a couple of still-warm croissants. My shadow would walk with me on the sand, at least twenty feet long. Hopeful gulls, smelling the croissants in their waxed paper, would circle overhead. And when I walked back, usually around five (although sometimes I stayed later—there was nothing waiting for me in Heaven's Bay, a town that mostly went sleepybye when summer was over), my shadow walked with me on the water. If the tide was in, it would waver on the surface, seeming to do a slow hula.

Although I can't be completely sure, I think the boy and the woman and their dog were there from the first time I took that walk. The shore between the town and the cheerful, blinking gimcrackery of Joyland was lined with summer homes, many of them expensive, most of them clapped shut after Labor Day. But not the biggest of them, the one that looked like a green wooden castle. A board-walk led from its wide back patio down to where the seagrass gave way to fine white sand. At the end of the boardwalk was a picnic table shaded by a bright green beach umbrella. In its shade, the boy sat in his wheelchair, wearing a baseball cap and covered from the waist down by a blanket even in the late afternoons, when the tempera-ture lingered in the seventies. I thought he was five or so, surely no older than seven. The dog, a Jack Russell terrier, either lay beside him or sat at his feet. The woman sat on one of the picnic table benches, sometimes reading a book, mostly just staring out at the water. She was very beautiful.

Going or coming, I always waved to them, and the boy waved back. She didn't, not at first. 1973 was the year of the OPEC oil embargo, the year Richard Nixon announced he was not a crook, the year Edward G. Robinson and Noel Coward died. It was Devin Jones's lost year. I was a twenty-one year-old virgin with literary aspirations. I possessed three pairs of bluejeans, four pairs of Jockey shorts, a clunker Ford (with a good radio), occasional suicidal ideations, and a broken heart.

Sweet, huh?

♥

The heartbreaker was Wendy Keegan, and she didn't deserve me. It's taken me most of my life to come to that conclusion, but you know the old saw; better late than never. She was from Portsmouth, New Hampshire; I was from South Berwick, Maine. That made her practically the girl next door. We had begun "going together" (as we used to say) during our freshman year at UNH—we actually met at the Freshman Mixer, and how sweet is that? Just like one of those pop songs.

We were inseparable for two years, went everywhere together and did everything together. Everything, that is, but "it." We were both work-study kids with University jobs. Hers was in the library; mine was in the Commons cafeteria. We were offered the chance to hold onto those jobs during the summer of 1972, and of course we did. The money wasn't great, but the togetherness was priceless. I assumed that would also be the deal during the summer of 1973, until Wendy announced that her friend Renee had gotten them jobs working at Filene's, in Boston.

"Where does that leave me?" I asked.

"You can always come down," she said. "I'll miss you like mad, but really, Dev, we could probably use some time apart."

A phrase that is very often a death-knell. She may have seen that idea on my face, because she stood on tiptoe and kissed me. "Absence makes the heart grow fonder," she said. "Besides, with my own place, maybe you can stay over." But she didn't quite look at me when she said that, and I never did stay over. Too many roommates, she said. Too little time. Of course such problems can be overcome, but somehow we never did, which should have told me something; in retrospect, it tells me a lot. Several times we had been very close to "it," but "it" just never quite happened. She always drew back, and I never pressed her. God help me, I was being gallant. I have wondered often since what would have changed (for good or for ill) had I not been. What I know now is that gallant young men rarely get pussy. Put it on a sampler and hang it in your kitchen.

♥

The prospect of another summer mopping cafeteria floors and loading elderly Commons dishwashers with dirty plates didn't hold much charm for me, not with Wendy seventy miles south, enjoying the bright lights of Boston, but it was steady work, which I needed, and I didn't have any other prospects. Then, in late February, one literally came down the dish-line to me on the conveyor belt.

Someone had been reading *Carolina Living* while he or she snarfed up that day's blue plate luncheon special, which happened to be Mexicali Burgers and Caramba Fries. He or she had left the magazine on the tray, and I picked it up along with the dishes. I almost tossed it in the trash, then didn't. Free reading material was, after all, free reading material. (I was a work-study kid, remember.) I stuck it in my back pocket and forgot about it until I got back to my dorm room. There it flopped onto the floor, open to the classified section at the back, while I was changing my pants.

Whoever had been reading the magazine had circled several job possibilities...although in the end, he or she must have decided none of them was quite right; otherwise *Carolina Living* wouldn't have come riding down the conveyor belt. Near the bottom of the page was an ad that caught my eye even though it hadn't been circled. In bold-face type, the first line read: WORK CLOSE TO HEAVEN! What English major could read that and not hang in for the pitch? And what glum twenty-one-year-old, beset with the growing fear that he might be losing his girlfriend, would not be attracted by the idea of working in a place called Joyland?

There was a telephone number, and on a whim, I called it. A week later, a job application landed in my dormitory mailbox. The attached letter stated that if I wanted full-time summer employment (which I did), I'd be doing many different jobs, most but not all custodial. I would have to possess a valid driver's license, and I would need to interview. I could do that on the upcoming spring break instead of going home to Maine for the week. Only I'd been planning to spend at least some of that week with Wendy. We might even get around to "it."

"Go for the interview," Wendy said when I told her. She didn't even hesitate. "It'll be an adventure."

"Being with you would be an adventure," I said.

"There'll be plenty of time for that next year." She stood on tiptoe and kissed me (she always stood on tiptoe). Was she seeing the other guy, even then? Probably not, but I'll bet she'd noticed him, because he was in her Advanced Sociology course. Renee St. Claire would have known, and probably would have told me if I'd asked—telling stuff was Renee's specialty, I bet she wore the priest out when she did the old confession bit—but some things you don't want to know. Like why the girl you loved with all your heart kept saying no to you, but tumbled into bed with the new guy at almost the first opportunity. I'm not sure anybody ever gets completely over their first love, and that still rankles. Part of me still wants to know what was *wrong* with me. What I was lacking. I'm in my sixties now, my hair is gray and I'm a prostate cancer survivor, but I still want to know why I wasn't good enough for Wendy Keegan.

♥

I took a train called the Southerner from Boston to North Carolina (not much of an adventure, but cheap), and a bus from Wilmington to Heaven's Bay. My interview was with Fred Dean, who was—among many other functions— Joyland's employment officer. After fifteen minutes of Q-and-A, plus a look at my driver's license and my Red Cross life-saving certificate, he handed me a plastic badge on a lanyard. It bore the word VISITOR, that day's date, and a cartoon picture of a grinning, blue-eyed German Shepherd who bore a passing resemblance to the famous cartoon sleuth, Scooby-Doo.

"Take a walk around," Dean said. "Ride the Carolina Spin, if you like. Most of the rides aren't up and running yet, but that one is. Tell Lane I said okay. What I gave you is a day-pass, but I want you back here by..." He looked at his watch. "Let's say one o'clock. Tell me then if you want the job. I've got five spots left, but they're all basically the same—as Happy Helpers."

"Thank you, sir."

He nodded, smiling. "Don't know how you'll feel about this place, but it suits me fine. It's a little old and a little rickety, but I find that charming. I tried Disney for a while; didn't like it. It's too...I don't know..."

"Too corporate?" I ventured.

"Exactly. Too corporate. Too buffed and shiny. So I came back to Joyland a few years ago. Haven't regretted it. We fly a bit more by the seat of our pants here—the place has a little of the old-time carny flavor. Go on, look around. See what you think. More important, see how you *feel*."

"Can I ask one question first?"

"Of course."

I fingered my day pass. "Who's the dog?"

His smile became a grin. "That's Howie the Happy Hound, Joyland's mascot. Bradley Easterbrook built Joyland, and the original Howie was his dog. Long dead now, but you'll still see a lot of him, if you work here this summer."

I did…and I didn't. An easy riddle, but the explanation will have to wait awhile.

♥

Joyland was an indie, not as big as a Six Flags park, and nowhere near as big as Disney World, but it was large enough to be impressive, especially with Joyland Avenue, the main drag, and Hound Dog Way, the secondary drag, almost empty and looking eight lanes wide. I heard the whine of power-saws and saw plenty of workmen—the largest crew swarming over the Thunderball, one of Joyland's two coasters—but there were no customers, because the park didn't open until June fifteenth. A few of the food concessions were doing business to take care of the workers' lunch needs, though, and an old lady in front of a star-studded tell-your-fortune kiosk was staring at me suspiciously. With one exception, everything else was shut up tight.

The exception of the Carolina Spin. It was a hundred and seventy feet tall (this I found out later), and turning very slowly. Out in front stood a tightly muscled guy in faded jeans, balding suede boots splotched with grease, and a strap-style tee shirt. He wore a derby hat tilted on his coal-black hair. A filterless cigarette was parked behind one ear. He looked like a cartoon carnival barker from an old-time newspaper strip. There was an open toolbox and a big portable radio on an orange crate beside him. The Faces were singing "Stay with Me." The guy was bopping to the beat, hands in his back pockets, hips moving side to side. I had a thought, absurd but perfectly clear: *When I grow up, I want to look just like this guy.*

He pointed to the pass. "Freddy Dean sent you, right? Told you everything else was closed, but you could take a ride on the big wheel."

"Yes, sir."

"A ride on the Spin means you're in. He likes the chosen few to get the aerial view. You gonna take the job?"

"I think so."

He stuck out his hand. "I'm Lane Hardy. Welcome aboard, kid."

I shook with him. "Devin Jones."

"Pleased to meet you."

He started up the inclined walk leading to the gently turning ride, grabbed a long lever that looked like a stick shift, and edged it back. The wheel came to a slow stop with one of the gaily painted cabins (the image of Howie the Happy Hound on each) swaying at the passenger loading dock.

"Climb aboard, Jonesy. I'm going to send you up where the air is rare and the view is much more than fair."

I climbed into the cabin and closed the door. Lane gave it a shake to make sure it was latched, dropped the safety bar, then returned to his rudimentary controls. "Ready for takeoff, cap'n?"

"I guess so."

"Amazement awaits." He gave me a wink and advanced the control stick. The wheel began to turn again and all at once he was looking up at me. So was the old lady by the fortune-telling booth. Her neck was craned and she was shading her eyes. I waved to her. She didn't wave back.

Then I was above everything but the convoluted dips and twists of the Thunderball, rising into the chilly early spring air, and feeling—stupid but true—that I was leaving all my cares and worries down below.

Joyland wasn't a theme park, which allowed it to have a little bit of everything. There was a secondary roller coaster called the Delirium Shaker and a water slide (Captain Nemo's Splash & Crash). On the far western side of the park was a special annex for the little ones called the Wiggle-Waggle Village. There was also a concert hall where most of the acts—this I also learned later—were either B-list C&W or the kind of rockers who peaked in the fifties or sixties. I remember that Johnny Otis and Big Joe Turner did a show there together. I had to ask Brenda Rafferty, the head accountant who was also a kind of den mother to the Hollywood Girls, who they were. Bren thought I was dense; I thought she was old; we were both probably right.

Lane Hardy took me all the way to the top and then stopped the wheel. I sat in the swaying car, gripping the safety bar, and looking out at a brand-new world. To the west was the North Carolina flatland, looking incredibly green to a New England kid who was used to thinking of March as nothing but true spring's cold and muddy precursor. To the east was the ocean, a deep metallic blue until it broke in creamy-white pulses on the beach where I would tote my abused heart up and down a few months hence. Directly below me was the good-natured jumble of Joyland—the big rides and small ones, the concert hall and concessions, the souvenir shops and the Happy Hound Shuttle, which took customers to the adjacent motels and, of course, the beach. To the north was Heaven's Bay. From high above the park (upstairs, where the air is rare), the town looked like a nestle of children's blocks from which four church steeples rose at the major points of the compass.

The wheel began to move again. I came down feeling like a kid in a Rudyard Kipling story, riding on the nose of an elephant. Lane Hardy brought me to a stop, but didn't bother to unlatch the car's door for me; I was, after all, almost an employee.

"How'd you like it?"

"Great," I said.

"Yeah, it ain't bad for a grandma ride." He reset his derby so it slanted the other way and cast an appraising eye over me. "How tall are you? Six-three?"

"Six-four."

"Uh-huh. Let's see how you like ridin all six-four of you on the Spin in the middle of July, wearin the fur and singin 'Happy Birthday' to some spoiled-rotten little snothole with cotton candy in one hand and a meltin Kollie Kone in the other."

"Wearing what fur?"

But he was headed back to his machinery and didn't answer. Maybe he couldn't hear me over his radio, which was now blasting "Crocodile Rock." Or maybe he just wanted my future occupation as one of Joyland's cadre of Happy Hounds to come as a surprise.

♥

I had over an hour to kill before meeting with Fred Dean again, so I strolled up Hound Dog Way toward a lunch-wagon that looked like it was doing a pretty good business. Not everything at Joyland was canine-themed, but plenty of stuff was, including this particular eatery, which was called Pup-A-Licious. I was on a ridiculously tight budget for this little job-hunting expedition, but I thought I could afford a couple of bucks for a chili-dog and a paper cup of French fries.

When I reached the palm-reading concession, Madame Fortuna planted herself in my path. Except that's not quite right, because she was only Fortuna between May fifteenth and Labor Day. During those sixteen weeks, she dressed in long skirts, gauzy, layered blouses, and shawls decorated with various cabalistic symbols. Gold hoops hung from her ears, so heavy they dragged the lobes down, and she talked in a thick Romany accent that made her sound like a character from a 1930s fright-flick, the kind featuring mist-shrouded castles and howling wolves.

During the rest of the year she was a widow from Brooklyn who collected Hummel figures and liked movies (especially the weepy-ass kind where some chick gets cancer and dies beautifully). Today she was smartly put together in a black pantsuit and low heels. A rose-pink scarf around her throat added a touch of color. As Fortuna, she sported masses of wild gray locks, but that was a wig, and still stored under its own glass dome in her little Heaven's Bay house. Her actual hair was a cropped cap of dyed black. The *Love Story* fan from Brooklyn and Fortuna the Seer only came together in one respect: both fancied themselves psychic.

"There is a shadow over you, young man," she announced.

I looked down and saw she was absolutely right. I was standing in the shadow of the Carolina Spin. We both were.

"Not that, stupidnik. Over your future. You will have a hunger."

I had a bad one already, but a Pup-A-Licious footlong would soon take care of it. "That's very interesting, Mrs… um…"

"Rosalind Gold," she said, holding out her hand. "But you can call me Rozzie. Everyone does. But during the season…" She fell into character, which meant she sounded like Bela Lugosi with breasts. "Doorink the season, I am… *Fortuna!*"

I shook with her. If she'd been in costume as well as in character, half a dozen gold bangles would have clattered on her wrist. "Very nice to meet you." And, trying on the same accent: "I am…*Devin!*"

She wasn't amused. "An Irish name?"

"Right."

"The Irish are full of sorrow, and many have the sight. I don't know if you do, but you will meet someone who does."

Actually, I was full of happiness…along with that surpassing desire to put a Pup-A-Licious pup, preferably loaded with chili, down my throat. This was feeling like an adventure. I told myself I'd probably feel less that way when I was swabbing out toilets at the end of a busy day, or cleaning puke from the seats of the Whirly Cups, but just then everything seemed perfect.

"Are you practicing your act?"

She drew herself up to her full height, which might have been five-two. "Is no act, my lad." She said *ect* for *act*. "Jews are the most psychically sensitive race on earth. This is a thing everyone knows." She dropped the accent. "Also, Joyland beats hanging out a palmistry shingle on Second Avenue. Sorrowful or not, I like you. You give off good vibrations."

"One of my very favorite Beach Boys songs."

"But you are on the edge of great sorrow." She paused, doing the old emphasis thing. "And, perhaps, danger."

"Do you see a beautiful woman with dark hair in my future?" Wendy was a beautiful woman with dark hair.

"No," Rozzie said, and what came next stopped me dead. "She is in your past."

Ohh-kay.

I walked around her in the direction of Pup-A-Licious, being careful not to touch her. She was a charlatan, I didn't have a single doubt about that, but touching her just then still seemed like a lousy idea.

No good. She walked with me. "In your future is a little girl and a little boy. The boy has a dog."

"A Happy Hound, I bet. Probably named Howie."

She ignored this latest attempt at levity. "The girl wears a red hat and carries a doll. One of these children has the sight. I don't know which. It is hidden from me."

I hardly heard that part of her spiel. I was thinking of the previous pronouncement, made in a flat Brooklyn accent: *She is in your past.*

Madame Fortuna got a lot of stuff wrong, I found out, but she *did* seem to have a genuine psychic touch, and on the day I interviewed for a summer at Joyland, she was hitting on all cylinders…

Read the rest today!
JOYLAND is available now
from your favorite bookseller.
For more information, visit
www.HardCaseCrime.com

Acclaim For the Work
of STEPHEN KING!

"Excellent, psychologically textured…Stephen King is so widely acknowledged as America's master of paranormal terrors that you can forget his real genius is for the everyday."
— *New York Times Book Review*

"King has written…a novel that's as hauntingly touching as it is just plain haunted…one of his freshest and most frightening works to date."
— *Entertainment Weekly*

"Extraordinarily vivid…an impressive tour de force, a sensitive character study that holds the reader rapt."
— *Playboy*

"Stephen King is superb."
— *Time*

"Mr. King makes palpable the longing and regret that arise out of calamity, and deftly renders the kindness and pettiness that can mark small-town life."
— *Wall Street Journal*

"King is a master at crafting a story and creating a sense of place."
— *USA Today*

"A thoroughly compelling thriller."
— *Esquire*

"Don't start this one on a school night…You'll be up till dawn."
  —*People*

"As brilliant a dark dream as has ever been dreamed in this century."
  —*Palm Beach Post*

"A great book…A landmark in American literature."
  —*Chicago Sun-Times*

"Stephen King is an immensely talented storyteller of seemingly inexhaustible gifts."
  —*Interview*

"A rare blend of luminous prose, thought-provoking themes and masterful storytelling."
  —*San Diego Union Tribune*

"Not only immensely popular but immensely talented, a modern-day counterpart to Twain, Hawthorne, Dickens."
  —*Publishers Weekly*

"He's a master storyteller. Gather around the pages of his literary campfire and he'll weave you a darn good yarn."
  —*Houston Chronicle*

"King surpasses our expectations, leaves us spellbound and hungry for the next twist of plot."
  —*Boston Globe*

"Top shelf. You couldn't go wrong with a King book."
  —*Michael Connelly*

"Stephen King is the Winslow Homer of blood."
  —*New Yorker*

"King has invented genres, reinvented them, then stepped outside what he himself has accomplished...Stephen King, like Mark Twain, is an American genius."
—*Greg Iles*

"Stephen King is much more than just a horror fiction writer. And I believe that he's never been given credit for taking American literature and stretching its boundaries."
—*Gloria Naylor*

"To my mind, King is one of the most underestimated novelists of our time."
—*Mordechai Richler, Vancouver Sun*

"King possesses an incredible sense of story...[He is] a gifted writer of intensely felt emotions, a soulful writer in control of a spare prose that never gets in the way of the story...I, for one (of millions), wait impatiently to see where this king of storytellers takes us next."
—*Ridley Pearson*

"An absorbing, constantly surprising novel filled with true narrative magic."
—*Washington Post*

"It grabs you and holds you and won't let go...a genuine page turner."
—*Chattanooga Times*

"Blending philosophy with a plot that moves at supersonic speed while showcasing deeply imagined characters...an impressive sensitivity to what has often loosely been called the human condition."
—*Newsday*

I stashed my basket of dirty rags and Turtle Wax by the exit door in the arcade. It was ten past noon, but right then food wasn't what I was hungry for. I walked slowly along the track and into Horror House.

I had to duck my head when I passed beneath the Screaming Skull, even though it was now pulled up and locked in its home position. My footfalls echoed on a wooden floor painted to look like stone. I could hear my breathing. It sounded harsh and dry. I was scared, okay? Tom had told me to stay away from this place, but Tom didn't run my life any more than Eddie Parks did.

Between the Dungeon and the Torture Chamber, the track descended and described a double-S curve where the cars picked up speed and whipped the riders back and forth. Horror House was a dark ride, but when it was in operation, this stretch was the only completely dark part. It had to be where the girl's killer had cut her throat and dumped her body. How quick he must have been, and how certain of exactly what he was going to do!

I walked slowly down the double-S, thinking it would not be beyond Eddie to hear me and shut off the overhead work-lights as a joke. To leave me in here to feel my way past the murder site with only the sound of the wind and that one slapping board to keep me company. And suppose…just suppose…a young girl's hand reached out in that darkness and took mine…?

JOYLAND

by **Stephen King**

A HARD CASE CRIME NOVEL

A HARD CASE CRIME BOOK
(HCC-112)
First Hard Case Crime edition: June 2013

Published by

Titan Books
A division of Titan Publishing Group Ltd
144 Southwark Street
London
SE1 0UP

in collaboration with Winterfall LLC

ISBN 978-1-78116-264-4

Design direction by Max Phillips
www.maxphillips.net

Typeset by Swordsmith Productions

The name "Hard Case Crime" and the Hard Case Crime logo are trademarks of Winterfall LLC. Hard Case Crime books are selected and edited by Charles Ardai.

Printed and bound in Great Britain by CPI Group (UK) Ltd, Croydon, CR0 4YY

Visit us on the web at www.HardCaseCrime.com

For Donald Westlake

♥

I had a car, but on most days in that fall of 1973 I walked to Joyland from Mrs. Shoplaw's Beachside Accommodations in the town of Heaven's Bay. It seemed like the right thing to do. The only thing, actually. By early September, Heaven Beach was almost completely deserted, which suited my mood. That fall was the most beautiful of my life. Even forty years later I can say that. And I was never so unhappy, I can say that, too. People think first love is sweet, and never sweeter than when that first bond snaps. You've heard a thousand pop and country songs that prove the point; some fool got his heart broke. Yet that first broken heart is always the most painful, the slowest to mend, and leaves the most visible scar. What's so sweet about that?

♥

Through September and right into October, the North Carolina skies were clear and the air was warm even at seven in the morning, when I left my second-floor apartment by the outside stairs. If I started with a light jacket on, I was wearing it tied around my waist before I'd finished half of the three miles between the town and the amusement park.

I'd make Betty's Bakery my first stop, grabbing a couple of still-warm croissants. My shadow would walk with me on the

sand, at least twenty feet long. Hopeful gulls, smelling the croissants in their waxed paper, would circle overhead. And when I
walked back, usually around five (although sometimes I stayed
later—there was nothing waiting for me in Heaven's Bay, a
town that mostly went sleepybye when summer was over), my
shadow walked with me on the water. If the tide was in, it would
waver on the surface, seeming to do a slow hula.

Although I can't be completely sure, I think the boy and the
woman and their dog were there from the first time I took that
walk. The shore between the town and the cheerful, blinking
gimcrackery of Joyland was lined with summer homes, many of
them expensive, most of them clapped shut after Labor Day.
But not the biggest of them, the one that looked like a green
wooden castle. A boardwalk led from its wide back patio down
to where the seagrass gave way to fine white sand. At the end
of the boardwalk was a picnic table shaded by a bright green
beach umbrella. In its shade, the boy sat in his wheelchair,
wearing a baseball cap and covered from the waist down by
a blanket even in the late afternoons, when the temperature
lingered in the seventies. I thought he was five or so, surely no
older than seven. The dog, a Jack Russell terrier, either lay
beside him or sat at his feet. The woman sat on one of the picnic
table benches, sometimes reading a book, mostly just staring
out at the water. She was very beautiful.

Going or coming, I always waved to them, and the boy waved
back. She didn't, not at first. 1973 was the year of the OPEC oil
embargo, the year Richard Nixon announced he was not a crook,
the year Edward G. Robinson and Noel Coward died. It was
Devin Jones's lost year. I was a twenty-one year-old virgin with
literary aspirations. I possessed three pairs of bluejeans, four

pairs of Jockey shorts, a clunker Ford (with a good radio), occasional suicidal ideations, and a broken heart.

Sweet, huh?

♥

The heartbreaker was Wendy Keegan, and she didn't deserve me. It's taken me most of my life to come to that conclusion, but you know the old saw; better late than never. She was from Portsmouth, New Hampshire; I was from South Berwick, Maine. That made her practically the girl next door. We had begun "going together" (as we used to say) during our freshman year at UNH—we actually met at the Freshman Mixer, and how sweet is that? Just like one of those pop songs.

We were inseparable for two years, went everywhere together and did everything together. Everything, that is, but "it." We were both work-study kids with University jobs. Hers was in the library; mine was in the Commons cafeteria. We were offered the chance to hold onto those jobs during the summer of 1972, and of course we did. The money wasn't great, but the togetherness was priceless. I assumed that would also be the deal during the summer of 1973, until Wendy announced that her friend Renee had gotten them jobs working at Filene's, in Boston.

"Where does that leave me?" I asked.

"You can always come down," she said. "I'll miss you like mad, but really, Dev, we could probably use some time apart."

A phrase that is very often a death-knell. She may have seen that idea on my face, because she stood on tiptoe and kissed me. "Absence makes the heart grow fonder," she said. "Besides, with my own place, maybe you can stay over." But she didn't quite look at me when she said that, and I never did stay over. Too many roommates, she said. Too little time. Of course such problems can be overcome, but somehow we never did, which should have told me something; in retrospect, it tells me a lot. Several times we had been very close to "it," but "it" just never quite happened. She always drew back, and I never pressed her. God help me, I was being gallant. I have wondered often since what would have changed (for good or for ill) had I not been. What I know now is that gallant young men rarely get pussy. Put it on a sampler and hang it in your kitchen.

♥

The prospect of another summer mopping cafeteria floors and loading elderly Commons dishwashers with dirty plates didn't hold much charm for me, not with Wendy seventy miles south, enjoying the bright lights of Boston, but it was steady work, which I needed, and I didn't have any other prospects. Then, in late February, one literally came down the dish-line to me on the conveyor belt.

Someone had been reading *Carolina Living* while he or she snarfed up that day's blue plate luncheon special, which happened to be Mexicali Burgers and Caramba Fries. He or she had left the magazine on the tray, and I picked it up along with the dishes. I almost tossed it in the trash, then didn't. Free reading material was, after all, free reading material. (I was a work-study kid, remember.) I stuck it in my back pocket and forgot about it until I got back to my dorm room. There it flopped onto the floor, open to the classified section at the back, while I was changing my pants.

Whoever had been reading the magazine had circled several

job possibilities...although in the end, he or she must have decided none of them was quite right; otherwise *Carolina Living* wouldn't have come riding down the conveyor belt. Near the bottom of the page was an ad that caught my eye even though it hadn't been circled. In boldface type, the first line read: WORK CLOSE TO HEAVEN! What English major could read that and not hang in for the pitch? And what glum twenty-one-year-old, beset with the growing fear that he might be losing his girl-friend, would not be attracted by the idea of working in a place called Joyland?

There was a telephone number, and on a whim, I called it. A week later, a job application landed in my dormitory mailbox. The attached letter stated that if I wanted full-time summer employment (which I did), I'd be doing many different jobs, most but not all custodial. I would have to possess a valid driver's license, and I would need to interview. I could do that on the upcoming spring break instead of going home to Maine for the week. Only I'd been planning to spend at least some of that week with Wendy. We might even get around to "it."

"Go for the interview," Wendy said when I told her. She didn't even hesitate. "It'll be an adventure."

"Being with you would be an adventure," I said.

"There'll be plenty of time for that next year." She stood on tiptoe and kissed me (she always stood on tiptoe). Was she seeing the other guy, even then? Probably not, but I'll bet she'd noticed him, because he was in her Advanced Sociology course. Renee St. Claire would have known, and probably would have told me if I'd asked—telling stuff was Renee's specialty, I bet she wore the priest out when she did the old confession bit—but some things you don't want to know. Like why the girl you loved with all your heart kept saying no to you, but tumbled into bed with the new guy at almost the first opportunity. I'm not sure anybody ever gets completely over their first love, and that still rankles. Part of me still wants to know what was *wrong* with me. What I was lacking. I'm in my sixties now, my hair is gray and I'm a prostate cancer survivor, but I still want to know why I wasn't good enough for Wendy Keegan.

♥

I took a train called the Southerner from Boston to North Carolina (not much of an adventure, but cheap), and a bus from Wilmington to Heaven's Bay. My interview was with Fred Dean, who was—among many other functions—Joyland's employment officer. After fifteen minutes of Q-and-A, plus a look at my driver's license and my Red Cross life-saving certificate, he handed me a plastic badge on a lanyard. It bore the word VISITOR, that day's date, and a cartoon picture of a grinning, blue-eyed German Shepherd who bore a passing resemblance to the famous cartoon sleuth, Scooby-Doo.

"Take a walk around," Dean said. "Ride the Carolina Spin, if you like. Most of the rides aren't up and running yet, but that one is. Tell Lane I said okay. What I gave you is a day-pass, but I want you back here by…" He looked at his watch. "Let's say one o'clock. Tell me then if you want the job. I've got five spots left, but they're all basically the same—as Happy Helpers."

"Thank you, sir."

He nodded, smiling. "Don't know how you'll feel about this place, but it suits me fine. It's a little old and a little rickety, but I find that charming. I tried Disney for a while; didn't like it. It's too…I don't know…"

"Too corporate?" I ventured.

"Exactly. Too corporate. Too buffed and shiny. So I came back to Joyland a few years ago. Haven't regretted it. We fly a bit more by the seat of our pants here—the place has a little of the old-time carny flavor. Go on, look around. See what you think. More important, see how you *feel*."

"Can I ask one question first?"

"Of course."

I fingered my day pass. "Who's the dog?"

His smile became a grin. "That's Howie the Happy Hound, Joyland's mascot. Bradley Easterbrook built Joyland, and the original Howie was his dog. Long dead now, but you'll still see a lot of him, if you work here this summer."

I did...and I didn't. An easy riddle, but the explanation will have to wait awhile.

♥

Joyland was an indie, not as big as a Six Flags park, and no-where near as big as Disney World, but it was large enough to be impressive, especially with Joyland Avenue, the main drag, and Hound Dog Way, the secondary drag, almost empty and looking eight lanes wide. I heard the whine of power-saws and saw plenty of workmen—the largest crew swarming over the Thunderball, one of Joyland's two coasters—but there were no customers, because the park didn't open until May fifteenth. A few of the food concessions were doing business to take care of the workers' lunch needs, though, and an old lady in front of a star-studded tell-your-fortune kiosk was staring at me suspiciously. With one exception, everything else was shut up tight.

The exception of the Carolina Spin. It was a hundred and

seventy feet tall (this I found out later), and turning very slowly. Out in front stood a tightly muscled guy in faded jeans, balding suede boots splotched with grease, and a strap-style tee shirt. He wore a derby hat tilted on his coal-black hair. A filterless cigarette was parked behind one ear. He looked like a cartoon carnival barker from an old-time newspaper strip. There was an open toolbox and a big portable radio on an orange crate beside him. The Faces were singing "Stay with Me." The guy was bopping to the beat, hands in his back pockets, hips moving side to side. I had a thought, absurd but perfectly clear: *When I grow up, I want to look just like this guy.*

He pointed to the pass. "Freddy Dean sent you, right? Told you everything else was closed, but you could take a ride on the big wheel."

"Yes, sir."

"A ride on the Spin means you're in. He likes the chosen few to get the aerial view. You gonna take the job?"

"I think so."

He stuck out his hand. "I'm Lane Hardy. Welcome aboard, kid."

I shook with him. "Devin Jones."

"Pleased to meet you."

He started up the inclined walk leading to the gently turning ride, grabbed a long lever that looked like a stick shift, and edged it back. The wheel came to a slow stop with one of the gaily painted cabins (the image of Howie the Happy Hound on each) swaying at the passenger loading dock.

"Climb aboard, Jonesy. I'm going to send you up where the air is rare and the view is much more than fair."

I climbed into the cabin and closed the door. Lane gave it a shake to make sure it was latched, dropped the safety bar, then returned to his rudimentary controls. "Ready for takeoff, cap'n?"

"I guess so."

"Amazement awaits." He gave me a wink and advanced the control stick. The wheel began to turn again and all at once he was looking up at me. So was the old lady by the fortune-telling booth. Her neck was craned and she was shading her eyes. I waved to her. She didn't wave back.

Then I was above everything but the convoluted dips and twists of the Thunderball, rising into the chilly early spring air, and feeling—stupid but true—that I was leaving all my cares and worries down below.

Joyland wasn't a theme park, which allowed it to have a little bit of everything. There was a secondary roller coaster called the Delirium Shaker and a water slide (Captain Nemo's Splash & Crash). On the far western side of the park was a special annex for the little ones called the Wiggle-Waggle Village. There was also a concert hall where most of the acts—this I also learned later—were either B-list C&W or the kind of rockers who peaked in the fifties or sixties. I remember that Johnny Otis and Big Joe Turner did a show there together. I had to ask Brenda Rafferty, the head accountant who was also a kind of den mother to the Hollywood Girls, who they were. Bren thought I was dense; I thought she was old; we were both probably right.

Lane Hardy took me all the way to the top and then stopped the wheel. I sat in the swaying car, gripping the safety bar, and looking out at a brand-new world. To the west was the North Carolina flatland, looking incredibly green to a New England kid who was used to thinking of March as nothing but true spring's cold and muddy precursor. To the east was the ocean, a deep metallic blue until it broke in creamy-white pulses on the beach where I would tote my abused heart up and down a few months hence. Directly below me was the good-natured jumble of Joyland—the big rides and small ones, the concert hall and concessions, the souvenir shops and the Happy Hound Shuttle, which took customers to the adjacent motels and, of course, the beach. To the north was Heaven's Bay. From high above the park (upstairs, where the air is rare), the town looked like a nestle of children's blocks from which four church steeples rose at the major points of the compass.

The wheel began to move again. I came down feeling like a kid in a Rudyard Kipling story, riding on the nose of an elephant. Lane Hardy brought me to a stop, but didn't bother to unlatch the car's door for me; I was, after all, almost an employee.

"How'd you like it?"

"Great," I said.

"Yeah, it ain't bad for a grandma ride." He reset his derby so it slanted the other way and cast an appraising eye over me. "How tall are you? Six-three?"

"Six-four."

"Uh-huh. Let's see how you like ridin all six-four of you on the Spin in the middle of July, wearin the fur and singin 'Happy Birthday' to some spoiled-rotten little snothole with cotton candy in one hand and a meltin Kollie Kone in the other."

"Wearing what fur?"

But he was headed back to his machinery and didn't answer. Maybe he couldn't hear me over his radio, which was now blasting "Crocodile Rock." Or maybe he just wanted my future occupation as one of Joyland's cadre of Happy Hounds to come as a surprise.

♥

I had over an hour to kill before meeting with Fred Dean again, so I strolled up Hound Dog Way toward a lunch-wagon that looked like it was doing a pretty good business. Not everything at Joyland was canine-themed, but plenty of stuff was, including this particular eatery, which was called Pup-A-Licious. I was on a ridiculously tight budget for this little job-hunting expedition, but I thought I could afford a couple of bucks for a chili-dog and a paper cup of French fries.

When I reached the palm-reading concession, Madame Fortuna planted herself in my path. Except that's not quite right, because she was only Fortuna between May fifteenth and Labor Day. During those sixteen weeks, she dressed in long skirts, gauzy, layered blouses, and shawls decorated with various cabalistic symbols. Gold hoops hung from her ears, so heavy they dragged the lobes down, and she talked in a thick Romany accent that made her sound like a character from a 1930s fright-flick, the kind featuring mist-shrouded castles and howling wolves.

During the rest of the year she was a widow from Brooklyn who collected Hummel figures and liked movies (especially the weepy-ass kind where some chick gets cancer and dies beautifully). Today she was smartly put together in a black pantsuit and low heels. A rose-pink scarf around her throat added a touch of color. As Fortuna, she sported masses of wild gray locks, but that was a wig, and still stored under its own glass dome in her little Heaven's Bay house. Her actual hair was a cropped cap of dyed black. The *Love Story* fan from Brooklyn and Fortuna the Seer only came together in one respect: both fancied themselves psychic.

"There is a shadow over you, young man," she announced.

I looked down and saw she was absolutely right. I was standing in the shadow of the Carolina Spin. We both were.

"Not that, stupidnik. Over your future. You will have a hunger."

I had a bad one already, but a Pup-A-Licious footlong would soon take care of it. "That's very interesting, Mrs…um…"

"Rosalind Gold," she said, holding out her hand. "But you can call me Rozzie. Everyone does. But during the season…" She fell into character, which meant she sounded like Bela Lugosi with breasts. "Doorink the season, I am…*Fortuna*!"

I shook with her. If she'd been in costume as well as in character, half a dozen gold bangles would have clattered on her wrist. "Very nice to meet you." And, trying on the same accent: "I am…*Devin*!"

She wasn't amused. "An Irish name?"

"Right."

"The Irish are full of sorrow, and many have the sight. I don't know if you do, but you will meet someone who does."

Actually, I was full of happiness…along with that surpassing desire to put a Pup-A-Licious pup, preferably loaded with chili, down my throat. This was feeling like an adventure. I told myself I'd probably feel less that way when I was swabbing out toilets at the end of a busy day, or cleaning puke from the seats of the Whirly Cups, but just then everything seemed perfect.

"Are you practicing your act?"

She drew herself up to her full height, which might have been five-two. "Is no act, my lad." She said *ect* for *act*. "Jews are the most psychically sensitive race on earth. This is a thing everyone knows." She dropped the accent. "Also, Joyland beats hanging out a palmistry shingle on Second Avenue. Sorrowful or not, I like you. You give off good vibrations."

"One of my very favorite Beach Boys songs."

"But you are on the edge of great sorrow." She paused, doing the old emphasis thing. "And, perhaps, danger."

"Do you see a beautiful woman with dark hair in my future?" Wendy was a beautiful woman with dark hair.

"No," Rozzie said, and what came next stopped me dead. "She is in your past."

Ohh-kay.

I walked around her in the direction of Pup-A-Licious, being careful not to touch her. She was a charlatan, I didn't have a single doubt about that, but touching her just then still seemed like a lousy idea.

No good. She walked with me. "In your future is a little girl and a little boy. The boy has a dog."

"A Happy Hound, I bet. Probably named Howie."

She ignored this latest attempt at levity. "The girl wears a red hat and carries a doll. One of these children has the sight. I don't know which. It is hidden from me."

I hardly heard that part of her spiel. I was thinking of the previous pronouncement, made in a flat Brooklyn accent: *She is in your past.*

Madame Fortuna got a lot of stuff wrong, I found out, but she *did* seem to have a genuine psychic touch, and on the day I interviewed for a summer at Joyland, she was hitting on all cylinders.

♥

I got the job. Mr. Dean was especially pleased by my Red Cross life-saving certificate, obtained at the YMCA the summer I turned sixteen. That was what I called my Boredom Summer.

In the years since, I've discovered there's a lot to be said for boredom.

I told Mr. Dean when my finals ended, and promised him that I'd be at Joyland two days later, ready for team assignment and training. We shook hands and he welcomed me aboard. I had a moment when I wondered if he was going to encourage me to do the Happy Hound Bark with him, or something equivalent, but he just wished me a good day and walked out of the office with me, a little man with sharp eyes and a lithe stride. Standing on the little cement-block porch of the employment office, listening to the pound of the surf and smelling the damp salt air, I felt excited all over again, and hungry for summer to begin.

"You're in the amusement business now, young Mr. Jones," my new boss said. "Not the carny business—not exactly, not the way we run things today—but not so far removed from it, either. Do you know what that means, to be in the amusement business?"

"No, sir, not exactly."

His eyes were solemn, but there was a ghost of a grin on his mouth. "It means the rubes have to leave with smiles on their faces—and by the way, if I ever hear *you* call the customers rubes, you're going to be out the door so fast you won't know what hit you. I can say it, because I've been in the amusement business since I was old enough to shave. They're rubes—no different from the redneck Okies and Arkies that rubbernecked their way through every carny I worked for after World War II. The people who come to Joyland may wear better clothes and drive Fords and Volkswagen microbuses instead of Farmall pickups, but the place turns em into rubes with their mouths hung open. If it doesn't, it's not doing its job. But to you, they're the conies. When *they* hear it, they think Coney Island. We know better. They're rabbits, Mr. Jones, nice plump fun-loving rabbits, hopping from ride to ride and shy to shy instead of from hole to hole."

He dropped me a wink and gave my shoulder a squeeze.

"The conies have to leave happy, or this place dries up and blows away. I've seen it happen, and when it does, it happens fast. It's an amusement park, young Mr. Jones, so pet the conies and give their ears only the gentlest of tugs. In a word, *amuse* them."

"Okay," I said…although I didn't know how much customer amusement I'd be providing by polishing the Devil Wagons (Joyland's version of Dodgem cars) or running a street-sweeper down Hound Dog Way after the gates closed.

"And don't you dare leave me in the lurch. Be here on the agreed-upon date, and five minutes before the agreed-upon time."

"Okay."

"There are two important showbiz rules, kiddo: always know where your wallet is…and *show up*."

♥

When I walked out beneath the big arch with WELCOME TO JOYLAND written on it in neon letters (now off) and into the mostly empty parking lot, Lane Hardy was leaning against one of the shuttered ticket booths, smoking the cigarette previously parked behind his ear.

"Can't smoke on the grounds anymore," he said. "New rule. Mr. Easterbrook says we're the first park in America to have it, but we won't be the last. Get the job?"

"I did."

"Congratulations. Did Freddy give you the carny spiel?"

"Sort of, yeah."

"Tell you about petting the conies?"

"Yeah."

"He can be a pain in the banana, but he's old-time showbiz, seen it all, most of it twice, and he's not wrong. I think you'll do okay. You've got a carny look about you, kid." He waved a hand at the park with its landmarks rising against the blameless blue sky: the Thunderball, the Delirium Shaker, the convoluted twists and turns of Captain Nemo's water slide, and—of course—the Carolina Spin. "Who knows, this place might be your future."

"Maybe," I said, although I already knew what my future was going to be: writing novels and the kind of short stories they publish in *The New Yorker*. I had it all planned out. Of course, I also had marriage to Wendy Keegan all planned out, and how we'd wait until we were in our thirties to have a couple of kids. When you're twenty-one, life is a roadmap. It's only when you get to be twenty-five or so that you begin to suspect you've been looking at the map upside down, and not until you're forty are you entirely sure. By the time you're sixty, take it from me, you're fucking lost.

"Did Rozzie Gold give you her usual bundle of Fortuna horseshit?"

"Um…"

Lane chuckled. "Why do I even ask? Just remember, kid, that ninety percent of everything she says really is horseshit. The other ten…let's just say she's told folks some stuff that rocked them back on their heels."

"What about you?" I asked. "Any revelations that rocked *you* back on your heels?"

He grinned. "The day I let Rozzie read my palm is the day I go back on the road, ride-jocking the tornado-and-chittlins circuit. Mrs. Hardy's boy doesn't mess with Ouija boards and crystal balls."

Do you see a beautiful woman with dark hair in my future? I'd asked.

No. She is in your past.

He was looking at me closely. "What's up? You swallow a fly?"

"It's nothing," I said.

"Come on, son. Did she feed you truth or horseshit? Live or Memorex? Tell your daddy."

"Definitely horseshit." I looked at my watch. "I've got a bus to catch at five, if I'm going to make the train to Boston at seven. I better get moving."

"Ah, you got plenty of time. Where you staying this summer?"

"I hadn't even thought about it."

"You might want to stop at Mrs. Shoplaw's on your way to the bus station. Plenty of people in Heaven's Bay rent to summer help, but she's the best. She's housed a lot of Happy Helpers over the years. Her place is easy to find; it's where Main Street ends at the beach. Great big rambler painted gray. You'll see the sign hanging from the porch. Can't miss it, because it's made out of shells and some're always falling off. MRS. SHOPLAW'S BEACHSIDE ACCOMMODATIONS. Tell her I sent you."

"Okay, I will. Thanks."

"If you rent there, you can walk down here on the beach if you want to save your gas money for something more important, like stepping out on your day off. That beach walk makes a pretty way to start the morning. Good luck, kid. Look forward to working with you." He held out his hand. I shook it and thanked him again.

Since he'd put the idea in my head, I decided to take the beach walk back to town. It would save me twenty minutes waiting for a taxi I couldn't really afford. I had almost reached the wooden stairs going down to the sand when he called after me.

"Hey, Jonesy! Want to know something Rozzie won't tell you?"

"Sure," I said.

"We've got a spook palace called Horror House. The old Roz-ola won't go within fifty yards of it. She hates the pop-ups and the torture chamber and the recorded voices, but the real reason is that she's afraid it really might be haunted."

"Yeah?"

"Yeah. And she ain't the only one. Half a dozen folks who work here claim to have seen her."

"Are you serious?" But this was just one of the questions you ask when you're flabbergasted. I could see he was.

"I'd tell you the story, but break-time's over for me. I've got some power-poles to replace on the Devil Wagons, and the safety inspection guys are coming to look at the Thunderball around three. What a pain in the ass those guys are. Ask Shoplaw. When it comes to Joyland, Emmalina Shoplaw knows more than I do. You could say she's a student of the place. Compared to her, I'm a newbie."

"This isn't a joke? A little rubber chicken you toss at all the new hires?"

"Do I look like I'm joking?"

He didn't, but he did look like he was having a good time. He even dropped me a wink. "What's a self-respecting amusement park without a ghost? Maybe you'll see her yourself. The rubes never do, that's for sure. Now hurry along, kiddo. Nail down a room before you catch the bus back to Wilmington. You'll thank me later."

♥

With a name like Emmalina Shoplaw, it was hard not to picture a rosy-cheeked landlady out of a Charles Dickens novel, one who went everywhere at a bosomy bustle and said things like *Lor' save us*. She'd serve tea and scones while a supporting cast of kind-hearted eccentrics looked on approvingly; she might even pinch my cheek as we sat roasting chestnuts over a crackling fire.

But we rarely get what we imagine in this world, and the gal who answered my ring was tall, fiftyish, flat-chested, and as pale as a frosted windowpane. She carried an old-fashioned beanbag ashtray in one hand and a smoldering cigarette in the other. Her mousy brown hair had been done up in fat coils that covered her ears. They made her look like an aging version of a princess in a Grimm's fairy tale. I explained why I was there.

"Going to work at Joyland, huh? Well, I guess you better come in. Do you have references?"

"Not apartment references, no—I live in a dorm. But I've got a work reference from my boss at the Commons. The Commons is the food-service cafeteria at UNH where I—"

"I know what a Commons is. I was born at night, but it wasn't last night." She showed me into the front parlor, a house-long room stuffed with mismatched furniture and dominated by a big table-model TV. She pointed at it. "Color. My renters are welcome to use it—and the parlor—until ten on weeknights and midnight on the weekends. Sometimes I join the kids for a movie or the Saturday afternoon baseball. We have pizza or I make popcorn. It's jolly."

Jolly, I thought. *As in jolly good*. And it sounded jolly good.

"Tell me, Mr. Jones, do you drink and get noisy? I consider that sort of behavior antisocial, although many don't."

"No, ma'am." I drank a little, but rarely got noisy. Usually after a beer or two, I just got sleepy.

"Asking if you use drugs would be pointless, you'd say no whether you do or not, wouldn't you? But of course that sort of thing always reveals itself in time, and when it does, I invite my renters to find fresh accommos. Not even pot, are we clear on that?"

"Yes."

She peered at me. "You don't *look* like a pothead."

"I'm not."

"I have space for four boarders, and only one of those places is currently taken. Miss Ackerley. She's a librarian. All my rents are single rooms, but they're far nicer than what you'd find at a motel. The one I'm thinking of for you is on the second floor. It has its own bathroom and shower, which those on the third floor do not. There's an outside staircase, too, which is convenient if you have a lady-friend. I have nothing against lady-friends, being both a lady and quite friendly myself. Do you have a lady-friend, Mr. Jones?"

"Yes, but she's working in Boston this summer."

"Well, perhaps you'll meet someone. You know what the song says—love is all around."

I only smiled at that. In the spring of '73, the concept of loving anyone other than Wendy Keegan seemed utterly foreign to me.

"You'll have a car, I imagine. There are just two parking spaces out back for four tenants, so every summer it's first come, first served. You're first come, and I think you'll do. If I find you don't, it's down the road you'll go. Does that strike you as fair?"

"Yes, ma'am."

"Good, because that's the way it is. I'll need the usual: first month, last month, damage deposit." She named a figure that also seemed fair. Nevertheless, it was going to make a shambles of my First New Hampshire Trust account.

"Will you take a check?"

"Will it bounce?"

"No, ma'am, not quite."

She threw back her head and laughed. "Then I'll take it, assuming you still want the room once you've seen it." She stubbed out her cigarette and rose. "By the way, no smoking upstairs—it's a matter of insurance. And no smoking in here, once there are tenants in residence. That's a matter of common politeness. Do you know that old man Easterbrook is instituting a no-smoking policy at the park?"

"I heard that. He'll probably lose business."

"He might at first. Then he might gain some. I'd put my money on Brad. He's a shrewd guy, carny-from-carny." I thought to ask her what that meant, exactly, but she had already moved on. "Shall we have a peek at the room?"

A peek at the second floor room was enough to convince me it would be fine. The bed was big, which was good, and the

window looked out on the ocean, which was even better. The
bathroom was something of a joke, so tiny that when I sat on
the commode my feet would be in the shower, but college students with only crumbs in their financial cupboards can't be
too picky. And the view was the clincher. I doubted if the rich
folks had a better one from their summer places along Heaven's
Row. I pictured bringing Wendy here, the two of us admiring
the view, and then…in that big bed with the steady, sleepy beat
of the surf outside…

"It." Finally, "it."

"I want it," I said, and felt my cheeks heat up. It wasn't just
the room I was talking about.

"I know you do. It's all over your darn face." As if she knew
what I was thinking, and maybe she did. She grinned—a big
wide one that made her almost Dickensian in spite of her flat
bosom and pale skin. "Your own little nest. Not the Palace of
Versailles, but your own. Not like having a dorm room, is it?
Even a single?"

"No," I admitted. I was thinking I'd have to talk my dad into
putting another five hundred bucks into my bank account, to
keep me covered until I started getting paychecks. He'd grouse
but come through. I just hoped I wouldn't have to play the
Dead Mom card. She had been gone almost four years, but Dad
carried half a dozen pictures of her in his wallet, and still wore
his wedding ring.

"Your own job and your own place," she said, sounding a bit
dreamy. "That's good stuff, Devin. Do you mind me calling you
Devin?"

"Make it Dev."

"All right, I will." She looked around the little room with its sharply sloping roof—it was under an eave—and sighed. "The thrill doesn't last long, but while it does, it's a fine thing. That sense of independence. I think you'll fit in here. You've got a carny look about you."

"You're the second person to tell me that." Then I thought of my conversation with Lane Hardy in the parking lot. "Third, actually."

"And I bet I know who the other two were. Anything else I can show you? The bathroom's not much, I know, but it beats having to take a dump in a dormitory bathroom while a couple of guys at the sinks fart and tell lies about the girls they made out with last night."

I burst into roars of laughter, and Mrs. Emmalina Shoplaw joined me.

♥

We descended by way of the outside stairs. "How's Lane Hardy?" she asked when we got to the bottom. "Still wearing that stupid beanie of his?"

"It looked like a derby to me."

She shrugged. "Beanie, derby, what's the diff?"

"He's fine, but he told me something…"

She was giving me a head-cocked look. Almost smiling, but not quite.

"He told me the Joyland funhouse—Horror House, he called it—is haunted. I asked him if he was pulling my leg, and he said he wasn't. He said you knew about it."

"Did he, now."

"Yes. He says that when it comes to Joyland, you know more than he does."

"Well," she said, reaching into the pocket of her slacks and bringing out a pack of Winstons, "I know a fair amount. My husband was chief of engineering down there until he took a heart attack and died. When it turned out his life insurance was lousy—and borrowed against to the hilt in the bargain—I started renting out the top two stories of this place. What else was I going to do? We just had the one kid, and now she's up in New York, working for an ad agency." She lit her cigarette, inhaled, and chuffed it back out as laughter. "Working on losing her southern accent, too, but that's another story. This overgrown monstrosity of a house was Howie's playtoy, and I never begrudged him. At least it's paid off. And I like staying connected to the park, because it makes me feel like I'm still connected to him. Can you understand that?"

"Sure."

She considered me through a rising raft of cigarette smoke, smiled, and shook her head. "Nah—you're being kind, but you're a little too young."

"I lost my Mom four years ago. My dad's still grieving. He says there's a reason *wife* and *life* sound almost the same. I've got school, at least, and my girlfriend. Dad's knocking around a house just north of Kittery that's way too big for him. He knows he should sell it and get a smaller one closer to where he works—we both know—but he stays. So yeah, I know what you mean."

"I'm sorry for your loss," Mrs. Shoplaw said. "Some day I'll open my mouth too wide and fall right in. That bus of yours, is it the five-ten?"

"Yes."

"Well, come on in the kitchen. I'll make you a toasted cheese and microwave you a bowl of tomato soup. You've got time. And I'll tell you the sad story of the Joyland ghost while you eat, if you want to hear it."

"Is it really a ghost story?"

"I've never been in that damn funhouse, so I don't know for sure. But it's a murder story. That much I *am* sure of."

♥

The soup was just Campbell's out of the can, but the toasted cheese was Muenster—my favorite—and tasted heavenly. She poured me a glass of milk and insisted I drink it. I was, Mrs. Shoplaw said, a growing boy. She sat down opposite me with her own bowl of soup but no sandwich ("I have to watch my girlish figure") and told me the tale. Some of it she'd gotten from the newspapers and TV reports. The juicier bits came from her Joyland contacts, of whom she had many.

"It was four years ago, which I guess would make it around the same time your mother died. Do you know what always comes first to my mind when I think about it? The guy's shirt. And the gloves. Thinking about those things gives me the creeps. Because it means he *planned* it."

"You might be kind of starting in the middle," I said.

Mrs. Shoplaw laughed. "Yeah, I suppose I am. The name of your supposed ghost is Linda Gray, and she was from Florence. That's over South Carolina way. She and her boyfriend—if that's what he was; the cops checked her background pretty closely and found no trace of him—spent her last night on earth at the Luna Inn, half a mile south of here along the beach. They entered Joyland around eleven o'clock the next day. He bought them day passes, using cash. They rode some rides and then had a late lunch at Rock Lobster, the seafood place down by the concert hall. That was just past one o'clock. As for the time of death, you probably know how they establish it…contents of the stomach and so on…"

"Yeah." My sandwich was gone, and I turned my attention to the soup. The story wasn't hurting my appetite any. I was twenty-one, remember, and although I would have told you different, down deep I was convinced I was never going to die. Not even my mother's death had been able to shake that core belief.

"He fed her, then he took her on the Carolina Spin—a slow ride, you know, easy on the digestion—and then he took her into Horror House. They went in together, but only he came out. About halfway along the course of the ride, which takes about nine minutes, he cut her throat and threw her out beside the monorail track the cars run on. Threw her out like a piece of trash. He must have known there'd be a mess, because he was wearing two shirts, and he'd put on a pair of yellow work-gloves. They found the top shirt—the one that would have caught most of the blood—about a hundred yards farther along from the body. The gloves a little farther along still."

I could see it: first the body, still warm and pulsing, then the shirt, then the gloves. The killer, meanwhile, sits tight and fin-ishes the ride. Mrs. Shoplaw was right, it *was* creepy.

"When the ride ended, the son of a bee just got out and walked away. He mopped up the car—that shirt they found was soaking—but he didn't get quite all of the blood. One of the Helpers spotted some on the seat before the next ride started and cleaned it up. Didn't think twice about it, either. Blood on amusement park rides isn't unusual; mostly it's some kid who gets overexcited and has a nose-gusher. You'll find out for your-self. Just make sure you wear your own gloves when you do the cleanup, in case of diseases. They have em at all the first-aid stations, and there are first-aid stations all over the park."

"Nobody noticed that he got off the ride without his date?"

"Nope. This was mid-July, the very height of the season, and the place was a swarming madhouse. They didn't find the body until one o'clock the next morning, long after the park was closed and the Horror House work-lights were turned on. For the graveyard shift, you know. You'll get your chance to experi-ence that; all the Happy Helper crews get cleanup duty one week a month, and you want to catch up on your sleep ahead of time, because that swing-shift's a booger."

"People rode past her until the park closed and didn't see her?"

"If they did, they thought it was just part of the show. But probably the body went unnoticed. Remember, Horror House is a dark ride. The only one in Joyland, as it happens. Other parks have more."

A dark ride. That struck a shivery chord, but it wasn't strong enough to keep me from finishing my soup. "What about a description of him? Maybe from whoever served them at the restaurant?"

"They had better than that. They had pictures. You want to believe the police made sure they got on TV and printed in the newspapers."

"How did that happen?"

"The Hollywood Girls," Mrs. Shoplaw said. "There are always half a dozen working the park when it's going full-blast. There's never been anything close to a cooch joint at Joyland, but old man Easterbrook didn't spend all those years in rolling carnies for nothing. He knows people like a little dash of sex appeal to go with the rides and the corndogs. There's one Hollywood Girl on each Helper team. You'll get yours, and you and the rest of the guys on your team will be expected to keep a big-brotherly eye out in case anyone bothers her. They run around in these short green dresses and green high heels and cutie-pie green hats that always make me think of Robin Hood and his Merry Men. Only they're the Merry Chicks. They tote Speed Graphic cameras, like the kind you see in old movies, and they take pictures of the rubes." She paused. "Although I'd advise you against calling the customers that yourself."

"Already been warned by Mr. Dean," I said.

"Figures. Anyhow, the Hollywood Girls are told to concentrate on family groups and dating couples who look over twenty-one. Kids younger than that usually aren't interested in souvenir photos; they'd rather spend their money on food and arcade games. So the deal is, the girls snap first, then approach." She did a breathy little Marilyn Monroe voice. " 'Hello, welcome to Joyland, I'm Karen! If you'd like a copy of the picture I just took, give me your name and check at the Hollywood Photo Booth on Hound Dog Way as you exit the park.' Like that.

"One of them took a picture of Linda Gray and her boyfriend at the Annie Oakley Shootin' Gallery, but when she approached, the guy gave her the brushoff. A *hard* brushoff. She told the cops later that he looked like he would've taken her camera and broken it, if he thought he could get away with it. Said his eyes gave her chills. Hard and gray, she said." Mrs. Shoplaw smiled and shrugged. "Only it turned out he was wearing sunglasses. You know how some girls like to dramatize."

As a matter of fact, I did. Wendy's friend Renee could turn a routine trip to the dentist into a horror-movie scenario.

"That was the best picture, but not the only one. The cops went through all the Hollywood Girl snaps from that day and found the Gray girl and her friend in the background of at least four others. In the best of those, they're standing in line for the Whirly Cups, and he's got his hand on her keister. Pretty chummy for someone none of her family or friends had ever seen before."

"Too bad there aren't closed-circuit TV cameras," I said. "My lady-friend got a job at Filene's in Boston this summer, and she says they've got a few of those cameras, and are putting in more. To foil shoplifters."

"A day will come when they have em everywhere," she said. "Just like in that science fiction book about the Thought Police. I don't look forward to it, either. But they'll never have them in rides like Horror House. Not even infrared ones that see in the dark."

"No?"

"Nope. There's no Tunnel of Love at Joyland, but Horror House is most definitely the Tunnel of Grope. My husband told me once that a day when the graveyard shift cleanup crew didn't find at least three pairs of panties beside the track was a slow day, indeed.

"But they did have that one great photo of the guy at the shooting gallery. A portrait, almost. It ran in the papers and on TV for a week. Him snuggled up to her hip to hip, showing her how to hold the rifle, the way the guys always do. Everyone in both Carolinas must have seen it. She's smiling, but he looks dead serious."

"With his gloves and knife in his pockets the whole time," I said. Marveling at the idea.

"Razor."

"Huh?"

"He used a straight razor or something like it, that's what the medical examiner figured. Anyway, they had those photos, including the one great one, and you know what? You can't make his face out in any of them."

"Because of the sunglasses."

"For starters. Also a goatee that covered his chin, and a baseball cap, the kind with a long bill, that shaded what little of his face the sunglasses and goatee didn't cover. Could have been anyone. Could have been you, except you're dark-haired instead of blond and don't have a bird's head tattooed on one of your hands. This guy did. An eagle or maybe a hawk. It showed up very clearly in the Shootin' Gallery pic. They ran a blowup of the tat in the paper for five days running, hoping someone would recognize it. Nobody did."

"No leads at the inn where they stayed the night before?"

"Uh-uh. He showed a South Carolina driver's license when he checked in, but it was stolen a year before. No one even saw her. She must have waited in the car. She was a Jane Doe for almost a week, but the police released a full-face sketch. Made her look like she was just sleeping, not dead with her throat cut. Someone—a friend she went to nursing school with, I think it was—saw it and recognized it. She told the girl's parents. I can't imagine how they must have felt, coming up here in their car and hoping against hope that when they got to the morgue, it would turn out to be someone else's well-loved child." She shook her head slowly. "Kids are such a risk, Dev. Did that ever cross your mind?"

"I guess so."

"Which means it hasn't. Me…I think if they turned back that sheet and it was my daughter lying there, I'd lose my mind."

"You don't think Linda Gray really haunts the funhouse, do you?"

"I can't answer that, because I hold no opinion on the after-life, pro or con. My feeling is I'll find that stuff out when I get there, and that's good enough for me. All I know is that lots of people who work at Joyland claim to have seen her standing beside the track, wearing what she had on when they found her: blue skirt and blue sleeveless blouse. None of them would have seen those colors in the photos they released to the public, because the Speed Graphics the Hollywood Girls use only shoot black-and-white. Easier and cheaper to develop, I guess."

"Maybe the color of her clothes was mentioned in the articles."

She shrugged. "Might have been; I don't remember. But several people have also mentioned that the girl they saw standing by the track was wearing a blue Alice band, and that *wasn't* in the news stories. They held it back for almost a year, hoping to use it on a likely suspect if they came up with one."

"Lane said the rubes never see her."

"No, she only shows up after hours. It's mostly Happy Helpers on the graveyard shift who see her, but I know at least one safety inspector from Raleigh who claims he did, because I had a drink with him at the Sand Dollar. Guy said she was just standing there on his ride-through. He thought it was a new pop-up until she raised her hands to him, like this."

Mrs. Shoplaw held her hands out with the palms upturned, a supplicatory gesture.

"He said it felt like the temperature dropped twenty degrees.

A cold pocket, he called it. When he turned and looked back, she was gone."

I thought of Lane, in his tight jeans, scuffed boots, and tilted tuff-boy derby. *Truth or horseshit?* he'd asked. *Live or Memorex?* I thought the ghost of Linda Gray was almost certainly horseshit, but I hoped it wasn't. I hoped I would see her. It would be a great story to tell Wendy, and in those days, all my thoughts led back to her. If I bought this shirt, would Wendy like it? If I wrote a story about a young girl getting her first kiss while on a horseback ride, would Wendy enjoy it? If I saw the ghost of a murdered girl, would Wendy be fascinated? Maybe enough to want to come down and see for herself?

"There was a follow-up story in the Charleston *News and Courier* about six months after the murder," Mrs. Shoplaw said. "Turns out that since 1961, there have been four similar murders in Georgia and the Carolinas. All young girls. One stabbed, three others with their throats cut. The reporter dug up at least one cop who said all of them could have been killed by the guy who murdered Linda Gray."

"Beware the Funhouse Killer!" I said in a deep announcer-type voice.

"That's exactly what the paper called him. Hungry, weren't you? You ate everything but the bowl. Now I think you'd better write me that check and beat feet to the bus station, or you're apt to be spending the night on my sofa."

Which looked comfortable enough, but I was anxious to get back north. Two days left in spring break, and then I'd be back at school with my arm around Wendy Keegan's waist.

I took out my checkbook, scribbled, and by so doing rented a one-room apartment with a charming ocean view that Wendy Keegan—my lady-friend—never got a chance to sample. That room was where I sat up some nights with my stereo turned down low, playing Jimi Hendrix and the Doors, having those occasional thoughts of suicide. They were sophomoric rather than serious, just the fantasies of an over-imaginative young man with a heart condition...or so I tell myself now, all these years later, but who really knows?

When it comes to the past, *everyone* writes fiction.

♥

I tried to reach Wendy from the bus station, but her stepmom said she was out with Renee. When the bus got to Wilmington I tried again, but she was still out with Renee. I asked Nadine— the stepmom—if she had any idea where they might have gone. Nadine said she didn't. She sounded as if I were the most un-interesting caller she'd gotten all day. Maybe all year. Maybe in her life. I got along well enough with Wendy's dad, but Nadine Keegan was never one of my biggest fans.

Finally—I was in Boston by then—I got Wendy. She sounded sleepy, although it was only eleven o'clock, which is the shank of the evening to most college students on spring break. I told her I got the job.

"Hooray for you," she said. "Are you on your way home?"

"Yes, as soon as I get my car." And if it didn't have a flat tire. In those days I was always running on baldies and it seemed one of them was always going flat. A spare, you ask? Pretty funny, *señor*. "I could spend the night in Portsmouth instead of going straight home and see you tomorrow, if—"

"Wouldn't be a good idea. Renee's staying over, and that's about all the company Nadine can take. You know how *sensitive* she is about company."

Some company, maybe, but I thought Nadine and Renee

had always gotten on like a house afire, drinking endless cups of coffee and gossiping about their favorite movie stars as if they were personal friends, but this didn't seem like the time to say so.

"Ordinarily I'd love to talk to you, Dev, but I was getting ready to turn in. Me n Ren had a busy day. Shopping and…things."

She didn't elaborate on the *things* part, and I found I didn't care to ask about them. Another warning sign.

"Love you, Wendy."

"Love you, too." That sounded perfunctory rather than fervent. *She's just tired*, I told myself.

I rolled north out of Boston with a distinct feeling of unease. Something about the way she had sounded? That lack of enthusiasm? I didn't know. I wasn't sure I wanted to know. But I wondered. Sometimes even now, all these years later, I wonder. She's nothing to me these days but a scar and a memory, someone who hurt me as young women will hurt young men from time to time. A young woman from another life. Still I can't help wondering where she was that day. What those *things* were. And if it was really Renee St. Clair she was with.

We could argue about what constitutes the creepiest line in pop music, but for me it's early Beatles—John Lennon, actually—singing *I'd rather see you dead, little girl, than to be with another man*. I could tell you I never felt that way about Wendy in the aftermath of the breakup, but it would be a lie. It was never a constant thing, but did I think of her with a certain malevolence in the aftermath of the breakup? Yes. There were long and sleepless nights when I thought she deserved something bad—maybe really bad—to happen to her for the way she hurt me. It dismayed me to think that way, but sometimes

I did. And then I would think about the man who went into Horror House with his arm around Linda Gray and wearing two shirts. The man with the bird on his hand and a straight razor in his pocket.

♥

In the spring of 1973—the last year of my childhood, when I look back on it—I saw a future in which Wendy Keegan was Wendy Jones...or perhaps Wendy Keegan-Jones, if she wanted to be modern and keep her maiden name in the mix. There would be a house on a lake in Maine or New Hampshire (maybe western Massachusetts) filled with the clatter-and-yell of a couple of little Keegan-Joneses, a house where I wrote books that weren't exactly bestsellers but popular enough to keep us comfortably and were—*very* important—well reviewed. Wendy would pursue her dream of opening a small clothing boutique (also well reviewed), and I would teach a few creative writing seminars, the kind gifted students vie to get into. None of this ever happened, of course, so it was fitting that the last time we were together as a couple was in the office of Professor George B. Nako, a man who never was.

In the fall of 1968, returning University of New Hampshire students discovered Professor Nako's "office" under the stairs in the basement of Hamilton Smith Hall. The space was papered with fake diplomas, peculiar watercolors labeled Albanian Art, and seating plans with such names as Elizabeth Taylor, Robert Zimmerman, and Lyndon Beans Johnson penciled into the squares. There were also posted themes from students who never existed. One, I remember, was titled "Sex Stars of the Orient." Another was called "The Early Poetry of Cthulhu: An

Analysis." There were three standing ashtrays. A sign taped to the underside of the stairs read: PROFESSOR NAKO SEZ: "THE SMOKING LAMP IS <u>ALWAYS</u> LIT!" There were a couple of ratty easy chairs and an equally ratty sofa, very handy for students in search of a comfy make-out spot.

The Wednesday before my last final was unseasonably hot and humid. Around one in the afternoon, thunderheads began to build up, and around four, when Wendy had agreed to meet me in George B. Nako's underground "office," the skies opened and it began to pour. I got there first. Wendy showed up five minutes later, soaked to the skin but in high good humor. Droplets of water sparkled in her hair. She threw herself into my arms and wriggled against me, laughing. Thunder boomed; the few hanging lights in the gloomy basement hallway flickered.

"Hug me hug me hug me," she said. "That rain is *so* cold."

I warmed her up and she warmed me up. Pretty soon we were tangled together on the ratty sofa, my left hand curled around her and cupping her braless breast, my right far enough up her skirt to brush against silk and lace. She let that one stay there for a minute or two, then sat up, moved away from me, and fluffed her hair.

"Enough of that," she said primly. "What if Professor Nako came in?"

"I don't think that's likely, do you?" I was smiling, but below the belt I was feeling a familiar throb. Sometimes Wendy would relieve that throb—she had become quite expert at what we used to call a "through-the-pants job"—but I didn't think this was going to be one of those days.

"One of his students, then," she said. "Begging for a last-chance passing grade. 'Please, Professor Nako, please-please-*please*, I'll do anything.' "

That wasn't likely, either, but the chances of being interrupted were good, she was right about that. Students were always dropping by to put up new bogus themes or fresh works of Albanian art. The sofa was make-out friendly, but the locale wasn't. Once, maybe, but not since the understairs nook had become a kind of mythic reference-point for students in the College of Liberal Arts.

"How was your sociology final?" I asked her.

"Okay. I doubt if I aced it, but I know I passed it and that's good enough for me. Especially since it's the last one." She stretched, fingers touching the zig-zag of the stairs above us and lifting her breasts most entrancingly. "I'm out of here in…" She looked at her watch. "…exactly one hour and ten minutes."

"You and Renee?" I had no great liking for Wendy's roommate, but knew better than to say so. The one time I had, Wendy and I had had a brief, bitter argument in which she accused me of trying to manage her life.

"That is correct, sir. She'll drop me at my dad and stepmom's. And in one week, we're official Filene's employees!"

She made it sound as if the two of them had landed jobs as pages at the White House, but I held my peace on that, too. I had other concerns. "You're still coming up to Berwick on Saturday, right?" The plan was for her to arrive in the morning, spend the day, and stay over. She'd be in the guest bedroom, of course, but that was only a dozen steps down the hall. Given the fact that we might not see each other again until fall, I thought the possibility of "it" happening was very strong. Of course, little children believe in Santa Claus, and UNH freshmen sometimes went a whole semester believing that George B. Nako was a real professor, teaching real English courses.

"Absoloodle." She looked around, saw no one, and slipped a hand up my thigh. When it reached the crotch of my jeans, she tugged gently on what she found there. "Come here, you."

So I got my through-the-pants job after all. It was one of her better efforts, slow and rhythmic. The thunder rolled, and at some point the sigh of the pouring rain became a hard, hollow rattle as it turned to hail. At the end she squeezed, heightening and prolonging the pleasure of my orgasm.

"Make sure to get good and wet when you go back to your dorm, or the whole world will know exactly what we were doing down here." She bounced to her feet. "I have to go, Dev. I've still got some things to pack."

"I'll pick you up at noon on Saturday. My dad's making his famous chicken casserole for supper."

She once more said *absoloodle*; like standing on her tiptoes to kiss me, it was a Wendy Keegan trademark. Only on Friday night I got a call from her saying that Renee's plans had changed and they were leaving for Boston two days early. "I'm sorry, Dev, but she's my ride."

"There's always the bus," I said, already knowing that wasn't going to work.

"I promised, honey. And we have tickets for *Pippin*, at the Imperial. Renee's dad got them for us, as a surprise." She paused. "Be happy for me. You're going all the way to North Carolina, and I'm happy for *you*."

"Happy," I said. "Roger-wilco."

"That's better." Her voice dropped, became confidential. "Next time we're together, I'll make it up to you. Promise."

That was a promise she never kept but one she never had to break, either, because I never saw Wendy Keegan after that day in Professor Nako's "office." There wasn't even a final phone call filled with tears and accusations. That was on Tom Kennedy's advice (we'll get to him shortly), and it was probably a good thing. Wendy might have been expecting such a call, maybe even wished for it. If so, she was disappointed.

I hope she was. All these years later, with those old fevers and deliriums long in my past, I still hope she was.

Love leaves scars.

♥

I never produced the books I dreamed of, those well-reviewed almost-bestsellers, but I do make a pretty good living as a writer, and I count my blessings; thousands are not so lucky. I've moved steadily up the income ladder to where I am now, working at *Commercial Flight*, a periodical you've probably never heard of.

A year after I took over as editor-in-chief, I found myself back on the UNH campus. I was there to attend a two-day symposium on the future of trade magazines in the twenty-first century. During a break on the second day, I strolled over to Hamilton Smith Hall on a whim and peeked under the basement stairs. The themes, celebrity-studded seating charts, and Albanian artwork were gone. So were the chairs, the sofa, and the standing ashtrays. And yet *someone* remembered. Scotch-taped to the underside of the stairs, where there had once been a sign proclaiming that the smoking lamp was always lit, I saw a sheet of paper with a single typed line in print so small I had to lean close and stand on tiptoe in order to read it:

Professor Nako now teaches at the Hogwarts School of Witchcraft and Wizardry.

Well, why not?

Why the fuck not?

As for Wendy, your guess is as good as mine. I suppose I could use Google, that twenty-first century Magic 8-Ball, to chase her down and find out if she ever realized *her* dream, the one of owning the exclusive little boutique, but to what purpose? Gone is gone. Over is over. And after my stint in Joyland (just down the beach from a town called Heaven's Bay, let's not forget that), my broken heart seemed a lot less important. Mike and Annie Ross had a lot to do with that.

♥

My dad and I ended up eating his famous chicken casserole with no third party in attendance, which was probably all right with Timothy Jones; although he tried to hide it out of respect for me, I knew his feelings about Wendy were about the same as mine about Wendy's friend Renee. At the time, I thought it was because he was a bit jealous of Wendy's place in my life. Now I think he saw her more clearly than I could. I can't say for sure; we never talked about it. I'm not sure men know how to talk about women in any meaningful way.

After the meal was eaten and the dishes washed, we sat on the couch, drinking beer, eating popcorn, and watching a movie starring Gene Hackman as a tough cop with a foot fetish. I missed Wendy—probably at that moment listening to the *Pippin* company sing "Spread a Little Sunshine"—but there are advantages to the two-guy scenario, such as being able to belch and fart without trying to cover it up.

The next day—my last at home—we went for a walk along the disused railroad tracks that passed through the woods behind the house where I grew up. Mom's hard and fast rule had been that my friends and I had to stay away from those tracks. The last GS&WM freight had passed along them ten years before, and weeds were growing up between the rusty ties, but that made no difference to Mom. She was convinced that if we played there, one last train (call it the Kid-Eating Special) would go bulleting through and turn us all to paste. Only she was the one who got hit by an unscheduled train—metastatic breast cancer at the age of forty-seven. One mean fucking express.

"I'll miss having you around this summer," my dad said.

"I'll miss you, too."

"Oh! Before I forget." He reached into his breast pocket and brought out a check. "Be sure to open an account and deposit it first thing. Ask them to speed the clearance, if they can."

I looked at the amount: not the five hundred I'd asked for, but a thousand. "Dad, can you afford this?"

"Yes. Mostly because you held onto your Commons job, and that saved me having to try and make up the difference. Think of it as a bonus."

I kissed his cheek, which was scratchy. He hadn't shaved that morning. "Thanks."

"Kid, you're more welcome than you know." He took a handkerchief from his pocket and wiped his eyes matter-of-factly, without embarrassment. "Sorry about the waterworks. It's hard when your kids go away. Someday you'll find that out for yourself, but hopefully you'll have a good woman to keep you company after they're gone."

I thought of Mrs. Shoplaw saying *Kids are such a risk*. "Dad, are you going to be okay?"

He put the handkerchief back in his pocket and gave me a

grin, sunny and unforced. "Call me once in a while, and I will
be. Also, don't let them put you to work climbing all over one of
their damned roller coasters."

That actually sounded sort of exciting, but I told him I wouldn't.

"And—" But I never heard what he meant to say next, advice or
admonition. He pointed. "Will you look at that!"

Fifty yards ahead of us, a doe had come out of the woods.
She stepped delicately over one rusty GS&WM track and onto
the railbed, where the weeds and goldenrod were so high they
brushed against her sides. She paused there, looking at us calmly,
ears cocked forward. What I remember about that moment was
the silence. No bird sang, no plane went droning overhead. If
my mother had been with us, she'd have had her camera and
would have been taking pictures like mad. Thinking of that
made me miss her in a way I hadn't in years.

I gave my father a quick, fierce hug. "I love you, Dad."

"I know," he said. "I know."

When I looked back, the deer was gone. A day later, so was I.

♥

When I got back to the big gray house at the end of Main Street
in Heaven's Bay, the sign made of shells had been taken down
and put in storage, because Mrs. Shoplaw had a full house for
the summer. I blessed Lane Hardy for telling me to nail down a
place to live. Joyland's summer troops had arrived, and every
rooming house in town was full.

I shared the second floor with Tina Ackerley, the librarian.
Mrs. Shoplaw had rented the accommodations on the third floor
to a willowy redheaded art major named Erin Cook and a stocky
undergrad from Rutgers named Tom Kennedy. Erin, who had

taken photography courses both in high school and at Bard, had
been hired as a Hollywood Girl. As for Tom and me…

"Happy Helpers," he said. "General employment, in other
words. That's what that guy Fred Dean checked on my application. You?"

"The same," I said. "I think it means we're janitors."

"I doubt it."

"Really? Why?"

"Because we're white," he said, and although we did our
share of clean-up chores, he turned out to be largely correct.
The custodial crew—twenty men and over thirty women who
dressed in coveralls with Howie the Happy Hound patches sewn
on the breast pockets—were all Haitians and Dominicans, and
almost surely undocumented. They lived in their own little village ten miles inland and were shuttled back and forth in a pair
of retired school buses. Tom and I were making four dollars an
hour; Erin a little more. God knows what the cleaners were
making. They were exploited, of course, and saying that there
were undocumented workers all over the south who had it far
worse doesn't excuse it, nor does pointing out that it was forty
years ago. Although there was this: they never had to put on the
fur. Neither did Erin.

Tom and I did.

♥

On the night before our first day at work, the three of us were
sitting in the parlor of *Maison* Shoplaw, getting to know each
other and speculating on the summer ahead. As we talked, the
moon rose over the Atlantic, as calmly beautiful as the doe my
father and I had seen standing on the old railroad tracks.

"It's an amusement park, for God's sake," Erin said. "How tough can it be?"

"Easy for you to say," Tom told her. "No one's going to expect you to hose down the Whirly Cups after every brat in Cub Scout Pack 18 loses his lunch halfway through the ride."

"I'll pitch in where I have to," she said. "If it includes mopping up vomit as well as snapping pictures, so be it. I need this job. I've got grad school staring me in the face next year, and I'm exactly two steps from broke."

"We all ought to try and get on the same team," Tom said— and, as it turned out, we did. All the work teams at Joyland had doggy names, and ours was Team Beagle.

Just then Emmalina Shoplaw entered the parlor, carrying a tray with five champagne flutes on it. Miss Ackerley, a beanpole with huge bespectacled eyes that gave her a Joyce Carol Oatesian look, walked beside her, bottle in hand. Tom Kennedy brightened. "Do I spy French ginger ale? That looks just a leetle too elegant to be supermarket plonk."

"Champagne it is," Mrs. Shoplaw said, "although if you're expecting *Moet et Chandon*, young Mr. Kennedy, you're in for a disappointment. This isn't Cold Duck, but it's not the high-priced spread, either."

"I can't speak for my new co-workers," Tom said, "but as someone who educated his palate on Apple Zapple, I don't think I'll be disappointed."

Mrs. Shoplaw smiled. "I always mark the beginning of summer this way, for good luck. It seems to work. I haven't lost a seasonal hire yet. Each of you take a glass, please." We did as we were told. "Tina, will you pour?"

When the flutes were full, Mrs. Shoplaw raised hers and we raised ours.

"Here is to Erin, Tom, and Devin," she said. "May they have a wonderful summer, and wear the fur only when the temperature is below eighty degrees."

We clinked glasses and drank. Maybe not the high-priced spread, but pretty damned good, and with enough left for us all to have another swallow. This time it was Tom who offered the toast. "Here's to Mrs. Shoplaw, who gives us shelter from the storm!"

"Why, thank you, Tom, that's lovely. It won't get you a discount on the rent, though."

We drank. I set my glass down feeling just the tiniest bit buzzy. "What is this about wearing the fur?" I asked.

Mrs. Shoplaw and Miss Ackerley looked at each other and smiled. It was the librarian who answered, although it wasn't really an answer at all. "You'll find out," she said.

"Don't stay up late, children," Mrs. Shoplaw advised. "You've got an early call. Your career in show business awaits."

♥

The call *was* early: seven AM, two hours before the park opened its doors on another summer. The three of us walked down the beach together. Tom talked most of the way. He always talked. It would have been wearisome if he hadn't been so amusing and relentlessly cheerful. I could see from the way Erin (walking in the surf with her sneakers dangling from the fingers of her left hand) looked at him that she was charmed and fascinated. I envied Tom his ability to do that. He was heavyset and at least three doors down from handsome, but he was energetic and possessed of the gift of gab I sadly lacked. Remember the old joke about the starlet who was so clueless she fucked the writer?

"Man, how much do you think the people who own those

places are worth?" he asked, waving an arm at the houses on Beach Row. We were just passing the big green one that looked like a castle, but there was no sign of the woman and the boy in the wheelchair that day. Annie and Mike Ross came later.

"Millions, probably," Erin said. "It ain't the Hamptons, but as my dad would say, it ain't cheeseburgers."

"The amusement park probably brings the property values down a little," I said. I was looking at Joyland's three most distinctive landmarks, silhouetted against the blue morning sky: Thunderball, Delirium Shaker, Carolina Spin.

"Nah, you don't understand the rich-guy mindset," Tom said. "It's like when they pass bums looking for handouts on the street. They just erase em from their field of vision. Bums? What bums? And that park, same deal—what park? People who own these houses live, like, on another plane of existence." He stopped, shading his eyes and looking at the green Victorian that was going to play such a large part in my life that fall, after Erin Cook and Tom Kennedy, by then a couple, had gone back to school. "That one's gonna be mine. I'll be expecting to take possession on…mmm…June first, 1987."

"I'll bring the champagne," Erin said, and we all laughed.

♥

I saw Joyland's entire crew of summer hires in one place for the first and last time that morning. We gathered in Surf Auditorium, the concert hall where all those B-list country acts and aging rockers performed. There were almost two hundred of us. Most, like Tom, Erin, and me, were college students willing to work for peanuts. Some of the full-timers were there, as well. I saw Rozzie Gold, today dressed for work in her gypsy duds and dangly earrings. Lane Hardy was up on stage, placing a mike at the podium and then checking it with a series of thudding finger-taps. His derby was present and accounted for, cocked at its usual just-so angle. I don't know how he picked me out in all those milling kids, but he did, and sketched a little salute off the tilted brim of his lid. I sent him one right back.

He finished his work, nodded, jumped off the stage, and took the seat Rozzie had been saving for him. Fred Dean walked briskly out from the wings. "Be seated, please, all of you be seated. Before you get your team assignments, the owner of Joyland—and your employer—would like to say a few words. Please give a hand to Mr. Bradley Easterbrook."

We did as we were told, and an old man emerged from the wings, walking with the careful, high-stepping strides of someone with bad hips, a bad back, or both. He was tall and amazingly thin, dressed in a black suit that made him look more like an undertaker than a man who owned an amusement park. His face was long, pale, covered with bumps and moles. Shaving must have been torture for him, but he had a clean one. Ebony hair that had surely come out of a bottle was swept back from his deeply lined brow. He stood beside the podium, his enormous hands—they seemed to be nothing but knuckles—clasped before him. His eyes were set deep in pouched sockets.

Age looked at youth, and youth's applause first weakened, then died.

I'm not sure what we expected; possibly a mournful foghorn voice telling us that the Red Death would soon hold sway over all. Then he smiled, and it lit him up like a jukebox. You could almost hear a sigh of relief rustle through the summer hires. I found out later that was the summer Bradley Easterbrook turned ninety-three.

"You guys," he said, "welcome to Joyland." And then, before stepping behind the podium, he actually bowed to us. He took several seconds adjusting the mike, which produced a series of amplified screeks and scronks. He never took his sunken eyes from us as he did it.

"I see many returning faces, a thing that always makes me happy. For you greenies, I hope this will be the best summer of your lives, the yardstick by which you judge all your future employment. That is no doubt an extravagant wish, but anyone who runs a place like this year in and year out must have a wide streak of extravagance. For certain you'll never have another job like it."

He surveyed us, giving the poor mike's articulated neck another twist as he did so.

"In a few moments, Mr. Dean and Mrs. Brenda Rafferty, who is queen of the front office, will give you your team assignments. There will be seven of you to a team, and you will be expected to act as a team and work as a team. Your team's tasks will be assigned by your team leader and will vary from week to week, sometimes from day to day. If variety is the spice of life, you will find the next three months very spicy, indeed. I hope you will keep one thought foremost in your mind, young ladies and gentlemen. Will you do that?"

He paused as if expecting us to answer, but nobody made a sound. We only looked at him, a very old man in a black suit and a white shirt open at the collar. When he spoke again, it might have been himself he was talking to, at least to begin with.

"This is a badly broken world, full of wars and cruelty and senseless tragedy. Every human being who inhabits it is served his or her portion of unhappiness and wakeful nights. Those of you who don't already know that will come to know it. Given such sad but undeniable facts of the human condition, you have been given a priceless gift this summer: you are here to sell fun. In exchange for the hard-earned dollars of your customers, you will parcel out happiness. Children will go home and dream of what they saw here and what they did here. I hope you will remember that when the work is hard, as it sometimes will be, or when people are rude, as they often will be, or when you feel your best efforts have gone unappreciated. This is a different world, one that has its own customs and its own language, which we simply call the Talk. You'll begin learning it today. As you learn to talk the Talk, you'll learn to walk the walk. I'm not going to explain that, because it can't be explained; it can only be learned."

Tom leaned close to me and whispered, "Talk the talk? Walk the walk? Did we just wander into an AA meeting?"

I hushed him. I had come in expecting to get a list of commandments, mostly *thou shalt nots*; instead I had gotten a kind of rough poetry, and I was delighted. Bradley Easterbrook surveyed us, then suddenly displayed those horsey teeth in another grin. This one looked big enough to eat the world. Erin Cook was staring at him raptly. So were most of the new summer hires. It was the way students stare at a teacher who offers a new and possibly wonderful way of looking at reality.

"I hope you'll enjoy your work here, but when you don't—when, for instance, it's your turn to wear the fur—try to remember how privileged you are. In a sad and dark world, we are a little island of happiness. Many of you already have plans for your lives—you hope to become doctors, lawyers, I don't know, politicians—"

"*OH-GOD-NO!*" someone shouted, to general laughter.

I would have said Easterbrook's grin could not possibly have widened, but it did. Tom was shaking his head, but he had also given in. "Okay, now I get it," he whispered in my ear. "This guy is the Jesus of Fun."

"You'll have interesting, fruitful lives, my young friends. You'll do many good things and have many remarkable experiences. But I hope you'll always look back on your time in Joyland as something special. We don't sell furniture. We don't sell cars. We don't sell land or houses or retirement funds. We have no political agenda. *We sell fun.* Never forget that. Thank you for your attention. Now go forth."

He stepped away from the podium, gave another bow, and left the stage in that same painful, high-stepping stride. He was gone almost before the applause began. It was one of the best speeches I ever heard, because it was truth rather than horse-shit. I mean, listen: how many rubes can put *sold fun for three months in 1973* on their resumes?

♥

All the team leaders were long-time Joyland employees who worked the carny circuit as showies in the off-season. Most were also on the Park Services Committee, which meant they had to deal with state and federal regulations (both very loose in 1973), and field customer complaints. That summer most of the complaints were about the new no-smoking policy.

Our team leader was a peppy little guy named Gary Allen, a

seventy-something who ran the Annie Oakley Shootin' Gallery. Only none of us called it that after the first day. In the Talk, a shooting gallery was a bang-shy and Gary was the bang-shy agent. The seven of us on Team Beagle met him at his joint, where he was setting out rifles on chains. My first official Joyland job—along with Erin, Tom, and the other four guys on the team—was putting the prizes on the shelves. The ones that got pride of place were the big fuzzy stuffed animals that hardly anyone ever won...although, Gary said, he was careful to give out at least one every evening when the tip was hot.

"I like the marks," he said. "Yes I do. And the marks I like the best are the points, by which I mean the purty girls, and the points I like the best are the ones who wear the low-cut tops and bend forrad to shoot like this." He snatched up a .22 modified to shoot BBs (it had also been modified to make a loud and satisfying bang with each trigger-pull) and leaned forward to demonstrate.

"When a guy does that, I notify em that they're foulin the line. The points? Never."

Ronnie Houston, a bespectacled, anxious-looking young man wearing a Florida State University cap, said: "I don't see any foul-line, Mr. Allen."

Gary looked at him, hands fisted on non-existent hips. His jeans seemed to be staying up in defiance of gravity. "Listen up, son, I got three things for you. Ready?"

Ronnie nodded. He looked like he wanted to take notes. He also looked like he wanted to hide behind the rest of us.

"First thing. You can call me Gary or Pops or come here you old sonofabitch, but I ain't no schoolteacher, so can the mister. Second thing. I never want to see that fucking schoolboy hat on

your head again. Third thing. The foul line is wherever I say
the foul line is on any given night. I can do that because it's in
my *myyyyynd*." He tapped one sunken, vein-gnarled temple to
make this point perfectly clear, then waved at the prizes, the
targets, and the counter where the conies—the rubes—laid down
their mooch. "This is all in my *myyyyynd. The shy is mental.*
Geddit?"

Ronnie didn't, but he nodded vigorously.

"Now whip off that turdish-looking schoolboy hat. Get you a
Joyland visor or a Howie the Happy Hound dogtop. Make it
Job One."

Ronnie whipped off his FSU lid with alacrity, and stuck it in
his back pocket. Later that day—I believe within the hour—he
replaced it with a Howie cap, known in the Talk as a dogtop.
After three days of ribbing and being called greenie, he took
his new dogtop out to the parking lot, found a nice greasy spot,
and trompled it for a while. When he put it back on, it had the
right look. Or almost. Ronnie Houston never got the *complete*
right look; some people were just destined to be greenies forever. I remember Tom sidling up to him one day and suggesting
that he needed to piss on it a little to give it that final touch that
means so much. When he saw Ronnie was on the verge of taking
him seriously, Tom backpedaled and said just soaking it in the
Atlantic would achieve the same effect.

Meanwhile, Pops was surveying us.

"Speaking of good-looking ladies, I perceive we have one
among us."

Erin smiled modestly.

"Hollywood Girl, darlin?"

"That's what Mr. Dean said I'd be doing, yes."

"Then you want to go see Brenda Rafferty. She's second-in-command around here, and she's also the park Girl Mom. She'll get you fitted up with one of those cute green dresses. Tell her you want yours extra-short."

"The hell I will, you old lecher," Erin said, and promptly joined him when he threw back his head and bellowed laughter.

"Pert! Sassy! Do I like it? I do! When you're not snappin pix of the conies, you come on back to your Pops and I'll find you something to do...but change out of the dress first. You don't get grease or sawdust on it. *Kapish*?"

"Yes," Erin said. She was all business again.

Pops Allen looked at his watch. "Park opens in one hour, kiddies, then you'll learn while you earn. Start with the rides." He pointed to us one by one, naming rides. I got the Carolina Spin, which pleased me. "Got time for a question or two, but no more'n that. Anybody got one or are you good to go?"

I raised my hand. He nodded at me and asked my name.

"Devin Jones, sir."

"Call me sir again and you're fired, lad."

"Devin Jones, Pops." I certainly wasn't going to call him *come here you old sonofoabitch*, at least not yet. Maybe when we knew each other better.

"There you go," he said, nodding. "What's on your mind, Jonesy? Besides that foine head of red hair?"

"What's carny-from-carny mean?"

"Means you're like old man Easterbrook. His father worked the carny circuit back in the Dust Bowl days, and his grandfather worked it back when they had a fake Indian show featuring Big Chief Yowlatcha."

"You *got* to be *kidding*!" Tom exclaimed, almost exultantly.

Pops gave him a cool stare that settled Tom down—a thing not always easy to do. "Son, do you know what history is?"

"Uh…stuff that happened in the past?"

"Nope," he said, tying on his canvas change-belt. "History is the collective and ancestral shit of the human race, a great big and ever-growin pile of crap. Right now we're standin at the top of it, but pretty soon we'll be buried under the doodoo of generations yet to come. That's why your folks' clothes look so funny in old photographs, to name but a single example. And, as someone who's destined to be buried beneath the shit of your children and grandchildren, I think you should be just a *leetle* more forgiving."

Tom opened his mouth, probably to make a smart comeback, then wisely closed it again.

George Preston, another member of Team Beagle, spoke up. "Are *you* carny-from-carny?"

"Nope. My daddy was a cattle rancher in Oregon; now my brothers run the spread. I'm the black sheep of the family, and damn proud of it. Okay, if there's nothing else, it's time to quit the foolishness and get down to business."

"Can I ask one thing more?" Erin asked.

"Only because you're purty."

"What does 'wearing the fur' mean?"

Pops Allen smiled. He placed his hands on the mooch-counter of his shy. "Tell me, little lady, do you have an idea what it *might* mean?"

"Well…yes."

The smile widened into a grin that showed every yellowing fang in our new team leader's mouth. "Then you're probably right."

♥

What did I do at Joyland that summer? Everything. Sold tickets. Pushed a popcorn wagon. Sold funnel cakes, cotton candy, and a zillion hot dogs (which we called Hound Dogs—you probably knew that). It was a Hound Dog that got my picture in the paper, as a matter of fact, although I wasn't the guy who sold that unlucky pup; George Preston did. I worked as a lifeguard, both on the beach and at Happy Lake, the indoor pool where the Splash & Crash water slide ended. I line-danced in the Wiggle-Waggle Village with the other members of Team Beagle to "Bird Dance Beat," "Does Your Chewing Gum Lose Its Flavor on the Bedpost Overnight," "Rippy-Rappy, Zippy-Zappy," and a dozen other nonsense songs. I also did time—most of it happy—as an unlicensed child-minder. In the Wiggle-Waggle, the approved rallying cry when faced with a bawling kiddie was "Let's turn that frown upside-down!" and I not only liked it, I got good at it. It was in the Wiggle-Waggle that I decided having kids at some point in the future was an actual Good Idea rather than a Wendy-flavored daydream.

I—and all the other Happy Helpers—learned to race from one side of Joyland to the other in nothing flat, using either the alleys behind the shys, joints, rides, and concessions or one of three service-tunnels known as Joyland Under, Hound Dog Under, and the Boulevard. I hauled trash by the ton, usually driving it in an electric cart down the Boulevard, a shadowy and sinister thoroughfare lit by ancient fluorescent bar-lights that stuttered and buzzed. I even worked a few times as a roadie, hauling amps and monitors when one of the acts showed up late and unsupported.

I learned to talk the Talk. Some of it—like bally for a free show, or gone larry for a ride that had broken down—was pure carny, and as old as the hills. Other terms—like points for purty girls and fumps for the chronic complainers—were strictly Joyland lingo. I suppose other parks have their own version of the Talk, but underneath it's always carny-from-carny. A hammersquash is a cony (usually a fump) who bitches about having to wait in line. The last hour of the day (at Joyland, that was ten PM to eleven) was the blow-off. A cony who loses at some shy and wants his mooch back is a mooch-hammer. The donniker is the bathroom, as in "Hey, Jonesy, hustle down to the donniker by the Moon Rocket—some dumb fump just puked in one of the sinks."

Running the concessions (known as joints) came easy to most of us, and really, anyone who can make change is qualified to push the popcorn wagon or work the counter of a souvenir shop. Learning to ride-jock wasn't much more difficult, but it was scary at first, because there were lives in your hands, many those of little children.

♥

"Here for your lesson?" Lane Hardy asked me when I joined him at the Carolina Spin. "Good. Just in time. Park opens in twenty minutes. We do it the way they do in the navy—see one, do one, teach one. Right now that heavyset kid you were standing next to—"

"Tom Kennedy."

"Okay. Right now Tom's over learning the Devil Wagons. At some point—probably this very day—he's gonna teach you how to run the ride, and you'll teach him how to run the Spin. Which, by the way, is an Aussie Wheel, meaning it runs counterclockwise."

"Is that important?"

"Nope," he said, "but I think it's interesting. There are only a few in the States. It has two speeds: slow and *really* slow."

"Because it's a grandma ride."

"Correctamundo." He demonstrated with the long stick shift I'd seen him operating on the day I got my job, then made me take over the stick with the bicycle handgrip at the top. "Feel it click when it's in gear?"

"Yes."

"Here's stop." He put his hand over mine and pulled the lever all the way up. This time the click was harder, and the enormous wheel stopped at once, the cars rocking gently. "With me so far?"

"I guess so. Listen, don't I need a permit or a license or something to run this thing?"

"You *got* a license, don't you?"

"Sure, a Maine driver's license, but—"

"In South Carolina, a valid DL's all you need. They'll get around to additional regulations in time—they always do—but for this year, at least, you're good to go. Now pay attention, because this is the most important part. Do you see that yellow stripe on the side of the housing?"

I did. It was just to the right of the ramp leading up to the ride.

"Each car has a Happy Hound decal on the door. When you see the Hound lining up with the yellow stripe, you pull stop, and there'll be a car right where the folks get on." He yanked the lever forward again. "See?"

I said I did.

"Until the wheel's tipsed—"

"What?"

"Loaded. Tipsed means loaded. Don't ask me why. Until the wheel's tipsed, you just alternate between super-slow and stop. Once you've got a full load—which you'll have most of the time, if we have a good season—you go to the normal slow speed. They get four minutes." He pointed to his suitcase radio. "It's my boomie, but the rule is when you run the ride, you control the tunes. Just no real blasting rock and roll— Who, Zep, Stones, stuff like that—until after the sun goes down. Got it?"

"Yeah. What about letting them off?"

"Exactly the same. Super-slow, stop. Super-slow, stop. Always line up the yellow stripe with the Happy Hound, and you'll always have a car right at the ramp. You should be able to get ten spins an hour. If the wheel's loaded each time, that's over seven hundred customers, which comes to almost a d-note."

"Which is what, in English?"

"Five hundred."

I looked at him uncertainly. "I won't really have to do this, will I? I mean, it's your ride."

"It's Brad Easterbrook's ride, kiddo. They all are. I'm just another employee, although I've been here a few years. I'll run the hoister most of the time, but not *all* of the time. And hey, stop sweating. There are carnies where half-drunk bikers covered with tattoos do this, and if they can, you can."

"If you say so."

Lane pointed. "Gates're open and here come the conies, rolling down Joyland Avenue. You're going to stick with me for the first three rides. Later on you teach the rest of your team, and that includes your Hollywood Girl. Okay?"

It wasn't even close to okay—I was supposed to send people a hundred and seventy feet in the air after a five-minute tutorial? It was insane.

He gripped my shoulder. "You can do this, Jonesy. So never mind 'if you say so.' Tell me it's okay."

"It's okay," I said.

"Good boy." He turned on his radio, now hooked to a speaker high on the Spin's frame. The Hollies began to sing "Long Cool Woman in a Black Dress" as Lane took a pair of rawhide gloves from the back pocket of his jeans. "And get you a pair of these— you're going to need them. Also, you better start learning how to pitch." He bent down, grabbed a hand-held mike from the ever-present orange crate, put one foot up, and began to work the crowd.

"Hey folks welcome in, time to take a little spin, hurry hurry, summer won't last forever, take a ride upstairs where the air is rare, this is where the fun begins, step over here and ride the Spin."

He lowered the mike and gave me a wink. "That's my pitch, more or less; give me a drink or three and it gets a lot better. You work out your own."

The first time I ran the Spin by myself, my hands were shaking with terror, but by the end of that first week I was running it like a pro (although Lane said my pitch needed a lot of work). I was also capable of running the Whirly Cups and the Devil Wagons...although ride-jocking the latter came down to little more than pushing the green START button, the red STOP button, and getting the cars untangled when the rubes got them stuck together against the rubber bumpers, which was at least four times during each four-minute ride. Only when you were running the Devil Wagons, you didn't call them rides; each run was a spree.

I learned the Talk; I learned the geography, both above and below ground; I learned how to run a joint, take over a shy, and award plushies to good-looking points. It took a week or so to get most of it down, and it was two weeks before I started getting comfortable. Wearing the fur, however, I understood by twelve-thirty on my first day, and it was just my luck—good or bad—that Bradley Easterbrook happened to be in Wiggle-Waggle Village at the time, sitting on a bench and eating his usual lunch of bean sprouts and tofu—hardly amusement park chow, but let's keep in mind that the man's food-processing system hadn't been new since the days of bathtub gin and flappers.

After my first impromptu performance as Howie the Happy Hound, I wore the fur a lot. Because I was good at it, you see. And Mr. Easterbrook *knew* I was good at it. I was wearing it a month or so later, when I met the little girl in the red hat on Joyland Avenue.

♥

That first day was a madhouse, all right. I ran the Carolina Spin with Lane until ten o'clock, then alone for the next ninety minutes while he rushed around the park putting out opening day fires. By then I no longer believed the wheel was going to malfunction and start running out of control, like the merry-go-round in that old Alfred Hitchcock movie. The most terrifying thing was how *trusting* people were. Not a single dad with kids in tow detoured to my pitch to ask if I knew what I was doing. I didn't get as many spins as I should have—I was concentrating so

hard on that damn yellow stripe that I gave myself a headache—
but every spin I did get was tipsed.

Erin came by once, pretty as a picture in her green Hollywood Girl dress, and took pictures of some of the family groups
waiting to get on. She took one of me, too—I still have it somewhere. When the wheel was turning again, she gripped me by
the arm, little beads of sweat standing out on her forehead, her
lips parted in a smile, her eyes shining.

"Is this great, or what?" she asked.

"As long as I don't kill anybody, yeah," I said.

"If some little kid falls out of a car, just make sure you catch
him." Then, having given me something new to obsess about,
she jogged off in search of new photo subjects. There was no
shortage of people willing to pose for a gorgeous redhead on a
summer morning. And she was right, actually. It was pretty
great.

Around eleven-thirty, Lane came back. By that point, I was
comfortable enough ride-jocking the Spin to turn the rudimentary controls over to him with some reluctance.

"Who's your team leader, Jonesy? Gary Allen?"

"That's right."

"Well, go on over to his bang-shy and see what he's got for
you. If you're lucky, he'll send you down to the boneyard for
lunch."

"What's the boneyard?"

"Where the help goes when they've got time off. Most carnies,
it's the parking lot or out behind the trucks, but Joyland's lux.
There's a nice break-room where the Boulevard and Hound
Dog Under connect. Take the stairs between the balloon-pitch
and the knife-show. You'll like it, but you only eat if Pop says it's

okay. I ain't getting in dutch with that old bastard. His team is his team; I got my own. You got a dinner bucket?"

"Didn't know I was supposed to bring one."

He grinned. "You'll learn. For today, stop at Ernie's joint—the fried chicken place with the big plastic rooster on top. Show him your Joyland ID card and he'll give you the company discount."

I did end up eating fried chicken at Ernie's, but not until two that afternoon. Pop had other plans for me. "Go by the costume shop—it's the trailer between Park Services and the carpentry shop. Tell Dottie Lassen I sent you. Damn woman's busting her girdle."

"Want me to help you reload first?" The Shootin' Gallery was also tipsed, the counter crowded with high school kids anxious to win those elusive plushies. More rubes (so I was already thinking of them) were lined up three deep behind the current shooters. Pop Allen's hands never stopped moving as he talked to me.

"What I want is for you to get on your pony and ride. I was doin this shit long before you were born. Which one are you, anyway, Jonesy or Kennedy? I know you're not the dingbat in the college-boy hat, but beyond that I can't remember."

"I'm Jonesy."

"Well, Jonesy, you're going to spend an edifying hour in the Wiggle-Waggle. It'll be edifying for the kiddies, anyhow. For you, maybe not so much." He bared his yellow fangs in a trademark Pop Allen grin, the one that made him look like an elderly shark. "Enjoy that fur suit."

♥

The costume shop was also a madhouse, filled with women running every whichway. Dottie Lassen, a skinny lady who needed a girdle like I needed elevator shoes, fell on me the second I walked through the door. She hooked her long-nailed fingers into my armpit and dragged me past clown costumes, cowboy costumes, a huge Uncle Sam suit (with stilts leaning beside it against the wall), a couple of princess outfits, a rack of Hollywood Girl dresses, and a rack of old-fashioned Gay Nineties bathing suits...which, I found out, we were condemned to wear when on lifeguard duty. At the very back of her crowded little empire were a dozen deflated dogs. Howies, in fact, complete with the Happy Hound's delighted stupid-and-loving-it grin, his big blue eyes, and his fuzzy cocked ears. Zippers ran down the backs of the suits from the neck to the base of the tail.

"Christ, you're a big one," Dottie said. "Thank God I got the extra-large mended last week. The last kid who wore it ripped it out under both arms. There was a hole under the tail, too. He must have been eating Mexican food." She snatched the XL Howie off the rack and slammed it into my arms. The tail curled around my leg like a python. "You're going to the Wiggle-Waggle, and I mean chop-fucking-chop. Butch Hadley was supposed to take care of that from Team Corgi—or so I thought—but he says his whole team's out with a key to the midway." I had no idea what that meant, and Dottie gave me no time to ask. She rolled her eyes in a way that indicated either good humor or the onset of madness, and continued. "You say 'What's the big deal?' I'll tell you what's the big deal, greenie: Mr. Easterbrook usually eats his lunch there, he *always* eats it there on the first day we're running full-out, and if there's no Howie, he'll be very disappointed."

"Like as in someone will get fired?"

"No, as in very disappointed. Stick around awhile and you'll know that's plenty bad enough. No one wants to disappoint him, because he's a great man. Which is nice, I suppose, but what's more important is he's a good guy. In this business, good guys are scarcer than hen's teeth." She looked at me and made a sound like a small animal with its paw caught in a trap. "Dear *Christ*, you're a big one. And green as grass. But it can't be helped."

I had a billion questions, but my tongue was frozen. All I could do was stare at the deflated Howie. Who stared back at me. Do you know what I felt like just then? James Bond, in the movie where he's tied to some kind of crazy exercise gadget. *Do you expect me to talk?* he asks Goldfinger, and Goldfinger replies, with chilling good humor, *No, Mr. Bond! I expect you to die!* I was tied to a happiness machine instead of an exercise machine, but hey, same idea. No matter how hard I worked to keep up on that first day, the damn thing just kept going faster.

"Take it down to the boneyard, kid. Please tell me you know where that is."

"I do." Thank God Lane had told me.

"Well, that's one for the home team, anyway. When you get there, strip down to your undies. If you wear more than that while you're wearing the fur, you'll roast. And…anybody ever tell you the First Rule of Carny, kid?"

I thought so, but it seemed safer to keep my mouth shut.

"Always know where your wallet is. This park isn't anywhere near as sleazy as some of the places I worked in the flower of my youth—thank God—but that's still the First Rule. Give it to me, I'll keep it for you."

I handed over my wallet without protest.

"Now go. But even before you strip down, drink a lot of water. I mean until your belly feels swollen. And don't eat anything, I don't care how hungry you are. I've had kids get heatstroke and barf in Howie suits, and the results ain't pretty. Suit almost always has to be thrown out. Drink, strip, put on the fur, get someone to zip you up, then hustle down the Boulevard to the Wiggle-Waggle. There's a sign, you can't miss it."

I looked doubtfully at Howie's big blue eyes.

"They're screen mesh," she said. "Don't worry, you'll see fine."

"But what do I *do*?"

She looked at me, at first unsmiling. Then her face—not just her mouth and eyes but her whole face—broke into a grin. The laugh that accompanied it was this weird honk that seemed to come through her nose. "You'll be fine," she said. People kept telling me that. "It's method acting, kiddo. Just find your inner dog."

♥

There were over a dozen new hires and a handful of old-timers having lunch in the boneyard when I arrived. Two of the greenies were Hollywood Girls, but I had no time to be modest. After gulping a bellyful from the drinking fountain, I shucked down to my Jockeys and sneakers. I shook out the Howie costume and stepped in, making sure to get my feet all the way down in the back paws.

"Fur!" one of the old-timers yelled, and slammed a fist down on the table. "Fur! Fur! Fur!"

The others took it up, and the boneyard rang with the chant

as I stood there in my underwear with a deflated Howie puddled around my shins. It was like being in the middle of a prison messhall riot. Rarely have I felt so exquisitely stupid…or so oddly heroic. It was showbiz, after all, and I was stepping into the breach. For a moment it didn't matter that I didn't know what the fuck I was doing.

"*Fur! Fur! FUR! FUR!*"

"*Somebody zip me the hell up!*" I shouted. "*I have to get down to the Wiggle-Waggle posthaste!*"

One of the girls did the honors, and I immediately saw why wearing the fur was such a big deal. The boneyard was air conditioned—all of Joyland Under was—but I was already popping hard sweat.

One of the old-timers came over and gave me a kindly pat on my Howie-head. "I'll give you a ride, son," he said. "Cart's right there. Jump in."

"Thanks." My voice was muffled.

"Woof-woof, Bowser!" someone called, and they all cracked up.

We rolled down the Boulevard with its spooky, stuttering fluorescent lights, a grizzled old guy in janitor's greens with a giant blue-eyed German Shepherd riding co-pilot. As he pulled up at the stairs marked with an arrow and the painted legend WIGWAG on the cinderblocks, he said: "Don't talk. Howie never talks, just gives hugs and pats em on the head. Good luck, and if you start feelin all swimmy, get the hell out. The kids don't want to see Howie flop over with heatstroke."

"I have no idea what I'm supposed to do," I said. "Nobody's told me."

I don't know if that guy was carny-from-carny or not, but he knew something about Joyland. "It don't matter. The kids all love Howie. *They'll* know what to do."

I clambered out of the cart, almost tripped over my tail, then grasped the string in the left front paw and gave it a yank to get the damn thing out of my way. I staggered up the stairs and fumbled with the lever of the door at the top. I could hear music, something vaguely remembered from my early childhood. I finally got the lever to go down. The door opened and bright Junelight flooded through Howie's screen-mesh blue eyes, momentarily dazzling me.

The music was louder now, being piped from overhead speakers, and I could put a name to it: "The Hokey Pokey," that all-time nursery school hit. I saw swings, slides, and teeter-totters, an elaborate jungle gym, and a roundy-round being pushed by a greenie wearing long fuzzy rabbit ears and a powder-puff tail stuck to the seat of his jeans. The Choo-Choo Wiggle, a toy train capable of dazzling speeds approaching four miles an hour, steamed by, loaded with little kids dutifully waving to their camera-toting parents. About a gazillion kids were boiling around, watched over by plenty of summer hires, plus a couple of full-time personnel who probably *did* have child-care licenses. These two, a man and a woman, were wearing sweatshirts that read WE LUV HAPPY KIDS. Dead ahead was the long daycare building called Howie's Howdy House.

I saw Mr. Easterbrook, too. He was sitting on a bench beneath a Joyland umbrella, dressed in his mortician's suit and eating his lunch with chopsticks. He didn't see me at first; he was looking at a crocodile line of children being led toward the Howdy House by a couple of greenies. The kiddies could be parked there (I found this out later) for a maximum of two hours while the parents either took their older kids on the bigger rides or had lunch at Rock Lobster, the park's class-A restaurant.

I also found out later that the eligibility ages for Howdy House ran from three to six. Many of the children now approaching looked pretty mellow, probably because they were daycare vets from families where both parents worked. Others weren't taking it so well. Maybe they'd managed to keep a stiff upper lip at first, hearing mommy and daddy say they'd all be back together in just an hour or two (as if a four-year-old has any real concept of what an hour is), but now they were on their own, in a noisy and confusing place filled with strangers and mommy and daddy nowhere in sight. Some of those were crying. Buried in the Howie costume, looking out through the screen mesh that served as eyeholes and already sweating like a pig, I thought I was witnessing an act of uniquely American child abuse. Why would you bring your kid—your *toddler*, for Christ's sake—to the jangling sprawl of an amusement park only to fob him or her off on a crew of strange babysitters, even for a little while?

The greenies in charge could see the tears spreading (toddler-angst is just another childhood disease, really, like measles), but their faces said they had no idea what to do about it. Why would they? It was Day One, and they had been thrown into the mix with as little preparation as I'd had when Lane Hardy walked away and left me in charge of a gigantic Ferris wheel. *But at least kids under eight can't get on the Spin without an adult*, I thought. *These little buggers are pretty much on their own.*

I didn't know what to do either, but felt I had to try something.

I walked toward the line of kids with my front paws up and wagging my tail like mad (I couldn't see it, but I could feel it). And just as the first two or three saw me and pointed me out, inspiration struck. It was the music. I stopped at the intersection of Jellybean Road and Candy Cane Avenue, which happened to be directly beneath two of the blaring speakers. Standing almost seven feet from paws to furry cocked ears, I'm sure I was quite a presence. I bowed to the kids, who were now all staring with open mouths and wide eyes. As they watched, I began to do the Hokey Pokey.

Sorrow and terror over lost parents were forgotten, at least for the time being. They laughed, some with tears still gleaming on their cheeks. They didn't quite dare approach, not while I was doing my clumsy little dance, but they crowded forward. There was wonder but no fear. They all knew Howie; those from the Carolinas had seen his afternoon TV show, and even those from far-flung exotic locales like St. Louis and Omaha had seen brochures and advertisements on the Saturday morning cartoons. They understood that although Howie was a *big* dog, he was a *good* dog. He'd never bite. He was their friend.

I put my left foot in; I put my left foot out; I put my left foot in and I shook it all about. I did the Hokey Pokey and I turned myself around, because—as almost every little kid in America knows—that's what it's all about. I forgot about being hot and uncomfortable. I didn't think about how my undershorts were sticking in the crack of my ass. Later I would have a bitch of a heat-headache, but just then I felt okay—really good, in fact. And you know what? Wendy Keegan never once crossed my mind.

When the music changed to the *Sesame Street* theme, I quit

dancing, dropped to one padded knee, and held out my arms like Al Jolson.

"*HOWWWIE!*" a little girl screamed, and all these years later I can still hear the perfect note of rapture in her voice. She ran forward, pink skirt swirling around her chubby knees. That did it. The orderly crocodile line dissolved.

The kids will know what to do, the old-timer had said, and how right he was. First they swarmed me, then they knocked me over, then they gathered around me, hugging and laughing. The little girl in the pink skirt kissed my snout repeatedly, shouting "Howie, Howie, Howie!" as she did it.

Some of the parents who had ventured into the Wiggle-Waggle to snap pictures were approaching, equally fascinated. I paddled my paws to get some space, rolled over, and got up before they could crush me with their love. Although just then I was loving them right back. For such a hot day, it was pretty cool.

I didn't notice Mr. Easterbrook reach into the jacket of his mortician's suit, bring out a walkie-talkie, and speak into it briefly. All I knew was that the *Sesame Street* music suddenly cut out and "The Hokey Pokey" started up again. I put my right paw in and my right paw out. The kids got into it right away, their eyes never leaving me, not wanting to miss the next move and be left behind.

Pretty soon we were all doing the Hokey Pokey at the inter-section of Jellybean and Candy Cane. The greenie minders joined in. I'll be goddamned if some of the parents didn't join in as well. I even put my long tail in and pulled my long tail out. Laughing madly, the kids turned around and did the same, only with invisible tails.

As the song wound down, I made an extravagant "Come on,

kids!" gesture with my left paw (inadvertently yanking my tail up so stringently I almost tore the troublesome fucker off) and led them toward Howdy House. They followed as willingly as the children of Hamelin followed the pied piper, and not one of them was crying. That actually wasn't the best day of my brilliant (if I do say so myself, and I do) career as Howie the Happy Hound, but it was right up there.

♥

When they were safely inside Howdy House (the little girl in the pink skirt stood in the door long enough to wave me a bye-bye), I turned around and the world seemed to keep right on turning when I stopped. Sweat sheeted into my eyes, doubling Wiggle-Waggle Village and everything in it. I wavered on my back paws. The entire performance, from my first Hokey Pokey moves to the little girl waving bye-bye, had only taken seven minutes—nine, tops—but I was totally fried. I started trudging back the way I had come, not sure what to do next.

"Son," a voice said. "Over here."

It was Mr. Easterbrook. He was holding open a door in the back of the Wishing Well Snack Bar. It might have been the door I'd come through, probably was, but then I'd been too anxious and excited to notice.

He ushered me inside, closed the door behind us, and pulled down the zipper at the back of the costume. Howie's surprisingly heavy head fell off my own, and my damp skin drank up the blessed air conditioning. My skin, still winter-white (it wouldn't stay that way for long), rashed out in goosebumps. I took big deep breaths.

"Sit down on the steps," he said. "I'll call for a ride in a minute, but right now you need to get your wind back. The first few turns as Howie are always difficult, and the performance you just gave was particularly strenuous. It was also extraordinary."

"Thanks." It was all I could manage. Until I was back inside the cool quiet, I hadn't realized how close to my limit I was. "Thanks very much."

"Head down if you feel faint."

"Not faint. Got a headache, though." I snaked one arm out of Howie and wiped my face, which was dripping. "You kinda rescued me."

"Maximum time wearing Howie on a hot day—I'm talking July and August, when the humidity is high and the temperature goes into the nineties—is fifteen minutes," Mr. Easterbrook said. "If someone tries to tell you different, send them directly to me. And you'll be well advised to swallow a couple of salt pills. We want you summer kids to work hard, but we don't want to kill you."

He took out his walkie-talkie and spoke briefly and quietly. Five minutes later, the old-timer showed up again in his cart, with a couple of Anacin and a bottle of blessedly cold water. In the meantime Mr. Easterbrook sat next to me, lowering himself to the top step leading down to the Boulevard with a glassy care that made me a trifle nervous.

"What's your name, son?"

"Devin Jones, sir."

"Do they call you Jonesy?" He didn't wait for me to reply. "Of course they do, it's the carny way, and that's all Joyland is, really—a thinly disguised carny. Places like this won't last much longer. The Disneys and Knott's Berry Farms are going to rule the amusement world, except maybe down here in the mid-south. Tell me, aside from the heat, how did you enjoy your first turn wearing the fur?"

"I liked it."

"Because?"

"Because some of them were crying, I guess."

He smiled. "And?"

"Pretty soon *all* of them would have been crying, but I stopped it."

"Yes. You did the Hokey Pokey. A splinter of genius. How did you know it would work?"

"I didn't." But actually...I did. On some level, I did.

He smiled. "At Joyland, we throw our new hires—our gree-nies—into the mix without much in the way of preparation, because in some people, some *gifted* people, it encourages a sort of spontaneity that's very special and valuable, both to us and to our patrons. Did you learn something about yourself just now?"

"Jeez, I don't know. Maybe. But...can I say something, sir?"

"Feel free."

I hesitated, then decided to take him at his word. "Sending those kids to daycare—daycare at an amusement park—that seems, I don't know, kind of mean." I added hastily, "Although the Wiggle-Waggle seems really good for little people. Really fun."

"You have to understand something, son. At Joyland, we're in the black this much." He held a thumb and forefinger only a smidge apart. "When parents know there's care for their wee ones—even for just a couple of hours—they bring the whole family. If they needed to hire a babysitter at home, they might not come at all, and our profit margin would disappear. I take

your point, but I have a point, too. Most of those little ones
have never been to a place like this before. They'll remember it
the way they'll remember their first movie, or their first day at
school. Because of you, they won't remember crying because
they were abandoned by their parents for a little while; they'll
remember doing the Hokey Pokey with Howie the Happy Hound,
who appeared like magic."

"I guess."

He reached out, not for me but for Howie. He stroked the
fur with his gnarled fingers as he spoke. "The Disney parks are
scripted, and I hate that. *Hate* it. I think what they're doing
down there in Orlando is fun-pimping. I'm a seat-of-the-pants
fan, and sometimes I see someone who's a seat-of-the-pants
genius. That could be you. Too early to tell for sure, but yes, it
could be you." He put his hands to the small of his back and
stretched. I heard an alarmingly loud series of cracking noises.
"Might I share your cart back to the boneyard? I think I've had
enough sun for one day."

"My cart is your cart." Since Joyland was his park, that was
literally true.

"I think you'll wear the fur a lot this summer. Most of the
young people see that as a burden, or even a punishment. I don't
believe that you will. Am I wrong?"

He wasn't. I've done a lot of jobs in the years since then, and
my current editorial gig—probably my last gig before retirement
seizes me in its claws—is terrific, but I never felt so weirdly
happy, so absolutely in-the-right-place, as I did when I was
twenty-one, wearing the fur and doing the Hokey Pokey on a
hot day in June.

Seat of the pants, baby.

♥

I stayed friends with Tom and Erin after that summer, and I'm friends with Erin still, although these days we're mostly email and Facebook buddies who sometimes get together for lunch in New York. I've never met her second husband. She says he's a nice guy, and I believe her. Why would I not? After being married to Mr. Original Nice Guy for eighteen years and having that yardstick to measure by, she'd hardly pick a loser.

In the spring of 1992, Tom was diagnosed with a brain tumor. He was dead six months later. When he called and told me he was sick, his usual ratchetjaw delivery slowed by the wrecking ball swinging back and forth in his head, I was stunned and depressed, the way almost anyone would be, I suppose, when he hears that a guy who should be in the very prime of life is instead approaching the finish line. You want to ask how a thing like that can be fair. Weren't there supposed to be a few more good things for Tom, like a couple of grandchildren and maybe that long-dreamed-of vacation in Maui?

During my time at Joyland, I once heard Pops Allen talk about burning the lot. In the Talk, that means to blatantly cheat the rubes at what's supposed to be a straight game. I thought of that for the first time in years when Tom called with his bad news.

But the mind defends itself as long as it can. After the first shock of such news dissipates, maybe you think, *Okay, it's bad, I get that, but it's not the final word; there still might be a chance. Even if ninety-five percent of the people who draw this particular card go down, there's still that lucky five percent. Also, doctors misdiagnose shit all the time. Barring those things, there's the occasional miracle.*

You think that, and then you get the follow-up call. The woman who makes the follow-up call was once a beautiful young girl who ran around Joyland in a flippy green dress and a silly Sherwood Forest hat, toting a big old Speed Graphic camera, and the conies she braced hardly ever said no. How could they say no to that blazing red hair and eager smile? How could anyone say no to Erin Cook?

Well, God said no. God burned Tom Kennedy's lot, and He burned hers in the process. When I picked up the phone at five-thirty on a gorgeous October afternoon in Westchester, that girl had become a woman whose voice, blurry with the tears, sounded old and tired to death. "Tom died at two this afternoon. It was very peaceful. He couldn't talk, but he was aware. He...Dev, he squeezed my hand when I said goodbye."

I said, "I wish I could have been there."

"Yes." Her voice wavered, then firmed. "Yes, that would have been good."

You think *Okay, I get it, I'm prepared for the worst*, but you hold out that small hope, see, and that's what fucks you up. That's what kills you.

I talked to her, I told her how much I loved her and how much I had loved Tom, I told her yes, I'd be at the funeral, and if there was anything I could do before then, she should call. Day or night. Then I hung up the phone and lowered my head and bawled my goddam eyes out.

The end of my first love doesn't measure up to the death of one old friend and the bereavement of the other, but it followed the same pattern. Exactly the same. And if it seemed like the end of the world to me—first causing those suicidal ideations (silly and halfhearted though they may have been) and then a seismic shift in the previously unquestioned course of my life—you have to understand I had no scale by which to judge it. That's called being young.

♥

As June wore on, I started to understand that my relationship with Wendy was as sick as William Blake's rose, but I refused to believe it was *mortally* sick, even when the signs became increasingly clear.

Letters, for instance. During my first week at Mrs. Shoplaw's, I wrote Wendy four long ones, even though I was run off my feet at Joyland and came drag-assing into my second-floor room each night with my head full of new information and new experiences, feeling like a kid dropped into a challenging college course (call it The Advanced Physics of Fun) halfway through the semester. What I got in return was a single postcard with Boston Common on the front and a very peculiar collaborative message on the back. At the top, written in a hand I didn't recognize, was this: **Wenny writes the card while Rennie drives the bus!** Below, in a hand I *did* recognize, Wendy—or Wenny, if you like; I hated it, myself—had written breezily: **Whee! We is salesgirls off on a venture to Cape Cod! It's a party! Hoopsie muzik! Don't worry I held the wheel while Ren wrote her part. Hope your good. W.**

Hoopsie muzik? Hope your good? No love, no do you miss me, just *hope your good?* And although, judging by the bumps and jags and inkblots, the card had been written while on the move in Renee's car (Wendy didn't have one), they both sounded either stoned or drunk on their asses. The following week I sent four more letters, plus an Erin-photo of me wearing the fur. From Wendy, nothing in reply.

You start to worry, then you start to get it, then you know. Maybe you don't want to, maybe you think that lovers as well as doctors misdiagnose shit all the time, but in your heart you know.

Twice I tried calling her. The same grumpy girl answered both times. I imagined her wearing harlequin glasses, an ankle-length granny dress, and no lipstick. Not there, she said the first time. Out with Ren. Not there and not likely to be there in the future, Grumpy Girl said the second time. Moved.

"Moved where?" I asked, alarmed. This was in the parlor of *Maison* Shoplaw, where there was a long-distance honor sheet beside the phone. My fingers were holding the big old-fashioned receiver so tightly they had gone numb. Wendy was going to college on a patchwork magic carpet of scholarships, loans, and work-study employment, the same as me. She couldn't afford a place on her own. Not without help, she couldn't.

"I don't know and don't care," Grumpy Girl said. "I got tired of all the drinking and hen-parties at two in the morning. Some of us actually like to get a little sleep. Strange but true."

My heart was beating so hard I could feel it pulsing in my temples. "Did Renee go with her?"

"No, they had a fight. Over that guy. The one who helped Wennie move out." She said *Wennie* with a kind of bright contempt that made me sick to my stomach. Surely it wasn't the guy part that made me feel that way; *I* was her guy. If some friend, someone she'd met at work, had pitched in and helped her move her stuff, what was that to me? Of course she could have guy friends. I had made at least one *girl* friend, hadn't I?

"Is Renee there? Can I talk to her?"

"No, she had a date." Some penny must have finally dropped, because all at once Grumpy Girl got interested in the conversation. "Heyyy, is your name Devin?"

I hung up. It wasn't something I planned, just something I did. I told myself I hadn't heard Grumpy Girl all of a sudden change into *Amused* Grumpy Girl, as if there was some sort of joke going on and I was part of it. Maybe even the butt of it. As I believe I have said, the mind defends itself as long as it can.

♥

Three days later, I got the only letter I received from Wendy Keegan that summer. The last letter. It was written on her stationery, which was deckle-edged and featured happy kittens playing with balls of yarn. It was the stationery of a fifth-grade girl, although that thought didn't occur to me until much later. There were three breathless pages, mostly saying how sorry she was, and how she had fought against the attraction but it was just hopeless, and she knew I would be hurt so I probably shouldn't call her or try to see her for a while, and she hoped we could be good friends after the initial shock wore off, and he was a nice guy, he went to Dartmouth, he played lacrosse, she knew I'd like him, maybe she could introduce him to me when the fall semester started, etc. etc. fucking etc.

That night I plopped myself down on the sand fifty yards or so from Mrs. Shoplaw's Beachside Accommodations, planning to get drunk. At least, I thought, it wouldn't be expensive. In those days, a sixpack was all it took to get me pie-eyed. At some point Tom and Erin joined me, and we watched the waves roll in together: the three Joyland Musketeers.

"What's wrong?" Erin asked.

I shrugged, the way you do when it's small shit but annoying shit, all the same. "Girlfriend broke up with me. Sent me a Dear John letter."

"Which in your case," Tom said, "would be a Dear Dev letter."

"Show a little compassion," Erin told him. "He's sad and hurt and trying not to show it. Are you too much of a dumbass to see that?"

"No," Tom said. He put his arm around my shoulders and briefly hugged me against him. "I'm sorry for your pain, pal. I feel it coming off you like a cold wind from Canada or maybe even the Arctic. Can I have one of your beers?"

"Sure."

We sat there for quite a while, and under Erin's gentle questioning, I spilled some of it, but not all of it. I *was* sad. I *was* hurt. But there was a lot more, and I didn't want them to see it. This was partly because I'd been raised by my parents to believe barfing your feelings on other people was the height of impoliteness, but mostly because I was dismayed by the depth and strength of my jealousy. I didn't want them to even guess at that lively worm (he was from *Dartmouth*, oh God *yes*, he'd probably pledged the best frat and drove a Mustang his folks had given him as a high school graduation present). Nor was jealousy the worst of it. The worst was the horrifying realization—that night it was just starting to sink in—that I had been really and truly rejected for the first time in my life. She was through with me, but I couldn't imagine being through with her.

Erin also took a beer, and raised the can. "Let's toast the next one to come along. I don't know who she'll be, Dev, only that meeting you will be her lucky day."

"Hear-hear!" Tom said, raising his own can. And, because he was Tom, he felt compelled to add "Where-where!" and "There-there!"

I don't think either of them realized, then or all the rest of the summer, how fundamentally the ground under my feet had shifted. How lost I felt. I didn't want them to know. It was more than embarrassing; it seemed shameful. So I made myself smile, raised my own can of suds, and drank.

At least with them to help me drink the six, I didn't have to wake up the next morning hungover as well as heartbroke. That was good, because when we got to Joyland that morning, I found out from Pop Allen that I was down to wear the fur that afternoon on Joyland Avenue—three fifteen-minute shifts at three, four, and five. I bitched for form's sake (everybody was supposed to bitch about wearing the fur) but I was glad. I liked being mobbed by the kids, and for the next few weeks, playing Howie also had a bitter sort of amusement value. As I made my tail-wagging way down Joyland Avenue, followed by crowds of laughing children, I thought it was no wonder Wendy had dumped me. Her new boyfriend went to Dartmouth and played lacrosse. Her old one was spending the summer in a third-tier amusement park. Where he played a dog.

♥

Joyland summer.

I ride-jockeyed. I flashed the shys in the mornings—meaning I restocked them with prizes—and ran some of them in the afternoons. I untangled Devil Wagons by the dozen, learned how to fry dough without burning my fingers off, and worked on my pitch for the Carolina Spin. I danced and sang with the other greenies on the Wiggle-Waggle Village's Story Stage. Several times Fred Dean sent me to scratch the midway, a true sign of trust because it meant picking up the noon or five PM take from the various concessions. I made runs to Heaven's Bay or Wilmington when some piece of machinery broke down and stayed late on Wednesday nights—usually along with Tom, George Preston, and Ronnie Houston—to lube the Whirly Cups and a vicious, neck-snapping ride called the Zipper. Both of those babies drank oil the way camels drink water when they get to the next oasis. And, of course, I wore the fur.

In spite of all this, I wasn't sleeping for shit. Sometimes I'd lie on my bed, clap my elderly, taped-up headphones over my ears, and listen to my Doors records. (I was particularly partial to such cheerful tunes as "Cars Hiss By My Window," "Riders on the Storm," and—of course—"The End.") When Jim Morrison's voice and Ray Manzarek's mystic, chiming organ weren't enough to sedate me, I'd creep down the outside staircase and walk on the beach. Once or twice I *slept* on the beach. At least there were no bad dreams when I did manage to get under for a little while. I don't remember dreaming that summer at all.

I could see bags under my eyes when I shaved in the morning, and sometimes I'd feel lightheaded after a particularly strenuous turn as Howie (birthday parties in the overheated bedlam of Howdy House were the worst), but that was normal; Mr. Easterbrook had told me so. A little rest in the boneyard always put me right again. On the whole, I thought I was *representing*, as they say nowadays. I learned different on the first Monday in July, two days before the Glorious Fourth.

♥

My team—Beagle—reported to Pop Allen's shy first thing, as always, and he gave us our assignments as he laid out the pop-guns. Usually our early chores involved toting boxes of prizes (MADE IN TAIWAN stamped on most of them) and flashing shys until Early Gate, which was what we called opening. That morning, however, Pop told me that Lane Hardy wanted me. This was a surprise; Lane rarely showed his face outside the bone-yard until twenty minutes or so before Early Gate. I started that way, but Pop yelled at me.

"Nah, nah, he's at the simp-hoister." This was a derogatory term for the Ferris wheel he would have known better than to use if Lane had actually been there. "Beat feet, Jonesy. Got a lot to do today."

I beat feet, but saw no one at the Spin, which stood tall, still, and silent, waiting for the day's first customers.

"Over here," a woman called. I turned to my left and saw Rozzie Gold standing outside her star-studded fortune-telling shy, all kitted out in one of her gauzy Madame Fortuna rigs. On her head was an electric blue scarf, the knotted tail of which fell almost to the small of her back. Lane was standing beside her in *his* usual rig: faded straight-leg jeans and a skin-tight strappy tee-shirt perfect for showing off his fully loaded guns. His derby was tilted at the proper wiseguy angle. Looking at him, you'd believe he didn't have a brain in his head, but he had plenty.

Both dressed for show, and both wearing bad-news faces. I ran quickly through the last few days, trying to think of anything I'd done that might account for those faces. It crossed my mind that Lane might have orders to lay me off…or even fire me. But at the height of the summer? And wouldn't that be Fred Dean's or Brenda Rafferty's job? Also, why was Rozzie here?

"Who died, guys?" I asked.

"Just as long as it isn't you," Rozzie said. She was getting into character for the day and sounded funny: half Brooklyn and half Carpathian Mountains.

"Huh?"

"Walk with us, Jonesy," Lane said, and immediately started down the midway, which was largely deserted ninety minutes before Early Gate; no one around but a few members of the janitorial staff—gazoonies, in the Talk, and probably not a green card among them—sweeping up around the concessions: work that should have been done the night before. Rozzie made room for me between them when I caught up. I felt like a crook being escorted to the pokey by a couple of cops.

"What's this about?"

"You'll see," Rozzie/Fortuna said ominously, and pretty soon I did. Next to Horror House—the two connected, actually—was Mysterio's Mirror Mansion. Next to the agent's booth was a regular mirror with a sign over it reading SO YOU WON'T FORGET HOW YOU **REALLY** LOOK. Lane took me by one arm, Rozzie by the other. Now I really did feel like a perp being brought in for booking. They placed me in front of the mirror.

"What do you see?" Lane asked.

"Me," I said, and then, because that didn't seem to be the answer they wanted: "Me needing a haircut."

"Look at your clothes, silly boy," Rozzie said, pronouncing the last two words *seely poy*.

I looked. Above my yellow workboots I saw jeans (with the recommended brand of rawhide gloves sticking out of the back pocket), and above my jeans was a blue chambray workshirt, faded but reasonably clean. On my head was an admirably battered Howie dogtop, the finishing touch that means so much.

"What about them?" I said. I was starting to get a little mad.

"Kinda hangin on ya, aren't they?" Lane said. "Didn't used to. How much weight you lost?"

"Jesus, I don't know. Maybe we ought to go see Fat Wally." Fat Wally ran the guess-your-weight joint.

"Is not funny," Fortuna said. "You can't wear that damn dog costume half the day under the hot summer sun, then swallow two more salt pills and call it a meal. Mourn your lost love all you want, but eat while you do it. *Eat*, dammit!"

"Who's been talking to you? Tom?" No, it wouldn't have been him. "Erin. She had no business—"

"No one has been talking to me," Rozzie said. She drew herself up impressively. "I have the sight."

"I don't know about the sight, but you've got one hell of a nerve."

All at once she reverted to Rozzie. "I'm not talking about psychic sight, kiddo, I'm talking about ordinary woman-sight. You think I don't know a lovestruck Romeo when I see one? After all the years I've been gigging palms and peeping the crystal? *Hah*!" She stepped forward, her considerable breastworks leading the way. "I don't care about your love life; I just don't want to see you taken to the hospital on July Fourth— when it's supposed to hit ninety-five in the shade, by the way— with heat prostration or something worse."

Lane took off his derby, peered into it, and re-set it on his head cocked the other way. "What she won't come right out and say because she has to protect her famous crusty reputation is we all like you, kid. You learn fast, you do what's asked of you,

you're honest, you don't make no trouble, and the kids love you like mad when you're wearing the fur. But you'd have to be blind not to see something's wrong with you. Rozzie thinks girl trouble. Maybe she's right. Maybe she ain't."

Rozzie gave him a haughty dare-you-doubt-me stare.

"Maybe your parents are getting a divorce. Mine did, and it damn near killed me. Maybe your big brother got arrested for selling dope—"

"My mother's dead and I'm an only child," I said sulkily.

"I don't care what you are in the straight world," he said. "This is Joyland. The *show*. And you're one of us. Which means we got a right to care about you, whether you like it or not. So get something to eat."

"Get a *lot* to eat," Rozzie said. "Now, noon, all day. *Every* day. And try to eat something besides fried chicken where, I tell you what, there's a heart attack in every drumstick. Go in Rock Lobster and tell them you want a take-out of fish and salad. Tell them to make it a double. Get your weight up so you don't look like the Human Skeleton in a ten-in-one." She turned her gaze on Lane. "It's a girl, of course it is. Anybody can see that."

"Whatever it is, stop fucking *pining*," Lane said.

"Such language to use around a lady," Rozzie said. She was sounding like Fortuna again. Soon she'd come out with *Ziss is vat za spirits vant*, or something equivalent.

"Ah, blow it out," Lane said, and walked back toward the Spin.

When he was gone, I looked at Rozzie. She really wasn't much in the mother-figure department, but right then she was what I had. "Roz, does *everyone* know?"

She shook her head. "Nah. To most of the old guys, you're
just another greenie jack-of-all-trades...although not as green
as you were three weeks ago. But many people here like you,
and they see something is wrong. Your friend Erin, for one.
Your friend Tom for another." She said *friend* like it rhymed
with *rent*. "I am another friend, and as a friend I tell you that
you can't fix your heart. Only time can do that, but you can fix
your body. Eat!"

"You sound like a Jewish mother joke," I said.

"I *am* a Jewish mother, and believe me, it's no joke."

"*I'm* the joke," I said. "I think about her all the time."

"That you can't help, at least for now. But you must turn
your back on the other thoughts that sometimes come to you."

I think my mouth dropped open. I'm not sure. I know I stared.
People who've been in the business as long as Rozzie Gold had
been back then—they are called *mitts* in the Talk, for their
palmistry skills—have their ways of picking your brains so that
what they say sounds like the result of telepathy, but usually it's
just close observation.

Not always, though.

"I don't understand."

"Give those morbid records a rest, do you understand that?"
She looked grimly into my face, then laughed at the surprise
she saw there. "Rozzie Gold may be just a Jewish mother and
grandmother, but Madame Fortuna sees much."

So did my landlady, and I found out later—after seeing Rozzie
and Mrs. Shoplaw having lunch together in Heaven's Bay on one
of Madame Fortuna's rare days off—that they were close friends
who had known each other for years. Mrs. Shoplaw dusted my
room and vacuumed the floor once a week; she would have seen

my records. As for the rest—those famous suicidal ideations that sometimes came to me—might not a woman who had spent most of her life observing human nature and watching for psychological clues (called *tells* both in the Talk and big-league poker) guess that a sensitive young man, freshly dumped, might entertain thoughts of pills and ropes and riptide undertows?

"I'll eat," I promised. I had a thousand things to do before Early Gate, but mostly I was just anxious to be away from her before she said something totally outrageous like *Her name is Vendy, and you still think of her ven you mess-turbate.*

"Also, drink big glass of milk before you go to bed." She raised an admonitory finger. "No coffee; milk. Vill help you sleep."

"Worth a try," I said.

She went back to Roz again. "The day we met, you asked if I saw a beautiful woman with dark hair in your future. Do you remember that?"

"Yes."

"What did I say?"

"That she was in my past."

Rozzie gave a single nod, hard and imperious. "So she is. And when you want to call her and beg for a second chance—you will, you will—show a little spine. Have a little self-respect. Also remember that the long-distance is expensive."

Tell me something I don't know, I thought. "Listen, I really have to get going, Roz. Lots to do."

"Yes, a busy day for all of us. But before you go, Jonesy—have you met the boy yet? The one with the dog? Or the girl who wears the red hat and carries the doll? I told you about them, too, when we met."

"Roz, I've met a billion kids in the last—"

"You haven't, then. Okay. You will." She stuck out her lower lip and blew, stirring the fringe of hair that stuck out from beneath her scarf. Then she seized my wrist. "I see danger for you, Jonesy. Sorrow and danger."

I thought for a moment she was going to whisper something like *Beware the dark stranger! He rides a unicycle!* Instead, she let go of me and pointed at Horror House. "Which team turns that unpleasant hole? Not yours, is it?"

"No, Team Doberman." The Dobies were also responsible for the adjacent attractions: Mysterio's Mirror Mansion and the Wax Museum. Taken together, these three were Joyland's half-hearted nod to the old carny spook-shows.

"Good. Stay out of it. It's haunted, and a boy with bad thoughts needs to be visiting a haunted house like he needs arsenic in his mouthwash. *Kapish*?"

"Yeah." I looked at my watch.

She got the point and stepped back. "Watch for those kids. And watch your step, boychick. There's a shadow over you."

♥

Lane and Rozzie gave me a pretty good jolt, I'll admit it. I didn't stop listening to my Doors records—not immediately, at least—but I made myself eat more, and started sucking down three milkshakes a day. I could feel fresh energy pouring into my body as if someone had turned on a tap, and I was very grateful for that on the afternoon of July Fourth. Joyland was tipsed and I was down to wear the fur ten times, an all-time record.

Fred Dean himself came down to give me the schedule, and to hand me a note from old Mr. Easterbrook. *If it becomes too much, stop at once and tell your team leader to find a sub.*

"I'll be fine," I said.

"Maybe, but make sure Pop sees this memo."

"Okay."

"Brad likes you, Jonesy. That's rare. He hardly ever notices the greenies unless he sees one of them screw up."

I liked him, too, but didn't say so to Fred. I thought it would have sounded suck-assy.

♥

All my July Fourth shifts were tenners, not bad even though most ten-minute shifts actually turned out to be fifteenies, but the heat was crushing. *Ninety-five in the shade*, Rozzie had said, but by noon that day it was a hundred and two by the thermometer that hung outside the Park Ops trailer. Luckily for me, Dottie Lassen had repaired the other XL Howie suit and I could swap between the two. While I was wearing one, Dottie would have the other turned as inside-out as it would go and hung in front of three fans, drying the sweat-soaked interior.

At least I could remove the fur by myself; by then I'd discovered the secret. Howie's right paw was actually a glove, and when you knew the trick, pulling down the zipper to the neck of the costume was a cinch. Once you had the head off, the rest was cake. This was good, because I could change by myself behind a pull-curtain. No more displaying my sweaty, semi-transparent undershorts to the costume ladies.

As the bunting-draped afternoon of July Fourth wore on, I was excused from all other duties. I'd do my capering, then retreat to Joyland Under and collapse on the ratty old couch in the boneyard for a while, soaking up the air conditioning. When I felt revived, I'd use the alleys to get to the costume shop and swap one fur for the other. Between shifts I guzzled pints of water and quarts of unsweetened iced tea. You won't believe I was having fun, but I was. Even the brats were loving me that day.

So: quarter to four in the afternoon. I'm jiving down Joyland Avenue—our midway—while the overhead speakers blast out Daddy Dewdrop's "Chick-A-Boom, Chick-A-Boom, Don'tcha Just Love It." I'm giving out hugs to the kiddies and Awesome August coupons to the adults, because Joyland's business always dropped off as the summer wound down. I'm posing for pictures (some taken by Hollywood Girls, most by hordes of sweat-soaked, sunburned Parent Paparazzi), and trailing adoring kids after me in cometary splendor. I'm also looking for the nearest door to Joyland Under, because I'm pretty well done up. I have just one more turn as Howie scheduled today, because Howie the Happy Hound never shows his blue eyes and cocked ears after sundown. I don't know why; it was just a show tradition.

Did I notice the little girl in the red hat before she fell down on the baking pavement of Joyland Avenue, writhing and jerking? I think so but can't say for sure, because passing time adds false memories and modifies real ones. I surely wouldn't have noticed the Pup-A-Licious she was waving around, or her bright red Howie dogtop; a kid at an amusement park with a hotdog is hardly a unique sighting, and we must have sold a thousand red Howie hats that day. If I did notice her, it was because of the doll she held curled to her chest in the hand not holding her mustard-smeared Pup. It was a big old Raggedy Ann. Madame Fortuna had suggested I be on the lookout for a little girl with a doll only two days before, so maybe I did notice her. Or maybe I was only thinking of getting off the midway before I fell down in a faint. Anyway, her doll wasn't the problem. The Pup-A-Licious she was eating—*that* was the problem.

I only *think* I remember her running toward me (hey, they all did), but I know what happened next, and why it happened. She had a bite of her Pup in her mouth, and when she drew in breath to scream *HOWWWIE*, she pulled it down her throat. Hot dogs: the perfect choking food. Luckily for her, just enough of Rozzie Gold's Fortuna bullshit had stuck in my head for me to act quickly.

When the little girl's knees buckled, her expression of happy ecstasy turning first to surprise and then terror, I was already reaching behind me and grabbing the zipper with my paw-glove. The Howie-head tumbled off and lolled to the side, revealing the red face and sweat-soaked, clumpy hair of Mr. Devin Jones. The little girl dropped her Raggedy Ann. Her hat fell off. She began clawing at her neck.

"Hallie?" a woman cried. "Hallie, what's *wrong*?"

Here's more Luck in Action: I not only knew what was wrong, I knew what to do. I'm not sure you'll understand how fortunate that was. This is 1973 we're talking about, remember, and Henry Heimlich would not publish the essay that would give the Heimlich Maneuver its name for another full year. Still, it's always been the most commonsense way to deal with choking, and we had learned it during our first and only orientation session before beginning work in the UNH Commons. The teacher was a tough old veteran of the restaurant wars who had lost his Nashua coffee shop a year after a new McDonald's went up nearby.

"Just remember, it won't work if you don't do it hard," he told us. "Don't worry about breaking a rib if you see someone dying in front of you."

I saw the little girl's face turning purple and didn't even think about her ribs. I seized her in a vast, furry embrace, with my tail-pulling left paw jammed against the bony arch in her midsection where her ribs came together. I gave a single hard squeeze, and a yellow-smeared chunk of hotdog almost two inches long came popping out of her mouth like a cork from a champagne bottle. It flew nearly four feet. And no, I didn't break any of her ribs. Kids are flexible, God bless 'em.

I wasn't aware that I and Hallie Stansfield—that was her name—were hemmed in by a growing circle of adults. I certainly wasn't aware that we were being photographed dozens of times, including the shot by Erin Cook that wound up in the Heaven's Bay *Weekly* and several bigger papers, including the Wilmington *Star-News*. I've still got a framed copy of that photo in an attic box somewhere. It shows the little girl dangling in the arms of this weird man/dog hybrid with one of its two heads lolling on its shoulder. The girl is holding out her arms to her mother, perfectly caught by Erin's Speed Graphic just as Mom collapses to her knees in front of us.

All of that is a blur to me, but I remember the mother sweeping the little girl up into her own arms and the father saying *Kid, I think you saved her life*. And I remember—this is as clear as crystal—the girl looking at me with her big blue eyes and saying, "Oh poor Howie, your head fell off."

♥

The all-time classic newspaper headline, as everyone knows, is MAN BITES DOG. The *Star-News* couldn't equal that, but the one over Erin's picture gave it a run for its money: DOG SAVES GIRL AT AMUSEMENT PARK.

Want to know my first snarky urge? To clip the article and send it to Wendy Keegan. I might even have done it, had I not looked so much like a drowned muskrat in Erin's photo. I did send it to my father, who called to say how proud of me he was. I could tell by the tremble in his voice that he was close to tears.

"God put you in the right place at the right time, Dev," he said.

Maybe God. Maybe Rozzie Gold, aka Madame Fortuna. Maybe a little of both.

The next day I was summoned to Mr. Easterbrook's office, a pine-paneled room raucous with old carny posters and photographs. I was particularly taken by a photo that showed a straw-hatted agent with a dapper mustache standing next to a test-your-strength shy. The sleeves of his white shirt were rolled up, and he was leaning on a sledgehammer like it was a cane: a total dude. At the top of the ding-post, next to the bell, was a sign reading KISS HIM, LADY, HE'S A HE-MAN!

"Is that guy you?" I asked.

"It is indeed, although I only ran the ding-show for a season. It wasn't to my taste. Gaff jobs never have been. I like my games straight. Sit down, Jonesy. You want a Coke or anything?"

"No, sir. I'm fine." I was, in fact, sloshing with that morning's milkshake.

"I'll be perfectly blunt. You gave this show twenty thousand dollars' worth of good publicity yesterday afternoon, and I still can't afford to give you a bonus. If you knew…but never mind." He leaned forward. "What I *can* do is owe you a favor. If you need one, ask. I'll grant it if it's in my power. Will that do?"

"Sure."

"Good. And would you be willing to make one more appearance—as Howie—with the little girl? Her parents want to thank you in private, but a public appearance would be an excellent thing for Joyland. Entirely your call, of course."

"When?"

"Saturday, after the noon parade. We'd put up a platform at the intersection of Joyland and Hound Dog Way. Invite the press."

"Happy to," I said. I liked the idea of being in the newspapers again, I will admit. It had been a tough summer on my ego and self-image, and I'd take all the turnaround I could get.

He rose to his feet in his glassy, unsure way, and offered me his hand. "Thank you again. On behalf of that little girl, but also on behalf of Joyland. The accountants who run my damn life will be very happy about this."

♥

When I stepped out of the office building, which was located with the other administrative buildings in what we called the backyard, my entire team was there. Even Pop Allen had come. Erin, dressed for success in Hollywood Girl green, stepped forward with a shiny metal crown of laurels made from Campbell's Soup cans. She dropped to one knee. "For you, my hero."

I would have guessed I was too sunburned to flush, but that turned out not to be true. "Oh Jesus, get up."

"Savior of little girls," Tom Kennedy said. "Not to mention savior of our place of employment getting its ass sued off and possibly having to shut its doors."

Erin bounced to her feet, stuck the ludicrous soup-can crown on my head, then gave me a big old smackaroonie. Everyone on Team Beagle cheered.

"Okay," Pop said when it died down. "We can all agree that you're a knight in shining ah-mah, Jonesy. You are also not the first guy to save a rube from popping off on the midway. Could we maybe all get back to work?"

I was good with that. Being famous was fun, but the don't-get-a-swelled-head message of the tin laurels wasn't lost on me.

♥

I was wearing the fur that Saturday, on the makeshift platform at the center of our midway. I was happy to take Hallie in my arms, and she was clearly happy to be there. I'd guess there were roughly nine miles of film burned as she proclaimed her love for her favorite doggy and kissed him again and again for the cameras.

Erin was in the front row with her camera for a while, but the news photogs were bigger and all male. Soon they shunted her away to a less favorable position, and what did they all want? What Erin had already gotten, a picture of me with my Howie-head off. That was one thing I wouldn't do, although I'm sure none of Fred, Lane, or Mr. Easterbrook himself would have penalized me for it. I wouldn't do it because it would have flown in the face of park tradition: Howie *never* took off the fur in public; to do so would have been like outing the Tooth Fairy. I'd done it when Hallie Stansfield was choking, but that was the necessary exception. I would not deliberately break the rule. So I guess I was carny after all (although not carny-from-carny, never that).

Later, dressed in my own duds again, I met with Hallie and her parents in the Joyland Customer Service Center. Close-up, I could see that Mom was pregnant with number two, although she probably had three or four months of eating pickles and ice cream still ahead of her. She hugged me and wept some more. Hallie didn't seem overly concerned. She sat in one of the plastic chairs, swinging her feet and looking at old copies of *Screen Time*, speaking the names of the various celebrities in the declamatory voice of a court page announcing visiting royalty. I patted Mom's back and said there-there. Dad didn't cry, but the tears were standing in his eyes as he approached me and held out a check in the amount of five hundred dollars, made out to me. When I asked what he did for a living, he said he had started his own contracting firm the year before—just now little, but gettin on our feet pretty good, he told me. I considered that, factored in one kid here plus another on the way, and tore up the check. I told him I couldn't take money for something that was just part of the job.

You have to remember I was only twenty-one.

♥

There were no weekends *per se* for Joyland summer help; we got a day and a half every nine, which meant they were never the same days. There was a sign-up sheet, so Tom, Erin, and I almost always managed to get the same downtime. That was why we were together on a Wednesday night in early August, sitting around a campfire on the beach and having the sort of meal that can only nourish the very young: beer, burgers, barbecue-flavored potato chips, and coleslaw. For dessert we had s'mores that Erin cooked over the fire, using a grill she borrowed from Pirate Pete's Ice Cream Waffle joint. It worked pretty well.

We could see other fires—great leaping bonfires as well as

cooking fires—all the way down the beach to the twinkling metropolis of Joyland. They made a lovely chain of burning jewelry. Such fires are probably illegal in the twenty-first century; the powers that be have a way of outlawing many beautiful things made by ordinary people. I don't know why that should be, I only know it is.

While we ate, I told them about Madame Fortuna's prediction that I would meet a boy with a dog and a little girl in a red hat who carried a doll. I finished by saying, "One down and one to go."

"Wow," Erin said. "Maybe she really *is* psychic. A lot of people have told me that, but I didn't really—"

"Like who?" Tom demanded.

"Well…Dottie Lassen in the costume shop, for one. Tina Ackerley, for another. You know, the librarian Dev creeps down the hall to visit at night?"

I flipped her the bird. She giggled.

"Two is not a lot," Tom said, speaking in his Hot Shit Professor voice.

"Lane Hardy makes three," I said. "He says she's told people stuff that rocked them back on their heels." In the interest of total disclosure, I felt compelled to add: "Of course he also said that ninety percent of her predictions are total crap."

"Probably closer to ninety-five," said the Hot Shit Professor. "Fortune telling's a con game, boys and girls. An Ikey Heyman, in the Talk. Take the hat thing. Joyland dogtops only come in three colors—red, blue, and yellow. Red's by far the most popular. As for the doll, c'mon. How many little kids bring some sort of toy to the amusement park? It's a strange place, and a favorite toy is a comfort thing. If she hadn't choked on her hotdog right in front of you, if she'd just given Howie a big old hug and passed on, you would have seen some other little girl wearing a red dogtop and carrying a doll and said, 'Aha! Madame Fortuna really *can* see the future, I must cross her palm with silver so she will tell me more.' "

"You're such a cynic," Erin said, giving him an elbow. "Rozzie Gold would never try taking money from someone in the show."

"She didn't ask for money," I said, but I thought what Tom said made a lot of sense. It was true she had known (or *seemed* to know) that my dark-haired girl was in my past, not my future, but that could have been no more than a guess based on percentages—or the look on my face when I asked.

"Course not," Tom said, helping himself to another s'more. "She was just practicing on you. Staying sharp. I bet she's told a lot of other greenies stuff, too."

"Would you be one of them?" I asked.

"Well…no. But that means nothing."

I looked at Erin, who shook her head.

"She also thinks Horror House is haunted," I said.

"I've heard that one, too," Erin said. "By a girl who got murdered in there."

"Bullshit!" Tom cried. "Next you'll be telling me it was the Hook, and he still lurks behind the Screaming Skull!"

"There really was a murder," I said. "A girl named Linda Gray. She was from Florence, South Carolina. There are pictures of her and the guy who killed her at the shooting gallery and standing in line at the Spin. No hook, but there was a tattoo of a bird on his hand. A hawk or an eagle."

That silenced him, at least for the time being.

"Lane Hardy said that Roz only *thinks* Horror House is

haunted, because she won't go inside and find out for sure. She won't even go near it, if she can help it. Lane thinks that's ironic, because he says it really *is* haunted."

Erin made her eyes big and round and scooted a little closer to the fire—partly for effect, mostly I think so that Tom would put his arm around her. "He's *seen*—?"

"I don't know. He said to ask Mrs. Shoplaw, and she gave me the whole story." I ran it down for them. It was a good story to tell at night, under the stars, with the surf rolling and a beach-fire just starting to burn down to coals. Even Tom seemed fascinated.

"Does *she* claim to have seen Linda Gray?" he asked when I finally ran down. "La Shoplaw?"

I mentally replayed her story as told to me on the day I rented the room on the second floor. "I don't think so. She would have said."

He nodded, satisfied. "A perfect lesson in how these things work. Everyone *knows* someone who's seen a UFO, and everyone *knows* someone who's seen a ghost. Hearsay evidence, inadmissible in court. Me, I'm a Doubting Thomas. Geddit? Tom Kennedy, Doubting Thomas?"

Erin threw him a much sharper elbow. "We get it." She looked thoughtfully into the fire. "You know what? Summer's two-thirds gone, and I've never been in the Joyland scream-shy a single time, not even the baby part up front. It's a no-photo zone. Brenda Rafferty told us it's because lots of couples go in there to make out." She peered at me. "What are you grinning about?"

"Nothing." I was thinking of La Shoplaw's late husband going through the place after Late Gate and picking up cast-off panties.

"Have either of you guys been in?"

We both shook our heads. "HH is Dobie Team's job," Tom said.

"Let's do it tomorrow. All three of us in one car. Maybe we'll see her."

"Go to Joyland on our day off when we could spend it on the beach?" Tom asked. "That's masochism at its very finest."

This time in spite of giving him an elbow, she poked him in the ribs. I didn't know if they were sleeping together yet, but it seemed likely; the relationship had certainly become very physical. "Poop on that! As employees we get in free, and what does the ride take? Five minutes?"

"I think a little longer," I said. "Nine or ten. Plus some time in the baby part. Say fifteen minutes, all told."

Tom put his chin on her head and looked at me through the fine cloud of her hair. "Poop on that, she says. You can tell that here is a young woman with a fine college education. Before she started hanging out with sorority girls, she would have said *shitsky* and left it at that."

"The day I start hanging out with that bunch of half-starved mix-n-match sluts will be the day I crawl up my own ass and die!" For some reason, this vulgarity pleased me to no end. Possibly because Wendy was a veteran mix-n-matcher. "You, Thomas Patrick Kennedy, are just afraid we *will* see her, and you'll have to take back all those things you said about Madame Fortuna and ghosts and UFOs and—"

Tom raised his hands. "I give up. We'll get in the line with the rest of the rubes—the conies, I mean—and take the Horror House tour. I only insist it be in the afternoon. I need my beauty rest."

"You certainly do," I said.

"Coming from someone who looks like you, that's pretty funny. Give me a beer, Jonesy."

I gave him a beer.

"Tell us how it went with the Stansfields," Erin said. "Did they blubber all over you and call you their hero?"

That was pretty close, but I didn't want to say so. "The parents were okay. The kid sat in the corner, reading *Screen Time* and saying she spied Dean Martin with her little eye."

"Forget the local color and cut to the chase," Tom said. "Did you get any money out of it?"

I was preoccupied with thoughts of how the little girl announcing the celebrities with such reverence could have been in a flatline coma instead. Or in a casket. Thus distracted, I answered honestly. "The guy offered me five hundred dollars, but I wouldn't take it."

Tom goggled. "Say *what*?"

I looked down at the remains of the s'more I was holding. Marshmallow was drooling onto my fingers, so I tossed it into the fire. I was full, anyway. I was also embarrassed, and pissed off to be feeling that way. "The man's trying to get a little business up and running, and based on the way he talked about it, it's at the point where it could go either way. He's also got a wife and a kid and another kid coming soon. I didn't think he could afford to be giving money away."

"*He* couldn't? What about *you*?"

I blinked. "What about me?"

To this day I don't know if Tom was genuinely angry or faking it. I think he might have started out faking, then gathered steam as full understanding of what I'd done struck him. I have no idea exactly what his home situation was, but I know he was living from paycheck to paycheck, and had no car. When he wanted to take Erin out, he borrowed mine...and was careful —punctilious, I should say—about paying for the gas he used. Money mattered to him. I never got the sense it completely owned him, but yes, it mattered to him a great deal.

"You're going to school on a wing and a prayer, same as Erin and me, and working at Joyland isn't going to land any of us in a limousine. What's wrong with you? Did your mother drop you on your head when you were a baby?"

"Take it easy," Erin said.

He paid no attention. "Do you *want* to spend the fall semester next year getting up early so you can pull dirty breakfast dishes off a Commons conveyor belt? You must, because five hundred a semester is about what it pays at Rutgers. I know, because I checked before lucking into a tutoring gig. You know how I made it through freshman year? Writing papers for rich frat-boys majoring in Advanced Beerology. If I'd been caught, I could have been suspended for a semester or tossed completely. I'll tell you what your grand gesture amounted to: giving away twenty hours a week you could have spent studying." He heard himself ranting, stopped, and raised a grin. "Or chatting up lissome females."

"*I'll* give you lissome," Erin said, and pounced on him. They went rolling across the sand, Erin tickling and Tom yelling (with a notable lack of conviction) for her to get off. That was fine with me, because I did not care to pursue the issues Tom had raised. I had already made up my mind about some things, it seemed, and all that remained was for my conscious mind to get the news.

♥

The next day, at quarter past three, we were in line at Horror House. A kid named Brady Waterman was agenting the shy. I remember him because he was also good at playing Howie. (But not as good as I was, I feel compelled to add…strictly in the cause of honesty.) Although quite stout at the beginning of the summer, Brady was now slim and trim. As a diet program, wearing the fur had Weight Watchers beat six ways to Tulsa.

"What are you guys doing here?" he asked. "Isn't it your day off?"

"We had to see Joyland's one and only dark ride," Tom said, "and I'm already feeling a satisfying sense of dramatic unity— Brad Waterman and Horror House. It's the perfect match."

He scowled. "You're all gonna try to cram into one car, aren'tcha?"

"We have to," Erin told him. Then she leaned close to one of Brad's juggy ears and whispered, "It's a Truth or Dare thing."

As Brad considered this, he touched the tip of his tongue to the middle of his upper lip. I could see him calculating the possibilities.

The guy behind us spoke up. "Kids, could you move the line along? I understand there's air conditioning inside, and I could use some."

"Go on," Brad told us. "Put an egg in your shoe and beat it." Coming from Brad, this was Rabelaisian wit.

"Any ghosts in there?" I asked.

"Hundreds, and I hope they all fly right up your ass."

♥

We started with Mysterio's Mirror Mansion, pausing briefly to regard ourselves drawn tall or smashed squat. With that minor giggle accomplished, we followed the tiny red dots on the bottoms of certain mirrors. These led us directly to the Wax Museum. Given this secret roadmap, we arrived well ahead of the rest of the current group, who wandered around, laughing and bumping into the various angled panes of glass.

To Tom's disappointment, there were no murderers in the Wax Museum, only pols and celebs. A smiling John F. Kennedy and a jumpsuited Elvis Presley flanked the doorway. Ignoring the PLEASE DO NOT TOUCH sign, Erin gave Elvis's guitar a strum. "Out of tu—" she began, then recoiled as Elvis jerked to life and began singing "Can't Help Falling in Love with You."

"Gotcha!" Tom said gleefully, and gave her a hug.

Beyond the Wax Museum was a doorway leading to the Barrel and Bridge Room, which rumbled with machinery that sounded dangerous (it wasn't) and stuttered with strobe lights of conflicting colors. Erin crossed to the other side on the shaking, tilting Billy Goat's Bridge while the macho men accompanying her dared the Barrel. I stumbled my way through, reeling like a drunk but only falling once. Tom stopped in the middle, stuck out his hands and feet so he looked like a paperdoll, and made a complete three-sixty that way.

"Stop it, you goof, you'll break your neck!" Erin called.

"He won't even if he falls," I said. "It's padded."

Tom rejoined us, grinning and flushed to the roots of his hair. "That woke up brain cells that have been asleep since I was three."

"Yeah, but what about all the ones it killed?" Erin asked.

Next came the Tilted Room and beyond that was an arcade filled with teenagers playing pinball and Skee-Ball. Erin watched the Skee-Ball for a while, with her arms folded beneath her breasts and a disapproving look on her face. "Don't they know that's a complete butcher's game?"

"People come here to be butched," I said. "It's part of the attraction."

Erin sighed. "And I thought *Tom* was a cynic."

On the far side of the arcade, beneath a glowing green skull, was a sign reading: HORROR HOUSE LIES BEYOND! BEWARE! PREGNANT WOMEN AND THOSE WITH SMALL CHILDREN MAY EXIT LEFT.

We walked into an antechamber filled with echoing recorded cackles and screams. Pulsing red light illuminated a single steel track and a black tunnel entrance beyond. From deep within it came rumbles, flashing lights, and more screams. These were not recorded. From a distance, they didn't sound particularly happy, but probably they were. Some, at least.

Eddie Parks, proprietor of Horror House and boss of Team Doberman, walked over to us. He was wearing rawhide gloves and a dogtop so old it was faded to no color at all (although it turned blood red each time the lights pulsed). He gave us a dismissive sniff. "Must have been a damn boring day off."

"Just wanted to see how the other half lives," Tom said.

Erin gave Eddie her most radiant smile. It was not returned.

"Three to a car, I guess. That what you want?"

"Yes," I said.

"Fine with me. Just remember that the rules apply to you, same as anyone else. Keep your fuckin hands inside."

"Yessir," Tom said, and gave a little salute. Eddie looked at him the way a man might look at a new species of bug and walked back to his controls, which consisted of three shifter-knobs sticking out of a waist-high podium. There were also a few buttons illuminated by a Tensor lamp bent low to minimize its less-than-ghostly white light.

"Charming guy," Tom muttered.

Erin hooked an arm into Tom's right elbow and my left, drawing us close. "Does anyone like him?" she murmured.

"No," Tom said. "Not even his own team. He's already fired two of them."

The rest of our group started to catch up just as a train filled with laughing conies (plus a few crying kids whose parents probably should have heeded the warning and exited from the arcade) arrived. Erin asked one of the girls if it was scary.

"The scary part was trying to keep *his* hands where they belong," she said, then squealed happily as her boyfriend first kissed her neck and then pulled her toward the arcade.

We climbed aboard. Three of us in a car designed for two made for an extremely tight fit, and I was very aware of Erin's thigh pressing against mine, and the brush of her breast against my arm. I felt a sudden and far from unpleasant southward tingle. I would argue that—fantasies aside—the majority of men are monogamous from the chin up. Below the belt-buckle, however, there's a wahoo stampeder who just doesn't give a shit.

"Hands inside the *caaa*!" Eddie Parks was yelling in a bored-to-death monotone that was the complete antithesis of a cheerful Lane Hardy pitch. "Hands inside the *caaa*! You got a kid under three feet, put im in your lap or get out of the *caaa*! Hold still and watch for the *baaa*!"

The safety bars came down with a clank, and a few girls tuned up with preparatory screams. Clearing their vocal cords for dark-ride arias to come, you might say.

There was a jerk, and we rode into Horror House.

♥

Nine minutes later we got out and exited through the arcade with the rest of the tip. Behind us, we could hear Eddie exhorting his next bunch to keep their hands inside the *caaa* and watch for the *baaa*. He never gave us a look.

"The dungeon part wasn't scary, because all the prisoners were Dobies," Erin said. "The one in the pirate outfit was Billy Ruggerio." Her color was high, her hair was mussed from the blowers, and I thought she had never looked so pretty. "But the Screaming Skull really got me, and the Torture Chamber…my God!"

"Pretty gross," I agreed. I'd seen a lot of horror movies during my high school years, and thought of myself as inured, but seeing an eye-bulging head come rolling down an inclined trough from the guillotine had jumped the shit out of me. I mean, the mouth was still moving.

Out on Joyland Avenue again, we spotted Cam Jorgensen from Team Foxhound selling lemonade. "Who wants one?" Erin asked. She was still bubbling over. "I'm buying!"

"Sure," I said.

"Tom?"

He shrugged his assent. Erin gave him a quizzical look, then ran to get the drinks. I glanced at Tom, but he was watching the Rocket go around and around. Or maybe looking through it.

Erin came back with three tall paper cups, half a lemon bobbing on top of each. We took them to the benches in Joyland Park, just down from the Wiggle-Waggle, and sat in the shade. Erin was talking about the bats at the end of the ride, how she knew they were just wind-up toys on wires, but bats had always scared the hell out of her and—

There she broke off. "Tom, are you okay? You haven't said a

word. Not sick to your stomach from turning in the Barrel, are you?"

"My stomach's fine." He took a sip of his lemonade, as if to prove it. "What was she wearing, Dev? Do you know?"

"Huh?"

"The girl who got murdered. Laurie Gray."

"*Linda* Gray."

"Laurie, Larkin, Linda, whatever. What was she wearing? Was it a full skirt—a long one, down to her shins—and a sleeveless blouse?"

I looked at him closely. We both did, initially thinking it was just another Tom Kennedy goof. Only he didn't look like he was goofing. Now that I really examined him, what he looked like was scared half to death.

"Tom?" Erin touched his shoulder. "Did you see her? Don't joke, now."

He put his hand over hers but didn't look at her. He was looking at me. "Yeah," he said, "long skirt and sleeveless blouse. You know, because La Shoplaw told you."

"What color?" I asked.

"Hard to tell with the lights changing all the time, but I think blue. Blouse and skirt both."

Then Erin got it. "Holy shit," she said in a kind of sigh. The high color was leaving her cheeks in a hurry.

There was something else. Something the police had held back for a long time, according to Mrs. Shoplaw.

"What about her hair, Tom? Ponytail, right?"

He shook his head. Took a small sip of his lemonade. Patted his mouth with the back of his hand. His hair hadn't gone gray, he wasn't all starey-eyed, his hands weren't shaking, but he still didn't look like the same guy who'd joked his way through the Mirror Mansion and the Barrel and Bridge Room. He looked like a guy who'd just gotten a reality enema, one that had flushed all the junior-year-summer-job bullshit out of his system.

"Not a ponytail. Her hair long, all right, but she had a thing across the top of her head to keep it out of her face. I've seen a billion of em, but I can't remember what girls call it."

"An Alice band," Erin said.

"Yeah. I think that was blue, too. She was holding out her hands." He held his out in the exact same way Emmalina Shoplaw had held hers out on the day she told me the story. "Like she was asking for help."

"You already know this stuff from Mrs. Shoplaw," I said. "Isn't that right? Tell us, we won't be mad. Will we, Erin?"

"No, uh-uh."

But Tom shook his head. "I'm just telling you what I saw. Neither of you saw her?"

We had not, and said so.

"Why me?" Tom asked plaintively. "Once we were inside, I wasn't even thinking of her. I was just having fun. So *why me*?"

♥

Erin tried to get more details while I drove us back to Heaven's Bay in my heap. Tom answered the first two or three of her questions, then said he didn't want to talk about it anymore in an abrupt tone I'd never heard him use with Erin before. I don't think she had, either, because she was quiet as a mouse for the rest of the ride. Maybe they talked about it some more between themselves, but I can tell you that he never spoke of it again to me until about a month before he died, and then only briefly. It was near the end of a phone conversation that had been painful because of his halting, nasal voice and the way he sometimes got confused.

"At least…I know…there's *something*," he said. "I saw…for myself…that summer. In the Hasty Hut." I didn't bother to correct him; I knew what he meant. "Do you…remember?"

"I remember," I said.

"But I don't know…the *something*…if it's good…or bad." His dying voice filled with horror. "The way she…Dev, *the way she held out her hands*…"

Yes.

The way she held out her hands.

♥

The next time I had a full day off, it was nearly the middle of August, and the tide of conies was ebbing. I no longer had to jink and juke my way up Joyland Avenue to the Carolina Spin …and to Madame Fortuna's shy, which stood in its revolving shadow.

Lane and Fortuna—she was all Fortuna today, in full gypsy kit—were talking together by the Spin's control station. Lane saw me and tipped his derby widdershins, which was his way of acknowledging me.

"Look what the cat drug in," he said. "How ya be, Jonesy?"

"Fine," I said, although this wasn't strictly true. The sleepless nights had come back now that I was only wearing the fur four or five times a day. I lay in my bed waiting for the small hours to get bigger, window open so I could hear the incoming surf, thinking about Wendy and her new boyfriend. Also thinking about the girl Tom had seen standing beside the tracks in Horror

House, in the fake brick tunnel between the Dungeon and the Chamber of Torture.

I turned to Fortuna. "Can I talk to you?"

She didn't ask why, just led me to her shy, swept aside the purple curtain that hung in the doorway, and ushered me in. There was a round table covered with a rose-pink cloth. On it was Fortuna's crystal, now draped. Two simple folding chairs were positioned so that seer and supplicant faced each other over the crystal (which, I happened to know, was underlit by a small bulb Madame Fortuna could operate with her foot). On the back wall was a giant silk-screened hand, fingers spread and palm out. On it, neatly labeled, were the Seven: lifeline, heartline, headline, loveline (also known as the Girdle of Venus), sunline, fateline, healthline.

Madame Fortuna gathered her skirts and seated herself. She motioned for me to do the same. She did not undrape her crystal, nor did she invite me to cross her palm with silver so that I might know the future.

"Ask what you came to ask," she said.

"I want to know if the little girl was just an informed guess or if you really knew something. Saw something."

She looked at me, long and steadily. In Madame Fortuna's place of business, there was a faint smell of incense instead of popcorn and fried dough. The walls were flimsy, but the music, the chatter of the conies, and the rumble of the rides all seemed very far away. I wanted to look down, but managed not to.

"Actually, you want to know if I'm a fraud. Isn't that so?"

"I…ma'am, I honestly don't know *what* I want."

At that she smiled. It was a good one—as if I had passed

some sort of test. "You're a sweet boy, Jonesy, but like so many sweet boys, you're a punk liar."

I started to reply; she hushed me with a wave of her ring-heavy right hand. She reached beneath her table and brought out her cashbox. Madame Fortuna's readings were free—all part of your admission fee, ladies and gentlemen, boys and girls—but tips were encouraged. And legal under North Carolina law. When she opened the box, I saw a sheaf of crumpled bills, mostly ones, something that looked suspiciously like a punch-board (*not* legal under North Carolina law), and a single small envelope. Printed on the front was my name. She held it out. I hesitated, then took it.

"You didn't come to Joyland today just to ask me that," she said.

"Well…"

She waved me off again. "You know *exactly* what you want. In the short term, at least. And since the short term is all any of us have, who is Fortuna—or Rozzie Gold, for that matter—to argue with you? Go now. Do what you came here to do. When it's done, open that and read what I've written." She smiled. "No charge to employees. Especially not good kids like you."

"I don't—"

She rose in a swirl of skirts and a rattle of jewelry. "Go, Jonesy. We're finished here."

♥

I left her tight little booth in a daze. Music from two dozen shys and rides seemed to hit me like conflicting winds, and the sun was a hammer. I went directly to the administration building (actually a doublewide trailer), gave a courtesy knock, went in, and said hello to Brenda Rafferty, who was going back and forth between an open account book and her faithful adding machine.

"Hello, Devin," she said. "Are you taking care of your Hollywood Girl?"

"Yes, ma'am, we all watch out for her."

"Dana Elkhart, isn't it?"

"Erin Cook, ma'am."

"Erin, of course. Team Beagle. The redhead. What can I do for you?"

"I wonder if I could speak to Mr. Easterbrook."

"He's resting, and I hate to disturb him. He had an awful lot of phone calls to make earlier, and we still have to go over some numbers, much as I hate to bother him with them. He tires very easily these days."

"I wouldn't be long."

She sighed. "I suppose I could see if he's awake. Can you tell me what it's about?"

"A favor," I said. "He'll understand."

♥

He did, and only asked me two questions. The first was if I was sure. I said I was. The second…

"Have you told your parents yet, Jonesy?"

"It's just me and my dad, Mr. Easterbrook, and I'll do that tonight."

"Very well, then. Put Brenda in the picture before you leave. She'll have all the necessary paperwork, and you can fill it out…" Before he could finish, his mouth opened and he displayed his horsey teeth in a vast, gaping yawn. "Excuse me, son. It's been a tiring day. A tiring *summer*."

"Thank you, Mr. Easterbrook."

He waved his hand. "Very welcome. I'm sure you'll be a great addition, but if you do this without your father's consent, I shall be disappointed in you. Close the door on your way out, please."

I tried not to see Brenda's frown as she searched her file cabinets and hunted out the various forms Joyland, Inc. required for full-time employment. It didn't matter, because I felt her disapproval anyway. I folded the paperwork, stuck it in the back pocket of my jeans, and left.

Beyond the line of donnikers at the far end of the backyard was a little grove of blackgum trees. I went in there, sat down with my back against one, and opened the envelope Madame Fortuna had given me. The note was brief and to the point.

You're going to Mr. Easterbrook to ask if you can stay on at the park after Labor Day. You know he will not refuse your request.

She was right, I wanted to know if she was a fraud. Here was her answer. And yes, I had made up my mind about what came next in the life of Devin Jones. She had been right about that, too.

But there was one more line.

You saved the little girl, but dear boy! You can't save everyone.

♥

After I told my dad I wasn't going back to UNH—that I needed a year off from college and planned to spend it at Joyland—there was a long silence at the southern Maine end of the line. I thought he might yell at me, but he didn't. He only sounded tired. "It's that girl, isn't it?"

I'd told him almost two months earlier that Wendy and I were "taking some time off," but Dad saw right through that. Since then, he hadn't spoken her name a single time in our weekly phone conversations. Now she was just *that girl*. After the first couple of times he said it I tried a joke, asking if he thought I'd been going out with Marlo Thomas. He wasn't amused. I didn't try again.

"Wendy's part of it," I admitted, "but not all of it. I just need some time off. A breather. And I've gotten to like it here."

He sighed. "Maybe you do need a break. At least you'll be working instead of hitchhiking around Europe, like Dewey Michaud's girl. Fourteen months in youth hostels! Fourteen and counting! Ye gods! She's apt to come back with ringworm and a bun in the oven."

"Well," I said, "I think I can avoid both of those. If I'm careful."

"Just make sure you avoid the hurricanes. It's supposed to be a bad season for them."

"Are you really all right with this, Dad?"

"Why? Did you want me to argue? Try to talk you out of it? If that's what you want, I'm willing to give it a shot, but I know what your mother would say—if he's old enough to buy a legal drink, he's old enough to start making decisions about his life."

I smiled. "Yeah. That sounds like her."

"As for me, I guess I don't want you going back to college if you're going to spend all your time mooning over that girl and letting your grades go to hell. If painting rides and fixing up concessions will help get her out of your system, probably that's a good thing. But what about your scholarship and loan package, if you want to go back in the fall of '74?"

"It won't be a problem. I've got a 3.2 cume, which is pretty persuasive."

"That girl," he said in tones of infinite disgust, and then we moved on to other topics.

♥

I was still sad and depressed about how things had ended with Wendy, he was right about that, but I had begun the difficult trip (*the journey*, as they say in the self-help groups these days) from denial to acceptance. Anything like true serenity was still over the horizon, but I no longer believed—as I had in the long, painful days and nights of June—that serenity was out of the question.

Staying had to do with other things that I couldn't even begin to sort out, because they were piled helter-skelter in an untidy stack and bound with the rough twine of intuition. Hallie Stansfield was there. So was Bradley Easterbrook, way back at the beginning of the summer, saying *we sell fun*. The sound of the ocean at night was there, and the way a strong onshore breeze would make a little song when it blew through the struts of the Carolina Spin. The cool tunnels under the park were there. So was the Talk, that secret language the other greenies would have forgotten by the time Christmas break rolled around. I didn't want to forget it; it was too rich. I felt that Joyland had something more to give me. I didn't know what, just…s'more.

But mostly—this is weird, I have examined and re-examined my memories of those days to make sure it's a true memory, and it seems to be—it was because it had been our Doubting Thomas to see the ghost of Linda Gray. It had changed him in small but fundamental ways. I don't think Tom *wanted* to change —I think he was happy just as he was—but *I* did.

I wanted to see her, too.

♥

During the second half of August, several of the old-timers—
Pop Allen for one, Dottie Lassen for another—told me to pray
for rain on Labor Day weekend. There was no rain, and by
Saturday afternoon I understood what they meant. The conies
came back in force for one final grand hurrah, and Joyland was
tipsed to the gills. What made it worse was that half of the
summer help was gone by then, headed back to their various
schools. The ones who were left worked like dogs.

Some of us didn't just work *like* dogs, but *as* dogs—one dog
in particular. I saw most of that holiday weekend through the
mesh eyes of Howie the Happy Hound. On Sunday I climbed
into that damned fur suit a dozen times. After my second-to-
last turn of the day, I was three-quarters of the way down the
Boulevard beneath Joyland Avenue when the world started to
swim away from me in shades of gray. *Shades of* Linda *Gray*, I
remember thinking.

I was driving one of the little electric service-carts with the
fur pushed down to my waist so I could feel the air conditioning on my sweaty chest, and when I realized I was losing it,
I had the good sense to pull over to the wall and take my foot
off the rubber button that served as the accelerator. Fat Wally
Schmidt, who ran the guess-your-weight shy, happened to be
taking a break in the boneyard at the time. He saw me parked
askew and slumped over the cart's steering bar. He got a pitcher
of icewater out of the fridge, waddled down to me, and lifted
my chin with one chubby hand.

"Hey greenie. You got another suit, or is that the only one
that fits ya?"

"Theresh another one," I said. I sounded drunk. "Cossume
shop. Ex'ra large."

"Oh hey, that's good," he said, and dumped the pitcher over my head. My scream of surprise echoed up and down the Boulevard and brought several people running.

"What the *fuck*, Fat Wally?"

He grinned. "Wakes ya up, don't it? Damn right it does. Labor Day weekend, greenie. That means ya labor. No sleepin on the job. Thank yer lucky stars n bars it ain't a hunnert and ten out there."

If it *had* been a hunnert and ten, I wouldn't be telling this story; I would have died of a baked brain halfway through a Happy Howie Dance on the Wiggle-Waggle Story Stage. But Labor Day itself was actually cloudy, and featured a nice seabreeze. I got through it somehow.

Around four o'clock that Monday, as I was climbing into the spare fur for my final show of the summer, Tom Kennedy strolled into the costume shop. His dogtop and filthy sneakers were gone. He was wearing crisply pressed chinos (*wherever were you keeping them*, I wondered), a neatly tucked-in Ivy League shirt, and Bass Weejuns. Rosy-cheeked son of a bitch had even gotten a haircut. He looked every inch the up-and-coming college boy with his eye on the business world. You never would have guessed that he'd been dressed in filthy Levis only two days before, displaying at least an inch of ass-cleavage as he crawled under the Zipper with an oil-bucket and cursing Pop Allen, our fearless Team Beagle leader, every time he bumped his head on a strut.

"You on your way?" I asked.

"That's a big ten-four, good buddy. I'm taking the train to Philly at eight tomorrow morning. I've got a week at home, then it's back to the grind."

"Good for you."

"Erin's got some stuff to finish up, but then she's meeting me in Wilmington tonight. I booked us a room at a nice little bed and breakfast."

I felt a dull throb of jealousy at that. "Good deal."

"She's the real thing," he said.

"I know."

"So are you, Dev. We'll stay in touch. People say that and don't mean it, but I do. We *will* stay in touch." He held out his hand.

I took it and shook it. "That's right, we will. You're okay, Tom, and Erin's the total package. You take care of her."

"No problem there." He grinned. "Come spring semester, she's transferring to Rutgers. I already taught her the Scarlet Knights fight song. You know, 'Upstream, Redteam, Redteam, Upstream—' "

"Sounds complex," I said.

He shook his finger at me. "Sarcasm will get you nowhere in this world, boy. Unless you're angling for a writing job at *Mad* magazine, that is."

Dottie Lassen called, "Maybe you could shorten up the farewells and keep the tears to a minimum? You've got a show to do, Jonesy."

Tom turned to her and held out his arms. "Dottie, how I love you! How I'll *miss* you!"

She slapped her bottom to show just how much this moved her and turned away to a costume in need of repair.

Tom handed me a scrap of paper. "My home address, school address, phone numbers for both. I expect you to use them."

"I will."

"You're really going to give up a year you could spend drinking beer and getting laid to scrape paint here at Joyland?"

"Yep."

"Are you crazy?"

I considered this. "Probably. A little. But getting better."

I was sweaty and his clothes were clean, but he gave me a brief hug just the same. Then he headed for the door, pausing to give Dottie a kiss on one wrinkled cheek. She couldn't cuss at him—her mouth was full of pins at the time—but she shooed him away with a flap of her hand.

At the door, he turned back to me. "You want some advice, Dev? Stay away from…" He finished with a head-jerk, and I knew well enough what he meant: Horror House. Then he was gone, probably thinking about his visit home, and Erin, the car he hoped to buy, and Erin, the upcoming school year, and Erin. Upstream, Redteam, Redteam, Upstream. Come spring semester, they could chant it together. Hell, they could chant it that very night, if they wanted to. In Wilmington. In bed. Together.

♥

There was no punch-clock at the park; our comings and goings were supervised by our team leaders. After my final turn as Howie on that first Monday in September, Pop Allen told me to bring him my time-card.

"I've got another hour," I said.

"Nah, someone's waiting at the gate to walk you back." I knew who the someone had to be. It was hard to believe there was a soft spot in Pop's shriveled-up raisin of a heart for anyone, but there was, and that summer Miss Erin Cook owned it.

"You know the deal tomorrow?"

"Seven-thirty to six," I said. And no fur. What a blessing.

"I'll be running you for the first couple of weeks, then I'm off to sunny Florida. After that, you're Lane Hardy's responsibility. And Freddy Dean, I guess, if he happens to notice you're still around."

"Got it."

"Good. I'll sign your card and then you're ten-forty-two." Which meant the same thing in the Talk as it did on the CBs that were so popular then: *End of tour.* "And Jonesy? Tell that girl to send me a postcard once in a while. I'll miss her."

He wasn't the only one.

♥

Erin had also begun making the transition back from Joyland Life to Real Life. Gone were the faded jeans and tee-shirt with the sassy rolled-to-the-shoulder sleeves; ditto the green Hollywood Girl dress and Sherwood Forest hat. The girl standing in the scarlet shower of neon just outside the gate was wearing a silky blue sleeveless blouse tucked into a belted A-line skirt. Her hair was pinned back and she looked gorgeous.

"Walk me up the beach," she said. "I'll just have time to catch the bus to Wilmington. I'm meeting Tom."

"He told me. But never mind the bus. I'll drive you."

"Would you do that?"

"Sure."

We walked along the fine white sand. A half-moon had risen in the sky, and it beat a track across the water. Halfway to Heaven's Beach—it was, in fact, not far from the big green Victorian that played such a part in my life that fall—she took my hand, and we walked that way. We didn't say much until we reached the steps leading up to the beach parking lot. There she turned to me.

"You'll get over her." Her eyes were on mine. She wasn't wearing makeup that night, and didn't need any. The moonlight was her makeup.

"Yes," I said. I knew it was true, and part of me was sorry. It's hard to let go. Even when what you're holding onto is full of thorns, it's hard to let go. Maybe especially then.

"And for now this is the right place for you. I feel that."

"Does Tom feel it?"

"No, but he never felt about Joyland the way you do…and the way I did this summer. And after what happened that day in the funhouse…what he saw…"

"Do the two of you ever talk about that?"

"I tried. Now I leave it alone. It doesn't fit into his philosophy of how the world works, so he's trying to make it gone. But I think he worries about you."

"Do *you* worry about me?"

"About you and the ghost of Linda Gray, no. About you and the ghost of that Wendy, a little."

I grinned. "My father no longer speaks her name. Just calls her 'that girl.' Erin, would you do me a favor when you get back to school? If you have time, that is?"

"Sure. What is it?"

I told her.

♥

She asked if I would drop her at the Wilmington bus station instead of taking her directly to the B&B Tom had booked. She said she'd rather take a taxi there. I started to protest that it was a waste of money, then didn't. She looked flustered, a trifle embarrassed, and I guessed it had something to do with not wanting to climb out of my car just so she could drop her clothes and climb into the sack with Tom Kennedy two minutes later.

When I pulled up opposite the taxi stand, she put her hands on the sides of my face and kissed my mouth. It was a long and thoroughly thorough kiss.

"If Tom hadn't been there, *I* would have made you forget that stupid girl," she said.

"But he was," I said.

"Yes. He was. Stay in touch, Dev."

"Remember what I asked you to do. If you get a chance, that is."

"I'll remember. You're a sweet man."

I don't know why, but that made me feel like crying. I smiled instead. "Also, admit it, I made one hell of a Howie."

"That you did. Devin Jones, savior of little girls."

For a moment I thought she was going to kiss me again, but she didn't. She slid out of my car and ran across the street to the taxis, skirt flying. I sat there until I saw her climb into the back of a Yellow and drive away. Then I drove away myself, back to Heaven's Beach, and Mrs. Shoplaw's, and my autumn at Joyland —both the best and worst autumn of my life.

Were Annie and Mike Ross sitting at the end of the green Victorian's boardwalk when I headed down the beach to the park on that Tuesday after Labor Day? I remember the warm croissants I ate as I walked, and the circling gulls, but of them I can't be completely sure. They became such an important part of the scenery—such a landmark—that it's impossible to pinpoint the first time I actually noticed their presence. Nothing screws with memory like repetition.

Ten years after the events I'm telling you about, I was (for my sins, maybe) a staff writer on *Cleveland* magazine. I used to do most of my first-draft writing on yellow legal pads in a coffee shop on West Third Street, near Lakefront Stadium, which was the Indians' stomping grounds back then. Every day at ten, this young woman would come in and get four or five coffees, then take them back to the real estate office next door. I couldn't tell you the first time I saw her, either. All I know is that one day I *saw* her, and realized that she sometimes glanced at me as she went out. The day came when I returned that glance, and when she smiled, I did, too. Eight months later we were married.

Annie and Mike were like that; one day they just became a real part of my world. I always waved, the kid in the wheelchair always waved back, and the dog sat watching me with his ears cocked and the wind ruffling his fur. The woman was blonde and beautiful—high cheekbones, wide-set blue eyes, and full lips, the kind that always look a little bruised. The boy in the wheelchair wore a White Sox cap that came down over his ears. He looked very sick. His smile was healthy enough, though. Whether I was going or coming, he always flashed it. Once or twice he even flashed me the peace sign, and I sent it right back. I had become part of his landscape, just as he had become part of mine. I think even Milo, the Jack Russell, came to recognize me as part of the landscape. Only Mom held herself apart. Often when I passed, she never even looked up from whatever book she was reading. When she did she didn't wave, and she certainly never flashed the peace sign.

♥

I had plenty to occupy my time at Joyland, and if the work wasn't as interesting and varied as it had been during the summer, it was steadier and less exhausting. I even got a chance to reprise my award-winning role as Howie, and to sing a few more choruses of "Happy Birthday to You" in the Wiggle-Waggle Village, because Joyland was open to the public for the first three weekends in September. Attendance was way down, though, and I didn't jock a single tipsed ride. Not even the Carolina Spin, which was second only to the merry-go-round as our most popular attraction.

"Up north in New England, most parks stay open weekends until Halloween," Fred Dean told me one day. We were sitting on a bench and eating a nourishing, vitamin-rich lunch of chili burgers and pork rinds. "Down south in Florida, they run year-round. We're in a kind of gray zone. Mr. Easterbrook tried pushing for a fall season back in the sixties—spent a bundle on a big advertising blitz—but it didn't work very well. By the time the nights start getting nippy, people around here start thinking about county fairs and such. Also, a lot of our vets head south or out west for the winter." He looked down the empty expanse of Hound Dog Way and sighed. "This place gets kind of lonely this time of year."

"I like it," I said, and I did. That was my year to embrace loneliness. I sometimes went to the movies in Lumberton or Myrtle Beach with Mrs. Shoplaw and Tina Ackerley, the librarian with the goo-goo-googly eyes, but I spent most evenings in my room, re-reading *The Lord of the Rings* and writing letters to Erin, Tom, and my dad. I also wrote a fair amount of poetry, which I am now embarrassed even to think about. Thank God I burned it. I added a new and satisfyingly grim record to my

small collection—*The Dark Side of the Moon*. In the Book of
Proverbs we are advised that "as a dog returns to its vomit, so a
fool repeats his folly." That autumn I returned to *Dark Side*
again and again, only giving Floyd the occasional rest so I could
listen to Jim Morrison once more intone, "This is the end, beautiful friend." Such a really bad case of the twenty-ones—I know,
I know.

At least there was plenty at Joyland to occupy my days. The
first couple of weeks, while the park was still running part-
time, were devoted to fall cleaning. Fred Dean put me in charge
of a small crew of gazoonies, and by the time the CLOSED FOR
THE SEASON sign went up out front, we had raked and cut
every lawn, prepared every flowerbed for winter, and scrubbed
down every joint and shy. We slapped together a prefab corru-
gated metal shed in the backyard and stored the food carts (called
grub-rollers in the Talk) there for the winter, each popcorn
wagon, Sno-Cone wagon, and Pup-a-Licious wagon snugged
under its own green tarp.

When the gazoonies headed north to pick apples, I started
the winterizing process with Lane Hardy and Eddie Parks, the
ill-tempered vet who ran Horror House (and Team Doberman)
during the season. We drained the fountain at the intersection
of Joyland Avenue and Hound Dog Way, and had moved on to
Captain Nemo's Splash & Crash—a much bigger job—when
Bradley Easterbrook, dressed for traveling in his black suit,
came by.

"I'm off to Sarasota this evening," he told us. "Brenda Rafferty
will be with me, as usual." He smiled, showing those horse
teeth of his. "I'm touring the park and saying my thank-yous.
To those who are left, that is."

"Have a wonderful winter, Mr. Easterbrook," Lane said.

Eddie muttered something that sounded to me like *eat a wooden ship*, but was probably *have a good trip*.

"Thanks for everything," I said.

He shook hands with the three of us, coming to me last. "I hope to see you again next year, Jonesy. I think you're a young man with more than a little carny in his soul."

But he didn't see me the following year, and nobody saw him. Mr. Easterbrook died on New Year's Day, in a condo on John Ringling Boulevard, less than half a mile from where the famous circus winters.

"Crazy old bastid," Parks said, watching Easterbrook walk to his car, where Brenda was waiting to receive him and help him in.

Lane gave him a long, steady look, then said: "Shut it, Eddie."

Eddie did. Which was probably wise.

♥

One morning, as I walked to Joyland with my croissants, the Jack Russell finally trotted down the beach to investigate me.

"Milo, come back!" the woman called.

Milo turned to look at her, then looked back at me with his bright black eyes. On impulse, I tore a piece from one of my pastries, squatted, and held it out to him. Milo came like a shot.

"Don't you feed him!" the woman called sharply.

"Aw, Mom, get over it," the boy said.

Milo heard her and didn't take the shred of croissant…but he did sit up before me with his front paws held out. I gave him the bite.

"I won't do it again," I said, getting up, "but I couldn't let a good trick go to waste."

The woman snorted and went back to her book, which was thick and looked arduous. The boy called, "We feed him all the time. He never puts on weight, just runs it off."

Without looking up from her book, Mom said: "What do we know about talking to strangers, Mike-O?"

"He's not exactly a stranger when we see him every day," the boy pointed out. Reasonably enough, at least from my point of view.

"I'm Devin Jones," I said. "From down the beach. I work at Joyland."

"Then you won't want to be late." Still not looking up.

The boy shrugged at me—*whattaya gonna do*, it said. He was pale and as bent-over as an old man, but I thought there was a lively sense of humor in that shrug and the look that went with it. I returned the shrug and walked on. The next morning I took care to finish my croissants before I got to the big green Victorian so Milo wouldn't be tempted, but I waved. The kid, Mike, waved back. The woman was in her usual place under the green umbrella, and she had no book, but—as per usual—she didn't wave to me. Her lovely face was closed. *There is nothing here for you*, it said. *Go on down to your trumpery amusement park and leave us alone.*

So that was what I did. But I continued to wave, and the kid waved back. Morning and night, the kid waved back.

♥

The Monday after Gary "Pop" Allen left for Florida—bound for Alston's All-Star Carnival in Jacksonville, where he had a job waiting as shy-boss—I arrived at Joyland and found Eddie Parks, my least favorite old-timer, sitting in front of Horror

House on an apple-box. Smoking was *verboten* in the park, but with Mr. Easterbrook gone and Fred Dean nowhere in evidence, Eddie seemed to feel it safe to flout the rule. He was smoking with his gloves on, which would have struck me as strange if he ever took them off, but he never seemed to.

"There you are, kiddo, and only five minutes late." Everyone else called me either Dev or Jonesy, but to Eddie I was just *kiddo*, and always would be.

"I've got seven-thirty on the nose," I said, tapping my watch.

"Then you're slow. Why don't you drive from town, like everybody else? You could be here in five minutes."

"I like the beach."

"I don't give a tin shit what you like, kiddo, just get here on time. This isn't like one of your college classes, when you can duck in and out anytime you want to. This is a *job*, and now that the Head Beagle is gone, you're gonna work like it's a job."

I could have pointed out that Pop had told me Lane Hardy would be in charge of my schedule after he, Pop, was gone, but kept my lip zipped. No sense making a bad situation worse. As to why Eddie had taken a dislike to me, that was obvious. Eddie was an equal-opportunity disliker. I'd go to Lane if life with Eddie got too hard, but only as a last resort. My father had taught me—mostly by example—that if a man wanted to be in charge of his life, he had to be in charge of his problems.

"What have you got for me, Mr. Parks?"

"Plenty. I want you to get a tub of Turtle Wax from the supply shed to start with, and don't be lingerin down there to shoot the shit with any of your pals, either. Then I want you to go on in Horra and wax all them cars." Except, of course, he said it *caaas*. "You know we wax em once the season's over, don't you?"

"Actually I didn't."

"Jesus Christ, you kids." He stomped on his cigarette butt, then lifted the apple-box he was sitting on enough to toss it under. As if that would make it gone. "You want to really put some elbow-grease into it, kiddo, or I'll send you back in to do it again. You got that?"

"I got it."

"Good for you." He stuck another cigarette in his gob, then fumbled in his pants pocket for his lighter. With the gloves on, it took him awhile. He finally got it, flicked back the lid, then stopped. "What are you looking at?"

"Nothing," I said.

"Then get going. Flip on the house lights so you can see what the fuck you're doing. You know where the switches are, don't you?"

I didn't, but I'd find them without his help. "Sure."

He eyed me sourly. "Ain't you the smart one." *Smaaat*.

♥

I found a metal box marked LTS on the wall between the Wax Museum and the Barrel and Bridge Room. I opened it and flipped up all the switches with the heel of my hand. Horror House should have lost all of its cheesy/sinister mystique with all the house lights on, but somehow didn't. There were still shadows in the corners, and I could hear the wind—quite strong that morning—blowing outside the joint's thin wooden walls and rattling a loose board somewhere. I made a mental note to track it down and fix it.

I had a wire basket swinging from one hand. It was filled with clean rags and a giant economy-size can of Turtle Wax. I carried it through the Tilted Room—now frozen on a starboard slant—and into the arcade. I looked at the Skee-Ball machines and remembered Erin's disapproval: *Don't they know that's a complete butcher's game?* I smiled at the memory, but my heart was beating hard. I knew what I was going to do when I'd finished my chore, you see.

The cars, twenty in all, were lined up at the loading point. Ahead, the tunnel leading into the bowels of Horror House was lit by a pair of bright white work lights instead of flashing strobes. It looked a lot more prosaic that way.

I was pretty sure Eddie hadn't so much as swiped the little cars with a damp rag all summer long, and that meant I had to start by washing them down. Which also meant fetching soap powder from the supply shed and carrying buckets of water from the nearest working tap. By the time I had all twenty cars washed and rinsed off, it was break-time, but I decided to work right through instead of going out to the backyard or down to the boneyard for coffee. I might meet Eddie at either place, and I'd listened to enough of his grouchy bullshit for one morning. I set to work polishing instead, laying the Turtle Wax on thick and then buffing it off, moving from car to car, making them shine in the overhead lights until they looked new again. Not that the next crowd of thrill-seekers would notice as they crowded in for their nine-minute ride. My own gloves were ruined by the time I was finished. I'd have to buy a new pair at the hardware store in town, and good ones didn't come cheap. I amused myself briefly by imagining how Eddie would react if I asked him to pay for them.

I stashed my basket of dirty rags and Turtle Wax (the can now mostly empty) by the exit door in the arcade. It was ten past noon, but right then food wasn't what I was hungry for. I tried to stretch the ache out of my arms and legs, then went back to the loading-point. I paused to admire the cars gleaming mellowly beneath the lights, then walked slowly along the track and into Horror House proper.

I had to duck my head when I passed beneath the Screaming Skull, even though it was now pulled up and locked in its home position. Beyond it was the Dungeon, where the live talent from Eddie's Team Doberman had tried (and mostly succeeded) in scaring the crap out of children of all ages with their moans and howls. Here I could straighten up again, because it was a tall room. My footfalls echoed on a wooden floor painted to look like stone. I could hear my breathing. It sounded harsh and dry. I was scared, okay? Tom had told me to stay away from this place, but Tom didn't run my life any more than Eddie Parks did. I had the Doors, and I had Pink Floyd, but I wanted more. I wanted Linda Gray.

Between the Dungeon and the Torture Chamber, the track descended and described a double-S curve where the cars picked up speed and whipped the riders back and forth. Horror House was a dark ride, but when it was in operation, this stretch was the only completely dark part. It had to be where the girl's killer had cut her throat and dumped her body. How quick he must have been, and how certain of exactly what he was going to do! Beyond the last curve, riders were dazzled by a mix of stuttering, multi-colored strobes. Although Tom had never said it in so many words, I was positive it was where he had seen what he'd seen.

I walked slowly down the double-S, thinking it would not be beyond Eddie to hear me and shut off the overhead work-lights as a joke. To leave me in here to feel my way past the murder site with only the sound of the wind and that one slapping board to keep me company. And suppose…just suppose…a young girl's hand reached out in that darkness and took mine, the way Erin had taken my hand that last night on the beach?

The lights stayed on. No bloody shirt and gloves appeared beside the track, glowing spectrally. And when I came to what I felt sure was the right spot, just before the entrance to the Torture Chamber, there was no ghost-girl holding her hands out to me.

Yet something was there. I knew it then and I know it now. The air was colder. Not cold enough to see my breath, but yes, definitely colder. My arms and legs and groin all prickled with gooseflesh, and the hair at the nape of my neck stiffened.

"Let me see you," I whispered, feeling foolish and terrified. Wanting it to happen, hoping it wouldn't.

There was a sound. A long, slow sigh. Not a human sigh, not in the least. It was as if someone had opened an invisible steam-valve. Then it was gone. There was no more. Not that day.

♥

"Took you long enough," Eddie said when I finally reappeared at quarter to one. He was seated on the same apple-box, now with the remains of a BLT in one hand and a Styrofoam cup of coffee in the other. I was filthy from the neck down. Eddie, on the other hand, looked fresh as a daisy.

"The cars were pretty dirty. I had to wash them before I could wax them."

Eddie hawked back phlegm, twisted his head, and spat. "If you want a medal, I'm fresh out. Go find Hardy. He says it's time to drain the irry-gation system. That should keep a lag-ass like you busy until quittin time. If it don't, come see me and I'll find something else for you to do. I got a whole list, believe me."

"Okay." I started off, glad to be going.

"Kiddo!"

I turned back reluctantly.

"Did you see her in there?"

"Huh?"

He grinned unpleasantly. "Don't 'huh' me. I know what you were doin. You weren't the first, and you won't be the last. Did you see her?"

"Have *you* ever seen her?"

"Nope." He looked at me, sly little gimlet eyes peering out of a narrow sunburned face. How old was he? Thirty? Sixty? It was impossible to tell, just as it was impossible to tell if he was speaking the truth. I didn't care. I just wanted to be away from him. He gave me the creeps.

Eddie raised his gloved hands. "The guy who did it wore a pair of these. Did you know that?"

I nodded. "Also an extra shirt."

"That's right." His grin widened. "To keep the blood off. And it worked, didn't it? They never caught him. Now get out of here."

♥

When I got to the Spin, only Lane's shadow was there to greet me. The man it belonged to was halfway up the wheel, climbing the struts. He tested each steel crosspiece before he put his weight on it. A leather toolkit hung on one hip, and every now and then he reached into it for a socket wrench. Joyland only had a single dark ride, but almost a dozen so-called high rides, including the Spin, the Zipper, the Thunderball, and the Delirium Shaker. There was a three-man maintenance crew that checked them each day before Early Gate during the season, and of course there were visits (both announced and unannounced) from the North Carolina State Inspector of Amusements, but Lane said a ride-jock who didn't check his ride himself was both lazy and irresponsible. Which made me wonder when Eddie Parks had last ridden in one of his own *caaas* and safety-checked the *baaas*.

Lane looked down, saw me, and shouted: "Did that ugly sonofabitch ever give you a lunch break?"

"I worked through it," I called back. "Lost track of time." But now I *was* hungry.

"There's some tuna-and-macaroni salad in my doghouse, if you want it. I made up way too much last night."

I went into the little control shack, found a good-sized Tupperware container, and popped it open. By the time Lane was back on the ground, the tuna-and-macaroni was in my stomach and I was tamping it down with a couple of leftover Fig Newtons.

"Thanks, Lane. That was tasty."

"Yeah, I'll make some guy a good wife someday. Gimme some of those Newtons before they all go down your throat."

I handed over the box. "How's the ride?"

"The Spin is tight and the Spin is right. Want to help me work on the engine for a while after you've digested a little?"

"Sure."

He took off his derby and spun it on his finger. His hair was pulled back in a tight little ponytail, and I noticed a few threads of white in the black. They hadn't been there at the start of the summer—I was quite sure of it. "Listen, Jonesy, Eddie Parks is carny-from-carny, but that doesn't change the fact that he's one mean-ass sonofabitch. In his eyes, you got two strikes against you: you're young and you've been educated beyond the eighth grade. When you get tired of taking his shit, tell me and I'll get him to back off."

"Thanks, but I'm okay for now."

"I know you are. I've been watching how you handle yourself, and I'm impressed. But Eddie's not your average bear."

"He's a bully," I said.

"Yeah, but here's the good news: like with most bullies, you scratch the surface and find pure chickenshit underneath. Usually not very far underneath, either. There are people on the show he's afraid of, and I happen to be one of them. I've whacked his nose before and I don't mind whacking it again. All I'm saying is that if the day comes when you want a little breathing room, I'll see that you get it."

"Can I ask you a question about him?"

"Shoot."

"Why does he always wear those gloves?"

Lane laughed, stuck his derby on his head, and gave it the correct tilt. "Psoriasis. His hands are scaly with it, or so he says—I can't tell you the last time I actually saw them. He says without the gloves, he scratches them until they bleed."

"Maybe that's what makes him so bad-tempered."

"I think it's more likely the other way around—the bad temper made the bad skin." He tapped his temple. "Head controls body, that's what I believe. Come on, Jonesy, let's get to work."

♥

We finished putting the Spin right for its long winter's nap, then moved on to the irrigation system. By the time the pipes were blown out with compressed air and the drains had swallowed several gallons of antifreeze, the sun was lowering toward the trees west of the park and the shadows were lengthening.

"That's enough for today," Lane said. "More than enough. Bring me your card and I'll sign it."

I tapped my watch, showing him it was only quarter past five.

He shook his head, smiling. "I've got no problem writing six on the card. You did twelve hours' worth today, kiddo. Twelve easy."

"Okay," I said, "but don't call me kiddo. That's what *he* calls me." I jerked my head toward Horror House.

"I'll make a note of it. Now bring me your card and buzz off."

♥

The wind had died a little during the afternoon, but it was still warm and breezy when I set off down the beach. On many of those walks back to town I liked to watch my long shadow on the waves, but that evening I mostly watched my feet. I was tired out. What I wanted was a ham and cheese sandwich from Betty's Bakery and a couple of beers from the 7-Eleven next door. I'd go back to my room, settle into my chair by the window, and read me some Tolkien as I ate. I was deep into *The Two Towers*.

What made me look up was the boy's voice. The breeze was in my favor, and I could hear him clearly. *"Faster, Mom! You've almost g—"* He was temporarily stopped by a coughing fit. Then: *"You've almost got it!"*

Mike's mother was on the beach tonight instead of beneath

her umbrella. She was running toward me but didn't see me, because she was looking at the kite she was holding over her head. The string ran back to the boy, seated in his wheelchair at the end of the boardwalk.

Wrong direction, Mom, I thought.

She released the kite. It rose a foot or two, wagged naughtily from side to side, then took a dive into the sand. The breeze kicked up and it went skittering. She had to chase it down.

"*Once more!*" Mike called. "*That time—*" Cough-cough-cough, harsh and bronchial. "*That time you almost had it!*"

"No, I didn't." She sounded tired and pissed off. "Goddamned thing hates me. Let's go in and get some sup—"

Milo was sitting beside Mike's wheelchair, watching the evening's activities with bright eyes. When he saw me, he was off like a shot, barking. As I watched him come, I remembered Madame Fortuna's pronouncement on the day I first met her: *In your future is a little girl and a little boy. The boy has a dog.*

"Milo, come back!" Mom shouted. Her hair had probably started that evening tied up, but after several experiments in aviation, it hung around her face in strings. She pushed it away wearily with the backs of her hands.

Milo paid no attention. He skidded to a stop in front of me with his front paws spraying sand, and did his sitting-up thing. I laughed and patted his head. "That's all you get, pal—no croissants tonight."

He barked at me once, then trotted back to Mom, who was standing ankle-deep in the sand, breathing hard and eyeing me with mistrust. The captured kite hung down by her leg.

"See?" she said. "That's why I didn't want you to feed him.

He's a terrible beggar, and he thinks anybody who gives him a scrap is his friend."

"Well, I'm a friendly sort of guy."

"Good to know," she said. "Just don't feed our dog anymore." She was wearing pedal pushers and an old blue tee-shirt with faded printing on the front. Judging from the sweat-stains on it, she had been trying to get the kite airborne for quite some time. Trying hard, and why not? If I had a kid stuck in a wheelchair, I'd probably want to give him something that would fly, too.

"You're going the wrong way with that thing," I said. "And you don't need to run with it, anyway. I don't know why everybody thinks that."

"I'm sure you're quite the expert," she said, "but it's late and I have to get Mike his supper."

"Mom, let him try," Mike said. "Please?"

She stood for a few more seconds with her head lowered and escaped locks of her hair—also sweaty—clumped against her neck. Then she sighed and held the kite out to me. Now I could read the printing on her shirt: CAMP PERRY MATCH COMPETITION (PRONE) 1959. The front of the kite was a lot better, and I had to laugh. It was the face of Jesus.

"Private joke," she said. "Don't ask."

"Okay."

"You get one try, Mr. Joyland, and then I'm taking him in for his supper. He can't get chilled. He was sick last year, and he still hasn't gotten over it. He thinks he has, but he hasn't."

It was still at least seventy-five on the beach, but I didn't point this out; Mom was clearly not in the mood for further contradictions. Instead I told her again that my name was Devin

Jones. She raised her hands and then let them flop: *Whatever you say, bub*.

I looked at the boy. "Mike?"

"Yes?"

"Reel in the string. I'll tell you when to stop."

He did as I asked. I followed, and when I was even with where he sat, I looked at Jesus. "Are you going to fly this time, Mr. Christ?"

Mike laughed. Mom didn't, but I thought I saw her lips twitch.

"He says he is," I told Mike.

"Good, because—" Cough. Cough-cough-cough. She was right, he wasn't over it. Whatever *it* was. "Because so far he hasn't done anything but eat sand."

I held the kite over my head, but facing Heaven's Bay. I could feel the wind tug at it right away. The plastic rippled. "I'm going to let go, Mike. When I do, start reeling in the string again."

"But it'll just—"

"No, it won't just. But you have to be quick and careful." I was making it sound harder than it was, because I wanted him to feel cool and capable when the kite went up. It would, too, as long as the breeze didn't die on us. I really hoped that wouldn't happen, because I thought Mom had meant what she said about me getting only one chance. "The kite will rise. When it does, start paying out the twine again. Just keep it taut, okay? That means if it starts to dip, you—"

"I pull it in some more. I get it. God's sake."

"Okay. Ready?"

"Yeah!"

Milo sat between Mom and me, looking up at the kite.

"Okay, then. Three…two…one…lift-off."

The kid was hunched over in his chair and the legs beneath his shorts were wasted, but there was nothing wrong with his hands and he knew how to follow orders. He started reeling in, and the kite rose at once. He began to pay the string out—at first too much, and the kite sagged, but he corrected and it started going up again. He laughed. "I can feel it! I can feel it in my hands!"

"That's the wind you feel," I said. "Keep going, Mike. Once it gets up a little higher, the wind will own it. Then all you have to do is not let go."

He let out the twine and the kite climbed, first over the beach and then above the ocean, riding higher and higher into that September day's late blue. I watched it awhile, then chanced looking at the woman. She didn't bristle at my gaze, because she didn't see it. All her attention was focused on her son. I don't think I ever saw such love and such happiness on a person's face. Because *he* was happy. His eyes were shining and the coughing had stopped.

"Mommy, it feels like it's *alive*!"

It is, I thought, remembering how my father had taught me to fly a kite in the town park. I had been Mike's age, but with good legs to stand on. *As long as it's up there, where it was made to be, it really is.*

"Come and feel it!"

She walked up the little slope of beach to the boardwalk and stood beside him. She was looking at the kite, but her hand was stroking his cap of dark brown hair. "Are you sure, honey? It's your kite."

"Yeah, but you have to try it. It's incredible!"

She took the reel, which had thinned considerably as the twine paid out and the kite rose (it was now just a black diamond, the face of Jesus no longer visible) and held it in front of her. For a moment she looked apprehensive. Then she smiled. When a gust tugged the kite, making it wag first to port and then to starboard above the incoming waves, the smile widened into a grin.

After she'd flown it for a while, Mike said: "Let *him*."

"No, that's okay," I said.

But she held out the reel. "We insist, Mr. Jones. You're the flightmaster, after all."

So I took the twine, and felt the old familiar thrill. It tugged the way a fishing-line does when a fair-sized trout has taken the hook, but the nice thing about kite-flying is nothing gets killed.

"How high will it go?" Mike asked.

"I don't know, but maybe it shouldn't go much higher tonight. The wind up there is stronger, and might rip it. Also, you guys need to eat."

"Can Mr. Jones eat supper with us, Mom?"

She looked startled at the idea, and not in a good way. Still, I saw she was going to agree because I'd gotten the kite up.

"That's okay," I said. "I appreciate the invitation, but it was quite a day at the park. We're battening down the hatches for winter, and I'm dirt from head to toe."

"You can wash up in the house," Mike said. "We've got, like, seventy bathrooms."

"Michael Ross, we do not!"

"Maybe seventy-five, with a Jacuzzi in each one." He started laughing. It was a lovely, infectious sound, at least until it turned to coughing. The coughing became whooping. Then, just as Mom was starting to look really concerned (I was already there), he got it under control.

"Another time," I said, and handed him the reel of twine. "I love your Christ-kite. Your dog ain't bad, either." I bent and patted Milo's head.

"Oh…okay. Another time. But don't wait too long, because—"

Mom interposed hastily. "Can you go to work a little earlier tomorrow, Mr. Jones?"

"Sure, I guess."

"We could have fruit smoothies right here, if the weather's nice. I make a mean fruit smoothie."

I bet she did. And that way, she wouldn't have to have a strange man in the house.

"Will you?" Mike asked. "That'd be cool."

"I'd love to. I'll bring a bag of pastries from Betty's."

"Oh, you don't have to—" she began.

"My pleasure, ma'am."

"Oh!" She looked startled. "I never introduced myself, did I? I'm Ann Ross." She held out her hand.

"I'd shake it, Mrs. Ross, but I really am filthy." I showed her my hands. "It's probably on the kite, too."

"You should have given Jesus a mustache!" Mike shouted, and then laughed himself into another coughing fit.

"You're getting a little loose with the twine there, Mike," I said. "Better reel it in." And, as he started doing it, I gave Milo a farewell pat and started back down the beach.

"Mr. Jones," she called.

I turned back. She was standing straight, with her chin raised. Sweat had molded the shirt to her, and she had great breasts.

"It's *Miss* Ross. But since I guess we've now been properly introduced, why don't you call me Annie?"

"I can do that." I pointed at her shirt. "What's a match competition? And why is it prone?"

"That's when you shoot lying down," Mike said.

"Haven't done it in ages," she said, in a curt tone that suggested she wanted the subject closed.

Fine with me. I tipped Mike a wave and he sent one right back. He was grinning. Kid had a great grin.

Forty or fifty yards down the beach, I turned around for another look. The kite was descending, but for the time being the wind still owned it. They were looking up at it, the woman with her hand on her son's shoulder.

Miss, I thought. *Miss, not Mrs. And is there a mister with them in the big old Victorian with the seventy bathrooms?* Just because I'd never seen one with them didn't mean there wasn't one, but I didn't think so. I thought it was just the two of them. On their own.

♥

I got no clarification from Annie Ross the next morning, but plenty of dish from Mike. I also got one hell of a nice fruit smoothie. She said she made the yogurt herself, and it was layered with fresh strawberries from God knows where. I brought croissants and blueberry muffins from Betty's Bakery. Mike skipped the pastries, but finished his smoothie and asked for another. From the way his mother's mouth dropped open, I gathered that this was an astounding development. But not, I guessed, in a bad way.

"Are you sure you can eat another one?"

"Maybe just half," he said. "What's the deal, Mom? You're the one who says fresh yogurt helps me move my bowels."

"I don't think we need to discuss your bowels at seven in the morning, Mike." She got up, then cast a doubtful glance my way.

"Don't worry," Mike said brightly, "if he tries to kiddie-fiddle me, I'll tell Milo to sic 'im."

Color bloomed in her cheeks. *"Michael Everett Ross!"*

"Sorry," he said. He didn't look sorry. His eyes were sparkling.

"Don't apologize to me, apologize to Mr. Jones."

"Accepted, accepted."

"Will you keep an eye on him, Mr. Jones? I won't be long."

"I will if you'll call me Devin."

"Then I'll do that." She hurried up the boardwalk, pausing once to look over her shoulder. I think she had more than half a mind to come back, but in the end, the prospect of stuffing a few more healthy calories into her painfully thin boy was too much for her to resist, and she went on.

Mike watched her climb the steps to the back patio and sighed. "Now I'll have to eat it."

"Well...yeah. You asked for it, right?"

"Only so I could talk to you without her butting in. I mean, I love her and all, but she's always butting in. Like what's wrong with me is this big shameful secret we have to keep." He shrugged. "I've got muscular dystrophy, that's all. That's why I'm in the wheelchair. I *can* walk, you know, but the braces and crutches are a pain in the butt."

"I'm sorry," I said. "That stinks, Mike."

"I guess, but I can't remember *not* having it, so what the hell. Only it's a special kind of MD. Duchenne's muscular dystrophy, it's called. Most kids who have it croak in their teens or early twenties."

So, you tell me—what do you say to a ten-year-old kid who's just told you he's living under a death sentence?

"But." He raised a teacherly finger. "Remember her talking about how I was sick last year?"

"Mike, you don't have to tell me all this if you don't want to."

"Yeah, except I do." He was looking at me with clear intensity. Maybe even urgency. "Because you want to know. Maybe you even need to know."

I was thinking of Fortuna again. Two children, she had told me, a girl in a red hat and a boy with a dog. She said one of them had the sight, but she didn't know which. I thought that now I did.

"Mom said I think I got over it. Do I sound like I got over it?"

"Nasty cough," I ventured, "but otherwise…" I couldn't think how to finish. *Otherwise your legs are nothing but sticks? Otherwise you look like your mom and I could tie a string to the back of your shirt and fly you like a kite? Otherwise if I had to bet on whether you or Milo would live longer, I'd put my money on the dog?*

"I came down with pneumonia just after Thanksgiving, okay? When I didn't improve after a couple of weeks in the hospital, the doctor told my mom I was probably going to die and she ought to, you know, get ready for that."

But he didn't tell her in your hearing, I thought. *They'd never have a conversation like that in your hearing.*

"I hung in, though." He said this with some pride. "My grandfather called my mom—I think it was the first time they'd talked in a long time. I don't know who told him what was going on, but he has people everywhere. It could have been any of them."

People everywhere sounded kind of paranoid, but I kept my mouth shut. Later I found out it wasn't paranoid at all. Mike's grandfather *did* have them everywhere, and they all saluted Jesus, the flag, and the NRA, although possibly not in that order.

"Grampa said I got over the pneumonia because of God's will. Mom said he was full of bullshit, just like when he said me having DMD in the first place was God's punishment. She said I was just one tough little sonofabitch, and God had nothing to do with it. Then she hung up on him."

Mike might have heard her end of that conversation, but not Grampa's, and I doubted like hell if his mother had told him. I didn't think he was making it up, though. I found myself hoping Annie wouldn't hurry back. This wasn't like listening to Madame Fortuna. What she had, I believed (and still do, all these years later), was some small bit of authentic psychic ability amped up by a shrewd understanding of human nature and then packaged in glittering carny bullshit. Mike's thing was clearer. Simpler. *Purer*. It wasn't like seeing the ghost of Linda Gray, but it was akin to that, okay? It was touching another world.

"Mom said she'd never come back here, but here we are. Because I wanted to come to the beach and because I wanted to fly a kite and because I'm never going to make twelve, let alone my early twenties. It was the pneumonia, see? I get steroids, and they help, but the pneumonia combined with the Duchenne's MD fucked up my lungs and heart permanently."

He looked at me with a child's defiance, watching for how I'd react to what is now so coyly referred to as "the f-bomb." I didn't react, of course. I was too busy processing the sense to worry about his choice of words.

"So," I said. "I guess what you're saying is an extra fruit smoothie won't help."

He threw back his head and laughed. The laughter turned into the worst coughing fit yet. Alarmed, I went to him and pounded his back…but gently. It felt as if there were nothing under there but chicken bones. Milo barked once and put his paws up on one of Mike's wasted legs.

There were two pitchers on the table, water in one and fresh-squeezed orange juice in the other. Mike pointed to the water and I poured him half a glass. When I tried to hold it for him, he gave me an impatient look—even with the coughing fit still wracking him—and took it himself. He spilled some on his shirt, but most of it went down his throat, and the coughing eased.

"That was a bad one," he said, patting his chest. "My heart's going like a bastard. Don't tell my mother."

"Jesus, kid! Like she doesn't know?"

"She knows too much, that's what I think," Mike said. "She knows I might have three more good months and then four or five really bad ones. Like, in bed all the time, not able to do anything but suck oxygen and watch *MASH* and *Fat Albert*. The only question is whether or not she'll let Grammy and Grampa Ross come to the funeral." He'd coughed hard enough to make his eyes water, but I didn't mistake that for tears. He was bleak, but in control. Last evening, when the kite went up and he felt it tugging the twine, he had been younger than his age. Now I was watching him struggle to be a lot older. The scary thing was how well he was succeeding. His eyes met mine, dead-on. "She knows. She just doesn't know that *I* know."

The back door banged. We looked and saw Annie crossing the patio, heading for the boardwalk.

"Why would *I* need to know, Mike?"

He shook his head. "I don't have any idea. But you can't talk about it to Mom, okay? It just upsets her. I'm all she's got." He said this last not with pride but a kind of gloomy realism.

"All right."

"Oh, one other thing. I almost forgot." He shot a glance at her, saw she was only halfway down the boardwalk, and turned back to me. "It's not white."

"What's not white?"

Mike Ross looked mystified. "No idea. When I woke up this morning, I remembered you were coming for smoothies, and that came into my head. I thought *you'd* know."

Annie arrived. She had poured a mini-smoothie into a juice glass. On top was a single strawberry.

"Yum!" Mike said. "Thanks, Mom!"

"You're very welcome, hon."

She eyed his wet shirt but didn't mention it. When she asked me if I wanted some more juice, Mike winked at me. I said more juice would be great. While she poured, Mike fed Milo two heaping spoonfuls of his smoothie.

She turned back to him, and looked at the smoothie glass, now half empty. "Wow, you really *were* hungry."

"Told you."

"What were you and Mr. Jones—Devin—talking about?"

"Nothing much," Mike said. "He's been sad, but he's better now."

I said nothing, but I could feel heat rising in my cheeks. When I dared a look at Annie, she was smiling.

"Welcome to Mike's world, Devin," she said, and I must have looked like I'd swallowed a goldfish, because she burst out laughing. It was a nice sound.

♥

That evening when I walked back from Joyland, she was standing at the end of the boardwalk, waiting for me. It was the first time I'd seen her in a blouse and skirt. And she was alone. That was a first, too.

"Devin? Got a second?"

"Sure," I said, angling up the sandy slope to her. "Where's Mike?"

"He has physical therapy three times a week. Usually Janice—she's his therapist—comes in the morning, but I arranged for her to come this evening instead, because I wanted to speak to you alone."

"Does Mike know that?"

Annie smiled ruefully. "Probably. Mike knows far more than he should. I won't ask what you two talked about after he got rid of me this morning, but I'm guessing that his...insights... come as no surprise to you."

"He told me why he's in a wheelchair, that's all. And he mentioned he had pneumonia last Thanksgiving."

"I wanted to thank you for the kite, Dev. My son has very restless nights. He's not in pain, exactly, but he has trouble breathing when he's asleep. It's like apnea. He has to sleep in a semi-sitting position, and that doesn't help. Sometimes he stops breathing completely, and when he does, an alarm goes off and wakes him up. Only last night—after the kite—he slept right through. I even went in once, around two AM, to make sure the monitor wasn't malfunctioning. He was sleeping like a baby. No restless tossing and turning, no nightmares—he's prone to them—and no moaning. It was the kite. It satisfied him in a way nothing else possibly could. Except maybe going to that damned amusement park of yours, which is completely out of the question." She stopped, then smiled. "Oh, shit. I'm making a speech."

"It's all right," I said.

"It's just that I've had so few people to talk to. I have house-keeping help—a very nice woman from Heaven's Bay—and of course there's Janice, but it's not the same." She took a deep breath. "Here's the other part. I was rude to you on several occasions, and with no cause. I'm sorry."

"Mrs....Miss..." Shit. "Annie, you don't have anything to apologize for."

"Yes. I do. You could have just walked on when you saw me struggling with the kite, and then Mike wouldn't have gotten that good night's rest. All I can say is that I have problems trusting people."

This is where she invites me in for supper, I thought. But she didn't. Maybe because of what I said next.

"You know, he *could* come to the park. It'd be easy to arrange, and with it closed and all, he could have the run of the place."

Her face closed up hard, like a hand into a fist. "Oh, no. Absolutely not. If you think that, he didn't tell you as much about his condition as I thought he did. Please don't mention it to him. In fact, I have to insist."

"All right," I said. "But if you change your mind..."

I trailed off. She wasn't going to change her mind. She looked at her watch, and a new smile lit her face. It was so brilliant you could almost overlook how it never reached her eyes. "Oh boy, look how late it's getting. Mike will be hungry after his PE, and I haven't done a thing about supper. Will you excuse me?"

"Sure."

I stood there watching her hurry back down the boardwalk to the green Victorian—the one I was probably never going to see the inside of, thanks to my big mouth. But the idea of taking Mike through Joyland had seemed so right. During the summer, we had groups of kids with all sorts of problems and disabilities—crippled kids, blind kids, cancer kids, kids who were mentally challenged (what we called *retarded* back in the unenlightened 70s). It wasn't as though I expected to stick Mike in the front car of the Delirium Shaker and then blast him off. Even if the Shaker hadn't been buttoned up for the winter, I'm not a total idiot.

But the merry-go-round was still operational, and surely he could ride that. Ditto the train that ran through the Wiggle-Waggle Village. I was sure Fred Dean wouldn't mind me touring the kid through Mysterio's Mirror Mansion, either. But no. No. He was her delicate hothouse flower, and she intended to keep it that way. The thing with the kite had just been an aberration, and the apology a bitter pill she felt she had to swallow.

Still, I couldn't help admiring how quick and lithe she was, moving with a grace her son would never know. I watched her bare legs under the hem of her skirt and thought about Wendy Keegan not at all.

♥

I had the weekend free, and you know what happened. I guess the idea that it always rains on the weekends must be an illusion, but it sure doesn't *seem* like one; ask any working stiff who ever planned to go camping or fishing on his days off.

Well, there was always Tolkien. I was sitting in my chair by the window on Saturday afternoon, moving ever deeper into the mountains of Mordor with Frodo and Sam, when Mrs. Shoplaw knocked on the door and asked if I'd like to come down to the parlor and play Scrabble with her and Tina Ackerley. I am not at all crazy about Scrabble, having suffered many humiliations at the hands of my aunts Tansy and Naomi, who each have a huge mental vocabulary of what I still think of as "Scrabble shit-words"—stuff like *suq*, *tranq*, and *bhoot* (an Indian ghost, should you wonder). Nevertheless, I said I'd love to play. Mrs. Shoplaw was my landlady, after all, and diplomacy takes many forms.

On our way downstairs, she confided, "We're helping Tina bone up. She's quite the Scrabble-shark. She's entered in some sort of tournament in Atlantic City next weekend. I believe there is a cash prize."

It didn't take long—maybe four turns—to discover that our resident librarian could have given my aunts all the game they could handle, and more. By the time Miss Ackerley laid down *nubility* (with the apologetic smile all Scrabble-sharks seem to have; I think they must practice it in front of their mirrors), Emmalina Shoplaw was eighty points behind. As for me...well, never mind.

"I don't suppose either of you know anything about Annie and Mike Ross, do you?" I asked during a break in the action (both women seemed to feel a need to study the board a *looong* time before laying down so much as a single tile). "They live on Beach Row in the big green Victorian?"

Miss Ackerley paused with her hand still inside the little brown bag of letters. Her eyes were big, and her thick lenses made them even bigger. "Have *you* met them?"

"Uh-huh. They were trying to fly a kite...well, *she* was...and

I helped out a little. They're very nice. I just wondered...the two of them all alone in that big house, and him pretty sick..."

The look they exchanged was pure incredulity, and I started to wish I hadn't raised the subject.

"She *talks* to you?" Mrs. Shoplaw asked. "The Ice Queen actually *talks* to you?"

Not only talked to me, but gave me a fruit smoothie. Thanked me. Even apologized to me. But I said none of that. Not because Annie really had iced up when I presumed too much, but because to do so would have seemed disloyal, somehow.

"Well, a little. I got the kite up for them, that's all." I turned the board. It was Tina's, the pro kind with its own little built-in spindle. "Come on, Mrs. S. Your turn. Maybe you'll even make a word that's in my puny vocabulary."

"Given the correct positioning, *puny* can be worth seventy points," Tina Ackerley said. "Even more, if a *y*-word is connected to *pun*."

Mrs. Shoplaw ignored both the board and the advice. "You know who her father is, of course."

"Can't say I do." Although I *did* know she was on the outs with him, and big-time.

"Buddy Ross? As in *The Buddy Ross Hour of Power*? Ring any bells?"

It did, vaguely. I thought I might have heard some preacher named Ross on the radio in the costume shop. It kind of made sense. During one of my quick-change transformations into Howie, Dottie Lassen had asked me—pretty much out of a clear blue sky—if I had found Jesus. My first impulse had been to tell her that I didn't know He was lost, but I restrained it.

"One of those Bible-shouters, right?"

"Next to Oral Roberts and that Jimmy Swaggart fellow, he's just about the biggest of them," Mrs. S. said. "He broadcasts from this gigantic church—God's Citadel, he calls it—in Atlanta. His radio show goes out all over the country, and now he's getting more and more into TV. I don't know if the stations give him the time free, or if he has to buy it. I'm sure he can afford it, especially late at night. That's when the old folks are up with their aches and pains. His shows are half miracle healings and half pleas for more love-offerings."

"Guess he didn't have any luck healing his grandson," I said.

Tina withdrew her hand from the letter-bag with nothing in it. She had forgotten about Scrabble for the time being, which was a good thing for her hapless victims. Her eyes were sparkling. "You don't know any of this story, do you? Ordinarily I don't believe in gossip, but…" She dropped her voice to a confidential tone pitched just above a whisper. "…but since you've *met* them, I could tell you."

"Yes, please," I said. I thought one of my questions—how Annie and Mike came to be living in a huge house on one of North Carolina's ritziest beaches—had already been answered. It was Grampa Buddy's summer retreat, bought and paid for with love-offerings.

"He's got two sons," Tina said. "They're both high in his church—deacons or assistant pastors, I don't know what they call them exactly, because I don't go for that holy rolling stuff. The daughter, though, *she* was different. A sporty type. Horseback riding, tennis, archery, deer hunting with her father, quite a bit of competition shooting. All that got in the papers after her trouble started."

Now the CAMP PERRY shirt made sense.

"Around the time she turned eighteen, it all went to hell—
quite literally, as he saw it. She went to what they call 'a secular-
humanist college,' and by all accounts she was quite the wild
child. Giving up the shooting competitions and tennis tourna-
ments was one thing; giving up the church-going for parties
and liquor and men was quite another. Also…" Tina lowered
her voice. "*Pot-smoking.*"

"Gosh," I said, "not that!"

Mrs. Shoplaw gave me a look, but Tina didn't notice. "Yes!
That! She got into the newspapers, too, those tabloids, because
she was pretty and rich, but mostly because of her father. And
being fallen-away. That's what they call it. She was a scandal to
that church of his, wearing mini-skirts and going braless and all.
Well, you know what those fundamentalists preach is straight
out of the Old Testament, all that about the righteous being
rewarded and sinners being punished even unto the seventh
generation. And she did more than hit the party circuit down
there in Green Witch Village." Tina's eyes were now so huge
they looked on the verge of tumbling from their sockets and
rolling down her cheeks. "*She quit the NRA and joined the
American Atheist Society!*"

"Ah. And did *that* get in the papers?"

"Did it ever! Then she got pregnant, no surprise there, and
when the baby turned out to have some sort of problem…cere-
bral palsy, I think—"

"Muscular dystrophy."

"Whatever it is, her father was asked about it on one of his
crusade things, and do you know what he said?"

I shook my head, but thought I could make a pretty good
guess.

"He said that God punishes the unbeliever and the sinner. He said his daughter was no different, and maybe her son's affliction would bring her back to God."

"I don't think it's happened yet," I said. I was thinking of the Jesus-kite.

"I can't understand why people use religion to hurt each other when there's already so much pain in the world," Mrs. Shoplaw said. "Religion is supposed to *comfort*."

"He's just a self-righteous old prig," Tina said. "No matter how many men she might have been with or how many joints of pot she might have smoked, she's still his daughter. And the child is still his grandson. I've seen that boy in town once or twice, either in a wheelchair or tottering along in those cruel braces he has to wear if he wants to walk. He seems like a perfectly nice boy, and she was sober. Also wearing a bra." She paused for further recollection. "I think."

"Her father might change," Mrs. Shoplaw said, "but I doubt it. Young women and young men grow up, but old women and old men just grow older and surer they've got the right on their side. Especially if they know scripture."

I remembered something my mother used to say. "The devil can quote scripture."

"And in a pleasing voice," Mrs. Shoplaw agreed moodily. Then she brightened. "Still, if the Reverend Ross is letting them use his place on Beach Row, maybe he's willing to let bygones be bygones. It *might* have crossed his mind by now that she was only a young girl, maybe not even old enough to vote. Dev, isn't it your turn?"

It was. I made *tear*. It netted me four points.

♥

My drubbing wasn't merciful, but once Tina Ackerley really got rocking, it was relatively quick. I returned to my room, sat in my chair by the window, and tried to rejoin Frodo and Sam on the road to Mount Doom. I couldn't do it. I closed the book and stared out through the rain-wavery glass at the empty beach and the gray ocean beyond. It was a lonely prospect, and at times like that, my thoughts had a way of turning back to Wendy—wondering where she was, what she was doing, and who she was with. Thinking about her smile, the way her hair fell against her cheek, the soft rise of her breasts in one of her seemingly endless supply of cardigan sweaters.

Not today. Instead of Wendy, I found myself thinking of Annie Ross and realizing I'd developed a small but powerful crush on her. The fact that nothing could come of it—she had to be ten years older than me, maybe twelve—only seemed to make things worse. Or maybe I mean better, because unrequited love *does* have its attractions for young men.

Mrs. S. had suggested that Annie's holier-than-thou father might be willing to let bygones be bygones, and I thought she might have something there. I'd heard that grandchildren had a way of softening stiff necks, and he might want to get to know the boy while there was still time. He could have found out (from the people he had everywhere) that Mike was smart as well as crippled. It was even possible he'd heard rumors that Mike had what Madame Fortuna called "the sight." Or maybe all that was too rosy. Maybe Mr. Fire-and-Brimstone had given her the use of the house in exchange for a promise that she'd keep her mouth shut and not brew up any fresh pot-and-miniskirt scandals while he was making the crucial transition from radio to television.

I could speculate until the cloud-masked sun went down, and not be sure of anything on Buddy Ross's account, but I thought I could be sure about one thing on Annie's: she was *not* ready to let bygones be bygones.

I got up and trotted downstairs to the parlor, fishing a scrap of paper with a phone number on it out of my wallet as I went. I could hear Tina and Mrs. S. in the kitchen, chattering away happily. I called Erin Cook's dorm, not expecting to get her on a Saturday afternoon; she was probably down in New Jersey with Tom, watching Rutgers football and singing the Scarlet Knights' fight song.

But the girl on phone duty said she'd get her, and three minutes later, her voice was in my ear.

"Dev, I was going to call you. In fact, I want to come down and see you, if I can get Tom to go along. I think I can, but it wouldn't be next weekend. Probably the one after."

I checked the calendar hanging on the wall and saw that would be the first weekend in October. "Have you actually found something out?"

"I don't know. Maybe. I love to do research, and I really got into this. I've piled up lots of background stuff for sure, but it's not like I solved the murder of Linda Gray in the college library, or anything. Still…there are things I want to show you. Things that trouble me."

"Trouble you why? Trouble you how?"

"I don't want to try explaining over the phone. If I can't persuade Tom to come down, I'll put everything in a big manila envelope and send it to you. But I think I can. He wants to see you, he just doesn't want anything to do with my little investigation. He wouldn't even look at the photos."

I thought she was being awfully mysterious, but decided to

let it go. "Listen, have you heard of an evangelist named Buddy Ross?"

"Buddy—" She burst into giggles. "*The Buddy Ross Hour of Power*! My gramma listens to that old faker all the time! He pretends to pull goat stomachs out of people and claims they're tumors! Do you know what Pop Allen would say?"

"Carny-from-carny," I said, grinning.

"Right you are. What do you want to know about him? And why can't you find out for yourself? Did your mother get scared by a card catalogue while she was carrying you?"

"Not that I know of, but by the time I get off work, the Heaven's Bay library is closed. I doubt if they've got *Who's Who*, anyway. I mean, it's only one room. It's not about him, anyway. It's about his two sons. I want to know if they have any kids."

"Why?"

"Because his daughter has one. He's a great kid, but he's dying."

A pause. Then: "What are you into down there now, Dev?"

"Meeting new people. Come on down. I'd love to see you guys again. Tell Tom we'll stay out of the funhouse."

I thought that might make her laugh, but it didn't. "Oh, he will. You couldn't get him within thirty yards of the place."

We said our goodbyes, I wrote the length of my call on the honor sheet, then went back upstairs and sat by the window. I was feeling that strange dull jealousy again. Why had Tom Kennedy been the one to see Linda Gray? Why him and not me?

♥

The Heaven's Bay weekly paper came out on Thursdays, and the headline on the October fourth edition read JOYLAND EMPLOYEE SAVES SECOND LIFE. I thought that was an exaggeration. I'll take full credit for Hallie Stansfield, but only part of it for the unpleasant Eddie Parks. The rest—not neglecting a tip of the old Howie-hat to Lane Hardy—belongs to Wendy Keegan, because if she hadn't broken up with me in June, I would have been in Durham, New Hampshire that fall, seven hundred miles from Joyland.

I certainly had no idea that more life-saving was on the agenda; premonitions like that were strictly for folks like Rozzie Gold and Mike Ross. I was thinking of nothing but Erin and Tom's upcoming visit when I arrived at the park on October first, after another rainy weekend. It was still cloudy, but in honor of Monday, the rain had stopped. Eddie was seated on his apple-box throne in front of Horror House, and smoking his usual morning cigarette. I raised my hand to him. He didn't bother to raise his in return, just stomped on his butt and leaned over to raise the apple-box and toss it under. I'd seen it all fifty times or more (and sometimes wondered how many butts were piled up beneath that box), but this time, instead of lifting the apple-box, he just went right on leaning.

Was there a look of surprise on his face? I can't say. By the time I realized something was wrong, all I could see was his faded and grease-smeared dogtop as his head dropped between his knees. He kept going forward, and ended up doing a complete somersault, landing on his back with his legs splayed out and his face up to the cloudy sky. And by then the only thing on it was a knotted grimace of pain.

I dropped my lunchsack, ran to him, and fell on my knees beside him. "Eddie? What is it?"

"Ticka," he managed.

For a moment I thought he was talking about some obscure

disease engendered by tick-bites, but then I saw the way he was clutching the left side of his chest with his gloved right hand.

The pre-Joyland version of Dev Jones would simply have yelled for help, but after four months of talking the Talk, *help* never even crossed my mind. I filled my lungs, lifted my head, and screamed *"HEY, RUBE!"* into the damp morning air as loud as I could. The only person close enough to hear was Lane Hardy, and he came fast.

The summer employees Fred Dean hired didn't have to know CPR when they signed on, but they had to learn. Thanks to the life-saving class I'd taken as a teenager, I already knew. The half-dozen of us in that class had learned beside the YMCA pool, working on a dummy with the unlikely name of Herkimer Saltfish. Now I had a chance to put theory into practice for the first time, and do you know what? It wasn't really that much different from the clean-and-jerk I'd used to pop the hotdog out of the little Stansfield girl's throat. I wasn't wearing the fur, and there was no hugging involved, but it was still mostly a matter of applying hard force. I cracked four of the old bastard's ribs and broke one. I can't say I'm sorry, either.

By the time Lane arrived, I was kneeling alongside Eddie and doing closed chest compressions, first rocking forward with my weight on the heels of my hands, then rocking back and listening to see if he'd draw in a breath.

"Christ," Lane said. "Heart attack?"

"Yeah, I'm pretty sure. Call an ambulance."

The closest phone was in the little shack beside Pop Allen's Shootin' Gallery—his doghouse, in the Talk. It was locked, but Lane had the Keys to the Kingdom: three masters that opened everything in the park. He ran. I went on doing CPR, rocking back and forth, my thighs aching now, my knees barking about their long contact with the rough pavement of Joyland Avenue. After each five compressions I'd slow-count to three, listening for Eddie to inhale, but there was nothing. No joy in Joyland, not for Eddie. Not after the first five, not after the second five, not after half a dozen fives. He just lay there with his gloved hands at his sides and his mouth open. Eddie fucking Parks. I stared down at him as Lane came sprinting back, shouting that the ambulance was on its way.

I'm not doing it, I thought. *I'll be damned if I'll do it*.

Then I leaned forward, doing another compression on the way, and pressed my mouth to his. It wasn't as bad as I feared; it was worse. His lips were bitter with the taste of cigarettes, and there was the stink of something else in his mouth—God help me, I think it was jalapeno peppers, maybe from a breakfast omelet. I got a good seal, though, pinched his nostrils shut, and breathed down his throat.

I did that five or six times before he started breathing on his own again. I stopped the compressions to see what would happen, and he kept going. Hell must have been full that day, that's all I can figure. I rolled him onto his side in case he vomited. Lane stood beside me with a hand on my shoulder. Shortly after that, we heard the wail of an approaching siren.

Lane hurried to meet them at the gate and direct them. Once he was gone, I found myself looking at the snarling green monster-faces decorating the façade of Horror House. COME IN IF YOU DARE was written above the faces in drippy green letters. I found myself thinking again of Linda Gray, who had gone in alive and had been carried out hours later, cold and dead. I think my mind went that way because Erin was coming with information. Information that *troubled* her. I also thought of the girl's killer.

Could have been you, Mrs. Shoplaw had said. *Except you're dark-haired instead of blond and don't have a bird's head tattooed on one of your hands. This guy did. An eagle or maybe a hawk.*

Eddie's hair was the premature gray of the lifelong heavy smoker, but it could have been blond four years ago. And he always wore gloves. Surely he was too old to have been the man who had accompanied Linda Gray on her last dark ride, *surely*, but...

The ambulance was very close but not quite here, although I could see Lane at the gate, waving his hands over his head, making hurry-up gestures. Thinking what the hell, I stripped off Eddie's gloves. His fingers were lacy with dead skin, the backs of his hands red beneath a thick layer of some sort of white cream. There were no tattoos.

Just psoriasis.

♥

As soon as he was loaded up and the ambulance was heading back to the tiny Heaven's Bay hospital, I went into the nearest donniker and rinsed my mouth again and again. It was a long time before I got rid of the taste of those damn jalapeno peppers, and I have never touched one since.

When I came out, Lane Hardy was standing by the door. "That was something," he said. "You brought him back."

"He won't be out of the woods for a while, and there might be brain damage."

"Maybe yes, maybe no, but if you hadn't been there, he'd have been in the woods permanently. First the little girl, now the dirty old man. I may start calling you Jesus instead of Jonesy, because you sure are the savior."

"You do that, and I'm DS." That was Talk for *down south*, which in turn meant turning in your time-card for good.

"Okay, but you did all right, Jonesy. In fact, I gotta say you rocked the house."

"The *taste* of him," I said. "God!"

"Yeah, I bet, but look on the bright side. With him gone, you're free at last, free at last, thank God Almighty, you're free at last. I think you'll like it better that way, don't you?"

I certainly did.

From his back pocket, Lane drew out a pair of rawhide gloves. Eddie's gloves. "Found these laying on the ground. Why'd you take em off him?"

"Uh…I wanted to let his hands breathe." That sounded primo stupid, but the truth would have sounded even stupider. I couldn't believe I'd entertained the notion of Eddie Parks being Linda Gray's killer for even a moment. "When I took my life-saving course, they told us that heart attack victims need all the free skin they can get. It helps, somehow." I shrugged. "It's supposed to, at least."

"Huh. You learn a new thing every day." He flapped the gloves. "I don't think Eddie's gonna be back for a long time—if at all— so you might as well stick these in his doghouse, yeah?"

"Okay," I said, and that's what I did. But later that day I went and got them again. Something else, too.

♥

I didn't like him, we're straight on that, right? He'd given me
no reason to like him. He had, so far as I knew, given not one
single Joyland employee a reason to like him. Even old-timers
like Rozzie Gold and Pop Allen gave him a wide berth. Nevertheless, I found myself entering the Heaven's Bay Community
Hospital that afternoon at four o'clock, and asking if Edward
Parks could have a visitor. I had his gloves in one hand, along
with the something else.

The blue-haired volunteer receptionist went through her
paperwork twice, shaking her head, and I was starting to think
Eddie had died after all when she said, "Ah! It's Edwin, not
Edward. He's in Room 315. That's ICU, so you'll have to check
at the nurse's station first."

I thanked her and went to the elevator—one of those huge
ones big enough to admit a gurney. It was slower than old cold
death, which gave me plenty of time to wonder what I was
doing here. If Eddie needed a visit from a park employee, it
should have been Fred Dean, not me, because Fred was the
guy in charge that fall. Yet here I was. They probably wouldn't
let me see him, anyway.

But after checking his chart, the head nurse gave me the okay.
"He may be sleeping, though."

"Any idea about his—?" I tapped my head.

"Mental function? Well…he was able to give us his name."

That sounded hopeful.

He was indeed asleep. With his eyes shut and that day's
late-arriving sun shining on his face, the idea that he might
have been Linda Gray's date a mere four years ago was even
more ludicrous. He looked at least a hundred, maybe a hundred

and twenty. I saw I needn't have brought his gloves, either. Someone had bandaged his hands, probably after treating the psoriasis with something a little more powerful than whatever OTC cream he'd been using on them. Looking at those bulky white mittens made me feel a queer, reluctant pity.

I crossed the room as quietly as I could, and put the gloves in the closet with the clothes he'd been wearing when he was brought in. That left me with the other thing—a photograph that had been pinned to the wall of his cluttered, tobacco-smelling little shack next to a yellowing calendar that was two years out of date. The photo showed Eddie and a plain-faced woman standing in the weedy front yard of an anonymous tract house. Eddie looked about twenty-five. He had his arm around the woman. She was smiling at him. And—wonder of wonders—he was smiling back.

There was a rolling table beside his bed with a plastic pitcher and a glass on it. This I thought rather stupid; with his hands bandaged the way they were, he wasn't going to be pouring anything for a while. Still, the pitcher could serve one useful purpose. I propped the photo against it so he'd see it when he woke up. With that done, I started for the door.

I was almost there when he spoke in a whispery voice that was a long way from his usual ill-tempered rasp. "Kiddo."

I returned—not eagerly—to his bedside. There was a chair in the corner, but I had no intention of pulling it over and sitting down. "How you feeling, Eddie?"

"Can't really say. Hard to breathe. They got me all taped up."

"I brought you your gloves, but I see they already…" I nodded at his bandaged hands.

"Yeah." He sucked in air. "If anything good comes out of this, maybe they'll fix em up. Fuckin itch all the time, they do." He looked at the picture. "Why'd you bring that? And what were you doin in my doghouse?"

"Lane told me to put your gloves in there. I did, but then I thought you might want them. And you might want the picture. Maybe she's someone you'd want Fred Dean to call?"

"Corinne?" He snorted. "She's been dead for twenty years. Pour me some water, kiddo. I'm as dry as ten-year dogshit."

I poured, and held the glass for him, and even wiped the corner of his mouth with the sheet when he dribbled. It was all a lot more intimate than I wanted, but didn't seem so bad when I remembered that I'd been soul-kissing the miserable bastard only hours before.

He didn't thank me, but when had he ever? What he said was, "Hold that picture up." I did as he asked. He looked at it fixedly for several seconds, then sighed. "Miserable scolding backbiting cunt. Walking out on her for Royal American Shows was the smartest thing I ever did." A tear trembled at the corner of his left eye, hesitated, then rolled down his cheek.

"Want me to take it back and pin it up in your doghouse, Eddie?"

"No, might as well leave it. We had a kid, you know. A little girl."

"Yeah?"

"Yeah. She got hit by a car. Three years old she was, and died like a dog in the street. That miserable cunt was yakking on the phone instead of watching her." He turned his head aside and closed his eyes. "Go on, get outta here. Hurts to talk, and I'm tired. Got a elephant sitting on my chest."

"Okay. Take care of yourself."

He grimaced without opening his eyes. "That's a laugh. How e'zacly am I s'posed to do that? You got any ideas? Because I haven't. I got no relatives, no friends, no savings, no *in*-surance. What am I gonna do now?"

"It'll work out," I said lamely.

"Sure, in the movies it always does. Go on, get lost."

This time I was all the way out the door before he spoke again.

"You shoulda let me die, kiddo." He said it without melo-drama, just as a passing observation. "I coulda been with my little girl."

♥

When I walked back into the hospital lobby I stopped dead, at first not sure I was seeing who I thought I was seeing. But it was her, all right, with one of her endless series of arduous novels open in front of her. This one was called *The Dissertation*.

"Annie?"

She looked up, at first wary, then smiling as she recognized me. "Dev! What are you doing here?"

"Visiting a guy from the park. He had a heart attack today."

"Oh, my God, I'm so sorry. Is he going to be all right?"

She didn't invite me to sit down next to her, but I did, anyway. My visit to Eddie had upset me in ways I didn't understand, and my nerves were jangling. It wasn't unhappiness and it wasn't sorrow. It was a queer, unfocused anger that had some-thing to do with the foul taste of jalapeno peppers that still seemed to linger in my mouth. And with Wendy, God knew why. It was wearying to know I wasn't over her, even yet. A broken arm would have healed quicker. "I don't know. I didn't talk to a doctor. Is *Mike* all right?"

"Yes, it's just a regularly scheduled appointment. A chest X-ray and a complete blood count. Because of the pneumonia, you know. Thank God he's over it now. Except for that lingering cough, Mike's fine." She was still holding her book open, which probably meant she wanted me to go, and that made me angrier. You have to remember that was the year *everyone* wanted me to go, even the guy whose life I'd saved.

Which is probably why I said, "*Mike* doesn't think he's fine. So who am I supposed to believe here, Annie?"

Her eyes widened with surprise, then grew distant. "I'm sure I don't care who or what you believe, Devin. It's really not any of your business."

"Yes it is." That came from behind us. Mike had rolled up in his chair. It wasn't the motorized kind, which meant he'd been turning the wheels with his hands. Strong boy, cough or no cough. He'd buttoned his shirt wrong, though.

Annie turned to him, surprised. "What are you doing here? You were supposed to let the nurse—"

"I told her I could do it on my own and she said okay. It's just a left and two rights from radiology, you know. I'm not blind, just dy—"

"Mr. Jones was visiting a friend of his, Mike." So now I had been demoted back to Mr. Jones. She closed her book with a snap and stood up. "He's probably anxious to get home, and I'm sure you must be ti—"

"I want him to take us to the park." Mike spoke calmly enough, but his voice was loud enough to make people look around. "*Us.*"

"Mike, you know that's not—"

"To Joyland. To *Joy*…Land." Still calm, but louder still. Now everyone was looking. Annie's cheeks were flaming. "I want you both to take me." His voice rose louder still. *"I want you to take me to Joyland before I die."*

Her hand covered her mouth. Her eyes were huge. Her words, when they came, were muffled but understandable. "Mike…you're not going to *die*, who told you…" She turned on me. "Do I have you to thank for putting that idea in his head?"

"Of course not." I was very conscious that our audience was growing—it now included a couple of nurses and a doctor in blue scrubs and booties—but I didn't care. I was still angry. "*He* told *me*. Why would that surprise you, when you know all about his intuitions?"

That was my afternoon for provoking tears. First Eddie, now Annie. Mike was dry-eyed, though, and he looked every bit as furious as I felt. But he said nothing as she grabbed the handles of his wheelchair, spun it around, and drove it at the door. I thought she was going to crash into them, but the magic eye got them open just in time.

Let them go, I thought, but I was tired of letting women go. I was tired of just letting things happen to me and then feeling bad about them.

A nurse approached me. "Is everything all right?"

"No," I said, and followed them out.

♥

Annie had parked in the lot adjacent to the hospital, where a sign announced THESE TWO ROWS RESERVED FOR THE HANDI-CAPPED. She had a van, I saw, with plenty of room for the folded-up wheelchair in back. She had gotten the passenger door open, but Mike was refusing to get out of the chair. He was gripping the handles with all his strength, his hands dead white.

"Get in!" she shouted at him.

Mike shook his head, not looking at her.

"*Get in, dammit!*"

This time he didn't even bother to shake his head.

She grabbed him and yanked. The wheelchair had its brake on and tipped forward. I grabbed it just in time to keep it from going over and spilling them both into the open door of the van.

Annie's hair had fallen into her face, and the eyes peering through it were wild: the eyes, almost, of a skittish horse in a thunderstorm. "*Let go! This is all your fault! I never should have—*"

"Stop," I said. I took hold of her shoulders. The hollows there were deep, the bones close to the surface. I thought, *She's been too busy stuffing calories into him to worry about herself.*

"*LET ME G—*"

"I don't want to take him away from you," I said. "Annie, that's the last thing I want."

She stopped struggling. Warily, I let go of her. The novel she'd been reading had fallen to the pavement in the struggle. I bent down, picked it up, and put it into the pocket on the back of the wheelchair.

"Mom." Mike took her hand. "It doesn't have to be the last good time."

Then I understood. Even before her shoulders slumped and the sobs started, I understood. It wasn't the fear that I'd stick him on some crazy-fast ride and the burst of adrenaline would kill him. It wasn't fear that a stranger would steal the damaged heart she loved so well. It was a kind of atavistic belief—a *mother's* belief—that if they never started doing certain last things, life would go on as it had: morning smoothies at the end of the boardwalk, evenings with the kite at the end of the boardwalk, all of it in a kind of endless summer. Only it was October now and the beach was deserted. The happy screams of teenagers on the Thunderball and little kids shooting down the Splash & Crash water slide had ceased, there was a nip in the air as the days drew down. No summer is endless.

She put her hands over her face and sat down on the passenger seat of the van. It was too high for her, and she almost slid off. I caught her and steadied her. I don't think she noticed.

"Go on, take him," she said. "I don't give a fuck. Take him parachute-jumping, if you want. Just don't expect me to be a part of your…your *boys' adventure*."

Mike said, "I can't go without you."

That got her to drop her hands and look at him. "Michael, you're all I've got. Do you understand that?"

"Yes," he said. He took one of her hands in both of his. "And you're all *I've* got."

I could see by her face that the idea had never crossed her mind, not really.

"Help me get in," Mike said. "Both of you, please."

When he was settled (I don't remember fastening his seatbelt, so maybe this was before they were a big deal), I closed the door and walked around the nose of the van with her.

"His chair," she said distractedly. "I have to get his chair."

"I'll put it in. You sit behind the wheel and get yourself ready to drive. Take a few deep breaths."

She let me help her in. I had her above the elbow, and I

could close my whole hand around her upper arm. I thought of telling her she couldn't live on arduous novels alone, and thought better of it. She had been told enough this afternoon.

I folded the wheelchair and stowed it in the cargo compartment, taking longer with the job than I needed to, giving her time to compose herself. When I went back to the driver's side, I half-expected to find the window rolled up, but it was still down. She had wiped her eyes and nose, and pushed her hair into some semblance of order.

I said, "He can't go without you, and neither can I."

She spoke to me as if Mike weren't there and listening. "I'm so afraid for him, all the time. He sees so much, and so much of it hurts him. That's what the nightmares are about, I know it. He's such a great kid. Why can't he just get well? Why this? Why *this*?"

"I don't know," I said.

She turned to kiss Mike's cheek. Then she turned back to me. Drew in a deep, shaky breath and let it out. "So when do we go?" she asked.

♥

The Return of the King was surely not as arduous as *The Dissertation*, but that night I couldn't have read *The Cat in the Hat*. After eating some canned spaghetti for supper (and largely ignoring Mrs. Shoplaw's pointed observations about how some young people seem determined to mistreat their bodies), I went up to my room and sat by the window, staring out at the dark and listening to the steady beat-and-retreat of the surf.

I was on the verge of dozing when Mrs. S. knocked lightly on my door and said, "You've got a call, Dev. It's a little boy."

I went down to the parlor in a hurry, because I could think of only one little boy who might call me.

"Mike?"

He spoke in a low voice. "My mom is sleeping. She said she was tired."

"I bet she was," I said, thinking of how we'd ganged up on her.

"I know we did," Mike said, as if I had spoken the thought aloud. "We had to."

"Mike…can you read minds? Are you reading mine?"

"I don't really know," he said. "Sometimes I see things and hear things, that's all. And sometimes I get ideas. It was my idea to come to Grampa's house. Mom said he'd never let us, but I knew he would. Whatever I have, the special thing, I think it came from him. He heals people, you know. I mean, sometimes he fakes it, but sometimes he really does."

"Why did you call, Mike?"

He grew animated. "About Joyland! Can we really ride the merry-go-round and the Ferris wheel?"

"I'm pretty sure."

"Shoot in the shooting gallery?"

"Maybe. If your mother says so. All this stuff is contingent on your mother's approval. That means—"

"I know what it means." Sounding impatient. Then the child's excitement broke through again. "That is so awesome!"

"None of the fast rides," I said. "Are we straight on that? For one thing, they're buttoned up for the winter." The Carolina Spin was, too, but with Lane Hardy's help, it wouldn't take forty minutes to get it running again. "For another—"

"Yeah, I know, my heart. The Ferris wheel would be enough for me. We can see it from the end of the boardwalk, you know. From the top, it must be like seeing the world from my kite."

I smiled. "It is like that, sort of. But remember, only if your mom says you can. She's the boss."

"We're *going* for her. She'll know when we get there." He sounded eerily sure of himself. "And it's for you, Dev. But mostly it's for the girl. She's been there too long. She wants to leave."

My mouth dropped open, but there was no danger of drooling; my mouth had gone entirely dry. "How—" Just a croak. I swallowed again. "How do you know about her?"

"I don't know, but I think she's why I came. Did I tell you it's not white?"

"You did, but you said you didn't know what that meant. Do you now?"

"Nope." He began to cough. I waited it out. When it cleared, he said, "I have to go. My mom's getting up from her nap. Now she'll be up half the night, reading."

"Yeah?"

"Yeah. I really hope she lets me go on the Ferris wheel."

"It's called the Carolina Spin, but people who work there just call it the hoister." Some of them—Eddie, for instance— actually called it the chump-hoister, but I didn't tell him that. "Joyland folks have this kind of secret talk. That's part of it."

"The hoister. I'll remember. Bye, Dev."

The phone clicked in my ear.

♥

This time it was Fred Dean who had the heart attack.

He lay on the ramp leading to the Carolina Spin, his face blue and contorted. I knelt beside him and started chest compressions.

When there was no result from that, I leaned forward, pinched his nostrils shut, and jammed my lips over his. Something tickled across my teeth and onto my tongue. I pulled back and saw a black tide of baby spiders pouring from his mouth.

I woke up half out of bed, the covers pulled loose and wound around me in a kind of shroud, heart pumping, clawing at my own mouth. It took several seconds for me to realize there was nothing in there. Nonetheless, I got up, went to the bathroom, and drank two glasses of water. I may have had worse dreams than the one that woke me at three o'clock on that Tuesday morning, but if so, I can't remember them. I re-made my bed and laid back down, convinced there would be no more sleep for me that night. Yet I had almost dozed off again when it occurred to me that the big emotional scene the three of us had played out at the hospital yesterday might have been for nothing.

Sure, Joyland was happy to make special arrangements for the lame, the halt, and the blind—what are now called "special needs children"—during the season, but the season was over. Would the park's undoubtedly expensive insurance policy still provide coverage if something happened to Mike Ross in October? I could see Fred Dean shaking his head when I made my request and saying he was very sorry, but—

It was chilly that morning, with a strong breeze, so I took my car, parking beside Lane's pickup. I was early, and ours were the only vehicles in Lot A, which was big enough to hold five hundred cars. Fallen leaves tumbled across the pavement, making an insectile sound that reminded me of the spiders in my dream.

Lane was sitting in a lawn chair outside Madame Fortuna's shy (which would soon be disassembled and stored for the winter), eating a bagel generously smeared with cream cheese. His derby was tilted at its usual insouciant angle, and there was a cigarette parked behind one ear. The only new thing was the denim jacket he was wearing. Another sign, had I needed one, that our Indian summer was over.

"Jonesy, Jonesy, lookin lonely. Want a bagel? I got extra."

"Sure," I said. "Can I talk to you about something while I eat it?"

"Come to confess your sins, have you? Take a seat, my son." He pointed to the side of the fortune-telling booth, where another couple of folded lawn chairs were leaning.

"Nothing sinful," I said, opening one of the chairs. I sat down and took the brown bag he was offering. "But I made a promise and now I'm afraid I might not be able to keep it."

I told him about Mike, and how I had convinced his mother to let him come to the park—no easy task, given her fragile emotional state. I finished with how I'd woken up in the middle of the night, convinced Fred Dean would never allow it. The only thing I didn't mention was the dream that had awakened me.

"So," Lane said when I'd finished. "Is she a fox? The mommy?"

"Well…yeah. Actually she is. But that isn't the reason—"

He patted my shoulder and gave me a patronizing smile I could have done without. "Say nummore, Jonesy, say nummore."

"Lane, she's ten years older than I am!"

"Okay, and if I had a dollar for every babe I ever took out who was ten years *younger*, I could buy me a steak dinner at Hanratty's in the Bay. Age is just a number, my son."

"Terrific. Thanks for the arithmetic lesson. Now tell me if I stepped in shit when I told the kid he could come to the park and ride the Spin and the merry-go-round."

"You stepped in shit," he said, and my heart sank. Then he raised a finger. "*But*."

"But?"

"Have you set a date for this little field trip yet?"

"Not exactly. I was thinking maybe Thursday." Before Erin and Tom showed up, in other words.

"Thursday's no good. Friday, either. Will the kid and his foxy mommy still be here next week?"

"I guess so, but—"

"Then plan on Monday or Tuesday."

"Why wait?"

"For the paper." Looking at me as if I were the world's biggest idiot.

"Paper…?"

"The local rag. It comes out on Thursday. When your latest lifesaving feat hits the front page, you're going to be Freddy Dean's fair-haired boy." Lane tossed the remains of his bagel into the nearest litter barrel—two points—and then raised his hands in the air, as if framing a newspaper headline. " 'Come to Joyland! We not only sell fun, we save lives!' " He smiled and tilted his derby the other way. "Priceless publicity. Fred's gonna owe you another one. Take it to the bank and say thanks."

"How would the paper even find out? I can't see Eddie Parks telling them." Although if he did, he'd probably want them to make sure the part about how I'd practically crushed his ribcage made Paragraph One.

He rolled his eyes. "I keep forgetting what a Jonesy-come-lately you are to this part of the world. The only articles anybody actually reads in that catbox-liner are the Police Beat and the Ambulance Calls. But ambulance calls are pretty dry. As a special favor to you, Jonesy, I'll toddle on down to the *Banner* office on my lunch break and tell the rubes all about your heroism. They'll send someone out to interview you pronto."

"I don't really want—"

"Oh gosh, a Boy Scout with a merit badge in modesty. Save it. You want the kid to get a tour of the park, right?"

"Yes."

"Then do the interview. Also smile pretty for the camera."

Which—if I may jump ahead—is pretty much what I did.

As I was folding up my chair, he said: "Our Freddy Dean might have said fuck the insurance and risked it anyway, you know. He doesn't look it, but he's carny-from-carny himself. His father was a low-pitch jack-jaw on the corn circuit. Freddy told me once his pop carried a Michigan bankroll big enough to choke a horse."

I knew low-pitch, jack-jaw, and corn circuit, but not Michigan bankroll. Lane laughed when I asked him. "Two twenties on the outside, the rest either singles or cut-up green paper. A great gag when you want to attract a tip. But when it comes to Freddy himself, that ain't the point." He re-set his derby yet again.

"What is?"

"Carnies have a weakness for good-looking points in tight skirts and kids down on their luck. They also have a strong allergy to rube rules. Which includes all the bean-counter bullshit."

"So maybe I wouldn't have to—"

He raised his hands to stop me. "Better not to have to find out. Do the interview."

♥

The *Banner*'s photographer posed me in front of the Thunder-ball. The picture made me wince when I saw it. I was squinting and thought I looked like the village idiot, but it did the job; the paper was on Fred's desk when I came in to see him on Friday morning. He hemmed and hawed, then okayed my request, as long as Lane promised to stick with us while the kid and his mother were in the park.

Lane said okay to that with no hemming or hawing. He said he wanted to see my girlfriend, then burst out laughing when I started to fulminate.

Later that day, I told Annie Ross I'd set up a tour of the park the following Tuesday morning, if the weather was good—Wednesday or Thursday if it wasn't. Then I held my breath.

There was a long pause, followed by a sigh.

Then she said okay.

♥

That was a busy Friday. I left the park early, drove to Wilmington, and was waiting when Tom and Erin stepped off the train. Erin ran the length of the platform, threw herself into my arms, and kissed me on both cheeks and the tip of my nose. She made a lovely armful, but it's impossible to mistake sisterly kisses for anything other than what they are. I let her go and allowed Tom to pull me into an enthusiastic back-thumping manhug. It was as if we hadn't seen each other in five years instead of five weeks. I was a working stiff now, and although I had put on my best chinos and a sport-shirt, I looked it. Even with my grease-spotted jeans and sun-faded dogtop back in the closet of my room at Mrs. S.'s, I looked it.

"It's so great to see you!" Erin said. "My God, what a tan!"

I shrugged. "What can I say? I'm working in the northernmost province of the Redneck Riviera."

"You made the right call," Tom said. "I never would have believed it when you said you weren't going back to school, but you made the right call. Maybe *I* should have stayed at Joyland."

He smiled—that I-French-kissed-the-Blarney-Stone smile of his that could charm the birdies down from the trees—but it didn't quite dispel the shadow that crossed his face. He could never have stayed at Joyland, not after our dark ride.

They stayed the weekend at Mrs. Shoplaw's Beachside Accommodations (Mrs. S. was delighted to have them, and Tina Ackerley was delighted to see them) and all five of us had a hilarious half-drunk picnic supper on the beach, with a roaring bonfire to provide warmth. But on Saturday afternoon, when it came time for Erin to share her troubling information with me, Tom declared his intention to whip Tina and Mrs. S. at Scrabble and sent us off alone. I thought that if Annie and Mike were at the end of their boardwalk, I'd introduce Erin to them. But the day was chilly, the wind off the ocean was downright cold, and the picnic table at the end of the boardwalk was deserted. Even the umbrella was gone, taken in and stored for the winter.

At Joyland, all four parking lots were empty save for the little fleet of service trucks. Erin—dressed in a heavy turtleneck sweater and wool pants, carrying a slim and very businesslike briefcase with her initials embossed on it—raised her eyebrows when I produced my keyring and used the biggest key to open the gate.

"So," she said. "You're one of them now."

That embarrassed me—aren't we all embarrassed (even if we don't know why) when someone says we're one of *them*?

"Not really. I carry a gate-key in case I get here before anyone else, or if I'm the last to leave, but only Fred and Lane have all the Keys to the Kingdom."

She laughed as if I'd said something silly. "The key to the gate *is* the key to the kingdom, that's what I think." Then she sobered and gave me a long, measuring stare. "You look older, Devin. I thought so even before we got off the train, when I saw you waiting on the platform. Now I know why. You went to work and we went back to Never Never Land to play with the Lost Boys and Girls. The ones who will eventually turn up in suits from Brooks Brothers and with MBAs in their pockets."

I pointed to the briefcase. "That would go with a suit from Brooks Brothers...if they really make suits for women, that is."

She sighed. "It was a gift from my parents. My father wants me to be a lawyer, like him. So far I haven't gotten up the nerve to tell him I want to be a freelance photographer. He'll blow his stack."

We walked up Joyland Avenue in silence—except for the bonelike rattle of the fallen leaves. She looked at the covered rides, the dry fountain, the frozen horses on the merry-go-round, the empty Story Stage in the deserted Wiggle-Waggle Village.

"Kind of sad, seeing it this way. It makes me think mortal thoughts." She looked at me appraisingly. "We saw the paper. Mrs. Shoplaw made sure to leave it in our room. You did it again."

"Eddie? I just happened to be there." We had reached Madame Fortuna's shy. The lawn chairs were still leaning against it. I unfolded two and gestured for Erin to sit down. I sat beside her, then pulled a pint bottle of Old Log Cabin from the pocket of my jacket. "Cheap whiskey, but it takes the chill off."

Looking amused, she took a small nip. I took one of my own, screwed on the cap, and stowed the bottle in my pocket. Fifty yards down Joyland Avenue—our midway—I could see the tall false front of Horror House and read the drippy green letters: COME IN IF YOU DARE.

Her small hand gripped my shoulder with surprising strength. "You saved the old bastard. You did. Give yourself some credit, you."

I smiled, thinking of Lane saying I had a merit badge in modesty. Maybe; giving myself credit for stuff wasn't one of my strong points in those days.

"Will he live?"

"Probably. Freddy Dean talked to some doctors who said blah-blah-blah, patient must give up smoking, blah-blah-blah, patient must give up eating French fries, blah-blah-blah, patient must begin a regular exercise regimen."

"I can just see Eddie Parks jogging," Erin said.

"Uh-huh, with a cigarette in his mouth and a bag of pork rinds in his hand."

She giggled. The wind gusted and blew her hair around her face. In her heavy sweater and businesslike dark gray pants, she didn't look much like the flushed American beauty who'd run around Joyland in a little green dress, smiling her pretty Erin smile and coaxing people to let her take their picture with her old-fashioned camera.

"What have you got for me? What did you find out?"

She opened her briefcase and took out a folder. "Are you absolutely sure you want to get into this? Because I don't think you're going to listen, say 'Elementary, my dear Erin,' and spit out the killer's name like Sherlock Holmes."

If I needed evidence that Sherlock Holmes I wasn't, my wild idea that Eddie Parks might have been the so-called Funhouse Killer was it. I thought of telling her that I was more interested in putting the victim to rest than I was in catching the killer, but it would have sounded crazy, even factoring in Tom's experience. "I'm not expecting that, either."

"And by the way, you owe me almost forty dollars for inter-library loan fees."

"I'm good for it."

She poked me in the ribs. "You better be. I'm not working my way through school for the fun of it."

She settled her briefcase between her ankles and opened the folder. I saw Xeroxes, two or three pages of typewritten notes, and some glossy photographs that looked like the kind the conies got when they bought the Hollywood Girls' pitch. "Okay, here we go. I started with the Charleston *News and Courier* article you told me about." She handed me one of the Xeroxes. "It's a Sunday piece, five thousand words of specula-tion and maybe eight hundred words of actual info. Read it later if you want, I'll summarize the salient points.

"Four girls. Five if you count *her*." She pointed down the midway at Horror House. "The first was Delight Mowbray, DeeDee to her friends. From Waycross, Georgia. White, twenty-one years old. Two or three days before she was killed, she told her good friend Jasmine Withers that she had a new boyfriend, older and very handsome. She was found beside a trail on the edge of the Okefenokee Swamp on August 31st, 1961, nine days after she disappeared. If the guy had taken her into the swamp, even a little way, she might not have been found for a much longer time."

"If ever," I said. "A body left in there would have been gator-bait in twenty minutes."

"Gross but true." She handed me another Xerox. "This is the story from the Waycross *Journal-Herald*." There was a photo. It showed a somber cop holding up a plaster cast of tire tracks. "The theory is that he dumped her where he cut her throat. The tire tracks were made by a truck, the story says."

"Dumped her like garbage," I said.

"Also gross but true." She handed me another Xeroxed newspaper clipping. "Here's number two. Claudine Sharp, from Rocky Mount, right here in NC. White, twenty-three years old. Found dead in a local theater. August second, 1963. The movie being shown was *Lawrence of Arabia*, which happens to be very long and very loud. The guy who wrote the story quotes 'an unnamed police source' as saying the guy probably cut her throat during one of the battle scenes. Pure speculation, of course. He left a bloody shirt and gloves, then must have walked out in the shirt he was wearing underneath."

"That just about has to be the guy who killed Linda Gray," I said. "Don't you think so?"

"It sure sounds like it. The cops questioned all her friends, but Claudine hadn't said anything about a new boyfriend."

"Or who she was going to the movies with that night? Not even to her parents?"

Erin gave me a patient look. "She was twenty-three, Dev, not fourteen. She lived all the way across town from her parents. Worked in a drugstore and had a little apartment above it."

"You got all that from the newspaper story?"

"Of course not. I also made some calls. Practically dialed my fingers off, if you want to know the truth. You owe me for the long-distance, too. More about Claudine Sharp later. For now, let's move on. Victim number three—according to the *News and Courier* story—was a girl from Santee, South Carolina. Now we're up to 1965. Eva Longbottom, age nineteen. Black. Disappeared on July fourth. Her body was found nine days later by a couple of fishermen, lying on the north bank of the Santee River. Raped and stabbed in the heart. The others were neither black nor raped. You can put her in the Funhouse Killer column if you want to, but I'm doubtful, myself. Last victim—before Linda Gray—was her."

She handed me what had to be a high school yearbook photo of a beautiful golden-haired girl. The kind who's the head cheerleader, the Homecoming Queen, dates the football quarterback...and is *still* liked by everyone.

"Darlene Stamnacher. Probably would have changed her last name if she'd gotten into the movie biz, which was her stated goal. White, nineteen. From Maxton, North Carolina. Disappeared on June 29th, 1967. Found two days later, after a massive search, inside a roadside lean-to in the sugar-pine williwags south of Elrod. Throat cut."

"Christ, she's beautiful. Didn't she have a steady boyfriend?"

"A girl this good-looking, why do you even ask? And that's where the police went first, only he wasn't around. He and three of his buddies had gone camping in the Blue Ridge, and they could all vouch for him. Unless he flapped his arms and flew back, it wasn't him."

"Then came Linda Gray," I said. "Number five. If they were all murdered by the same guy, that is."

Erin raised a teacherly finger. "And only five if all the guy's victims have been found. There could have been others in '62, '64, '66...you get it."

The wind gusted and moaned through the struts of the Spin.

"Now for the things that trouble me," Erin said...as if five dead girls weren't troubling enough. From her folder she took another Xerox. It was a flier—a shout, in the Talk—advertising something called *Manly Wellman's Show of 1000 Wonders*. It showed a couple of clowns holding up a parchment listing some of the wonders, one of which was AMERICA'S FINEST COLLECTION OF **FREAKS**! AND **ODDITIES**! There were also rides, games, fun for the kiddies, and THE WORLD'S SCARIEST FUNHOUSE!

Come in if you dare, I thought.

"You got this from interlibrary loan?" I asked.

"Yes. I've decided you can get anything by way of interlibrary loan, if you're willing to dig. Or maybe I should say cock an ear, because it's really the world's biggest jungle telegraph. This ad appeared in the Waycross *Journal-Herald*. It ran during the first week of August, 1961."

"The Wellman carny was in Waycross when the first girl disappeared?"

"Her name was DeeDee Mowbray, and no—it had moved on by then. But it was there when DeeDee told her girlfriend that she had a new boyfriend. Now look at this. It's from the Rocky Mount *Telegram*. Ran for a week in mid-July of 1963. Standard advance advertising. I probably don't even need to tell you that."

It was another full-pager shouting *Manly Wellman's Show of 1000 Wonders*. Same two clowns holding up the same parchment, but two years after the stop in Waycross, they were also promising a ten thousand dollar cover-all Beano game, and the word *freaks* was nowhere to be seen.

"Was the show in town when the Sharp girl was killed in the movie theater?"

"Left the day before." She tapped the bottom of the sheet. "All you have to do is look at the dates, Dev."

I wasn't as familiar with the timeline as she was, but I didn't bother defending myself. "The third girl? Longbottom?"

"I didn't find anything about a carny in the Santee area, and I sure wouldn't have found anything about the Wellman show, because it went bust in the fall of 1964. I found that in *Outdoor Trade and Industry*. So far as I or any of my many librarian helpers could discover, it's the only trade magazine that covers the carny and amusement park biz."

"Jesus, Erin, you should forget photography and find yourself a rich writer or movie producer. Hire on as his research assistant."

"I'd rather take pictures. Research is too much like work. But don't lose the thread here, Devin. There was no carny in the Santee area, true, but the Eva Longbottom murder doesn't look like the other four, anyway. Not to me. No rape in the others, remember?"

"That you know of. Newspapers are coy about that stuff."

"That's right, they say molested or sexually assaulted instead of raped, but they get the point across, believe me."

"What about Darlene Shoemaker? Was there—"

"*Stamnacher*. These girls were murdered, Dev, the least you can do is get their names right."

"I will. Give me time."

She put a hand over mine. "Sorry. I'm throwing this at you all at once, aren't I? I've had weeks to brood over it."

"Have you been?"

"Sort of. It's pretty awful."

She was right. If you read a whodunit or see a mystery movie, you can whistle gaily past whole heaps of corpses, only interested in finding out if it was the butler or the evil stepmother. But these had been real young women. Crows had probably ripped their flesh; maggots would have infested their eyes and squirmed up their noses and into the gray meat of their brains.

"Was there a carny in the Maxton area when the Stamnacher girl was killed?"

"No, but there was a county fair about to start in Lumberton —that's the nearest town of any size. Here."

She handed me another Xerox, this one advertising the Robeson County Summer Fair. Once again, Erin tapped the sheet. This time she was calling my attention to a line reading 50 **SAFE** RIDES PROVIDED BY SOUTHERN STAR AMUSEMENTS. "I also looked Southern Star up in *Outdoor Trade and Industry*. The company's been around since after World War II. They're based in Birmingham and travel all over the south, putting up rides. Nothing so grand as the Thunderball or the Delirium Shaker, but they've got plenty of chump-shoots, and the jocks to run them."

I had to grin at that. She hadn't forgotten all the Talk, it seemed. Chump-shoots were rides that could be easily put up or taken down. If you've ever ridden the Krazy Kups or the Wild Mouse, you've been on on a chump-shoot.

"I called the ride-boss at Southern Star. Said I'd worked at Joyland this summer, and was doing a term paper on the amusement industry for my sociology class. Which I just might do, you know. After all this, it would be a slam-dunk. He told me what I'd already guessed, that there's a big turnover in their line of work. He couldn't tell me offhand if they'd picked anyone up from the Wellman show, but he said it was likely—a couple of roughies here, a couple of jocks there, maybe a ride-monkey or two. So the guy who killed DeeDee and Claudine could have been at that fair, and Darlene Stamnacher could have met him. The fair wasn't officially open for business yet, but lots of townies gravitate to the local fairgrounds to watch the ride-monkeys and the local gazoonies do the setup." She looked at me levelly. "And I think that's just what happened."

"Erin, is the carny link in the story the *News and Courier* published after Linda Gray was killed? Or maybe I should call it the amusement link."

"Nope. Can I have another nip from your bottle? I'm cold."

"We can go inside—"

"No, it's this murder stuff that makes me cold. Every time I go over it."

I gave her the bottle, and after she'd taken her nip, I took one of my own. "Maybe *you're* Sherlock Holmes," I said. "What about the cops? Do you think they missed it?"

"I don't know for sure, but I think…they did. If this was a detective show on TV, there'd be one smart old cop—a Lieutenant Columbo type—who'd look at the big picture and put it together, but I guess there aren't many guys like that in real life. Besides, the big picture is hard to see because it's scattered across three states and eight years. One thing you can be sure of is that if he ever worked at Joyland, he's long gone. I'm sure the turnover at an amusement park isn't as fast as it is in a road company like

Southern Star Amusements, but there are still plenty of people leaving and coming in."

I knew that for myself. Ride-jocks and concession shouters aren't exactly the most grounded people, and gazoonies went in and out like the tide.

"Now here's the other thing that troubles me," she said, and handed me her little pile of eight-by-ten photos. Printed on the white border at the bottom of each was PHOTO TAKEN BY YOUR JOYLAND "HOLLYWOOD GIRL."

I shuffled through them, and felt in need of another nip when I realized what they were: the photos showing Linda Gray and the man who had killed her. "Jesus God, Erin, these aren't newspaper pix. Where'd you get them?"

"Brenda Rafferty. I had to butter her up a little, tell her what a good mom she'd been to all us Hollywood Girls, but in the end she came through. These are fresh prints made from negatives she had in her personal files and loaned to me. Here's something interesting, Dev. You see the headband the Gray girl's wearing?"

"Yes." An Alice band, Mrs. Shoplaw had called it. A *blue* Alice band.

"Brenda said they fuzzed that out in the shots they gave to the newspapers. They thought it would help them nail the guy, but it never did."

"So what troubles you?"

God knew all of the pictures troubled me, even the ones where Gray and the man she was with were just passing in the background, only recognizable by her sleeveless blouse and Alice band and his baseball cap and dark glasses. In only two of them were Linda Gray and her killer sharp and clear. The first showed them at the Whirly Cups, his hand resting casually on the swell of Gray's bottom. In the other—the best of the lot—they were at the Annie Oakley Shootin' Gallery. Yet in neither was the man's face really visible. I could have passed him on the street and not known him.

Erin plucked up the Whirly Cups photo. "Look at his hand."

"Yeah, the tattoo. I see it, and I heard about it from Mrs. S. What do you make it to be? A hawk or an eagle?"

"I think an eagle, but it doesn't matter."

"Really?"

"Really. Remember I said I'd come back to Claudine Sharp? A young woman getting her throat cut in the local movie theater—during *Lawrence of Arabia*, no less—was big news in a little town like Rocky Mount. The *Telegram* ran with it for almost a month. The cops turned up exactly one lead, Dev. A girl Claudine went to high school with saw her at the snackbar and said hello. Claudine said hi right back. The girl said there was a man in sunglasses and a baseball cap next to her, but she never thought the guy was with Claudine, because he was a lot older. The only reason she noticed him at all was because he was wearing sunglasses in a movieshow…and because he had a tattoo on his hand."

"The bird."

"No, Dev. It was a Coptic cross. Like this." She took out another Xerox sheet and showed me. "She told the cops she thought at first it was some kind of Nazi symbol."

I looked at the cross. It was elegant, but looked nothing at all like a bird. "Two tats, one on each hand," I said at last. "The bird on one, the cross on the other."

She shook her head and gave me the Whirly Cups photo again. "Which hand's got the bird on it?"

He was standing on Linda Gray's left, encircling her waist. The hand resting on her bottom…

"The right."

"Yes. But the girl who saw him in the movie theater said the *cross* was on his right."

I considered this. "She made a mistake, that's all. Witnesses do it all the time."

"Sure they do. My father could talk all day on that subject. But look, Dev."

Erin handed me the Shootin' Gallery photo, the best of the bunch because they weren't just passing in the background. A roving Hollywood Girl had seen them, noted the cute pose, and snapped them, hoping for a sale. Only the guy had given her the brushoff. A *hard* brushoff, according to Mrs. Shoplaw. That made me remember how she had described the photo: *Him snuggled up to her hip to hip, showing her how to hold the rifle, the way guys always do.* The version Mrs. S. saw would have been a fuzzy newspaper reproduction, made up of little dots. This was the original, so sharp and clear I almost felt I could step into it and warn the Gray girl. He *was* snuggled up to her, his hand over hers on the barrel of the beebee-shooting .22, helping her aim.

It was his *left* hand. And there was no tattoo on it.

Erin said, "You see it, don't you?"

"There's nothing to see."

"That's the point, Dev. That's exactly the point."

"Are you saying that it was two different guys? That one with a cross on his hand killed Claudine Sharp and *another* one—a guy with a bird on his hand—killed Linda Gray? That doesn't seem very likely."

"I couldn't agree more."

"Then what are you saying?"

"I thought I saw something in one of the photos, but I wasn't sure, so I took the print and the negative to a grad student named Phil Hendron. He's a darkroom genius, practically lives in the Bard Photography Department. You know those clunky Speed Graphics we carried?"

"Sure."

"They were mostly for effect—cute girls toting old-fashioned cameras—but Phil says they're actually pretty terrific. You can do a lot with the negs. For example…"

She handed me a blow-up of the Whirly Cups pic. The Hollywood Girl's target had been a young couple with a toddler between them, but in this enlarged version they were hardly there. Now Linda Gray and her murderous date were at the center of the image.

"Look at his hand, Dev. Look at the tattoo!"

I did, frowning. "It's a little hard to see," I complained. "The hand's blurrier than the rest."

"I don't think so."

This time I held the photo close to my eyes. "It's…Jesus, Erin. Is it the ink? Is it running? Just a little?"

She gave me a triumphant smile. "July of 1969. A hot night in Dixie. Almost everybody was sweating buckets. If you don't believe me, look at some of the other pictures and note the perspiration rings. Plus, he had something else to be sweaty about, didn't he? He had murder on his mind. An audacious one, at that."

I said, "Oh, shit. Pirate Pete's."

She pointed a forefinger at me. "Bingo."

Pirate Pete's was the souvenir shop outside the Splash & Crash, proudly flying a Jolly Roger from its roof. Inside you could get the usual stuff—tee-shirts, coffee mugs, beach towels, even a pair of swim-trunks if your kid forgot his, everything imprinted with the Joyland logo. There was also a counter where you could get a wide assortment of fake tattoos. They came on decals. If you didn't feel capable of applying it yourself, Pirate Pete (or one of his greenie minions) would do it for a small surcharge.

Erin was nodding. "I doubt he got it there—that would have been dumb, and this guy isn't dumb—but I'm sure it's not a real tattoo, any more than the Coptic cross the girl saw in that Rocky Mount movie theater was a real tattoo." She leaned forward and gripped my arm. "You know what I think? I think he does it because it draws attention. People notice the tattoo and everything else just…" She tapped the indistinct shapes that had been the actual subject of this photo before her friend at Bard blew it up.

I said, "Everything else about him fades into the background."

"Yup. Later he just washes it off."

"Do the cops know?"

"I have no idea. You could tell them—not me, I'm going back to school—but I'm not sure they'd care at this late date."

I shuffled through the photos again. I had no doubt that Erin had actually discovered something, although I *did* doubt it would, by itself, be responsible for the capture of the Funhouse Killer. But there was something else about the photos. *Something.* You know how sometimes a word gets stuck on the tip of your tongue and just won't come off? It was like that.

"Have there been any murders like these five—or these four, if we leave out Eva Longbottom—since Linda Gray? Did you check?"

"I tried," she said. "The short answer is I don't think so, but I can't say for sure. I've read about fifty murders of young girls and women—fifty at least—and haven't found any that fit the parameters." She ticked them off. "Always in summer. Always as a result of a dating situation with an unknown older man. Always the cut throat. And always with some sort of carny connec—"

"Hello, kids."

We looked up, startled. It was Fred Dean. Today he was wearing a golfing shirt, bright red baggies, and a long-billed cap with HEAVEN'S BAY COUNTRY CLUB stitched in gold thread above the brim. I was a lot more used to seeing him in a suit, where informality consisted of pulling down his tie and popping the top button of his Van Heusen shirt. Dressed for the links, he looked absurdly young. Except for the graying wings of hair at his temples, that was.

"Hello, Mr. Dean," Erin said, standing up. Most of her paperwork—and some of the photographs—were still clutched in one hand. The folder was in the other. "I don't know if you remember me—"

"Of course I do," he said, approaching. "I never forget a Hollywood Girl, but sometimes I *do* mix up the names. Are you Ashley or Jerri?"

She smiled, put her paperwork back in the folder, and handed it to me. I added the photos I was still holding. "I'm Erin."

"Of course. Erin Cook." He dropped me a wink, which was even weirder than seeing him in old-fashioned golfing baggies. "You have excellent taste in young ladies, Jonesy."

"I do, don't I?" It seemed too complicated to tell him that Erin was actually Tom Kennedy's girlfriend. Fred probably wouldn't remember Tom anyway, never having seen him in a flirty green dress and high heels.

"I just stopped by to get the accounts books. Quarterly IRS payments coming up. Such a pain in the hindquarters. Enjoying your little alumna visit, Erin?"

"Yes, sir, very much."

"Coming back next year?"

She looked a trifle uncomfortable at that, but stuck gamely to the truth. "Probably not."

"Fair enough, but if you change your mind, I'm sure Brenda Rafferty can find a place for you." He switched his attention to me. "This boy you plan to bring to the park, Jonesy. Have you set a date with his mother?"

"Tuesday. Wednesday or Thursday if it's rainy. The kid can't be out in the rain."

Erin was looking at me curiously.

"I advise you stick to Tuesday," he said. "There's a storm coming up the coast. Not a hurricane, thank God, but a tropical disturbance. Lots of rain and gale-force winds is what they're saying. It's supposed to arrive mid-morning on Wednesday."

"Okay," I said. "Thanks for the tip."

"Nice to see you again, Erin." He tipped his cap to her and started off toward the back lot.

Erin waited until he was out of sight before bursting into giggles. "Those *pants*. Did you see those *pants*?"

"Yeah," I said. "Pretty wild." But I was damned if I was going to laugh at them. Or him. According to Lane, Fred Dean held Joyland together with spit, baling wire, and account-book wizardry. That being the case, I thought he could wear all the golf baggies he wanted. And at least they weren't checks.

"What's this about bringing some kid to the park?"

"Long story," I said. "I'll tell you while we walk back."

So I did, giving her the Boy-Scout-majoring-in-modesty

version and leaving out the big argument at the hospital. Erin listened without interruption, asking only one question, just as we reached the steps leading up from the beach. "Tell me the truth, Dev—is mommy foxy?"

People kept asking me that.

♥

That night Tom and Erin went out to Surfer Joe's, a beer-and-boogie bar where they had spent more than a few off-nights during the summer. Tom invited me along, but I heeded that old saying about two being company and three being you-know-what. Besides, I doubted if they'd find the same raucous, party-hearty atmosphere. In towns like Heaven's Bay, there's a big difference between July and October. In my role as big brother, I even said so.

"You don't understand, Dev," Tom said. "Me n Erin don't go *looking* for the fun; we *bring* the fun. It's what we learned last summer."

Nevertheless, I heard them coming up the stairs early, and almost sober, from the sound of them. Yet there were whispers and muffled laughter, sounds that made me feel a little lonely. Not for Wendy; just for *someone*. Looking back on it, I suppose even that was a step forward.

I read through Erin's notes while they were gone, but found nothing new. I set them aside after fifteen minutes and went back to the photographs, crisp black-and-white images TAKEN BY YOUR JOYLAND "HOLLYWOOD GIRL." At first I just shuffled through them; then I sat on the floor and laid them out in a square, moving them from place to place like a guy trying to put a puzzle together. Which was, I suppose, exactly what I was doing.

Erin was troubled by the carny connection and the tattoos that probably weren't real tattoos at all. Those things troubled me as well, but there was something else. Something I couldn't quite get. It was maddening because I felt like it was staring me right in the face. Finally I put all but two of the photos back in the folder. The key two. These I held up, looking first at one, then at the other.

Linda Gray and her killer waiting in line at the Whirly Cups.

Linda Gray and her killer at the Shootin' Gallery.

Never mind the goddam tattoo, I told myself. *It's not that. It's something else.*

But what else could it be? The sunglasses masked his eyes. The goatee masked his lower face, and the slightly tilted bill of the baseball cap shaded his forehead and eyebrows. The cap's logo showed a catfish peering out of a big red C, the insignia of a South Carolina minor league team called the Mudcats. Dozens of Mudcat lids went through the park every day at the height of the season, so many that we called them fishtops instead of dogtops. The bastard could hardly have picked a more anonymous lid, and surely that was the idea.

Back and forth I went, from the Whirly Cups to the Shootin' Gallery and then back to the Whirly Cups again. At last I tossed the photos in the folder and threw the folder on my little desk. I read until Tom and Erin came in, then went to bed.

Maybe it'll come to me in the morning, I thought. *I'll wake up and say, "Oh shit, of course."*

The sound of the incoming waves slipped me into sleep. I dreamed I was on the beach with Annie and Mike. Annie and I were standing with our feet in the surf, our arms around each other, watching Mike fly his kite. He was paying out twine and running after it. He could do that because there was nothing wrong with him. He was fine. I had only dreamed that stuff about Duchenne's muscular dystrophy.

I woke early because I'd forgotten to pull down the shade. I went to the folder, pulled out those two photographs, and stared at them in the day's first sunlight, positive I'd see the answer.

But I didn't.

♥

A harmony of scheduling had allowed Tom and Erin to travel from New Jersey to North Carolina together, but when it comes to train schedules, harmony is the exception rather than the rule. The only ride they got together on Sunday was the one from Heaven's Bay to Wilmington, in my Ford. Erin's train left for upstate New York and Annandale-on-Hudson two hours before Tom's Coastal Express was due to whisk him back to New Jersey.

I tucked a check in her jacket pocket. "Interlibrary loans and long distance."

She fished it out, looked at the amount, and tried to hand it back. "Eighty dollars is too much, Dev."

"Considering all you found out, it's not enough. Take it, Lieutenant Columbo."

She laughed, put it back in her pocket, and kissed me goodbye —another brother-sister quickie, nothing like the one we'd shared that night at the end of the summer. She spent considerably longer in Tom's arms. Promises were made about Thanksgiving at Tom's parents' home in western Pennsylvania. I could tell he didn't want to let her go, but when the loudspeakers announced

Joyland

Something in his voice made me look up in a hurry. His cheeks were even more flushed than usual. I put the menu down.

"This stuff you've had Erin doing…I think it should stop. It's bothering her, and I think she's been neglecting her coursework." He laughed, glanced out the window at the train-station bustle, looked back at me. "I sound more like her dad than her boyfriend, don't I?"

"You sound concerned, that's all. Like you care for her."

"*Care* for her? Buddy, I'm head-over-heels in love. She's the most important thing in my life. What I'm saying here isn't jealousy talking, though. I don't want you to get that idea. Here's the thing: if she's going to transfer and still hold onto her financial aid, she can't let her grades slip. You see that, don't you?"

Yes, I could see that. I could see something else, too, even if Tom couldn't. He wanted her away from Joyland in mind as well as body, because something had happened to him there that he couldn't understand. Nor did he want to, which in my opinion made him sort of a fool. That dour flush of envy ran through me again, causing my stomach to clench around the food it was trying to digest.

Then I smiled—it was an effort, I won't kid you about that— and said, "Message received. As far as I'm concerned, our little research project is over." *So relax, Thomas. You can stop thinking about what happened in Horror House. About what you saw there.*

"Good. We're still friends, right?"

I reached across the table. "Friends to the end," I said.

We shook on it.

♥

The Wiggle-Waggle Village's Story Stage had three backdrops: Prince Charming's Castle, Jack's Magic Beanstalk, and a starry night sky featuring the Carolina Spin outlined in red neon. All three had sun-faded over the course of the summer. I was in the Wiggle-Waggle's small backstage area on Monday morning, touching them up (and hoping not to *fuck* them up—I was no Van Gogh) when one of the part-time gazoonies arrived with a message from Fred Dean. I was wanted in his office.

I went with some unease, wondering if I was going to get a reaming for bringing Erin into the park on Saturday. I was surprised to find Fred dressed not in one of his suits or his amusing golf outfit, but in faded jeans and an equally faded Joyland tee-shirt, the short sleeves rolled to show some real muscle. There was a paisley sweatband cinched around his brow. He didn't look like an accountant or the park's chief employment officer; he looked like a ride-jock.

He registered my surprise and smiled. "Like the outfit? I must admit I do. It's the way I dressed when I caught on with the Blitz Brothers show in the Midwest, back in the fifties. My mother was okay with the Blitzies, but my dad was horrified. And *he* was carny."

"I know," I said.

He raised his eyebrows. "Really? Word gets around, doesn't it? Anyway, there's a lot to do this afternoon."

"Just give me a list. I'm almost done painting the backdrops in the—"

"Not at all, Jonesy. You're signing out at noon today, and I don't want to see you until tomorrow morning at nine, when you turn up with your guests. Don't worry about your paycheck, either. I'll see you're not docked for the hours you miss."

"What's this about, Fred?"

He gave me a smile I couldn't interpret. "It's a surprise."

♥

That Monday was warm and sunny, and Annie and Mike were having lunch at the end of the boardwalk when I walked back to Heaven's Bay. Milo saw me coming and raced to meet me.

"Dev!" Mike called. "Come and have a sandwich! We've got plenty!"

"No, I really shouldn't—"

"We insist," Annie said. Then her brow furrowed. "Unless you're sick, or something. I don't want Mike to catch a bug."

"I'm fine, just got sent home early. Mr. Dean—he's my boss—wouldn't tell me why. He said it was a surprise. It's got something to do with tomorrow, I guess." I looked at her with some anxiety. "We're still on for tomorrow, right?"

"Yes," she said. "When I surrender, I surrender. Just…we're not going to tire him out. Are we, Dev?"

"*Mom*," Mike said.

She paid him no mind. "*Are* we?"

"No, ma'am." Although seeing Fred Dean dressed up like a carny road dog, with all those unsuspected muscles showing,

had made me uneasy. Had I made it clear to him how fragile
Mike's health was? I thought so, but—

"Then come on up here and have a sandwich," she said. "I
hope you like egg salad."

♥

I didn't sleep well on Monday night, half-convinced that the
tropical storm Fred had mentioned would arrive early and
wash out Mike's trip to the park, but Tuesday dawned cloud-
less. I crept down to the parlor and turned on the TV in time to
get the six forty-five weathercast on WECT. The storm was still
coming, but the only people who were going to feel it today
were the ones living in coastal Florida and Georgia. I hoped
Mr. Easterbrook had packed his galoshes.

"You're up early," Mrs. Shoplaw said, poking her head in
from the kitchen. "I was just making scrambled eggs and bacon.
Come have some."

"I'm not that hungry, Mrs. S."

"Nonsense. You're still a growing boy, Devin, and you need
to eat. Erin told me what you've got going on today, and I think
you're doing a wonderful thing. It will be fine."

"I hope you're right," I said, but I kept thinking of Fred Dean
in his work-clothes. Fred, who'd sent me home early. Fred, who
had a surprise planned.

♥

We had made our arrangements at lunch the day before, and
when I turned my old car into the driveway of the big green
Victorian at eight-thirty on Tuesday morning, Annie and Mike
were ready to go. So was Milo.

"Are you sure nobody will mind us bringing him?" Mike had asked on Monday. "I don't want to get into trouble."

"Service dogs are allowed in Joyland," I said, "and Milo's going to be a service dog. Aren't you, Milo?"

Milo had cocked his head, apparently unfamiliar with the service dog concept.

Today Mike was wearing his huge, clanky braces. I moved to help him into the van, but he waved me off and did it himself. It took a lot of effort and I expected a coughing fit, but none came. He was practically bouncing with excitement. Annie, looking impossibly long-legged in Lee Riders, handed me the van keys. "You drive." And lowering her voice so Mike wouldn't hear: "I'm too goddam nervous to do it."

I was nervous, too. I'd bulldozed her into this, after all. I'd had help from Mike, true, but I was the adult. If it went wrong, it would be on me. I wasn't much for prayer, but as I loaded Mike's crutches and wheelchair into the back of the van, I sent one up that nothing would go wrong. Then I backed out of the driveway, turned onto Beach Drive, and drove past the bill-board reading BRING YOUR KIDS TO JOYLAND FOR THE TIME OF THEIR LIVES!

Annie was in the passenger seat, and I thought she had never looked more beautiful than she did that October morning, in her faded jeans and a light sweater, her hair tied back with a hank of blue yarn.

"Thank you for this, Dev," she said. "I just hope we're doing the right thing."

"We are," I said, trying to sound more confident than I felt. Because, now that it was a done deal, I had my doubts.

♥

The Joyland sign was lit up—that was the first thing I noticed. The second was that the summertime get-happy music was playing through the loudspeakers: a sonic parade of late sixties and early seventies hits. I had intended to park in one of the Lot A handicapped spaces—they were only fifty feet or so from the park entrance—but before I could do so, Fred Dean stepped through the open gate and beckoned us forward. Today he wasn't wearing just any suit but the three-piecer he saved for the occasional celebrity who rated a VIP tour. The suit I had seen, but never the black silk top hat, which looked like the kind you saw diplomats wearing in old newsreel footage.

"Is this usual?" Annie asked.

"Sure," I said, a trifle giddily. None of it was usual.

I drove through the gate and onto Joyland Avenue, pulling up next to the park bench outside the Wiggle-Waggle Village where I had once sat with Mr. Easterbrook after my first turn as Howie.

Mike wanted to get out of the van the way he'd gotten in: by himself. I stood by, ready to catch him if he lost his balance, while Annie hoisted the wheelchair out of the back. Milo sat at my feet, tail thumping, ears cocked, eyes bright.

As Annie rolled the wheelchair up, Fred approached in a cloud of aftershave. He was…resplendent. There's really no other word for it. He took off his hat, bowed to Annie, then held out a hand. "You must be Mike's mother." You have to re-member that Ms. wasn't common usage back then, and, nervous as I was, I took a moment to appreciate how deftly he had avoided the Miss/Mrs. dichotomy.

"I am," she said. I don't know if she was flustered by his courtliness or by the difference in the way they were dressed—she amusement-park casual, he state-visit formal—but flustered she was. She shook his hand, though. "And this young man—"

"—is Michael." He offered his hand to the wide-eyed boy standing there in his steel supports. "Thank you for coming today."

"You're welcome…I mean, thank *you*. Thank you for having us." He shook Fred's hand. "This place is *huge*."

It wasn't, of course; Disney World is huge. But to a ten-year-old who had never been to an amusement park, it had to look that way. For a moment I could see it through his eyes, see it new, and my doubts about bringing him began to melt away.

Fred bent down to examine the third member of the Ross family, hands on his knees. "And you're Milo!"

Milo barked.

"Yes," Fred said, "and I am equally pleased to meet you." He held out his hand, waiting for Milo to raise his paw. When he did, Fred shook it.

"How do you know our dog's name?" Annie asked. "Did Dev tell you?"

He straightened, smiling. "He did not. I know because this is a magic place, my dear. For instance." He showed her his empty hands, then put them behind his back. "Which hand?"

"Left," Annie said, playing along.

Fred brought out his left hand, empty.

She rolled her eyes, smiling. "Okay, right."

This time he brought out a dozen roses. Real ones. Annie and Mike gasped. Me too. All these years later, I have no idea how he did it.

"Joyland is for children, my dear, and since today Mike is the only child here, the park belongs to him. These, however, are for you."

She took them like a woman in a dream, burying her face in the blooms, smelling their sweet red dust.

"I'll put them in the van for you," I said.

She held them a moment longer, then passed them to me.

"Mike," Fred said, "do you know what we sell here?"

He looked uncertain. "Rides? Rides and games?"

"We sell *fun*. So what do you say we have some?"

♥

I remember Mike's day at the park—Annie's day, too—as if it happened last week, but it would take a correspondent much more talented than I am to tell you how it *felt*, or to explain how it could have ended the last hold Wendy Keegan still held over my heart and my emotions. All I can say is what you already know: some days are treasure. Not many, but I think in almost every life there are a few. That was one of mine, and when I'm blue—when life comes down on me and everything looks tawdry and cheap, the way Joyland Avenue did on a rainy day—I go back to it, if only to remind myself that life isn't always a butcher's game. Sometimes the prizes are real. Sometimes they're precious.

Of course not all the rides were running, and that was okay, because there were a lot of them Mike couldn't handle. But more than half of the park was operational that morning—the lights, the music, even some of the shys, where half a dozen gazoonies were on duty selling popcorn, fries, sodas, cotton candy, and Pup-A-Licious dogs. I have no idea how Fred and Lane pulled it off in a single afternoon, but they did.

We started in the Village, where Lane was waiting beside the engine of the Choo-Choo Wiggle. He was wearing a pillowtick engineer's cap instead of his derby, but it was cocked at the same insouciant angle. Of course it was. "All aboard! This is the ride that makes kids happy, so get on board and make it snappy. Dogs ride free, moms ride free, kids ride up in the engine with me."

He pointed at Mike, then to the passenger seat in the engine. Mike got out of his chair, set his crutches, then tottered on them. Annie started for him.

"No, Mom. I'm okay. I can do it."

He got his balance and clanked to where Lane was standing—a real boy with robot legs—and allowed Lane to boost him into the passenger seat. "Is that the cord that blows the whistle? Can I pull it?"

"That's what it's there for," Lane said, "but watch out for pigs on the tracks. There's a wolf in the area, and they're scared to death of him."

Annie and I sat in one of the cars. Her eyes were bright. Roses all her own burned in her cheeks. Her lips, though tightly pressed together, were trembling.

"You okay?" I asked her.

"Yes." She took my hand, laced her fingers through mine, and squeezed almost tight enough to hurt. "Yes. Yes. Yes."

"Controls green across the board!" Lane cried. "Check me on that, Michael!"

"Check!"

"Watch out for what on the tracks?"

"Pigs!"

"Kid, you got style that makes me smile. Give that yell-rope a yank and we're off!"

Mike yanked the cord. The whistle howled. Milo barked. The airbrakes chuffed, and the train began to move.

Choo-Choo Wiggle was strictly a zamp ride, okay? All the

rides in the Village were zamps, meant mostly for boys and girls between the ages of three and seven. But you have to remember how seldom Mike Ross had gotten out, especially since his pneumonia the year before, and how many days he had sat with his mother at the end of that boardwalk, listening to the rumble of the rides and the happy screams coming from down the beach, knowing that stuff wasn't for him. What *was* for him was more gasping for air as his lungs failed, more coughing, a gradual inability to walk even with the aid of crutches and braces, and finally the bed where he would die, wearing diapers under his PJs and an oxygen mask over his face.

Wiggle-Waggle Village was sort of depopulated with no greenies to play the fairy-tale parts, but Fred and Lane had reactivated all the mechanicals: the magic beanstalk that shot out of the ground in a burst of steam; the witch cackling in front of the Candy House; the Mad Hatter's tea party; the nightcap-wearing wolf who lurked beneath one of the underpasses and sprang at the train as it passed. As we rounded the final turn, we passed three houses all kids know well—one of straw, one of sticks, and one of bricks.

"Watch out for pigs!" Lane cried, and just then they came waddling onto the tracks, uttering amplified oinks. Mike shrieked with laughter and yanked the whistle. As always, the pigs escaped …barely.

When we pulled back into the station, Annie let go of my hand and hurried up to the engine. "Are you okay, hon? Want your inhaler?"

"No, I'm fine." Mike turned to Lane. "Thanks, Mr. Engineer!"

"My pleasure, Mike." He held out a hand, palm up. "Slap me five if you're still alive."

Mike did, and with gusto. I doubt if he'd ever felt more alive.

"Now I've got to move on," Lane said. "Today I am a man of many hats." He dropped me a wink.

♥

Annie vetoed the Whirly Cups but allowed Mike—not without apprehension—to ride the Chair-O-Planes. She gripped my arm even harder than she had my hand when his chair rose thirty feet above the ground and began to tilt, then loosened up again when she heard him laughing.

"God," she said, "look at his *hair*! How it flies out behind him!" She was smiling. She was also crying, but didn't seem aware of it. Nor of my arm, which had found its way around her waist.

Fred was running the controls, and knew enough to keep the ride at half-speed, rather than bringing it all the way up to full, which would have had Mike parallel to the ground, held in only by centrifugal force. When he finally came back to earth, the kid was too dizzy to walk. Annie and I each took an arm and guided him to the wheelchair. Fred toted Mike's crutches.

"Oh, man." It seemed to be all he could say. "Oh man, oh man."

The Dizzy Speedboats—a land ride in spite of the name— was next. Mike rode over the painted water in one with Milo, both of them clearly loving it. Annie and I took another one. Although I had been working at Joyland for over four months by then, I'd never been on this ride, and I yelled the first time I saw us rushing prow-first at Mike and Milo's boat, only to shear off at the last second.

"*Wimp!*" Annie shouted in my ear.

When we got off, Mike was breathing hard but still not

coughing. We rolled him up Hound Dog Way and grabbed sodas. The gazoonie refused to take the fivespot Annie held out. "Everything's on the house today, ma'am."

"Can I have a Pup, Mom? And some cotton candy?"

She frowned, then sighed and shrugged. "Okay. Just as long as you understand that stuff is still off-limits, buster. Today's an exception. And no more fast rides."

He wheeled ahead to the Pup-A-Licious shy, his own pup trotting beside him. She turned to me. "It's not about nutrition, if that's what you're thinking. If he gets sick to his stomach, he might vomit. And vomiting is dangerous for kids in Mike's condition. They—"

I kissed her, just a gentle brush of my lips across hers. It was like swallowing a tiny drop of something incredibly sweet. "Hush," I said. "Does he look sick?"

Her eyes got very large. For a moment I felt positive that she was going to slap me and walk away. The day would be ruined and it would be my own stupid goddam fault. Then she smiled, looking at me in a speculative way that made my stomach feel light. "I bet you could do better than that, if you had half a chance."

Before I could think of a reply, she was hurrying after her son. It really would have made no difference if she'd hung around, because I was totally flummoxed.

♥

Annie, Mike, and Milo crowded into one car of the Gondola Glide, which crossed above the whole park on a diagonal. Fred Dean and I rode beneath them in one of the electric carts, with Mike's wheelchair tucked in back.

"Seems like a terrific kid," Fred commented.

"He is, but I never expected you to go all-out like this."

"That's for you as much as for him. You've done the park more good than you seem to know, Dev. When I told Mr. Easterbrook I wanted to go big, he gave me the green light."

"You called him?"

"I did indeed."

"That thing with the roses...how'd you pull it off?"

Fred shot his cuffs and looked modest. "A magician never tells his secrets. Don't you know that?"

"Did you have a card-and-bunny-gig when you were with Blitz Brothers?"

"No, sir, I did not. All I did with the Blitzies was ride-jock and drag the midway. And, although I did not have a valid driver's license, I also drove a truck on a few occasions when we had to DS from some rube-ranch or other in the dead of night."

"So where did you learn the magic?"

Fred reached behind my ear, pulled out a silver dollar, dropped it into my lap. "Here and there, all around the square. Better goose it a little, Jonesy. They're getting ahead of us."

♥

From Skytop Station, where the gondola ride ended, we went to the merry-go-round. Lane Hardy was waiting. He had lost the engineer's cap and was once more sporting his derby. The park's loudspeakers were still pumping out rock and roll, but under the wide, flaring canopy of what's known in the Talk as the spinning jenny, the rock was drowned out by the calliope playing "A Bicycle Built for Two." It was recorded, but still sweet and old-fashioned.

Before Mike could mount the dish, Fred dropped to one knee and regarded him gravely. "You can't ride the jenny without a Joyland hat," he said. "We call em dogtops. Got one?"

"No," Mike said. He still wasn't coughing, but dark patches had begun to creep out beneath his eyes. Where his cheeks weren't flushed with excitement, he looked pale. "I didn't know I was supposed to…"

Fred took off his own hat, peered inside, showed it to us. It was empty, as all magicians' top hats must be when they are displayed to the audience. He looked into it again, and brightened. "Ah!" He brought out a brand new Joyland dogtop and put it on Mike's head. "Perfect! Now which beast do you want to ride? A horse? The unicorn? Marva the Mermaid? Leo the Lion?"

"Yes, the lion, please!" Mike cried. "Mom, you ride the tiger right next to me!"

"You bet," she said. "I've always wanted to ride a tiger."

"Hey, champ," Lane said, "lemme help you up the ramp."

While he did that, Annie lowered her voice and spoke to Fred. "Not a lot more, okay? It's all great, a day he'll never forget, but—"

"He's fading," Fred said. "I understand."

Annie mounted the snarling, green-eyed tiger next to Mike's lion. Milo sat between them, grinning a doggy grin. As the merry-go-round started to move, "A Bicycle Built for Two" gave way to "Twelfth Street Rag." Fred put his hand on my shoulder. "You'll want to meet us at the Spin—we'll make that his last ride—but you need to visit the costume shop first. And put some hustle into it."

I started to ask why, then realized I didn't need to. I headed for the back lot. And yes, I put some hustle into it.

♥

That Tuesday morning in October of 1973 was the last time I wore the fur. I put it on in the costume shop and used Joyland Under to get back to the middle of the park, pushing one of the electric carts as fast as it would go, my Howie-head bouncing up and down on one shoulder. I surfaced behind Madame Fortuna's shy, just in time. Lane, Annie, and Mike were coming up the midway. Lane was pushing Mike's chair. None of them saw me peering around the corner of the shy; they were looking at the Carolina Spin, their necks craned. Fred saw me, though. I raised a paw. He nodded, then turned and raised his own paw to who-ever was currently watching from the little sound booth above Customer Services. Seconds later, Howie-music rolled from all the speakers. First up was Elvis, singing "Hound Dog."

I leaped from cover, going into my Howie-dance, which was kind of a fucked-up soft-shoe. Mike gaped. Annie clapped her hands to her temples, as if she'd suddenly been afflicted with a monster headache, then started laughing. I believe what fol-lowed was one of my better performances. I hopped and skipped around Mike's chair, hardly aware that Milo was doing the same thing, only in the other direction. "Hound Dog" gave way to the Rolling Stones version of "Walking the Dog." That's a pretty short song, which was good—I hadn't realized how out of shape I was.

I finished by throwing my arms wide and yelling: "*Mike! Mike! Mike!*" That was the only time Howie ever talked, and all I can say in my defense is that it really sounded more like a bark.

Mike rose from his chair, opened his arms, and fell forward. He knew I'd catch him, and I did. Kids half his age had given me the Howie-Hug all summer long, but no hug had ever felt so good. I only wished I could turn him around and squeeze him the way I had Hallie Stansfield, expelling what was wrong with him like an aspirated chunk of hotdog.

Face buried in the fur, he said: "You make a really good Howie, Dev."

I rubbed his head with one paw, knocking off his dogtop. I couldn't reply as Howie—barking his name was as close as I could come to that—but I was thinking, *A good kid deserves a good dog. Just ask Milo.*

Mike looked up into Howie's blue mesh eyes. "Will you come on the hoister with us?"

I gave him an exaggerated nod and patted his head again. Lane picked up Mike's new dogtop and stuck it back on his head.

Annie approached. Her hands were clasped demurely at her waist, but her eyes were full of merriment. "Can I unzip you, Mr. Howie?"

I wouldn't have minded, but of course I couldn't let her. Every show has its rules, and one of Joyland's—hard and fast—was that Howie the Happy Hound was *always* Howie the Happy Hound. You never took off the fur where the conies could see.

♥

I ducked back into Joyland Under, left the fur in the cart, and rejoined Annie and Mike at the ramp leading up to the Carolina Spin. Annie looked up nervously and said, "Are you sure you want to do this, Mike?"

"Yes! It's the one I want to do most!"

"All right, then. I guess." To me she added: "I'm not terrified of heights, but they don't exactly thrill me."

Lane was holding a car door open. "Climb aboard, folks. I'm

going to send you up where the air is rare." He bent down and scruffed Milo's ears. "You're sittin this one out, fella."

I sat on the inside, nearest the wheel. Annie sat in the middle, and Mike on the outside, where the view was best. Lane dropped the safety bar, went back to the controls, and reset his derby on a fresh slant. "Amazement awaits!" he called, and up we went, rising with the stately calm of a coronation procession.

Slowly, the world opened itself beneath us: first the park, then the bright cobalt of the ocean on our right and all of the North Carolina lowlands on our left. When the Spin reached the top of its great circle, Mike let go of the safety bar, raised his hands over his head, and shouted, *"We're flying!"*

A hand on my leg. Annie's. I looked at her and she mouthed two words: *Thank you*. I don't know how many times Lane sent us around—more spins than the usual ride, I think, but I'm not sure. What I remember best was Mike's face, pale and full of wonder, and Annie's hand on my thigh, where it seemed to burn. She didn't take it away until we slowed to a stop.

Mike turned to me. "Now I know what my kite feels like," he said.

So did I.

♥

When Annie told Mike he'd had enough, the kid didn't object. He was exhausted. As Lane helped him into his wheelchair, Mike held out a hand, palm up. "Slap me five if you're still alive."

Grinning, Lane slapped him five. "Come back anytime, Mike."

"Thanks. It was so great."

Lane and I pushed him up the midway. The booths on both sides were shut up again, but one of the shys was open: Annie

Oakley's Shootin' Gallery. Standing at the chump board, where Pop Allen had stood all summer long, was Fred Dean in his three-piece suit. Behind him, chain-driven rabbits and ducks traveled in opposite directions. Above them were bright yellow ceramic chicks. These were stationary, but very small.

"Like to try your shooting skill before you exit the park?" Fred asked. "There are no losers today. Today *ev*-rybody wins a prize."

Mike looked around at Annie. "Can I, mom?"

"Sure, honey. But not long, okay?"

He tried to get out of the chair, but couldn't. He was too tired. Lane and I propped him up, one on each side. Mike picked up a rifle and took a couple of shots, but he could no longer steady his arms, even though the gun was light. The beebees struck the canvas backdrop and clicked into the gutter at the bottom.

"Guess I suck," he said, putting the rifle down.

"Well, you didn't exactly burn it up," Fred allowed, "but as I said, today everyone wins a prize." With that, he handed over the biggest Howie on the shelf, a top stuffy that even sharp-shooters couldn't earn without spending eight or nine bucks on reloads.

Mike thanked him and sat back down, looking overwhelmed. That damn stuffed dog was almost as big as he was. "You try, Mom."

"No, that's okay," she said, but I thought she wanted to. It was something in her eyes as she measured the distance between the chump board and the targets.

"Please?" He looked first at me, then at Lane. "She's really good. She won the prone shooting tournament at Camp Perry before I was born and came in second twice. Camp Perry's in Ohio."

"I don't—"

Lane was already holding out one of the modified .22s. "Step right up. Let's see your best Annie Oakley, Annie."

She took the rifle and examined it in a way few of the conies ever did. "How many shots?"

"Ten a clip," Fred said.

"If I'm going to do this, can I shoot two clips?"

"As many as you want, ma'am. Today's your day."

"Mom used to also shoot skeet with my grampa," Mike told them.

Annie raised the .22 and squeezed off ten shots with a pause of perhaps two seconds between each. She knocked over two moving ducks and three of the moving bunnies. The teensy ceramic chicks she ignored completely.

"A crack shot!" Fred crowed. "Any prize on the middle shelf, your pick!"

She smiled. "Fifty percent isn't anywhere near crack. My dad would have covered his face for shame. I'll just take the reload, if that's okay."

Fred took a paper cone from under the counter—a wee shoot, in the Talk—and put the small end into a hole on top of the gag rifle. There was a rattle as another ten beebees rolled in.

"Are the sights on these trigged?" she asked Fred.

"No, ma'am. All the games at Joyland are straight. But if I told you Pop Allen—the man who usually runs this shy—spent long hours sighting them in, I'd be a liar."

Having worked on Pop's team, I knew that was disingenuous, to say the least. Sighting in the rifles was the *last* thing Pop would do. The better the rubes shot, the more prizes Pop had to give away…and he had to buy his own prizes. All the shy-bosses did. They were cheap goods, but not *free* goods.

"Shoots left and high," she said, more to herself than to us. Then she raised the rifle, socked it into the hollow of her right shoulder, and triggered off ten rounds. This time there was no discernable pause between shots, and she didn't bother with the ducks and bunnies. She aimed for the ceramic chicks and exploded eight of them.

As she put the gun back on the counter, Lane used his bandanna to wipe a smutch of sweat and grime from the back of his neck. He spoke very softly as he did this chore. "Jesus Horatio Christ. Nobody gets eight peeps."

"I only nicked the last one, and at this range I should have had them all." She wasn't boasting, just stating a fact.

Mike said, almost apologetically: "Told you she was good." He curled a fist over his mouth and coughed into it. "She was thinking about the Olympics, only then she dropped out of college."

"You really *are* Annie Oakley," Lane said, stuffing his bandanna back into a rear pocket. "Any prize, pretty lady. You pick."

"I already have my prize," she said. "This has been a wonderful, wonderful day. I can never thank you guys enough." She turned in my direction. "And *this* guy. Who actually had to talk me into it. Because I'm a fool." She kissed the top of Mike's head. "But now I better get my boy home. Where's Milo?"

We looked around and saw him halfway down Joyland Avenue, sitting in front of Horror House with his tail curled around his paws.

"Milo, come!" Annie called.

His ears pricked up but he didn't come. He didn't even turn in her direction, just stared at the façade of Joyland's only dark ride. I could almost believe he was reading the drippy, cobweb-festooned invitation: COME IN IF YOU DARE.

While Annie was looking at Milo, I stole a glance at Mike. Although he was all but done in from the excitements of the day, his expression was hard to mistake. It was satisfaction. I know it's crazy to think he and his Jack Russell had worked this out in advance, but I did think it.

I still do.

"Roll me down there, Mom," Mike said. "He'll come with me."

"No need for that," Lane said. "If you've got a leash, I'm happy to go get him."

"It's in the pocket on the back of Mike's wheelchair," Annie said.

"Um, probably not," Mike said. "You can check but I'm pretty sure I forgot it."

Annie checked while I thought, *In a pig's ass you forgot.*

"Oh, Mike," Annie said reproachfully. "Your dog, your responsibility. How many times have I told you?"

"Sorry, Mom." To Fred and Lane he said, "Only we hardly ever use it because Milo *always* comes."

"Except when we need him to." Annie cupped her hands around her mouth. "Milo, come *on*! Time to go home!" Then, in a much sweeter voice: "Biscuit, Milo! Come get a biscuit!"

Her coaxing tone would have brought me on the run—probably with my tongue hanging out—but Milo didn't budge.

"Come *on* Dev," Mike said. As if I were also in on the plan but had missed my cue, somehow. I grabbed the wheelchair's handles and rolled Mike down Joyland Avenue toward the fun-house. Annie followed. Fred and Lane stayed where they were, Lane leaning on the chump board among the laid-out popguns on their chains. He had removed his derby and was spinning it on one finger.

When we got to the dog, Annie regarded him crossly. "What's wrong with you, Milo?"

Milo thumped his tail at the sound of Annie's voice, but didn't look at her. Nor did he move. He was on guard and intended to stay that way unless he was hauled away.

"Michael, *please* make your dog heel so we can go home. You need to get some r—"

Two things happened before she could finish. I'm not exactly sure of the sequence. I've gone over it often in the years since then—most often on nights when I can't sleep—and I'm still not sure. I *think* the rumble came first: the sound of a ride-car starting to roll along its track. But it might have been the pad-lock dropping. It's even possible that both things happened at the same time.

The big American Master fell off the double doors below the Horror House façade and lay on the boards, gleaming in the October sunshine. Fred Dean said later that the shackle must not have been pushed firmly into the locking mechanism, and the vibration of the moving car caused it to open all the way. This made perfect sense, because the shackle was indeed open when I checked it.

Still bullshit, though.

I put that padlock on myself, and remember the click as the shackle clicked into place. I even remember tugging on it to make sure it caught, the way you do with a padlock. And all that begs a question Fred didn't even *try* to answer: with the Horror House breakers switched off, how could that car have gotten rolling in the first place? As for what happened next...

Here's how a trip through Horror House ended. On the far side of the Torture Chamber, just when you thought the ride was over and your guard was down, a screaming skeleton (nick-named Hagar the Horrible by the greenies) came flying at you, seemingly on a collision course with your car. When it pulled away, you saw a stone wall dead ahead. Painted there in fluo-rescent green was a rotting zombie and a gravestone with END OF THE LINE printed on it. Of course the stone wall split open just in time, but that final double-punch was extremely effec-tive. When the car emerged into the daylight, making a semi-circle before going back in through another set of double doors and stopping, even grown men were often screaming their heads off. Those final shrieks (always accompanied by gales of oh-shit-you-got-me laughter) were Horror House's best adver-tisement.

There were no screams that day. Of course not, because when the double doors banged open, the car that emerged was empty. It rolled through the semicircle, bumped lightly against the next set of double doors, and stopped.

"O-*kay*," Mike said. It was a whisper so low that I barely heard it, and I'm sure Annie didn't—all her attention had been drawn to the car. The kid was smiling.

"What made it do that?" Annie asked.

"I don't know," I said. "Short-circuit, maybe. Or some kind of power surge." Both of those explanations sounded good, as long as you didn't know about the breakers being off.

I stood on my tiptoes and peered into the stalled car. The

first thing I noticed was that the safety bar was up. If Eddie Parks or one of his greenie minions forgot to lower it, the bar was supposed to snap down automatically once the ride was in motion. It was a state-mandated safety feature. The bar being up on this one made a goofy kind of sense, though, since the only rides in the park that had power that morning were the ones Lane and Fred had turned on for Mike.

I spotted something beneath the semicircular seat, something as real as the roses Fred had given Annie, only not red.

It was a blue Alice band.

♥

We headed back to the van. Milo, once more on best behavior, padded along beside Mike's wheelchair.

"I'll be back as soon as I get them home," I told Fred. "Put in some extra hours."

He shook his head. "You're eighty-six for today. Get to bed early, and be here tomorrow at six. Pack a couple of extra sandwiches, because we'll all be working late. Turns out that storm's moving a little faster than the weather forecasters expected."

Annie looked alarmed. "Should I pack some stuff and take Mike to town, do you think? I'd hate to when he's so tired, but—"

"Check the radio this evening," Fred advised. "If NOAA issues a coastal evacuation order, you'll hear it in plenty of time, but I don't think that'll happen. This is just going to be your basic cap of wind. I'm a little worried about the high rides, that's all— the Thunderball, the Shaker, and the Spin."

"They'll be okay," Lane said. "They stood up to Agnes last year, and that was a bona fide hurricane."

"Does this storm have a name?" Mike asked.

"They're calling it Gilda," Lane said. "But it's no hurricane, just a little old subtropical depression."

Fred said, "Winds are supposed to start picking up around midnight, and the heavy rain'll start an hour or two later. Lane's probably right about the big rides, but it's still going to be a busy day. Have you got a slicker, Dev?"

"Sure."

"You'll want to wear it."

♥

The weather forecast we heard on WKLM as we left the park eased Annie's mind. The winds generated by Gilda weren't expected to top thirty miles an hour, with occasionally higher gusts. There might be some beach erosion and minor flooding inland, but that was about it. The dj called it "great kite-flying weather," which made us all laugh. We had a history now, and that was nice.

Mike was almost asleep by the time we arrived back at the big Victorian on Beach Row. I lifted him into his wheelchair. It wasn't much of a chore; I'd put on muscle in the last four months, and with those horrible braces off, he couldn't have weighed seventy pounds. Milo once more paced the chair as I rolled it up the ramp and into the house.

Mike needed the toilet, but when his mother tried to take over the wheelchair handles, Mike asked if I'd do it, instead. I rolled him into the bathroom, helped him to stand, and eased down his elastic-waisted pants while he held onto the grab bars.

"I hate it when she has to help me. I feel like a baby."

Maybe, but he pissed with a healthy kid's vigor. Then, as he leaned forward to push the flush handle, he staggered and almost took a header into the toilet bowl. I had to catch him.

"Thanks, Dev. I already washed my hair once today." That made me laugh, and Mike grinned. "I wish we *were* going to have a hurricane. That'd be boss."

"You might not think so if it happened." I was remembering Hurricane Doria, two years before. It hit New Hampshire and Maine packing ninety-mile-an-hour winds, knocking down trees all over Portsmouth, Kittery, Sanford, and the Berwicks. One big old pine just missed our house, our basement flooded, and the power had been out for four days.

"I wouldn't want stuff to fall down at the park, I guess. That's just about the best place in the world. That I've ever been, anyway."

"Good. Hold on, kid, let me get your pants back up. Can't have you mooning your mother."

That made him laugh again, only the laughter turned to coughing. Annie took over when we came out, rolling him down the hall to the bedroom. "Don't you sneak out on me, Devin," she called back over her shoulder.

Since I had the afternoon off, I had no intention of sneaking out on her if she wanted me to stay awhile. I strolled around the parlor, looking at things that were probably expensive but not terribly interesting—not to a young man of twenty-one, anyway. A huge picture window, almost wall-to-wall, saved what would otherwise have been a gloomy room, flooding it with light. The window looked out on the back patio, the boardwalk, and the ocean. I could see the first clouds feathering in from the southeast, but the sky overhead was still bright blue. I remember thinking that I'd made it to the big house after all, although I'd probably never have a chance to count all the bathrooms. I remember thinking about the Alice band, and wondering if Lane would see it when he put the wayward car back under cover. What else was I thinking? That I had seen a ghost after all. Just not of a person.

Annie came back. "He wants to see you, but don't stay long."

"Okay."

"Third door on the right."

I went down the hall, knocked lightly, and let myself in. Once you got past the grab bars, the oxygen tanks in the corner, and the leg braces standing at steely attention beside the bed, it could have been any boy's room. There was no baseball glove and no skateboard propped against the wall, but there were posters of Mark Spitz and Miami Dolphins running back Larry Csonka. In the place of honor above the bed, the Beatles were crossing Abbey Road.

There was a faint smell of liniment. Mike looked very small in the bed, all but lost under a green coverlet. Milo was curled up, nose to tail, beside him, and Mike was stroking his fur absently. It was hard to believe this was the same kid who had raised his hands triumphantly over his head at the apogee of the Carolina Spin. He didn't look sad, though. He looked almost radiant.

"Did you see her, Dev? Did you see her when she left?"

I shook my head, smiling. I had been jealous of Tom, but not of Mike. Never of Mike.

"I wish my grampa had been there. He would have seen her, and heard what she said when she left."

"What *did* she say?"

"Thanks. She meant both of us. And she told you to be careful. Are you sure you didn't hear her? Even a little?"

I shook my head again. No, not even a little.

"But you *know*." His face was too pale and tired, the face of a boy who was very sick, but his eyes were alive and healthy. "You *know*, don't you?"

"Yes." Thinking of the Alice band. "Mike, do you know what happened to her?"

"Someone killed her." Very low.

"I don't suppose she told you…"

But there was no need to finish. He was shaking his head.

"You need to sleep," I said.

"Yeah, I'll feel better after a nap. I always do." His eyes closed, then slowly opened again. "The Spin was the best. The hoister. It's like flying."

"Yes," I said. "It is like that."

This time when his eyes closed, they didn't re-open. I walked to the door as quietly as I could. As I put my hand on the knob, he said, "Be careful, Dev. It's not white."

I looked back. He was sleeping. I'm sure he was. Only Milo was watching me. I left, closing the door softly.

♥

Annie was in the kitchen. "I'm making coffee, but maybe you'd rather have a beer? I've got Blue Ribbon."

"Coffee would be fine."

"What do you think of the place?"

I decided to tell the truth. "The furnishings are a little elderly for my taste, but I never went to interior decorating school."

"Nor did I," she said. "Never even finished college."

"Join the club."

"Ah, but you will. You'll get over the girl who dumped you, and you'll go back to school, and you'll finish, and you'll march off into a brilliant future."

"How do you know about—"

"The girl? One, you might as well be wearing a sandwich board. Two, Mike knows. He told me. He's been *my* brilliant future. Once upon a time I was going to major in anthropology. I was going to win a gold medal at the Olympics. I was going to see strange and fabulous places and be the Margaret Mead of my generation. I was going to write books and do my best to earn back my father's love. Do you know who he is?"

"My landlady says he's a preacher."

"Indeed he is. Buddy Ross, the man in the white suit. He also has a great head of white hair. He looks like an older version of the Man from Glad in the TV ads. Mega church; big radio presence; now TV. Offstage, he's an asshole with a few good points." She poured two cups of coffee. "But that's pretty much true of all of us, isn't it? I think so."

"You sound like someone with regrets." It wasn't the politest thing to say, but we were beyond that. I hoped so, at least.

She brought the coffee and sat down opposite me. "Like the song says, I've had a few. But Mike's a great kid, and give my father this—he's taken care of us financially so I could be with Mike full-time. The way I look at it, checkbook love is better than no love at all. I made a decision today. I think it happened when you were wearing that silly costume and doing that silly dance. While I was watching Mike laugh."

"Tell me."

"I decided to give my father what he wants, which is to be

invited back into my son's life before it's too late. He said terrible things about how God caused Mike's MD to punish me for
my supposed sins, but I've got to put that behind me. If I wait
for an apology, I'll be waiting a long time…because in his heart,
Dad still believes that's true."

"I'm sorry."

She shrugged, as if it were of no matter. "I was wrong about
not letting Mike go to Joyland, and I've been wrong about holding
onto my old grudges and insisting on some sort of fucked-up
quid pro quo. My son isn't goods in a trading post. Do you think
thirty-one's too old to grow up, Dev?"

"Ask me when I get there."

She laughed. "*Touché*. Excuse me a minute."

She was gone for almost five. I sat at the kitchen table, sipping
my coffee. When she came back, she was holding her sweater
in her right hand. Her stomach was tanned. Her bra was a pale
blue, almost matching her faded jeans.

"Mike's fast asleep," she said. "Would you like to go upstairs
with me, Devin?"

♥

Her bedroom was large but plain, as if, even after all the months
she had spent here, she'd never fully unpacked. She turned to
me and linked her arms around my neck. Her eyes were very
wide and very calm. A trace of a smile touched the corners of her
mouth, making soft dimples. "'I bet you could do better, if you
had half a chance.' Remember me saying that?"

"Yes."

"Is that a bet I'd win?"

Her mouth was sweet and damp. I could taste her breath.

She drew back and said, "It can only be this once. You have to understand that."

I didn't want to, but I did. "Just as long as it's not…you know…"

She was really smiling now, almost laughing. I could see teeth as well as dimples. "As long as it's not a thank-you fuck? It's not, believe me. The last time I had a kid like you, I was a kid myself." She took my right hand and put it on the silky cup covering her left breast. I could feel the soft, steady beat of her heart. "I must not have let go of all my daddy issues yet, because I feel delightfully wicked."

We kissed again. Her hands dropped to my belt and un-buckled it. There was the soft rasp as my zipper went down, and then the side of her palm was sliding along the hard ridge beneath my shorts. I gasped.

"Dev?"

"What?"

"Have you ever done this before? Don't you dare lie to me."

"No."

"Was she an idiot? This girl of yours?"

"I guess we both were."

She smiled, slipped a cool hand inside my underwear, and gripped me. That sure hold, coupled with her gently moving thumb, made all of Wendy's efforts at boyfriend satisfaction seem very minor league. "So you're a virgin."

"Guilty as charged."

"Good."

♥

It *wasn't* just the once, and that was lucky for me, because the first time lasted I'm going to say eight seconds. Maybe nine. I got inside, that much I did manage, but then everything spurted everywhere. I may have been more embarrassed once—the time I blew an ass-trumpet while taking communion at Methodist Youth Camp—but I don't think so.

"Oh God," I said, and put a hand over my eyes.

She laughed, but there was nothing mean about it. "In a weird way, I'm flattered. Try to relax. I'm going downstairs for another check on Mike. I'd just as soon he didn't catch me in bed with Howie the Happy Hound."

"Very funny." I think if I'd blushed any harder, my skin would have caught on fire.

"I think you'll be ready again when I come back. It's the nice thing about being twenty-one, Dev. If you were seventeen, you'd probably be ready now."

She came back with a couple of sodas in an ice bucket, but when she slipped out of her robe and stood there naked, Coke was the last thing I wanted. The second time was quite a bit better; I think I might have managed four minutes. Then she began to cry out softly, and I was gone. But what a way to go.

♥

We drowsed, Annie with her head pillowed in the hollow of my shoulder. "Okay?" she asked.

"So okay I can't believe it."

I didn't see her smile, but I felt it. "After all these years, this bedroom finally gets used for something besides sleeping."

"Doesn't your father ever stay here?"

"Not for a long time, and I only started coming back because

Mike loves it here. Sometimes I can face the fact that he's almost certainly going to die, but mostly I can't. I just turn away from it. I make deals with myself. 'If I don't take him to Joyland, he won't die. If I don't make it up with my father so Dad can come and see him, he won't die. If we just stay here, he won't die.' A couple of weeks ago, the first time I had to make him put on his coat to go down to the beach, I cried. He asked me what was wrong, and I told him it was my time of the month. He knows what that is."

I remembered something Mike had said to her in the hospital parking lot: *It doesn't have to be the last good time*. But sooner or later the last good time would come around. It does for all of us.

She sat up, wrapping the sheet around her. "Remember me saying that Mike turned out to be my future? My brilliant career?"

"Yes."

"I can't think of another one. Anything beyond Michael is just …blank. Who said that in America there are no second acts?"

I took her hand. "Don't worry about act two until act one is over."

She slipped her hand free and caressed my face with it. "You're young, but not entirely stupid."

It was nice of her to say, but I certainly felt stupid. About Wendy, for one thing, but that wasn't the only thing. I found my mind drifting to those damn pictures in Erin's folder. Something about them…

She lay back down. The sheet slipped away from her nipples, and I felt myself begin to stir again. Some things about being twenty-one *were* pretty great. "The shooting gallery was fun. I forgot how good it is, sometimes, just to have that eye-and-hand thing going on. My father put a rifle in my hands for the first time when I was six. Just a little single-shot .22. I loved it."

"Yeah?"

She was smiling. "Yeah. It was our thing, the thing that worked. The *only* thing, as it turned out." She propped herself up on an elbow. "He's been selling that hellfire and brimstone shit since he was a teenager, and it's not just about the money—he got a triple helping of backroads gospel from his own parents, and I have no doubt he believes every word of it. You know what, though? He's still a southern man first and a preacher second. He's got a custom pickup truck that cost fifty thousand dollars, but a pickup truck is still a pickup truck. He still eats biscuits and gravy at Shoney's. His idea of sophisticated humor is Minnie Pearl and Junior Samples. He loves songs about cheatin and honky-tonkin. And he loves his guns. I don't care for his brand of Jesus and I have no interest in owning a pickup truck, but the guns…that he passed on to his only daughter. I go bang-bang and feel better. Shitty legacy, huh?"

I said nothing, only got out of bed and opened the Cokes. I gave one to her.

"He's probably got fifty guns at his full-time place in Savannah, most of them valuable antiques, and there's another half a dozen in the safe here. I've got two rifles of my own at my place in Chicago, although I hadn't shot at a target for two years before today. If Mike dies…" She held the Coke bottle to the middle of her forehead, as if trying to soothe a headache. "*When* Mike dies, the first thing I'm going to do is get rid of them all. They'd be too much temptation."

"Mike wouldn't want—"

"No, of course not, I know that, but it's not *all* about him. If

I could believe—like my holy-hat father—that I was going to find Mike waiting outside the golden gates to show me in after I die, that would be one thing. But I don't. I tried my ass off to believe that when I was a little girl, and I couldn't. God and heaven lasted about four years longer than the Tooth Fairy, but in the end, I couldn't. I think there's just darkness. No thought, no memory, no love. Just darkness. Oblivion. That's why I find what's happening to him so hard to accept."

"Mike knows it's more than oblivion," I said.

"What? Why? Why do you think that?"

Because she was there. He saw her, and he saw her go. Because she said thank you. And I know because I saw the Alice band, and Tom saw her.

"Ask him," I said. "But not today."

She put her Coke aside and studied me. She was wearing the little smile that put dimples at the corners of her mouth. "You've had seconds. I don't suppose you'd be interested in thirds?"

I put my own Coke down beside the bed. "As a matter of fact…"

She held out her arms.

♥

The first time was embarrassing. The second time was good. The third…man, the third time was the charm.

♥

I waited in the parlor while Annie dressed. When she came downstairs, she was back in her jeans and sweater. I thought of the blue bra just beneath the sweater, and damned if I didn't feel that stirring again.

"Are we good?" she said.

"Yes, but I wish we could be even better."

"I wish that, too, but this is as good as it's ever going to get. If you like me as much as I like you, you'll accept that. Can you?"

"Yes."

"Good."

"How much longer will you and Mike be here?"

"If the place doesn't blow away tonight, you mean?"

"It won't."

"A week. Mike's got a round of specialists back in Chicago starting on the seventeenth, and I want to get settled before then." She drew in a deep breath. "And talk to his grandpa about a visit. There'll have to be some ground rules. No Jesus, for one."

"Will I see you again before you leave?"

"Yes." She put her arms around me and kissed me. Then she stepped away. "But not like this. It would confuse things too much. I know you get that."

I nodded. I got it.

"You better go now, Dev. And thank you. It was lovely. We saved the best ride for last, didn't we?"

That was true. Not a dark ride but a bright one. "I wish I could do more. For you. For Mike."

"So do I," she said, "but that's not the world we live in. Come by tomorrow for supper, if the storm's not too bad. Mike would love to see you."

She looked beautiful, standing there barefooted in her faded jeans. I wanted to take her in my arms, and lift her, and carry her into some untroubled future.

Instead, I left her where she was. *That's not the world we live in*, she'd said, and how right she was.

How right she was.

♥

About a hundred yards down Beach Row, on the inland side of the two-lane, there was a little cluster of shops too tony to be called a strip mall: a gourmet grocery, a salon called Hair's Looking at You, a drugstore, a branch of the Southern Trust, and a restaurant called Mi Casa, where the Beach Row elite no doubt met to eat. I didn't give those shops so much as a glance when I drove back to Heaven's Bay and Mrs. Shoplaw's. If ever I needed proof that I didn't have the gift that Mike Ross and Rozzie Gold shared, that was it.

♥

Go to bed early, Fred Dean had told me, and I did. I lay on my back with my hands behind my head, listening to the waves as I had all summer long, remembering the touch of her hands, the firmness of her breasts, the taste of her mouth. Mostly it was her eyes I thought about, and the fan of her hair on the pillow. I didn't love her the way I loved Wendy—that sort of love, so strong and stupid, only comes once—but I loved her. I did then and still do now. For her kindness, mostly, and her patience. Some young man somewhere may have had a better initiation into the mysteries of sex, but no young man ever had a sweeter one.

Eventually, I slept.

♥

It was a banging shutter somewhere below that woke me. I picked my watch up from the night table and saw it was quarter of one. I didn't think there was going to be any more sleep for me until that banging stopped, so I got dressed, started out the door, then returned to the closet for my slicker. When I got

downstairs, I paused. From the big bedroom down the hall
from the parlor, I could hear Mrs. S. sawing wood in long, noisy
strokes. No banging shutter was going to break her rest.

It turned out I didn't need the slicker, at least not yet, because
the rain hadn't started. The wind was strong, though; it had to
be blowing twenty-five already. The low, steady thud of the surf
had become a muted roar. I wondered if the weather boffins
had underestimated Gilda, thought of Annie and Mike in the
house down the beach, and felt a tickle of unease.

I found the loose shutter and re-fastened it with the hook-
and-eye. I let myself back in, went upstairs, undressed, and lay
down again. This time sleep wouldn't come. The shutter was
quiet, but there was nothing I could do about the wind moaning
around the eaves (and rising to a low scream each time it gusted).
Nor could I turn off my brain, now that it was running again.

It's not white, I thought. That meant nothing to me, but it
wanted to mean something. It wanted to connect with something I'd seen at the park during our visit.

There's a shadow over you, young man. That had been Rozzie
Gold, on the day that I'd met her. I wondered how long she had
worked at Joyland, and where she had worked before. Was she
carny-from-carny? And what did it matter?

One of these children has the sight. I don't know which.

I knew. Mike had seen Linda Gray. And set her free. He had,
as they say, shown her the door. The one she hadn't been able
to find herself. Why else would she have thanked him?

I closed my eyes and saw Fred at the Shootin' Gallery, re-
splendent in his suit and magic top hat. I saw Lane holding out
one of the .22s chained to the chump board.

Annie: *How many shots?*

Fred: *Ten a clip. As many as you want. Today's your day.*

My eyes flew open as several things came crashing together in my mind. I sat up, listening to the wind and the agitated surf. Then I turned on the overhead light and got Erin's folder out of my desk drawer. I laid the photographs on the floor again, my heart pounding. The pix were good but the light wasn't. I dressed for the second time, shoved everything back into the folder, and made another trip downstairs.

A lamp hung above the Scrabble table in the middle of the parlor, and I knew from the many evenings I'd gotten my ass kicked that the light it cast was plenty bright. There were sliding doors between the parlor and the hall leading to Mrs. S.'s quarters. I pulled them shut so the light wouldn't disturb her. Then I turned on the lamp, moved the Scrabble box to the top of the TV, and laid my photos out. I was too agitated to sit down. I bent over the table instead, arranging and re-arranging the photographs. I was about to do that for the third time when my hand froze. I saw it. I saw *him*. Not proof that would stand up in court, no, but enough for me. My knees came unhinged, and I sat down after all.

The phone I'd used so many times to call my father—always noting down the time and duration on the guest-call honor sheet when I was done—suddenly rang. Only in that windy early morning silence, it sounded more like a scream. I lunged at it and picked up the receiver before it could ring again.

"H-H-Hel—" It was all I could manage. My heart was pounding too hard for more.

"It's you," the voice on the other end said. He sounded both amused and pleasantly surprised. "I was expecting your land-lady. I had a story about a family emergency all ready."

I tried to speak. Couldn't.

"Devin?" Teasing. *Cheerful.* "Are you there?"

"I…just a second."

I held the phone to my chest, wondering (it's crazy how your mind can work when it's put under sudden stress) if he could hear my heart at his end of the line. On mine, I listened for Mrs. Shoplaw. I heard her, too: the muted sound of her continuing snores. It was a good thing I'd closed the parlor doors, and a better thing that there was no extension in her bedroom. I put the phone back to my ear and said, "What do you want? Why are you calling?"

"I think you know, Devin…and even if you didn't, it's too late now, isn't it?"

"Are you psychic, too?" It was stupid, but right then my brain and my mouth seemed to be running on separate tracks.

"That's Rozzie," he said. "Our Madame Fortuna." He actually laughed. He sounded relaxed, but I doubt if he was. Killers don't make telephone calls in the middle of the night if they're relaxed. Especially if they can't be sure of who's going to answer the phone.

But he had a story, I thought. *This guy's a Boy Scout, he's crazy but always prepared. The tattoo, for instance. That's what takes your eye when you look at those photos. Not the face. Not the baseball cap.*

"I knew what you were up to," he said. "I knew even before the girl brought you that folder. The one with the pictures in it. Then today…with the pretty mommy and the crippled kid… have you told them, Devin? Did they help you work it out?"

"They don't know anything."

The wind gusted. I could hear it at his end, too…as if he were outside. "I wonder if I can believe you."

"You can. You absolutely can." Looking down at the pictures. Tattoo Man with his hand on Linda Gray's ass. Tattoo Man helping her aim her rifle at the Shootin' Gallery.

Lane: *Let's see your best Annie Oakley, Annie.*

Fred: *A crack shot!*

Tattoo Man in his fishtop cap and dark glasses and sandy blond goatee. You could see the bird tattoo on his hand because the rawhide gloves had stayed in his back pocket until he and Linda Gray were in Horror House. Until he had her in the dark.

"I wonder," he said again. "You were in that big old house for a long time this afternoon, Devin. Were you talking about the pictures the Cook girl brought, or were you just fucking her? Maybe it was both. Mommy's a tasty piece, all right."

"They don't know anything," I repeated. I was speaking low and fixing my gaze on the closed parlor doors. I kept expecting them to open and to see Mrs. S. standing there in her night-gown, her face ghostly with cream. "Neither do I. Not that I could prove."

"Probably not, but it would only be a matter of time. You can't unring the bell. Do you know that old saying?"

"Sure, sure." I didn't, but at that moment I would have agreed with him if he'd declared that Bobby Rydell (a yearly performer at Joyland) was president.

"Here's what you're going to do. You're going to come to Joyland, and we'll talk this out, face to face. Man to man."

"Why would I do that? That would be pretty crazy, if you're who I—"

"Oh, you know I am." He sounded impatient. "And *I* know that if you went to the police, they'd find out I came onboard at Joyland only a month or so after Linda Gray was killed. Then they'd put me with the Wellman show and Southern Star Amusements, and there goes the ballgame."

"So why don't I call them right now?"

"Do you know where I am?" Anger was creeping into his voice. No—venom. "Do you know where I am right now, you nosy little sonofabitch?"

"Joyland, probably. In admin."

"Not at all. I'm at the shopping center on Beach Row. The one where the rich bitches go to buy their macrobiotics. Rich bitches like your girlfriend."

A cold finger began to trace its course—its very slow course—down the length of my spine from the nape of my neck to the crack of my ass. I said nothing.

"There's a pay phone outside the drugstore. Not a booth, but that's okay because it isn't raining yet. Just windy. That's where I am. I can see your girlfriend's house from where I'm standing. There's a light on in the kitchen—probably the one she leaves on all night—but the rest of the house is dark. I could hang up this phone and be there in sixty seconds."

"There's a burglar alarm!" I didn't know if there was or not.

He laughed. "At this point, do you think I give a shit? It won't stop me from cutting her throat. But first I'll make her watch me do it to the little cripple."

You won't rape her, though, I thought. *You wouldn't even if there was time. I don't think you can.*

I came close to saying it, but didn't. As scared as I was, I knew that goading him right now would be a very bad idea.

"You were so nice to them today," I said stupidly. "Flowers… prizes…the rides…"

"Yeah, all the rube shit. Tell me about the car that came popping out of the funhouse shy. What was *that* about?"

"I don't know."

"I think you do. Maybe we'll discuss it. At Joyland. I know

your Ford, Jonesy. It's got the flickery left headlight and the cute little pinwheel on the antenna. If you don't want me in that house cutting throats, you're going to get in it right now, and you're going to drive down Beach Row to Joyland."

"I—"

"Shut up when I'm talking to you. When you pass the shopping center, you'll see me standing by one of the park trucks. I'll give you four minutes to get here from the time I hang up the phone. If I don't see you, I'll kill the woman and the kid. Understand?"

"I…"

"Do you understand?"

"Yes!"

"I'll follow you to the park. Don't worry about the gate; it's already open."

"So you'll either kill me or them. I get to choose. Is that it?"

"Kill you?" He sounded honestly surprised. "I'm not going to kill you, Devin. That would only make my position worse. No, I'm going to do a fade. It won't be the first time, and it probably won't be the last. What I want is to talk. I want to know how you got onto me."

"I could tell you that over the phone."

He laughed. "And spoil your chance to overpower me and be Howie the Hero again? First the little girl, then Eddie Parks, and the pretty mommy and her crippled-up brat for the exciting climax. How could you pass that up?" He stopped laughing. "Four minutes."

"I—"

He hung up. I stared down at the glossy photos. I opened the drawer in the Scrabble table, took out one of the pads, and

fumbled for the mechanical pencil Tina Ackerley always insisted
on using to keep score. I wrote: *Mrs. S. If you're reading this,
something has happened to me. I know who killed Linda Gray.
Others, too.*

I wrote his name in capital letters.

Then I ran for the door.

♥

My Ford's starter spun and sputtered and did not catch. Then it
began to slow. All summer I'd been telling myself I had to get a
new battery, and all summer I'd found other things to spend
my money on.

My father's voice: *You're flooding it, Devin.*

I took my foot off the gas and sat there in the dark. Time
seemed to be racing, racing. Part of me wanted to run back
inside and call the police. I couldn't call Annie because I didn't
have her fucking phone number, and given her famous father,
it would be unlisted. Did *he* know that? Probably not, but he
had the luck of the devil. As brazen as he was, the murdering
son of a bitch should have been caught three or four times already, but hadn't been. Because he had the luck of the devil.

She'll hear him breaking in and she'll shoot him.

Only the guns were in the safe, she'd said so. Even if she got
one, she'd probably find the bastard holding his straight-razor
to Mike's throat when she confronted him.

I turned the key again, and with my foot off the accelerator
and the carb full of gas, my Ford started up at once. I backed
down the driveway and turned toward Joyland. The circular
red neon of the Spin and the blue neon swoops of the Thunderball stood out against low, fast-running clouds. Those two rides
were always lit on stormy nights, partly as a beacon for ships at

sea, partly to warn away any low-flying small aircraft bound for the Parish County Airport.

Beach Row was deserted. Sheets of sand blew across it with every gust of wind, some of those gusts strong enough to shake my car. Dunelets were already starting to build up on the macadam. In my headlights, they looked like skeleton fingers.

When I passed the shopping center, I saw a single figure standing in the middle of the parking lot next to one of the Joyland maintenance trucks. He raised a hand to me as I went past and gave a single solemn wave.

The big Victorian on the beach side came next. There *was* a light on in the kitchen. I thought it was the fluorescent over the sink. I remembered Annie coming into the room with her sweater in her hand. Her tanned stomach. The bra almost the same color as her jeans. *Would you like to go upstairs with me, Devin?*

Lights bloomed in my rearview mirror and pulled up close. He was using his brights and I couldn't see the vehicle behind them, but I didn't have to. I knew it was the maintenance truck, just as I knew he had been lying when he said he wasn't going to kill me. The note I'd left for Mrs. Shoplaw would still be there in the morning. She would read it, and the name I had written there. The question was how long it would take her to believe it. He was such a charmer, him with his rhyming patter, winning smile, and cocked derby lid. Why, all the women loved Lane Hardy.

♥

The gates were open, as promised. I drove through them and tried to park in front of the now-shuttered Shootin' Gallery. He gave his horn a brief blip and flashed his lights: *Drive on.* When I got to the Spin, he flashed his lights again. I turned off my

Ford, very aware that I might never start it again. The hoister's red neon cast a blood-colored light over the dashboard, the seats, my own skin.

The truck's headlights went out. I heard the door open and shut. And I heard the wind blowing through the Spin's struts—tonight that sound was a harpy's screech. There was a steady, almost syncopated rattling sound, as well. The wheel was shaking on its tree-thick axle.

The Gray girl's killer—and DeeDee Mowbray's, and Claudine Sharp's, and Darlene Stamnacher's—walked to my car and tapped on the window with the barrel of a pistol. With his other hand he made a beckoning gesture. I opened the door and got out.

"You said you weren't going to kill me." It sounded as weak as my legs felt.

Lane smiled his charming smile. "Well…we'll see which way the flow's gonna go. Won't we?"

Tonight his derby was cocked to the left and pulled down tight so it wouldn't fly off. His hair, let loose from its workday ponytail, blew around his neck. The wind gusted and the Spin gave an unhappy screech. The red glow of the neon flickered across his face as it shook.

"Don't worry about the hoister," he said. "If it was solid it might blow over, but the wind shoots right through the struts. You've got other things to worry about. Tell me about the funhouse car. That's what I really want to know. How'd you do that? Was it some kind of remote gadget? I'm very interested in those things. They're the wave of the future, that's what I think."

"There was no gadget."

He didn't seem to hear me. "Also what was the point? Was it

supposed to flush me out? If it was, you didn't need to bother. I was already flushed."

"*She* did it," I said. I didn't know if that was strictly true, but I had no intention of bringing Mike into this conversation. "Linda Gray. Didn't you see her?"

The smile died. "Is that the best you can manage? The old ghost-in-the-funhouse story? You'll have to do a little better than that."

So he hadn't seen her any more than I had. But I think he knew there was *something*. I'll never know for sure, but I think that was why he offered to go after Milo. He hadn't wanted us anywhere near Horror House.

"Oh, she was there. I saw her headband. Remember me looking in? It was under the seat."

He lashed out so suddenly I didn't even have a chance to get my hand up. The barrel of the gun slammed across my forehead, opening a gash. I saw stars. Then blood poured into my eyes and I saw only that. I staggered back against the rail beside the ramp leading to the Spin and gripped it to keep from falling down. I swiped at my face with the sleeve of my slicker.

"I don't know why you'd bother trying to spook me with a campfire story at this late date," he said, "and I don't appreciate it. You know about the headband because there was a picture of it in the folder your nosy college-cunt girlfriend brought you." He smiled. There was nothing charming about this one; it was all teeth. "Don't kid a kidder, kiddo."

"But…you didn't *see* the folder." The answer to that one was a simple deduction even with my head ringing. "Fred saw it. And told you. Didn't he?"

"Yep. On Monday. We were having lunch together in his

office. He said that you and the college cunt were playing Hardy Boys, although he didn't put it quite that way. He thought it was sort of cute. I didn't, because I'd seen you stripping off Eddie Parks's gloves after he had his heart attack. That's when *I* knew you were playing Hardy Boys. That folder…Fred said the cunt had pages of notes. I knew it was only a matter of time before she put me with Wellman's and Southern Star."

I had an alarming picture of Lane Hardy riding the train to Annandale with a straight razor in his pocket. "Erin doesn't know anything."

"Oh, relax. Do you think I'm going after her? Apply some strain and use your brain. And take a little stroll while you do it. Up the ramp, champ. You and I are going for a ride. Up there where the air is rare."

I started to ask him if he was crazy, but that would have been sort of a stupid question at this late date, wouldn't it?

"What have you got to grin about, Jonesy?"

"Nothing," I said. "You don't really want to go up with the wind blowing like this, do you?" But the Spin's engine was running. I hadn't been aware of it over the wind, the surf, and the eerie scream of the ride itself, but now that I was listening, I heard it: a steady rumble. Almost a purr. Something fairly obvious came to me: he was probably planning to turn the gun on himself after he finished with me. Maybe you think that should have occurred to me sooner, because crazy people have a way of doing that—you read about it in the paper all the time. Maybe you'd be right. But I was under a lot of stress.

"Old Carolina's safe as houses," he said. "I'd go up in her if the wind was blowing sixty instead of just thirty. It blew at least that hard when Carla skimmed past the coast two years ago, and she was just fine."

"How are you going to put it in gear if we're both in the car?"

"Get in and see. Or…" He lifted the gun. "Or I can shoot you right here. I'm good with it either way."

I walked up the ramp, opened the door of the car currently sitting at the loading station, and started to climb in.

"No, no, no," he said. "You want to be on the outside. Better view. Stand aside, Clyde. And put your hands in your pockets."

Lane sidled past me, the gun leveled. More blood was trickling into my eyes and down my cheeks, but I didn't dare take a hand from my slicker pocket to wipe it off. I could see how white his finger was on the trigger of the pistol. He sat down on the inside of the car.

"*Now* you."

I got in. I didn't see any choice.

"And close the door, that's what it's there for."

"You sound like Dr. Seuss," I said.

He grinned. "Flattery will get you nowhere. Close the door or I'll put a bullet in your knee. You think anyone will hear it over this wind? I don't."

I closed the door. When I looked at him again, he had the pistol in one hand and a square metal gadget in the other. It had a stubby antenna. "Told you, I love these gadgets. This one's your basic garage door-opener with a couple of small modifications. Sends a radio signal. Showed it to Mr. Easterbrook this spring, told him it was the perfect thing for wheel maintenance when there wasn't a greenie or a gazoonie around to run the ground-side controls. He said I couldn't use it because it hasn't been safety-approved by the state commission. Cautious old sonofa-bitch. I was going to patent it. Too late now, I guess. Take it."

I took it. It *was* a garage door opener. A Genie. My dad had one almost exactly like it.

"See the button with the up arrow?"

"Yes."

"Push it."

I put my thumb on the button, but didn't push it. The wind was strong down here; how much stronger up there, where the air was rare? *We're flying!* Mike had shouted.

"Push it or take one in the knee, Jonesy."

I pushed the button. The Spin's motor geared down at once, and our car began to rise.

"Now throw it over the side."

"*What?*"

"Throw it over the side or you get one in the knee and you'll never two-step again. I'll give you a three-count. One…t—"

I threw his controller over the side. The wheel rose and rose into the windy night. To my right I could see the waves pounding in, their crests marked by foam so white it looked phosphorescent. On the left, the land was dark and sleeping. Not a single set of headlights moved on Beach Row. The wind gusted. My blood-sticky hair flew back from my forehead in clumps. The car rocked. Lane threw himself forward, then back, making the car rock more…but the gun, now pointed at my side, never wavered. Red neon skimmed lines along the barrel.

He shouted, *"Not so much like a grandma ride tonight, is it, Jonesy?"*

It sure wasn't. Tonight the staid old Carolina Spin was terrifying. As we reached the top, a savage gust shook the wheel so hard I heard our car rattling on the steel supports that held it. Lane's derby flew off into the night.

"Shit! Well, there's always another one."

Lane, how are we going to get off? The question rose behind my lips, but I didn't ask. I was too afraid he'd tell me we weren't, that if the storm didn't blow the Spin over and if the power didn't go out, we'd still be going around and around when Fred got here in the morning. Two dead men on Joyland's chump-hoister. Which made my next move rather obvious.

Lane was smiling. "You want to try for the gun, don't you? I can see it in your eyes. Well, it's like Dirty Harry said in that movie—you have to ask yourself if you feel lucky."

We were going down now, the car still rocking but not quite so much. I decided I didn't feel lucky at all.

"How many have you killed, Lane?"

"None of your fucking business. And since I have the gun, I think I should get to ask the questions. How long have you known? Quite a while, right? At least since the college cunt showed you the pictures. You just held off so the cripple could get his day at the park. Your mistake, Jonesy. A rube's mistake."

"I only figured it out tonight," I said.

"Liar, liar, pants on fire."

We swept past the ramp and started up again. I thought, *He's probably going to shoot me when the car's at the top. Then he'll either shoot himself or push me out, slide over, and jump onto the ramp when the car comes back down. Take his chances on not breaking a leg or a collarbone.* I was betting on the murder-suicide scenario, but not until his curiosity was satisfied.

I said, "Call me stupid if you want, but don't call me a liar. I kept looking at the pictures, and I kept seeing something in them, something familiar, but until tonight I couldn't quite figure out what it was. It was the hat. You were wearing a fishtop baseball cap in the photos, not a derby, but it was tilted one way when you and the Gray girl were at the Whirly Cups, and the other when you were at the Shootin' Gallery. I looked at the rest, the ones where the two of you are only in the background, and saw the same thing. Back and forth, back and forth. You do it all the time. You don't even think about it."

"That's *all*? A fucking tilted cap?"

"No."

We were reaching the top for the second time, but I thought I was good for at least one more turn. He wanted to hear this. Then the rain started, a hard squall that turned on like a shower spigot. *At least it'll wash the blood off my face*, I thought. When I looked at him, I saw that wasn't all it was washing off.

"One day I saw you with your hat off and I thought your hair was showing the first strands of white." I was almost yelling to be heard over the wind and the rush of the rain. It was coming sideways, hitting us in the face. "Yesterday I saw you wiping the back of your neck. I thought it was dirt. Then tonight, after I got the thing about the cap, I started thinking about the fake bird tattoo. Erin saw how the sweat made it run. I guess the cops missed that."

I could see my car and the maintenance truck, growing larger as the Spin neared the bottom of its circle for the second time. Beyond them, something large—a wind-loosened swatch of canvas, maybe—was blowing up Joyland Avenue.

"It wasn't dirt you were wiping off, it was dye. It was running, just like the tattoo ran. Like it's running now. It's all over your neck. It wasn't strands of white hair I saw, it was strands of *blond*."

He wiped his neck and looked at the black smear on his palm. I almost went for him then, but he raised the gun and all at once I was looking into a black eye. It was small but terrible.

"I *used* to be blond," he said, "but under the black I'm mostly gray now. I've lived a stressful life, Jonesy." He smiled ruefully, as though this were some sad joke we were both in on.

We were going up again, and I had just a moment to think that the thing I'd seen blowing up the midway—what I'd taken for a big square of loose canvas—could have been a car with its headlights out. It was crazy to hope, but I hoped, anyway.

The rain slashed at us. My slicker rippled. Lane's hair flew like a ragged flag. I hoped I could keep him from pulling the trigger for at least one more spin. Maybe two? Possible but not probable.

"Once I let myself think of you as Linda Gray's killer—and it wasn't easy, Lane, not after the way you took me in and showed me the ropes—I could see past the hat and sunglasses and face-hair. I could see *you*. You weren't working here—"

"I was running a forklift in a warehouse in Florence." He wrinkled his nose. "Rube work. I hated it."

"You were working in Florence, you met Linda Gray in Florence, but you knew all about Joyland over here in NC, didn't you? I don't know if you're carny-from-carny, but you've never been able to stay away from the shows. And when you suggested a little road trip, she went along with it."

"I was her secret boyfriend. I told her I had to be. Because I was older." He smiled. "She bought it. They all do. You'd be surprised how much the young ones will buy."

You sick fuck, I thought. *You sick, sick fuck.*

"You brought her to Heaven's Bay, you stayed at a motel, and then you killed her here at Joyland even though you must have known about the Hollywood Girls running around with their cameras. Bold as brass. That was part of the kick, wasn't it? Sure it was. You did it on a ride full of conies—"

"Rubes," he said. The hardest gust yet shook the Spin, but he seemed not to feel it. Of course, he was on the inside of the wheel where things were a little calmer. "Call em what they are. They're just rubes, all of them. They see nothing. It's like their eyes are connected to their assholes instead of their brains. Everything goes right through."

"You get off on the risk, don't you? That's why you came back and hired on."

"Not even a month later." His smile widened. "All this time I've been right under their noses. And you know what? I've been…you know, good…ever since that night in the funhouse. All the bad stuff was behind me. I could have gone on being good. I like it here. I was building a life. I had my gadget, and I was going to patent it."

"Oh, I think sooner or later you would have done it again." We were back at the top. The wind and rain pelted us. I was shivering. My clothes were soaked; Lane's cheeks were dark with hair-dye. It ran down his skin in tendrils. *His mind is like that*, I thought. *On the inside, where he never smiles.*

"No. I was cured. I have to do you, Jonesy, but only because you stuck your nose in where it doesn't belong. It's too bad, because I liked you. I really did."

I thought he was telling the truth, which made what was happening even more horrible.

We were going back down. The world below was windy and rain-soaked. There had been no car with its headlights out, only a blowing piece of canvas that for a moment looked like

that to my yearning mind. The cavalry wasn't coming. Thinking
it was would only get me killed. I had to do this myself, and the
only chance I had was to make him mad. *Really* mad.

"You get off on risk, but you don't get off on rape, do you? If
you did, you would have taken them to some isolated place.
I think what your secret girlfriends have between their legs
scares you limp. What do you do later? Lie in bed and jack off
thinking about how brave you are, killing defenseless girls?"

"Shut up."

"You can fascinate them, but you can't fuck them." The wind
shouted; the car rocked. I was going to die and at that moment
I didn't give shit one. I didn't know how angry I was making
him, but I was angry enough for both of us. "What happened to
make you this way? Did your mother put a clothespin on your
peepee when you went weewee in the corner? Did Uncle Stan
make you give him a blowjob? Or was it—"

"*Shut up!*" He rose into a crouch, gripping the safety bar in
one hand and pointing the gun at me with the other. A stroke of
lightning lit him up: staring eyes, lank hair, working mouth.
And the gun. "*Shut your dirty mou—*"

"*DEVIN, DUCK!*"

I didn't think about it, I just did it. There was a whipcrack
report, an almost liquid sound in the blowing night. The bullet
must have gone right past me, but I didn't hear it or feel it, the
way characters do in books. The car we were in swept past the
loading point and I saw Annie Ross standing on the ramp with a
rifle in her hands. The van was behind her. Her hair was blowing
around her bone-white face.

We started up again. I looked at Lane. He was frozen in his
crouch, his mouth ajar. Black dye ran down his cheeks. His eyes

were rolled up so only the bottom half of the irises showed. Most of his nose was gone. One nostril hung down by his upper lip, but the rest of it was just a red ruin surrounding a black hole the size of a dime.

He sat down on the seat, hard. Several of his front teeth rattled out of his mouth when he did. I plucked the gun from his hand and tossed it over the side. What I was feeling right then was...nothing. Except in some very deep part of me, where I had begun to realize this might not be my night to die, after all.

"Oh," he said. Then he said "Ah." Then he slumped forward, chin on chest. He looked like a man considering his options, and very carefully.

There was more lightning as the car reached the top. It illuminated my seatmate in a stutter of blue fire. The wind blew and the Spin moaned in protest. We were coming down again.

From below, almost lost in the storm: *"Dev, how do I stop it?"*

I first thought of telling her to look for the remote control gadget, but in the storm she could hunt for half an hour and still not find it. Even if she did, it might be broken or lying shorted out in a puddle. Besides, there was a better way.

"Go to the motor!" I shouted. *"Look for the red button! RED BUTTON, ANNIE! It's the emergency stop!"*

I swept past her, registering the same jeans and sweater she'd worn earlier, both now soaked and plastered to her. No jacket, no hat. She had come in a hurry, and I knew who had sent her. How much simpler it would have been if Mike had focused on Lane at the start. But Rozzie never had, even though she'd known him for years, and I was to find out later that Mike never focused on Lane Hardy at all.

I was going back up again. Beside me, Lane's soaking hair

was dripping black rain into his lap. *"Wait until I come back down!"*

"*What?*"

I didn't bother trying again; the wind would have drowned it out. I could only hope she wouldn't hammer on the red button while I was at the top of the ride. As the car rose into the worst of the storm the lightning flashed again, and this time there was an accompanying crack of thunder. As if it had roused him—perhaps it had—Lane lifted his head and looked at me. *Tried* to look at me; his eyes had come back level in their sockets, but were now pointing in opposite directions. That terrible image has never left my mind, and still comes to me at the oddest times: going through turnpike tollbooths, drinking a cup of coffee in the morning with the CNN anchors baying bad news, getting up to piss at three AM, which some poet or other has rightly dubbed the Hour of the Wolf.

He opened his mouth and blood poured out. He made a grinding insectile sound, like a cicada burrowing into a tree. A spasm shook him. His feet tap-danced briefly on the steel floor of the car. They stilled, and his head dropped forward again.

Be dead, I thought. *Please be dead this time.*

As the Spin started down again, a bolt of lightning struck the Thunderball; I saw the tracks light up briefly. I thought, *That could have been me*. The hardest gust of wind yet struck the car. I held on for dear life. Lane flopped like a big doll.

I looked down at Annie—her white face staring up, her eyes squinted against the rain. She was inside the rail, standing next to the motor. So far, so good. I put my hands around my mouth. *"The red button!"*

"*I see it!*"

"Wait until I tell you!"

The ground was coming up. I grabbed the bar. When the late (at least I hoped he was) Lane Hardy was at the control stick, the Spin always came to an easy halt, the cars up top swaying gently. I had no idea what an emergency stop would be like, but I was going to find out.

"Now, Annie! Push it now!"

It was a good thing I was holding on. My car stopped dead about ten feet from the unloading point and still five feet above the ground. The car tilted. Lane was thrown forward, his head and torso flopping over the bar. Without thinking, I grabbed his shirt and pulled him back. One of his hands flopped into my lap and I flung it away with a grunt of disgust.

The bar wouldn't unlock, so I had to wriggle out from beneath it.

"Be careful, Dev!" Annie was standing beside the car, holding up her hands, as if to catch me. She had propped the rifle she'd used to end Hardy's life against the motor housing.

"Step back," I said, and threw one leg over the side of the car. More lightning flashed. The wind howled and the Spin howled back. I got hold of a strut and swung out. My hands slipped on the wet metal and I dropped. I went to my knees. A moment later she was pulling me to my feet.

"Are you all right?"

"Yes."

I wasn't, though. The world was swimming, and I was on the edge of a faint. I lowered my head, gripped my legs just above the knees, and began taking deep breaths. For a moment it could have gone either way, but then things began to solidify. I stood up again, careful not to move too fast.

It was hard to tell with the rain bucketing down, but I was

pretty sure she was crying. "I had to do it. He was going to kill you. Wasn't he? Please, Dev, say he was going to kill you. Mike *said* he was, and—"

"You can quit worrying about that, believe me. And I wouldn't have been his first. He's killed four women." I thought of Erin's speculation about the years when there had been no bodies— none discovered, at least. "Maybe more. *Probably* more. We have to call the police. There's a phone in—"

I started to point toward Mysterio's Mirror Mansion, but she grabbed my arm. "No. You can't. Not yet."

"Annie—"

She thrust her face close to mine, almost kissing distance, but kissing was the last thing on her mind. "How did I get here? Am I supposed to tell the police that a ghost showed up in my son's room in the middle of the night and told him you'd die on the Ferris wheel if I didn't come? Mike can't be a part of this, and if you tell me I'm being an overprotective mom, I'll...I'll kill you myself."

"No," I said. "I won't tell you that."

"So how did I get here?"

At first I didn't know. You have to remember that I was still scared myself. Only scared doesn't cover it. Scared isn't even in the ballpark. I was in shock. Instead of Mysterio's, I led her to her van and helped her sit behind the wheel. Then I went around and got in on the passenger side. By then I had an idea. It had the virtue of simplicity, and I thought it would fly. I shut the door and took my wallet out of my hip pocket. I almost dropped it on the floor when I opened it; I was shaking like crazy. Inside there were plenty of things to write on, but I had nothing to write with.

"Please tell me you have a pen or a pencil, Annie."

"Maybe in the glove compartment. *You'll* have to call the police, Dev. I have to get back to Mike. If they arrest me for leaving the scene or something...or for murder..."

"Nobody's going to arrest you, Annie. You saved my life." I was pawing through the glove compartment as I talked. There was an owner's manual, piles of gasoline credit card receipts, Rolaids, a bag of M&Ms, even a Jehovah's Witnesses pamphlet asking if I knew where I was going to spend the afterlife, but no pen or pencil.

"You can't wait...in a situation like that...that's what I was always told..." Her words came in chunks because her teeth were chattering. "Just aim...and squeeze before you can...you know...second-guess yourself...it was supposed to go between his eyes, but...the wind...I guess the wind..."

She shot out a hand and gripped my shoulder hard enough to hurt. Her eyes were huge.

"Did I hit you, too, Dev? There's a gash in your forehead and blood on your shirt!"

"You didn't hit me. He pistol-whipped me a little, that's all. Annie, there's nothing in here to write w—"

But there was: a ballpoint at the very back of the glove compartment. Printed on the barrel, faded but still legible, was LET'S GO KROGERING! I won't say that pen saved Annie and Mike Ross serious police trouble, but I know it saved them a lot of questions about what had brought Annie to Joyland on such a dark and stormy night.

I passed her the pen and a business card from my wallet, blank side up. Earlier, sitting in my car and terribly afraid that my failure to buy a new battery was going to get Annie and Mike killed, I'd thought I could go back into the house and call her…only I didn't have her number. Now I told her to write it down. "And below the number, write *Call if plans change*."

While she did, I started the van's engine and turned the heater on full blast. She returned the card. I tucked it into my wallet, shoved the wallet back into my pocket, and tossed the pen into the glove compartment. I took her in my arms and kissed her cold cheek. Her trembling didn't stop, but it eased.

"You saved my life," I said. "Now let's make sure nothing happens to you *or* Mike because you did. Listen very carefully."

She listened.

♥

Six days later, Indian summer came back to Heaven's Bay for a brief final fling. It was perfect weather for a noon meal at the end of the Ross boardwalk, only we couldn't go there. Newsmen and photographers had it staked out. They could do that because, unlike the two acres surrounding the big green Victorian, the beach was public property. The story of how Annie had taken out Lane Hardy (known then and forever after as The Carny Killer) with one shot had gone nationwide.

Not that the stories were bad. Quite the opposite. The Wilmington paper had led with DAUGHTER OF EVANGELIST BUDDY ROSS BAGS CARNY KILLER. The *New York Post* was more succinct: HERO MOM! It helped that there were file photos from Annie's salad days where she looked not just gorgeous but smoking hot. *Inside View*, the most popular of the supermarket tabloids back then, put out an extra edition. They had unearthed a photo of Annie at seventeen, taken after a shooting competition at Camp Perry. Clad in tight jeans, an NRA tee-shirt, and cowboy boots, she was standing with an antique Purdey shotgun broken over one arm and holding up a blue ribbon in her free hand. Next to the smiling girl was a mug-shot of Lane Hardy at twenty-one, after an arrest in San Diego—under his real name, which was Leonard Hopgood—for indecent exposure. The two pix made a terrific contrast. The headline: BEAUTY AND THE BEAST.

Being a minor hero myself, I got some mention in the North Carolina papers, but in the tabloids I was hardly mentioned. Not sexy enough, I guess.

Mike thought having a HERO MOM was cool. Annie loathed the whole circus and couldn't wait for the press to move on to the next big thing. She'd gotten all the newspaper coverage she wanted in the days when she had been the holy man's wild child, famous for dancing on the bars in various Greenwich Village dives. So she gave no interviews, and we had our farewell picnic in the kitchen. There were actually five of us, because Milo was under the table, hoping for scraps, and Jesus—on the face of Mike's kite—was propped in the extra chair.

Their bags were in the hall. When the meal was done, I would drive them to Wilmington International. A private jet, laid on by Buddy Ross Ministries, Inc., would fly them back to Chicago and out of my life. The Heaven's Bay police department (not to mention the North Carolina State Police and maybe even the FBI) would undoubtedly have more questions for her, and she'd probably be back at some point to testify before a grand jury, but she'd be fine. She was the HERO MOM, and thanks to that promotional pen from Kroger's in the back of the van's glove compartment, there would never be a photo of Mike in the *Post* below a headline reading PSYCHIC SAVIOR!

Our story was simple, and Mike played no part in it. I had gotten interested in the murder of Linda Gray because of the legend that her ghost haunted the Joyland funhouse. I had enlisted the help of my research-minded friend and summer co-worker, Erin Cook. The photographs of Linda Gray and her killer had reminded me of someone, but it wasn't until after Mike's day at Joyland that the penny dropped. Before I could call the police, Lane Hardy had called me, threatening to kill Annie and Mike if I didn't come to Joyland on the double. So much truth, and only one little lie: I had Annie's phone number so I could call her if plans for Mike's visit to the park changed. (I produced the card for the lead detective, who barely glanced at it.) I said I called Annie from Mrs. Shoplaw's before leaving for Joyland, telling her to lock her doors, call the cops, and stay put. She *did* lock the doors, but didn't stay put. Nor did she call the police. She was terrified that if Hardy saw blue flashing lights, he'd kill me. So she'd taken one of the guns from the safe and followed Lane with her headlights off, hoping to surprise him. Which she did. Thus, HERO MOM.

"How's your father taking all this, Dev?" Annie asked.

"Aside from saying he'd come to Chicago and wash your cars for life, if you wanted?" She laughed, but my father had actually said that. "He's fine. I'm heading back to New Hampshire next month. We'll have Thanksgiving together. Fred asked me to stay on until then, help him get the park buttoned up, and I agreed. I can still use the money."

"For school?"

"Yeah. I guess I'll go back for the spring semester. Dad's sending me an application."

"Good. That's where you need to be, not painting rides and replacing lightbulbs in an amusement park."

"You'll really come to see us in Chicago, right?" Mike asked. "Before I get too sick?"

Annie stirred uneasily, but said nothing.

"I have to," I said, and pointed to the kite. "How else am I going to return that? You said it was just a loan."

"Maybe you'll get to meet my grandpa. Other than being crazy about Jesus, he's pretty cool." He gave his mother a sideways glance. "*I* think so, anyway. He's got this great electric train set in his basement."

I said, "Your grandfather may not want to see me, Mike. I almost got your mother in a whole peck of trouble."

"He'll know you didn't mean to. It wasn't your fault that you worked with that guy." Mike's face grew troubled. He put down his sandwich, picked up a napkin, and coughed into it. "Mr. Hardy seemed really nice. He took us on the rides."

A lot of girls thought he was really nice, too, I thought. "You never had a…a vibe about him?"

Mike shook his head and coughed some more. "No. I liked him. And I thought he liked me."

I thought of Lane on the Carolina Spin, calling Mike a crippled brat.

Annie put a hand on Mike's wand of a neck and said, "Some people hide their real faces, hon. Sometimes you can tell when they're wearing masks, but not always. Even people with powerful intuitions can get fooled."

I had come for lunch, and to take them to the airport, and to say goodbye, but I had another reason, as well. "I want to ask you something, Mike. It's about the ghost who woke you up and told you I was in trouble at the park. Is that okay? Will it upset you?"

"No, but it's not like on TV. There wasn't any white see-through thing floating around and going *whooo-ooo*. I just woke up…and the ghost was there. Sitting on my bed like a real person."

"I wish you wouldn't talk about this," Annie said. "Maybe it's not upsetting him, but it's sure as hell upsetting me."

"I just have one more question, and then I'll let it go."

"Fine." She began to clear the table.

Tuesday we had taken Mike to Joyland. Not long after midnight on Wednesday morning, Annie had shot Lane Hardy on the Carolina Spin, ending his life and saving mine. The next day had been taken up by police interviews and dodging reporters. Then, on Thursday afternoon, Fred Dean had come to see me, and his visit had nothing to do with Lane Hardy's death.

Except I thought it did.

"Here's what I want to know, Mike. Was it the girl from the funhouse? Was she the one who came and sat on your bed?"

Mike's eyes went wide. "Gosh, no! She's gone. When they go, I don't think they ever come back. It was a *guy*."

♥

In 1991, shortly after his sixty-third birthday, my father suffered a fairly serious heart attack. He spent a week in Portsmouth General Hospital and was then sent home, with stern warnings about watching his diet, losing twenty pounds, and cutting out the evening cigar. He was one of those rare fellows who actually followed the doctor's orders, and at this writing he's eighty-five and, except for a bad hip and dimming eyesight, still good to go.

In 1973, things were different. According to my new research assistant (Google Chrome), the average stay back then was two weeks—the first in ICU, the second on the Cardiac Recovery floor. Eddie Parks must have done okay in ICU, because while Mike was touring Joyland on that Tuesday, Eddie was being moved downstairs. That was when he had the second heart attack. He died in the elevator.

♥

"What did he say to you?" I asked Mike.

"That I had to wake up my mom and make her go to the park right away, or a bad man was going to kill you."

Had this warning come while I was still on the phone with Lane, in Mrs. Shoplaw's parlor? It couldn't have come much later, or Annie wouldn't have made it in time. I asked, but Mike didn't know. As soon as the ghost went—that was the word Mike used; it didn't disappear, didn't walk out the door or use the window, it just *went*—he had thumbed the intercom beside his bed. When Annie answered his buzz, he'd started screaming.

"That's enough," Annie said, in a tone that brooked no refusal. She was standing by the sink with her hands on her hips.

"I don't mind, Mom." *Cough-cough*. "Really." *Cough-cough-cough*.

"She's right," I said. "It's enough."

Did Eddie appear to Mike because I saved the bad-tempered old geezer's life? It's hard to know anything about the motivations of those who've Gone On (Rozzie's phrase, the caps always implied by lifted and upturned palms), but I doubt it. His reprieve only lasted a week, after all, and he sure didn't spend those last few days in the Caribbean, being waited on by topless honeys. But…

I had come to visit him, and except maybe for Fred Dean, I was the only one who did. I even brought him a picture of his ex-wife. Sure, he'd called her a miserable scolding backbiting cunt, and maybe she was, but at least I'd made the effort. In the end, so had he. For whatever reason.

As we drove to the airport, Mike leaned forward from the back seat and said, "You want to know something funny, Dev? He never once called you by name. He just called you the kiddo. I guess he figured I'd know who he meant."

I guessed so, too.

Eddie fucking Parks.

♥

Those are things that happened once upon a time and long ago, in a magical year when oil sold for eleven dollars a barrel. The year I got my damn heart broke. The year I lost my virginity. The year I saved a nice little girl from choking and a fairly nasty old man from dying of a heart attack (the first one, at least). The year a madman almost killed me on a Ferris wheel. The year I wanted to see a ghost and didn't…although I guess at least one of them saw me. That was also the year I learned to talk a secret language, and how to dance the Hokey Pokey in a dog costume. The year I discovered that there are worse things than losing the girl.

The year I was twenty-one, and still a greenie.

The world has given me a good life since then, I won't deny it, but sometimes I hate the world, anyway. Dick Cheney, that apologist for waterboarding and for too long chief preacher in the Holy Church of Whatever It Takes, got a brand-new heart while I was writing this—how about that? He lives on; other people have died. Talented ones like Clarence Clemons. Smart ones like Steve Jobs. Decent ones like my old friend Tom Kennedy. Mostly you get used to it. You pretty much have to. As W. H. Auden pointed out, the Reaper takes the rolling in money, the screamingly funny, and those who are very well hung. But that isn't where Auden starts his list. He starts with the innocent young.

Which brings us to Mike.

♥

I took a seedy off-campus apartment when I went back to school for the spring semester. One chilly night in late March, as I was cooking a stir-fry for myself and this girl I was just about crazy for, the phone rang. I answered it in my usual jokey way: "Wormwood Arms, Devin Jones, proprietor."

"Dev? It's Annie Ross."

"Annie! Wow! Hold on a second, just let me turn down the radio."

Jennifer—the girl I was just about crazy for—gave me an inquiring look. I shot her a wink and a smile and picked up the phone. "I'll be there two days after spring break starts, and you can tell him that's a promise. I'm going to buy my ticket next wee—"

"Dev. Stop. Stop."

I picked up on the dull sorrow in her voice and all my happiness at hearing from her collapsed into dread. I put my forehead against the wall and closed my eyes. What I really wanted to close was the ear with the phone pressed to it.

"Mike died last evening, Dev. He…" Her voice wavered, then steadied. "He spiked a fever two days ago, and the doctor said we ought to get him into the hospital. Just to be safe, he said. He seemed to be getting better yesterday. Coughing less. Sitting up and watching TV. Talking about some big basketball tournament. Then…last night…" She stopped. I could hear the rasp of her breath as she tried to get herself under control. I was also trying, but the tears had started. They were warm, almost hot.

"It was very sudden," she said. Then, so softly I could barely hear: "My heart is breaking."

There was a hand on my shoulder. Jennifer's. I covered it

with my own. I wondered who was in Chicago to put a hand on Annie's shoulder.

"Is your father there?"

"On a crusade. In Phoenix. He's coming tomorrow."

"Your brothers?"

"George is here now. Phil's supposed to arrive on the last flight from Miami. George and I are at the…place. The place where they…I can't watch it happen. Even though it's what he wanted." She was crying hard now. I had no idea what she was talking about.

"Annie, what can I do? Anything. Anything at all."

She told me.

♥

Let's end on a sunny day in April of 1974. Let's end on that short stretch of North Carolina beach that lies between the town of Heaven's Bay and Joyland, an amusement park that would close its doors two years later; the big parks finally drove it to bankruptcy in spite of all Fred Dean's and Brenda Rafferty's efforts to save it. Let's end with a pretty woman in faded jeans and a young man in a University of New Hampshire sweatshirt. The young man is holding something in one hand. Lying at the end of the boardwalk with his snout on one paw is a Jack Russell terrier who seems to have lost all his former bounce. On the picnic table, where the woman once served fruit smoothies, there's a ceramic urn. It looks sort of like a vase missing its bouquet. We're not quite ending where we began, but close enough.

Close enough.

♥

"I'm on the outs with my father again," Annie said, "and this time there's no grandson to hold us together. When he got back from his damn crusade and found out I'd had Mike cremated, he was furious." She smiled wanly. "If he hadn't stayed for that last goddam revival, he might have talked me out of it. Probably would have."

"But it's what Mike wanted."

"Strange request for a kid, isn't it? But yes, he was very clear. And we both know why."

Yes. We did. The last good time always comes, and when you see the darkness creeping toward you, you hold on to what was bright and good. You hold on for dear life.

"Did you even ask your dad…?"

"To come? Actually I did. It's what Mike would have wanted. Daddy refused to participate in what he called 'a pagan cere-mony.' And I'm glad." She took my hand. "This is for us, Dev. Because we were here when he was happy."

I raised her hand to my lips, kissed it, gave it a brief squeeze, then let it go. "He saved my life as much as you did, you know. If he hadn't woken you up…if he'd even hesitated—"

"I know."

"Eddie couldn't have done anything for me without Mike. I don't see ghosts, or hear them. Mike was the medium."

"This is hard," she said. "Just…so hard to let him go. Even the little bit that's left."

"Are you sure you want to go through with it?"

"Yes. While I still can."

She took the urn from the picnic table. Milo raised his head to look at it, then lowered it back to his paw. I don't know if he understood Mike's remains were inside, but he knew Mike was gone, all right; that he knew damned well.

I held out the Jesus kite with the back to her. There, as per Mike's instructions, I had taped a small pocket, big enough to hold maybe half a cup of fine gray ash. I held it open while Annie tipped the urn. When the pocket was full, she planted the urn in the sand between her feet and held out her hands. I gave her the reel of twine and turned toward Joyland, where the Carolina Spin dominated the horizon.

I'm flying, he'd said that day, lifting his arms over his head. No braces to hold him down then, and none now. I believe that Mike was a lot wiser than his Christ-minded grandfather. Wiser than all of us, maybe. Was there ever a crippled kid who didn't want to fly, just once?

I looked at Annie. She nodded that she was ready. I lifted the kite and let it go. It rose at once on a brisk, chilly breeze off the ocean. We followed its ascent with our eyes.

"You," she said, and held out her hands. "This part is for you, Dev. He said so."

I took the twine, feeling the pull as the kite, now alive, rose above us, nodding back and forth against the blue. Annie picked up the urn and carried it down the sandy slope. I guess she dumped it there at the edge of the ocean, but I was watching the kite, and once I saw the thin gray streamer of ash running away from it, carried into the sky on the breeze, I let the string go free. I watched the untethered kite go up, and up, and up. Mike would have wanted to see how high it would go before it disappeared, and I did, too.

I wanted to see that, too.

August 24, 2012

AUTHOR'S NOTE

Carny purists (I'm sure there are such) are even now preparing to write and inform me, with varying degrees of outrage, that much of what I call "the Talk" doesn't exist: that rubes were never called conies, for instance, and that pretty girls were never called points. Such purists would be correct, but they can save their letters and emails. Folks, that's why they call it fiction.

And anyway, most of the terms here really are carnival lingo, an argot both rich and humorous. The Ferris wheel was known as the chump-hoister or the simp-hoister; kiddie rides were known as zamp rides; leaving town in a hurry was indeed called burning the lot. These are just a few examples. I am indebted to *The Dictionary of Carny, Circus, Sideshow & Vaudeville Lingo*, by Wayne N. Keyser. It's posted on the internet. You can go there and check out a thousand other terms. Maybe more. You can also order his book, *On the Midway*.

Charles Ardai edited this book. Thanks, man.

Stephen King

"King has invented genres, reinvented them, then stepped outside what he himself has accomplished...Stephen King, like Mark Twain, is an American genius."

—*Greg Iles*

"Stephen King is much more than just a horror fiction writer. And I believe that he's never been given credit for taking American literature and stretching its boundaries."

—*Gloria Naylor*

"To my mind, King is one of the most underestimated novelists of our time."

—*Mordechai Richler, Vancouver Sun*

"King possesses an incredible sense of story...[He is] a gifted writer of intensely felt emotions, a soulful writer in control of a spare prose that never gets in the way of the story...I, for one (of millions), wait impatiently to see where this king of storytellers takes us next."

—*Ridley Pearson*

"An absorbing, constantly surprising novel filled with true narrative magic."

—*Washington Post*

"It grabs you and holds you and won't let go...a genuine page turner."

—*Chattanooga Times*

"Blending philosophy with a plot that moves at supersonic speed while showcasing deeply imagined characters...an impressive sensitivity to what has often loosely been called the human condition."

—*Newsday*

Marsden's house came into view. It was like one of those Hollywood Hills mansions you see in the movies: big and jutting out over the drop. The side facing us was all glass.

"The house that heroin built." Liz sounded vicious.

There was one more curve before we came to the paved yard in front of the house. Liz drove around it and I saw a man in front of the double garage where Marsden's fancy cars were. I opened my mouth to say it must be Teddy, the gatekeeper, but then I saw his mouth was gone.

And given the red hole where his mouth had been, he hadn't died a natural death.

Like I said, this is a horror story...

**HARD CASE CRIME BOOKS
BY STEPHEN KING:**

THE COLORADO KID
JOYLAND
LATER

**SOME OTHER HARD CASE CRIME BOOKS
YOU WILL ENJOY:**

THE COCKTAIL WAITRESS *by James M. Cain*
BRAINQUAKE *by Samuel Fuller*
THIEVES FALL OUT *by Gore Vidal*
QUARRY *by Max Allan Collins*
SINNER MAN *by Lawrence Block*
SO NUDE, SO DEAD *by Ed McBain*
THE KNIFE SLIPPED *by Erle Stanley Gardner*
SNATCH *by Gregory Mcdonald*
THE LAST STAND *by Mickey Spillane*
UNDERSTUDY FOR DEATH *by Charles Willeford*
CHARLESGATE CONFIDENTIAL *by Scott Von Doviak*
SO MANY DOORS *by Oakley Hall*
A BLOODY BUSINESS *by Dylan Struzan*
THE TRIUMPH OF THE SPIDER MONKEY
by Joyce Carol Oates
BLOOD SUGAR *by Daniel Kraus*
DOUBLE FEATURE *by Donald E. Westlake*
ARE SNAKES NECESSARY?
by Brian De Palma and Susan Lehman
KILLER, COME BACK TO ME *by Ray Bradbury*

LATER

by **Stephen King**

A HARD CASE CRIME NOVEL

A HARD CASE CRIME BOOK
(HCC-147)
First Hard Case Crime edition: March 2021

Published by

Titan Books
A division of Titan Publishing Group Ltd
144 Southwark Street
London SE1 0UP

in collaboration with Winterfall LLC

Print edition ISBN 978-1-78909-649-1
E-book ISBN 978-1-78909-650-7

Design direction by Max Phillips
www.maxphillips.net

Typeset by Swordsmith Productions

The name "Hard Case Crime" and the Hard Case Crime logo are trademarks of Winterfall LLC. Hard Case Crime books are selected and edited by Charles Ardai.

Printed and bound by CPI Group (UK) Ltd, Croydon, CR0 4YY

A CIP catalogue record for this title is available from the British Library

Visit us on the web at www.HardCaseCrime.com

For Chris Lotts

"There are only so many tomorrows."

—MICHAEL LANDON

LATER

I don't like to start with an apology—there's probably even a rule against it, like never ending a sentence with a preposition —but after reading over the thirty pages I've written so far, I feel like I have to. It's about a certain word I keep using. I learned a lot of four-letter words from my mother and used them from an early age (as you will find out), but this is one with five letters. The word is *later*, as in "Later on" and "Later I found out" and "It was only later that I realized." I know it's repetitive, but I had no choice, because my story starts when I still believed in Santa Claus and the Tooth Fairy (although even at six I had my doubts). I'm twenty-two now, which makes this later, right? I suppose when I'm in my forties—always assuming I make it that far—I'll look back on what I thought I understood at twenty-two and realize there was a lot I didn't get at all. There's always a later, I know that now. At least until we die. Then I guess it's all *before that*.

My name is Jamie Conklin, and once upon a time I drew a Thanksgiving turkey that I thought was the absolute cat's ass. Later—and not much later—I found out it was more like the stuff that comes out of the cat's ass. Sometimes the truth really sucks.

I think this is a horror story. Check it out.

I

I was coming home from school with my mother. She was holding my hand. In the other hand I clutched my turkey, the ones we made in first grade the week before Thanksgiving. I was so proud of mine I was practically shitting nickels. What you did, see, was put your hand on a piece of construction paper and then trace around it with a crayon. That made the tail and body. When it came to the head, you were on your own.

I showed mine to Mom and she's all yeah yeah yeah, right right right, totally great, but I don't think she ever really saw it. She was probably thinking about one of the books she was trying to sell. "Flogging the product," she called it. Mom was a literary agent, see. It used to be her brother, my Uncle Harry, but Mom took over his business a year before the time I'm telling you about. It's a long story and kind of a bummer.

I said, "I used Forest Green because it's my favorite color. You knew that, right?" We were almost to our building by then. It was only three blocks from my school.

She's all yeah yeah yeah. Also, "You play or watch *Barney* and *The Magic Schoolbus* when we get home, kiddo, I've got like a zillion calls to make."

So *I* go yeah yeah yeah, which earned me a poke and a grin. I loved it when I could make my mother grin because even at six I knew that she took the world very serious. Later on I found out part of the reason was me. She thought she might be raising a crazy kid. The day I'm telling you about was the one when she decided for sure I wasn't crazy after all. Which must have been sort of a relief and sort of not.

"You don't talk to anybody about this," she said to me later that day. "Except to me. And maybe not even me, kiddo. Okay?"

I said okay. When you're little and it's your mom, you say okay to everything. Unless she says it's bedtime, of course. Or to finish your broccoli.

We got to our building and the elevator was still broken. You could say things might have been different if it had been working, but I don't think so. I think that people who say life is all about the choices we make and the roads we go down are full of shit. Because check it, stairs or elevator, we still would have come out on the third floor. When the fickle finger of fate points at you, all roads lead to the same place, that's what I think. I may change my mind when I'm older, but I really don't think so.

"Fuck this elevator," Mom said. Then, "You didn't hear that, kiddo."

"Hear what?" I said, which got me another grin. Last grin for her that afternoon, I can tell you. I asked her if she wanted me to carry her bag, which had a manuscript in it like always, that day a big one, looked like a five-hundred-pager (Mom always sat on a bench reading while she waited for me to get out of school, if the weather was nice). She said, "Sweet offer, but what do I always tell you?"

"You have to tote your own burden in life," I said.

"Correctamundo."

"Is it Regis Thomas?" I asked.

"Yes indeed. Good old Regis, who pays our rent."

"Is it about Roanoke?"

"Do you even have to ask, Jamie?" Which made me snicker. *Everything* good old Regis wrote was about Roanoke. That was the burden he toted in life.

We went up the stairs to the third floor, where there were two other apartments plus ours at the end of the hall. Ours was the fanciest one. Mr. and Mrs. Burkett were standing outside 3A, and I knew right away something was wrong because Mr. Burkett was smoking a cigarette, which I hadn't seen him do before and was illegal in our building anyway. His eyes were bloodshot and his hair was all crazied up in gray spikes. I always called him mister, but he was actually Professor Burkett, and taught something smart at NYU. English and European Literature, I later found out. Mrs. Burkett was dressed in a nightgown and her feet were bare. That nightgown was pretty thin. I could see most of her stuff right through it.

My mother said, "Marty, what's wrong?"

Before he could say anything back, I showed him my turkey. Because he looked sad and I wanted to cheer him up, but also because I was so proud of it. "Look, Mr. Burkett! I made a turkey! Look, Mrs. Burkett!" I held it up for her in front of my face because I didn't want her to think I was looking at her stuff.

Mr. Burkett paid no attention. I don't think he even heard me. "Tia, I have some awful news. Mona died this morning."

My mother dropped her bag with the manuscript inside it between her feet and put her hand over her mouth. "Oh, no! Tell me that's not true!"

He began to cry. "She got up in the night and said she
wanted a drink of water. I went back to sleep and she was on
the couch this morning with a comforter pulled up to her
chin and so I tiptoed to the kitchen and put on the coffee
because I thought the pleasant smell would w-w-wake...
would wake..."

He really broke down then. Mom took him in her arms
the way she did me when I hurt myself, even though Mr.
Burkett was about a hundred (seventy-four, I found out
later).

That was when Mrs. Burkett spoke to me. She was hard to
hear, but not as hard as some of them because she was still
pretty fresh. She said, "Turkeys aren't green, James."

"Well mine is," I said.

My mother was still holding Mr. Burkett and kind of
rocking him. They didn't hear her because they couldn't,
and they didn't hear me because they were doing adult
things: comforting for Mom, blubbering for Mr. Burkett.

Mr. Burkett said, "I called Dr. Allen and he came and said
she probably had a soak." At least that's what I thought he
said. He was crying so much it was hard to tell. "He called
the funeral parlor. They took her away. I don't know what I'll
do without her."

Mrs. Burkett said, "My husband is going to burn your
mother's hair with his cigarette if he doesn't look out."

And sure enough, he did. I could smell the singeing hair,
a kind of beauty shop smell. Mom was too polite to say anything about it, but she made him let go of her, and then she
took the cigarette from him and dropped it on the floor and
stepped on it. I thought that was a groady thing to do,

extreme litterbugging, but I didn't say anything. I got that it was a special situation.

I also knew that talking to Mrs. Burkett any more would freak him out. Mom, too. Even a little kid knows certain basic things if he's not soft in the attic. You said please, you said thank you, you didn't flap your weenie around in public or chew with your mouth open, and you didn't talk to dead folks when they were standing next to living folks who were just starting to miss them. I only want to say, in my own defense, that when I saw her I didn't know she was dead. Later on I got better at telling the difference, but back then I was just learning. It was her nightgown I could see through, not her. Dead people look just like living people, except they're always wearing the clothes they died in.

Meanwhile, Mr. Burkett was rehashing the whole thing. He told my mother how he sat on the floor beside the couch and held his wife's hand till that doctor guy came and again till the mortician guy came to take her away. "Conveyed her hence" was what he actually said, which I didn't understand until Mom explained it to me. And at first I thought he said *beautician*, maybe because of the smell when he burned Mom's hair. His crying had tapered off, but now it ramped up again. "Her rings are gone," he said through his tears. "Both her wedding ring and her engagement ring, that big diamond. I looked on the night table by her side of the bed, where she puts them when she rubs that awful-smelling arthritis cream into her hands—"

"It does smell bad," Mrs. Burkett admitted. "Lanolin is basically sheep dip, but it really helps."

I nodded to show I understood but didn't say anything.

"—and on the bathroom sink, because sometimes she leaves them there…I've looked *everywhere*."

"They'll turn up," my mother soothed, and now that her hair was safe, she took Mr. Burkett in her arms again. "They'll turn up, Marty, don't you worry about that."

"*I miss her so much! I miss her already!*"

Mrs. Burkett flapped a hand in front of her face. "I give him six weeks before he's asking Dolores Magowan out to lunch."

Mr. Burkett was blubbing, and my mother was doing her soothing thing like she did to me whenever I scraped my knee or this one time when I tried to make her a cup of tea and slopped hot water on my hand. Lots of noise, in other words, so I took a chance but kept my voice low.

"Where are your rings, Mrs. Burkett? Do you know?"

They have to tell you the truth when they're dead. I didn't know that at the age of six; I just assumed all grownups told the truth, living *or* dead. Of course back then I also believed Goldilocks was a real girl. Call me stupid if you want to. At least I didn't believe the three bears actually talked.

"Top shelf of the hall closet," she said. "Way in the back, behind the scrapbooks."

"Why there?" I asked, and my mother gave me a strange look. As far as she could see, I was talking to the empty doorway…although by then she knew I wasn't quite the same as other kids. After a thing that happened in Central Park, not a nice thing—I'll get to it—I overheard her telling one of her editor friends on the phone that I was "fey." That scared the shit out of me, because I thought she meant she was changing my name to Fay, which is a girl's name.

"I don't have the slightest idea," Mrs. Burkett said. "By then I suppose I was having the stroke. My thoughts would have been drowning in blood."

Thoughts drowning in blood. I never forgot that.

Mom asked Mr. Burkett if he wanted to come down to our apartment for a cup of tea ("or something stronger"), but he said no, he was going to have another hunt for his wife's missing rings. She asked him if he would like us to bring him some Chinese take-out, which my mother was planning for dinner, and he said that would be good, thank you Tia.

My mother said de nada (which she used almost as much as yeah yeah yeah and right right right), then said we'd bring it to his apartment around six, unless he wanted to eat with us in ours, which he was welcome to do. He said no, he'd like to eat in his place but he would like us to eat with him. Except what he actually said was *our* place, like Mrs. Burkett was still alive. Which she wasn't, even though she was there.

"By then you'll have found her rings," Mom said. She took my hand. "Come on, Jamie. We'll see Mr. Burkett later, but for now let's leave him alone."

Mrs. Burkett said, "Turkeys aren't green, Jamie, and that doesn't look like a turkey anyway. It looks like a blob with fingers sticking out of it. You're no Rembrandt."

Dead people have to tell the truth, which is okay when you want to know the answer to a question, but as I said, the truth can really suck. I started to be mad at her, but just then she started to cry and I couldn't be. She turned to Mr. Burkett and said, "Who'll make sure you don't miss the belt loop in the back of your pants now? Dolores Magowan? I should smile and kiss a pig." She kissed his cheek…or kissed *at* it, I couldn't really tell which. "I loved you, Marty. Still do."

Mr. Burkett raised his hand and scratched the spot where her lips had touched him, as if he had an itch. I suppose that's what he thought it was.

2

So yeah, I see dead people. As far as I can remember, I always have. But it's not like in that movie with Bruce Willis. It can be interesting, it can be scary sometimes (the Central Park dude), it can be a pain in the ass, but mostly it just *is*. Like being left-handed, or being able to play classical music when you're like three years old, or getting early-onset Alzheimer's, which is what happened to Uncle Harry when he was only forty-two. At age six, forty-two seemed old to me, but even then I understood it's young to wind up not knowing who you are. Or what the names of things are—for some reason that's what always scared me the most when we went to see Uncle Harry. His thoughts didn't drown in blood from a busted brain vessel, but they drowned, just the same.

Mom and me trucked on down to 3C, and Mom let us in. Which took some time, because there are three locks on the door. She said that's the price you pay for living in style. We had a six-room apartment with a view of the avenue. Mom called it the Palace on Park. We had a cleaning woman who came in twice a week. Mom had a Range Rover in the parking garage on Second Avenue, and sometimes we went up to Uncle Harry's place in Speonk. Thanks to Regis Thomas and a few other writers (but mostly good old Regis), we were living high on the hog. It didn't last, a depressing development I will discuss all too soon. Looking back on it, I sometimes think my life was like a Dickens novel, only with swearing.

Mom tossed her manuscript bag and purse on the sofa and sat down. The sofa made a farting noise that usually made us laugh, but not that day. "Jesus-fuck," Mom said, then raised a hand in a stop gesture. "You—"

"I didn't hear it, nope," I said.

"Good. I need to have an electric shock collar or something that buzzes every time I swear around you. That'd teach me." She stuck out her lower lip and blew back her bangs. "I've got another two hundred pages of Regis's latest to read—"

"What's this one called?" I asked, knowing the title would have *of Roanoke* in it. They always did.

"*Ghost Maiden of Roanoke*," she said. "It's one of his better ones, lots of se...lots of kissing and hugging."

I wrinkled my nose.

"Sorry, kiddo, but the ladies love those pounding hearts and torrid thighs." She looked at the bag with *Ghost Maiden of Roanoke* inside, secured with the usual six or eight rubber bands, one of which always snapped and made Mom give out some of her best swears. Many of which I still use. "Now I feel like I don't want to do anything but have a glass of wine. Maybe the whole bottle. Mona Burkett was a prize pain in the ass, he might actually be better off without her, but right now he's gutted. I hope to God he's got relatives, because I don't relish the idea of being Comforter in Chief."

"She loved him, too," I said.

Mom gave me a strange look. "Yeah? You think?"

"I know. She said something mean about my turkey, but then she cried and kissed him on the cheek."

"You imagined that, James," she said, but half-heartedly. She knew better by then, I'm sure she did, but grownups have a tough time believing, and I'll tell you why. When they find out as kids that Santa Claus is a fake and Goldi-locks isn't a real girl and the Easter Bunny is bullshit—just three examples, I could give more—it makes a complex and they stop believing anything they can't see for them-selves.

"Nope, didn't imagine it. She said I'd never be Rembrandt. Who is that?"

"An artist," she said, and blew her bangs back again. I don't know why she didn't just cut them or wear her hair a different way. Which she could, because she was really pretty.

"When we go down there to eat, don't you dare say any-thing to Mr. Burkett about what you think you saw."

"I won't," I said, "but she was right. My turkey sucks." I felt bad about that.

I guess it showed, because she held out her arms. "Come here, kiddo."

I came and hugged her.

"Your turkey is beautiful. It's the most beautiful turkey I ever saw. I'm going to put it up on the refrigerator and it will stay there forever."

I hugged as tight as I could and put my face in the hollow of her shoulder so I could smell her perfume. "I love you, Mom."

"I love you too, Jamie, a million bunches. Now go play or watch TV. I need to roll some calls before ordering the Chinese."

"Okay." I started for my room, then stopped. "She put her rings on the top shelf of the hall closet, behind some scrapbooks."

My mother stared at me with her mouth open. "Why would she do that?"

"I asked her and she said she didn't know. She said by then her thoughts were drownding in blood."

"Oh my God," Mom whispered, and put her hand to her neck.

"You should figure out a way to tell him when we have the Chinese. Then he won't worry about it. Can I have General Tso's?"

"Yes," she said. "And brown rice, not white."

"Right right right," I said, and went to play with my Legos. I was making a robot.

3

The Burketts' apartment was smaller than ours, but nice. After dinner, while we were having our fortune cookies (mine said *A feather in the hand is better than a bird in the air*, which makes no sense at all), Mom said, "Have you checked the closets, Marty? For her rings, I mean?"

"Why would she put her rings in a closet?" A sensible enough question.

"Well, if she was having a stroke, she might not have been thinking too clearly."

We were eating at the little round table in the kitchen nook. Mrs. Burkett was sitting on one of the stools at the counter and nodded vigorously when Mom said that.

"Maybe I'll check," Mr. Burkett said. He sounded pretty vague. "Right now I'm too tired and upset."

"You check the bedroom closet when you get around to it," Mom said. "I'll check the one in the hall right now. A little stretching will do me good after all that sweet and sour pork."

Mrs. Burkett said, "Did she think that up all by herself? I didn't know she was that smart." Already she was getting hard to hear. After awhile I wouldn't be able to hear her at all, just see her mouth moving, like she was behind a thick pane of glass. Pretty soon after that she'd be gone.

"My mom's plenty smart," I said.

"Never said she wasn't," Mr. Burkett said, "but if she finds those rings in the front hall closet, I'll eat my hat."

Just then my mother said "Bingo!" and came in with the rings on the palm of one outstretched hand. The wedding ring was pretty ordinary, but the engagement ring was as big as an eyeball. A real sparkler.

"Oh my God!" Mr. Burkett cried. "How in God's name…?"

"I prayed to St. Anthony," Mom said, but cast a quick glance my way. And a smile. "'Tony, Tony, come around! Something's lost that must be found!' And as you see, it worked."

I thought about asking Mr. Burkett if he wanted salt and pepper on his hat, but didn't. It wasn't the right time to be funny, and besides, it's like my mother always says—nobody loves a smartass.

4

The funeral was three days later. It was my first one, and interesting, but not what you'd call fun. At least my mother didn't have to be Comforter in Chief. Mr. Burkett had a sister and brother to take care of that. They were old, but not as old as he was. Mr. Burkett cried all the way through the service and the sister kept handing him Kleenex. Her purse seemed to be full of them. I'm surprised she had room for anything else.

That night mom and I had pizza from Domino's. She had wine and I had Kool-Aid as a special treat for being good at the funeral. When we were down to the last piece of the pie, she asked me if I thought Mrs. Burkett had been there.

"Yeah. She was sitting on the steps leading up to the place where the minister and her friends talked."

"The pulpit. Could you…" She picked up the last slice, looked at it, then put it down and looked at me. "Could you see through her?"

"Like a movie ghost, you mean?"

"Yes. I suppose that is what I mean."

"Nope. She was all there, but still in her nightgown. I was surprised to see her, because she died three days ago. They don't usually last that long."

"They just disappear?" Like she was trying to get it straight in her mind. I could tell she didn't like talking about it, but I was glad she was. It was a relief.

"Yeah."

"What was she doing, Jamie?"

"Just sitting there. Once or twice she looked at her coffin, but mostly she looked at him."

"At Mr. Burkett. Marty."

"Right. She said something once, but I couldn't hear. Pretty soon after they die, their voices start to fade away, like turning down the music on the car radio. After awhile you can't hear them at all."

"And then they're gone."

"Yes," I said. There was a lump in my throat, so I drank the rest of my Kool-Aid to make it go away. "Gone."

"Help me clean up," she said. "Then we can watch an episode of *Torchwood*, if you want."

"Yeah, cool!" In my opinion *Torchwood* wasn't really cool, but getting to stay up an hour after my usual bedtime was way cool.

"Fine. Just as long as you understand we're not going to make a practice of it. But I need to tell you something first, and it's very serious, so I want you to pay attention. *Close* attention."

"Okay."

She got down on one knee, so our faces were more or less level and took hold of me by the shoulders, gently but firmly. "Never tell anyone about seeing dead people, James. *Never*."

"They wouldn't believe me anyway. You never used to."

"I believed *something*," she said. "Ever since that day in Central Park. Do you remember that?" She blew back her bangs. "Of course you do. How could you forget?"

"I remember." I only wished I didn't.

She was still on her knee, looking into my eyes. "So here it is. People not believing is a good thing. But someday somebody might. And that might get the wrong kind of talk going, or put you in actual danger."

"Why?"

"There's an old saying that dead men tell no tales, Jamie. But they *can* talk to you, can't they? Dead men *and* women. You say they have to answer questions, and give truthful answers. As if dying is like a dose of sodium pentothal."

I had no clue what that was and she must have seen it on my face because she said to never mind that, but to remember what Mrs. Burkett had told me when I asked about her rings.

"So?" I said. I liked being close to my mom, but I didn't like her looking at me in that intense way.

"Those rings were valuable, especially the engagement ring. People die with secrets, Jamie, and there are always people who want to know those secrets. I don't mean to scare you, but sometimes a scare is the only lesson that works."

Like the man in Central Park was a lesson about being careful in traffic and always wearing your helmet when you were on your bike, I thought…but didn't say.

"I won't talk about it," I said.

"Not ever. Except to me. If you need to."

"Okay."

"Good. We have an understanding."

She got up and we went in the living room and watched TV. When the show was over, I brushed my teeth and peed and washed my hands. Mom tucked me in and kissed me and said what she always said: "Sweet dreams, pleasant repose, all the bed and all the clothes."

Most nights that was the last time I saw her until morning. I'd hear the clink of glass as she poured herself a second glass of wine (or a third), then jazz turned way down low as she started reading some manuscript. Only I guess moms must have an extra sense, because that night she came back in and sat on my bed. Or maybe she just heard me crying, although I was trying my best to keep it on the down-low. Because, as she also always said, it's better to be part of the solution instead of part of the problem.

"What's wrong, Jamie?" she asked, brushing back my hair. "Are you thinking about the funeral? Or Mrs. Burkett being there?"

"What would happen to me if you died, Mom? Would I have to go live in an orphanage home?" Because it sure as shit wouldn't be with Uncle Harry.

"Of course not," Mom said, still brushing my hair. "And it's what we call a moot point, Jamie, because I'm not going to die for a long time. I'm thirty-five years old, and that means I still have over half my life ahead of me."

"What if you get what Uncle Harry's got, and have to live in that place with him?" The tears were streaming down my face. Having her stroke my forehead made me feel better, but it also made me cry more, who knows why. "That place smells bad. It smells like *pee!*"

"The chance of that happening is so teensy that if you put it next to an ant, the ant would look like Godzilla," she said. That made me smile and feel better. Now that I'm older I know she was either lying or misinformed, but the gene that triggers what Uncle Harry had—early-onset Alzheimer's—swerved around her, thank God.

"I'm not going to die, *you're* not going to die, and I think there's a good chance that this peculiar ability of yours will fade when you get older. So…are we good?"

"We're good."

"No more tears, Jamie. Just sweet dreams and—"

"Pleasant repose, all the bed and all the clothes," I finished.

"Yeah yeah yeah." She kissed my forehead and left. Leaving the door open a little bit, as she always did.

I didn't want to tell her it wasn't the funeral that had made me cry, and it wasn't Mrs. Burkett, either, because she wasn't scary. Most of them aren't. But the bicycle man in Central Park scared the shit out of me. He was *gooshy*.

5

We were on the 86th Street Transverse, heading for Wave Hill in the Bronx, where one of my preschool friends was having a big birthday party. ("Talk about spoiling a kid rotten," Mom said.) I had my present to give Lily in my lap. We went around a curve and saw a bunch of people standing in the street. The accident must have just happened. A man was lying half on the pavement and half on the sidewalk with a twisted-up bicycle beside him. Someone had put a jacket over his top half. His bottom half was wearing black bike shorts with red stripes up the sides, and a knee brace, and sneakers with blood all over them. It was on his socks and legs, too. We could hear approaching sirens.

Standing next to him was the same man in the same bike shorts and knee brace. He had white hair with blood in it. His face was caved in right down the middle, I think maybe from where he hit the curb. His nose was like in two pieces and so was his mouth.

Cars were stopping and my mother said, "Close your eyes." It was the man lying on the ground she was looking at, of course.

"He's dead!" I started to cry. "That man is dead!"

We stopped. We had to. Because of the other cars in front of us.

"No, he's not," Mom said. "He's asleep, that's all. It's what happens sometimes when someone gets banged hard. He'll be fine. Now close your eyes."

I didn't. The smashed-up man raised a hand and waved at me. They know when I see them. They always do.

"His face is in *two pieces!*"

Mom looked again to be sure, saw the man was covered down to his waist, and said, "Stop scaring yourself, Jamie. Just close your—"

"He's *there!*" I pointed. My finger was trembling. *Everything* was trembling. "Right *there*, standing next to himself!"

That scared her. I could tell by the way her mouth got all tight. She laid on her horn with one hand. With the other she pushed the button that rolled down her window and started waving at the cars ahead of her. "*Go!*" she shouted. "*Move! Stop staring at him, for Christ's sake, this isn't a fucking movie!*"

They did, except for the one right in front of her. That guy was leaning over and taking a picture with his phone. Mom pulled up and bumped his fender. He gave her the bird. My mother backed up and pulled into the other lane to go around. I wish I'd also given him the bird, but I was too freaked out.

Mom barely missed a police car coming the other way and drove for the far side of the park as fast as she could. She was almost there when I unbuckled my seatbelt. Mom yelled at me not to do that but I did it anyway and buzzed down my window and kneeled on the seat and leaned out and blew groceries all down the side of the car. I couldn't help it. When we got to the Central Park West side, Mom pulled over and wiped off my face with the sleeve of her blouse. She might have worn that blouse again, but if she did I don't remember it.

"God, Jamie. You're white as a sheet."

"I couldn't help it," I said. "I never saw anyone like that before. There were *bones* sticking right out of his no-nose—" Then I ralphed again, but managed to get most of that one on the street instead of on our car. Plus there wasn't as much.

She stroked my neck, ignoring someone (maybe the man who gave us the finger) who honked at us and drove around our car. "Honey, that's just your imagination. He was covered up."

"Not the one on the ground, the one standing beside him. He *waved* at me."

She stared at me for a long time, seemed like she was going to say something, then just buckled my seatbelt. "I think maybe we should skip the party. How does that sound to you?"

"Good," I said. "I don't like Lily anyway. She sneaky-pinches me during Story Time."

We went home. Mom asked me if I could keep down a cup of cocoa and I said I could. We drank cocoa together in the living room. I still had Lily's present. It was a little doll in a sailor suit. When I gave it to Lily the next week, instead of sneaky-pinching me, she gave me a kiss right on the mouth. I got teased about that and never minded a bit.

While we were drinking our cocoa (she might have put a little something extra in hers), Mom said, "I promised myself when I was pregnant that I'd never lie to my kid, so here goes. Yeah, that guy was probably dead." She paused. "No, he *was* dead. I don't think even a bike helmet would have saved him, and I didn't see one."

No, he wasn't wearing a helmet. Because if he'd been wearing it when he got hit (it was a taxi that did it, we found out), he would have been wearing it as he stood beside his body. They're always wearing what they had on when they died.

"But you only imagined you saw his face, honey. You couldn't have. Someone covered him up with a jacket. Someone very kind."

"He was wearing a tee-shirt with a lighthouse on it," I said. Then I thought of something else. It was only a little bit cheery, but after something like that, I guess you take what you can get. "At least he was pretty old."

"Why do you say that?" She was looking at me oddly. Looking back on it, I think that was when she started to believe, at least a little bit.

"His hair was white. Except for the parts with the blood in it, that is."

I started to cry again. My mother hugged me and rocked me and I went to sleep while she was doing it. I tell you what, there's nothing like having a mother around when you're thinking of scary shit.

We got the *Times* delivered to our door. My mother usually read it at the table in her bathrobe while we ate breakfast, but the day after the Central Park man she was reading one of her manuscripts instead. When breakfast was over, she told me to get dressed and maybe we'd ride the Circle Line, so it must have been a Saturday. I remember thinking it was the first weekend the Central Park man was dead in. That made it real all over again.

I did what she said, but first I went into her bedroom while she was in the shower. The newspaper was on the bed, open to the page where they put dead folks who are famous enough for the *Times*. The picture of the Central Park man was there. His name was Robert Harrison. At four I was already reading at a third-grade level, my mother was very proud of that, and there were no tough words in the headline of the story, which was all I read: CEO OF LIGHTHOUSE FOUNDATION DIES IN TRAFFIC ACCIDENT.

I saw a few more dead people after that—the saying about how in life we are in death is truer than most people know—and sometimes I said something to Mom, but mostly I didn't because I could see it upset her. It wasn't until Mrs. Burkett died and Mom found her rings in the closet that we really talked about it again.

That night after she left my room I thought I wouldn't be able to sleep, and if I did I would dream about the Central Park man with his split-open face and bones sticking out of his nose, or about my mother in her coffin, but also sitting on the steps to the pulpit, where only I could see her. But so far as I can remember, I didn't dream about anything. I got up the next morning feeling good, and Mom was feeling good, and we joked around like we sometimes did, and she stuck my turkey on the fridge and then put a big smackeroo on it, which made me giggle, and she walked me to school, and Mrs. Tate told us about dinosaurs, and life went on for two years in the good ways it usually did. Until, that is, everything fell apart.

6

When Mom realized how bad things were, I heard her talking to Anne Staley, her editor friend, about Uncle Harry on the phone. Mom said, "He was soft even before he went soft. I realize that now."

At six I wouldn't have had a clue. But by then I was eight going on nine, and I understood, at least partly. She was talking about the mess her brother had gotten himself—and her—into even before the early-onset Alzheimer's carried off his brains like a thief in the night.

I agreed with her, of course; she was my mother, and it was us against the world, a team of two. I hated Uncle Harry for the jam we were in. It wasn't until later, when I was twelve or maybe even fourteen, that I realized my mother was also partly to blame. She might have been able to get out while there was still time, probably could have, but she didn't. Like Uncle Harry, who founded the Conklin Literary Agency, she knew a lot about books but not enough about money.

She even got two warnings. One was from her friend Liz Dutton. Liz was an NYPD detective, and a great fan of Regis Thomas's Roanoke series. Mom met her at a launch party for one of those books, and they clicked. Which turned out to be not so good. I'll get to it, but for now I'll just say that Liz told my mother that the Mackenzie Fund was too good to be true. This might have been around the time Mrs. Burkett died, I'm not sure about that, but I know it was before the fall of 2008, when the economy went belly-up. Including our part of it.

Uncle Harry used to play racquetball at some fancy club near Pier 90, where the big boats dock. One of the friends he played with was a Broadway producer who told him about the Mackenzie Fund. The friend called it a license to coin money, and Uncle Harry took him seriously about that. Why wouldn't he? The friend had produced like a bazillion musicals that ran on Broadway for a bazillion years, plus also all over the country, and the royalties just poured in. (I knew exactly what royalties were—I was a literary agent's kid.)

Uncle Harry checked it out, talked to some big bug who worked for the Fund (although not to James Mackenzie himself, because Uncle Harry was just a small bug in the great scheme of things), and put in a bunch of money. The returns were so good that he put in more. And more. When he got the Alzheimer's—and he went downhill really fast—my mother took over all the accounts, and she not only stuck with the Mackenzie Fund, she put even more money into it.

Monty Grisham, the lawyer who helped with contracts back then, not only told her not to put in more, he told her to get out while the getting was good. That was the other warning she got, and not long after she took over the Conklin Agency. He also said that if a thing looked too good to be true, it probably was.

I'm telling you everything I found out in little driblets and drablets—like that overheard conversation between Mom and her editor pal. I'm sure you get that, and I'm sure you don't need me to tell you that the Mackenzie Fund was actually a big fat Ponzi scheme. The way it worked was Mackenzie and his merry band of thieves took in mega-millions and paid back big percentage returns while skimming off most of the investment dough. They kept it going by roping in new investors, telling each one how special he or she was because only a select few were allowed into the Fund. The select few, it turned out, were thousands, everyone from Broadway producers to wealthy widows who stopped being wealthy almost overnight.

A scheme like that depends on investors being happy with their returns and not only leaving their initial investments in the Fund but putting in more. It worked okay for awhile, but when the economy crashed in 2008, almost everybody in the Fund asked for their money back and the money wasn't there. Mackenzie was a piker compared to Madoff, the king of Ponzi schemes, but he gave old Bern a run for his money;

after taking in over twenty billion dollars, all he had in the Mackenzie accounts was a measly fifteen million. He went to jail, which was satisfying, but as Mom sometimes said, "Grits ain't groceries and revenge don't pay the bills."

"We're okay, we're okay," she told me when Mackenzie started showing up on all the news channels and in the *Times*. "Don't worry, Jamie." But the circles under her eyes said that *she* was plenty worried, and she had plenty of reasons to be.

Here's more of what I found out later: Mom only had about two hundred grand in assets she could put her hands on, and that included the insurance policies on her and me. What she had on the liability side of the ledger, you don't want to know. Just remember our apartment was on Park Avenue, the agency office was on Madison Avenue, and the extended care home where Uncle Harry was living ("If you can call that living," I can hear my mother adding) was in Pound Ridge, which is about as expensive as it sounds.

Closing the office on Madison was Mom's first move. After that she worked out of the Palace on Park, at least for awhile. She paid some rent in advance by cashing in those insurance policies I mentioned, including her brother's, but that would only last eight or ten months. She rented Uncle Harry's place in Speonk. She sold the Range Rover ("We don't really need a car in the city anyway, Jamie," she said) and a bunch of first edition books, including a signed Thomas Wolfe of *Look Homeward, Angel*. She cried over that one and said she didn't get half of what it was worth, because the rare book market was also in the toilet, thanks to a bunch of sellers as desperate for cash as she was. Our Andrew Wyeth painting went, too. And every day she cursed James Mackenzie for the thieving, money-grubbing, motherfucking, cock-sucking, bleeding hemorrhoid on legs that he was. Sometimes she also cursed Uncle Harry, saying he'd be living behind a garbage dumpster by the end of the year and it would serve him right. And, to be fair, later on she cursed herself for not listening to Liz and Monty.

"I feel like the grasshopper who played all summer instead of working," she said to me one night. January or February of 2009, I think. By then Liz was staying over sometimes, but not that night. That might have been the first time I noticed there were threads of gray in my mom's pretty red hair. Or maybe I remember because she started to cry and it was my turn to comfort her, even though I was just a little kid and didn't really know how to do it.

That summer we moved out of the Palace on Park and into a much smaller place on Tenth Avenue. "Not a dump," Mom said, "and the price is right." Also: "I'll be damned if I'll move out of the city. That would be waving the white flag. I'd start losing clients."

The agency moved with us, of course. The office was in what I suppose would have been my bedroom if things hadn't been so fucking dire. My room was an alcove adjacent to the kitchen. It was hot in the summer and cold in the winter, but at least it smelled good. I think it used to be the pantry.

She moved Uncle Harry to a facility in Bayonne. The less said about that place the better. The only good thing about it, I suppose, was that poor old Uncle Harry didn't know where he was, anyway; he would have pissed his pants just as much if he'd been in the Beverly Hilton.

Other things I remember about 2009 and 2010: My mother stopped getting her hair done. She stopped lunching with friends and only lunched with clients of the agency if she really had to (because she was the one who always got stuck with the check). She didn't buy many new clothes, and the ones she did buy were from discount stores. And she started drinking more wine. A lot more. There were nights when she and her friend Liz—the Regis Thomas fan and detective I told you about—would get pretty soused together. The next day Mom would be red-eyed and snappy, puttering around in her office in her pajamas. Sometimes she'd sing, "Crappy days are here again, the skies are fucking drear again." On those days it was a relief to go to school. A *public* school, of course; my private school days were over, thanks to James Mackenzie.

There were a few rays of light in all that gloom. The rare book market might have been in the shithouse, but people were reading regular books again—novels to escape and self-help books because, let's face it, in 2009 and '10, a lot of people needed to help themselves. Mom was always a big mystery reader, and she had been building up that part of the Conklin stable ever since taking over for Uncle Harry. She had ten or maybe even a dozen mystery authors. They weren't big-ticket guys and gals, but their fifteen percent brought in enough to pay the rent and keep the lights on in our new place.

Plus, there was Jane Reynolds, a librarian from North Carolina. Her novel, a mystery titled *Dead Red*, came in over the transom, and Mom just raved about it. There was an auction for who would get to publish it. All the big companies took part, and the rights ended up selling for two million dollars. Three hundred thousand of those scoots were ours, and my mother began to smile again.

"It will be a long time before we get back to Park Avenue," she said, "and we've got a lot of climbing to do before we get out of the hole Uncle Harry dug for us, but we just might make it."

"I don't want to go back to Park Avenue anyway," I said. "I like it here."

She smiled and hugged me. "You're my little love." She held me at arms' length and studied me. "Not so little anymore, either. Do you know what I'm hoping, kiddo?"

I shook my head.

"That Jane Reynolds turns out to be a book-a-year babe. And that the movie of *Dead Red* gets made. Even if neither of those things happen, there's good old Regis Thomas and his Roanoke Saga. He's the jewel in our crown."

Only *Dead Red* turned out to be like a final flash of sunlight before a big storm moves in. The movie never got made, and the publishers who bid on the book got it wrong, as they sometimes do. The book flopped, which didn't hurt us financially—the money was paid—but other stuff happened and that three hundred grand vanished like dust in the wind.

First, Mom's wisdom teeth went to hell and got infected. She had to have them all pulled. That was bad. Then Uncle Harry, troublesome Uncle Harry, still not fifty years old, tripped in the Bayonne care facility and fractured his skull. That was a lot worse.

Mom talked to the lawyer who helped her with book

contracts (and took a healthy bite of our agency fee for his trouble). He recommended another lawyer who specialized in liability and negligence suits. That lawyer said we had a good case, and maybe we did, but before the case got anywhere near a courtroom, the Bayonne facility declared bankruptcy. The only one who made money out of that was the fancy slip-and-fall lawyer, who banked just shy of forty thousand dollars.

"Those billable hours are a bitch," Mom said one night when she and Liz Dutton were well into their second bottle of wine. Liz laughed because it wasn't her forty thousand. Mom laughed because she was squiffed. I was the only one who didn't see the humor in it, because it wasn't just the lawyer's bills. We were on the hook for Uncle Harry's medical bills as well.

Worst of all, the IRS came after Mom for back taxes Uncle Harry owed. He had been putting off that other uncle— Sam—so he could dump more money into the Mackenzie Fund. Which left Regis Thomas.

The jewel in our crown.

7

Now check this out.

It's the fall of 2009. Obama is president, and the economy is slowly getting better. For us, not so much. I'm in the third grade, and Ms. Pierce has me doing a fractions problem on the board because I'm good at shit like that. I mean I was doing percentages when I was seven—literary agent's kid, remember. The kids behind me are restless because it's that funny little stretch of school between Thanksgiving and Christmas. The problem is as easy as soft butter on toast, and I'm just finishing when Mr. Hernandez, the assistant principal, sticks his head in. He and Ms. Pierce have a brief murmured conversation, and then Ms. Pierce asks me to step out into the hall.

My mother is waiting out there, and she's as pale as a glass of milk. *Skim* milk. My first thought is that Uncle Harry, who now has a steel plate in his skull to protect his useless brain, has died. Which in a gruesome way would actually be good, because it would cut down on expenses. But when I ask, she says Uncle Harry—by then living in a third-rate care home in Piscataway (he kept moving further west, like some fucked-up brain-dead pioneer)—is fine.

Mom hustles me down the hall and out the door before I can ask any more questions. Parked at the yellow curb where parents drop off their kids and pick them up in the afternoon is a Ford sedan with a bubble light on the dash. Standing beside it in a blue parka with NYPD on the breast is Liz Dutton.

Mom is rushing me toward the car, but I dig in my heels and make her stop. "What is it?" I ask. "Tell me!" I'm not crying, but the tears are close. There's been a lot of bad news since we found out about the Mackenzie Fund, and I don't think I can stand any more, but I get some. Regis Thomas is dead.

The jewel just fell out of our crown.

8

I have to stop here and tell you about Regis Thomas. My mother used to say that most writers are as weird as turds that glow in the dark, and Mr. Thomas was a case in point.

The Roanoke Saga—that's what he called it—consisted of nine books when he died, each one as thick as a brick. "Old Regis always serves up a heaping helping," Mom said once. When I was eight, I snitched a copy of the first one, *Death Swamp of Roanoke*, off one of the office shelves and read it. No problem there. I was as good at reading as I was at math and seeing dead folks (it's not bragging if it's true). Plus *Death Swamp* wasn't exactly *Finnegans Wake*.

I'm not saying it was badly written, don't get that idea; the man could tell a tale. There was plenty of adventure, lots of scary scenes (especially in the Death Swamp), a search for buried treasure, and a big hot helping of good old S-E-X. I learned more about the true meaning of sixty-nine in that book than a kid of eight should probably know. I learned something else as well, although I only made a conscious connection later. It was about all those nights Mom's friend Liz stayed over.

I'd say there was a sex scene every fifty pages or so in *Death Swamp*, including one in a tree while hungry alligators crawled around beneath. We're talking *Fifty Shades of Roanoke*. In my early teens Regis Thomas taught me to jack off, and if that's too much information, deal with it.

The books really were a saga, in that they told one continuing story with a cast of continuing characters. They were strong men with fair hair and laughing eyes, untrustworthy men with shifty eyes, noble Indians (who in later books became noble Native Americans), and gorgeous women with firm, high breasts. Everyone—the good, the bad, the firm-breasted—was randy all the time.

The heart of the series, what kept the readers coming back (other than the duels, murders, and sex, that is) was the titanic secret that had caused all the Roanoke settlers to disappear. Had it been the fault of George Threadgill, the chief villain? Were the settlers dead? Was there really an ancient city beneath Roanoke full of ancient wisdom? What did Martin Betancourt mean when he said "Time is the key" before expiring? What did that cryptic word *croatoan*, found carved on a palisade of the abandoned community, really mean? Millions of readers slavered to know the answers to those questions. To anyone far in the future finding that hard to believe, I'd simply tell you to hunt up something by Judith Krantz or Harold Robbins. Millions of people read their stuff, too.

Regis Thomas's characters were classic projection. Or maybe I mean wish fulfillment. He was a little wizened dude whose author photo was routinely altered to make his face look a little less like a lady's leather purse. He didn't come to New York City because he couldn't. The guy who wrote about fearless men hacking their way through pestilent swamps, fighting duels, and having athletic sex under the stars was an agoraphobe bachelor who lived alone. He was also incredibly paranoid (so said my mother) about his work.

No one saw it until it was done, and after the first two volumes were such rip-roaring successes, staying at the top of the bestseller lists for months, that included a copyeditor. He insisted that they be published as he wrote them, word for golden word.

He wasn't a book-a-year author (that literary agent's El Dorado), but he was dependable; a book with *of Roanoke* in the title would appear every two or three years. The first four came during Uncle Harry's tenure, the next five in Mom's. That included *Ghost Maiden of Roanoke*, which Thomas announced was the penultimate volume. The last book in the series, he promised, would answer all the questions his loyal readers had been asking ever since those first expeditions into the Death Swamp. It would also be the longest book in the series, maybe seven hundred pages. (Which would allow the publisher to tack an extra buck or two onto the purchase price.) And once Roanoke and all its mysteries were put to rest, he had confided to my mother on one of her visits to his upstate New York compound, he intended to begin a multi-volume series focused on the *Mary Celeste*.

It all sounded good until he dropped dead at his desk with only thirty or so pages of his magnum opus completed. He had been paid a cool three million in advance, but with no book, the advance would have to be paid back, including our share. Only our share was either gone or spoken for. This, as you may have guessed, was where I came in.

Okay, back to the story.

9

As we approached the unmarked police car (I knew what it was, I'd seen it lots of times, parked in front of our building with the sign reading POLICE OFFICER ON CALL on the dash), Liz held open the side of her parka to show me her empty shoulder holster. This was a kind of joke between us. No guns around my son, that was Mom's hard and fast rule. Liz always showed me the empty holster when she was wearing it, and I'd seen it plenty of times on the coffee table in our living room. Also on the night table on the side of the bed my mother didn't use, and by the age of nine, I had a pretty good idea of what that meant. *Death Swamp of Roanoke* included some steamy stuff going on between Laura Goodhugh and Purity Betancourt, the widow of Martin Betancourt (pure she wasn't).

"What's *she* doing here?" I asked Mom when we got to the car. Liz was right there, so I guess it was an impolite thing to say, if not downright rude, but I had just been jerked out of class and been told before we even got outside that our meal ticket had been revoked.

"Get in, Champ," Liz said. She always called me Champ. "Time's a-wasting."

"I don't want to. We're having fish sticks for lunch."

"Nope," Liz said, "we're having Whoppers and fries. I'm buying."

"Get in," my mother said. "Please, Jamie."

So I got in the back. There were a couple of Taco Bell wrappers on the floor and a smell that might have been microwave popcorn. There was also another smell, one I associated with our visits to Uncle Harry in his various care homes, but at least there was no metal grill between the back and the front, like I'd seen on some of the police shows Mom watched (she was partial to *The Wire*).

Mom got in front and Liz pulled out, pausing at the first red light to turn on the dashboard flasher. It went *blip-blip-blip*, and even without any siren, cars moved out of her way and we were on the FDR lickety-split.

My mother turned around and looked at me from between the seats with an expression that scared me. She looked desperate. "Could he be at his house, Jamie? I'm sure they've taken his body away to the morgue or the funeral parlor, but could he still be there?"

The answer to that was I didn't know, but I didn't say that or anything else at first. I was too amazed. And hurt. Maybe even mad, I don't remember for sure about that, but the amazement and hurt I remember very well. She had told me never to tell anybody about seeing dead people, and I never had, but then *she* did. She told Liz. That was why Liz was here, and would soon be using her blipping dashboard light to shift traffic out of our way on the Sprain Brook Parkway.

At last I said, "How long has she known?"

I saw Liz wink at me in the rearview mirror, the kind of wink that said *we've got a secret*. I didn't like it. It was Mom and me who were supposed to have the secret.

Mom reached over the seat and grasped me by the wrist.

Her hand was cold. "Never mind that, Jamie, just tell me if he could still be there."

"Yeah, I guess. If that's where he died."

Mom let go of me and told Liz to go faster, but Liz shook her head.

"Not a good idea. We might pick up a police escort, and they'd want to know what the big deal was. Am I supposed to tell them we need to talk to a dead guy before he disappears?" I could tell by the way she said it that she didn't believe a word of what Mom had told her, she was just humoring her. Joshing her along. That was okay with me. As for Mom, I don't think she cared what Liz thought, as long as she got us to Croton-on-Hudson.

"As fast as you can, then."

"Roger that, Tee-Tee." I never liked her calling Mom that, it's what some kids in my class called having to go to the bathroom, but Mom didn't seem to mind. On that day she wouldn't have cared if Liz called her Bonnie Boobsalot. Probably wouldn't even have noticed.

"Some people can keep secrets and some people can't," I said. I couldn't help myself. So I guess I was mad.

"Stop it," my mother said. "I can't afford to have you sulking."

"I'm not sulking," I said sulkily.

I knew she and Liz were tight, but she and I were supposed to be even tighter. She could have at least asked me what I thought about the idea before spilling our greatest secret some night when she and Liz were in bed after climbing what Regis Thomas called "the ladder of passion."

"I can see you're upset, and you can be pissed off at me later, but right now I need you, kiddo." It was like she had forgotten Liz was there, but I could see Liz's eyes in the rearview mirror and knew she was listening to every word.

"Okay." She was scaring me a little. "Chill, Mom."

She ran her hand through her hair and gave her bangs a yank for good measure. "This is so unfair. Everything that's happened to us…that's still happening…is so fucking fucked up!" She ruffled my hair. "You didn't hear that."

"Yes I did," I said. Because I was still mad, but she was right. Remember what I said about being in a Dickens novel, only with swears? You know why people read books like that? Because they're so happy that fucked-up shit isn't happening to them.

"I've been juggling bills for two years now and never dropped a single one. Sometimes I had to let the little ones go to pay the big ones, sometimes I let the big ones go to pay a bunch of little ones, but the lights stayed on and we never missed a meal. Right?"

"Yeah yeah yeah," I said, thinking it might raise a smile. It didn't.

"But now…" She gave her bangs another yank, leaving them all clumpy. "*Now* half a dozen things have come due at once, with goddam Infernal Revenue leading the pack. I'm drowning in a sea of red ink and I was expecting Regis to save me. Then the son of a bitch dies! At the age of fifty-nine! Who dies at fifty-nine if they're not a hundred pounds overweight or using drugs?"

"People with cancer?" I said.

Mom gave a watery snort and yanked her poor bangs.

"Easy, Tee," Liz murmured. She laid her palm against the side of Mom's neck, but I don't think Mom felt it.

"The book could save us. The book, the whole book, and

nothing but the book." She gave a wild laugh that scared me even more. "I know he only had a couple of chapters done, but nobody else knows it, because he didn't talk to anybody but my brother before Harry got sick and now me. He didn't outline or keep notes, Jamie, because he said it straitjacketed the creative process. Also because he didn't have to. He always knew where he was going."

She took my wrist again and squeezed so hard she left bruises. I saw them later that night.

"He *still* might know."

10

We did the drive-thru at the Tarrytown Burger King, and I got a Whopper, as promised. Also a chocolate shake. Mom didn't want to stop, but Liz insisted. "He's a growing boy, Tee. He needs chow even if you don't."

I liked her for that, and there were other things I liked her for, but there were also things I didn't like. Big things. I'll get to that, I'll have to, but for now let's just say my feelings about Elizabeth Dutton, Detective 2nd Grade, NYPD, were complicated.

She said one other thing before we got to Croton-on-Hudson, and I need to mention it. She was just making conversation, but it turned out to be important later (I know, that word again). Liz said Thumper had finally killed someone.

The man who called himself Thumper had been on the local news every now and then over the last few years, especially on NY1, which Mom watched most nights while she

was making supper (and sometimes while we were eating, if
it had been an interesting news day). Thumper's "reign of
terror"—thanks, NY1—had actually been going on even
before I was born, and he was sort of an urban legend. You
know, like Slender Man or The Hook, only with explosives.

"Who?" I said. "Who did he kill?"

"How long until we get there?" Mom asked. She had no
interest in Thumper; she had her own fish to fry.

"A guy who made the mistake of trying to use one of
Manhattan's few remaining phone booths," Liz said, ignoring
my mother. "Bomb Squad thinks it went off the second he
lifted the receiver. Two sticks of dynamite—"

"Do we have to talk about this?" Mom asked. "And why is
every goddam light *red*?"

"Two sticks of dynamite taped under the little ledge where
people can put their change," Liz went on, undeterred.
"Thumper's a resourceful SOB, got to give him that. They're
going to crank up another task force—this will be the third
since 1996—and I'm going to try for it. I was on the last one,
so I've got a shot, and I can use the OT."

"Light's green," Mom said. "Go."

Liz went.

11

I was still eating a few last French fries (cold by then, but I
didn't mind) when we turned onto a little dead-end street
called Cobblestone Lane. There might have been cobble-
stones on it once, but now it was just smooth tar. The house

at the end of it was Cobblestone Cottage. It was a big stone house with fancy carved shutters and moss on the roof. You heard me, moss. Crazy, right? There was a gate, but it was open. There were signs on the gateposts, which were the same gray stone as the house. One said DO NOT TRESPASS, WE ARE TIRED OF HIDING THE BODIES. The other showed a snarling German Shepherd and said BEWARE ATTACK DOG.

Liz stopped and looked at my mother, eyebrows raised.

"The only body Regis ever buried was his pet parakeet, Francis," Mom said. "Named after Francis Drake, the explorer. And he never had a dog."

"Allergies," I said from the back seat.

Liz drove up to the house, stopped, and turned off the blippy dashboard light. "Garage doors are shut and I see no cars. Who's here?"

"Nobody," Mom said. "The housekeeper found him. Mrs. Quayle. Davina. She and a part-time gardener were the whole staff. Nice woman. She called me right after she called for an ambulance. *Ambulance* made me wonder if she was sure he was really dead, and she said she was, because she worked in a nursing home before coming to work for Regis, but he still had to go to the hospital first. I told her to go home as soon as the body was removed. She was pretty freaked out. She asked about Frank Wilcox, he's Regis's business manager, and I said I'd get in touch with him. In time I will, but the last time I spoke to Regis, he told me Frank and his wife were in Greece."

"Press?" Liz asked. "He was a bestselling writer."

"Jesus-God, I don't know." Mom looked around wildly, as

if expecting to see reporters hiding in the bushes. "I don't see any."

"They may not even know yet," Liz said. "If they do, if they heard it on a scanner, they'll go after the cops and EMTs first. The body's not here so the story's not here. We've got some time, so calm down."

"I'm staring bankruptcy in the face, I've got a brother who may live in a home for the next thirty years, and a boy who might like to go to college someday, so don't tell me to calm down. Jamie, do you see him? You know what he looks like, right? Tell me you see him."

"I know what he looks like, but I don't see him," I said.

Mom groaned and slapped the heel of her palm against her poor clumped-up bangs.

I grabbed for the door handle, and surprise surprise, there wasn't one. I told Liz to let me out and she did. We all got out.

"Knock on the door," Liz said. "If no one answers, we'll go around and boost Jamie up so he can look in the windows."

We could do that because the shutters—with fancy little ornamental doodads carved into them—were all open. My mother ran to try the door, and for the moment Liz and I were alone.

"You don't really think you can see dead people like the kid in that movie, do you, Champ?"

I didn't care if she believed me or not, but something about her tone—as if this was all a big joke—pissed me off. "Mom told you about Mrs. Burkett's rings, didn't she?"

Liz shrugged. "That might have been a lucky guess. You didn't happen to see any dead folks on the way here, did you?"

I said no, but it can be hard to tell unless you talk to them...or they talk to you. Once when me and Mom were on the bus I saw a girl with cuts in her wrists so deep they looked like red bracelets, and I was pretty sure *she* was dead, although she was nowhere near as gooshy as the Central Park man. And just that day, as we drove out of the city, I spotted an old woman in a pink bathrobe standing on the corner of Eighth Avenue. When the sign turned to WALK, she just stood there, looking around like a tourist. She had those roller things in her hair. She might have been dead, but she also might have been a live person just wandering around, the way Mom said Uncle Harry used to do sometimes before she had to put him in that first care home. Mom told me that when Uncle Harry started doing that, sometimes in his pj's, she gave up thinking he might get better.

"Fortune tellers guess lucky all the time," Liz said. "And there's an old saying about how even a stopped clock is right twice a day."

"So you think my mother's crazy and I'm helping her be crazy?"

She laughed. "That's called *enabling*, Champ, and no, I don't think that. What I think is she's upset and grasping at straws. Do you know what that means?"

"Yeah. That she's crazy."

Liz shook her head again, more emphatically this time. "She's under a lot of stress. I totally get it. But making things up won't help her. I hope *you* get *that*."

Mom came back. "No answer, and the door's locked. I tried it."

"Okay," Liz said. "Let's go window-peeking."

We walked around the house. I could look in the dining room windows, because they went all the way to the ground, but I was too short for most of the other ones. Liz made a hand-step so I could look into those. I saw a big living room with a wide-screen TV and lots of fancy furniture. I saw a dining room with a table long enough to seat the starting team of the Mets, plus maybe their bullpen pitchers. Which was crazy for a guy who hated company. I saw a room that Mom called the small parlor, and around back was the kitchen. Mr. Thomas wasn't in any of the rooms.

"Maybe he's upstairs. I've never been up there, but if he died in bed…or in the bathroom…he might still be…"

"I doubt if died on the throne, like Elvis, but I suppose it's possible."

That made me laugh, calling the toilet the throne always made me laugh, but I stopped when I saw Mom's face. This was serious business, and she was losing hope. There was a kitchen door, and she tried the knob, but it was locked, just like the front door.

She turned to Liz. "Maybe we could…"

"Don't even think about it," Liz said. "No way are we breaking in, Tee. I've got enough problems at the Department without setting off a recently deceased bestselling author's security system and trying to explain what we're doing here when the guys from Brinks or ADT show up. Or the local cops. And speaking of the cops…he died alone, right? The housekeeper found him?"

"Yes, Mrs. Quayle. She called me, I told you that—"

"The cops will want to ask her some questions. Probably

doing it right now. Or maybe the medical examiner. I don't know how they do things in Westchester County."

"Because he's famous? Because they think someone might have *murdered* him?"

"Because it's routine. And yeah, because he's famous, I suppose. The point is, I'd like for us to be gone when they show up."

Mom's shoulders slumped. "Nothing, Jamie? No sign of him?"

I shook my head.

Mom sighed and looked at Liz. "Maybe we should check the garage?"

Liz gave her a shrug that said *it's your party*.

"Jamie? What do you think?"

I couldn't imagine why Mr. Thomas would be hanging out in his garage, but I guessed it was possible. Maybe he had a favorite car. "I guess we should. As long as we're here."

We started for the garage, but then I stopped. There was a gravel path beyond Mr. Thomas's swimming pool, which had been drained. The path was lined with trees, but because it was late in the season and most of the leaves were gone, I could see a little green building. I pointed to it. "What's that?"

Mom gave her forehead another slap. I was starting to worry she might give herself a brain tumor, or something. "Oh my God, *La Petite Maison dans le Bois*! Why didn't I think of it first?"

"What's that?" I asked.

"His study! Where he writes! If he's anywhere, it would be there! Come on!"

She grabbed my hand and ran me around the shallow end of the pool, but when we got to where the gravel path started, I set my feet and stopped. Mom kept going, and if Liz hadn't grabbed me by the shoulder, I probably would have face-planted.

"Mom? *Mom!*"

She turned around, looking impatient. Except that's not the right word. She looked halfway to crazy. "Come on! I'm telling you if he's anywhere *here*, it will be *there!*"

"You need to calm down, Tee," Liz said. "We'll check out his writing cabin, and then I think we should go."

"*Mom!*"

My mother ignored me. She was starting to cry, which she hardly ever did. She didn't do it even when she found out how much the IRS wanted, that day she just pounded her fists on her desk and called them a bunch of bloodsucking bastards, but she was crying now. "You go if you want, but we're staying here until Jamie's sure it's a bust. This might be just a pleasure jaunt for you, humoring the crazy lady—"

"That's unfair!"

"—but this is my *life* we're talking about—"

"I know that—"

"—and Jamie's life, and—"

"*MOM!*"

One of the worst things about being a kid, maybe the very worst, is how grownups ignore you when they get going on their shit. "*MOM! LIZ! BOTH OF YOU! STOP!*"

They stopped. They looked at me. There we stood, two women and a little boy in a New York Mets hoodie, beside a drained pool on an overcast November day.

I pointed to the gravel path leading to the little house in the woods where Mr. Thomas wrote his Roanoke books.

"He's right there," I said.

12

He came walking toward us, which didn't surprise me. Most of them, not all but most, are attracted to living people for awhile, like bugs to a bug-light. That's kind of a horrible way to put it, but it's all I can think of. I would have known he was dead even if I didn't *know* he was dead, because of what he was wearing. It was a chilly day, but he was dressed in a plain white tee, baggy shorts, and those strappy sandals Mom calls Jesus shoes. Plus there was something else, something weird: a yellow sash with a blue ribbon pinned to it.

Liz was saying something to my mother about how there was no one there and I was just pretending, but I paid no attention. I pulled free of Mom's hand and walked toward Mr. Thomas. He stopped.

"Hello, Mr. Thomas," I said. "I'm Jamie Conklin. Tia's son. I've never met you."

"Oh, come on," Liz said from behind me.

"Be quiet," Mom said, but some of Liz's skepticism must have gotten through, because she asked me if I was sure Mr. Thomas was really there.

I ignored this, too. I was curious about the sash he was wearing. Had been wearing when he died.

"I was at my desk," he said. "I always wear my sash when I'm writing. It's my good luck charm."

"What's the blue ribbon for?"

"The Regional Spelling Bee I won when I was in the sixth

grade. Spelled down kids from twenty other schools. I lost in the state competition, but I got this blue ribbon for the Regional. My mother made the sash and pinned the ribbon on it."

In my opinion I thought that was sort of a weird thing to still be wearing, since sixth grade must have been a zillion years ago for Mr. Thomas, but he said it without any embarrassment or self-consciousness. Some dead people can feel love—remember me telling you about Mrs. Burkett kissing Mr. Burkett's cheek?—and they can feel hate (something I found out in due time), but most of the other emotions seem to leave when they die. Even the love never seemed all that strong to me. I don't like to tell you this, but hate stays stronger and lasts longer. I think when people see ghosts (as opposed to dead people), it's because they are hateful. People think ghosts are scary because they *are*.

I turned back to Mom and Liz. "Mom, did you know Mr. Thomas wears a sash when he writes?"

Her eyes widened. "That was in the *Salon* interview he did five or six years ago. He's wearing it now?"

"Yeah. It's got a blue ribbon on it. From—"

"The spelling bee he won! In the interview, he laughed and called it 'my silly affectation.'"

"Maybe so," Mr. Thomas said, "but most writers have silly affectations and superstitions. We're like baseball players that way, Jimmy. And who can argue with nine straight *New York Times* bestsellers?"

"I'm Jamie," I said.

Liz said, "You told Champ there about the interview, Tee.

Must have. Or he read it himself. He's a hell of a good reader. He knew, that's all, and he—"

"*Be quiet*," my mother said fiercely. Liz raised her hands, like surrendering.

Mom stepped up beside me, looking at what to her was just a gravel path with nobody on it. Mr. Thomas was standing right in front of her with his hands in the pockets of his shorts. They were loose, and I hoped he wouldn't push down on his pockets too hard, because it looked to me like he wasn't wearing any undies.

"Tell him what I told you to tell him!"

What Mom wanted me to tell him was that he had to help us or the thin financial ice we'd been walking on for a year or more was going to break and we'd drown in a sea of debt. Also that the agency had begun to bleed clients because some of her writers knew we were in trouble and might be forced to close. Rats deserting a sinking ship was what she called them one night when Liz wasn't there and Mom was into her fourth glass of wine.

I didn't bother with all that blah-de-blah, though. Dead people have to answer your questions—at least until they disappear—and they have to tell the truth. So I just cut to the chase.

"Mom wants to know what *The Secret of Roanoke* is about. She wants to know the whole story. Do you *know* the whole story, Mr. Thomas?"

"Of course." He shoved his hands deeper into his pockets, and now I could see a little line of hair running down the middle of his stomach from below his navel. I didn't want to see that, but I did. "I always have *everything* before I write *anything*."

"And keep it all in your head?"

"I have to. Otherwise someone might steal it. Put it on the Internet. Spoil the surprises."

If he'd been alive, that might have come out sounding paranoid. Dead, he was just stating a fact, or what he believed was a fact. And hey, I thought he had a point. Computer trolls were always spilling stuff on the Net, everything from boring shit like political secrets to the really important things, like what was going to happen in the season finale of *Fringe*.

Liz walked away from me and Mom, sat on one of the benches beside the pool, crossed her legs, and lit a cigarette. She had apparently decided to let the lunatics run the asylum. That was okay with me. Liz had her good points, but that morning she was basically in the way.

"Mom wants you to tell me everything," I said to Mr. Thomas. "I'll tell her, and she'll write the last *Roanoke* book. She'll say you sent her almost all of it before you died, along with notes about how to finish the last couple of chapters."

Alive, he would have howled at the idea of someone else finishing his book; his work was the most important thing in his life and he was very possessive of it. But now the rest of him was lying on a mortician's table somewhere, dressed in the khaki shorts and the yellow sash he'd been wearing as he wrote his last few sentences. The version of him talking to me was no longer jealous or possessive of his secrets.

"Can she do that?" was all he asked.

Mom had assured me (and Liz) on the way out to Cobblestone Cottage that she really could do that. Regis Thomas insisted that no copyeditor should sully a single one of his precious words, but in fact Mom had been copyediting his books for years without telling him—even back when Uncle Harry was still in his right mind and running the business. Some of the changes were pretty big, but he never knew… or at least never said anything. If anyone in the world could copy Mr. Thomas's style, it was my mother. But style wasn't the problem. The problem was *story*.

"She can," I said, because it was simpler than telling him all of that.

"Who is that other woman?" Mr. Thomas asked, pointing at Liz.

"That's my mother's friend. Her name is Liz Dutton." Liz looked up briefly, then lit another cigarette.

"Are she and your mother fucking?" Mr. Thomas asked.

"Pretty sure, yeah."

"I thought so. It's how they look at each other."

"What did he say?" Mom asked anxiously.

"He asked if you and Liz were close friends," I said. Kind of lame, but all I could think of on the spur of the moment. "So will you tell us *The Secret of Roanoke*?" I asked Mr. Thomas. "I mean the whole book, not just the secret part."

"Yes."

"He says yes," I told Mom, and she took both her phone and a little tape recorder out of her bag. She didn't want to miss a single word.

"Tell him to be as detailed as he can."

"Mom says to be—"

"I heard her," Mr. Thomas said. "I'm dead, not deaf." His shorts were lower than ever.

"Cool," I said. "Listen, maybe you better pull up your shorts, Mr. Thomas, or your willy's gonna get chilly."

He pulled up his shorts so they hung off his bony hips. "Is it chilly? It doesn't feel that way to me." Then, with no change in tone: "Tia is starting to look old, Jimmy."

I didn't bother to tell him again that my name was Jamie. Instead I looked at my mother and holy God, she *did* look old. Was starting to, anyway. When had that happened?

"Tell us the story," I said. "Begin at the beginning."

"Where else?" Mr. Thomas said.

13

It took an hour and a half, and by the time we were done, I was exhausted and I think Mom was, too. Mr. Thomas looked just the same at the end as when we started, standing there with that somehow sorry yellow sash falling down over his poochy belly and low-slung shorts. Liz parked her car between the gateposts with the dashboard light blipping, which was probably a good idea, because the news of Mr. Thomas's death had begun to spread, and people were showing up out front to snap pictures of Cobblestone Cottage. Once she came back to ask how much longer we'd be and Mom just waved her off, told her to inspect the grounds or something, but mostly Liz hung in.

It was stressful as well as exhausting, because our future depended on Mr. Thomas's book. It wasn't fair for me to have to bear the weight of that responsibility, not at nine, but there was no choice. I had to repeat everything Mr. Thomas said to Mom—or rather to Mom's recording devices—and Mr. Thomas had plenty to say. When he told me he was able to keep everything in his head, he wasn't just blowing smoke. And Mom kept asking questions, mostly for clarification. Mr. Thomas didn't seem to mind (didn't seem to care one way or the other, actually), but the way Mom was dragging things out started bugging the shit out of me. Also, my mouth got wickedly dry. When Liz brought me her leftover Coke from Burger King, I gulped down the few swallows that were left and gave her a hug.

"Thank you," I said, handing back the paper cup. "I needed that."

"Very welcome." Liz had stopped looking bored. Now she looked thoughtful. She couldn't see Mr. Thomas, and I don't think she still totally believed he was there, but she knew *something* was going on, because she'd heard a nine-year-old boy spieling out a complicated plot featuring half a dozen major characters and at least two dozen minor ones. Oh, and a threesome (under the influence of bulbous canary grass supplied by a helpful Native American of the Nottoway People) consisting of George Threadgill, Purity Betancourt, and Laura Goodhugh. Who ended up getting pregnant. Poor Laura always got the shitty end of the stick.

At the end of Mr. Thomas's summary, the big secret came out, and it was a dilly. I'm not going to tell you what it was. Read the book and find out for yourself. If you haven't read it already, that is.

"Now I'll tell you the last sentence," Mr. Thomas said. He seemed as fresh as ever...although "fresh" is probably the wrong word to use with a dead person. His voice had started to fade, though. Just a little. "Because I always write that first. It's the beacon I row to."

"Last sentence coming up," I told Mom.

"Thank God," she said.

Mr. Thomas raised one finger, like an old-time actor getting ready to give his big speech. "'On that day, a red sun went down over the deserted settlement, and the carved word that would puzzle generations glowed as if limned in blood: CROATOAN.' Tell her *croatoan* in capital letters, Jimmy."

I told her (although I didn't know exactly what "limbed in blood" meant), then asked Mr. Thomas if we were done. Just as he said we were, I heard a brief siren from out front—two whoops and a blat.

"Oh God," Liz said, but not in a panicky way; more like she had been expecting it. "Here we go."

She had her badge clipped to her belt and unzipped her parka so it would show. Then she went out front and came back with two cops. They were also wearing parkas, with Westchester County Police patches on them.

"Cheese it, the cops," Mr. Thomas said, which I didn't understand at all. Later, when I asked Mom, she told me it was slang from the olden days of the 1950s.

"This is Ms. Conklin," Liz said. "She's my friend and was Mr. Thomas's agent. She asked me to run her up here, because she was concerned someone might take the opportunity to steal souvenirs."

"Or manuscripts," my mother added. The little tape recorder was safe in her bag and her phone was in the back pocket of her jeans. "One in particular, the last book in a cycle of novels Mr. Thomas was writing."

Liz gave her a look that said *enough, already*, but my mother continued.

"He just finished it, and millions of people will want to read it. I felt it my duty to make sure they get the chance."

The cops didn't seem all that interested; they were here to look at the room where Mr. Thomas had died. Also to make sure the people who had been observed on the grounds had a good reason to be there.

"I believe he died in his study," Mom said, and pointed toward *La Petite Maison*.

"Uh-huh," one of the cops said. "That's what we heard. We'll check it out." He had to bend down with his hands on his knees to get face time with me; I was pretty shrimpy in those days. "What's your name, son?"

"James Conklin." I gave Mr. Thomas a pointed look. "*Jamie*. This is my mother." I took her hand.

"Are you playing hooky today, Jamie?"

Before I could answer, Mom cut in, smooth as silk. "I usually pick him up when he gets out of school, but I thought I might not get back in time today, so we swung by to get him. Didn't we, Liz?"

"Roger that," Liz said. "Officers, we didn't check the study, so I can't tell you if it's locked or not."

"Housekeeper left it open with the body inside," the one who'd talked to me said. "But she gave me her keys and we'll lock up after we have a quick look around."

"You might tell them there was no foul play," Mr. Thomas said. "I had a heart attack. Hurt like the devil."

I was going to tell them no such thing. I was only nine, but that didn't make me stupid.

"Is there also a key to the gate?" Liz asked. She was being all pro now. "Because it was open when we arrived."

"There is, and we'll lock it when we leave," the second cop said. "Good move parking your car there, detective."

Liz spread her hands, as if to say it was all in a day's work. "If you're set, we'll get out of your way."

The cop who had spoken to me said, "We should know what that valuable manuscript looks like so we can make sure it's safe."

This was a ball my mother could carry. "He sent the original to me just last week. On a thumb drive. I don't think there's another copy. He was pretty paranoid."

"I was," Mr. Thomas admitted. His shorts were sinking again.

"Glad you were here to keep an eye out," the second cop said. He and the other one shook hands with Mom and Liz, also with me. Then they started down the gravel path to the little green building where Mr. Thomas had died. Later on I found out a whole lot of writers died at their desks. Must be a Type A occupation.

"Let's go, Champ," Liz said. She tried to take my hand, but I wouldn't let her.

"Go stand over by the swimming pool for a minute," I said. "Both of you."

"Why?" Mom asked.

I looked at my mother in a way I don't think I ever had before—as if she was stupid. And right then, I thought she *was* being stupid. Both of them were. Not to mention rude as fuck.

"Because you got what you wanted and I need to say thank you."

"Oh my God," Mom said, and slapped her brow again. "What was I thinking? Thank you, Regis. So much."

Mom was directing her thank-you to a flower bed, so I took her arm and turned her. "He's over here, Mom."

She said another thank you, to which Mr. Thomas didn't respond. He didn't seem to care. Then she walked over to where Liz was standing by the empty pool, lighting another cigarette.

I didn't really need to say thank you, by then I knew that dead people don't give much of a shit about things like that, but I said thanks anyway. It was only polite, and besides, I wanted something else.

"My mom's friend," I said. "Liz?"

Mr. Thomas didn't reply, but he looked at her.

"She still mostly thinks I'm making it up about seeing you. I mean, she knows something weird happened, because no kid could make up that whole story—by the way, I loved what happened to George Threadgill—"

"Thank you. He deserved no better."

"But she'll work it around in her head so in the end she's got it the way she wants it."

"She will rationalize."

"If that's what you call it."

"It is."

"Well, is there any way you can show her you're here?" I was thinking about how Mr. Burkett scratched his cheek when his wife kissed him.

"I don't know. Jimmy, do you have any idea what comes next for me?"

"I'm sorry, Mr. Thomas. I don't."

"I suppose I will find out for myself."

He walked toward the pool where he'd never swim again. Someone might fill it when warm weather returned, but by then he would be long gone. Mom and Liz were talking quietly and sharing Liz's cigarette. One of the things I didn't like about Liz was how she'd gotten my mother smoking again. Only a little, and only with her, but still.

Mr. Thomas stood in front of Liz, drew in a deep breath, and blew it out. Liz didn't have bangs to blow on, her hair was pulled back tight and tied in a ponytail, but she still slitted her eyes the way you will when the wind gusts in your face, and recoiled. She would have fallen into the pool, I think, if Mom hadn't grabbed her.

I said, "Did you feel that?" Stupid question, of course she had. "That was Mr. Thomas."

Who was now walking away from us, back toward his study.

"Thanks again, Mr. Thomas!" I called. He didn't turn, but raised a hand to me before putting it back in the pocket of his shorts. I was getting an excellent view of his plumber's crack (that's what Mom called it when she spotted a guy wearing low-riding jeans), and if that's also too much information for you, too bad. We made him tell us—in one hour!—everything it had taken him months of thinking to come up with. He couldn't say no, and maybe that gave him the right to show us his ass.

Of course I was the only one who could see it.

14

It's time to talk about Liz Dutton, so check it out. Check *her* out.

She was about five-six, my mom's height, with shoulder-length black hair (when it wasn't yanked back in her cop-approved ponytail, that was), and she had what some of the boys in my fourth grade class would call—as if they had any idea what they were talking about—a "smokin' hot bod." She had a great smile and gray eyes that were usually warm. Unless she was mad, that is. When she was mad, those gray eyes could turn as cold as a sleety day in November.

I liked her because she could be kind, like when my mouth and throat were so dry and she gave me what was left in that Burger King Coke without me having to ask her (my mother was just fixated on getting the ins and outs of Mr. Thomas's unwritten last book). Also, she would sometimes bring me a Matchbox car to add to my growing collection and once in awhile would get right down on the floor beside me and we'd play together. Sometimes she'd give me a hug and ruffle my hair. Sometimes she'd tickle me until I screamed for her to stop or I'd pee myself…which she called "watering my Jockeys."

I *didn't* like her because sometimes, especially after our trip to Cobblestone Cottage, I'd look up and catch her studying me like I was a bug on a slide. There was no warmth in her gray eyes then. Or she'd tell me my room was a mess, which in fairness it usually was, although my mom didn't seem to mind. "It hurts my eyes," Liz would say. Or, "Are you going to live that way all your life, Jamie?" She also thought I was too old for a nightlight, but my mother put an end to *that* discussion, just saying "Leave him alone, Liz. He'll give it up when he's ready."

The biggest thing? She stole a lot of my mother's attention and affection that I used to get. Much later, when I read some of Freud's theories in a sophomore psych class, it occurred to me that as a kid I'd had a classic mother fixation, seeing Liz as a rival.

Well, duh.

Of *course* I was jealous, and I had good reason to be. I had no father, didn't even know who the fuck he was because my mother wouldn't talk about him. Later I found out she had good reason for *that*, but at the time all I knew was that it was "You and me against the world, Jamie." Until Liz came along, that was. And remember this, I didn't have a whole lot of Mom even *before* Liz, because Mom was too busy trying to save the agency after she and Uncle Harry got fucked by James Mackenzie (I hated that he and I had the same first name). Mom was always mining for gold in the slush pile, hoping to come across another Jane Reynolds.

I would have to say that liking and disliking were pretty evenly balanced on the day we went to Cobblestone Cottage, with liking slightly ahead for at least four reasons: Matchbox cars and trucks were not to be sneezed at; sitting between them on the sofa and watching *The Big Bang Theory* was fun and cozy; I wanted to like who my mother liked; Liz made her happy. Later (there it is again), not so much.

That Christmas was excellent. I got cool presents from both of them, and we had an early lunch at Chinese Tuxedo before Liz had to go to work. Because, she said, "Crime never takes a holiday." So Mom and me went to the old place on Park Avenue.

Mom stayed in touch with Mr. Burkett after we moved, and sometimes the three of us hung out. "Because he's lonely," Mom said, "but also because why, Jamie?"

"Because we like him," I said, and that was true.

We had Christmas dinner in his apartment (actually turkey sandwiches with cranberry sauce from Zabar's) because his daughter was on the west coast and couldn't come back. I found out more about that later.

And yes, because we liked him.

As I may have told you, Mr. Burkett was actually *Professor* Burkett, now Emeritus, which I understood to mean that he was retired but still allowed to hang around NYU and teach the occasional class in his super-smart specialty, which happened to be E and E—English and European Literature. I once made this mistake of calling it Lit and he corrected me, saying *lit* was either for lights or being drunk.

Anyway, even with no stuffing and only carrots for veg, it was a nice little meal, and we had more presents after. I gave Mr. Burkett a snow globe for his collection. I later found out it had been his wife's collection, but he admired it, thanked me, and put it on the mantel with the others. Mom gave him a big book called *The New Annotated Sherlock Holmes*, because back when he was working full time, he'd taught a course called Mystery and Gothic in English Fiction.

He gave Mom a locket that he said had belonged to his

wife. Mom protested and said he should save it for his daughter. Mr. Burkett said that Siobhan had gotten all the good pieces of Mona's jewelry, and besides, "If you snooze, you lose." Meaning, I guess, that if his daughter (from the sound of it, I thought her name was *Shivonn*) couldn't bother to come east, she could go whistle. I sort of agreed with that, because who knew how many more Christmases she might have her father around? He was older than God. Besides, I had a soft spot for fathers, not having one myself. I know they say you can't miss what you've never had, and there's some truth to that, but I knew I was missing *something*.

My present from Mr. Burkett was also a book. It was called *Twenty Unexpurgated Fairy Tales*.

"Do you know what *unexpurgated* means, Jamie?" Once a professor, always a professor, I guess.

I shook my head.

"What do you reckon?" He was leaning forward with his big gnarly hands between his skinny thighs, smiling. "Can you guess from the context of the title?"

"Uncensored? Like R-rated?"

"Nailed it," he said. "Well done."

"I hope there's not a lot of sex in them," Mom said. "He reads at high school level, but he's only nine."

"No sex, just good old violence," Mr. Burkett said (I never called him *professor* in those days, because it seemed stuck-up somehow). "For instance, in the original tale of Cinderella, which you'll find here, the wicked stepsisters—"

Mom turned to me and stage-whispered, "Spoiler alert."

Mr. Burkett was not to be deterred. He was in full teaching mode. I didn't mind, it was interesting.

"In the original, the wicked stepsisters cut off their toes in their efforts to make the glass slipper fit."

"Eww!" I said this in a way that meant *gross, tell me more*.

"And the glass slipper wasn't glass at all, Jamie. That seems to have been a translation error which has been immortalized by Walt Disney, that homogenizer of fairy tales. The slipper was actually made of squirrel fur."

"Wow," I said. Not as interesting as the stepsisters cutting off their toes, but I wanted to keep him rolling.

"In the original story of the Frog King, the princess doesn't kiss the frog. Instead, she—"

"No more," Mom said. "Let him read the stories and find out for himself."

"Always best," Mr. Burkett agreed. "And perhaps we'll discuss them, Jamie."

You mean you'll *discuss them while I listen*, I thought, but that would be okay.

"Should we have hot chocolate?" Mom asked. "It's also from Zabar's, and they make the best. I can reheat it in a jiff."

"Lay on, Macduff," Mr. Burkett said, "and damn'd be him that first cries, 'Hold, enough!' " Which meant yes, and we had it with whipped cream.

In my memory that's the best Christmas I had as a kid, from the Santa pancakes Liz made in the morning to the hot chocolate in Mr. Burkett's apartment, just down the hall from where Mom and I used to live. New Year's Eve was also fine, although I fell asleep on the couch between Mom and Liz before the ball dropped. All good. But in 2010, the arguments started.

Before that, Liz and my mother used to have what Mom called "spirited discussions," mostly about books. They liked many of the same writers (they bonded over Regis Thomas, remember) and the same movies, but Liz thought my mother was too focused on things like sales and advances and various writers' track records instead of the stories. And she actually laughed at the works of a couple of Mom's clients, calling them "subliterate." To which my mother responded that those subliterate writers paid the rent and kept the lights on. (Kept them *lit*.) Not to mention paying for the care home where Uncle Harry was marinating in his own pee.

Then the arguments began to move away from the more or less safe ground of books and films and get more heated. Some were about politics. Liz loved this Congress guy, John Boehner. My mother called him John Boner, which is what some kids of my acquaintance called a stiffy. Or maybe she meant to pull a boner, but I don't really think so. Mom thought Nancy Pelosi (another politician, which you probably know as she's still around) was a brave woman working in "a boys' club." Liz thought she was your basic liberal dingleberry.

The biggest fight they ever had about politics was when Liz said she didn't completely believe Obama had been born in America. Mom called her stupid and racist. They were in the bedroom with the door shut—that was where most of their arguments happened—but their voices were raised and I could hear every word from the living room. A few minutes later, Liz left, slamming the door on her way out, and didn't come back for almost a week. When she did, they made up. In the bedroom. With the door closed. I heard that, too, because the making-up part was pretty noisy. Groans and laughter and squeaky bedsprings.

They argued about police tactics, too, and this was still a few years before Black Lives Matter. That was a sore point with Liz, as you might guess. Mom decried what she called "racial profiling," and Liz said you can only draw a profile if the features are clear. (Didn't get that then, don't get it now.) Mom said when black people and white people were sentenced for the same type of crime, it was the black people who got hit with the heaviest sentences, and sometimes the white people didn't do time at all. Liz countered by saying, "You show me a Martin Luther King Boulevard in any city, and I'll show you a high crime area."

The arguments started to come closer together, and even at my tender age I knew one big reason why—they were drinking too much. Hot breakfasts, which my mother used to make twice or even three times a week, pretty much ceased. I'd come out in the morning and they'd be sitting there in their matching bathrobes, hunched over mugs of coffee, their faces pale and their eyes red. There'd be three, sometimes four, empty bottles of wine in the trash with cigarette butts in them.

My mother would say, "Get some juice and cereal for yourself while I get dressed, Jamie." And Liz would tell me not to make a lot of noise because the aspirin hadn't kicked in yet, her head was splitting, and she either had roll-call or was on stakeout for some case or other. Not the Thumper task force, though; she didn't get on that.

I'd drink my juice and eat my cereal quiet as a mouse on those mornings. By the time Mom was dressed and ready to walk me to school (ignoring Liz's comment that I was now

big enough to make that walk by myself), she was starting to
come around.

All of this seemed normal to me. I don't think the world
starts to come into focus until you're fifteen or sixteen; up
until then you just take what you've got and roll with it.
Those two hungover women hunched over their coffee was
just how I started my day on some mornings that eventually
became lots of mornings. I didn't even notice the smell of
wine that began to permeate everything. Only part of me
must have noticed, because years later, in college, when my
roomie spilled a bottle of Zinfandel in the living room of our
little apartment, it all came back and it was like getting hit in
the face with a plank. Liz's snarly hair. My mother's hollow
eyes. How I knew to close the cupboard where we kept the
cereal *slowly* and *quietly*.

I told my roomie I was going down to the 7-Eleven to get
a pack of cigarettes (yes, I eventually picked up that particular bad habit), but basically I just had to get away from that
smell. Given a choice between seeing dead folks—yes, I still
see them—and the memories brought on by the smell of
spilled wine, I'd pick the dead folks.

Any day of the fucking week.

15

My mother spent four months writing *The Secret of Roanoke*
with her trusty tape recorder always by her side. I asked her
once if writing Mr. Thomas's book was like painting a picture. She thought about it and said it was more like one of
those Paint by Numbers kits, where you just followed the

directions and ended up with something that was supposedly "suitable for framing."

She hired an assistant so she could work on it pretty much full time. She told me on one of our walks home from school —which was just about the only fresh air she ever got during the winter of 2009 and 2010—that she couldn't afford to hire an assistant and couldn't afford not to. Barbara Means was fresh out of the English program at Vassar, and was willing to toil in the agency at bargain-basement wages for the experience, and she was actually pretty good, which was a big help. I liked her big green eyes, which I thought were beautiful.

Mom wrote, Mom rewrote, Mom read the *Roanoke* books and little else during those months, wanting to immerse herself in Regis Thomas's style. She listened to my voice. She rewound and fast forwarded. She filled in the picture. One night, deep into their second bottle of wine, I heard her tell Liz that if she had to write another sentence containing a phrase such as "firm thrusting breasts tipped with rosy nipples," she might lose her mind. She also had to field calls from the trades—and once from Page Six of the *New York Post*—about the state of the final Thomas book, because all sorts of rumors were flying around. (All this came back to me, and vividly, when Sue Grafton died without writing the final book of her alphabet series of mysteries.) Mom said she hated the lying.

"Ah, but you're so good at it," I remember Liz saying, which earned her one of the cold looks I saw from my mother more and more in the final year of their relationship.

She lied to Regis's editor as well, telling her Regis had

instructed her not long before he died that the manuscript of *Secret* should be withheld from everyone (except Mom, of course) until 2010, "in order to build reader interest." Liz said she thought that was a little bit shaky, but Mom said it would fly. "Fiona never edited him, anyway," she said. Meaning Fiona Yarbrough, who worked for Doubleday, Mr. Thomas's publisher. "Her only job was writing Regis a letter after she got each new manuscript, telling him that he'd outdone himself this time."

Once the book was finally turned in, Mom spent a week pacing and snapping at everyone (I was not excluded from said snappery), waiting for Fiona to call and say *Regis didn't write this book, it doesn't sound a bit like him, I think* you *wrote it, Tia*. But in the end it was fine. Either Fiona never guessed or didn't care. Certainly the reviewers never guessed when the book was crashed into production and appeared in the fall of 2010.

Publishers Weekly: "Thomas saved the best for last!"

Kirkus Reviews: "Fans of sweet-savage historical fiction will once more be in bodice-ripping clover."

Dwight Garner, in *The New York Times*: "The trudging, flavorless prose is typical Thomas: the rough equivalent of a heaping plate of food from an all-you-can-eat buffet in a dubious roadside restaurant."

Mom didn't care about the reviews; she cared about the huge advance and the refreshed royalties from the previous *Roanoke* volumes. She bitched mightily about only getting fifteen percent when she had written the whole thing, but got a small measure of revenge by dedicating it to herself. "Because I deserve it," she said.

"I'm not so sure," Liz said. "When you think about it, Tee, you were just the secretary. Maybe you should have dedicated it to Jamie."

This earned Liz another of my mom's cold looks, but I thought Liz had something there. Although when you *really* thought about it, I was also just the secretary. It was still Mr. Thomas's book, dead or not.

16

Now check this out: I told you at least some of the reasons why I liked Liz, and there were probably a few more. I told you all the reasons I *didn't* like Liz, and there were probably a few more of those, too. What I never considered until later (yup, there's that word again) was the possibility that she didn't like *me*. Why would I? I was used to being loved, almost blasé about it. I was loved by my mother and my teachers, especially Mrs. Wilcox, my third-grade teacher, who hugged me and said she'd miss me on the day school let out. I was loved by my best friends Frankie Ryder and Scott Abramowitz (although of course we didn't talk or even think about it that way). And don't forget Lily Rhinehart, who once put a big smackeroo on my mouth. She also gave me a Hallmark card before I changed schools. It had a sad-looking puppy on the front and inside it said *I'LL MISS YOU EVERY DAY YOU'RE AWAY*. She signed it with a little heart over the *i* in her name. Also x's and o's.

Liz at least *liked* me, at least for awhile, I'm sure of it. But that began to change after Cobblestone Cottage. That was when she started to see me as a freak of nature. I think—no, I *know*—that was when Liz started to be scared of me, and it's hard to like what you're scared of. Maybe impossible.

Although she thought nine was old enough for me to walk home from school by myself, Liz sometimes came for me instead of Mom if Liz was working what she called "the swing shift," which started at four in the morning and ended at noon. It was a shift detectives tried to avoid, but Liz got it quite a bit. That was another thing that I never wondered about then, but later (there it is again, yeah yeah yeah, right right right) I realized that she wasn't exactly liked by her bosses. Or trusted. It didn't have anything to do with the relationship she had with my mother; when it came to sex, the NYPD was slowly moving into the 21st century. It wasn't the drinking, either, because she wasn't the only cop who liked to put it away. But certain people she worked with had begun to suspect that Liz was a dirty cop. And—spoiler alert!—they were right.

17

I need to tell you about two particular times Liz got me after school. On both occasions she was in her car—not the one we took out to Cobblestone Cottage, but the one she called her personal. The first time was in 2011, while she and Mom were still a thing. The second was in 2013, a year or so after they stopped being a thing. I'll get to that, but first things first.

I came out of school that day in March with my backpack

slung over just one shoulder (which was how the cool sixth-grade boys did it) and Liz was waiting for me at the curb in her Honda Civic. On the yellow part of the curb, as a matter of fact, which was for handicapped people, but she had her little POLICE OFFICER ON CALL sign for that…which, you could argue, should have told me something about her character even at the tender age of eleven.

I got in, trying not to wrinkle my nose at the smell of stale cigarette smoke that not even the little pine tree air-freshener hanging from the rearview mirror could hide. By then, thanks to *The Secret of Roanoke*, we had our own apartment and didn't have to live in the agency anymore, so I was expecting a ride home, but Liz turned toward downtown instead.

"Where are we going?" I asked.

"Little field trip, Champ," she said. "You'll see."

The field trip was to Woodlawn Cemetery, in the Bronx, final resting place of Duke Ellington, Herman Melville, and Bartholomew "Bat" Masterson, among others. I know about them because I looked it up, and later wrote a report about Woodlawn for school. Liz drove in from Webster Avenue and then just started cruising up and down the lanes. It was nice, but it was also a little scary.

"Do you know how many people are planted here?" she asked, and when I shook my head: "Three hundred thousand. Less than the population of Tampa, but not by much. I checked it out on Wikipedia."

"Why are we here? Because it's interesting, but I've got homework." This wasn't a lie, but I only had, like, a half-hour's worth. It was a bright sunshiny day and she seemed normal enough—just Liz, my mom's friend—but still, this was sort of a freaky field trip.

She totally ignored the homework gambit. "People are being buried here all the time. Look to your left." She pointed and slowed from twenty-five or so to a bare creep. Where she was pointing, people were standing around a coffin placed over an open grave. Some kind of minister was standing at the head of the grave with an open book in his hand. I knew he wasn't a rabbi, because he wasn't wearing a beanie.

Liz stopped the car. Nobody at the service paid any attention. They were absorbed in whatever the minister was saying.

"You see dead people," she said. "I accept that now. Hard not to, after what happened at Thomas's place. Do you see any here?"

"No," I said, more uneasy than ever. Not because of Liz, but because I'd just gotten the news that we were currently surrounded by 300,000 dead bodies. Even though I knew the dead went away after a few days—a week at most—I almost expected to see them standing beside their graves or right on top of them. Then maybe converging on us, like in a fucking zombie movie.

"Are you sure?"

I looked at the funeral (or graveside service, or whatever you call it). The minister must have started a prayer, because all the mourners had bowed their heads. All except one, that was. He was just standing there and looking unconcernedly up at the sky.

"That guy in the blue suit," I said finally. "The one who's

not wearing a tie. He might be dead, but I can't be sure. If there's nothing wrong with them when they die, nothing that *shows*, they look pretty much like anyone else."

"I don't see a man without a tie," she said.

"Well okay then, he's dead."

"Do they always come to their burials?" Liz asked.

"How should I know? This is my first graveyard, Liz. I saw Mrs. Burkett at her funeral, but I don't know about the graveyard, because me and Mom didn't go to that part. We just went home."

"But you see *him*." She was staring at the funeral party like she was in a trance. "You could go over there and talk to him, the way you talked to Regis Thomas that day."

"I'm not going over there!" I don't like to say I squawked this, but I pretty much did. "In front of all his friends? In front of his wife and kids? You can't make me!"

"Mellow out, Champ," she said, and ruffled my hair. "I'm just trying to get it straight in my mind. How did he get here, do you think? Because he sure didn't take an Uber."

"I don't know. I want to go home."

"Pretty soon," she said, and we continued our cruise of the cemetery, passing tombs and monuments and about a billion regular gravestones. We passed three more graveside ceremonies in progress, two small like the first one, where the star of the show was attending sight unseen, and one humungous one, where about two hundred people were gathered on a hillside and the guy in charge (beanie, check—plus a cool-looking shawl) was using a microphone. Each time Liz asked me if I could see the dead person and each time I told her I didn't have a clue.

"You probably wouldn't tell me if you did," she said. "I can tell you're in a pissy mood."

"I'm not in a pissy mood."

"You are, though, and if you tell Tee I brought you out here, we'll probably have a fight. I don't suppose you could tell her we went for ice cream, could you?"

We were almost back to Webster Avenue by then and I was feeling a little better. Telling myself Liz had a right to be curious, that anyone would be. "Maybe if you actually bought me one."

"Bribery! That's a Class B felony!" She laughed, gave my hair a ruffle, and we were pretty much all right again.

We left the cemetery and I saw a young woman in a black dress sitting on a bench and waiting for her bus. A little girl in a white dress and shiny black shoes was sitting beside her. The girl had golden hair and rosy cheeks and a hole in her throat. I waved to her. Liz didn't see me do it; she was waiting for a break in traffic so she could make her turn. I didn't tell her what I saw. That night Liz left after dinner to either go to work or go back to her own place, and I almost told my mother. In the end I didn't. In the end I kept the little girl with the golden hair to myself. Later I would think that the hole in her throat was from the little girl choking on food and they cut into her throat so she could breathe but it was too late. She was sitting there beside her mother and her mother didn't know. But I knew. I saw. When I waved to her, she waved back.

18

While we were eating our ice cream at Lickety Split (Liz phoned my mother to tell her where we were and what we were up to), Liz said, "It must be so strange, what you can do. So *weird*. Doesn't it freak you out?"

I thought of asking her if it freaked her out to look up at night and see the stars and know they go on forever and ever, but didn't bother. I just said no. You get used to marvelous things. You take them for granted. You can try not to, but you do. There's too much wonder, that's all. It's everywhere.

19

I'll tell you about the other time Liz picked me up from school very soon, but first I have to tell you about the day they broke up. That was a scary morning, believe me.

I woke up that day even before my alarm clock went off, because Mom was yelling. I'd heard her mad before, but never *that* mad.

"You brought it into the apartment? Where I live with my *son*?"

Liz answered something, but it was little more than a mumble and I couldn't hear.

"Do you think that matters to me?" Mom shouted. "On

the cop shows that's what they call *serious weight*! I could go to jail as an accessory!"

"Don't be dramatic," Liz said. Louder now. "There was never any chance of—"

"That doesn't matter!" Mom yelled. "It was here! It still *is* here! On the fucking table beside the fucking sugar bowl! You brought drugs into my house! *Serious weight!*"

"Would you stop saying that? This isn't an episode of *Law and Order*." Now Liz was also getting loud. Getting mad. I stood with one ear pressed against my bedroom door, barefoot and dressed in my pajamas, my heart starting to pound. This wasn't a discussion or even an argument. This was more. Worse. "If you hadn't been going through my pockets—"

"Searching your stuff, is that what you think? I was trying to do you a *favor*! I was going to take your extra uniform coat to the cleaners along with my wool skirt. How long has it been there?"

"Only a little while. The guy it belongs to is out of town. He's going to be back tomor—"

"How long?"

Liz's reply was again too low for me to hear.

"Then why bring it here? I don't understand that. Why not put it in the gun safe at your place?"

"I don't…" She stopped.

"Don't what?"

"Don't actually *have* a gun safe. And there have been break-ins in my building. Besides, I was going to be here. We were going to spend the week together. I thought it would save me a trip."

"Save you a trip?"

To this Liz made no reply.

"No gun safe in your apartment. How many other things have you been lying to me about?" Mom didn't sound mad anymore. At least not right then. She sounded hurt. Like she wanted to cry. I felt like going out and telling Liz to leave my mother alone, even if my mother had started it by finding whatever she'd found—the *serious weight*. But I just stood there, listening. Trembling, too.

Liz mumbled some more.

"Is this why you're in trouble at the Department? Are you using as well as...I don't know *couriering* the stuff? *Distributing* the stuff?"

"I'm not using and I'm not distributing!"

"Well, you're passing it on!" Mom's voice was rising again. "That sounds like distributing to me." Then she went back to what was really troubling her. Well, not the only thing, but the one that was troubling her the most. "You brought it into my *apartment*. Where my *son* is. You lock your gun in your car, I always insisted on that, but now I find *two pounds of cocaine* in your spare jacket." She actually laughed, but not the way people do when something is funny. "Your spare *police* jacket!"

"It's not two pounds." Sounding sulky.

"I grew up weighing meat in my father's market," Mom said. "I know two pounds when I've got it in my hand."

"I'll get it out," she said. "Right now."

"You do that, Liz. Posthaste. And you can come back to get your things. By appointment. When I'm here and Jamie's not. Otherwise never."

"You don't mean that," Liz said, but even through the

door I could tell she didn't believe what she was saying.

"I absolutely do. I'm going to do you a favor and not report what I found to your watch captain, but if you ever show your face here again—except for that one time to pick up your shit—I will. That's a promise."

"You're throwing me out? Really?"

"Really. Take your dope and fuck off."

Liz started to cry. That was horrible. Then, after she was gone, Mom started to cry and that was even worse. I went out into the kitchen and hugged her.

"How much of that did you hear?" Mom asked, and before I could answer: "All of it, I imagine. I'm not going to lie to you, Jamie. Or gloss it over. She had dope, a lot of dope, and I never want you to say a word about it, okay?"

"Was it really cocaine?" I had also been crying, but didn't realize it until I heard my voice come out all husky.

"It was. And since you already know so much, I might as well tell you I tried it in college, just a couple of times. I tasted what was in the Baggie I found, and my tongue went numb. It was coke, all right."

"But it's gone. She took it."

Moms know what kids are scared of, if they're good moms. A critic might call that a romantic notion, but I think it's just a practical fact. "She did and we're fine. It was a nasty way to start the day, but it's over. We'll draw a line under it and move on."

"Okay, but…is Liz really not your friend anymore?"

Mom used a dishtowel to wipe her face. "I don't think she's been my friend for quite awhile now. I just didn't know it. Now get ready for school."

That night while I was doing my homework, I heard a *glug-glug-glug* coming from the kitchen and smelled wine. The smell was a lot stronger than usual, even on nights when Mom and Liz put away a lot of vino. I came out of my room to see if she'd spilled a bottle (although there had been no crash of glass) and saw Mom standing over the sink with a jug of red wine in one hand and a jug of white in the other. She was pouring it down the drain.

"Why are you throwing it away? Did it go bad?"

"In a manner of speaking," she said. "I think it started to go bad about eight months ago. It's time to stop."

I found out later that my mother went to AA for awhile after she broke up with Liz, then decided she didn't need it. ("Old men pissing and moaning about a drink they took thirty years ago," she said.) And I don't think she quit completely, because once or twice I thought I smelled wine on her breath when she kissed me goodnight. Maybe from dinner with a client. If she kept a bottle in the apartment, I never knew where she stashed it (not that I looked very hard). What I do know is that in the years that followed, I never saw her drunk and I never saw her hungover. That was good enough for me.

20

I didn't see Liz Dutton for a long time after that, a year or maybe a little more. I missed her at first, but that didn't last long. When the feeling came, I just reminded myself she screwed my mom over, and bigtime. I kept waiting for Mom to have another sleepover friend, but she didn't. Like ever. I asked her once, and she said, "Once burned, twice shy. We're okay, that's the important thing."

And we were. Thanks to Regis Thomas—27 weeks on the *New York Times* bestseller list—and a couple new clients (one of them discovered by Barbara Means, who was by then full-time and actually ended up getting her name on the door in 2017), the agency was back on a firm footing. Uncle Harry returned to the care home in Bayonne (same facility, new management), which wasn't great but better than it had been. Mom was no longer cross in the morning and she got some new clothes. "Have to," she told me once that year. "I've lost fifteen pounds of wine-weight."

I was in middle school by then, which sucked in some respects, was okay in others, and came with one excellent perk: student athletes with no class during the last period of the day could go to the gym, the art room, the music room, or sign out. I only played JV basketball, and the season was over, but I still qualified. Some days I checked out the art room, because this foxy chick named Marie O'Malley occasionally hung out there. If she wasn't working on one of her watercolors, I just went home. Walked if it was nice (on my own, it should go without saying), took the bus if it was nasty.

On the day Liz Dutton came back into my life, I didn't even bother looking for Marie, because I'd gotten a new Xbox for my birthday and I wanted to hit it. I was all the way down the walk and shouldering my backpack (no more one-armed tote for me; sixth grade was in the prehistoric past) when she called to me.

"Hey, Champ, what the haps, bambino?"

She was leaning against her personal, legs crossed at the ankles, wearing jeans and a low-cut blouse. It was a blazer over the blouse instead of a parka, but it still had NYPD on the breast and she flapped it open in the old way to show me her shoulder holster. Only this time it wasn't empty.

"Hi, Liz," I mumbled. I looked down at my shoes and made a right turn onto the street.

"Hold on, I need to talk to you."

I stopped, but I didn't turn back to her. Like she was Medusa and one look at her snaky head would turn me to stone. "I don't think I should. Mom would be mad."

"She doesn't need to know. Turn around, Jamie. Please. Looking at nothing but your back is just about killing me."

She sounded like she really felt bad, and that made me feel bad. I turned around. The blazer was closed again, but I could see the bulge of her gun just the same.

"I want you to take a ride with me."

"Not a good idea," I said. I was thinking of this girl named Ramona Sheinberg. She was in a couple of my classes at the beginning of the year, but then she was gone and my friend Scott Abramowitz told me her father snatched her during a custody suit and took her to someplace where there was no extradition. Scott said he hoped it was at least a place with palm trees.

"I need what you can do, Champ," she said. "I really do."

I didn't reply to that, but she must have seen I was wavering, because she gave me a smile. It was a nice one that lit up those gray eyes of hers. They weren't a bit sleety that day. "Maybe it will come to nothing, but I want to try. I want *you* to try."

"Try what?"

She didn't answer, not then, just held out a hand to me. "I helped your mother when Regis Thomas died. Won't you help me now?"

Technically, I was the one who helped my mother that day, Liz just gave us a quick ride up the Sprain Brook Parkway, but she *had* stopped to buy me a Whopper when Mom just wanted to push on. And she gave me the rest of her Coke when my mouth was so dry from talking. So I got in the car. I didn't feel good about it, but I did it. Adults have power, especially when they beg, and that's what Liz was doing.

I asked Liz where we were going, and she said Central Park to start with. Maybe a couple of other places after that. I said if I didn't get home by five, Mom would be worried. Liz told me she'd try to get me back before then, but this was very important.

That's when she told me what it was about.

21

The guy who called himself Thumper set his first bomb in Eastport, a Long Island town not all that far from Speonk, one-time home of Uncle Harry's Cabin (literary joke). This was in 1996. Thumper dropped a stick of dynamite hooked up to a timer in a trash can outside the restrooms of the King Kullen Supermarket. The timer was nothing but a cheap alarm clock, but it worked. The dynamite went off at 9 PM, just as the supermarket was closing. Three people were hurt, all store employees. Two of them suffered only superficial injuries, but the third guy was coming out of the men's when the bomb blew. He lost an eye and his right arm up to the elbow. Two days later, a note came in to the Suffolk County Police Department. It was typed on an IBM Selectric. It said, *How do you like my work so far? More to come! THUMPER*.

Thumper set nineteen bombs before he actually killed anybody. "*Nineteen!*" Liz exclaimed. "And it wasn't as if he wasn't trying. He set them all over the five boroughs, and a couple in New Jersey—Jersey City and Fort Lee—for good measure. All dynamite, Canadian manufacture."

But the score of the maimed and wounded was high. It had been closing in on fifty when he finally killed the man who picked the wrong Lexington Avenue pay phone. Every kaboom was followed by a note to the police responsible for the area where said kaboom occurred, and the notes were always the same: *How do you like my work so far? More to come! THUMPER*.

Before Richard Scalise (that was the pay phone man's name), a long period of time went by before each new explosion. The two closest were six weeks apart. The longest delay was close to a year. But after Scalise, Thumper sped up. The bombs became bigger and the timers more sophisticated. Nineteen explosions between 1996 and 2009—twenty, counting the pay phone bomb. Between 2010 and the pretty May day in 2013 when Liz came back into my life, he set ten more, wounding twenty and killing three. By then, Thumper wasn't just an urban legend, or an NY1 staple; by then he was nationwide.

He was good at avoiding security cameras, and those he couldn't avoid just showed a guy in a coat, sunglasses, and a

Yankees cap pulled down low. He kept his head low, too. Some white hair showed around the sides and back of the cap, but that could have been a wig. Over the seventeen years of his "reign of terror," three different task forces were organized to catch him. The first one disbanded during a long break in his "reign," when the police assumed he was finished. The second disbanded after a big shakeup in the department. The third started in 2011, when it became clear Thumper had gone into overdrive. Liz didn't tell me all this on our way to Central Park; I found it out later, as I did so many other things.

Finally, two days ago, they got the break in the case they'd been waiting and hoping for. Son of Sam was caught by a parking ticket. Ted Bundy got caught because he forgot to put his headlights on. Thumper—real name Kenneth Alan Therriault—was nailed because a building super had a minor accident on trash day. He was wheeling a dolly loaded with garbage cans down an alley to the pickup point out front. He hit a pothole and one of the cans spilled. When he went to clean up the mess, he found a bundle of wires and a yellow scrap of paper with CANACO printed on it. He might not have called the police if that had been all, but it wasn't. Attached to one of the wires was a Dyno Nobel blasting cap.

We got to Central Park and parked with a bunch of regular cop cars (another thing I found out later is that Central Park has its own precinct, the 22nd). Liz put her little cop sign on the dashboard and we walked down 86th Street for a little while before turning onto a path that led to the Alexander Hamilton Monument. That's one thing I didn't find out later; I just read the fucking sign. Or plaque. Whatever.

"The super took a picture of the wires, the scrap of paper, and the blasting cap with his phone, but the task force didn't get it until the next day."

"Yesterday," I said.

"Right. As soon as we saw it, we knew we had our guy."

"Sure, because of the blasting cap."

"Yeah, but not just that. The scrap of paper? Canaco is a Canadian company that manufactures dynamite. We got a list of all the building's tenants, and eliminated most of them without any fieldwork, because we knew we were looking for a male, probably single, and probably white. There were only six tenants who checked all those boxes, and only one guy who'd ever worked in Canada."

"Googled 'em, right?" I was getting interested.

"Right you are. Among other things, we found Kenneth Therriault has dual citizenship, U.S. and Canada. He worked all sorts of construction jobs up there in the great white north, plus fracking and oil shale sites. He was Thumper, pretty much had to be."

I only got a quick look at Alexander Hamilton, just enough to read the sign and note his fancy pants. Liz had me by the hand and was leading me toward a path a little way beyond the statue. Pulling me, actually.

"We went in with a SWAT team, but his crib was empty. Well, not *empty* empty, all his stuff was there, but he was gone. The super didn't keep his big discovery to himself, unfortunately, although he was told to. He blabbed to some of the residents, and the word spread. One of the things we found in the apartment was an IBM Selectric."

"That's a typewriter?"

She nodded. "Those babies used to come with different type elements for different fonts. The one in the machine matched Thumper's notes."

Before we get to the path and the bench that wasn't there, I need to tell you some other stuff I found out later. She was telling the truth about how Therriault finally tripped over his dick, but she kept talking about *we*. *We* this and *we* that, but Liz wasn't a part of the Thumper task force. She *had* been part of the second task force, the one that ended in the big departmental shakeup when everybody was running around like chickens with their heads cut off, but by 2013 all Liz Dutton had left in the NYPD was a toehold, and only that much because cops have a kickass union. The rest of her was already out the door. Internal Affairs was circling like buzzards around fresh roadkill, and on the day she picked me up from school, she wouldn't have been put on a task force dedicated to catching serial litterbugs. She needed a miracle, and I was supposed to be it.

"By today," she went on, "every cop in the boroughs had Kenneth Therriault's name and description. Every way out of the city was being monitored by human eyeballs as well as cameras—and as I'm sure you know, there's plenty of cameras. Nailing this guy, dead or alive, became our number one priority, because we were afraid he might decide to go out in a blaze of glory. Maybe setting off a bomb in front of Saks Fifth Avenue, or in Grand Central. Only he did us a favor."

She stopped and pointed at a spot beside the path. I noticed the grass was beaten down, as if a lot of people had been standing there.

"He came into the park, he sat down on a bench, and he blew his brains out with a Ruger .45 ACP."

I looked at the spot, awestruck.

"The bench is at the NYPD Forensics Lab in Jamaica, but this is where he did it. So here's the big question. Do you see him? Is he here?"

I looked around. I had no clue what Kenneth Alan Therriault looked like, but if he'd blown his brains out, I didn't think I could miss him. I saw some kids throwing a Frisbee for their dog to chase (the dog was off his leash, a Central Park no-no), I saw a couple of lady runners, a couple of 'boarders, and a couple of old guys further down the path reading newspapers, but I didn't see any guy with a hole in his head, and I told her that.

"Fuck," Liz said. "Well, all right. We've got two more chances, at least that I can see. He worked as an orderly at City of Angels Hospital on 70th—quite a comedown from his construction days, but he was in his seventies—and the apartment building where he lived is in Queens. Which do you think, Champ?"

"I think I want to go home. He might be anyplace."

"Really? Didn't you say they hang around places where they spent time when they were alive? Before they, I don't know, pop off for good?"

I couldn't remember if I'd said that to her, exactly, but it was true. Still, I was feeling more and more like Ramona Sheinberg. Kidnapped, in other words. "Why bother? He's dead, right? Case closed."

"Not quite." She bent down to look me in the eye. She didn't have to bend so far in 2013, because I was getting taller.

Nowhere near the six feet I am now, but a couple of inches. "There was a note pinned to his shirt. It said, *There's one more, and it is a big one. Fuck you and see you in hell.* It was signed *THUMPER*."

Well, that kind of changed things.

22

We went to City of Angels first, because it was closer. There was no guy with a hole in his head out front, just some smokers, so we went in through the Emergency Room entrance. A lot of people were sitting around in there, and one guy was bleeding from the head. The wound looked like a laceration to me rather than a bullet hole, and he was younger than Liz said Kenneth Therriault was, but I asked Liz if she could see him, just to be sure. She said she could.

We went to the desk, where Liz showed her badge and identified herself as an NYPD detective. She asked if there was a room where the custodians put their stuff and changed their clothes for their shifts. The lady at the desk said there was, but the other police had already been there and cleaned out Therriault's locker. Liz asked if they were still there and the lady said no, the last of them left hours ago.

"I'd like to grab a quick peek, anyway," Liz said. "Tell me how to get there."

The lady said to take the elevator down to B level and turn right. Then she smiled at me and said, "Are you helping your mom in her investigations today, young man?"

I thought of saying *Well, she's not my mom, but I guess I*

am helping because she hopes that if Mr. Therriault is still hanging around, I'll see him. Of course that wouldn't fly, so I was stuck.

Liz wasn't. She explained that the school nurse thought I might have mono, so this seemed like a chance to get me checked out and visit Therriault's place of work at the same time. Two birds with one stone type of deal.

"You'd probably do better with your own doctor," the desk lady said. "This place is a madhouse today. You'll wait for hours."

"That's probably best," Liz agreed. I thought how natural she sounded, and what a smooth liar she was. I couldn't decide if I was grossed out or admiring. I guess a little of both.

The desk lady leaned forward. I was fascinated by how her extremely large bazams shoved her papers forward. It made me think of an icebreaker boat I'd seen in a movie. She lowered her voice. "Everyone was shocked, let me tell you. Ken was the oldest of all the orderlies, and the nicest. Hardworking and willing to please. If someone asked him to do something, he was always happy to do it. And with a smile. To think we were working with a *killer*! Do you know what it proves?"

Liz shook her head, clearly impatient for us to be on our way.

"That you never know," the desk lady said. She spoke like someone who's imparting a great truth. "You just never know!"

"He was good at covering up, all right," Liz said, and I thought, *It takes one to know one.*

In the elevator, I asked, "If you're on a task force, how come you're not *with* the task force?"

"Don't be dumb, Champ. Was I supposed to take *you* to the task force? Having to make up a story about you at the desk was bad enough." The elevator stopped. "If anyone asks about you, remember why you're here."

"Mono."

"Right."

But there was no one to ask. The custodian's room was empty. It had yellow tape saying POLICE INVESTIGATION KEEP OUT across the door. Liz and I ducked under it, her holding my hand. There were benches, a few chairs, and about two dozen lockers. Also a fridge, a microwave, and a toaster oven. There was an open box of Pop Tarts by the toaster oven, and I thought I wouldn't have minded a Pop Tart just then. But there was no Kenneth Therriault.

The lockers had names stuck to them in DymoTape. Liz opened Therriault's, using a handkerchief because of the leftover fingerprint powder. She did it slowly, like she expected him to be hiding inside like the boogeyman in a kid's closet. Therriault was sort of a boogeyman, but he wasn't in there. It was empty. The cops took everything.

Liz said fuck again. I looked at my phone to check the time. It was twenty past three.

"I know, I know," she said. Her shoulders were slumped, and although I resented the way she'd just scooped me up and taken me away, I couldn't help feeling a little sorry for her. I remembered Mr. Thomas saying my mom looked older, and now I thought my mom's lost friend looked older, too. Thinner. And I had to admit I also felt some admiration, because she was trying to do the right thing and save lives. She was like the hero of a movie, the lone wolf who means to solve the case on her own. Maybe she did care about the innocent people who might be vaporized in Thumper's last bomb. Probably she did. But I know now she was also concerned with saving her job. I don't like to think it was her major concern, but in light of what happened later—I'll get to it—I have to think it was.

"Okay, one more shot. And stop looking at your dumb phone, Champ. I know what time it is, and no matter how much trouble you're in if I don't get you home before your mother shows up, I'll be in more."

"She'll probably take Barbara out for a drink before she goes home, anyway. Barbara works for the agency now." I don't know why I said that, exactly. Because I also wanted to save innocent lives, I suppose, although that seemed rather academic to me, because I didn't think we were going to find Kenneth Therriault. I think it was because Liz looked so beaten down. So backed into a corner.

"Well, that's a lucky break," Liz said. "All we need is one more."

23

The Frederick Arms was twelve or fourteen stories high, gray brick, with bars on the windows of the first- and second-floor apartments. To a kid who grew up in the Palace on Park, it looked more like that *Shawshank Redemption* prison than an apartment building. And Liz knew right away that we were never going to get inside, let alone to Kenneth Therriault's apartment. The place was swarming with cops. Lookie-loos were standing in the middle of the street, as close to the police sawhorse barricades as they could get, snapping photos. TV news vans were parked on both sides of the block with their antennas up and cables snaking everywhere. There was even a Channel 4 helicopter hovering overhead.

"Look," I said. "Stacy-Anne Conway! She's on NY1!"

"Ask me if I give a shit," Liz said.

I didn't.

We had been lucky not to run into reporters at Central Park or City of Angels, and I realized the only reason we hadn't was because they were all here. I looked at Liz and saw a tear trickling down one of her cheeks. "Maybe we can go to his funeral," I said. "Maybe he'll be there."

"He'll probably be cremated. Privately, at the city's expense. No relatives. He outlived them all. I'll take you home, Champ. Sorry to drag you all this way."

"That's okay," I said, and patted her hand. I knew Mom wouldn't like me doing that, but Mom wasn't there.

Liz pulled a U-turn and headed back toward the Queens-boro bridge. A block away from the Frederick Arms, I glanced at a little grocery on my side and said, "Oh my God. There he is."

She snapped a wide-eyed glance at me. "Are you sure? Are you *sure*, Jamie?"

I leaned forward and vomited between my sneakers. That was all the answer she needed.

24

I can't really say if he was as bad as the Central Park man, that was a long time ago. He could have been worse. Once you've seen what can happen to a human body that's suffered an act of violence—accident, suicide, murder—maybe it doesn't even matter. Kenneth Therriault, alias Thumper, was bad, okay? Really bad.

There were benches on either side of the grocery's door, so people could eat the snacks they bought, I suppose. Therriault was sitting on one of them with his hands on the thighs of his khaki pants. People were passing by, headed for whatever they were headed for. A black kid with a skateboard under his arm went into the store. A lady came out with a steaming paper cup of coffee. Neither of them glanced at the bench where Therriault was sitting.

He must have been right-handed, because that side of his head didn't look too bad. There was a hole in his temple, maybe the size of a dime, maybe a little smaller, surrounded by a dark corona that was either bruising or gunpowder. Probably gunpowder. I doubt if his body had time to muster enough blood to make a bruise.

The real damage was on the left, where the bullet exited. The hole on that side was almost as big as a dessert plate and surrounded by irregular fangs of bone. The flesh on his head was swelled, like from a gigantic infection. His left eye had been yanked sideways and bulged from its socket. Worst of all, gray stuff had dripped down his cheek. That was his brain.

"Don't stop," I said. "Just keep going." The smell of puke was strong in my nose and the taste of it was in my mouth, all slimy. "Please, Liz, I can't."

She swerved to the curb in front of a fire hydrant near the end of the block instead. "You have to. And I have to. Sorry, Champ, but we have to know. Now pull yourself together so people don't stare at us and think I've been abusing you."

But you are, I thought. *And you won't stop until you get what you want.*

The taste in my mouth was the ravioli I'd eaten in the school caff. As soon as I realized that I opened the door, leaned out, and puked some more. Like on the day of the Central Park man, when I never made it to Lily's birthday party at fancy-shmancy Wave Hill. That was *déjà vu* I could have done without.

"Champ? *Champ!*"

I turned to her and she was holding out a wad of Kleenex (show me a woman without Kleenex in her purse and I'll show you no one at all). "Wipe your mouth and then get out of the car. Try to look normal. Let's get this done."

I could see she meant it—we weren't going to leave until she had what she wanted. *Man up*, I thought. *I can do this. I have to, because lives are at stake.*

I wiped my mouth and got out. Liz put her little sign on the dashboard—the police version of Get Out of Jail Free—and came around to where I was standing on the sidewalk, staring into a laundromat at a woman folding clothes. That wasn't very interesting, but at least it kept me from looking at the ruined man up the street. For the time being, anyway. Soon I'd have to. Worse—oh God—I'd have to talk to him. If he even *could* talk.

I held out my hand without thinking. Thirteen was probably too old to be holding hands with a woman the people passing by would assume was my mother (if they bothered thinking about us at all), but when she took it, I was glad. Glad as hell.

We started back to the store. I wished we'd had miles to walk, but it was only half a block.

"Where is he, exactly?" she asked in a low voice.

I risked a look to make sure he hadn't moved. Nope, he was still on the bench, and now I could look directly into the crater where there had once been thoughts. His ear was still on, but it was crooked and I found myself remembering a Mr. Potato Head I'd had when I was four or five. My stomach clenched again.

"Get it together, Champ."

"Don't call me that anymore," I managed to say. "I hate it."

"Duly noted. Where is he?"

"Sitting on the bench."

"The one on this side of the door, or—"

"This side, yeah."

I was looking at him again, we were close now so I couldn't help it, and I saw an interesting thing. A man came out of the store with a newspaper under his arm and a hot dog in one hand. The hot dog was in one of those foil bags that's supposed to keep them hot (believe that and you'll believe the moon is made of green cheese). He started to sit down on the other bench, already pulling his hot dog out of the bag. Then he stopped, looked either at me and Liz or the other bench, and walked on down the block to eat his pup somewhere else. He didn't see Therriault—he would have run if he had, most likely screaming his head off—but I think he *felt* him. No, I don't just think it, I know it. I wish I'd paid more attention at the time, but I was upset, as I'm sure you understand. If you don't, you're an idiot.

Therriault turned his head. It was a relief because the move hid the worst of the exit wound. It wasn't a relief because his face was normal on one side and all bloated out of shape on the other, like that guy Two-Face in the Batman comics. Worst of all, now he was looking at me.

I see them and they know I do. It's always been that way.

"Ask him where the bomb is," Liz said. She was speaking from the corner of her mouth, like a spy in a comedy.

A woman with a baby in a Papoose carrier came up the sidewalk. She gave me a distrustful glance, maybe because I looked funny or maybe because I smelled of puke. Maybe both. I was past the point of caring. All I wanted was to do what Liz Dutton had brought me here to do, then get the fuck out. I waited until the woman with the baby went inside.

"Where's the bomb, Mr. Therriault? The last bomb?"

At first he didn't reply and I was thinking *okay, his brains are blown out, he's here but he can't talk, end of story.* Then he spoke up. The words didn't exactly match the movements of his mouth and it came to me that he was talking from somewhere else. Like on a time-delay from hell. That scared the shit out of me. If I'd known that was when something awful came into him and took him over, it would have been even worse. But *do* I know that? Like for sure? No, but I almost know it.

"I don't want to tell you."

That stunned me to silence. I had never gotten such a reply from a dead person before. True, my experience was limited, but up until then I would have said they had to tell you the truth first time, every time.

"What did he say?" Liz asked. Still talking from the corner of her mouth.

I ignored her and spoke to Therriault again. Since there was no one around, I spoke louder, enunciating every word the way you would for a person who was deaf or only had a shaky grasp on English. "Where…is…the last…bomb?"

I also would have said that the dead can't feel pain, that they are beyond it, and Therriault certainly did not seem to be suffering from the cataclysmic self-inflicted wound in his head, but now his half-bloated face twisted as if I were burning him or stabbing him in the belly instead of just asking him a question.

"Don't want to *tell* you!"

"What did he—" Liz began again, but then the lady with the baby came back out. She had a lottery ticket. The baby in the Papoose had a Kit-Kat finger which he was smearing all over his face. Then he looked at the bench where Therriault was sitting and started crying. The mom must have thought her kid was looking at me, because she gave me another glance, *mega* distrustful this time, and hurried on her way.

"Champ…Jamie, I mean…"

"Shut up," I said. Then, because my mother would have hated me talking to any grownup like that, "Please."

I looked back to Therriault. His grimace of pain made his ruined face look more ruined than ever, and all at once I decided I didn't care. He had maimed enough people to fill a hospital ward, he had killed people, and if the note he'd pinned to his shirt wasn't a lie, he had died trying to kill even more. I decided I *hoped* he was suffering.

"Where…is it…you…motherfucker?"

He clasped his hands around his middle, bent over like he had cramps, groaned. Then he gave it up. "King Kullen. The King Kullen Supermarket in Eastport."

"Why?"

"Seemed right to finish where I started," he said, and drew a circle in the air with one finger. "Complete the circle."

"No, why do it at all? Why set all those bombs?"

He smiled, and the way it kind of squelched the bloated side of his face? I still see that, and I'll never be able to un-see it.

"Because," he said.

"Because what?"

"Because I felt like it," he said.

25

When I told Liz everything Therriault had said, she was excited and nothing else. I could understand that, she wasn't the one looking at a man who'd pretty much blown off one whole side of his head. She told me she had to go into the store and get some stuff.

"And leave me here with *him*?"

"No, go back down the street. Wait by the car. I'll only be a minute."

Therriault was sitting there looking at me with the eye

that was more or less regular and the one that was all stretched out. I could feel his gaze. It made me think of the time I went to camp and got fleas and had to have this special stinky shampoo like five times before they were all gone.

Shampoo wouldn't fix the way Therriault made me feel, only getting away from him would do that, so I did what Liz said. I walked as far as the laundromat and looked in at the woman who was still folding clothes. She saw me and gave me a wave. That brought back the little girl with the hole in her throat, and how *she* had waved to me, and for one horrible moment I thought the laundromat lady was also dead. Only a dead person wouldn't be folding clothes, they only stood around. Or sat around, like Therriault. So I gave her a return wave. I even tried to smile.

Then I turned back to the store. I told myself it was to see if Liz was coming out yet, but that wasn't why. I was looking to see if Therriault was still looking at me. He was. He raised one hand, palm up, three fingers tucked into his palm, one finger pointing. He curled it once, then twice. Very slowly. *Come here, boy.*

I walked back, my legs seeming to move of their own accord. I didn't want to, but couldn't seem to help myself.

"She doesn't care about you," Kenneth Therriault said. "Not a fig. Not one single *fig*. She's using you, boy."

"Fuck you, we're saving lives." There was no one passing by, but even if somebody had been, he or she wouldn't have heard me. He had stolen all of my voice but a whisper.

"What she's saving is her job."

"You don't know that, you're just some random psycho." Still only a whisper, and I felt on the verge of peeing myself.

He didn't say anything, only grinned. That was his answer.

Liz came out. She had one of those cheap plastic bags they gave you in stores like that back then. She looked at the bench, where the ruined man she couldn't see was sitting, and then at me. "What are you doing here, Cha…Jamie? I told you to go to the car." And before I could answer, quick and harsh, like I was a perp in a TV cop show interrogation room: "Did he tell you something else?"

That you only care about saving your job, I thought of saying. *But maybe I already knew that.*

"No," I said. "I want to go home, Liz."

"We will. We will. As soon as I do one more thing. Two, actually, I've also got to get your mess out of my car." She put an arm around my shoulders (like a good mom would) and walked me up past the laundromat. I would have waved to the clothes-folding lady again, but her back was turned.

"I set something up. I didn't really think I'd have a chance to use it, but thanks to you…"

When we were next to her car, she took a flip-phone out of the store bag. It was still in its blister pack. I leaned against the window of a shoe repair place and watched her fiddle with it until she got it working. It was now quarter past four. If Mom went for a drink with Barbara, we could still get back before she came home…but could I keep the afternoon's adventures to myself? I didn't know, and right then it didn't seem that important. I wished Liz could at least have driven around the corner, I thought she could have smelled my puke for that long after what I'd done for her, but she was too wound up. Plus, there was the bomb to consider. I thought of all the movies I'd seen where the clock is counting down to nothing and the hero is wondering whether to cut the red wire or the blue one.

Now she was calling.

"Colton? Yes, this is m…shut up, just listen. It's time to do your thing. You owe me a favor, a big one, and this is it. I'm going to tell you exactly what to say. Record it, then…*shut up, I said!*"

She sounded so vicious that I took a step back. I'd never heard Liz like that, and realized that I was seeing her for the first time in her other life. The police life where she dealt with scumbuckets.

"Record it, then write it down, then call me back. Do it right away." She waited. I snuck a look back at the store. Both benches were empty. That should have been a relief, but somehow I didn't feel relieved.

"Ready? Okay." Liz closed her eyes, shutting out everything but what she wanted to say. She spoke slowly and carefully. " 'If Ken Therriault was really Thumper…' I'll break in there and say I want to record this. You wait until I say 'Go ahead, start again.' Got that?" She listened until Colton—whoever he was—said he got it. You say, 'If Ken Therriault was really Thumper, he was always talking about finishing where he started. I'm calling you because we talked in 2008. I kept your card.' You got that?" Another pause. Liz nodding. "Good. I'll say who is this, and you hang up. Do it right away, this is time-sensitive. Screw it up and I'll fuck you bigtime. You know I can."

She ended the call. She paced around on the sidewalk. I snuck another look at the benches. Empty. Maybe Therriault —whatever remained of him—was heading back home to check out the scene at the good old Frederick Arms.

The drumbeat intro to "Rumor Has It" came from the pocket of Liz's blazer. She took out her real phone and said hello. She listened, then said, "Hold on, I want to record this." She did that, then said, "Go ahead, start again."

Once the script was played out, she ended the call and put her phone away. "It's not as strong as I'd like," she said. "But will they care?"

"Probably not, once they find the bomb," I said. Liz gave a little start, and I realized she had been talking to herself. Now that I'd done what she wanted, I was just baggage.

She had a roll of paper towels and a can of air freshener in the bag. She cleaned up my puke, dropped it in the gutter (hundred-dollar fine for littering, I found out later), and then sprayed the car with something that smelled like flowers.

"Get in," she told me.

I'd been turned away so I didn't have to look at what remained of my lunchtime ravioli (as far as cleaning up the mess went, I thought she owed me that), but when I turned back to get in the car, I saw Kenneth Therriault standing by the trunk. Close enough to reach out and touch me, and still grinning. I might have screamed, but when I saw him I was between breaths and my chest wouldn't seem to expand and grab another one. It was as if all the muscles had gone to sleep.

"I'll be seeing you," Therriault said. The grin widened and I could see a cake of dead blood between his teeth and cheek. "*Champ*."

26

We only drove three blocks before she stopped again. She took out her phone (her real one, not the burner), then looked at me and saw I was shaking. I maybe could have used a hug then, but all I got was a pat on the shoulder, presumably sympathetic. "Delayed reaction, kiddo. Know all about it. It'll pass."

Then she made a call, identified herself as Detective Dutton, and asked for Gordon Bishop. She must have been told he was on the job, because Liz said, "I don't care if he's on Mars, patch me through. This is Priority One."

She waited, tapping the fingers of her free hand on the steering wheel. Then she straightened up. "It's Dutton, Gordo…no, I know I'm not, but you need to hear this. I just got a tip about Therriault from someone I interviewed when I *was* on it…no, I don't know who. You need to check out the King Kullen in Eastport…where he started, right. It makes a degree of sense if you think about it." Listening. Then: "Are you kidding? How many people did we interview back then? A hundred? Two hundred? Listen, I'll play you the message. I recorded it, assuming my phone worked."

She knew it had; she'd checked it on our short three-block drive. She played it for him and when it was done, she said, "Gordo? Did you…shit." She ended the call. "He hung up." Liz gave me a grim smile. "He hates my guts, but he'll check. He knows it'll be on him if he doesn't."

Detective Bishop did check, because by then they'd had time to start digging into Kenneth Therriault's past, and they'd found a nugget that stood out in light of Liz's "anonymous tip." Long before his career in construction and his post-retirement career as an orderly at City of Angels, Therriault had grown up in the town of Westport, which is, natch, next door to Eastport. As a high school senior, he'd worked as a bag boy and shelf stocker at King Kullen. Where he was caught shoplifting. The first time he did it, Therriault was warned. The second time he got canned. But stealing, it seemed, was a hard habit to break. Later in life he moved on to dynamite and blasting caps. A good supply of both was later found in a Queens storage locker. All of it old, all of it from Canada. I guess the border searches were a lot less thorough in those days.

"Can we go home now?" I asked Liz. "Please?"

"Yes. Are you going to tell your mother about this?"

"I don't know."

She smiled. "It was a rhetorical question. Of course you will. And that's okay, doesn't bother me in the slightest. Do you know why?"

"Because nobody would believe it."

She patted my hand. "That's right, Champ. Hole in one."

27

Liz dropped me off on the corner and sped away. I walked down to our building. My mother and Barbara hadn't gone for that drink after all, Barb had a cold and said she was going home right after work. Mom was on the steps with her phone in her hand.

She flew down the steps when she saw me coming and grabbed me in a panicky hug that squeezed the breath out of me. "Where the fuck were you, James?" She only called me that when she was super-pissed, which you might have already guessed. "How could you be so thoughtless? I've been calling *everyone*, I was starting to think you'd been kidnapped, I even thought of calling…"

She quit hugging and held me at arms' length. I could see she had been crying and was starting to again and that made me feel really bad, even though none of it had been my fault. I think only your mother can truly make you feel lower than whale shit.

"Was it Liz?" And without waiting for an answer: "It was." Then, in a low and deadly voice: "That *bitch*."

"I had to go with her, Mom," I said. "I really had to."

Then I started to cry, too.

28

We went upstairs. Mom made coffee and gave me a cup. My first, and I've been a fool for the stuff ever since. I told her almost everything. How Liz had been waiting outside school. How she told me lives depended on finding Thumper's last bomb. How we went to the hospital, and to Therriault's building. I even told her how awful Therriault looked with half his head blown out of shape on one side. What I didn't tell her was how I'd turned around to see him standing be-hind Liz's car, close enough to grab my arm…if dead people

can grab, a thing I never wanted to find out one way or the
other. And I didn't tell her what he'd said, but that night
when I went to bed it clanged in my head like a cracked bell:
"I'll be seeing you...*Champ*."

Mom kept saying *okay* and *I understand*, all the time
looking more distressed. But she had to know what was happening on Long Island, and so did I. She turned on the TV
and we sat on the couch to watch. Lewis Dodley of NY1 was
doing a stand-up on a street with police sawhorses blocking
it off. "Police appear to be taking this tip very seriously," he
was saying. "According to a source in the Suffolk County
Police Department—"

I remembered the news helicopter flying over the Frederick
Arms and figured it must have had enough time to chopper
out to Long Island, so I grabbed the remote from my mother's
lap and flipped over to Channel 4. And there, sure enough,
was the roof of the King Kullen supermarket. The parking
lot was full of police cars. Parked by the main doors was a
big van that just about had to belong to the Bomb Squad. I
saw two helmeted cops with a pair of dogs on harnesses
going inside. The chopper was too high to see if the Bomb
Squad cops were wearing bulletproof vests and flak jackets
as well as helmets, but I'm sure they were. Not the dogs,
though. If Thumper's bomb went off while they were inside,
the dogs would be blown to mush.

The reporter in the chopper was saying, "We've been told
that all customers and store personnel have been safely evac-
uated. Although it's possible this is just another false alarm,
there have been many during Thumper's reign of terror—"
(Yup, he actually said that) "—taking these things seriously
is always the wisest course. All we know now is that this was

the site of Thumper's first bomb, and that no bomb has been found yet. Let's send it back to the studio."

The chromo behind the news anchors had a picture of Therriault, maybe his City of Angels ID, because he looked pretty old. He was no movie star, but he looked a hell of a lot better than he had sitting on that bench. Liz's manufactured tip might not have been taken so seriously had it not caused one of the older detectives in the department to recall a case from his childhood, that of George Metesky, dubbed the Mad Bomber by the press. Metesky planted thirty-three pipe bombs during his own reign of terror, which lasted from 1940 to 1956, and the seed was a similar grudge, in his case against Consolidated Edison.

Some quick researcher in the news department had also made the connection, and Metesky's face came up next on the chromo behind the anchors, but Mom didn't bother looking at the old guy…who, I thought, looked weirdly like Therriault in his orderly's uniform. She had grabbed her phone, then went muttering into her bedroom for her address book, presumably having deleted Liz's number after their argument about the *serious weight*.

A commercial for some pill came on, so I crept to her bedroom door to listen. If I'd waited I wouldn't have heard jack shit, because that call didn't last long. "It's Tia, Liz. Listen to me and don't say a word. I'm going to keep this to myself, for reasons that should be obvious to you. But if you ever bother my son again, if he even *sees* you, I will burn your life to the ground. You know I can do it. All it would take is one single push. *Stay away from Jamie*."

I scurried back to the couch and pretended to be absorbed

in the next commercial. Which turned out to be as useless as tits on a bull.

"You heard that?"

Her eyes were burning, telling me not to lie. I nodded.

"Good. If you see her again, you run like hell. Home. And tell me. Do you understand?"

I nodded again.

"Okay, right right right. I'm ordering take-out. Do you want pizza or Chinese?"

29

The cops found and defused Thumper's last bomb that Wednesday night, around eight o'clock. Mom and me were watching *Person of Interest* on TV when the station broke in with a special bulletin. The sniffer dogs had made lots of passes without finding anything, and their Bomb Squad handlers were about to take them out when one of them alerted in the housewares aisle. They'd been in that one several times before and there was no place on the shelves to hide a bomb, but one of the cops happened to look up and saw a ceiling panel just slightly out of place. That's where the bomb was, between the ceiling and the roof. It was tied to a girder with stretchy orange cord, like the kind bungee jumpers use.

Therriault really blew his wad on that one—sixteen sticks of dynamite and a dozen blasting caps. He'd moved far beyond alarm clocks; the bomb was hooked up to a digital timer very much like the ones in those movies I'd been thinking about (one of the cops took a picture after it was disarmed, and it was in the next day's *New York Times*). It was set to go off at 5 PM on Friday, when the store was always busiest. The next day on NY1 (we were back to Mom's fave) one of the Bomb Squad guys said it would have brought the whole roof down. When asked how many people might have been killed in such a blast, he only shook his head.

That Thursday night as we ate dinner, my mother said, "You did a good thing, Jamie. A *fine* thing. Liz did too, whatever her reasons might have been. It makes me think of something Marty said once." She meant Mr. Burkett, actually Professor Burkett, still Emeritus and still hanging in.

"What did he say?"

"'Sometimes God uses a broken tool.' It was from one of the old English writers he used to teach."

"He always asks me what I'm learning in school," I said, "and he always shakes his head like he's thinking I'm getting a bad education."

Mom laughed. "There's a man who's *stuffed* with education, and he's still totally sharp and in focus. Remember when we had Christmas dinner with him?"

"Sure, turkey sandwiches with cranberry dressing, the best! Plus hot chocolate!"

"Yes, that was a good night. It will be a shame when he passes on. Eat up, there's apple crisp for dessert. Barbara made it. And Jamie?"

I looked at her.

"Could we not talk about this anymore. Just kind of…put it behind us?"

I thought she wasn't just talking about Liz, or even

Therriault; she was also talking about how I could see dead folks. It was what our computer teacher might have called *a global request*, and it was all right with me. More than all right, actually. "Sure."

Right then, sitting in our brightly lit kitchen nook and eating pizza, I really thought we could put it behind us. Only I was wrong. I didn't see Liz Dutton for another two years, and hardly ever thought about her, but I saw Ken Therriault again that very night.

As I said at the beginning, this is a horror story.

30

I was almost asleep when two cats started yowling their heads off and I jerked fully awake. We were on the fifth floor and I might not have heard it—and the clatter of a trashcan that followed—if my window hadn't been cracked to let in some fresh air. I got up to shut it and froze with my hands on the sash. Therriault was standing across the street in the spreading glow of a streetlamp, and I knew right away that the cats hadn't been yowling because they were fighting. They had been yowling because they were scared. The baby in the Papoose carrier had seen him; so had those cats. He scared them on purpose. He knew I would come to the window, just as he knew Liz called me Champ.

He grinned from his half-destroyed head.

He beckoned.

I closed the window and thought about going into my mother's room to get in bed with her, only I was too big for that, and there would be questions. So I pulled the shade instead. I went back to my own bed and lay there, looking up into the dark. Nothing like this had ever happened to me before. No dead person had ever followed me home like a fucking stray dog.

Never mind, I thought. *In three or four days, he'll be gone like all of them are gone. A week at most. And it's not like he can* hurt *you*.

But could I be sure of that? Lying there in the dark, I realized I didn't. *Seeing* dead folks didn't mean *knowing* dead folks.

At last I went back to the window and peeked around the shade, sure he'd still be there. Maybe he'd even beckon again. One finger pointing…and then curling. *Come here. Come to me*, Champ.

No one was under the streetlight. He was gone. I went back to bed, but it took me a long time to go to sleep.

31

I saw him again on Friday, outside of school. There were quite a few parents waiting for their kids—there always are on Fridays, probably because they're going somewhere for the weekend—and they didn't see Therriault, but they must have felt him, because they gave the place where he was standing a wide berth. No one was pushing a baby in a carriage, but if someone had been, I knew that baby would be looking at the empty spot on the sidewalk and bawling its head off.

I went back inside and looked at some posters outside the

office, wondering what to do. I supposed I'd have to talk to him, find out what he wanted, and I made up my mind to do it right then, while there were people around. I didn't think he could hurt me, but I didn't *know*.

I used the boys' room first because all at once I really had to pee, but when I was standing at the urinal, I couldn't squeeze out even a single drop. So I went out, holding my backpack by the strap instead of wearing it. I had never been touched by a dead person, not once, I didn't know if they *could* touch, but if Therriault tried to touch me—or grab me—I intended to hit him with a sackful of books.

Only he was gone.

A week went by, then two. I relaxed, figuring he had to be past his sell-by date.

I was on the YMCA junior swim team, and on a Saturday in late May we had our final practice for an upcoming meet in Brooklyn, which would take place the following weekend. Mom gave me ten dollars for something to eat afterwards and told me—as she always did—to make sure I locked my locker so no one would steal the money or my watch (although why anyone would want to steal a lousy Timex I have no idea). I asked her if she was coming to the meet. She looked up from the manuscript she was reading and said, "For the fourth time, Jamie, *yes*. I'm coming to the meet. It's on my calendar."

It was only the second time I'd asked (or maybe the third), but I didn't tell her that, only kissed her on the cheek and headed down the hall to the elevator. When the doors opened, Therriault was in there, grinning his grin and staring at me from his good eye and the stretched-out one. There was a piece of paper pinned to his shirt. The suicide note was on it.

The note was always on it and the blood spattered across it was always fresh.

"Your mother has cancer, Champ. From the cigarettes. She'll be dead in six months."

I was frozen in place with my mouth hanging open.

The elevator doors rolled shut. I made some kind of sound —a squeak, a moan, I don't know—and leaned back against the wall so I wouldn't fall down.

They have to tell you the truth, I thought. *My mother is going to die.*

But then my head cleared a little and a better thought came. I grasped it like a drowning man clutching at a floating piece of wood. *But maybe they only have to tell the truth if you ask them questions. Otherwise, maybe they can tell you any kind of fake shit they want.*

I didn't want to go to swim practice after that, but if I didn't Coach might call Mom to ask where I'd been. Then *she* would want to know where I had been, and what was I going to tell her? That I was afraid that Thumper would be waiting for me on the corner? Or in the lobby of the Y? Or (somehow this was the most horrible) in the shower room, unseen by naked boys rinsing off the chlorine?

Was I going to tell her she had fucking *cancer*?

So I went, and as you might guess, I swam for shit. Coach told me to get my head on straight, and I had to pinch my armpit to keep from bursting into tears. I had to pinch it really hard.

When I got home, Mom was still deep in her manuscript. I hadn't seen her smoking since Liz left, but I knew she sometimes drank when I wasn't there—with her authors and various editors—so I sniffed at her when I kissed her, and didn't smell anything but a little perfume. Or maybe face cream, since it was Saturday. Some kind of lady stuff, anyway.

"Are you coming down with a cold, Jamie? You dried off well after swimming, didn't you?"

"Yeah. Mom, you're not smoking anymore, are you?"

"So *that's* it." She put aside the manuscript and stretched. "No, I haven't had one since Liz left."

Since you kicked her out, I thought.

"Have you been to the doctor lately? To get a checkup?"

She looked at me quizzically. "What's this about? You've got that crease between your brows."

"Well," I said, "you're the only parent I've got. If something happened to you, I couldn't exactly go live with Uncle Harry, could I?"

She made a funny face at that, then laughed and hugged me. "I'm fine, kiddo. Had the old annual checkup two months ago, as a matter of fact. Passed with flying colors."

And she looked okay. In the pink, as the saying goes. Hadn't lost any more weight that I could see, and wasn't coughing her brains out. Although cancer didn't just have to be in a person's throat or lungs, I knew that.

"Well...that's good. I'm glad."

"That makes two of us. Now make your mom a cup of coffee and let me finish this manuscript."

"Is it a good one?"

"As a matter of fact, it is."

"Better than Mr. Thomas's *Roanoke* books?"

"Much better, but not as commercial, alas."

"Can I have a cup of coffee?"

She sighed. "Half a cup. Now let me read."

32

During my last test in math that year, I looked out the window and saw Kenneth Therriault standing on the basketball court. He did his grinning-and-beckoning thing. I looked back at my paper, then looked up again. Still there, and closer. He turned his head so I could get a good look at the purple-black crater, plus the bone-fangs sticking up all around it. I looked down at my paper again, and when I looked up the third time, he was gone. But I knew he'd be back. He wasn't like the others. He was *nothing* like the others.

By the time Mr. Laghari told us to turn in our papers, I still hadn't solved the last five problems. I got a D- on the test, and there was a note at the top: *This is disappointing, Jamie. You must do better. What do I say at least once in every class?* What he said was that if you fell behind in math, you could never catch up.

Math wasn't so special that way, although Mr. Laghari might think so. It was true for most classes. As if to underline the point, I bricked a history test later that day. Not because Therriault was standing at the blackboard or anything, but because I couldn't stop thinking he *might* be standing at the blackboard.

I got the idea he *wanted* me to do badly in my courses. You could laugh at that, but there's another old saying that goes it's not paranoid if it's true. A few lousy tests weren't going to stop me from passing everything, not that late in the year, and then it would be summer vacation, but what about next year, if he was still hanging around?

Also, what if he was getting stronger? I didn't want to believe that, but just the fact that he was still there suggested it might be true. That it probably was true.

Telling somebody might help, and Mom was the logical choice, she'd believe me, but I didn't want to scare her. She'd already been scared enough, when she thought the agency was going to go under and she wouldn't be able to take care of me and her brother. That I'd helped her out of that pickle might make her blame herself for the one I was in now. That made no sense to me, but it might to her. Besides, she wanted to put the whole seeing-dead-folks stuff behind her. And here's the thing: what could she do, even if I *did* tell her? Blame Liz for putting me with Therriault in the first place, but that was all.

I thought briefly of talking to Ms. Peterson, who was the school's guidance counselor, but she'd assume I was having hallucinations, maybe a nervous breakdown. She'd tell my mother. I even thought of going to Liz, but what could Liz do? Pull out her gun and shoot him? Good luck there, since he was already dead. Besides, I was done with Liz, or so I thought. I was on my own, and that was a lonely, scary place to be.

My mother came to the swim meet where I swam like shit in every event. On the way home she gave me a hug and told me everyone had an off day and I'd do better next time. I almost blurted everything out right then, ending with my fear—which I now felt was reasonably justified—that Kenneth Therriault was trying to ruin my life for screwing up his last

and biggest bomb. If we hadn't been in a taxi, I really might
have. Since we were, I just put my head on her shoulder as I
had when I was small and thought my hand-turkey was the
greatest work of art since the *Mona Lisa*. Tell you what, the
worst part of growing up is how it shuts you up.

33

When I headed out of our apartment on the last day of
school, Therriault was once again in the elevator. Grinning
and beckoning. He probably expected me to cringe back like
I had the first time I saw him in there, but I didn't. I was
scared, all right, but not *as* scared, because I was getting
used to him, the way you might get used to a growth or a
birthmark on your face, even if it was ugly. This time I was
more angry than scared, because he wouldn't leave me the
fuck alone.

Instead of cringing, I lunged forward and put my arm out
to stop the elevator doors. I wasn't going to get in with
him—Christ, no!—but I wasn't going to let the doors close
until I got a few answers.

"Does my mother really have cancer?"

Once again his face twisted like I was hurting him, and
once again I hoped I was.

"*Does my mother have cancer?*"

"I don't know." The way he was staring at me...you know
that old saying about if looks could kill?

"Then why did you say that?"

He was at the back of the car now, with his hands pressed

to his chest, as if *I* was scaring *him*. He turned his head, showing me that enormous exit wound, but if he thought that was going to make me let go of the door and step back, he was wrong. Horrible as it was, I'd gotten used to it.

"*Why did you say that?*"

"Because I hate you," Therriault said, and bared his teeth.

"Why are you still here? How *can* you be?"

"I don't know."

"Go away."

He said nothing.

"Go *away!*"

"I'm not going away. I'm never going away."

That scared the hell out of me and my arm flopped down to my side as if it had gained weight.

"Be seeing you, *Champ*."

The elevator doors rolled shut, but the car didn't go anywhere because there was no one to push any of the inside buttons. When I pushed the one on my side, the doors rolled open on an empty car, but I took the stairs anyway.

I'll get used to him, I thought. *I got used to the hole in his head and I'll get used to him. It's not like he can hurt me.*

But in some ways he'd hurt me already: the D- on my math test and screwing the pooch at the swim meet were just two examples. I was sleeping badly (Mom had already commented on the pouches under my eyes), and little noises, even a dropped book in study hall, made me jump. I kept thinking I'd open my closet to get a shirt and he'd be in there, my own personal boogeyman. Or under the bed, and what if he grabbed my wrist or my dangling foot while I was sleeping? I didn't think he could grab, but I wasn't sure of that, either, especially if he was getting stronger.

What if I woke up and he was lying in bed with me? Maybe even grabbing at my junk?

That was an idea that, once thought, couldn't be *un*thought.

And something else, something even worse. What if he was still haunting me—because that's what this was, all right—when I was twenty? Or forty? What if he was there when I died at eighty-nine, waiting to welcome me into the afterlife, where he would go on haunting me even after I was dead?

If this is what a good deed gets you, I thought one night, looking out my window and watching Thumper across the street under his streetlight, *I never want to do another one*.

34

In late June, Mom and I made our monthly visit to see Uncle Harry. He didn't talk much anymore and hardly ever went into the common room. Although he still wasn't fifty, his hair had gone snow white.

Mom said, "Jamie brought you rugelach from Zabar's, Harry. Would you like some?"

I held the bag up from my place in the doorway (I didn't really want to go all the way in), smiling and feeling a little like one of the models on *The Price is Right*.

Uncle Harry said *yig*.

"Does that mean yes?" Mom asked.

Uncle Harry said *ng*, and waved both hands at me. Which you didn't have to be a mind reader to know meant *no fucking cookies*.

"Would you like to go out? It's beautiful."

I wasn't sure Uncle Harry even knew what *out* was these days.

"I'll help you up," Mom said, and took his arm.

"No!" Uncle Harry said. Not *ng*, not *yig*, not *ug*, no. As clear as a bell. His eyes had gotten big and were starting to water. Then, also as clear as a bell, "Who's that?"

"It's Jamie. You know Jamie, Harry."

Only he didn't know me, not anymore, and it wasn't me he was looking at. He was looking over my shoulder. I didn't need to turn around to know what I was going to see there, but I did, anyway.

"What he's got is hereditary," Therriault said, "and it runs in the male line. You'll be like him, Champ. You'll be like him before you know it."

"Jamie?" Mom asked. "Are you okay?"

"Fine," I said, looking at Therriault. "I'm just fine."

But I wasn't, and Therriault's grin said he knew it, too.

"Go away!" Uncle Harry said. "Go away, go away, go away!"

So we did.

All three of us.

35

I had just about decided to tell my mother everything—I needed to let it out, even if it scared her and made her unhappy—when fate, as the saying is, took a hand. This was in July of 2013, about three weeks after our trip to see Uncle Harry.

My mother got a call early one morning, while she was

getting ready to go to the office. I was sitting at the kitchen
table, scarfing up Cheerios with one eye open. She came out
of her bedroom, zipping her skirt. "Marty Burkett had a
little accident last night. Tripped over something—going to
the toilet, I imagine—and strained his hip. He says he's fine,
and maybe he is, but maybe he's just trying to be macho."

"Yeah," I said, mostly because it's always safer to agree
with my mom when she's rushing around and trying to do
like three different things at once. Privately I was thinking
that Mr. Burkett was a little old to be a macho man, although
it was amusing to think of him starring in a movie like
Terminator: The Retirement Years. Waving his cane and proclaiming "I'll be back." I picked up my bowl and started to
slurp the milk.

"Jamie, how many times have I told you not to do that?"

I couldn't remember if she ever had, because quite a few
parental edicts, especially those concerning table manners,
had a tendency to slide by me. "How else am I supposed to
get it all?"

She sighed. "Never mind. I made a casserole for our supper,
but we could have burgers. If, that is, you could interrupt
your busy schedule of watching TV and playing games on
your phone long enough to take it to Marty. I can't, full
schedule. I don't suppose you'd be willing to do that? And
then call and tell me how he's doing?"

At first I didn't answer. I felt like I'd just been hit on the
head with a hammer. Some ideas are like that. Also, I felt
like a total dumbo. Why had I never thought of Mr. Burkett
before?

"Jamie? Earth to Jamie."

"Sure," I said. "Happy to do it."

"Really?"

"Really."

"Are you sick? Do you have a fever?"

"Ha-ha," I said. "Funny as a rubber crutch."

She grabbed her purse. "I'll give you cab fare—"

"Nah, just put the casserole thing in a carry-bag. I'll walk."

"Really?" she said again, looking surprised. "All the way to Park?"

"Sure. I can use the exercise." Not strictly true. What I needed was time to be sure my idea was a good idea, and how to tell my story if it was.

36

At this point I'm going to start calling Mr. Burkett Professor Burkett, because he taught me that day. He taught me a lot. But before the teaching, he *listened*. I've already said I knew I had to talk to somebody, but I didn't know what a relief it would be to unburden myself until I actually did it.

He came to the door hobbling on not just one cane, which I'd seen him use before, but two. His face lit up when he saw me, so I guess he was glad to get company. Kids are pretty self-involved (as I'm sure you know if you've ever been one yourself, ha-ha), and I only realized later that he must have been a lonely, lonely man in the years after Mona died. He had that daughter on the west coast, but if she came to visit, I never saw her; see statement above about kids and self-involvement.

"Jamie! You come bearing gifts!"

"Just a casserole," I said. "I think it's a Swedish pie."

"You may mean *shepherd's* pie. I'm sure it's delicious. Would you be kind enough to put it in the icebox for me? I've got these…" He lifted the canes off the floor and for one scary moment I thought he was going to face-plant right in front of me, but he got them braced again in time.

"Sure," I said, and went into the kitchen. I got a kick out of how he called the fridge the icebox and cars autos. He was totally old school. Oh, and he also called the telephone the telefungus. I liked that one so much I started using it myself. Still do.

Getting Mom's casserole into the icebox was no problem, because he had almost nothing in there. He stumped in after me and asked how I was doing. I shut the icebox door, turned to him, and said, "Not so well."

He raised his shaggy eyebrows. "No? What's the problem?"

"It's a pretty long story," I said, "and you'll probably think I'm crazy, but I have to tell somebody, and I guess you're elected."

"Is it about Mona's rings?"

My mouth dropped open.

Professor Burkett smiled. "I never quite believed that your mother just happened to find them in the closet. Too fortuitous. *Far* too fortuitous. It crossed my mind to think she put them there herself, but every human action is predicated on motive and opportunity, and your mother had neither. Also, I was too upset to really think about it that afternoon."

"Because you'd just lost your wife."

"Indeed." He raised one cane enough to touch the heel of his palm to his chest, where his heart was. That made me feel bad for him. "So what happened, Jamie? I suppose it's all water under the bridge at this point, but as a lifetime reader of detective stories, I like to know the answers to such questions."

"Your wife told me," I said.

He stared at me across the kitchen.

"I see the dead," I said.

He didn't reply for so long I got scared. Then he said, "I think I need something with caffeine. I think we both do. Then you can tell me everything that's on your mind. I long to hear it."

37

Professor Burkett was so old school that he didn't have tea bags, just loose tea in a cannister. While I waited for his hot pot to boil, he showed me where to find what he called a "tea ball" and instructed me on how much of the loose tea to put in. Brewing tea was an interesting process. I will always prefer coffee, but sometimes a pot of tea is just the thing. Making it feels *formal*, somehow.

Professor Burkett told me the tea had to steep for five minutes in freshly boiled water—no more and no less. He set the timer, showed me where the cups were, and then stumped into the living room. I heard his sigh of relief when he sat down in his favorite chair. Also a fart. Not a trumpet blast, more of an oboe.

I made two cups of tea and put them on a tray along with the sugar bowl and the Half and Half from the icebox (which neither of us used, probably a good thing since it was a month past its sell-by date). Professor Burkett took his black and smacked his lips over the first sip. "Kudos, Jamie. Perfect on your first try."

"Thanks." I sugared mine up liberally. My mom would have screamed at that third heaping spoonful, but Professor Burkett never said boo.

"Now tell me your tale. I've nothing but time."

"Do you believe me? About the rings?"

"Well," he said, "I believe that you believe. And I *know* that the rings were found; they're in my bank safety deposit box. Tell me, Jamie, if I asked your mother, would she corroborate your story?"

"Yes, but please don't do that. I decided to talk to you because I don't want to talk to her. It would upset her."

He sipped his tea with a hand that shook slightly, then put it down and looked at me. Or maybe even *into* me. I can still see those bright blue eyes peering out from beneath his shaggy every-whichway brows. "Then talk to me. Convince me."

Having rehearsed my story on my crosstown walk, I was able to keep it in a pretty straight line. I started with Robert Harrison—you know, the Central Park man—and moved on to seeing Mrs. Burkett, then all the rest. It took quite awhile. When I finished, my tea was down to just lukewarm (maybe even a little less), but I drank a bunch of it anyway, because my throat was dry.

Professor Burkett considered, then said, "Will you go into

my bedroom, Jamie, and bring me my iPad? It's on the night table."

His bedroom smelled sort of like Uncle Harry's room in the care home, plus some sharp aroma that I guessed was liniment for his strained hip. I got his iPad and brought it back. He didn't have an iPhone, just the landline telefungus that hung on the kitchen wall like something in an old movie, but he loved his pad. He opened it when I gave it to him (the start-up screen was a picture of a young couple in wedding outfits that I assumed was him and Mrs. Burkett) and started poking away at once.

"Are you looking up Therriault?"

He shook his head without looking up. "Your Central Park man. You say you were in preschool when you saw him?"

"Yes."

"So this would have been 2003…possibly 2004…ah, here it is." He read, bent over the pad and occasionally brushing his hair out of his eyes (he had a lot of it). At last he looked up and said, "You saw him lying there dead and also standing beside himself. Your mother would also confirm *that*?"

"She knew I wasn't lying because I knew what the guy was wearing on top, even though that part of him was covered up. But I really don't want—"

"Understood, totally understood. Now concerning Regis Thomas's last book. It was unwritten—"

"Yeah, except for the first couple of chapters. I think."

"But your mother was able to glean enough details to write the rest of it herself, using you as her medium?"

I hadn't thought of myself as a medium, but in a way he was right. "I guess. Like in *The Conjuring*." And off his puzzled expression: "It's a movie. Mr. Burkett…*Professor*…do you think I'm crazy?" I almost didn't care, because the relief of getting it all out there was so great.

"No," he said, but something—probably my expression of relief—caused him to raise a warning finger. "This is not to say I believe your story, at least not without corroboration from your mother, which I have agreed not to ask for. But I will go this far: I don't necessarily *disbelieve*. Mostly because of the rings, but also because that last Thomas book does indeed exist. Not that I've read it." He made a little face at that. "You say your mother's friend—*ex*-friend—could also corroborate the last and most colorful part of your story."

"Yes, but—"

He raised his hand, like he must have done a thousand times to babbling students in class. "You don't want me to speak to her, either, and I quite understand. I only met her once, and I didn't care for her. Did she really bring drugs into your home?"

"I didn't see them myself, but if my mom said she did, she did."

He put his pad aside and fondled his go-to cane, which had a big white knob on the top. "Then Tia is well rid of her. And this Therriault, who you say is haunting you. Is he here now?"

"No." But I looked around to be sure.

"You want to be rid of him, of course."

"Yes, but I don't know how to do it."

He sipped his tea, brooded over the cup, then set it down and fixed me with those blue eyes again. He was old; they weren't. "An interesting problem, especially for an elderly gentleman who's encountered all sorts of supernatural creatures in his reading life. The gothics are full of them, Frankenstein's monster and Count Dracula being just the pair who show up most frequently on movie marquees. There are many more in European literature and folk-tales. Let's presume, at least for the moment, that this Therriault isn't just in your head. Let's presume he actually exists."

I kept myself from protesting that he *did* exist. The professor already knew what I believed, he'd said so himself.

"Let us go a step further. Based on what you've told me about your other sightings of dead people—including my wife—all of them go away after a few days. Disappear to…" He waved his hand. "…to wherever. But not this Therriault. He's still around. In fact, you think he may be getting stronger."

"I'm pretty sure he is."

"If so, perhaps he's not really Kenneth Therriault at all anymore. Perhaps what remained of Therriault after death has been infested—that's the correct word, not possessed— by a demon." He must have seen my expression because he hastened to add, "We're just speculating here, Jamie. I'm going to speak frankly and say I think it far more likely that you're suffering from a localized fugue state that has caused hallucinations."

"In other words, crazy." At that point I was still glad I'd told him, but his conclusion was maximo depressing, even though I'd been more or less expecting it.

He waved a hand. "Bosh. I don't think that at all. You're obviously operating in the real world as well as ever. And I must admit your story is full of things that are hard to explain in strictly rational terms. I don't doubt that you accompanied Tia and her ex-friend to the deceased Mr. Thomas's home. Nor do I doubt that Detective Dutton took you to Therriault's place of employment and his apartment building. If she did those things—I am channeling Ellery Queen here, one of my favorite apostles of deduction—*she* must have believed in your mediumistic talents. Which in turn leads us back to Mr. Thomas's home, where Detective Dutton must have seen something to convince her of that in the first place."

"You lost me," I said.

"Never mind." He leaned forward. "All I'm saying is that although I lean toward the rational, the known, and the empiric—having never seen a ghost, or had a flash of precognition—I must admit there are elements of your story I can't dismiss out of hand. So let us say that Therriault, or something nasty that has inhabited what remains of Therriault, actually exists. The question then becomes: can you get rid of him?"

Now I was leaning forward, thinking of the book he'd given me, the one full of fairy tales that were really horror stories with very few happy endings. The stepsisters cut off their toes, the princess threw the frog against a wall—*splat!*—instead of kissing him, Red Riding Hood actually *encouraged* the big bad wolf to eat Grandma, so she could inherit Grandma's property.

"*Can* I? You've read all those books, there must be a way in at least one of them! Or…" A new idea struck me. "Exorcism! What about that?"

"Probably a nonstarter," Professor Burkett said. "I think a

priest would be more apt to send you to a child psychiatrist than an exorcist. If your Therriault exists, Jamie, you may be stuck with him."

I stared at him with dismay.

"But maybe that's all right."

"All right? How can it be all right?"

He lifted his cup, sipped, and set it down.

"Have you ever heard of the Ritual of Chüd?"

38

Now I'm twenty-two—almost twenty-three, in fact—and living in the land of later. I can vote, I can drive, I can buy booze and cigarettes (which I plan to quit soon). I understand that I'm still very young, and I'm sure that when I look back I'll be amazed (hopefully not disgusted) by how naïve and wet behind the ears I was. Still, twenty-two is light years from thirteen. I know more now, but I believe less. Professor Burkett would never have been able to work the same magic on me now that he did back then. Not that I'm complaining! Kenneth Therriault—I don't know what he really was, so let's stick with that for now—was trying to destroy my sanity. The professor's magic saved it. It may even have saved my life.

Later, when I researched the subject for an anthropology paper in college (NYU, of course), I discovered half of what he told me that day was actually true. The other half was bullshit. I have to give him credit for invention, though (full marks, Mom's British romance writer Philippa Stephens would have said). Check this out, and dig the irony: my

Uncle Harry wasn't even fifty and totally gaga, while Martin
Burkett, although in his eighties, could still be creative on
the fly...and all in service of a troubled boy who turned up
uninvited, bearing a casserole and a weird story.

The Ritual of Chüd, the professor said, was practiced by a
sect of Tibetan and Nepalese Buddhists. (True.)

They did it to achieve a sense of perfect nothingness and
the resulting state of serenity and spiritual clarity. (True.)

It was also considered useful in combating demons, both
those in the mind and the supernatural ones who invaded
from the outside. (A gray area.)

"Which makes it perfect for you, Jamie, because it covers
all the bases."

"You mean it can work even if Therriault's really not
there, and I'm just crazypants."

He gave me a look combining reproach and impatience
that he probably perfected in his teaching career. "Stop
talking and try listening, if you don't mind."

"Sorry." I was on my second cup of tea, and feeling wired.

With the groundwork laid, Professor Burkett now moved
into the land of make-believe...not that I knew the difference. He said that chüd was especially useful when one of
these high-country Buddhists encountered a yeti, also known
as the abominable snowman.

"Are those things real?" I asked.

"As with your Mr. Therriault, I can't say with any surety.
But—also as with you and your Mr. Therriault—I *can* say
that the Tibetans believe they are."

The professor went on to say that a person unfortunate
enough to meet a yeti would be haunted by it for the rest of

his life. Unless, that was, it could be engaged and bested in the Ritual of Chüd.

If you're following this, you know that if bullshit was an event in the Olympics, the judges would have given Professor Burkett all 10s for that one, but I was only thirteen and in a bad place. Which is to say I swallowed it whole. If part of me had an idea of what Professor Burkett was up to—I can't really remember—I shut it down. You have to remember how desperate I was. The idea of being followed around by Kenneth Therriault, aka Thumper, for the rest of my life—*haunted* by him, to use the professor's word—was the most horrible thing I could imagine.

"How does it work?" I asked.

"Ah, you'll like this. It's like one of the uncensored fairy tales in the book I gave you. According to the stories, you and the demon bind yourselves together by biting into each other's tongues."

He said this with a certain relish, and I thought, *Like it? Why would I* like *it?*

"Once this union has been accomplished, you and the demon have a battle of wills. This would occur telepathically, I assume, since it would be hard to talk while engaged in a…mmm…mutual tongue-bite. The first to withdraw loses all power over the winner."

I stared at him, my mouth open. I had been raised to be polite, especially around my mother's clients and acquaintances, but I was too grossed out to consider the social niceties. "If you think I'm going to—what?—french-kiss that guy, you're out of your mind! For one thing, he's *dead*, did you not get that?"

"Yes, Jamie, I believe I did."

"Besides, how would I even get him to do it? What would I say, come on over here, Ken honey, and slip me some tongue?"

"Are you finished?" Professor Burkett asked mildly, once again making me feel like the most clueless student in class. "I think the tongue-biting aspect is meant to be symbolic. The way chunks of Wonder Bread and little thimbles of wine are meant to be symbolic of Jesus's last supper with his disciples."

I didn't get that, not being much of a churchgoer, so I kept my mouth shut.

"Listen to me, Jamie. Listen very carefully."

I listened as if my life depended on it. Because I thought it did.

39

As I was preparing to leave (politeness had resurfaced and I didn't neglect to tell him thank you), the professor asked me if his wife had said anything else. Besides about where the rings were, that was.

By the time you're thirteen I think you've forgotten most of the things that have happened to you when you're six—I mean, that's more than half your life ago!—but I didn't have any trouble remembering that day. I could have told him how Mrs. Burkett threw shade about my green turkey but figured that wouldn't interest him. He wanted to know if she'd said anything about *him*, not what she'd said to me.

"You were hugging my mom and she said you were going to burn her hair with your cigarette. And you did. Guess you quit smoking, huh?"

"I allow myself three a day. I suppose I could have more, I'm not going to be cut down in my youth, but three is all I seem to want. Did she say anything else?"

"Um, that you'd be having lunch with some woman in a month or two. Her name might have been Debbie or Diana, something like that—"

"Dolores? Was it Dolores Magowan?" He was looking at me with new eyes, and all at once I wished we'd had this part of our conversation to start with. It would have gone a long way toward establishing my credibility.

"It might have been."

He shook his head. "Mona always thought I had eyes for that woman, God knows why."

"She said something about rubbing sheep-dip into her hands—"

"Lanolin," he said. "For her swollen joints. I'll be damned."

"There was one other thing, too. About how you always missed the back loop on your pants. I think she said 'Who'll do that now?' "

"My God," he said softly. "Oh my God. Jamie."

"Oh, and she kissed you. On the cheek."

It was just a little kiss, and years ago, but that sealed the deal. Because he also wanted to believe, I guess. If not in everything, in her. In that kiss. That she had been there.

I left while I was ahead.

40

I kept an eye out for Therriault on my way home—that was second nature to me by then—but didn't see him. Which was great, but I'd given up hoping that he was gone for good. He was a bad penny, and he'd turn up. I only hoped I would be ready for him when he did.

That night I got an email from Professor Burkett. *I did a little research with interesting results*, it said. *I thought you also might be interested*. There were three attachments, all three reviews of Regis Thomas's last book. The professor had highlighted the lines he had found interesting, leaving me to draw my own conclusions. Which I did.

From the Sunday *Times Book Review*: "Regis Thomas's swan song is the usual farrago of sex and swamp-tromping adventure, but the prose is sharper than usual; here and there one finds glimmers of actual writing."

From the *Guardian*: "Although the long-bruited Mystery of Roanoke won't be much of a surprise to readers of the series (who surely saw it coming), Thomas's narrative voice is livelier than one might expect from the previous volumes, where turgid exposition alternated with fervid and some-times comical sexual encounters."

From the *Miami Herald*: "The dialogue snaps, the pacing is crisp, and for once the lesbian liaison between Laura Goodhugh and Purity Betancourt feels real and touching, rather than like a prurient joke or a stroke fantasy. It's a great wind-up."

I couldn't show those reviews to my mother—they would have raised too many questions—but I was pretty sure she must have seen them herself, and I guessed they had made her as happy as they made me. Not only had she gotten away with it, she had put a shine on Regis Thomas's sadly tarnished reputation.

There were many nights in the weeks and months following my first encounter with Kenneth Therriault when I went to bed feeling unhappy and afraid. That night wasn't one of them.

41

I'm not sure how many times I saw him the rest of that summer, which should tell you something. If it doesn't, here it is in plain English: I was getting used to him. I never would have believed it on the day when I turned around and saw him standing by the trunk of Liz Dutton's car, close enough to touch me. I never would have believed it on the day when the elevator opened and he was in there, telling me my mother had cancer and grinning like it was the happiest news ever. But familiarity breeds contempt, so they say, and in this case the saying was true.

It no doubt helped that he never did show up in my closet or under my bed (which would have been worse, because when I was little I was sure that was where the monster was waiting to grab a dangling foot or arm). That summer I read *Dracula*—okay, not the actual book, but a kick-ass graphic novel I bought at Forbidden Planet—and in it Van Helsing said that a vampire couldn't come in unless you invited him.

If it was true of vampires, it stood to reason (at least to thirteen-year-old me it did) that it was true of other supernatural beings. Like the one inside of Therriault, keeping him from disappearing after a few days like all the other dead people. I checked Wikipedia to see if Mr. Stoker just made that up, but he didn't. It was in lots of the vampire legends. Now (later!) I can see it makes symbolic sense. If we have free will, then you have to invite evil in.

Here's something else. He had mostly stopped crooking that finger at me. For most of that summer he just stood at a distance, staring. The only time I *did* see him beckoning was kind of funny. If, that is, you can say anything about that undead motherfucker was funny.

Mom got us tickets to see the Mets play the Tigers on the last Sunday in August. The Mets lost big, but I didn't care, because Mom bagged a pair of awesome seats from one of her publisher friends (contrary to popular belief, literary agents *do* have friends). They were on the third base side, just two rows up from the field. It was during the seventh inning stretch, while the Mets were still keeping it close, that I saw Therriault. I looked around for the hotdog man, and when I looked back, my pal Thumper was standing near the third base coach's box. Same khaki pants. Same shirt with blood all down the left side and spattering the suicide note. Head blown open like somebody lit off a cherry bomb in there. Grinning. And yes, beckoning.

The Tigers infield was throwing the ball around, and just after I saw Therriault, a chuck from the shortstop to the third basemen went way wild. The crowd whooped and jeered the usual stuff—*nice throw busher, my grandmother can do better than that*—but I just sat there with my hands clamped so tight the nails were biting into my palms. The shortstop hadn't seen Therriault (he would have run into the outfield screaming if he had), but he *felt* him. I know he did.

And here's something else: the third base coach went to retrieve the ball, then backed off and let it roll into the dugout. Shagging it would have brought him right next to the thing only I could see. Did the guy feel a cold spot, like in a ghost movie? I don't think so. I think he felt, just for a second or two, that the world was trembling around him. Vibrating like a guitar string. I have reasons to think that.

Mom said, "Okay, Jamie? You're not getting sunstroke on me, are you?"

"I'm fine," I said, and clenched hands or not, I mostly was. "Do you see the hotdog man?"

She craned around and waved to the nearest vendor. Which gave me a chance to give Kenneth Therriault the finger. His grin turned into a snarl that showed all his teeth. Then he walked into the visitors' dugout, where the players who weren't on the field no doubt shuffled around on the bench to give him room, without any idea why they were doing it.

I sat back with a smile. I wasn't ready to think that I'd vanquished him—not with a cross or holy water but by flipping him the bird—but the idea did kind of tiptoe in.

People started to leave in the top of the ninth, after the Tigers scored seven and put the game out of reach. Mom asked me if I wanted to stay and watch the Mr. Met Dash and I shook my head. The Dash was strictly for little kids. I had done it once, back before Liz, back before that fucker James Mackenzie stole our money in his Ponzi scheme, even before the day Mona Burkett told me turkeys weren't green. Back when I was a little kid and the world was my oyster.

That seemed so long ago.

42

You may be asking yourself a question I never asked myself back then: *Why me? Why Jamie Conklin?* I have asked myself since, and I don't know. I can only guess. I think it was because I was different, and it—the it inside the shell of Therriault—hated me for it and wanted to hurt me, even destroy me if it could. I think, call me crazy if you want, I *offended* it somehow. And maybe there was something else. I think maybe—just maybe—the Ritual of Chüd had already begun.

I think that once it started fucking with me it couldn't stop.

As I said, just guessing here. Its reasons might have been something else entirely, as unknowable as it was to me. And as monstrous. As I said, this is a horror story.

43

I was still scared of Therriault, but I no longer thought that I might chicken out if an opportunity came to put Professor Burkett's ritual into practice. I only needed to be ready. For Therriault to get close, in other words, not just be across the street or standing near third base at Citi Field.

My chance came on a Saturday in October. I was going down to Grover Park to play touch football with a bunch of kids from my school. Mom left me a note that said she'd stayed up late reading Philippa Stephens's latest opus and was going to sleep in. I was to get my breakfast quietly, and no more than half a cup of coffee. I was to have a good time with my friends and not come home with a concussion or a broken arm. I was to be back by two at the very latest. She left me lunch money, which I folded carefully into my pocket. There was a PS: *Would it be a waste of time to ask you to eat something green, even a scrap of lettuce on a hamburger?*

Probably, Mom, probably, I thought as I poured myself a bowl of Cheerios and ate them (quietly).

When I left the apartment, Therriault wasn't on my mind. He spent less and less time there, and I used some of the newly available space to think about other things, mostly girls. I was dwelling on Valeria Gomez in particular as I walked down the hall to the elevator. Did Therriault decide to get close that day because he had a kind of window into my head, and knew he was far from my thoughts? Sort of a low-grade telepathy? I don't know that either.

I pushed the call button, wondering if Valeria would come to the game. It was quite possible because her brother Pablo played. I was deep in a daydream of how I caught a pass, evaded all would-be touchers, and sped into the end zone with the ball held high, but I still stepped back when the elevator arrived—that had become second nature to me. It was empty. I pushed for the lobby. The elevator went down and the door opened. There was a short stub of hallway, and then a door, locked from the inside, which gave on a little foyer. The door to the outside wasn't locked, so the mailman could come in and put the mail in the boxes. If Therriault had been out there, in the foyer, I couldn't have done what I did. But he wasn't in the foyer. He was inside, at the end of the hall, grinning away like doing so was going to be outlawed the day after tomorrow.

He started to say something, maybe one of his bullshit prophecies, and if I'd been thinking of him instead of Valeria, I probably would have either frozen in place or stumbled back into the elevator car, whamming on the DOOR CLOSE button for all I was worth. But I was being pissed at him for intruding on my fantasy and all I remember thinking was what Professor Burkett told me on the day I brought him the casserole.

"The tongue-biting in the Ritual of Chüd is only one ceremony before meeting an enemy," he said. "There are many. The Maoris do a war-cry dance as they face their opponents. Kamikaze pilots toasted each other and photographs of their targets with what they believed was magical saké. In ancient Egypt, members of warring houses struck each other on the forehead before getting out the knives and spears and bows. Sumo wrestlers clap each other on the shoulders. All come down to the same thing: *I meet you in combat, where one of us will best the other*. In other words, Jamie, don't bother sticking out your tongue. Just grab your demon and hold on for dear life."

Instead of freezing or cringing, I bolted thoughtlessly forward with my arms out, like I was about to embrace a long absent friend. I screamed, but I think only in my head, because nobody looked out from one of the ground-floor apartments to see what was going on. Therriault's grin—the one that always showed that lump of dead blood between his teeth and cheek—disappeared, and I saw an amazing, wonderful thing: he was afraid of me. He cringed back against the door to the foyer, but it opened the other way and he was pinned. I grabbed him.

I can't describe how it went down. I don't think a much more gifted writer than I am could, but I'll do the best I can. Remember what I said about the world trembling, or vibrating like a guitar string? That was what it was like on the outside of Therriault, and all around him. I could feel it shaking my teeth and jittering my eyeballs. Only there was something else, on the *inside* of Therriault. It was something that was using him as a vessel and keeping him from moving on to wherever dead people go when their connection to our world rots away.

It was a very bad thing, and it was yelling at me to let it go. Or to let Therriault go. Maybe there was no difference. It was furious with me, and scared, but mostly it was surprised. Being grabbed was the last thing it had expected.

It struggled and would have gotten away if Therriault hadn't been pinned against the door, I'm sure of that. I was a skinny kid, Therriault was easily five inches taller and would have outweighed me by at least a hundred pounds if he'd been alive, but he wasn't. The thing inside him *was* alive, and I was pretty sure it had come in when I was forcing Therriault to answer my questions outside that little store.

The vibration got worse. It was coming up through the floor. It was coming down from the ceiling. The overhead light was shaking and throwing liquid shadows. The walls seemed to be crawling first one way and then the other.

"Let me go," Therriault said, and even his voice was vibrating. It sounded like when you put waxed paper over a comb and blow on it. His arms flew out to either side, then closed in and clapped me on the back. It immediately became hard to breathe. "Let me go and I'll let you go."

"No," I said, and hugged him tighter. *This is it*, I remember thinking. *This is Chüd. I'm in mortal combat with a demon right here in the front hall of my New York apartment building.*

"I'll strangle the breath out of you," it said.

"You can't," I said, hoping I was right about that. I could still breathe, but they were mighty short breaths. I began to think I could see *into* Therriault. Maybe it was a hallucination brought on by the vibration and the sense that the world was on the verge of exploding like a delicate wine glass, but I don't think so. It wasn't his guts I was looking at but a light. It was bright and dark at the same time. It was something from outside the world. It was horrible.

How long did we stand there hugging each other? It could have been five hours or only ninety seconds. You could say five hours was impossible, someone would have come, but I think...I almost *know*...that we were outside of time. One thing I can say for sure is that the elevator doors didn't close as they are supposed to five seconds or so after the passengers get out. I could see the elevator's reflection over Therriault's shoulder and the doors stayed open the whole time.

At last it said, "Let me go and I'll never come back."

That was an extremely tasty idea, as I'm sure you'll understand, and I might have done it if the professor hadn't prepared me for this, as well.

It will try to bargain, he said. *Don't let it*. And then he told me what to do, probably thinking that the only thing I had to confront was some neurosis or complex or whatever psychological thing you want to call it.

"Not good enough," I said, and went on hugging.

I could see more and more into Therriault, and realized he really *was* a ghost. Probably all dead people are and I just saw them as solid. The more insubstantial he became, the brighter that darklight—that deadlight—shone. I don't have any idea what it was. I only knew I had caught it, and there's an old saying that goes *he who takes a tiger by the tail dare not let go*.

The thing inside Therriault was worse than any tiger.

"What do you want?" Gasping it. There was no breath in him, I surely would have felt it on my cheek and neck if there had been, but he was gasping just the same. In worse shape than I was, maybe.

"It's not enough for you to stop haunting me." I took a deep breath and said what Professor Burkett had told me to say, if I was able to engage my nemesis in the Ritual of Chüd. And even though the world was shivering around me, even though this thing had me in a death grip, it gave me pleasure to say it. Great pleasure. *Warrior's* pleasure.

"Now I'll haunt *you*."

"No!" Its grip tightened.

I was squeezed against Therriault even though Therriault was now nothing but a supernatural hologram.

"Yes." Professor Burkett told me to say something else if I got the chance. I later found out it was the amended title of a famous ghost story, which made it very fitting. "Oh, I'll whistle and you'll come to me, my lad."

"No!" It struggled. That vile pulsing light made me feel like puking, but I held on.

"Yes. I'll haunt you as much as I want, whenever I want, and if you don't agree I'll hold onto you until you die."

"I can't die! But you can!"

That was undoubtedly true, but at that moment I had never felt stronger. Plus, all the time Therriault was fading and he was that deadlight's toehold in our world.

I said nothing. Only clutched. And Therriault clutched me. It went on like that. I was getting cold, feet and hands losing sensation, but I held on. I meant to hold on forever if I had to. I was terrified of the thing that was inside Therriault, but it was trapped. Of course I was also trapped; that was the nature of the ritual. If I let go, it won.

At last it said, "I agree to your terms."

I loosened my grip, but only a little. "Are you lying?" A stupid question, you might say, except it wasn't.

"I can't." Sounding slightly petulant. "You know that."

"Say it again. Say you agree."

"I agree to your terms."

"You know that I can haunt you?"

"I know, but I'm not afraid of you."

Bold words, but as I'd already found out, Therriault could make as many untrue statements as he—*it*—wanted to. Statements weren't answers to questions. And anybody who has to *say* they're not afraid is lying. I didn't have to wait until later to learn that, I knew it at thirteen.

"Are you afraid of me?"

I saw that cramped expression on Therriault's face again, as if he was tasting something sour and unpleasant. Which was probably how telling the truth felt to the miserable son of a bitch.

"Yes. You're not like the others. You *see*."

"Yes what?"

"Yes I'm afraid of you!"

Sweet!

I let him go. "Get out of here, whatever you are, and go to wherever you go. Just remember if I call you, *you come*."

He whirled around, giving me one final look at the gaping hole in the left side of his head. He grabbed at the doorknob. His hand went through it and *didn't* go through it. Both at the same time. I know it's crazy, a paradox, but it happened. I saw it. The knob turned and the door opened. At the same time the overhead light blew out and glass tinkled down from the fixture. There were a dozen or so mailboxes in the foyer, and half of them popped open. Therriault gave me one last hateful look over his bloody shoulder, and then he was gone, leaving the front door open. I saw him go down the steps, not so much running as plunging. A guy speeding past on a bike, probably a messenger, lost his balance, fell over, and sprawled in the street, cursing.

I knew the dead could impact the living, that was no surprise. I'd seen it, but those impacts had always been *little* things. Professor Burkett had felt his wife's kiss. Liz had felt Regis Thomas blow on her face. But the things I'd just seen—the light that blew out, the jittery, vibrating doorknob that had turned, the messenger falling off his bike—were on an entirely different level.

The thing I'm calling the deadlight almost lost its host while I was holding on, but when I let go, it did more than regain Therriault; it got stronger. That strength must have come from me, but I didn't feel any weaker (like poor Lucy Westenra while Count Dracula was using her as his personal lunch-wagon). In fact I felt better than ever, refreshed and invigorated.

It was stronger, so what? I'd owned it, had made it my bitch.

For the first time since Liz had picked me up from school that day and taken me hunting for Therriault, I felt good again. Like someone who's had a serious illness and is finally on the mend.

44

I got back home around quarter past two, a little late but not where-have-you-been-I-was-so-worried late. I had a long scrape on one arm and the knee of my pants got torn when one of the high school boys bumped me and I went down hard, but I felt pretty damned fine just the same. Valeria wasn't there, but two of her girlfriends were. One of them said Valeria liked me and the other one said I should talk to her, maybe sit with her at lunch.

God, the possibilities!

I let myself in and saw that someone—probably Mr. Provenza, the building super—had closed the mailboxes that had popped open when Therriault left. Or, to put it more accurately, when it fled the scene. Mr. Provenza had also cleaned up the broken glass, and put a sign in front of the elevator that said TEMPORARILY OUT OF ORDER. That made me remember the day Mom and I came home from school, me clutching my green turkey, and found the elevator at the Palace on Park out of order. *Fuck this elevator*, Mom had said. Then: *You didn't hear that, kiddo*.

Old days.

I took the stairs and let myself in to find Mom had dragged her home office chair up to the living room window, where she was reading and drinking coffee. "I was just about to call you," she said, and then, looking down, "Oh my God, that's a new pair of jeans!"

"Sorry," I said. "Maybe you can patch them up."

"I have many skills, but sewing isn't one of them. I'll take them to Mrs. Abelson at Dandy Cleaners. What did you have for lunch?"

"A burger. With lettuce and tomato."

"Is that true?"

"I cannot tell a lie," I said, and of course that made me think of Therriault, and I gave a little shiver.

"Let me see your arm. Come over here where I can get a good look." I came over and displayed my battle scar. "No need of a Band-Aid, I guess, but you need to put on some Neosporin."

"Okay if I watch ESPN after I do that?"

"It would be if we had electricity. Why do you think I'm reading at the window instead of at my desk?"

"Oh. That must be why the elevator isn't working."

"Your powers of deduction stun me, Holmes." This was one of my mom's literary jokes. She has dozens of them. Maybe hundreds. "It's just our building. Mr. Provenza says something blew out all the breakers. Some kind of power surge. He said he's never seen anything like it. He's going to try to get it fixed by tonight, but I've got an idea we'll be running on candles and flashlights once it gets dark."

Therriault, I thought, but of course it wasn't. It was the deadlight thing that was now inhabiting Therriault. It blew the light fixture, it opened some of the mailboxes, and it fried the circuit breakers for good measure when it left.

I went into the bathroom to get the Neosporin. It was pretty dark in there, so I flipped the light switch. Habit's a bitch, isn't it? I sat on the sofa to spread antibiotic goo on my scrape, looking at the blank TV and wondering how many circuit breakers there were in an apartment building the size of ours, and how much power it would take to cook them all.

I could whistle for that thing. And if I did, would it come to the lad named Jamie Conklin? That was a lot of power for a kid who wouldn't even be able to get a driver's license for another three years.

"Mom?"

"What?"

"Do you think I'm old enough to have a girlfriend?"

"No, dear." Without looking up from her manuscript.

"When will I be old enough?"

"How does twenty-five sound?"

She started laughing and I laughed with her. Maybe, I thought, when I was twenty-five or so I'd summon Therriault and ask him to bring me a glass of water. But on second thought, anything *it* brought might be poison. Maybe, just for shits and giggles, I'd ask it to stand on its Therriault head, do a split, maybe walk on the ceiling. Or I could let it go.

Tell it to get buzzin', cousin. Of course I didn't have to wait until I was twenty-five, I could do that anytime. Only I didn't want to. Let it be *my* prisoner for awhile. That nasty, horrible light reduced to little more than a firefly in a jar. See how it liked that.

The electricity came back on at ten o'clock, and all was right with the world.

45

On Sunday, Mom proposed a visit to Professor Burkett to see how he was doing and to retrieve the casserole dish. "Also, we could bring him some croissants from Haber's."

I said that sounded good. She gave him a call and he said he'd love to see us, so we walked to the bakery and then hailed a cab. My mother refused to use Uber. She said they weren't New York. *Taxis* were New York.

I guess the miracle of healing goes on even when you're old, because Professor Burkett was down to only one cane and moving pretty well. Not apt to be running in the NYC Marathon again (if he ever had), but he gave Mom a hug at the door and I wasn't afraid he was going to face-plant when he shook my hand. He gave me a keen look, I gave him a slight nod, and he smiled. We understood each other.

Mom bustled around, setting out the croissants and pats of butter and the tiny pots of jam that came with them. We ate in the kitchen with the mid-morning sun slanting in. It was a nice little meal. When we were done, Mom transferred the remains of the casserole (which was most of it; I guess old folks don't eat much) to a Tupperware and washed her dish. She set it to dry and then excused herself to use the bathroom.

As soon as she was gone, Professor Burkett leaned across the table. "What happened?"

"He was in the foyer when I came out of the elevator yesterday. I didn't think about it, just rushed forward and grabbed him."

"He was there? This Therriault? You saw him? *Felt* him?" Still half-convinced it was all in my mind, you know. I could see it on his face, and really, who could blame him?

"Yeah. But it's not Therriault, not anymore. The thing inside, it's a light, tried to get away but I held on. It was scary, but I knew it would be bad for me if I let go. Finally, when it saw that Therriault was fading out, it—"

"Fading out? What do you mean?"

The toilet flushed. Mom wouldn't come back until she'd washed her hands, but that wouldn't take long.

"I told it what you told me to say, Professor. That if I whistled, it had to come to me. That it was my turn to haunt *it*. It agreed. I made it say it out loud, and it did."

My mother came back before he could ask any more questions, but I could see he looked troubled and was still thinking the whole confrontation had been in my mind. I got that but I was a little pissed just the same—I mean, he *knew* stuff, about the rings and Mr. Thomas's book—but looking back on it, I understand. Belief is a high hurdle to get over and I think it's even higher for smart people. Smart people know a lot, and maybe that makes them think they know everything.

"We ought to go, Jamie," Mom said. "I've got a manuscript to finish."

"You always have a manuscript to finish," I said, which made her laugh because it was true. There were to-read stacks in both the agency office and her home office, and both of them were always piled high. "Before we go, tell the professor what happened in our building yesterday."

She turned to Professor Burkett. "That was so strange, Marty. Every circuit breaker in the building blew out. All at once! Mr. Provenza—he's the super—said there must have been some kind of power surge. He said he'd never seen anything like it."

The professor looked startled. "Only your building?"

"Just ours," she agreed. "Come on, Jamie. Let's get out of here and let Marty rest."

Going out was an almost exact replay of going in. Professor Burkett gave me a keen look and I gave him a slight nod.

We understood each other.

46

That night I got an email from him, sent from his iPad. He was the only person of my acquaintance who ever used a salutation when he sent one, and wrote actual letters instead of stuff like *How r u* and *ROFL* and *IMHO*.

> *Dear Jamie,*
>   *After you and your mother left this morning, I did some research concerning the discovery of the bomb at the Eastport supermarket, a thing I should have done*

earlier. What I found was interesting. Elizabeth Dutton did not figure prominently in any of the news stories. The Bomb Squad got most of the credit (especially the dogs, because people love dogs; I believe the mayor may have actually given a dog a medal). She was mentioned only as "a detective who received a tip from an old source." I found it peculiar that she did not take part in the press conference following the successful defusing of the bomb, and that she did not receive an official commendation. She has, however, managed to keep her job. That may have been all the reward she wanted and all her superiors felt she deserved.

Given my research on this matter, plus the strange power outage in your building at the time of your confrontation with Therriault, plus other matters of which you have made me aware, I find myself unable to disbelieve the things you've told me.

I must add a word of caution. I did not care for the look of confidence on your face when you said it was your turn to haunt it, or that you could whistle for it and it would come. Perhaps it would, BUT I URGE YOU NOT TO DO IT. Tightrope walkers sometimes fall. Lion tamers can be mauled by cats they believed to be completely tamed. Under certain conditions, even the best dog may turn and bite his master.

My advice to you, Jamie, is to leave this thing alone.

With every good wish from your friend,
Prof. Martin Burkett (Marty)

PS: I am very curious to know the exact details of your

extraordinary experience. If you can come and see me, I would listen with great interest. I am assuming you still do not want to burden your mother with the story, since it seems that matters have come to a successful conclusion.

I wrote back right away. My response was much shorter, but I made sure to compose it as he had, like a snail-mail letter.

Dear Professor Burkett,
    I'd be glad to do that, but I can't until Wednesday because of a trip to the Metropolitan Museum of Art on Monday and intramural volleyball, boys against the girls, on Tuesday. If Wednesday is okay, I will come after school, like around 3:30, but I can only stay for an hour or so. I'll tell my mother I just wanted to visit you, which is true.
                    Yours in friendship,
                    James Conklin

Professor Burkett must have had his iPad in his lap (I could picture him sitting in his living room, with all its framed pictures of old times), because he replied at once.

Dear Jamie,
    Wednesday will be fine. I will look for you at three-thirty and will supply raisin cookies. Would you prefer tea or a soft drink to go with them?
                    Yours,
                    Marty Burkett

I didn't bother making my reply look like a snail-mail letter, just typed *I wouldn't mind a cup of coffee*. After thinking about that, I added *It's OK with my mom*. Which wasn't a total lie, and he actually sent me an emoji in return: a thumbs-up. I thought that was pretty hip.

I did speak with Professor Burkett again, but there were no drinks or snacks. He no longer used those things, because he was dead.

47

On Tuesday morning, I got another email from him. My mother got the same one, and so did several other people.

> *Dear friends and associates,*
>
> *I have received some bad news. David Robertson—old friend, colleague, and former department head—suffered a stroke at his retirement home on Siesta Key in Florida last evening and is now in Sarasota Memorial Hospital. He is not expected to live, or even to regain consciousness, but I have known Dave and his lovely wife Marie for over forty years and must make the trip, little as I want to, if only to offer comfort to his wife and attend the funeral, should it come to that. I will reschedule such appointments as I have upon my return.*
>
> *I will be in residence at Bentley's Boutique Hotel (such a name!) in Osprey for the length of my stay, and you can reach me there, but the best way to get in touch with me is still email. As most of you know, I do not carry a personal phone. I apologize for any inconvenience.*
>
> *Sincerely yours,*
> *Prof. Martin F. Burkett (Emeritus)*

"He's old school," I said to Mom as we ate our breakfast: grapefruit and yogurt for her, Cheerios for me.

She nodded. "He is, and there aren't many of his kind left. To rush to the bedside of a dying friend at his age…" She shook her head. "Remarkable. Admirable. And that email!"

"Professor Burkett doesn't write emails," I said. "He writes letters."

"True, but not what I was thinking of. Really, how many appointments and scheduled visitors do you think he has at his age?"

Well, there was one, I thought, but didn't say.

48

I don't know if the professor's old friend died or not. I only know that the professor did. He had a heart attack on the flight and was dead in his seat when the plane landed. He had another old friend who was his lawyer—he was one of the recipients of the professor's final email—and he was the one who got the call. He took charge of getting the body shipped back, but it was my mom who stepped up after that. She closed the office and made the funeral arrangements. I was proud of her for that. She cried and was sad because she had lost a friend. I was just as sad because I'd made her friend my own. With Liz gone, he'd been my only grown-up friend.

The funeral was at the Presbyterian church on Park Avenue, same as Mona Burkett's had been seven years before. My mother was outraged that the daughter—the one on the west coast—didn't attend. Later, just out of curiosity, I called up that last email from Professor Burkett and saw she hadn't been one of the recipients. The only three women who'd gotten it were my mother, Mrs. Richards (an old lady he was friendly with on the fourth floor of the Palace on Park), and Dolores Magowan, the woman Mrs. Burkett had mistakenly predicted her widower husband would soon be asking out to lunch.

I looked for the professor at the church service, thinking that if his wife had attended hers, he might attend his. He wasn't there, but this time we went to the cemetery service as well and I saw him sitting on a gravestone twenty or thirty feet away from the mourners but close enough to hear what was being said. During the prayer, I raised my hand and gave him a discreet wave. Not much more than a twiddle of the fingers, but he saw it, and smiled, and waved back. He was a regular dead person, not a monster like Kenneth Therriault, and I started to cry.

My mother put her arm around me.

49

That was on a Monday, so I never did get to the Metropolitan Museum of Art with my class. I got the day off school to go to the funeral, and when we got back, I told my mother I wanted to go for a walk. That I needed to think.

"That's fine…if you're okay. *Are* you okay, Jamie?"

"Yes," I said, and gave her a smile to prove it.

"Be back by five or I'll worry."

"I will be."

I got as far as the door before she asked me the question I'd been waiting for. "Was he there?"

I had thought about lying, like maybe that would spare her feelings, but maybe it would make her feel better, instead. "Yes. Not at the church but at the cemetery."

"How…how did he look?"

I told her he looked okay, and that was the truth. They're always wearing the clothes they had on when they died, which in Professor Burkett's case was a brown suit that was a little too big for him but still looked quite cool, in my humble opinion. I liked that he'd put on a suit for the plane ride, because it was another part of being old school. And he didn't have his cane, possibly because he wasn't holding it when he died or because he dropped it when the heart attack struck.

"Jamie? Could your old mom have a hug before you go out on your walk?"

I hugged her a long time.

50

I walked to the Palace on Park, much older and taller than the little boy who'd come from his school one fall day holding his mother's hand on one side and his green turkey on the other. Older, taller, and maybe even wiser, but still that same person. We change, and we don't. I can't explain it. It's a mystery.

I couldn't go inside the building, I had no key, but I didn't need to, because Professor Burkett was sitting on the steps in his brown traveling suit. I sat down beside him. An old lady walked by with a little fluffy dog. The dog looked at the professor. The old lady didn't.

"Hello, Professor."

"Hello, Jamie."

It had been five days since he died on the airplane, and his voice was doing that fade-out thing they do. As if he was talking to me from far away and getting farther all the time. And while he seemed as kind as ever, he also seemed sort of, I don't know, disconnected. Most of them do. Even Mrs. Burkett was that way, although she was chattier than most (and some don't talk at all, unless you ask them a question). Because they are watching the parade instead of marching in it? That's close, but still not quite right. It's as if they've got other, more important things on their minds, and for the first time I realized that my voice must be fading for him, as well. The whole world must be fading.

"Are you okay?"

"Yes."

"Did it hurt? The heart attack?"

"Yes, but it was over soon." He was looking out at the street, not at me. As if storing it up.

"Is there anything you need me to do?"

"Only one thing. Never call for Therriault. Because Therriault is gone. What would come is the thing that possessed him. I believe that in the literature, that sort of entity is called a walk-in."

"I won't, I promise. Professor, why could it even possess him in the first place? Because Therriault was evil to start with? Is that why?"

"I don't know, but it seems likely."

"Do you still want to hear what happened when I grabbed him?" I thought of his email. "The details?"

"No." This disappointed me but didn't surprise me. Dead people lose interest in the lives of the living. "Just remember what I've told you."

"I will, don't worry."

A faint shadow of irritation came into his voice. "I wonder. You were incredibly brave, but you were also incredibly lucky. You don't understand because you're just a child, but take my word for it. That thing is from outside the universe. There are horrors there that no man can conceive of. If you truck with it you risk death, or madness, or the destruction of your very soul."

I had never heard anyone talk about *trucking* with some-thing—I suppose it was another of the professor's old-school words, like icebox for refrigerator, but I got the gist. And if he meant to scare me, he had succeeded. The destruction of my *soul*? Jesus!

"I won't," I said. "I really won't."

He didn't reply. Just looked out at the street with his hands on his knees.

"I'll miss you, professor."

"All right." His voice was growing fainter all the time. Pretty soon I wouldn't be able to hear him at all, I'd only be able to see his lips moving.

"Can I ask you one more thing?" Stupid question. When you ask, they have to answer, although you might not always like what you hear.

"Yes."

I asked my question.

51

When I got home, my mother was making salmon the way we like it, wrapped in wet paper towels and steamed in the microwave. You wouldn't think anything so easy could taste good, but it does.

"Right on time," she said. "There's a bag-salad Caesar. Will you put it together for me?"

"Okay." I got it out of the fridge—the icebox—and opened the bag.

"Don't forget to wash it. The bag says it's already been washed, but I never trust that. Use the colander."

I got the colander, dumped in the lettuce, and used the sprayer. "I went to our old building," I said. I wasn't looking at her, I was concentrating on my job.

"I kind of thought you might. Was he there?"

"Yes. I asked him why his daughter never came to visit him and didn't even come to the funeral." I turned off the water. "She's in a mental institution, Mom. He says she'll be there for the rest of her life. She killed her baby, and then tried to kill herself."

My mother was getting ready to put the salmon in the microwave, but she set it on the counter instead and plopped down on one of the stools. "Oh my God. Mona told me she was an assistant in a biology lab at Caltech. She seemed so *proud*."

"Professor Burkett said she's cata-whatsit."

"Catatonic."

"Yeah. That."

My mother was looking down at our dinner-to-be, the salmon's pink flesh kind of glimmering through its shroud of paper towels. She seemed to be thinking very deeply. Then the vertical line between her eyebrows smoothed out.

"So now we know something we probably shouldn't. It's done and can't be undone. Everybody has secrets, Jamie. You'll find that out for yourself in time."

Thanks to Liz and Kenneth Therriault, I had found that out already, and I found out my mother's secret, too.

Later.

52

Kenneth Therriault disappeared from the news, replaced by other monsters. And because he had stopped haunting me, he also disappeared from the forefront of my mind. As that fall chilled into winter, I still had a tendency to step back from the elevator doors when they opened, but by the time I turned fourteen, that little tic had disappeared.

I saw other dead people from time to time (and there were probably some I missed, since they looked like normal people unless they died of injuries or you got right up close). I'll tell you about one, although it has nothing to do with my main story. He was a little boy no older than I had been on the day I saw Mrs. Burkett. He was standing on the divider that runs down the middle of Park Avenue, dressed in red shorts and a Star Wars tee-shirt. He was paper pale. His lips were blue.

And I think he was trying to cry, although there were no tears. Because he looked vaguely familiar, I crossed the downtown side of Park and asked him what was wrong. You know, besides being dead.

"I can't find my way home!"

"Do you know your address?"

"I live at 490 Second Avenue Apartment 16B." He ran it off like a recording.

"Okay," I said, "that's pretty close. Come on, kid. I'll take you there."

It was a building called Kips Bay Court. When we got there, he just sat down on the curb. He wasn't crying anymore, and he was starting to get that drifting-away look they all get. I didn't like to leave him there, but I didn't know what else to do. Before I left, I asked him his name and he said it was Richard Scarlatti. Then I knew where I'd seen him. His picture was on NY1. Some big boys drowned him in Swan Lake, which is in Central Park. Those boys all cried like blue fuck and said they had only been goofing around. Maybe that was true. Maybe I'll understand all that stuff later, but actually I don't think so.

53

By then we were doing well enough that I could have gone to a private school. My mother showed me brochures from the Dalton School and the Friends Seminary, but I chose to stay public and go to Roosevelt, home of the Mustangs. It was okay. Those were good years for Mom and me. She landed a super-big client who wrote stories about trolls and woods elves and noble guys who went on quests. I landed a girlfriend, sort of. Mary Lou Stein was kind of a goth intellectual in spite of her girl-next-door name and a huge cinephile. We went to the Angelika just about once every week and sat in the back row reading subtitles.

One day shortly after my birthday (I'd reached the grand old age of fifteen), Mom texted me and asked if I could drop by the agency office after school instead of going straight home—not a huge deal, she said, just some news she wanted to pass on in person.

When I got there she poured me a cup of coffee—unusual but not unheard-of by then—and asked if I remembered Jesus Hernandez. I told her I did. He had been Liz's partner for a couple of years, and a couple of times Mom brought me along when she and Liz had meals with Detective Hernandez and his wife. That was quite awhile ago, but it's hard to forget a six-foot-six detective named Jesus, even if it is pronounced *Hay-soos*.

"I loved his dreads," I said. "They were cool."

"He called to tell me Liz lost her job." Mom and Liz had been quits a long time by then, but Mom still looked sad. "She finally got caught transporting drugs. Quite a lot of heroin, Jesus says."

It hit me hard. Liz hadn't been good for my mother after awhile, and she sure as shit hadn't been good for me, but it was still a bummer. I remembered her tickling me until I almost wet my pants, and sitting between her and Mom on the couch, all of us making stupid cracks about the shows, and the time she took me to the Bronx Zoo and bought me a

cone of cotton candy bigger than my head. Also, don't forget
that she saved fifty or maybe even a hundred lives that would
have been lost if Thumper's last bomb had gone off. Her
motivation might have been good or bad, but those lives
were saved either way.

That overheard phrase from their last argument came to
me. *Serious weight*, Mom had said. "She isn't going to jail, is
she?"

Mom said, "Well, she's out on bail now, Jesus said, but in
the end...I think there's a good chance she will, honey."

"Oh, fuck." I thought of Liz in an orange jumpsuit, like
the women in that Netflix show my mother sometimes
watched.

She took my hand. "Right right right."

54

It was two or three weeks later when Liz kidnapped me. You
could say she did that the first time, with Therriault, but you
could call that a "soft snatch." This time it was the real deal.
She didn't force me into her car kicking and screaming, but
she still forced me. Which makes it kidnapping as far as I'm
concerned.

I was on the tennis team, and on my way home from a
bunch of practice matches (which our coach called "heats,"
for some dumb reason). I had my pack on my back and my
tennis duffle in one hand. I was headed for the bus stop and
saw a woman leaning against a beat-up Toyota and looking at
her phone. I walked past without a second glance. It never

occurred to me that this scrawny chick—straw-blonde hair blowing around the collar of an unzipped duffle coat, over-sized gray sweatshirt, beat-up cowboy boots disappearing into baggy jeans—was my mom's old friend. My mom's old friend had favored tapered slacks in dark colors and low-cut silk blouses. My mom's old friend wore her hair slicked back and pulled into a short stump of ponytail. My mom's old friend had looked healthy.

"Hey, Champ, not even a howya doin for an old friend?"

I stopped and turned back. For a moment I still didn't recognize her. Her face was bony and pale. There were blemishes, untouched by makeup, dotting her forehead. All the curves I'd admired—in a little-boy way, granted—were gone. The baggy sweatshirt beneath the coat showed only a hint of what had been generous breasts. At a guess, I'd say she was forty or even fifty pounds lighter and looked twenty years older.

"Liz?"

"None other." She gave me a smile, then obscured it by wiping her nose with the heel of her hand. *Strung out*, I thought. *She's strung out*.

"How are you?"

Maybe not the wisest question, but the only one I could think of under the circumstances. And I was careful to keep what I considered to be a safe distance from her, so I could outrun her if she tried anything weird. Which seemed like a possibility, because she *looked* weird. Not like actors pretending to be drug addicts on TV but like the real ones you saw from time to time, nodding out on park benches or in the doorways of abandoned buildings. I guess New York is a

lot better than it used to be, but dopers are still an occasional part of the scenery.

"How do I look?" Then she laughed, but not in a happy
way. "Don't answer that. But hey, we did a mitzvah once
upon a time, didn't we? I deserved more credit for that than
I got, but what the hell, we saved a bunch of lives."

I thought of all I'd been through because of her. And it
wasn't just because of Therriault, either. She had fucked up
my mom's life, too. Liz Dutton had put us both through a
bad time, and here she was again. A bad penny, turning up
when you least expected it. I got mad.

"You didn't deserve *any* of the credit. I was the one who
made him talk. And I paid a price for it. You don't want to
know."

She cocked her head. "Sure I do. Tell me about the price
you paid, Champ. A few bad dreams about the hole in his
head? You want bad dreams, take a look at three crispy crit-
ters in a burned-out SUV sometime, one of them just a kid
in a car seat. So what price did you pay?"

"Forget it," I said, and started walking again.

She reached out and grabbed the strap of my tennis
duffle. "Not so fast. I need you again, Champ, so saddle up."

"No way. And let go of my bag."

She didn't, so I pulled. There was nothing to her and she
went to her knees, letting out a small cry and losing her grip
on the strap.

A man who was passing stopped and gave me the look
adults give a kid when they see him doing something mean.
"You don't do that to a woman, kid."

"Fuck off," Liz told him, getting to her feet. "I'm police."

"Whatever, whatever," the man said, and got walking again. He didn't look back.

"You're not police anymore," I said, "and I'm not going anywhere with you. I don't even want to talk to you, so leave me alone." Still, I felt a little bad about pulling her so hard she went to her knees. I remembered her on her knees in our apartment, too, but because she was playing Matchbox cars with me. I tried to tell myself that was in another life, but it didn't work because it wasn't another life. It was my life.

"Oh, but you *are* coming. If you don't want the whole world to know who really wrote Regis Thomas's last book, that is. The big bestseller that pulled Tee away from bankruptcy just in time? The *posthumous* bestseller?"

"You wouldn't do that." Then, as the shock of what she'd said cleared away a little: "You *can't* do that. It would be your word against Mom's. The word of a drug trafficker. Plus a junkie, from the look of you, so who'd believe you? No one!"

She had put her phone in her back pocket. Now she took it out. "Tia wasn't the only one recording that day. Listen to this."

What I heard made my stomach drop. It was my voice—much younger, but mine—telling Mom that Purity would find the key she'd been looking for under a rotted stump on the path to Roanoke Lake.

Mom: "How does she know which stump?"

Pause.

Me: "Martin Betancourt chalked a cross on it."

Mom: "What does she do with it?"

Pause.

Me: "Takes it to Hannah Royden. They go into the swamp together and find the cave."

Mom: "Hannah makes the Seeking Fire? The stuff that almost got her hung as a witch?"

Pause.

Me: "That's right. And he says George Threadgill sneaks after them. And he says that looking at Hannah makes George tumescent. What's that, Mom?"

Mom: "Never mi—"

Liz stopped the recording there. "I got a lot more. Not all of it, but an hour, at least. No doubt about it, Champ—that's you telling your mother the plot of the book *she* wrote. And *you* would be a bigger part of the story. James Conklin, Boy Medium."

I stared at her, my shoulders sagging. "Why didn't you play that for me before? When we went looking for Therriault?"

She looked at me as if I was stupid. Probably because I was. "I didn't need to. Back then you were basically a sweet kid who wanted to do the right thing. Now you're fifteen, old enough to be a pain in the ass. Which could be your right as a teenager, I guess, but that's a discussion for another day. Right now the question is this: do you get in the car and take a ride with me, or do I go to this reporter I know on the *Post* and give him a juicy scoop about the literary agent who faked her dead client's last book with the help of her ESP son?"

"Take a ride where?"

"It's a mystery tour, Champ. Get in and find out."

I didn't see any choice. "Okay, but one thing. Stop calling me Champ, like I was your pet horse."

"Okay, Champ." She smiled. "Joking, just joking. Get in, Jamie."

I got in.

55

"Which dead person am I supposed to talk to this time? Whoever it is and whatever they know, I don't think it will keep you from going to jail."

"Oh, I'm not going to jail," she said. "I don't think I'd like the food, let alone the company."

We passed a sign pointing to the Cuomo Bridge, which everybody in New York still calls the Tappan Zee, or just the Tap. I didn't like that. "Where are we going?"

"Renfield."

The only Renfield I knew was the Count's fly-eating helper in *Dracula*. "Where's that? Someplace in Tarrytown?"

"Nope. Little town just north of New Paltz. It'll take us two or three hours, so settle back and enjoy the ride."

I stared at her, more than alarmed, almost horrified. "You've got to be kidding! I'm supposed to be home for *supper*!"

"Looks like Tia's going to be eating in solitary splendor tonight." She took a small bottle of whitish-yellow powder from the pocket of her duffle coat, the kind that has a little gold spoon attached to the cap. She unscrewed it one-handed, tapped some of the powder onto the back of the hand she was using to drive, and snorted it up. She screwed the cap back on—still one-handed—and repocketed the vial. The quick dexterity of the process spoke of long practice.

She saw my expression and smiled. Her eyes had a new brightness. "Never seen anyone do that before? What a sheltered life you've led, Jamie."

I had seen kids smoke the herb, had even tried it myself, but the harder stuff? No. I'd been offered ecstasy at a school dance and turned it down.

She ran the palm of her hand up over her nose again, not a charming gesture. "I'd offer you some, I believe in sharing, but this is my own special blend: coke and heroin two-to-one, with just a dash of fentanyl. I've built up a tolerance. It would blow your head off."

Maybe she did have a tolerance, but I could tell when it hit her. She sat up straighter and talked faster, but at least she was still driving straight and keeping to the speed limit.

"This is your mother's fault, you know. For years, all I did was carry dope from Point A, which was usually the 79th Street Boat Basin or Stewart Airport, to Point B, which could be anywhere in the five boroughs. At first it was mostly cocaine, but times changed because of OxyContin. That shit hooks people fast, I mean *kabang*. When their doctors stopped supplying it, the dopers bought it on the street. Then the price went up and they realized they could get about the same high from the big white nurse, and cheaper. So they went to that. It's what the man we're going to see supplied."

"The man who's dead."

She frowned. "Don't interrupt me, kiddo. You wanted to know, I'm telling you."

The only thing I could remember wanting to know was where we were going, but I didn't say that. I was trying not to be scared. It was working a little because this was still Liz, but not very much because this didn't seem like the Liz I'd known at all.

"Don't get high on your own supply, that's what they say, that's the mantra, but after Tia kicked me out, I started chipping a little. Just to keep from being too depressed. Then I started chipping a lot. After awhile you couldn't really call it chipping at all. I was using."

"My mom kicked you out because you brought junk into the house," I said. "It was your own fault." Probably would have been smarter to keep quiet, but I couldn't help it. Her trying to blame Mom for what she'd become made me mad all over again. In any case, she paid no attention.

"I'll tell you one thing, though, Cha—Jamie. I have never used the spike." She said this with a kind of defiant pride. "Never once. Because when you snort, you've got a shot at getting clean. Shoot that stuff, and you're never coming back."

"Your nose is bleeding." Just a trickle down that little gutter between her nose and upper lip.

"Yeah? Thanks." She wiped with the heel of her palm again, then turned to me for a second. "Did I get it all?"

"Uh-huh. Now look at the road."

"Yessir, Mr. Backseat Driver, sir," she said, and for just a moment she sounded like the old Liz. It didn't break my heart, but it squeezed it a little.

We drove. The traffic wasn't too bad for a weekday afternoon. I thought about my mother. She'd still be at the agency now, but she'd be home soon. At first she wouldn't worry. Then she would worry a little. Then she'd worry a lot.

"Can I call Mom? I won't tell her where I am, just that I'm okay."

"Sure. Go ahead."

I took my phone out of my pocket and then it was gone. She grabbed it with the speed of a lizard snaring a bug. Before I had even quite realized what was happening, she had opened her window and dropped it onto the highway.

"Why did you do that?" I shouted. "That was mine!"

"I'm glad you reminded me about your phone." Now we were following signs to I-87, the Thruway. "I totally forgot. They don't call it dope for nothing, you know." And she laughed.

I punched her on the shoulder. The car swerved, then straightened. Someone gave us a honk. Liz whipped another glance at me, and she wasn't smiling now. She had the look she probably got on her face when she was reading people their rights. You know, perps. "Hit me again, Jamie, and I'll hit you back in the balls hard enough to make you puke. God knows it wouldn't be the first time someone puked in this fucking beater."

"You want to try fighting me while you're driving?"

Now the smile came back, her lips parting just enough to show the tops of her teeth. "Try me."

I didn't. I didn't try anything, including (if you're wondering) yelling for the creature inhabiting Therriault, although it was now theoretically at my command—whistle and you'll come to me, my lad, remember that? The truth is, he—or *it*—never crossed my mind. I forgot, just like Liz forgot to take my phone at first, and I didn't even have a snoutful of dope to blame. I might not have done it, anyway. Who knew if it would actually come? And if it did…well, I was scared of Liz, but more scared of the deadlight thing. *Death, madness, the destruction of your very soul*, the professor had said.

"Think about it, kiddo. If you called and said you were fine but taking a little ride with your old friend Lizzy Dutton, do you think she'd just say 'Okay, Jamie, that's fine, make her buy you dinner?' "

I said nothing.

"She'd call the cops. But that isn't the biggest thing. I should have gotten rid of your cell right away, because she can track it."

My eyes widened. "Bull*shit* she can!"

Liz nodded, smiling again, eyes on the road again as we pulled past a double-box semi. "She put a locater app on the first phone she gave you, when you were ten. I was the one who told her how to hide it, so you wouldn't find it and get all pissy about it."

"I got a new phone two years ago," I muttered. There were tears prickling the corners of my eyes, I don't know why. I felt…I don't know the word. Wait a minute, maybe I do. *Whipsawed*. That's how I felt, whipsawed.

"You think she didn't put that app on the new one?" Liz gave a harsh laugh. "Are you kidding? You're her one and only, kiddo, her little princeling. She'll still be tracking you ten years from now, when you're married and changing your first kid's diapers."

"Fucking liar," I said, but I was talking to my own lap.

She snorted some more of her special blend once we were clear of the city, the movements just as agile and practiced, but this time the car *did* swerve a little, and we got another disapproving honk. I thought of some cop lighting us up, and at first I thought that would be good, that it would end this nightmare, but maybe it wouldn't be good. In her current wired-up state, Liz might try to outrun a cop, and manage to kill us both. I thought of the Central Park man. His face and upper body had been covered with somebody's jacket so the bystanders couldn't see the worst of it, but I had seen.

Liz brightened up again. "You'd make a hell of a detective, Jamie. With your particular skill, you'd be a star. No murderer would escape you, because you could talk to the vics."

This idea had actually occurred to me once or twice. James Conklin, Detective of the Dead. Or maybe *to* the Dead. I'd never figured out which sounded better.

"Not the NYPD, though," she continued. "Fuck those assholes. Go private. I could see your name on the door." She briefly raised both hands from the wheel, as if framing it.

Another honk.

"Drive the fucking car," I said, trying not to sound alarmed. It probably didn't work, because I *was* alarmed.

"Don't worry about me, Champ. I've forgotten more about driving than you'll ever learn."

"Your nose is bleeding again," I said.

She wiped it with the heel of her palm, then wiped it on her sweatshirt. Not for the first time, by the look of it. "Septum's gone," she said. "I'm going to fix it. Once I'm clean."

After that we were quiet for awhile.

56

After we got on the Thruway, Liz helped herself to another bump of her special blend. I'd say she was starting to scare me, but we were well past that point.

"Do you want to know how we got here? Me and you, Holmes and Watson off on another adventure?"

Adventure wasn't the word I would have picked, but I didn't say so.

"I can see by your face that you don't. That's okay. Long story, not very interesting, but I'll tell you this much—no kid ever said they wanted to grow up to be a bum, a college dean, or a dirty cop. Or to pick up garbage in Westchester county, which is what my brother-in-law does these days."

She laughed, although I didn't know then what was funny about being a garbageman.

"Here's something that *might* interest you. I've moved a lot of dope from Point A to Point B and got paid for it, but the blow your mother found in my coat pocket that time was a freebie for a friend. Ironic, when you think about it. By then IAD already had their eye on me. They weren't sure, but they were getting there. I was scared to death that Tee would spill the beans. That would have been the time to get out, but by then I couldn't." She paused, considering this. "Or wouldn't. Looking back it's hard to tell which. But it makes me think of something Chet Atkins said once. You ever heard of Chet Atkins?"

I shook my head.

"How soon the great are forgotten. Google him when you get back. Excellent guitarist, up there with Clapton and Knopfler. He was talking about how shitty he was at tuning his instrument. 'By the time I realized I was no good at this part of the job, I was too rich to quit.' Same with me and my career as a transporter. Tell you one other thing, since we're just passing the time on the good old New York Thruway. You think your mother was the only one who got hurt when the economy went tits-up in '08? Not true. I had a stock portfolio—teeny-weenie, but it was mine—and that went poof."

She passed another double box, being careful to use her blinker before swinging out and then tucking back in. Considering how much dope she'd ingested, I was amazed. Also grateful. I didn't want to be with her, but even more than that I didn't want to die with her.

"But the main thing was my sister Bess. She married this guy who worked for one of the big investment companies. Probably haven't heard of Bear Stearns any more than you've heard of Chet Atkins, right?"

I didn't know whether to nod my head or shake it, so I just sat there.

"Danny—my brother-in-law, now majoring in waste management—was just entry-level at Bear when Bess married him, but he had a clear path forward. Future was so bright he had to wear shades, if I may borrow from an old song. They bought a house in Tuckahoe Village. Hefty mortgage, but everyone assured them—me included, damn my eyes—that property values out that way had nowhere to go but up. Like the stock market. They got an au pair for their kid.

They got a junior membership in the country club. Were they overextended? Fuck, yes. Was Bessie able to look down on my paltry seventy grand a year? Ten-four. But you know what my father used to say?"

How would I? I thought.

"He used to say that if you try to outrun your own shadow, you're bound to fall on your face. Danny and Bess were talking about putting in a swimming pool when the bottom fell out. Bear Stearns specialized in mortgage securities, and all at once the paper they were holding was just paper."

She brooded on this as we passed a sign that said NEW PALTZ 59 POUGHKEEPSIE 70 and RENFIELD 78. We were a little over an hour away from our final destination, and just thinking that gave me the creeps, *Final Destination* being a particularly gory horror movie me and my friends had watched. Not up there with the *Saw* flicks, but still pretty fucking grim.

"Bear Stearns? What a joke. One week their shares were selling for over a hundred and seventy dollars a pop, the next they were going for ten bucks. JP Morgan Chase picked up the pieces. Other companies took the same long walk off the same short dock. The guys at the top made it through okay, they always do. The little guys and gals, not so much. Go on YouTube, Jamie, and you can find clips of people coming out of their fancy midtown office buildings with their whole careers in cardboard boxes. Danny Miller was one of those guys. Six months after joining the Green Hills Country club, he was riding on a Greenwise garbage truck. And he was one of the lucky ones. As for their house, underwater. Know what that means?"

It so happened that I did. "They owed more on it than it was worth."

"A-plus work, Cham…Jamie. Go to the head of the class. But it was the only asset they had, not to mention a place where Bess, Danny, and my niece Francine could lay down their heads at night without getting rained on. Bess said she had friends who were sleeping in their camper. Who do you think kicked in enough so they could keep up with the payments on that four-bedroom white elephant?"

"I'm guessing you did."

"Right. Bess stopped looking down on my seventy grand a year, I can tell you that. But was I able to do it on just my salary, plus all the overtime I could glom? No way. Because I got part-time work as security in a couple of clubs? *More* no way. But I met people there, made connections, got offers. Certain lines of work are recession-proof. Funeral parlors always make out. Repo companies and bail bondsmen. Liquor stores. And the dope biz. Because, good times or bad, people are going to want to get high. And okay, I like nice things. Won't apologize for it. I find nice things a comfort, and felt like I deserved them. I was keeping a roof over my sister's family's head, after all the years Bess high-hatted me because she was prettier, smarter, went to a real college instead of a community deal. And, of course, she was *hetero*." Liz almost snarled this last.

"What happened?" I asked. "How did you lose your job?"

"IAD blindsided me with a piss test I wasn't ready for. Not that they didn't know all along, they just couldn't get rid of me right away after I pitched in with Therriault. Wouldn't have looked good. So they waited, which I suppose was smart, and then when they had me in a box—at least they thought they did—they tried to turn me. Get me to wear a wire and all that good *Serpico* shit. But here's another saying, one I didn't learn from my father: snitches wind up in ditches. And they didn't know I had an ace up my sleeve."

"What ace?" You can think I was stupid if you want, but that was actually an honest question.

"You, Jamie. You're my ace. And ever since Therriault, I knew the time would come when I'd have to play it."

57

We drove through downtown Renfield, which must have had a big population of college kids, judging from all the bars, bookstores, and fast food restaurants on its single main street. On the other side, the road turned west and began to rise into the Catskills. After three miles or so, we came to a picnic area overlooking the Wallkill River. Liz turned in and killed the engine. We were the only ones there. She took out her little bottle of special blend, seemed about to unscrew the cap, then put it away. Her duffle coat pulled open and I saw more smears of dried blood on her sweatshirt. I thought about her saying her septum was gone. Thinking about how the powder she was snorting was eating into her flesh was worse than any *Final Destination* or *Saw* movie, because it was real.

"Time to tell you why I brought you here, kiddo. You need to know what to expect, and what I expect of you. I don't think we'll part friends, but maybe we can part on relatively good terms."

I doubt that was another thing I didn't say.

"If you want to know how the dope biz works, watch *The Wire*. It's set in Baltimore instead of New York, but the dope biz doesn't change much from place to place. It's a pyramid, like any other big-money organization. You've got your junior street dealers at the bottom, and most of them *are* juniors, so when they get popped they get tried as juveniles. In family court one day, back on the street corner the next. Then you've got your senior dealers, who service the clubs—where I got recruited—and the fat cats who save money by buying in bulk."

She laughed, and I didn't get why that was funny, either.

"Go up a little and you've got your suppliers, your junior executives to keep things running smoothly, your accountants, your lawyers, and then the top boys. It's all compartmentalized, or at least it's supposed to be. The people at the bottom know who's directly above them, but that's all they know. The people in the middle know everyone below them, but still only one layer above them. I was different. Outside the pyramid. Outside the, um, hierarchy."

"Because you were a transporter. Like in that Jason Statham movie."

"Pretty much. Transporters are supposed to know only two people, the ones we receive from at Point A and the ones we turn the load over to at Point B. Those at Point B are the senior distributors who start the dope flowing down the pyramid to its final destination, the users."

Final destination. There it was again.

"Only as a cop—dirty, but still a cop—I pay attention, okay? I don't ask many questions, doing that is dangerous, but I listen. Also, I have—had, anyway—access to NYPD and DEA databases. It wasn't hard to trace the pyramid all the way to the tippy-top. There are maybe a dozen people importing three major kinds of dope into the New York and New England territories, but the one I was working for lives right here in Renfield. Lived, I should say. His name is Donald Marsden, and when he filed his taxes, he listed *developer* as his former occupation and *retired* as his current one. He's retired, all right."

Lived, I should say. Retired.

It was Kenneth Therriault all over again.

"The kid gets the picture," Liz said. "Fantastic. Mind if I smoke? I shouldn't have another bump until this is over. Then I'll treat myself to a double. Really redline the old blood pressure."

She didn't wait for me to give permission, just lit up. But at least she rolled down her window to let the smoke out. Most of it, anyway.

"Donnie Marsden was known to his colleagues—his *crew*— as Donnie Bigs, for good reason. He was one fat fuck, pardon my political incorrectness. Three hundred ain't in it, dear— try four and a quarter. He was asking for it, and he got it yesterday. Cerebral hemorrhage. Blew his brains out and didn't even need a gun."

She dragged deep and shot smoke out her window. The daylight was still strong but the shadows were getting long. Soon the light would start to fade.

"A week before he stroked out, I got word through two of my old contacts—this would be Point B guys I stayed friendly with—that Donnie received a shipment from China. *Huge* shipment, they said. Not powder, pills. Knockoff OxyContin, a lot of it for Donnie Bigs's personal sale. Maybe as a kind of bonus. That'd be my guess, anyway, because there really *is* no top of the pyramid, Jamie. Even the boss has bosses."

This made me think of something Mom and Uncle Harry used to chant sometimes. They had learned it as kids, I guess, and Uncle Harry remembered it even when all of the important stuff had blown away. *Big fleas have little fleas upon their backs to bite em, and little fleas have lesser fleas, and so on ad infinitum.* I supposed I might chant that to my own kids. If I ever had the chance to have them, that was.

"Pills, Jamie! *Pills!*" She sounded enraptured, which was mondo creepy. "Easy to transport and easier to sell! *Huge* could mean two or three thousand, maybe *ten* thousand. And Rico—one of my Point B guys—says they're forties. You know what forties go for on the street? Never mind, I know you don't. Eighty a pill. And never mind sweating out a run with heroin in plastic garbage bags, I could carry these in a fucking suitcase."

Smoke slithered out between her lips and she watched it drift away toward the guardrails with their sign reading STAY BACK FROM THE EDGE.

"We're going to get those pills, Jamie. You're going to find out where he put them. My guys asked me to cut them in if I got a line on the stuff, and of course I said yes, but this is my deal. Besides, there might not be ten thousand tabs. There might only be eight thousand. Or eight hundred."

She cocked her head, then shook it. As if arguing with herself.

"There'll be a couple thousand. A couple thousand at least,

got to be. Probably more. Donnie's executive bonus for doing a good job of supplying his New York clientele. But if you start splitting that, pretty soon you're stuck with chump change, and I'm no chump. Got a little bit of a drug problem, but that doesn't make me a chump. You know what I'll do, Jamie?"

I shook my head.

"Make it out to the west coast. Disappear from this part of the world forever. New clothes, new hair color, new me. I'll find someone out there who can broker a deal for the Oxy. I may not get eighty a pill, but I'll get a lot, because Oxy is still the gold standard, and the Chinese shit is as good as the real stuff. Then I'm going to get myself a nice new identity to go with my new hair and clothes. I'll check into a rehab and get clean. Find a job, maybe the kind where I can start making up for the past. Atonement is what the Catholics call it. How does that sound to you?"

Like a pipe dream, I thought.

It must have showed on my face, because the happy smile she'd been wearing froze. "You don't think so? Fine. Just watch me."

"I don't want to watch you," I said. "I want to get the hell away from you."

She raised a hand and I cringed back in my seat, thinking she meant to give me a swat, but she only sighed and wiped her nose with it again. "How can I blame you for that? So let's make it happen. We're going to drive up to his house— last one on Renfield Road, all by its lonesome—and you're going to ask him where those pills are currently residing. My guess would be in his personal safe. If so, you'll ask him for the combination. He'll have to tell you, because dead people can't lie."

"I can't be sure of that," I said, a lie which proved I was still alive. "It's not like I've questioned hundreds of them. Mostly I don't talk to them at all. Why would I? They're dead."

"But Therriault told you where the bomb was, even though he didn't want to."

I couldn't argue with that, but there was another possibility. "What if the guy's not there? What if he's wherever his body went? Or, I don't know, maybe he's visiting his mom and dad in Florida. Maybe once they're dead they can teleport anywhere."

I thought that might shake her, but she didn't look upset at all. "Thomas was at his place, wasn't he?"

"That doesn't mean they *all* are, Liz!"

"I'm pretty sure Marsden will be." She sounded very sure of herself. She didn't understand that dead people can be unpredictable. "Let's do this. Then I'll grant you your fondest wish. You'll never have to see me again."

She said this in a sad way, like I was supposed to feel sorry for her, but I didn't. The only thing I felt about her was scared.

58

The road ran upward in a series of lazy S-turns. At first there were some houses with mailboxes beside the road, but they were farther and farther apart. The trees began to crowd in, their shadows meeting and making it seem later than it was.

"How many do you think there are?" Liz asked.

"Huh?"

"People like you. Ones who can see the dead."

"How should I know?"

"Did you ever run into another one?"

"No, but it isn't exactly the kind of thing you talk about. Like starting a conversation with 'Hey, do you see dead people?' "

"I suppose not. But you sure didn't get it from your mother." Like she was talking about the color of my eyes or my curly hair. "What about your father?"

"I don't know who he is. Or was. Or whatever." Talking about my father made me uneasy, probably because my mother refused to.

"You never asked?"

"Sure I asked. She doesn't answer." I turned in my seat to look at her. "She never said anything about it…about him…to you?"

"I asked and got what you got. Brick wall. Not like Tee at all."

More curves, tighter now. The Wallkill was far below us, glittering in the late afternoon sunshine. Or maybe it was early evening. I'd left my watch at home on my nightstand, and the dashboard clock said 8:15, which was totally fucked up. Meanwhile the quality of the road was deteriorating. Liz's car rumbled over crumbling patches and thudded into potholes.

"Maybe she was so drunk she doesn't remember. Or maybe she got raped." Neither idea had ever crossed my mind, and

I recoiled. "Don't look so shocked. I'm only guessing. And you're old enough to at least consider what your mom might have gone through."

I didn't contradict her out loud, but in my mind I did. In fact, I thought she was full of shit. Are you ever old enough to wonder if your life is the result of blackout sex in the backseat of some stranger's car, or that your mom was hauled into an alley and raped? I really don't think so. That Liz did probably said all I needed to know about what she'd become. Maybe what she was all along.

"Maybe the talent came from your dear old Daddy-O. Too bad you can't ask him."

I thought I wouldn't ask him anything if I ran across him. I thought I would just punch him in the mouth.

"On the other hand, maybe it came from nowhere. I grew up in this little New Jersey town and there was a family down the street from us, the Joneses. Husband, wife, and five kids in this little shacky trailer. The parents were dumb as stone boats and so were four of the kids. The fifth was a fucking genius. Taught himself the guitar at six, skipped two grades, went to high school at twelve. Where did *that* come from? You tell me."

"Maybe Mrs. Jones had sex with the mailman," I said. This was a line I'd heard at school. It made Liz laugh.

"You're a hot sketch, Jamie. I wish we could still be friends."

"Then maybe you should have acted like one," I said.

59

The tar ended abruptly, but the dirt beyond was actually better: hard-packed, oiled down, smooth. There was a big orange sign that said PRIVATE ROAD NO TRESPASSING.

"What if there are guys there?" I asked. "You know, like bodyguards?"

"If there were, they really would be guarding a body. But the body's gone, and the guy he had minding the gate will also be gone. There was no one else except for the gardener and the housekeeper. If you're imagining some action movie scenario with men in black suits and sunglasses and semi-autos guarding the kingpin, forget about it. The guy at the gate was the only one who was armed, and even if Teddy still happens to be there, he knows me."

"What about Mr. Marsden's wife?"

"No wife. She left five years ago." Liz snapped her fingers. "Gone with the wind. Poof."

We swung around another turn. A mountain all shaggy with fir trees loomed ahead, blotting out the western half of the sky. The sun shone through a valley notch but would soon be gone. In front of us was a gate made out of iron stakes. Closed. There was an intercom and a keypad on one side of it. On the other, inside the gate, was a little house, presumably where the gatekeeper spent his time.

Liz stopped, turned off the car, and pocketed the keys. "Sit still, Jamie. This will be over before you know it."

Her cheeks were flushed and her eyes were bright. A trickle of blood ran from one of her nostrils and she wiped it away. She got out and went to the intercom, but the car windows were closed and I couldn't tell what she was saying. Then she went to the gatehouse side and this time I *could* hear her, because she raised her voice. "Teddy? Are you in there? It's your buddy Liz. Hoping to pay my respects, but I need to know where!"

There was no answer and no one came out. Liz walked back to the other side of the gate. She took a piece of paper from her back pocket, consulted it, then punched some numbers into the keypad. The gate trundled slowly open. She came back to the car, smiling. "Looks like we've got the place to ourselves, Jamie."

She drove through. The driveway was tar, smooth as glass. There was another S-curve, and as Liz piloted through it, electric torches lit up on either side of the driveway. Later on I found out you call those kind of lights flambeaux. Or maybe that's only for torches like the mob waves when they're storming the castle in the old *Frankenstein* movies.

"Pretty," I said.

"Yeah, but look at that fucking thing, Jamie!"

On the other side of the S, Marsden's house came into view. It was like one of those Hollywood Hills mansions you see in the movies: big and jutting out over the drop. The side facing us was all glass. I imagined Marsden drinking his morning coffee and watching the sun rise. I bet he could see all the way to Poughkeepsie, maybe even beyond. On the other hand…a view of Poughkeepsie? Maybe not one to kill for.

"The house that heroin built." Liz sounded vicious. "All

the bells and whistles, plus a Mercedes and a Boxster in the garage. The stuff I lost my job for."

I thought of saying *you had a choice*, which is what my mom always said to me when I screwed up, but kept my mouth shut. She was wired like one of Thumper's bombs, and I didn't want to set her off.

There was one more curve before we came to the paved yard in front of the house. Liz drove around it and I saw a man standing in front of the double garage where Marsden's fancy cars were (they sure hadn't taken Donnie Bigs to the morgue in his Boxster). I opened my mouth to say it must be Teddy, the gatekeeper—the guy was thin, so it sure wasn't Marsden—but then I saw his mouth was gone.

"The Boxster's in there?" I asked, hoping my voice was more or less normal. I pointed at the garage and the man standing in front of it.

She took a look. "Yup, but if you were hoping for a ride, or even a look, you're going to be disappointed. We must be about our business."

She didn't see him. Only I saw him. And given the red hole where his mouth had been, he hadn't died a natural death.

Like I said, this is a horror story.

60

Liz killed the engine and got out. She saw me still sitting in the passenger seat, my feet planted amid a bunch of snack wrappers, and gave me a shake. "Come on, Jamie. Time to do your job. Then you're free."

I got out and followed her to the front door. On the way I snuck another glance at the man in front of the double garage. He must have known I was seeing him, because he raised a hand. I checked to make sure Liz wasn't looking at me and lifted my own in return.

Slate steps led to a tall wooden door with a lion's head knocker. Liz didn't bother with that, just took the piece of paper out of her pocket and punched more numbers into a keypad. The red light on it turned green and there was a thud as the door unlocked.

Had Marsden given those numbers to a lowly trans- porter? I didn't think so, and I didn't think whoever she'd heard about the pills from would have known them. I didn't like that she had them, and for the first time I thought of Therriault...or the thing that now lived in what remained of him. I had bested that thing in the Ritual of Chüd, and maybe it would come if I called, always supposing it had to honor the deal we'd made. But that was yet to be proven. I would only do it as a last resort in any case, because I was terrified of it.

"Go on in." Liz had put the piece of paper in her back pocket, and the hand that had been holding it went into the pocket of her duffle coat. I took one more glance at the man—Teddy, I assumed—standing by the garage. I looked at the bloody hole where his mouth had been and thought of the smears on Liz's sweatshirt. Maybe those had come from wiping her nose.

Or not.

"I said go in." Not an invitation.

I opened the door. There was no foyer or entrance hall,

just a huge main room. In the middle was a sunken area furnished with couches and chairs. I later found out that sort of thing is called a conversation pit. There was more expensive-looking furniture placed around it (maybe so folks could spectate on the conversations going on below), a bar that looked like it was on wheels, and stuff on the walls. I say *stuff* because it didn't look like art to me, just a bunch of splats and squiggles, but the splats were framed so I guess it was art to Marsden. There was a chandelier over the conversation pit that looked like it weighed at least five hundred pounds, and I wouldn't have wanted to sit under it. Beyond the conversation pit, on the far side of the room, was a swooping double staircase. The only one remotely like it I'd seen in real life, as opposed to in the movies or on TV, was at the Apple Store on Fifth Avenue.

"Quite the joint, isn't it?" Liz said. She shut the door— *THUD*—and bammed the heel of her hand on the bank of light switches beside it. More flambeaux came on, plus the chandelier. It was a beautiful thing and cast a beautiful light, but I was in no mood to enjoy it. I was becoming more and more sure that Liz had already been here, and shot Teddy before she came to get me.

She won't have to shoot me if she doesn't know I saw him, I told myself, and although this made a degree of sense, I knew I couldn't trust logic to get me through this. She was as high as a kite, practically vibrating. I thought again of Thumper's bombs.

"You didn't ask me," I said.

"Ask you what?"

"If he's here."

"Well, is he?" She didn't ask with any real concern in her voice, more like it was for form's sake. What was up with that?

"No," I said.

She didn't seem upset like she had been when we were hunting for Therriault. "Let's check the second floor. Maybe he's in the master bedroom, recalling all the happy times he spent there boinking his whores. There were many after Madeline left. Probably before, too."

"I don't want to go up there."

"Why not? The place isn't *haunted*, Jamie."

"It is if he's up there."

She considered this, then laughed. Her hand was still in the pocket of her jacket. "I suppose you have a point, but since it's him we're looking for, go on up. *Ándale, ándale.*"

I gestured to the hall leading away from the right side of the great room. "Maybe he's in the kitchen."

"Getting himself a snack? I don't think so. I think he's upstairs. Go on."

I thought about arguing some more, or point-blank refusing, but then her hand might come out of her jacket pocket and I had a pretty good idea of what would be in it. So I started up the right-hand staircase. The rail was cloudy green glass, smooth and cool. The steps were made out of green stone. There were forty-seven steps in all, I counted, and each one was probably worth the price of a Kia.

On the wall at the top of this set of stairs was a gilt-framed mirror that had to be seven feet tall. There was one just like it on the other side. I watched myself rise into the mirror with Liz behind me, looking over my shoulder.

"Your nose," I said.

"I see it." Both of her nostrils were bleeding now. She wiped her nose, then wiped her hand on her sweatshirt. "It's stress. Stress makes it happen because all the capillaries in there are fragile. Once we find Marsden and he tells us where the pills are, the stress will be relieved."

Did it bleed when you shot Teddy? I wondered. *How stressful was that, Liz?*

The hall at the top was actually a circular balcony, almost a catwalk, with a waist-high rail. Looking over it made my stomach feel funny. If you fell—or got pushed—you'd take a short ride straight down to the middle of the conversation pit, where the colorful rug wouldn't do much to cushion you from the stone floor beneath.

"Left turn, Jamie."

Which meant away from the balcony, and that was good. We went down a long hall with all the doors on the left, so whoever was in those rooms could dig the view. The only door that was open was halfway down. It was a circular library, every shelf crammed with books. My mother would have swooned with delight. There were chairs and a sofa in front of the only wall without books. That wall was a window, of course, curved glass looking out on a landscape that was now turning purple with dusk. I could see the nest of lights that must have been the town of Renfield, and I would have given almost anything to be there.

Liz didn't ask if Marsden was in the library, either. Didn't even give it a glance. We came to the end of the hall and she used the hand not in her jacket pocket to point at the last door. "I'm pretty sure he's in there. Open it."

I did, and sure enough, Donald Marsden was there, sprawled on a bed so big it looked like a triple, maybe even a quadruple, instead of a double. He was a quadruple himself, Liz had been right about that. To my child's eyes, the bulk of him was almost hallucinatory. A good suit might have disguised at least some of his flab, but he wasn't wearing a suit. He was wearing a pair of gigantic boxer shorts and nothing else. His immense girth, jumbo man-breasts, and flabby arms were crisscrossed with shallow cuts. His full moon of a face was bruised and one eye was swollen shut. There was a weird thing stuck in his mouth that I later learned (on one of those websites you don't want your mom to know about) was a ball-gag. His wrists had been handcuffed to the top bed-posts. Liz must have only brought two pairs of cuffs, because his ankles had been duct-taped to the bottom posts. She must have used a roll for each one.

"Behold the man of the house," Liz said.

His good eye blinked. You would say I should have known from the cuffs and the duct tape. I should have known because some of the cuts were still oozing. But I didn't. I was in shock and I didn't. Not until that single blink.

"He's alive!"

"I can fix that," Liz said. She took the gun out of her coat pocket and shot him in the head.

61

Blood and brains spattered the wall behind him. I screamed and ran out of the room, down the stairs, out the door, past Teddy, and down the hill. I ran all the way to Renfield. All of this in one second. Then Liz wrapped her arms around me.

"Steady, kiddo. Stead—"

I punched her in the stomach and heard her woof out a surprised breath. Then I was whirled and my arm was twisted up behind me. It hurt like blue fuck and I screamed some more. All of a sudden my feet were no longer holding me up. She'd swept them right out from under me and I went on my knees, yelling my head off with my arm twisted up so high that my wrist was touching my shoulderblade.

"Shut up!" Her voice, little more than a growl, was in my ear. This was the woman who had once played Matchbox cars with me, both of us down on our knees while my mother stirred spaghetti sauce in the kitchen, listening to oldies on Pandora. "Quit that squalling and I'll let you go!"

I did and she did. Now I was on my hands and knees, staring down at the rug, shaking all over.

"On your feet, Jamie."

I managed to do it, but I kept looking at the rug. I didn't want to look at the fat man with the top of his head gone.

"Is he here?"

I stared at the rug and said nothing. My hair was in my eyes. My shoulder throbbed.

"*Is he here?* Look around!"

I raised my head, hearing my neck creak as I did it. Instead of looking directly at Marsden—although I could still see him, he was too big to miss—I looked at the table beside his bed. There was a cluster of pill bottles on it. There was also a fat sandwich and a bottle of spring water.

"*Is he here?*" She slapped me on the back of my head.

I scoped the room. There was nobody but us and the fat man's corpse. Now I'd seen two men shot in the head.

Therriault had been bad, but at least I hadn't had to watch him die.

"No one," I said.

"Why not? Why isn't he here?" She sounded frantic. I couldn't think much then, I was too fucking terrified. It was only later, replaying that endless five minutes in Marsden's room, that I realized she was doubting the whole thing. In spite of Regis Thomas and his book, in spite of the bomb in the supermarket, she was afraid I couldn't see dead people at all, and she'd killed the only person who knew where that stash of pills was hidden.

"I don't know. I was never where someone actually died. Maybe…maybe it takes awhile. I don't know, Liz."

"Okay," she said. "We'll wait."

"Not in here, okay? Please, Liz, not where I have to look at him."

"In the hall, then. If I let go of you, are you going to be good?"

"Yes."

"Not going to try to run?"

"No."

"You better not, I'd hate to shoot you in the foot or the leg. That'd be the end of your tennis career. Back out."

I backed out and she backed out with me, so she could block me off if I tried to make a break for it. When we were in the hall, she told me to look around again. I did. Marsden wasn't there and I told her that.

"Damn." Then: "You saw the sandwich, didn't you?"

I nodded. A sandwich and a bottle of water for a man who was bound to his jumbo bed. Bound hand and foot.

"He loved his food," Liz said. "I ate with him in a restaurant once. He should have had a shovel instead of a fork and spoon. What a pig."

"Why would you leave him a sandwich he couldn't eat?"

"I wanted him to look at it, that's why. Just look. All day, while I went to get you and bring you back. And believe me, a shot in the head is just what he deserved. Do you have any idea how many people he killed with his…his happy poison?"

Who helped him? I thought, and of course didn't say.

"How long do you think he would have lived, anyway? Two years? Five? I've been in his bathroom, Jamie. He's got a double-wide toilet seat!" She made a sound somewhere between a laugh and a snort of disgust. "Okay, let's stroll down to the balcony. We'll see if he's in the great room. Slow."

I couldn't have gone fast if I'd wanted to, because my thighs were trembling and my knees felt like jelly.

"You know how I got the gate code? Marsden's UPS man. Guy has a hell of a coke habit, I could have slept with his wife if I'd wanted to, he'd've been happy to supply her if I kept supplying him. The house code I got from Teddy."

"Before you killed him."

"What else was I supposed to do?" Like I was the dumbest kid in class. "He could identify me."

So can I, I thought, and that brought me back to the thing this lad—me—could whistle for. I'd have to do it, but I still didn't want to. Because it might not work? Yeah, but not just that. Rub a magic lamp and get a genie, okay, good for you. Rub it and summon a demon—a deadlight—and God might know what would happen, but I didn't.

We reached the balcony with its low rail and high drop. I peered over.

"Is he down there?"

"No."

The gun prodded me in the small of my back. "Are you lying?"

"No!"

She gave a harsh sigh. "This isn't the way it's supposed to go."

"I don't know how it's supposed to go, Liz. For all I know, he could be outside talking with T—" I stopped.

She took hold of my shoulder and turned me around. There was blood all over her upper lip now—her stress must have been very high—but she was smiling. "You saw Teddy?"

I dropped my eyes. Which was answer enough.

"You sly dog." She actually laughed. "We'll go out and take a look if Marsden doesn't show in here, but for the time being, let's just wait a little. We can afford to. His latest whore is visiting her relatives in Jamaica or Barbados or somewhere with palm trees, and he doesn't get company during the week, does all his business by phone these days. He was just lying there when I came in, watching that *John Law* court show on TV. Christ, I wish he'd at least been wearing some pajamas, you know?"

I said nothing.

"He told me there were no pills, but I could see on his face that he was lying, so I secured him and then cut him a little. Thought that might loosen his tongue, and you know what he did? He *laughed* at me. Said yes, okay, there was Oxy, a lot of it, but he'd never tell me where it was. 'Why should I?' he said. 'You're going to kill me anyway.' That's when the penny dropped. Couldn't believe I hadn't thought of it before. *Muy stupido*." She hit the side of her head with the hand holding the gun.

"Me," I said. "I was the penny that dropped."

"Yes indeed. So I left him a sandwich and a bottle of water to admire and I went to New York and I got you and we drove back and nobody came and here we are, *so where the fuck is he?*"

"There," I said.

"What? *Where?*"

I pointed. She turned and of course saw nothing, but I could see for both of us. Donald Marsden, also known as Donnie Bigs, was standing in the doorway of his circular library. He was wearing nothing but his boxer shorts and the top of his head was pretty much gone and his shoulders were drenched with blood, but he was staring at me with the eye Liz hadn't punched shut in her fury and frustration.

I raised a tentative hand to him. He raised one of his in return.

62

"Ask him!" She was digging into my shoulder and breathing in my face. Neither was pleasant, but her breath was worse.

"Let go of me and I will."

I walked slowly toward Marsden. Liz followed close behind. I could feel her, *looming*.

I stopped about five feet away. "Where are the pills?"

He replied without hesitation, talking as all of them did—with the exception of Therriault, that was—as if it didn't really matter. And why would it? He didn't need pills anymore, not where he was and not where he was going. Assuming he was going anywhere.

"Some are on the table beside my bed, but most are in

the medicine cabinet. Topomax, Marinox, Inderal, Pepcid, Flomax…" Plus half a dozen more. Droning them off like a shopping list.

"What did he—"

"Be quiet," I said. For the moment I was in charge, although I knew that wouldn't last long. Would I be in charge if I called the thing inhabiting Therriault? That I didn't know. "I asked the wrong question."

I turned to look at her.

"I can ask the right one, but first you have to promise you're going to let me go once you get what you came for."

"Of course I am, Jamie," she said, and I knew she was lying. I'm not sure exactly *how* I knew, there was nothing logical about it, but it wasn't pure intuition. I think it had to do with the way her eyes shifted away from mine when she used my name.

I knew then I'd have to whistle.

Donald Marsden was still standing by the door of his library. I wondered briefly if he actually read the books in there, or if they were just for show. "She doesn't want your prescription stuff, she wants the Oxy. Where is it?"

What happened next had happened just once before. When I asked Therriault where he'd planted his last bomb. Marsden's words stopped matching the movements of his mouth, as if he was struggling against the imperative to answer. "I don't want to tell you."

Exactly what Therriault had said.

"Jamie! What—"

"Be quiet, I said! Give me a chance!" Then, to him: "Where is the Oxy?"

When pressed, Therriault had looked like he was in pain, and I think—don't know but *think*—that's when the deadlight-thing came in. Marsden didn't look to be in physical pain, but something emotional was going on there even though he was dead. He put his hands over his face like a child who's done something wrong and said, "Panic room."

"What do you mean? What's a panic room?"

"It's a place to go in case of a break-in." The emotion was gone, fast as it had come. Marsden was back to his shopping-list drone. "I have enemies. She was one. I just didn't know it."

"Ask him where it is!" Liz said.

I was pretty sure I knew that, but I asked, anyway. He pointed into the library.

"It's a secret room," I said, but since that wasn't a question, he made no response. "Is it a secret room?"

"Yes."

"Show me."

He went into the library, which was now shadowy. Dead people aren't ghosts, exactly, but as he went into that dimness, he sure looked like one. Liz had to feel around for the switch that turned on the overhead and more flambeaux, suggesting to me that she'd never spent any time in there, even though she was a reader. How many times had she actually been in this house? Maybe once or twice, maybe never. Maybe she only knew it from pictures and very careful questions to people who had been there.

Marsden pointed to a shelf of books. Because Liz couldn't see him, I copied his gesture and said, "That one."

She went to it and pulled. I might have run right then,

except she pulled me along with her. She was stoned and redlining with excitement, but she still had at least some of her cop instincts. She yanked on several shelves with her free hand, but nothing happened. She cursed and turned to me.

To forestall another shaking or arm-twisting, I asked Marsden the obvious question. "Is there a catch that opens it?"

"Yes."

"What's he saying, Jamie? Goddam it, what's he saying?"

Besides being scary as fuck, she was driving me crazy with her questions. She had forgotten to wipe her nose and now fresh blood was running over her upper lip, making her look like one of Bram Stoker's vampires. Which in my opinion she sort of was.

"Give me a chance, Liz." Then to Marsden: "Where's the catch?"

"Top shelf, on the right," Marsden said.

I told Liz. She stood on her toes, fumbled some more, and then there was a click. This time when she pulled, the bookcase swung out on hidden hinges, revealing a steel door, another keypad, and another small red light above the numbers. Liz didn't have to tell me what to ask next.

"What's the code?"

Once again he raised his hands and covered his eyes, that childish gesture that says *If I can't see you, you can't see me*. It was a sad gesture, but I couldn't afford to be touched by it, and not just because he was a drug baron whose product had undoubtedly killed hundreds, maybe even thousands of people, and hooked thousands more. I had enough problems of my own.

"What…is…the…code?" Enunciating each word, as I had with Therriault. This was different, but it was also the same.

He told me. He had to.

"73612," I said.

She punched in the numbers, still holding onto my arm. I almost expected a thump and a hiss, like an airlock opening in a science fiction movie, but the only thing that happened was the red light turning green. There was no handle or doorknob, so Liz pushed on the door and it swung open. The room inside was as black as a black cat's asshole.

"Ask him where the light switches are."

I did, and Marsden said, "There aren't any." He had dropped his hands again. His voice was already starting to fade. At that moment I thought maybe he was going so fast because he'd been murdered instead of dying a natural death or having an accident. Later on I changed my mind. I think he wanted to be gone before we found out what was in there.

"Try just stepping inside," I said.

She took a tentative step into the dark, never losing her hold on me, and overhead fluorescents came on. The room was stark. On the far side was an icebox (Professor Burkett's voice came back to me), a hotplate, and a microwave. To the left and right were shelves stacked with cheap canned food, stuff like Spam and Dinty Moore Beef Stew and King Oscar sardines. There were also pouches containing more food (later I found out those were what the army calls MREs, meals ready to eat), and sixpacks of water and beer. There was a landline telefungus on one of the lower shelves. In the middle of the room was a plain wooden table. There was a desktop computer on it, a printer, a thick folder, and a zippered shaving bag.

"Where's the Oxy?"

I asked. "He says they're in the dopp kit, whatever that is."

She seized the shaving bag, unzipped it, and turned it over. A bunch of pill bottles fell out, along with two or three small packets done up in Saran Wrap. Not exactly a treasure trove. She yelled, "What the fuck is *this*?"

I barely heard her. I had flipped open the folder beside the computer, for no other reason than it was there, and I was in shock. At first it was like I didn't even know what I was seeing, but of course I did. And I knew why Marsden hadn't wanted us to come in here, and why he could feel shame even though he was dead. It had nothing to do with drugs. I wondered if the woman I was looking at had the same ball-gag in her mouth. Poetic justice if she did.

"Liz," I said. My lips felt numb, like I'd gotten a shot of Novocain at the dentist.

"Is this all?" she was shouting. "Don't you fucking *dare* tell me this is all!" She twisted open one of the prescription bottles and dumped out the contents. There were maybe two dozen pills. "This isn't even Oxy, these are fucking *Darvons*!"

She had let go of me and I could have run right then, but I never even thought of it. Even the thought of whistling for Therriault had left my mind. "Liz," I said again.

She paid no attention. She was opening the bottles, one after the other. Different kinds of pills, but not a lot of them in any of the bottles. She was staring at some of the blue ones. "Roxies, okay, but this isn't even a *dozen*! Ask him where the rest are!"

"Liz, look at this." It was my voice, but seeming to come from far away.

"I said ask him—" She swung back and stopped, looking at what I was looking at.

It was a glossy photograph topping a thin stack of other glossy photographs. There were three people in it: two men and a woman. One of the men was Marsden. He wasn't even wearing his boxers. The other man was also naked. They were doing things to the woman with the gag in her mouth. I don't want to say, only that Marsden had a little blowtorch and the other man had one of those double-pronged meat forks.

"Shit," she whispered. "Oh, *shit*." She flipped through some more. They were unspeakable. She closed the folder. "It's her."

"Who?"

"Maddie. His wife. Guess she didn't run off after all."

Marsden was still outside in the library, but looking away from us. The back of his head was a ruin, like the left side of Therriault's had been, but I barely noticed. There are worse things than bullet wounds, a little something I found out that evening.

"They tortured her to death," I said.

"Yes, and had fun while they were doing it. Look at those big smiles. You still sorry I killed him?"

"You didn't kill him because of what he did to his wife," I said. "You didn't know about that. You killed him because of the dope."

She shrugged as if it didn't matter, and to her it probably didn't. She looked out of the panic room, where he came to look at his awful pictures, and across the library to the upstairs hall. "Is he still there?"

"Yes. In the doorway."

"At first he said there weren't any pills, but I knew he was lying. Then he said there were a lot. A *lot*!"

"Maybe he was lying when he said that. He could, because he wasn't dead yet."

"But he told you they were in the panic room! He was already dead then!"

"He didn't say how many." I asked Marsden, "That's all you've got?"

"That's all," he said. His voice was starting to drift.

"You told her you had a lot!"

He shrugged his bloody shoulders. "As long as she believed I had what she wanted, I thought she'd keep me alive."

"But that tip she heard about your getting a big private shipment—"

"Just bullshit," he said. "There's a lot of bullshit in this business. People say all sorts of shit just to hear themselves talk."

Liz shook her head when I told her what he'd said, not believing it. Not *wanting* to believe it because if she did, it meant all her west coast plans fell down. It meant she'd been conned.

"He's hiding something," she insisted. "Somehow. Somewhere. Ask him again where the rest of them are."

I opened my mouth to say that if there were more he would have told me already. Then—probably because the terrible pictures had slapped a dazed part of me awake—I had an idea. Maybe I could do some conning of my own, because she was certainly ready to be conned. If it worked, I might be able to get away from her without whistling up a demon.

She grabbed my shoulders and gave me a shake. "Ask him, I said!"

So I did. "Where's the rest of the dope, Mr. Marsden?"

"I told you, that's all there is." His voice was fading, fading. "I keep a few on hand for Maria, but she's in the Bahamas. Bimini."

"Oh, okay. That's more like it." I pointed to the shelves of canned goods. "See the cans of spaghetti on the top shelf?" There was no way she could miss them, there had to be at least thirty. Donnie Bigs must have really loved his Franco-American. "He said he hid some in those—not Oxy, they're something else."

She could have dragged me with her, but I was thinking there was a good chance she'd be too eager, and I was right. She ran to the shelves of canned goods. I waited until she was standing on her tiptoes and reaching up. Then I bolted out of the panic room and across the library. I wish I'd remembered to shut the door, but I didn't. Marsden was standing there and he looked solid, but I ran right through him. There was a moment of freezing cold, and my mouth filled with an oily taste I think was pepperoni. Then I was sprinting for the stairs.

There was a clatter of falling cans from behind me. "Get back here, Jamie! Get back!"

She came after me. I could hear her. I made it to where

those stairs swooped down, and looked over my shoulder. That was a mistake. I tripped. Out of other options, I pursed my lips to whistle, but I couldn't do anything but huff air. My mouth and lips were too dry. So I screamed instead.

"*THERRIAULT!*"

I started to crawl down the stairs headfirst with my hair in my eyes, but she grabbed my ankle.

"*THERRIAULT, HELP ME! GET HER OFF ME!*"

Suddenly everything—not just the balcony, not just the stairs, but all of the space above the great room and the conversation pit—filled with white light. I was looking back at Liz when it happened, and I squinted against the glare, all but blinded. It was coming from that tall mirror, and more was pouring out of the mirror on the other side of the balcony.

Liz's grip loosened. I grabbed one of the slate stairs and yanked on it as hard as I could. Down I went on my belly, like a kid on the world's bumpiest toboggan ride. I came to a stop about a quarter of the way down. Behind me, Liz was shrieking. I looked between my arm and my side, because of my position seeing her upside down. She was standing in front of the mirror. I don't know exactly what she saw, and that's good, because I might never have slept again. The light was enough—that brilliant no-color light that came glaring out of the mirror like a solar flare.

The deadlight.

Then I saw—I *think* I saw—a hand come out of the mirror and seize Liz by the neck. It yanked her against the glass and I heard it crack. She continued to shriek.

All the lights went out.

It was still the tag-end of dusk so it wasn't pitch dark in

the house, but it was getting close. The room below me was a well of shadows. Behind me, at the top of the curving staircase, Liz was shrieking and shrieking. I used the smooth glass railing to pull myself to my feet and managed to stumble my way down to the living room without falling.

Behind me, Liz stopped shrieking and began to laugh. I turned and saw her running down the stairs, just a dark shape laughing like the Joker in a Batman cartoon. She was going way too fast, and not looking *where* she was going. She weaved from side to side, bouncing off the railings, looking back over her shoulder at the mirror where the light was now fading away, like the filament in an old-fashioned light bulb when you turn it off.

"Liz, look out!"

I yelled that even though the only thing in the world I wanted was to get away from her. The warning was pure instinct, and it did no good. She overbalanced, fell forward, hit the stairs, tumbled, hit the stairs again, did another somersault, then slid all the way to the bottom. She went on laughing the first time she hit but stopped the second time. Like she was a radio and someone had turned her off. She lay face-up at the foot of the stairs with her head cocked, her nose bent sideways, one arm all the way up behind her to her neck, and her eyes staring off into the gloom.

"Liz?"

Nothing.

"Liz, are you okay?"

What a stupid question, and why did I care? That one I can answer. I wanted her to be alive because something was behind me. I didn't hear it but I knew it was there.

I knelt next to her and held a hand to her bloody mouth. There was no breath on my palm. Her eyes did not blink. She was dead. I got up, turned, and saw exactly what I expected: Liz standing there in her unzipped duffle coat and bloodstained sweatshirt. She wasn't looking at me. She was looking over my shoulder. She raised one of her hands and pointed, reminding me even in that terrible moment of the Ghost of Christmas Yet to Come pointing at Scrooge's tombstone.

Kenneth Therriault—what remained of him, at least— was coming down the stairs.

63

He was like a burned log with fire still inside. I don't know any other way to put it. He had turned black, but his skin was cracked in dozens of places and that brilliant deadlight shone through. It was coming out of his nose, his eyes, even his ears. When he opened his mouth, it came out of there, too.

He grinned and lifted his arms. "Let's try the ritual again and see who wins this time. I think you owe me that, since I saved you from her."

He hurried down the stairs toward me, ready for the big reunion scene. Instinct told me to turn tail and run, but something deeper told me to stand pat no matter how much I wanted to flee that oncoming horror. If I did, it would grab me from behind, wrap its charred arms around me, and that would be the end. It would win, and I would become its slave, bound to come when it called. It would possess me alive as it had possessed Therriault dead, which would be worse.

"Stop," I said, and the blackened husk of Therriault stopped at the foot of the stairs. Those outstretched arms were less than a foot from me.

"Go away. I'm done with you. Forever."

"You'll never be done with me." And then it said one more word, one that made my skin pebble with goosebumps and the hair stand up on the nape of my neck. "*Champ*."

"Wait and see," I said. Brave words, but I couldn't keep the tremble out of my voice.

Still the arms were outstretched, the blackened hands with their brilliant cracks inches from my neck. "If you really want to get rid of me for good, take hold. We'll do the ritual again, and it will be fairer, because this time I'm ready for you."

I was weirdly tempted, don't ask me why, but a part of me that was far beyond ego and deeper than instinct prevailed. You may beat the devil once—through providence, bravery, dumbass luck, or a combination of all—but not twice. I don't think anyone but saints beat the devil twice, and maybe not even them.

"Go." It was my turn to point like Scrooge's last ghost. I pointed at the door.

The thing raised Therriault's charred and sooty lip in a sneer. "You can't send me away, Jamie. Don't you realize that by now? We're bound to one another. You didn't think of the consequences. But here we are."

I repeated my one word. It was all I could squeeze out of a throat that suddenly felt like it was the width of a pin.

Therriault's body seemed poised to close the distance between us, to leap at me and close me in its awful embrace, but it didn't. Maybe it couldn't.

Liz shrank away as it passed her by. I expected it to go right through the door—as I had passed through Marsden— but whatever that thing was, it was no ghost. Its hand grasped the knob and turned it, more skin splitting and more light shining through. The door swung open.

It turned back to me. "Oh whistle and I'll come to you, my lad."

Then it left.

64

My legs were going to give out and the stairs were close, but I wasn't going to sit on them with Liz Dutton's broken body sprawled at their foot. I staggered to the conversation pit and collapsed into one of the chairs near it. I lowered my head and sobbed. Those were tears of horror and hysteria, but I think they were also—although I can't remember for sure—tears of joy. I was alive. I was in a dark house at the end of a private road with two corpses and two leftovers (Marsden was looking down at me from the balcony), but I was alive.

"Three," I said. "Three corpses and three leftovers. Don't forget Teddy."

I started laughing, but then I thought of Liz laughing pretty much the same way just before she died and made myself stop. I tried to think what I should do. I decided the first thing was to shut that fucking front door. Having those two revenants (a word I learned, you guessed it, later) staring at me wasn't pleasant, but I was used to dead people seeing me seeing them. What I really didn't like was the thought of Therriault out there somewhere, with the deadlight shining through his decaying skin. I'd told him to go, and he went… but what if he came back?

I walked past Liz and shut the door. When I came back I asked her what I should do. I didn't expect an answer, but I got one. "Call your mother."

I thought of the landline in the panic room, but I wasn't going back up those stairs and into that room. Not for a million bucks.

"Do you have your phone, Liz?"

"Yes." Sounding disinterested, like most of them do. Not all, though; Mrs. Burkett had had enough life left in her to offer criticism about the artistic merits of my turkey. And Donnie Bigs had tried to hide his stash of torture porn.

"Where is it?"

"In my jacket pocket."

I went to her body and reached into the righthand pocket of her duffle coat. I touched the butt of the gun she'd used to end Donald Marsden's life and drew my hand back as if I'd touched something hot. I tried the other one and got her phone. I turned it on.

"What's the passcode?"

"2665."

I punched it in, touched the New York City area code and the first three digits of Mom's number, then changed my mind and made a different call.

"911, what is your emergency?"

"I'm in a house with two dead people," I said. "One was murdered and the other one fell down the stairs."

"Is this a joke, son?"

"I wish it was. The woman who fell down the stairs kidnapped me and brought me here."

"What is your location?" Now the woman on the other end sounded engaged.

"It's at the end of a private road outside of Renfield, ma'am. I don't know how many miles or if there's a street number." Then I thought of what I should have said right away. "It's Donald Marsden's house. He's the man the woman murdered. She's the one who fell down the stairs. Her name is Liz Dutton. Elizabeth."

She asked me if I was okay, then told me to sit tight, officers were on the way. I sat tight and called my mother. That was a much longer conversation, and not always too clear because both of us were blubbering. I told her everything except about the deadlight thing. She would have believed me, but one of us having nightmares was enough. I just said Liz tripped chasing me and fell and broke her neck.

During our conversation, Donald Marsden came down the stairs and stood by the wall. One dead with the top of his head gone, the other dead with her head on sideways. Quite the pair they made. I told you this was a horror story, you were warned about that, but I was able to look at them without too much distress, because the worst horror was gone. Unless I wanted it back, that was. If I did, it would come.

All I had to do was whistle.

After fifteen very long minutes, I began to hear whooping sirens in the distance. After twenty-five, red and blue lights filled the windows. There were at least half a dozen cops, a regular posse. At first they were only dark shapes filling the door, blotting out any last traces of daylight, assuming there were any left. One of them asked where the goddam light switches were. Another one said "Got 'em," then swore when nothing happened.

"Who's here?" another called. "Any persons here, identify yourselves!"

I stood up and raised my hands, although I doubted if they could see anything but a dark shape moving around. "I'm here! My hands are up! The lights went out! I'm the kid who called!"

Flashlights came on, conflicting beams that strobed around and then centered on me. One of the cops came forward. A woman. She swerved around Liz, surely without knowing why she was doing it. At first her hand was on the butt of her holstered gun, but when she saw me she let go of it. Which was a relief.

She took a knee. "Are you alone in the house, son?"

I looked at Liz. I looked at Marsden, standing well away from the woman who had killed him. Even Teddy had arrived. He stood in the doorway the cops had vacated, perhaps drawn by the commotion, maybe just on a whim. The Three Undead Stooges.

"Yes," I said. "I'm the only one here."

65

The lady cop put an arm around my shoulders and led me outside. I started shivering. She probably thought it was from the night air but of course it wasn't. She slipped off her jacket and put it over my shoulders, but that wasn't good enough. I put my arms down the too-long sleeves and hugged it against me. It was heavy with cop-things in the pockets, but that was okay with me. The weight felt good.

There were three cruisers in the courtyard, two flanking Liz's little car and one behind it. As we stood there, another car pulled in, this one an SUV with RENFIELD CHIEF OF POLICE on the side. I guessed it would be a holiday for drunks and speeders downtown, because most of the town's force had to be right here.

Another cop came out the door and joined the lady cop. "What happened in there, kid?"

Before I could answer, the lady cop put a finger over my lips. I didn't mind; it actually felt sort of good. "No questions, Dwight. This boy's in shock. He needs medical attention."

A burly man in a white shirt with a badge hung around his neck—the Chief, I assumed—had gotten out of the SUV and was in time to hear this last. "You take him, Caroline. Get him looked at. Are there confirmed dead?"

"There's a body at the foot of the stairs. Looks like a woman. I can't confirm she's deceased, but from the way her head's turned—"

"Oh, she's dead, all right," I told them, then started crying.

"Go on, Caro," the Chief said. "Don't bother going all the way to County, either. Take him to MedNow. No questions until I get there. Also until we've got an adult who's responsible for him. Get his name?"

"Not yet," Officer Caroline said. "It's been crazy. There are no lights in there."

The Chief bent toward me, hands on his upper thighs, making me feel like I was five again. "What's your handle, son?"

So much for no questions, I thought. "Jamie Conklin, and it's my mother who's coming. Her name is Tia Conklin. I already called her."

"Uh-huh." He turned to Dwight. "Why are there no lights? All the houses on the way up here had power."

"Don't know, Chief."

I said, "They went out when she was running down the stairs after me. I think it's why she fell."

I could see he wanted to ask me more, but he just told Officer Caroline to get rolling. As she eased her way out of the courtyard and started down the curving driveway, I felt in my pants pockets and found Liz's phone, although I didn't remember putting it there. "Can I call my mom again and tell her we're going to the doc-in-the-box?"

"Sure."

As I made the call, I realized that if Officer Caroline found out I was using Liz's phone, I could be in trouble. She might well ask how come I knew the dead woman's passcode, and I wouldn't be able to give a good answer. In any case, she didn't ask.

Mom said she was in an Uber (which would probably cost a small fortune, so it was good the agency was back on a profitable basis) and they were making excellent time. She asked if I was really all right. I told her I really was, and that Officer Caroline was taking me to MedNow in Renfield, but just to get checked out. She told me not to answer any questions until she got there, and I said I wouldn't.

"I'm going to call Monty Grisham," she said. "He doesn't do this kind of legal work, but he'll know someone who does."

"I don't need a lawyer, Mom." Officer Caroline gave me a quick sideways glance when I said that. "I didn't do anything."

"If Liz murdered someone and you were there, you need one. There'll be an inquest…press…I don't know what-all. This is my fault. I brought that bitch into our house." Then she spat: "Fucking *Liz*!"

"She was good at first." This was true, but all at once I felt very, very tired. "I'll see you when you get here."

I ended the call and asked Officer Caroline how long it would take us to get to the doc-in-the-box. She said twenty minutes. I looked over my shoulder, through the mesh blocking off the back seat, suddenly sure that Liz would be there. Or—so much worse—Therriault. But it was empty.

"It's just you and me, Jamie," Officer Caroline said. "Don't worry."

"I'm not," I said, but there was one thing I *did* have to worry about, and thank God I remembered, or me and Mom might have been in a heap of trouble. I put my head against the window and half-turned away from her. "Going to take a little nap."

"You do that." There was a smile in her voice.

I *did* take a little nap. But first I powered up Liz's phone, hiding it with my body, and deleted the recording she'd made of me passing on the plot of *The Secret of Roanoke* to my mom. If they took the phone and found out it wasn't mine, I'd make something up. Or just say I couldn't remember, which would be safer. But they couldn't hear that recording.

No way.

66

The Chief and two other cops turned up at the MedNow place an hour or so after Officer Caroline and I got there. Also a guy in a suit who introduced himself as the county attorney. A doctor examined me and said I was basically fine, blood pressure a little high but considering what I'd been through, that wasn't surprising. He felt sure it would be normal again by morning and pronounced me "your basic healthy teenager." I happened to be your basic healthy teenager who could see dead folks, but I didn't go into that.

Me and the cops and the county attorney went into the staff break room to wait for my mother, and as soon as she got there, the questions started. That night we stayed at the Renfield Stardust Motel, and the next morning there were more questions. My mother was the one who told them she and Elizabeth Dutton had been in a relationship that ended when Mom discovered Liz was involved in the drug trade. I was the one who told them how Liz had scooped me up after tennis practice and took me to Renfield, where she was expecting to rob a big haul of Oxy from Mr. Marsden's house. He finally told her where the drugs were, and she killed him, either because she didn't get the jackpot she was expecting or because of the other stuff she found in that room. The pictures.

"There's one thing I don't understand," Officer Caroline said as I gave her back her jacket, which I had kept wearing. Mom gave her a wary, ready-to-protect-my-cub look, but Officer Caroline didn't see it. She was looking at me. "She tied the guy up—"

"She said she *secured* him. That was the word she used. Because she used to be a cop, I guess."

"Okay, she secured him. And according to what she told you—also according to what we found upstairs—she tuned up on him a little. But not all that much."

"Would you get to the point?" Mom said. "My son has been through a terrible experience and he's exhausted."

Officer Caroline ignored her. She was looking at me, and her eyes were very bright. "She could have done a lot more, tortured him until she got what she wanted, but instead she left him, drove all the way to New York City, kidnapped you, and brought you back. Why did she do that?"

"I don't know."

"You had a two-hour ride with her, and she never said?"

"All she said was she was glad to see me." I couldn't remember if she'd actually said that or not, so I guess it was technically a lie, but it didn't feel like one. I thought of those nights on the couch, sitting between them and watching *The Big Bang Theory*, all of us laughing our heads off, and I started to cry. Which got us out of there.

Once we were in the motel with the door shut and locked, Mom said, "If they ask you again, say that maybe she was planning to take you with her when she headed west. Can you do that?"

"Yes," I said. Wondering if maybe that idea had been knocking around someplace in Liz's mind all along. It wasn't a good thing to speculate on, but better than what I *had* thought (and still do today): that she planned to kill me.

I didn't sleep in the connecting room. I slept on the couch in Mom's. I dreamed that I was walking on a lonely country road under a sickle moon. *Don't whistle, don't whistle*, I told myself, but I did. I couldn't help myself. I was whistling "Let It Be." I remember that very clearly. I hadn't gotten through more than the first six or eight notes when I heard footsteps behind me.

I woke up with my hands clapped over my mouth, as if to stifle a scream. I've woken up the same way a few times in the years since, and it's never a scream I'm afraid of. I'm afraid I'll wake up whistling and the deadlight thing will be there.

Arms outstretched to hug.

67

There are plenty of drawbacks to being a kid; check it out. Zits, the agony of choosing the right clothes to wear to school so you don't get laughed at, and the mystery of girls are only three of them. What I found out after my trip to Donald Marsden's house (my kidnapping, to be perfectly blunt) was that there are also advantages.

One of them was not having to run a gauntlet of reporters and TV cameras at the inquest, because I didn't have to testify in person. I gave a video deposition instead, with the lawyer Monty Grisham found for me on one side and my mom on the other. The press knew who I was, but my name never appeared in the media because I was that magic thing, a minor. The kids at school found out (the kids at school almost always find out everything), but nobody ragged on me. I got respect instead. I didn't have to figure out how to talk to girls, because they came up to my locker and talked to me.

Best of all, there was no trouble about my phone—which was actually Liz's phone. It no longer existed, anyway. Mom tossed it down the incinerator, bon voyage, and told me to say I'd lost it if anyone asked. No one did. As for why Liz came to New York and snatched me, the police came to the conclusion Mom had already suggested, all on their own: Liz had wanted a kid with her when she went west, maybe figuring a woman traveling with a kid would attract less attention. No one seemed to consider the possibility that I'd try to escape, or at least yell for help when we stopped for gas and grub in Pennsylvania or Indiana or Montana. Of course I wouldn't do that. I'd be a docile little kidnap victim, just like Elizabeth Smart. Because I was a kid.

The newspapers played it big for a week or so, especially the tabloids, partly because Marsden was a "drug kingpin" but mostly because of the pictures found in his panic room. And Liz came off as sort of a hero, weird but true. EX-COP DIES AFTER SLAYING TORTURE PORN DON, blared the *Daily News*. No mention that she'd lost her job as the result of an IAD investigation and a positive drug test, but the fact that she'd been instrumental in locating Thumper's last bomb before it could kill a bunch of shoppers *was* mentioned. The *Post* must have gotten a reporter inside Marsden's house ("Cockroaches get in everywhere," Mom said), or maybe they had pix of the Renfield place on file, because their headline read INSIDE DONNIE BIGS' HOUSE OF HORRORS. My mother actually laughed at that one, saying that the *Post*'s understanding of the apostrophe was a nice parallel for their grasp of American politics.

"Not Bigs-apostrophe," she said when I asked. "Bigs-apostrophe-S."

Okay, Mom. Whatever.

68

Before long, other news drove Donnie Bigs's House of Horrors from the front pages of the tabs, and my renown at school faded. It was like Liz said about Chet Atkins, how soon they forget. I found myself once more faced with the problem of talking to girls instead of waiting for them to come up to my locker, all round-eyed with mascara and pursed up with lip gloss, to talk to me. I played tennis and tried out for the class play. I ended up only getting a part with two lines, but I put my heart into them. I played video games with my friends. I took Mary Lou Stein to the movies and kissed her. She kissed me back, which was excellent.

Cue the montage, complete with flipping calendar pages. It got to be 2016, then 2017. Sometimes I dreamed I was on that country road and would wake up with my hands over my mouth thinking *Did I whistle? Oh God, did I whistle?* But those dreams came less frequently. Sometimes I saw dead folks, but not too often and they weren't scary. Once my mother asked me if I still saw them and I said hardly ever, knowing it would make her feel better. That was something I wanted, because she had been through a hard time, too, and I got that.

"Maybe you're growing out of it," she said.

"Maybe I am," I agreed.

This brings us to 2018, with our hero Jamie Conklin over six feet tall, able to grow a goatee (which my mother fucking loathed), accepted at NYU, and almost old enough to vote. I *would* be old enough when the elections came around in November.

I was in my room, hitting the books for finals, when my phone buzzed. It was Mom, calling from the back of another Uber, this time on her way to Tenafly, where Uncle Harry was now residing.

"It's pneumonia again," she said, "and I don't think he's going to get better this time, Jamie. They told me to come, and they don't do that unless it's very serious." She paused, then said: "Mortal."

"I'll be there as fast as I can."

"You don't have to do that." The subtext being that I'd never really known him anyway, at least not when he was a smart guy building a career for himself and his sister in the world of tough New York publishing. Which can be a tough world indeed. Now that I was also working in the office— only a few hours a week, mostly filing—I knew that was true.

And it was true that I had only vague memories of a smart guy who should have stayed smart a lot longer, but it wasn't him I'd be going for.

"I'll take the bus." Which I could do with ease, because the bus was how we'd always gone to New Jersey in the days when Ubers and Lyfts were beyond our budget.

"Your tests…you have to study for your finals…"

"Books are a uniquely portable magic. I read that somewhere. I'll bring 'em. See you there."

"We may have to stay overnight," she said. "Are you sure?"

I said I was.

I don't know exactly where I was when Uncle Harry died. Maybe in New Jersey, maybe still crossing the Hudson, maybe even while I could see Yankee Stadium from my bird-beshitted bus window. All I know is that Mom was waiting for me outside the care home—his final care home— on a bench under a shade tree. She was dry-eyed, but she was smoking a cigarette and I hadn't seen her do that in a long time. She gave me a good strong hug and I gave it right back to her. I could smell her perfume, that old sweet smell of La Vie est Belle, which always took me back to my childhood. To that little boy who thought his green hand-turkey was just the cat's ass. I didn't have to ask.

"Not ten minutes before I got here," she said.

"Are you okay?"

"Yes. Sad, but also relieved that it's finally over. He lasted much longer than most people who suffer from what he had. You know what, I was sitting here thinking about three flies, six grounders. Do you know what that is?"

"I think so, yeah."

"The other boys didn't want to let me play because I was a girl, but Harry said if they wouldn't let me play, he wouldn't play, either. And he was popular. Always the most popular. So I was, as they say, the only girl in the game."

"Were you good?"

"I was terrific," she said, and laughed. Then she wiped at one of her eyes. Crying after all. "Listen, I need to talk to Mrs. Ackerman—she's the boss-lady here—and sign some papers. Then I need to go down to his room and see if there's anything I need to take right away. I can't imagine there is."

I felt a stirring of alarm. "He's not still…?"

"No, honey. There's a funeral home they use here. I'll make arrangements tomorrow about getting him to New York and the…you know, final stuff." She paused. "Jamie?"

I looked at her.

"You don't…you don't see him, do you?"

I smiled. "No, Ma."

She grabbed my chin. "How many times have I told you not to call me that? Who says maa?"

"Baby sheep," I said, then added, "Yeah yeah yeah."

That made her laugh. "Wait for me, hon. This won't take long."

She went inside and I looked at Uncle Harry, who was standing not ten feet away. He'd been there all along, wearing the pajamas he'd died in.

"Hey, Uncle Harry," I said.

No reply. But he was looking at me.

"Have you still got the Alzheimer's?"

"No."

"So you're okay now?"

He looked at me with the merest glint of humor. "I suppose so, if being dead fits into your definition of okay."

"She's going to miss you, Uncle Harry."

No reply, and I didn't expect one because it wasn't a question. I did have one, though. He probably didn't know the answer, but there's an old saying that goes if you never ask, you never get.

"Do you know who my father is?"

"Yes."

"Who? Who is it?"

"I am," Uncle Harry said.

69

Almost done now (and I remember when I thought thirty pages was a lot!), but not quite, so don't give up before you check this out:

My grandparents—my *only* set of grandparents, as it turns out—died on their way to a Christmas party. A guy full of too much Christmas cheer swerved across three lanes of a four-lane highway and hit them head-on. The drunk survived, as they so often do. My uncle (also my father, as it turns out) was in New York when he got the news, making the rounds of *several* Christmas parties, schmoozing publishers, editors, and writers. His agency was brand-new then, and Uncle Harry (dear old dad!) was kind of like a guy in the deep woods, tending a tiny pile of burning twigs and hoping for a campfire.

He came home to Arcola—that's a small town in Illinois—for the funeral. After it was over, there was a reception at the Conklins'. Lester and Norma had been well liked, so lots of people came. Some brought food. Some brought booze, which serves as godfather to a great many surprise babies. Tia Conklin, at that time not long out of college and working at her first job in an accounting firm, drank a good deal. So did her brother. Uh-oh, right?

After everybody goes home, Harry finds her in her room, lying on her bed in her slip, crying her heart out. Harry lies down beside her and takes her in his arms. Just for comfort, you understand, but one kind of comfort leads to another. Just that once, but once is enough, and six weeks later Harry—back in New York—gets a phone call. Not long after that, my pregnant mother joins the firm.

Would the Conklin Literary Agency have succeeded in that tough, competitive field without her, or would my father/uncle's little pile of twigs and leaves have fizzled out in a little runner of white smoke before he could begin to add the first bigger pieces of wood? Hard to say. When things took off, I was lying around in a bassinet, peeing in my Pampers and going goo-goo. But she was good at the job, that I know. If she hadn't been, the agency would have gone under later, when the bottom fell out of the financial markets.

Let me tell you, there are a lot of bullshit myths about babies born of incest, especially when it comes to father–daughter and sister–brother. Yes, there can be medical problems, and yes, the chances of those are a little higher when it comes to incest, but the idea that the majority of those babies are born with feeble minds, one eye, or club feet? Pure crap.

I did find out that one of the most common defects in babies from incestuous relationships is fused fingers or toes. I have scars on the insides of my second and third fingers on my left hand, from a surgical procedure to separate them when I was an infant. The first time I asked about those scars—I couldn't have been more than four or five—Mom told me the docs had done it before she brought me home from the hospital. "Easy-peasy," she said.

And of course there's that other thing I was born with, which might have something to do with the fact that once upon a time, while suffering from grief and alcohol, my parents got a little closer than a brother and sister should have done. Or maybe seeing dead people has nothing at all to do with that. Parents who can't carry a tune in a tin pail can produce a singing prodigy; illiterates can produce a great writer. Sometimes talent comes from nowhere, or so it seems.

Except, hold it, wait one.

That whole story is fiction.

I don't know how Tia and Harry became the parents of a bouncing baby boy named James Lee Conklin, because I never asked Uncle Harry for any of the details. He would have told me—the dead can't lie, as I think we have established—but I didn't want to know. After he said those two words—*I am*—I turned away and walked back into the care home to find my mother. He didn't follow, and I never saw him again. I thought he might come to his funeral, or turn up at the graveside ceremony, but he didn't.

On the way back to the city (on the bus, just like old times), Mom asked me if something was wrong. I said there wasn't, that I was just trying to get used to the idea that Uncle Harry was really gone. "It feels like when I lost one of my baby teeth," I said. "There's a hole in me and I keep feeling it."

"I know," she said, hugging me. "I feel the same way. But I'm not sad. I didn't expect to be, and I'm not. Because he's really been gone for a long time."

It was good to be hugged. I loved my mom and I love her still, but I lied to her that day, and not just by omission. It wasn't like *losing* a tooth; what I'd found out was like growing another tooth, one there wasn't room for in my mouth.

Certain things make the story I just told you seem more likely. Lester and Norma Conklin *were* killed by a drunk driver while on their way to a Christmas party. Harry *did* come back to Illinois for their funeral; I found an article in the Arcola *Record Herald* that says he gave the eulogy. Tia Conklin *did* quit her job and go to New York to help her brother in his new literary agency early the next year. And James Lee Conklin *did* make his debut nine months or so after the funeral, in Lenox Hill Hospital.

So yeah yeah yeah and right right right, it could all be just the way I told it. It has a fair amount of logic going for it. But it also could have been some other way, which I would like a lot less. The rape of a young woman who'd drunk herself unconscious, for instance, said act committed by her drunken, horny older brother. The reason I didn't ask is simple: I didn't want to know. Do I wonder if they discussed abortion? Sometimes. Am I worried that I have inherited more from my uncle/father than the dimples that show up when I smile, or the fact that I'm showing the first traces of white in my black hair at the tender age of twenty-two? To come right out and say it, am I worried that I may start to lose my mind at the still-tender age of thirty, or thirty-five, or forty? Yes. Of course I am. According to the Internet, my father–uncle suffered from EOFAD: early-onset familial Alzheimer's disease. It bides its time on genes PSEN1 and PSEN2, and so there's a test for it: spit in a test-tube and wait for your answer. I suppose I will take it.

Later.

Here's a funny thing—looking back over these pages, I see that the writing got better as I went along. Not trying to say I'm up there with Faulkner or Updike; what I *am* saying is that I improved by doing, which I suppose is the case with most things in life. I'll just have to hope I'll be better and stronger in other ways when I again meet the thing that took over Therriault. Because I will. I've not glimpsed it since that night in Marsden's house when whatever Liz saw in that mirror drove her insane, but it's still waiting. I sense that. Know it, actually, although I don't know what it is.

It doesn't matter. I won't live my life with the pending question of whether or not I'm going to lose my mind in middle age, and I won't live it with the shadow of that thing hanging over me, either. It has drained the color from too many days. The fact that I am a child of incest seems laughably unimportant compared to the black husk of Therriault with the deadlight shining out from the cracks in its skin.

I have done a lot of reading in the years since that thing asked me for a do-over contest, another Ritual of Chüd, and I've come across a lot of strange superstitions and odd legends—stuff that never made it into Regis Thomas's Roanoke books or Stoker's *Dracula*—and while there are plenty concerning the possession of the living by demons, I have never yet found one about a creature able to possess the dead. The closest I've come are stories about malevolent ghosts, and that's really not the same at all. So I have no idea what I'm dealing with. All I know is that I must deal with it. I'll whistle for it, it will come, we will join in a mutual hug instead of the ritual tongue-biting thing, and then...well. Then we'll see, won't we?

Yes we will. We'll see.

Later.

From the Author of
LATER...

Don't Miss Stephen King's
JOYLAND

College student Devin Jones took the summer job at Joyland hoping to forget the girl who broke his heart. But he wound up facing something far more terrible: the legacy of a vicious murder, the fate of a dying child, and dark truths about life—and what comes after—that would change his world forever.

A riveting story about love and loss, about growing up and growing old—and about those who don't get to do either because death comes for them before their time—JOYLAND is Stephen King at the peak of his storytelling powers. With all the emotional impact of King masterpieces such as *The Green Mile* and *The Shawshank Redemption*, JOYLAND is at once a mystery, a horror story, and a bittersweet coming-of-age novel, one that will leave even the most hard-boiled reader profoundly moved.

"Immensely appealing."
— Washington Post

"Tight and engrossing...a prize worth all your tokens and skeeball tickets."
— USA Today

**Read on for a preview—
or get a copy today
from your favorite
local or online bookseller!**

♥

I had a car, but on most days in that fall of 1973 I walked to
Joyland from Mrs. Shoplaw's Beachside Accommodations in
the town of Heaven's Bay. It seemed like the right thing to
do. The only thing, actually. By early September, Heaven
Beach was almost completely deserted, which suited my
mood. That fall was the most beautiful of my life. Even forty
years later I can say that. And I was never so unhappy, I can
say that, too. People think first love is sweet, and never
sweeter than when that first bond snaps. You've heard a
thousand pop and country songs that prove the point; some
fool got his heart broke. Yet that first broken heart is always
the most painful, the slowest to mend, and leaves the most
visible scar. What's so sweet about that?

♥

Through September and right into October, the North
Carolina skies were clear and the air was warm even at seven
in the morning, when I left my second-floor apartment by
the outside stairs. If I started with a light jacket on, I was

wearing it tied around my waist before I'd finished half of the three miles between the town and the amusement park.

I'd make Betty's Bakery my first stop, grabbing a couple of still-warm croissants. My shadow would walk with me on the sand, at least twenty feet long. Hopeful gulls, smelling the croissants in their waxed paper, would circle overhead. And when I walked back, usually around five (although sometimes I stayed later—there was nothing waiting for me in Heaven's Bay, a town that mostly went sleepybye when summer was over), my shadow walked with me on the water. If the tide was in, it would waver on the surface, seeming to do a slow hula.

Although I can't be completely sure, I think the boy and the woman and their dog were there from the first time I took that walk. The shore between the town and the cheerful, blinking gimcrackery of Joyland was lined with summer homes, many of them expensive, most of them clapped shut after Labor Day. But not the biggest of them, the one that looked like a green wooden castle. A boardwalk led from its wide back patio down to where the seagrass gave way to fine white sand. At the end of the boardwalk was a picnic table shaded by a bright green beach umbrella. In its shade, the boy sat in his wheelchair, wearing a baseball cap and covered from the waist down by a blanket even in the late afternoons, when the temperature lingered in the seventies. I thought he was five or so, surely no older than seven. The dog, a Jack Russell terrier, either lay beside him or sat at his feet. The woman sat on one of the picnic table benches, sometimes reading a book, mostly just staring out at the water. She was very beautiful.

Going or coming, I always waved to them, and the boy waved back. She didn't, not at first. 1973 was the year of the OPEC oil embargo, the year Richard Nixon announced he was not a crook, the year Edward G. Robinson and Noel Coward died. It was Devin Jones's lost year. I was a twenty-one year-old virgin with literary aspirations. I possessed three pairs of bluejeans, four pairs of Jockey shorts, a clunker Ford (with a good radio), occasional suicidal ideations, and a broken heart.

Sweet, huh?

♥

The heartbreaker was Wendy Keegan, and she didn't deserve me. It's taken me most of my life to come to that conclusion, but you know the old saw; better late than never. She was from Portsmouth, New Hampshire; I was from South Berwick, Maine. That made her practically the girl next door. We had begun "going together" (as we used to say) during our freshman year at UNH—we actually met at the Freshman Mixer, and how sweet is that? Just like one of those pop songs.

We were inseparable for two years, went everywhere together and did everything together. Everything, that is, but "it." We were both work-study kids with University jobs. Hers was in the library; mine was in the Commons cafeteria. We were offered the chance to hold onto those jobs during the summer of 1972, and of course we did. The money wasn't great, but the togetherness was priceless. I assumed that would also be the deal during the summer of 1973, until Wendy announced that her friend Renee had gotten them jobs working at Filene's, in Boston.

"Where does that leave me?" I asked.

"You can always come down," she said. "I'll miss you like mad, but really, Dev, we could probably use some time apart."

A phrase that is very often a death-knell. She may have seen that idea on my face, because she stood on tiptoe and kissed me. "Absence makes the heart grow fonder," she said. "Besides, with my own place, maybe you can stay over." But she didn't quite look at me when she said that, and I never did stay over. Too many roommates, she said. Too little time. Of course such problems can be overcome, but somehow we never did, which should have told me something; in retrospect, it tells me a lot. Several times we had been very close to "it," but "it" just never quite happened. She always drew back, and I never pressed her. God help me, I was being gallant. I have wondered often since what would have changed (for good or for ill) had I not been. What I know now is that gallant young men rarely get pussy. Put it on a sampler and hang it in your kitchen.

♥

The prospect of another summer mopping cafeteria floors and loading elderly Commons dishwashers with dirty plates didn't hold much charm for me, not with Wendy seventy miles south, enjoying the bright lights of Boston, but it was steady work, which I needed, and I didn't have any other prospects. Then, in late February, one literally came down the dish-line to me on the conveyor belt.

Someone had been reading *Carolina Living* while he or she snarfed up that day's blue plate luncheon special, which happened to be Mexicali Burgers and Caramba Fries.

He or she had left the magazine on the tray, and I picked it up along with the dishes. I almost tossed it in the trash, then didn't. Free reading material was, after all, free reading material. (I was a work-study kid, remember.) I stuck it in my back pocket and forgot about it until I got back to my dorm room. There it flopped onto the floor, open to the classified section at the back, while I was changing my pants.

Whoever had been reading the magazine had circled several job possibilities…although in the end, he or she must have decided none of them was quite right; otherwise *Carolina Living* wouldn't have come riding down the conveyor belt. Near the bottom of the page was an ad that caught my eye even though it hadn't been circled. In boldface type, the first line read: WORK CLOSE TO HEAVEN! What English major could read that and not hang in for the pitch? And what glum twenty-one-year-old, beset with the growing fear that he might be losing his girlfriend, would not be attracted by the idea of working in a place called Joyland?

There was a telephone number, and on a whim, I called it. A week later, a job application landed in my dormitory mailbox. The attached letter stated that if I wanted full-time summer employment (which I did), I'd be doing many different jobs, most but not all custodial. I would have to possess a valid driver's license, and I would need to interview. I could do that on the upcoming spring break instead of going home to Maine for the week. Only I'd been planning to spend at least some of that week with Wendy. We might even get around to "it."

"Go for the interview," Wendy said when I told her. She didn't even hesitate. "It'll be an adventure."

"Being with you would be an adventure," I said.

"There'll be plenty of time for that next year." She stood on tiptoe and kissed me (she always stood on tiptoe). Was she seeing the other guy, even then? Probably not, but I'll bet she'd noticed him, because he was in her Advanced Sociology course. Renee St. Claire would have known, and probably would have told me if I'd asked—telling stuff was Renee's specialty, I bet she wore the priest out when she did the old confession bit—but some things you don't want to know. Like why the girl you loved with all your heart kept saying no to you, but tumbled into bed with the new guy at almost the first opportunity. I'm not sure anybody ever gets completely over their first love, and that still rankles. Part of me still wants to know what was *wrong* with me. What I was lacking. I'm in my sixties now, my hair is gray and I'm a prostate cancer survivor, but I still want to know why I wasn't good enough for Wendy Keegan.

I took a train called the Southerner from Boston to North Carolina (not much of an adventure, but cheap), and a bus from Wilmington to Heaven's Bay. My interview was with Fred Dean, who was—among many other functions—Joyland's employment officer. After fifteen minutes of Q-and-A, plus a look at my driver's license and my Red Cross life-saving certificate, he handed me a plastic badge on a lanyard. It bore the word VISITOR, that day's date, and a cartoon picture of a grinning, blue-eyed German Shepherd who bore a passing resemblance to the famous cartoon sleuth, Scooby-Doo.

"Take a walk around," Dean said. "Ride the Carolina Spin, if you like. Most of the rides aren't up and running yet, but that one is. Tell Lane I said okay. What I gave you is a day-pass, but I want you back here by…" He looked at his watch. "Let's say one o'clock. Tell me then if you want the job. I've got five spots left, but they're all basically the same —as Happy Helpers."

"Thank you, sir."

He nodded, smiling. "Don't know how you'll feel about this place, but it suits me fine. It's a little old and a little rickety, but I find that charming. I tried Disney for a while; didn't like it. It's too…I don't know…"

"Too corporate?" I ventured.

"Exactly. Too corporate. Too buffed and shiny. So I came back to Joyland a few years ago. Haven't regretted it. We fly a bit more by the seat of our pants here—the place has a little of the old-time carny flavor. Go on, look around. See what you think. More important, see how you *feel*."

"Can I ask one question first?"

"Of course."

I fingered my day pass. "Who's the dog?"

His smile became a grin. "That's Howie the Happy Hound, Joyland's mascot. Bradley Easterbrook built Joyland, and the original Howie was his dog. Long dead now, but you'll still see a lot of him, if you work here this summer."

I did…and I didn't. An easy riddle, but the explanation will have to wait awhile.

♥

Joyland was an indie, not as big as a Six Flags park, and no-where near as big as Disney World, but it was large enough to be impressive, especially with Joyland Avenue, the main drag, and Hound Dog Way, the secondary drag, almost empty and looking eight lanes wide. I heard the whine of power-saws and saw plenty of workmen—the largest crew swarming over the Thunderball, one of Joyland's two coasters—but there were no customers, because the park didn't open until June fifteenth. A few of the food concessions were doing business to take care of the workers' lunch needs, though, and an old lady in front of a star-studded tell-your-fortune kiosk was staring at me suspiciously. With one exception, everything else was shut up tight.

The exception of the Carolina Spin. It was a hundred and seventy feet tall (this I found out later), and turning very slowly. Out in front stood a tightly muscled guy in faded jeans, balding suede boots splotched with grease, and a strap-style tee shirt. He wore a derby hat tilted on his coal-black hair. A filterless cigarette was parked behind one ear. He looked like a cartoon carnival barker from an old-time newspaper strip. There was an open toolbox and a big portable radio on an orange crate beside him. The Faces were singing "Stay with Me." The guy was bopping to the beat, hands in his back pockets, hips moving side to side. I had a thought, absurd but perfectly clear: *When I grow up, I want to look just like this guy*.

He pointed to the pass. "Freddy Dean sent you, right? Told you everything else was closed, but you could take a ride on the big wheel."

"Yes, sir."

"A ride on the Spin means you're in. He likes the chosen few to get the aerial view. You gonna take the job?"

"I think so."

He stuck out his hand. "I'm Lane Hardy. Welcome aboard, kid."

I shook with him. "Devin Jones."

"Pleased to meet you."

He started up the inclined walk leading to the gently turning ride, grabbed a long lever that looked like a stick shift, and edged it back. The wheel came to a slow stop with one of the gaily painted cabins (the image of Howie the Happy Hound on each) swaying at the passenger loading dock.

"Climb aboard, Jonesy. I'm going to send you up where the air is rare and the view is much more than fair."

I climbed into the cabin and closed the door. Lane gave it a shake to make sure it was latched, dropped the safety bar, then returned to his rudimentary controls. "Ready for takeoff, cap'n?"

"I guess so."

"Amazement awaits." He gave me a wink and advanced the control stick. The wheel began to turn again and all at once he was looking up at me. So was the old lady by the fortune-telling booth. Her neck was craned and she was shading her eyes. I waved to her. She didn't wave back.

Then I was above everything but the convoluted dips and twists of the Thunderball, rising into the chilly early spring air, and feeling—stupid but true—that I was leaving all my cares and worries down below.

Joyland wasn't a theme park, which allowed it to have a little bit of everything. There was a secondary roller coaster called the Delirium Shaker and a water slide (Captain Nemo's Splash & Crash). On the far western side of the park was a special annex for the little ones called the Wiggle-Waggle Village. There was also a concert hall where most of the acts—this I also learned later—were either B-list C&W or the kind of rockers who peaked in the fifties or sixties. I remember that Johnny Otis and Big Joe Turner did a show there together. I had to ask Brenda Rafferty, the head accountant who was also a kind of den mother to the Hollywood Girls, who they were. Bren thought I was dense; I thought she was old; we were both probably right.

Lane Hardy took me all the way to the top and then stopped the wheel. I sat in the swaying car, gripping the safety bar, and looking out at a brand-new world. To the west was the North Carolina flatland, looking incredibly green to a New England kid who was used to thinking of March as nothing but true spring's cold and muddy precursor. To the east was the ocean, a deep metallic blue until it broke in creamy-white pulses on the beach where I would tote my abused heart up and down a few months hence. Directly below me was the good-natured jumble of Joyland —the big rides and small ones, the concert hall and concessions, the souvenir shops and the Happy Hound Shuttle, which took customers to the adjacent motels and, of course, the beach. To the north was Heaven's Bay. From high above the park (upstairs, where the air is rare), the town looked like a nestle of children's blocks from which four church steeples rose at the major points of the compass.

The wheel began to move again. I came down feeling like a kid in a Rudyard Kipling story, riding on the nose of an elephant. Lane Hardy brought me to a stop, but didn't bother to unlatch the car's door for me; I was, after all, almost an employee.

"How'd you like it?"

"Great," I said.

"Yeah, it ain't bad for a grandma ride." He reset his derby so it slanted the other way and cast an appraising eye over me. "How tall are you? Six-three?"

"Six-four."

"Uh-huh. Let's see how you like ridin all six-four of you on the Spin in the middle of July, wearin the fur and singin 'Happy Birthday' to some spoiled-rotten little snothole with cotton candy in one hand and a meltin Kollie Kone in the other."

"Wearing what fur?"

But he was headed back to his machinery and didn't answer. Maybe he couldn't hear me over his radio, which was now blasting "Crocodile Rock." Or maybe he just wanted my future occupation as one of Joyland's cadre of Happy Hounds to come as a surprise.

♥

I had over an hour to kill before meeting with Fred Dean again, so I strolled up Hound Dog Way toward a lunch-wagon that looked like it was doing a pretty good business. Not everything at Joyland was canine-themed, but plenty of stuff was, including this particular eatery, which was called Pup-A-Licious. I was on a ridiculously tight budget for this little job-hunting expedition, but I thought I could afford a couple of bucks for a chili-dog and a paper cup of French fries.

When I reached the palm-reading concession, Madame Fortuna planted herself in my path. Except that's not quite right, because she was only Fortuna between May fifteenth and Labor Day. During those sixteen weeks, she dressed in long skirts, gauzy, layered blouses, and shawls decorated with various cabalistic symbols. Gold hoops hung from her ears, so heavy they dragged the lobes down, and she talked in a thick Romany accent that made her sound like a character from a 1930s fright-flick, the kind featuring mist-shrouded castles and howling wolves.

During the rest of the year she was a widow from Brooklyn who collected Hummel figures and liked movies (especially the weepy-ass kind where some chick gets cancer and dies beautifully). Today she was smartly put together in a black pantsuit and low heels. A rose-pink scarf around her throat added a touch of color. As Fortuna, she sported masses of wild gray locks, but that was a wig, and still stored under its own glass dome in her little Heaven's Bay house. Her actual hair was a cropped cap of dyed black. The *Love Story* fan from Brooklyn and Fortuna the Seer only came together in one respect: both fancied themselves psychic.

"There is a shadow over you, young man," she announced.

I looked down and saw she was absolutely right. I was standing in the shadow of the Carolina Spin. We both were.

"Not that, stupidnik. Over your future. You will have a hunger."

I had a bad one already, but a Pup-A-Licious footlong would soon take care of it. "That's very interesting, Mrs... um..."

"Rosalind Gold," she said, holding out her hand. "But you can call me Rozzie. Everyone does. But during the season..." She fell into character, which meant she sounded like Bela Lugosi with breasts. "Doorink the season, I am... *Fortuna*!"

I shook with her. If she'd been in costume as well as in

character, half a dozen gold bangles would have clattered on her wrist. "Very nice to meet you." And, trying on the same accent: "I am...*Devin*!"

She wasn't amused. "An Irish name?"

"Right."

"The Irish are full of sorrow, and many have the sight. I don't know if you do, but you will meet someone who does."

Actually, I was full of happiness...along with that surpassing desire to put a Pup-A-Licious pup, preferably loaded with chili, down my throat. This was feeling like an adventure. I told myself I'd probably feel less that way when I was swabbing out toilets at the end of a busy day, or cleaning puke from the seats of the Whirly Cups, but just then everything seemed perfect.

"Are you practicing your act?"

She drew herself up to her full height, which might have been five-two. "Is no act, my lad." She said *ect* for *act*. "Jews are the most psychically sensitive race on earth. This is a thing everyone knows." She dropped the accent. "Also, Joyland beats hanging out a palmistry shingle on Second Avenue. Sorrowful or not, I like you. You give off good vibrations."

"One of my very favorite Beach Boys songs."

"But you are on the edge of great sorrow." She paused, doing the old emphasis thing. "And, perhaps, danger."

"Do you see a beautiful woman with dark hair in my future?" Wendy was a beautiful woman with dark hair.

"No," Rozzie said, and what came next stopped me dead. "She is in your past."

Ohh-kay.

I walked around her in the direction of Pup-A-Licious, being careful not to touch her. She was a charlatan, I didn't have a single doubt about that, but touching her just then still seemed like a lousy idea.

No good. She walked with me. "In your future is a little girl and a little boy. The boy has a dog."

"A Happy Hound, I bet. Probably named Howie."

She ignored this latest attempt at levity. "The girl wears a red hat and carries a doll. One of these children has the sight. I don't know which. It is hidden from me."

I hardly heard that part of her spiel. I was thinking of the previous pronouncement, made in a flat Brooklyn accent: *She is in your past.*

Madame Fortuna got a lot of stuff wrong, I found out, but she *did* seem to have a genuine psychic touch, and on the day I interviewed for a summer at Joyland, she was hitting on all cylinders...

The Best of MWA Grand Master
DONALD E. WESTLAKE!

"A book by this guy is cause for happiness."
— STEPHEN KING

Forever and a Death

Based on Westlake's story for a James Bond movie that was never filmed! Millions will die to satisfy one man's hunger for gold—and revenge…

The Comedy Is Finished

When domestic terrorists kidnap a big-name comedian, it'll take more than quick wits for him to survive.

Memory

With his memory damaged after a brutal assault and the police hounding him, actor Paul Cole fights to rebuild his shattered life.

Brothers Keepers

"Thou Shalt Not Steal" is only the first commandment to be broken when the Crispinite monks of New York City try to save their monastery from the wrecking ball.

Help I Am Being Held Prisoner

A gang of convicts plots to use a secret tunnel not to escape from prison but to rob two banks while they have the perfect alibi: they couldn't have done it since they're already behind bars…

The Best in Graphic Novels From
HARD CASE CRIME!

The finest writers and artists team up to tell
searing crime stories in the visual medium:

Peepland
by CHRISTA FAUST & GARY PHILLIPS

In seedy, sordid 1980s Times Square, a peepshow performer finds evidence of a murder committed by the son of a wealthy real estate developer. But will she live to tell the tale?

Normandy Gold
by MEGAN ABBOTT & ALISON GAYLIN

A small-town sheriff comes to Washington, D.C. to investigate her sister's disappearance and winds up deep undercover in the world of politicians, call girls, and the deadliest of dirty tricks.

Quarry's War
by MAX ALLAN COLLINS

Once a Marine sniper in Vietnam, Quarry came home to find his wife cheating on him and no work for a man whose only job skill was killing. Enter the Broker, an agent for professional hit men. But when the Broker assigns Quarry to kill a former platoon mate, will Quarry carry out the contract or fall prey to an attack of conscience? From the author of *Road to Perdition*, one of the most acclaimed graphic novels of all time.

The Assignment
by **WALTER HILL**

Kidnapped and operated on by the vengeful sister of one of his victims, a professional killer emerges permanently altered—and with a thirst for revenge of his own. Inspired the movie starring Michelle Rodriguez and Sigourney Weaver.

The Girl with the Dragon Tattoo
by **STIEG LARSSON & SYLVAIN RUNBERG**

The entire saga of Lisbeth Salander, adapted in three graphic novels—plus a fourth volume, *The Girl Who Danced With Death*, telling an all-new story unavailable in any other format.

Babylon Berlin
by **VOLKER KUTSCHER**

In the years leading up to WWII, Berlin is a hotbed of crime and deception, intrigue and violence. Can one detective uncover its secrets and live to see justice done?

Ryuko, Vol. 1 & 2
by **ELDO YOSHIMIZU**

From acclaimed international artist Yoshimizu, the bloody story of a daughter of the Yakuza and her quest to learn her mother's fate and redeem her suffering.